I0582762

STICK IT

NORTHERN LEGACY

R.A. SMYTH

Stick It

Stick It Copyright © 2025 R.A. Smyth

All rights reserved. No part of this book may be reproduced, or stored in a retrieval system, or transmitted in any form or by any means, electronic, mechanical, photocopying, recording, or otherwise, without express written permission of the publisher.

The characters and events portrayed in this book are fictitious. Any similarity to real persons, living or dead, is coincidental and not intended by the author.

ISBN: 978-1-915456-30-4

Cover by Disturbed Valkyrie Designs
Interior Design by Nikki Epperson
Editing by Lunar Rose Editing Services.
Formatting by Rachel Smyth.

In a game built for men, I came to make history.

As the only girl on an all-male Division I hockey team, I'm not a
novelty—I'm a threat. A spark in a powder keg of testosterone.
But I didn't come to play nice. I came to dominate.

I didn't expect them...

The golden boy captain who carries the team on his shoulders.
The brooding guardian with a darkness that calls to me.
The hot and cold viper who kisses me breathless in dark corners
—then acts like it never happened.
And the quiet bruiser who speaks my language in video games.

I live with them. Train with them. Compete against them.
They're temptation wrapped in danger—
And the first ones to ever look at me like I belong.

But this game has enemies off the ice too.
And someone wants to break me for good.

Let them try.

Because I'm not just here to play.
I'm here to rewrite the rules and claim my legacy.

STICK IT PLAYLIST

Control – Halsey
Jealous – Labrinth
Everybody Wants to Rule the World – Lorde
All I Want – Kodaline
Slow Dancing in the Dark – Joji
Enemy – Imagine Dragons & JID
bad idea! – girl in red
You Should See Me in a Crown – Billie Eilish
The Night We Met – Lord Huron
Bury a Friend – Billie Eilish
no body, no crime – Taylor Swift ft. HAIM
Believer – Imagine Dragons

TRIGGER WARNINGS

- Bullying
- Death of a family member
- Attempted murder
- Violence
- Mental health struggles

*****

This book is a dark, contemporary, new adult reverse harem romance, meaning the FMC will end up with 3+ males.

The book is a standalone, meaning there is no cliffhanger. It is book one in an interconnected series of standalones.

This book ends in an HEA.

AUTHORS NOTE

This book was born in the dark.

I started writing *Stick It* during a period of personal loss — one of those seasons where the world tilts sideways and nothing feels steady beneath your feet. After experiencing a miscarriage at the start of this year, I felt helpless. Unmoored. Like I'd lost control over my own body, my own story. So I turned to the only thing I could still shape with my hands: words.

That's when Dylan showed up.

She's fierce. Defiant. Unapologetically driven. And completely, beautifully flawed. She came to me fully formed — a girl who didn't shrink when the world tried to make her small. A girl who fought back, even when the odds were impossible. Even when she was hurting.

In her, I found the strength I was struggling to hold onto.

But this story isn't just hers. It's also about the people who show up when everything else falls apart. The ones who don't try to fix you — they just stand with you. Who steady your spine when you're too tired to hold yourself up. That part of the story was inspired, in no small way, by the quiet strength of my husband and my parents, who have always been there for me.

I didn't set out to write about breaking barriers or rewriting rules, but maybe it was in me anyway — in the ache, in the fight, in the need to believe we can rise even when everything inside us feels broken.

These characters are messy. They make mistakes. They guard their pain. But they love hard. They hold each other accountable. They heal, slowly and imperfectly, together.

Thank you for holding space for them.

And for whatever you're carrying — whatever brought you to this story — I hope you found a spark of strength in these pages too.

With love,
    Rachel

To every woman who was told she couldn't.
Who dared to want more. To be more.
To the ones who refuse to shrink to fit the world around them.

You don't need permission to rise.
Break the rules. Shatter the glass.
Take. Up. Space.

Write your own damn legacy.

And if your story ends with four possessive hockey gods at your feet?
You earned it, babe.

PROLOGUE

THE SOUND of their laughter echoes in my ears, sharp and mocking. Like what I'd said was so ridiculous, it didn't deserve anything else.

We were doing one of those dumb icebreaker things in homeroom. *Say your name and what you want to be when you grow up.*

Most of the girls say they want to be a pop star or a vet. Maybe even a teacher.

When it's my turn, I don't even hesitate. "I want to play in the NHL."

There's a moment of silence so thick you could hear the kid at the front of the classroom shuffling in his chair.

Then the laughter started.

Especially from the boy two rows over—Brandon freaking McKay. "That's stupid. You're a girl."

I blink, stunned for a second. "So?"

He scoffs, turning in his chair so the whole class can hear him. "Girls don't play in the NHL. That's for *real* players."

My cheeks burn, but I lift my chin. "I *am* a real player."

"Yeah, in peewee league." He grins, and the others laugh with him.

My stomach twists. "For now."

"Even if you were good enough—which you're not—you still don't get to. Girls *don't belong* there." His voice is so sure it feels like a slap.

I try to say something back. I open my mouth, but nothing comes out. Because the way everyone's looking at me? It's as if they agree.

Like I'm stupid.

Like I'm *wrong*.

Like I'm *less*.

I wait until the bell rings and I'm out of the classroom before I let the tears fall. I hold it in all the way home.

Until I walk through the front door and see my dad in the kitchen, stirring something on the stove, still in his team hoodie.

"Hey, kiddo."

That's all it takes.

I drop my bag and crumble.

He's across the room in seconds, wrapping me in one of those hugs that squeezes all the sadness out. Like I'm a snow globe someone shook too hard, and he's the only one who knows how to make it settle again.

"What happened?"

I sniff, voice cracking. "They laughed at me."

His brow furrows. "Who did?"

"Everyone. In class. I said I wanted to play in the NHL and they laughed." My throat tightens. "They said I *can't*. That girls *don't*."

He doesn't speak right away. Just crouches so we're eye to eye, his hands warm on my shoulders.

Then he says, "Did they laugh because it's never been done?"

I nod.

He smiles. "Then that means *no one* knows what it'll look like when someone does."

I shake my head. "But, Dad...it's *never* happened."

"Not yet." His voice is steady. Unshakable. "But that doesn't mean it can't. And if anyone could be the first..." He cups my chin. "It's you."

My lip wobbles. "But what if I'm not good enough?"

His thumb brushes my cheek. "Then you work until you are. You show up earlier. Stay later. Train harder. You *bleed* for it, Princess. Because that dream?" He taps the center of my chest. "It's already yours."

I blink at him, tears spilling over again. But this time, they don't sting.

They burn.

Hot. Fierce.

I nod. "Okay."

"Say it."

"I'm going to play in the NHL."

ONE

THE SOUND of footsteps echoes off the concrete tunnel, sounding like the entire team is marching toward the rink and not a lone girl with her heart lodged in her throat. The faint glow of the emergency lights guides me forward until the vacuous arena unfolds before me. Cold, biting air stings my nostrils and fills my lungs, bringing me to life with every inhale. Inadvertently, a smile twists at the corners of my lips.

Stale popcorn.

Zamboni fumes.

And a hint of metallic copper...

The smells of my childhood.

Of the most important thing in my life.

Hockey.

Hockey is all that I have now. It is *everything*. It's what gets me out of bed in the morning. What keeps the dark thoughts at bay. It gives me a future to work toward—something to strive for.

Without it...well, I don't want to think about where I'd be without this sport.

Thankfully, I don't have to.

Feet rooted to the ground, my gaze roams over the battered

and scuffed boards, carrying stories of a thousand games. Over the vacant plastic chairs that seat the asses of hundreds of supporters as they scream on their team.

This place has seen more blood, sweat, and tears than most churches, and God knows, it's far more sacred.

As though walking through the Sistine Chapel, I hold my breath as I steadily make my way toward the edge of the rink, taking all of it in, barely daring to believe I'm *here*. My fingers brush the top of the board with the same tenderness a Van Gogh fanatic would show *The Starry Night*, tracing the lines of peeled paint with reverence.

This is where I watched my first-ever hockey game. Where my love of the sport began. It's been years since I was back here. Truthfully, I never thought I would step foot in this arena again.

Yet, here I stand on the precipice of change.

Hopefully, things will go better this time around...

Goosebumps pebble along my arms. The tank top and jean shorts I'm wearing do little to combat the cold as I stare out over the ice. In my mind's eye, I can see the players—a sea of Bermuda blue and silver—skating across the rink, skates cutting across the bold Steelhawks emblem in the center of the ice. I can hear the roar of the crowd. The ding of the buzzer as a goal is scored. The slam of a body hitting the boards.

An entire game plays out in front of me before I lift my gaze higher, climbing the tall walls of the arena until I reach the row of jerseys—previous players who have gone on to join the NHL. I scan the names, not daring to consider a future where *my* name could be on that wall.

My focus stalls on the final jersey, a lump rising in my throat.

"Let's hope I don't screw this one up, eh?"

My question is directed to ghosts, but it is a very *alive* voice that responds, making me jump out of my skin.

"How did I know I'd find you here instead of at home, *resting*?"

Spinning toward the voice, a reluctant smile grows across my face.

"Just wanted to get a feel of the place before chaos ensues tomorrow." Once he's close enough, I wrap my arms around him, and he envelops me in a hug that I can feel to my bones. "Thought you'd be long gone by now, tucked up in bed, old man."

He scoffs, pulling away to nudge me with his elbow. "That's Coach to you now."

I scrunch my nose. "Nope. Don't think I can do it." Leaning in, I say more softly, "You'll always be Bear to me."

He huffs an irritated laugh, but I catch the way the corners of his lips lift, the tenderness that momentarily softens his eyes.

"Not in public, if you know what's good for you."

Aaaand that gruff exterior is back.

Gesturing toward the closest row of plastic seats, he walks over to sit, and I join him. "You're ready, you know. I might have gotten you in the door, but you deserve a spot on this team. What spot that is, is up to you, but you. Deserve. This. Shot."

He reaches over to squeeze my hand, and I manage a wan smile.

"What if I mess it all up again?" My voice is pinched tight with nerves.

"You won't. You've learned from last year. Focus on the game, and your raw talent will speak for itself." A wistful smile plays along his lips. "Of course, if you don't go home and get some rest, you're going to play like shit tomorrow."

I gasp, my turn to smack the man who has been like an uncle to me my entire life. "How dare you! I could be out partying all night and *still* kick ass on the ice."

"Ha," he barks. "I *know* you got the email with my rulebook. No partying, and no drinking during the season."

"Yeah," I scoff. "I bet every single one of your players sits at home every Saturday night, with a can of Coke, playing board games. They're definitely *not* at a bar after every game—win or lose—*drinking.*"

He simply shakes his head. He knows damn well what his players get up to off the ice.

"Besides," I argue, "*technically*, we're in the preseason…"

"Don't get smart with me, kiddo, or your ass will be benched before you get the chance to show *anyone* what you can do."

I grin, our banter having loosened the nerves starting to tighten in my chest. Leaning in, he wraps an arm around my shoulder, pressing his lips to my temple. "It's good to have you home, D." His gaze flicks skyward. "He'd be so proud of you."

With a lump in my throat and comforting arms around me, I stare steadfastly out across the rink. *God, I hope so*, because the next time I'm here, I won't just be looking at the ice.

I'll be playing on it.

THE HEAVY DOORS of the arena slam shut behind me as I step out into the setting sun. Taking a moment, I pull on my sunglasses and stare out over the parking lot. There is only one other car here other than mine, but I know when tomorrow morning rolls around, it'll be packed with the vehicles of various members of the team—players, trainers, coaches.

Refusing to let the nerves in, I cross the parking lot to my car and climb behind the wheel. The heat of the leather seats presses against the backs of my thighs, and I immediately blast the A/C. Glancing in my rearview mirror, I can't see past my belongings piled high in the back seat. Everything from my previous dorm room is haphazardly crammed into the confined space. I'm pretty sure I heard a light bulb smash at one point... Shit, I hope it wasn't one of my mugs. I don't think I could deal with a shattered mug on top of everything else right now.

Goddammit, I knew I should have taken better care when putting everything in the car. I was just so fucking ready to get out of there. With Blackstone State University only being a fifteen-minute drive from my old one, I easily could have made several trips back and forth instead of stuffing everything I had into one carload...

But nope. There was no way in hell you could pay me to step foot back on Northern Summit's campus.

Please don't let it be one of the mugs!

Sending up a silent prayer, I know I can't sit in the BSU parking lot all night. It's time to really get this fresh start underway.

Starting the engine, I pull out through the campus gates and head toward Athletes Row, the street where all student-athletes are housed. Why? Because it's the closest one to the sports center.

Blackstone is a small college town, so it only takes a few minutes before I turn onto the correct street, slowing as I check the numbers on each house for number 91—where I'll live for at least the next nine months. Even though the academic year doesn't start for another two weeks, the street is busy with other athletic students moving in since we all typically start back a week before everyone else.

With my window down to allow the pleasant August breeze to blow through my hair, I catch the upbeat tune from a speaker set up in the front lawn of a house as I drive past. Another house has two girls working together to carry an armchair inside, with a group of guys sitting outside the house opposite, beer in hand as they enjoy the last wisps of sunshine for the day.

Not that it gets cold at night at this time of year in Vermont. While our winters are bitingly cold, our summer days are *hot*, and our evenings blissfully pleasant.

Halfway down the street, I find the house I've been assigned to and pull up to the curb outside. My fingers tap absently against the wheel as I stare up at the three-story Victorian structure.

The house stands tall and stately, its pale clapboard siding weathered just enough to suggest history without neglect. Deep, Bermuda blue shutters frame the windows, and the steeply pitched roofline gives it a quaint, almost storybook charm. Despite its age, the house feels welcoming, like it has witnessed countless fresh starts and quiet triumphs. Against my better judgment, a flicker of hope stirs in my chest, a nervous energy simmering just beneath my skin.

Not one to put something off once I've set my mind to it, I blow out one final breath before I mutter, "Here goes nothing," and climb out of the car.

I twirl the keys around my finger as I make my way up the drive, the soles of my Converse slapping against the asphalt as I eye the large bay window that overlooks the front yard. I don't see any movement from within. Perhaps no one is home? Refusing to acknowledge the butterflies in my stomach, I stuff my keys into my pocket so I can't fiddle with them before ascending the front porch steps and rapping my knuckles against the faded wood of the front door.

Straining to listen, I don't hear any noise from inside the house. I can't decide if I'd prefer someone to be home so we can get this over with and I can collapse onto my bed, or if I'm grateful for the extra moments to gather myself.

Before returning to my car, I decide to try once more. I knock again, harder this time. Not expecting anyone to answer, I turn my back to the door and instead look out over the street, watching other co-eds laugh around with one another while they haul in suitcases or relax on folding chairs on the front lawn.

"Hi? Can I help you?"

"Jesus." I nearly jump out of my skin, my hand moving to rest over my thundering heart as I whirl to...

Whatever I was going to do or say is instantly forgotten as I stare dumbfounded at the sexiest, half-naked man I've ever seen leaning on the now open door. He's all cut muscle and casual confidence—abs tight, chest broad, and arms that make my knees forget how to function. Not to mention the swirls of black ink decorating his left pec and arm. I can't look away, he's *that* good-looking. I'm not even exaggerating. I grew up watching hockey—*playing* hockey with a bunch of boys. Believe me, I have seen *plenty* of hot, strong, powerful bodies, but *none* that come attached to the face of an angel.

A cheeky, smirking, mischievous angel.

Dammit, I've totally been caught gawking.

Striking green eyes dance with mirth, framed by thick, dark lashes that leave me envious. His sharp nose sits slightly crooked on his face, giving him a ruggedness that matches his tats. Freckles dance across his cheekbones, and red hair curls messily around his head.

All of it melds together to form a breathtaking scene.

No one—and I mean *no one*—has the right to look that good.

"Most call me Finn, but, sweet cheeks, you can feel free to call me anything you want."

His suggestive tone has my jaw snapping shut, and I can only hope no drool leaked out as I crash-land back in reality.

A reality where I'm standing on *Finn O'Rourke's* doorstep. The Steelhawks' number-one right winger. Oh yes, I know precisely who Finn O'Rourke is. I've just never had the...plea-sure?...of seeing him out of his gear.

And*God*, I wish that were still the case. At least then, I'd know he wouldn't be starring in my fantasies when I fall into bed at night.

"Uh, I think I must have the wrong house." I deliberately look everywhere and anywhere but into those hypnotizing eyes.

"What a happy accident for you," he teases with a lascivious smirk that...*nope!*

Ignoring him, I stuff my hand in my pocket, finding the scrap of paper with the address of my new accommodation. Scanning it, I frown. "Number ninety-one?" I mutter to myself before lifting my head, finally daring to meet his gaze. "Is this number ninety-one?"

"The one and only."

I frown. "Are you sure?"

His laugh is deep and melodic, like being dipped in dark chocolate. "Pretty sure. Only been living here for three years."

Shit.

He must see something in my expression because he drops the whole flirtatious act, finally pushing himself off the door-frame to stand upright.

"You sure you've got the right street?" he asks more seriously.

"Is there another Athletes Row?" My voice is higher than I'd like, and panic starts to tighten my throat.

"Nope. Just the one."

Fuck. Shit. Fuck, fuck, fuck.

I spin away from him, needing a moment to process. To break. To scream at the universe for fucking me over...*again.* Just in a brand-new and creative way.

Fate, you heinous bitch!

"Hey, it's okay." His fingers brush my shoulder, and I flinch away. He instantly drops his hand, stuffing both into the pockets of his sweats. "I'm sure we can get this sorted out. What's your name?" His softened tone only serves to make tears gather in my eyes. I force them back.

Nope, this is not happening here.

I will get through this just as I have gotten through every-thing else...and then I'll cry silently into my pillow when I'm alone.

"Dylan," I inform him when I finally regain control of my vocal cords. "My name is Dylan."

His eyes widen in surprise before a cheerful grin splits his face in two, showing straight white teeth that have no business belonging to a hockey player. They must all be fake. I bet he keeps them in a jar on his bedside table at night.

Strangely, believing that makes me feel marginally better.

"There's obviously been some mix-up. We're waiting for a new roommate called Dylan. Admin must have gotten you mixed up." He waves his hand dismissively. "I bet he's having the time of his life thinking he's rooming with the girls' swim team for the year." My lips twitch slightly, and catching it, his emerald eyes sparkle. "Lucky for you, that means you get to chill with me and my buddies tonight." He wags his eyebrows sugges-tively. "And in the morning, you can go to admin and sort it all out."

The color drains from my face at the mention of more of them. *Oh gods, which other team members does he live with?* Because I *know* whoever else lives in this house is also a hockey player. That's how BSU does it.

"Hey." Misinterpreting my distress, his hands fly up, fingers spread, palms forward. I notice that he carefully ensures he's an arm's length away from me. "I just meant you can have Dylan's —the other Dylan's—room until tomorrow. You can lock your-self in there, and you don't have to say a word to any of us. That's cool. Or you can go to a hotel," he continues. "That's cool, too. I was only offering 'cause I didn't know your situation or..."

Okay, it's actually kinda adorable when he does that. I've watched Finn O'Rourke many times on the ice, and not once has he ever shown anything other than unwavering confidence and blatant determination.

"It's fine," I interrupt with a tight smile. "I'll stay."

His shoulders drop from his ears as he visibly relaxes.

Grinning broadly, he steps aside and ushers me in. "Welcome to the hottest house on campus."

Fantastic, and I'm the one about to be tested in the flames... literally.

Because, you see, I've already pieced together what Finn has yet to.

That there is. No. *Male.* Dylan.

And soon enough, he—and whichever other Steelhawks live here—are going to realize that not only am I their new roommate, but I'm also their new teammate.

Yup, that's right. I'm about to be the only girl on an all-boys Division One hockey team.

What could possibly go wrong?

From experience...absolutely everything.

TWO

"GET IN THE CAR, or I'm leaving without your sorry asses," I bellow from the front door, keys in hand. When I don't immediately hear the thunder of shoes coming down the stairs, I glance at my watch in exasperation. "Guys!"

They know today, of all days, it's imperative that we are early.

Turning on my heel, I've just decided to leave their lazy asses behind when the hurried smack of footsteps against the stairs has me mumbling a "Finally."

"Sorry, sorry, we're here," Jax apologizes, his long legs striding past me as he walks out the front door, duffel bag thrown over his shoulder. Finn is on his heels, gracing me with a remorseless smirk. I give him a deadpan stare in return.

"Where the fuck is Reed?" I growl, already marching out of the house. He's got until I reverse out of the driveway to get his ass in the car. Otherwise, he can *walk* to the damn rink. Well, run, if he wants to make it on time for practice.

The others climb in, and I crank the engine. The final one of our foursome comes jogging out of the house as I start reversing.

"Seriously?" he snarks, practically diving into the back seat. "You were going to leave without me?"

I merely shrug, ignoring all of them as I pull onto the road. Initially, I'm lost in my thoughts, on centering my mind as I navigate the familiar streets toward the Steelhawks' arena.

It's the first day of a new year. My final one as a BSU student. My last first day as a college athlete. Yet it's not nostalgia or longing that I feel as I flick on my indicator and turn into the arena parking lot.

No, it's ironclad determination. Steely resolve.

To dominate. To win. To succeed.

Failure is not an option—not on the ice and definitely not off it.

"I'm telling you, man, she was *fit*." Finn's statement breaks my concentration. Doors slam as we all clamber out of the car.

Jax scoffs as we grab our bags from the trunk before walking as a group toward the back entrance. "I still think you're making the whole thing up."

Finn makes a noise in outrage, but Reed pipes up before he can protest. "I checked that room before we left, and there was no one there."

Is that what he was doing when I was telling him to hurry up? Checking up on some chick who was accidentally given our house as her accommodation? My jaw tics in irritation.

"She's an athlete," Finn argues. "She's probably at a team meeting or something."

"At 6 a.m.?" Reed throws back skeptically. "No one else's coach is a sadist."

"It's not my fault you guys decided to stop at a bar for a beer —without inviting me, by the way—and missed the entire thing." Finn's patience wears thin, that fiery redhead temper of his beginning to spark.

"You're telling me a girl had the chance to spend the night

with the best of the Steelhawks, and she tucked herself away in a bedroom?" Reed scoffs. "Yeah, I'm not buying it."

Finn shrugs, but it's a little stiff. "Not like she gave me enough time to tell her anything. The second she was over the threshold, she asked me where the spare room was and high-tailed it up there. She probably had no idea whose house she slept in last night."

Jax and Reed continue their argument with Finn, but I let their bickering wash over me as we step into the arena and make a beeline for the locker room to get ready for our first practice of the most important season of my life.

The one that will determine whether I get drafted into the NHL or prove my dad right—that I'm *not* good enough—and go crawling back on my hands and knees to his small mechanic business in butt-fuck nowhere, begging for a minimum-wage job.

I shake my head, dispelling that miserable thought.

No. This year is *our* year.

It's *my* year.

My year to lead our team to victory. To impress the scouts and be a first pick at the draft. To step up and prove I can be the leader Coach expects. Become the player I've been training my entire life to be.

This is the year I'll prove my father wrong. Prove—

My internal pep talk comes to a screeching halt as I open the locker room door, finding...a *girl* in my domain. One with a small, upturned nose and high cheekbones that look carved out of marble. Wavy, chestnut brown hair falls past her shoulders, and hazel-green eyes, golden flecks glinting beneath the harsh fluorescent lights, bounce warily over the four of us as she lifts her head at our sudden appearance. Her full lips are pressed into a flat, no-nonsense line, robbing them of any softness.

Nothing about her expression is welcoming, but that doesn't

stop her from being, well, beautiful. Her facial features, somehow sharp and soft at the same time, draw me in as I stare unblinkingly into those emerald depths.

"Who the fuck are you?"

The curt words are out of my mouth before I can reel them back in. But seriously? Today, of all days, some woman has to sneak into our locker room. Which one of my idiotic teammates fucked the crazy chick?

A low whistle comes from behind me, Finn craning to see past my broad shoulders. "Dylan?" He smacks one of the others. "I told you she was real! Wait...what are you doing here?"

Dylan?

My eyes narrow, and suddenly, I'm seeing her differently. As she unhurriedly gets to her feet, facing off against us, I rake my gaze over her again. Slower this time, noticing the details I missed before. There's nothing delicate about the way she stands, feet planted and shoulders squared. Her posture is tense, chin lifted as though ready for a fight. Those hazel eyes? They're not soft or doe-like; they're sharp, calculating. Astute. Like she's already assessed every single one of us and decided how great of a threat we are. Her lips are still pressed into that grim line, but it's not nervousness—it's determination.

Then there's what she's wearing: practice gear.

No, Dylan has not found herself in the boys' locker room by accident. Nor is she some puck bunny or crazed groupie hoping for a good time or an autograph.

She's got on black hockey pants with the familiar padding, a Bermuda blue jersey with the Steelhawks logo stretched over her chest. Her elbows and knees are already strapped with protective gear, and her gloves sit on the bench beside her. She's not fully suited up—no helmet or skates yet—but she's ready. Like she *belongs* here.

Except she doesn't.

"If you're looking for the girls' hockey team, they practice at the rink in town," Finn continues, likely seeing what I am but interpreting it differently.

"She's not here for the girls' team," I state succinctly.

Those sharp eyes snap to mine, her face giving nothing away. Silence stretches between us. The guys have stepped up beside me, forming a semicircle in front of her. The only sound in the room is the swish of the door as other team members arrive, slipping inside and standing quietly off to the side as they take in the strange confrontation.

"Are you?"

Coach had told us we were getting a junior transfer, but the only information he'd volunteered was a name.

A name that perfectly suits the five-foot-eight storm standing before me, hazel eyes burning with fire and determination like she's spent her entire life proving herself to people like us. There's a wariness there too, a guarded edge, but it only sharpens the challenge pouring off her in waves. This isn't just some transfer. This is a player who's here to take what she wants, and it's pretty damn clear she doesn't care if she has to fight us to get it.

"No."

That one word is delivered with crisp curtness, her tone unforgiving. Unrepentant of the mayhem her presence here is about to unleash.

I can feel the guys bristle around me, the tension only escalating when those plump lips hitch up in a mocking smirk.

"I'm your new left winger."

Fuck. Me.

This can't be happening.

Of all the years, Coach chooses the one where *I'm* the captain to bring a girl onto the team.

Chaos erupts at her declaration, the locker room falling into pandemonium. Everyone talks over one another, shouting "Hell no" and "You can't be serious" until the noise becomes a pounding in my skull. The entire time, the girl—*Dylan*—stands there, watching it all with shrewd vigilance. She knows exactly what sort of bomb she's just set off, and yet there's not an ounce of remorse in her expression.

Her eyes make their way back to mine, our gazes latching on. I don't have a clue what she's thinking, her facial expressions giving nothing away. Yet, the longer I stare into those liquid green-and-gold pools, the more distant the uproar around us becomes. It's almost as though I'm being pulled away—away from my team and from what matters.

Requiring more force than I'll ever admit, I wrench my gaze away and bellow, "Enough!"

The room falls deathly quiet, everyone turning to see what their captain has to say. Scanning the faces of men I've played alongside for the last number of years, a lump forms in my throat at the confidence shining back at me. These men trust me to fix this. To make it right.

The problem is, I don't have the first fucking clue how to do that.

When I woke up this morning, prepared to deliver my first speech as captain, I did not expect to face *this*.

"Cap," Matthews, a second-line sophomore, starts. "Tell us this isn't true. We can't seriously be expected to play with a girl on the team. We'll be a laughingstock!"

Thankfully, Coach chooses that moment to make an appearance, saving me from having to tell the team I'm as clueless as they are.

Gaze flicking around the room, he grunts, "Good, you're all here. And I see you've met the newest addition."

"Coach," Reed interjects. "This can't be for real."

"What can't be for real?" Coach challenges.

Looking at Coach as though he's going senile—and perhaps he is; he is getting up there in years after all—Reed flings his arm out toward Dylan. "You can't seriously be putting a girl on the team."

"I am, and I have."

Well, fuck. There goes any possibility that this was all one big misunderstanding. I'd really been hoping the girl was just batshit crazy or masterfully pulling off some sorority dare.

"She'll be crushed the first time someone checks her," Reed continues, undeterred.

"Your concern is noted and appreciated, Reed." Clearly, Coach is not registering the hostility blazing from his eyes. Reed is not pointing out how easy it would be for any of us to snap a bone in her lithe little body out of *concern*. "However, the decision has been made. If Dylan is incapable of hacking it on the ice, then she is free to withdraw from her position. Until such a time, she is as much a member of this team as anyone else in this room, and I expect her to be treated as such." When his words are met with stony silence, he snaps, "Do I make myself clear?!"

Choruses of "Yes, Coach," and "Yes, sir" deafen the room, and Coach nods in approval. "Good, then get changed. I want to see every single one of you out there in five minutes or you'll be doing suicides for the rest of practice."

He breezes out through the locker room door as quickly as he appeared. I hadn't wanted to question him in front of everyone else, but unable to let it go, I chase after him.

"Coach," I call, jogging down the hall to catch up with him. "I don't understand." Searching his eyes, I question, "Is this some sort of publicity stunt?" Why else would he allow a girl on the team? "'Cause Reed is right. She's going to get herself hurt out there. Not to mention that she will make a blatant weak point that all of our opponents will attack. No other team will take us seriously, and we can kiss our chance at making it to the Frozen Four goodbye."

There had been a hint of humor in Coach's eyes when I started talking, but it had burnt out by the end of my little speech.

"I can assure you, Maddox, I would *never* put someone's health at risk—nor the success of this team—for a mere *publicity stunt*." He practically spits the words at me. "As for our chances of making it to the championships." He points a calloused finger at the closed locker room door. "I believe *that girl* is our best shot of making it this year."

He must see the doubt written all over my face because he turns to face me fully. "Ethan, you're their captain. That team in there will look to *you* for guidance. They'll follow *your* lead. I've told Dylan that she has to bring her A game, to impress not only me but all of you. But she won't even get a shot at doing that if every single guy in there is out to get her. Prove to me that you're the captain this team needs. That you can be the captain I know you're capable of."

With that hard-hitting statement, he walks off, leaving me staring after him with no idea how the fuck to move forward.

THREE

UNSURPRISINGLY, things went downhill after my warm welcome in the locker room. Everyone on the team gave me such a wide berth throughout practice that you'd think I was carrying the bubonic plague.

Despite the distance, from the second practice began, with dynamic warm-ups and drills, I felt eyes on me. It didn't matter whether I was sitting on the bench while the defense ran drills or on the ice performing wrist shots. I was constantly being watched. Assessed. Judged.

I'd forgotten how exhausting it is. As if an early morning practice after a restless night's sleep in the new house I now share with *four* of my teammates isn't exhausting enough.

By the time practice ended, I was so done with peopling for the day.

Except I couldn't go back to my room and hide out there. I wasn't yet ready to face my new roommates. Their outrage. Their questions. *Hell no.* Yesterday, I'd deliberately hightailed it to my room as soon as Finn invited me inside. I couldn't have sat downstairs with him and the others once they returned and pretended I wasn't who I am. Nor was I comfortable admitting the truth. I'd wanted the news to come out the way it did—on territory I was familiar with. In a setting where I felt confident. Where *I* was in control.

However, because I hid away in my room last night, I didn't get the chance to suss out who else I'd be living with. But I'd hazard a guess they're the three other Steelhawks who entered the locker room with Finn this morning: Ethan Maddox, Jaxon "Jax" Keller, and Kyle Reed—my archnemesis since it's his spot I plan on taking. Sorry, Kyle. I'd say it's nothing personal, but I'm pretty sure he won't see it that way when he gets beat out by a girl.

To say I'm intimidated to be sleeping under the same roof as *three* of the prime NHL draft picks for this season would be an understatement. I've admired Ethan's hand-stick coordination from afar for years now. And the way he moves down the ice is just... I'd love to know how someone his size can move with such explosive agility. It should be impossible, and yet Ethan Maddox makes the impossible possible.

Plus, have you seen that guy when he takes his helmet off? *Delicious.* That's literally the best word to describe him. He is a *tall* glass of water in the height of summer. Wavy brown hair that he's never quite able to contain. Pale blue eyes that pierce right through you. Sharp jawline with a five-o'clock shadow that makes me shiver, imagining how it would feel against my skin. Today was my first time seeing him up close without his helmet and gear on, and he was even more spectacular than I could have imagined. I struggled to keep my eyes off him.

Of course, any time I managed to rip my gaze away, it would land on either Finn or Jax. Both as cruelly hot, and also star players and shoo-ins for the NHL. Their talent on the ice is unmatched. So is their talent off the ice...or so I hear. Finn has playboy written all over him, and his reputation as a ladies' man precedes him.

Where it's evident that Finn uses his charisma and flirty winks to get what he wants, Jax is his opposite. He's quiet, contemplative. He didn't say a word this morning, yet I could tell he was taking in the entire confrontation, assessing it from a hundred different angles.

He's built like a tank, towering above the other players and easily twice as wide as I am. With jet-black hair and matching eyes. He paints an intimidating picture. One that has me hoping I don't run into him some night on my way to the bathroom. It's always the quiet ones you need to watch out for, so I'll be keeping a close eye on Mr. Tall, Dark, and Broody.

I was surprised to see Kyle with them. He's not in the same league as the others, although, I guess, considering they're all seniors, it makes sense that they live together. Truthfully, if Kyle wasn't my competition, I'd have no idea who he was. He doesn't stand out on the ice. Not the way the others do. Don't get me wrong, he's a good player, but I'm better.

Which is why, in a few short weeks when Bea—*Coach*—announces the lines for this year, he'll be relegated to second while I'll be sitting up front in first.

Having delayed the inevitable long enough, it's early evening when I pull up to the curb out front of the house. If I want to avoid sleeping in my car tonight, I need to go in and get the second standoff of the day out of the way.

Who knows, maybe it won't be as bad as the first one.

Ha, yeah. Who am I kidding?

It's bad enough that I'm invading their team, but now I'm also invading their home life? They are going to be pissed with a capital P. And I can't totally blame them. Change is challenging. To have that change happen on two fronts isn't easy to deal with. I just hope when they go away and think about it and allow the reality of the situation to settle in, that they'll stop being so defensive about having someone who doesn't have a certain appendage dangling between her legs invading their territory.

Opening the front door, I walk into a narrow hallway. Coats are hung up on hooks, shoes are haphazardly kicked to the side, and duffel bags are dropped ceremoniously by the door. I'm hit in the face with the stench of sweat, my face scrunching. *Jesus.* How long have those duffels been sitting there? Can men not grasp the concept of sticking their sweaty gear in the washing machine as soon as they get home?

The hallway opens into a large living room with two three-seater sofas and a smaller cuddle chair. A ridiculously large TV is hung on the wall with game consoles lined up beneath it. I was too frenzied last night to take anything more in before bolting up the stairs, so I take the time now to run my eyes over the dark wood paneling, the thick brown window frames, and cream walls.

The hardwood floor beneath my feet is scraped and scarred from decades of abuse, and everything screams masculinity, but the space is surprisingly cozy, with light flooding the room through the large bay window.

On my right is the kitchen with wooden cupboards and granite countertops. A large island sits in the middle of the room, barstools along one side, and a kitchen table that seats six set to the left. Other than this morning's dishes stacked in the sink, the place is surprisingly clean and tidy.

I know they haven't explicitly cleaned up for me, and some of the tension leaves my shoulders. *At least they aren't complete slobs.* I hadn't realized until now that I'd been worried about that, but I can live with smelly practice gear as long as the house is clean.

While I've been taking in the space I'll be calling home for the rest of the year, all four of them have been watching *me*. I'd made a point of ignoring their presence in the living room, but now I've nowhere left to look but at them.

Slowly, taking a bolstering breath, I swivel my gaze in their direction. Finn and Kyle sit side by side on one of the sofas, elbows on their knees and gaming controllers forgotten in their hands as they stare at me with wary and reserved expressions. Jax is lounging on the other sofa, arm slung over the back of the cushion. He's attempting to be casual, but there's no hiding the calculating look in his eyes.

Ethan is the only one who has gotten to his feet. His posture is closed off, with his muscular arms crossed over his broad chest and lips pressed into a flat line.

I watch them, and they watch me, no one breaking the tense silence. Perhaps they're as unsure about what to say as I am.

"You didn't think to say anything last night?" Finn practically growls, tossing his controller carelessly onto the coffee table.

Or not.

"It made sense to do it with the entire team present." I can see the argument blazing in his eyes before he even opens his mouth, and I cut him off. "Besides, I was as caught off guard seeing you as you were me."

His brow furrows. "So you knew who I was then?"

"Kind of essential to know who I'll be lining up with, don't you think?"

A scoff has my gaze snapping to Kyle, my jaw setting. Shifting my attention to their captain, I state, "Ethan Maddox. Center and this year's captain. Twenty-six goals last season. Thirty-nine assists. Second in the conference for points per game, right behind that winger from Valehurst. You're one of the smartest players on the ice—rarely penalized, never out of position. You can control the tempo of a game almost single-handedly."

His jaw tightens, but there's a flicker of surprise in his eyes. I keep going.

"Finn," I say next, shifting my focus to him. The smirk he'd been wearing falters a little. "Right wing. You led the league in blocked shots last season—ninety-one total. You stood in front of more pucks than most goalies do in a season. You play like a wrecking ball—doesn't matter if it's an opponent or a wall, you're going through it. Nobody hits harder or fights dirtier when it counts, and every guy on this team knows it."

Long gone is Finn's smirk, his lips slightly parted in surprise, even as he crosses his arms over his chest.

Next, I turn to Jax. He doesn't look amused. "You're the anchor," I tell him. "Best defenseman in the division. You make every play look easy, like you see the game three steps ahead of everyone else. You led the team in ice time last season, and it wasn't even close. Whether it's a power play or penalty kill, you're the guy they trust to shut it down. Without you, this team wouldn't win half the games they do."

Unlike the others, Jax shows no outward reaction, but his gaze never breaks from mine, telling me he heard every word.

Finally, I look at Kyle. His lip curls in a sneer. "And you," I say, my voice calm. "Left wing. Eighteen points. Third in the league for turnovers. But you're a grinder. You get into the dirty areas and screen goalies like it's second nature. When you're in front of the net, you make it almost impossible for the other team to see the puck." A smugness enters Kyle's eyes, but I don't let him sit in it for too long. "That said," I continue, keeping my tone light, like I'm just making an observation and not that I've obsessed over his abilities and skills to ensure I can do better. Play harder. "If you focused on improving your positioning on rebounds, you'd probably double your scoring. And if you tightened up your puck management on zone entries, you'd create more opportunities for your line."

If I thought he was sneering at me before, he's now outright glaring. "Oh, is that so?" His voice drips with sarcasm.

I don't allow myself to get swept into an argument with him. I already know he's the type to tell me I'm wrong until he's blue in the face, even though everyone in this room knows I'm right—not that they'd admit it out loud.

Instead, I shift my attention back to their captain. The man I need to impress upon that I'm here, and I'm not going anywhere. That I *will* prove myself, and he should get on board already and let me do my thing.

"I know who you all are," I finish, letting my gaze sweep over them. "I've studied your games, your stats, your plays. I've studied every facet of every member of this team."

My declaration is met with silence until a jeer cracks through the air like a whip. I don't even need to look to know who it came from.

"Reciting some easily obtained stats proves nothing," Kyle states, collapsing back against the sofa as though done with this entire conversation. "If anything, it makes me think you're a crazed fan or obsessed groupie, rather than a genuine player."

The muscle in my jaw tics. One thing I know already, Kyle and I are *not* going to get along.

As if sensing the escalating tension between us, Ethan interjects, "Seems a little unfair that you know all about us, and we know next to nothing about you."

My gaze slides to his, holding that sharp, blue stare before I nod. "Four goals, eleven assists. Fifteen points total last season."

Ethan raises an eyebrow, and Finn's lips twitch like he's holding back a laugh. Kyle doesn't even bother; he snorts outright. "Not exactly first-line numbers," he taunts.

"No," I agree calmly, not allowing any frustration to show on my face. "They're not. But you can only do so much when your entire team is working against you."

"Entire team?" Finn interrupts, confused.

"Wait." It's the first time Jax has spoken, his voice a low baritone that throws me for a second. As though he just delivered something deep and meaningful, everyone in the room turns to look at him, but he continues looking at *me*, head tilted to one side. I can practically see the cogs spinning as he puts the puzzle pieces together. "You're the Northern Summit girl." A disbelieving laugh slips past his lips. "I can't believe I didn't see it before."

Dismissing me, he turns to his buddies. "The girl on the NSU team."

All of their heads snap back to mine.

"Jesus, they've been the laughingstock of the league these past two years," Kyle sneers.

"They've been playing like shit," Ethan observes, eyes narrowed on me as if it's *my* fault. If men didn't have such fragile egos, we'd have dominated the league, and my stats would be ranked up there with Ethan's, Finn's, and Jaxon's. So don't put that shit on me!

"Fuck me, what the hell is Coach thinking?" Groaning, Kyle buries his face in his hands.

"Look," Ethan says, lips pursed in consideration. "I don't know what your game is, but this is our senior year. Our last one playing college hockey. *Our shot* to secure a career in the NHL. It's nothing personal, but I refuse to let anything interfere with that. You might be a decent enough player, but you don't belong on this team."

A decent enough player?! I've never been so insulted.

"That isn't your call to make, *Captain*," I tell him flatly, before shaking off my irritation. Huffing an exhale, I say in a calmer tone, "Look, we don't have to like each other. We don't even need to get along. You play your game, and I'll play mine, and we'll all get what we want this season."

Sensing that this conversation will only go downhill if I hang around any longer, I step back into the hall before turning and fleeing up the stairs. Let them think what they want. I didn't come here to butt heads with obtuse hockey players. I came here to *prove* myself.

Which is exactly what I'm going to do.

I just wish I didn't have to live here, under the same roof as all of them. Unfortunately, I don't have a choice. I stopped by administration after practice, but the woman behind the desk barely spared me a glance before telling me there was no available housing and essentially implying I either suck it up or find private accommodation. I spent the rest of the afternoon scouring the web for listings, but everything near campus was already taken. So it looks like I'm stuck living with four guys who hate me.

As I close my bedroom door behind me, a sinking stone settles in my gut. Letting my head fall back against the wood, I close my eyes and send up a silent prayer that this year doesn't end up like the others—with a team sabotaging my every move, cutting me off from plays altogether, and having to fight just to touch the puck.

All I want is to play hockey. Why is that so damn difficult?

FOUR

"DRINKS AT THE STANLEY!" Finn declares to the locker room. It's Saturday, and we've just finished our final practice of the week.

The room descends into chaos, guys hooting and hollering while others bang their fists against the doors of their lockers. From the corner of my eye, I catch sight of Dylan, stripped to her sports bra and tight shorts that mold to her thighs and ass like a second skin that she wears underneath her gear. Grabbing her towel and a change of clothes, she hightails it to the showers without sparing any of us a glance. Despite being surrounded by people she barely knows, she's at ease in a locker room full of guys who tower over her. Or at least, she does an excellent job of acting like she is.

Other than at practices, I've barely seen her all week. She's out of the house before any of us get up in the mornings, and she somehow manages to sneak in at night without anyone noticing. It's clear she's avoiding us, although I'm not sure how long she thinks she can keep that up for.

Tensions are brewing—at home *and* on the ice.

After that first day, when she blew the minds of every Steelhawks player by announcing she was the new addition to the team, Ethan pulled us all aside and told us to simply ignore her. His order had been met with scoffs and challenges. Even I was skeptical. I mean, has he *seen* her? With her sharp eyes that don't miss a thing and her tight, lithe body, Dylan Carter is *impossible* to ignore.

He convinced the guys by wisely reminding them that until Roster Day, there's no point in worrying about her. After all, she might not even be placed. She could end up warming the bench for the entire season, never seeing a minute of ice time.

The only problem with Cap's logic is that...she's *good.* Seriously fucking good on the ice. I know I'm not the only one unable to take my eyes off her when she's got skates on her feet and a stick in her hand. The way she handles the puck and weaves around behemoth players as though they are practice dummies. I don't know if it's her lighter frame that makes her so damn quick, but in the time it takes to blink, she's across the rink, ready to sink the puck in the opponent's net. While I'd never say it aloud, she's the fastest forward we've got.

And I'm not the only one who has noticed.

As the week has progressed and we've seen more and more of what she's capable of, some of the other guys have started to grow antsy. They're nervous—as many of them should be. It's clear she's gunning for their spots. It wouldn't surprise me if Coach put her on the third line. Heck, maybe even the second.

The room is abuzz with chatter, everyone happy to see the end of a long week. More than a few of my teammates are moving stiffly, freshmen still adjusting to the rigorous preseason schedule, and more senior students making it obvious they slacked in their conditioning over the summer—idiots.

Someone who has no issue moving with grace and stealth? Dylan Carter. She has breezed through the entire week as though two grueling practices a day, plus daily strength training and cardio workouts, are the norm.

"Ready to go?" Ethan claps me on the shoulder. He's changed out of his gear into a pair of formfitting jeans and a loose T-shirt. I realize I'd been distracted watching Dylan tie up her laces and pack up. Even now, I watch as she throws her bag over her shoulder and strides toward the door. She doesn't say goodbye to anyone, and no one else notices her slip quietly from the room.

Shaking her from my thoughts, I face Ethan. "Yeah, man. A drink sounds good."

Half an hour later, the team has commandeered all three booths along the back wall of The Stanley. The bar is steadily filling up—thanks to social media, any students already on campus know we're here. They flock to us like birds to water. It'll only get worse when the school year starts, which is why I agreed to come out tonight, when it's quieter. I can't deal with the craziness when it's full throttle.

I'm sitting in the middle of our group, elbows on the table, my beer sweating against my palm as I listen to the guys unwind.

"So there I am, half asleep on the bus," Finn regales, grinning like he's already cracking himself up. His voice carries easily over the music and noise around us. He's got the entire table's attention, like always, his hands gesticulating wildly as he tells his story. "And Griff decides it's the perfect time to dump a bottle of water on my head. Not just a splash—no. Full-on arctic shower."

Griffin, seated a few spots down, leans back against the booth, his smirk unapologetic.

"I wake up choking, thinking I'm drowning, and who's standing over me? Griffin. Laughing his ass off like a damn psycho."

The team descends into hoots of laughter, a couple of guys slapping the table.

"I don't know how you didn't kill him," Kyle retorts, shaking his head.

"Ha." He tried.

Griffin grins savagely.

"Fucker knew I was out to get him." Finn shakes his head, before pointing a finger at Griffin. "I *will* get you—one day, when you least expect it."

There's a primal gleam in Griffin's eye. Nothing that maniac enjoys more than a challenge. "Bring it, O'Rourke."

"Might wanna sleep with one eye open this season," Finn taunts. He might be smiling, but there's a viciousness behind it that lets me know he's not joking.

Ethan shakes his head at their back-and-forth, but he doesn't comment. He knows as well as any of us that, as important as it is to focus on the game, it's vital that we all let off steam. So long as their antics don't get out of hand, he'll let it slide.

"We're gonna crush it this year," a sophomore whose name I can't remember says, smirking as he leans in. "All the way, baby."

"Hell yes!" Kyle raises his glass, the rest of the guys following as they stamp their feet, and a cheering of "Steelhawks! Steelhawks! Steelhawks!" commences until the entire bar joins in the chant.

"No one is touching us this year," Kyle continues, shouting to be heard. "Not Northern Summit, not Eastwick, not Blackharbor, and not whoever we face in the NCAAs—"

"Yeah," a freshman player snorts, "because having a girl on the NSU team worked so well for them. What a joke." He shakes his head, and murmurs of agreement go up from the guys as the tension shifts.

Kyle leans forward, his grin sharp. "Yeah, well, good thing Coach isn't that dumb. No way he gives her a starting spot."

"What if he does?" someone asks him.

He shrugs, his tone light but laced with something darker. "We'll fix his mistake."

His words hang in the air, and I use my position as the silent observer to suss out the other players at the table. Some are frowning, not entirely on board with Kyle's insinuation, but more than a few look as though they agree.

I meet Ethan's gaze. His eyes are dark with the same tension. For the most part, Kyle is all talk, but there's been the odd occasion where he's taken shit too far. In that look, we both silently agree that we need to keep an eye on him. None of us are happy about having Dylan on the team, and I have no idea how it will work if Coach actually gives her a position, but that doesn't mean we want any harm to come to her. Hell, part of the reason for *not* wanting her on the team is because she's bound to get hurt. It's only a matter of time before a larger player crashes into her and she breaks a bone. It's just *reckless* on her part. Stupid.

Ethan's chair creaks as he sits forward, his jaw tight as he surveys the players gathered around us. "You want to win this year?" he asks. His voice is low, calm, but it cuts through the table with sharp precision.

Kyle freezes, his grin faltering, and the freshman straightens in his seat. The whole table goes silent.

Ethan's gaze sweeps the group, sharp and assessing. "Then focus on *your* game. Not hers. Not anyone else's."

He nods toward the freshman. "Fletcher, you've got speed, but your corners are sloppy. Work on that. And, Matthews—" Ah, that's the sophomore's name. "—Coach already told you you're not reading the plays fast enough. Fix it."

Matthews nods, all of the guys' postures shifting under their captain's scrutiny. Even Kyle doesn't argue, though I can see his jaw clench as he sips his beer.

"Do your job," Ethan finishes, leaning back again. "The rest will take care of itself."

The table goes quiet for a beat before Finn breaks it, leaning over to clap Fletcher on the back. "Guess you're running suicides all next week, huh?"

The tension snaps, and the laughter returns, the conversation moving on. The guys start talking about their summers. I only contribute to the conversation when someone asks a direct question. Otherwise, I nurse my beer and observe.

The table slowly empties as the night wears on, guys peeling off one by one. By the time I decide to call it, half the team's either at a dartboard or chasing hookups. I push back my chair and drain the last of my drink.

"You heading out?" Ethan asks, disengaging from his conversation with a junior player to look my way as I stand from the table.

"Yeah."

"All right. It was good to have you out with us." He knows well enough by now that this isn't my scene. Crowds. People. I'd far rather be set up in the living room with a beer and my headset on while I play *Call of Duty*. I give him a curt nod. "See you at home." He returns to his conversation as I stride away from the table, the crowd parting to let me through.

I catch sight of Finn sucking face with some girl at the bar. His mischievous smirk gets him into any girl's panties faster than anyone I know, and I shake my head as I move past him.

"You leaving?" Griffin steps into my path, blocking my exit. He's got a girl glued to his side, sucking on his neck like she's a vampire and he's her next meal.

"Yeah," I grunt.

"Missing out, bro. I'm sure Misty here would be down to share."

The girl detaches her lips from his neck long enough to correct, "Missy." Her gaze flicks my way, running up and down my broad six-foot-four frame before smirking lasciviously. "The more, the merrier."

She reaches out to touch my arm, and I shift so her hand falls short. Why the fuck do girls think they have the right to touch you? If I did that to her, I'd be hauled into the police station under sexual assault charges.

"Maybe some other time." Or never.

Unfazed, Griff winks at me as he hauls her off, the two of them disappearing into the crowd and granting me free passage to the exit.

I'm already socialed out for the entire year.

WALKING INTO THE HOUSE, I drop my keys onto the small table by the door before stopping in my tracks at the faint glow from the TV. Stepping into the doorway, I pause. Dylan is sitting on the couch, pizza box open on the coffee table, her legs tucked under her. She's focused, eyes locked on the screen where game footage plays—*our* game footage from last season. I remember this game against Blackharbor. The forward line is currently on the ice, Ethan leading a rush.

She's not just watching it, though—she's studying it. Leaning forward slightly like she's memorizing every play, every movement with that same look of focused concentration she wears on the ice.

With her distracted, I allow myself a moment to take her in. She's casually dressed in sweats and an oversized T-shirt, her feet bare and hair scraped back into a messy bun on the top of her head. There's not a stitch of makeup on her face. In fact, I haven't seen her wear makeup once. It's not what I'm used to when it comes to girls. Most of the girls that hang around the team are dolled up to the nines in skirts short enough to intentionally show off whatever color G-string they are wearing and a face caked with enough makeup that you wouldn't have a hope of recognizing them without it. Even most female athletes put on makeup when they aren't at practice or in the sports center. But not Dylan.

She must feel my eyes on her as her head snaps toward me. For a second, she stares, like a deer caught in the headlights. Then she moves. Quickly and efficiently, she grabs the pizza box and the remote, planning to run for it.

"You don't have to go." The words are out before I've fully thought them through.

She pauses, frowning slightly.

I shrug, stepping farther into the room. "It's your house too. You don't have to hide."

Still frozen in place, pizza box in hand and remote pointed at the TV, her gaze flicks over my shoulder.

"It's just me," I tell her. "The others are still out. Probably will be for a while longer." I don't know why I say *that*. I have no idea when the others will be home. For all I know, Finn has picked up some girl and is bringing her back here as we speak. Ethan will stay at the bar until the last of the team heads out, and who the fuck knows with Kyle.

She hesitates for a second longer, and I expect her to grab the last of her belongings and leave. But then she exhales, slowly places the pizza box back on the table, as if she's liable to change her mind at any second, and sinks down onto the sofa.

Cautiously, as though approaching a wild animal, I move to sit on the chair across from her. An awkward silence settles between us. Lifting my chin toward the screen, I ask her, "This what you do every night? Watch game footage?"

She looks at me, her expression unreadable. "I do whatever I have to do to be the best." Her voice is calm, but there's an edge to it. Like she feels she has to defend herself. Justify her actions.

I nod. I mean, I get it. We all watch game footage. Maybe not every night, but the guys and I frequently sit down to review tapes when the season gets underway. Truth be told, if I were joining a new team, I'd be doing the same thing she is.

Leaning back in the seat, I spread my legs, posture relaxed, as I shift my focus to the television. "Last season, huh?"

She pauses momentarily, and I feel her eyes on me before she presses play, relaxing—although not as much as before—into the sofa.

The footage resumes, the game back in play. Every so often, she pauses it, pointing out moves or plays.

"See here?" Ethan has just sped down the ice, weaving past two defensemen like they don't exist. Finn trails a few paces behind, perfectly positioned for the pass that never comes. Instead, Ethan cuts too close to the net and takes a desperate shot, which the goalie deflects with ease.

Dylan's finger is pointed at the screen. "Ethan's great on the rush, but he hesitates for just a second too long before passing. It gives the defense time to adjust. Finn should have had that puck, and the team would have been up early in the game."

Not waiting for any comment or retort from me, she presses play on the remote, and the game continues. Nothing in particular stands out until the puck ricochets off the boards, skidding toward where Reed is camped out on the blue line, stick raised for a slap shot. However, he hesitates, his eyes fixed on a defender instead of the puck. By the time he adjusts, it's too late, and the opposing team clears it.

Pausing, Dylan rewinds, replaying Reed's hesitation in slow

motion. I can't look away as she stares captivated at the screen, her head tilted and lips slightly parted, drinking in everything that's happening. "Kyle's got a strong shot, but he doesn't always read the ice well enough to know where the puck will end up," she accurately deduces, talking mostly to herself rather than me, before absently pressing play again.

While the game unfolds, I watch her, not the TV. She's sharp. Scary sharp. It's not just that she sees everything; it's that she knows how to fix it. Knows how to exploit every weakness like she's playing chess while everyone else is still figuring out checkers. She's breaking down our game with the precision of someone who's lived and breathed hockey her entire life.

And suddenly, I know. She's going to make the roster.

There's no way Coach is benching her. She's too good. Too valuable.

I glance back at the screen before she can catch me staring, but my thoughts are spinning. She might be good—*great*—but she's still a girl. She doesn't have the strength to take a hit from someone like Reed, let alone Ethan. Or me. And if the other teams catch wind that we've got a girl on the ice? They'll go after her. They'll break her.

That's if Reed or the other guys don't get to her first. The way they talked tonight—it wasn't just locker room bravado. It was a warning. Unease settles in my stomach as I watch her dissect another play. Because no matter how good she is, no matter how sharp her instincts are, I can already see the cracks forming.

This team isn't ready for her, and if Coach puts her on the roster, it won't just be the other teams trying to tear her apart—it'll be us.

FIVE

I PUSH open the gym door and stride inside without hesitation, knowing Griffin Price—the Steelhawks' goalie—will already be in the weights area, midway through his workout. It might be 5 a.m., but while every other player is grabbing an extra hour of sleep before a brutal practice session, Griffin and I are the only ones glutton enough for punishment to squeeze in a workout beforehand.

The first day I walked in here and saw him, I nearly turned around and left. I hadn't expected anyone else to be up at this hour, and I definitely wasn't thrilled about being alone in the same room as one of the guys from the team.

However, he barely spared me a glance as I stood frozen in the doorway in indecision, and after a momentary debate, I marched over to the treadmill. I knew to be wary, but no way was I letting this team keep me out of the weights room.

I deliberately left my earbuds out, not trusting that he wouldn't ambush me when I was distracted with my workout, but from the corner of my eye, I'd watched while he finished his sets in the weights area before walking out. All without even seeming to realize I was there.

Since then, he's ignored me, and I've ignored him, and it's been...fantastic, really. It sounds like I'm insane, to consider being left alone is as good as it gets, but for me, it's the truth. I couldn't even set foot in the gym at Northern Summit without being hassled and jeered. When that didn't put me off, the guys had escalated, smearing peanut butter over the weights bar, messing with the machines, and even removing all the weight plates from the room. Once, they actually managed to rig the treadmill so it wouldn't stop when I pressed the button. And when I tried to slow it down, it sped up until I was going so fast I thought I would pass out.

They played it all off as normal hazing, of course. But I knew. I could see it in their eyes. They didn't want me there, and they were willing to do whatever it took to get me to leave.

Unfortunately, they eventually succeeded.

And not in a way I ever thought they would.

Shaking my head to dispel those thoughts, I focus on my workout, first jumping onto the treadmill. I start with a warm-up jog to loosen my muscles and get the blood pumping before amping up the pace until I'm breathing hard and sweat sticks to my black sports bra.

I might be comfortable wearing my earbuds now, but I keep one eye on Griffin as he goes through his rounds of squats before moving on to bench presses.

He's shirtless, wearing only loose basketball shorts that hug his trim waist before falling to his knees. With the angle of the weights bench, I have the perfect view of his hard, sculpted chest, the straining of his biceps as he pushes his arms straight into the air. There isn't an ounce of fat on him, the ridges of every muscle plain to see and begging to be licked.

It doesn't help that, judging by the amount of weight he's lifting, he could easily bench-press *me*. There's just something so *hot* about a guy who could effortlessly lift you over his head.

On day three of this peaceful arrangement of ours, I noticed he had his nipples pierced, a loop hanging from each of the taut nubs.

On day five, I discovered he had a tattoo—a long, thin line of some design I've never quite been able to make out, running from his armpit to the waistband of his shorts.

I'm staring at that little strip of black ink now, trying to decipher the lines and squiggles. I'm so caught up in working it out that I don't realize he's stopped lifting the weights bar.

Or that he's staring directly at me.

My red-from-exertion cheeks turn beetroot, and I snap my gaze away, staring steadfastly at the treadmill screen as the miles slowly tick up.

God, I can't believe he caught me looking. How embarrassing!

I hope he doesn't think I'm interested now. Because I'm not. Hockey guys—maybe even athletes in general—are *not* my type, and my number one life rule is officially *do not date people you are on the same team as.*

It's the same as not dating your co-worker.

It gets messy...and fast.

Been there, done that, got the mental scars to prove it.

Doesn't mean I can't quietly admire from afar. From a distance where my heart and judgment aren't at risk. Besides playing hockey at a professional level far superior to what I'd achieve on the girls' team, all the eye candy is the only other benefit to my situation.

Except for when they all whip off their towels after a shower in the locker room. If you ever wondered if a girl could see too much dick, the answer is yes. *Yes,* you most certainly can have too much dick in your face, *especially* arrogant hockey player dick. The juvenile idiots grinding their hips like that's going to entice me to jump aboard.

I deliberately force myself not to look Griffin's way until I reach the five-mile mark—the length of my typical morning runs. Then, wanting to be sure the coast is clear and he isn't lurking around waiting for me to finish, I cast a surreptitious glance around the gym.

Finding it empty, I sigh in relief. Griffin must have finished and left while I was beating myself up. I'd worry I'd scared him out of the room, but a guy like that...no way he was put off by a little awkward gawking.

I may not know much about Griffin, except that he's one of the best college hockey goalies in the country *and* a strange enigma. He seems to me like he's a bit of a loner, but he partakes in the locker room banter and occasionally goes out with the guys. There's always something...*sharp* beneath his exterior, though. Something calculating. *Predatory.* Like he's the apex animal, and we're all just mice dancing to his tune until he decides to snap our necks.

Still, his self-confidence is on par with every other Division One hockey player I've ever met, so I don't stress that he'll have read more into my staring than that it was a passing glance—a moment of distraction.

Which is precisely what it was.

Relaxing fully for the first time since I arrived at the sports center, I finish up on the treadmill and move on to the weights portion of my workout.

AFTER A LONG PRACTICE, during which I was once again ignored by every single member of the team—quite a feat for Finn since we were paired together for drills—I'm off to my first class at BSU.

Working toward a double major in sports management and

sports analytics means that every moment not spent training is spent in the classroom, studying, or completing some assignment.

I knew it would be a lot when I took both on at the beginning of my sophomore year, but since a college player getting into the NHL is around one in four thousand, the chances of a *woman* making it into the league are inordinately less likely.

In fact, the word most commonly used when I express my goals is *impossible*.

However, I find I quite enjoy the challenge of overcoming impossible odds. Much like becoming the only girl in the country to make it onto a boys' Division One college hockey team. I might have had a helping hand from Bear this season, but I made it onto the NSU team all on my own. In fact, I went out of my way to ensure it was only *my* skills and ability that were taken into consideration when they held tryouts for the team.

Since then, my determination to shove it in everyone's face who says it isn't possible has only grown. Still, I'm not an idiot. I know I might be fighting to achieve something that will never happen. I'm prepared for failure, or as prepared as one can be when they have their dream ripped out from beneath them. But if I can't *be* a hockey player, the next best thing is to work with them. With the teams. The league.

As a woman in male sports, no matter what career path I choose, it will be an uphill battle. However, if I can impress them before I have to sit down for an interview and they realize I'm actually a *girl*—yes, I totally plan on using my gender-neutral name to get ahead because a woman needs to use every tool at her disposal to get what she wants in this world—then hopefully they'll see past the tits and lack of a dick and realize I'm more fucking capable than half the men they interview.

Of course, if I can't even get a team of boys to let me play alongside them, what hope do I have of ever having a professional relationship with any of them?

Still, the silent treatment I've been getting from the Steelhawks is a giant leap in the right direction compared to my old team. Although I'm not sure how much longer that will hold up. While I'd happily take an entire season of them icing me out so long as they're willing to play alongside me, I highly doubt I will be so lucky. Especially once Roster Day rolls around.

The twisting in my gut says this is the calm before the storm. I can only hope this one doesn't completely destroy me.

My morning classes are uneventful—mostly the professors explaining the agenda for the semester and what is expected from us. I notice some gazes darting my way, hushed whispers behind hands, but I largely ignore them. It's nothing I'm not used to.

I'm packing up my things after my Data Visualization for Athletes class when a shadow falls over my desk. Lifting my head, I have to crane my neck to look up into the face of the man towering over me. Except, when I finally meet his eyes, he's not staring at my face.

No. His gaze slowly rises over my body, lingering longer than is appropriate on my hips and chest before finally—*finally*—coming to rest on my face. His expression is less than impressed.

"So you're the girl who thinks she can hack it with the boys."

Ah, so it's one of those conversations. What fun.

My gaze flicks from his below-average-looking face to the two equally large and intimidating buddies at his back, both staring at me with curious skepticism. I don't recognize any of their faces, but that doesn't mean they aren't players on the team. Or they could play a different sport at BSU. Equally, they could just be your regular run-of-the-mill, misogynistic douchebags.

Whoever they are, they've picked the wrong girl to mess with.

Even though I'm five-foot-eight and taller than most women, since I'm typically surrounded by hockey players, I'm often the shortest person in the room. So their height doesn't bother me. What does is the fact that they are crowding me, standing while I sit.

Snatching my backpack off the table, my chair scrapes against the floor as I stand. I still have to look up into their faces, but that's nothing new.

"Nope," I say casually.

In mirror symmetry to one another, all three of their brows flatten, and I can see the wheels rotating furiously in their empty heads. *Do we have the right girl? Are the rumors false? I wonder what's for lunch in the cafeteria.*

Putting them out of their misery, I smile slyly. "I *know* I can hack it with the boys."

Before their minds can finish spinning and they can come up with some stupid retort that will bounce off my now hardened-in-steel-and-flames exterior, I shove through them and down the steps of the lecture theatre.

"There are girls' and boys' teams for a reason!" one of them yells after me.

Ignoring them, I shove through the doors, hearing them clang shut behind me as I storm off. They might be right, but the world of sports is changing. It's not as black and white as it once was. The number of female coaches on professional male sporting teams has increased exponentially over the last few years, with last season showing *fifteen* full-time female coaches on various NFL teams.

It's not just the coaching and support staff, either. Fabiola da

Silva is an inline skating savant who regularly competes against men—and kicks their ass. And despite how these small-minded college kids get on, I am *not* the first woman to join a male sports team. Throughout history, women have proven they can play at the same level as men. Hell, assuming I get a spot, I wouldn't even be the first woman to play in the NHL. That supreme achievement goes to Manon Rhéaume who was the goaltender for Tampa Bay Lightning in 1992–1993. She might have only played in exhibition games, but she proved women have just as much of a place in pro-sports leagues as men.

And she's not the only one.

Charlotte Cagigos is a French ice hockey player who plays on an otherwise all-male Division One team.

All over the world, women are stepping into previously male-dominated roles and sports and proving we are just as capable as they are.

Sure, when it comes to hockey, both those women were goalies—a position that offered them the most safety against larger, more aggressive players, but I've never been one to follow in someone else's footsteps. I want to blaze my own path. Plus, goaltending was *not* for me. I hated being stuck near the net and missing out on all the action at the opposite end of the ice.

After my run-in with the intimidating trio, I feel eyes on me more prevalently for the remainder of the day, and I *know* the hushed whispers are about me.

The *woman* on the *men's* hockey team.

The girl who dares defy tradition.

The bitch who's going to prove to them we're entering an entirely different world where women can kick ass just as hard as men.

❄

Now that classes have started, we're limited to one training session a day. However, I've never been a fan of just *one* daily practice. Once a day is for those who aren't committed. For those who are in this game for the status, the attention, the girls.

Since as far back as I can remember, I've always trained twice a day—plus a cardio and weights session. Sunday is the only day where I'll maybe—*maybe*—only get on the ice once.

So, after a grueling day of class introductions and being gawked at, I head to the arena.

The rink is cold, and the chill seeps through my hoodie as I enter the arena. The ice is only half lit up, the lights casting long shadows across the boards and giving the place an almost eerie stillness.

While I love seeing the stands packed, breathing in the heady buzz of psyched fans as they scream and cheer, listening to the shudder of bodies being slammed against the boards, skates slicing over ice, and the puck whizzing down the rink, I think I love this stillness more.

Some of my fondest memories are in this stillness.

Of watching my dad skate with the kind of ease that made it look effortless.

Him teaching me, one wobbling step at a time.

Before I can get too caught up in traveling down memory lane, I move toward the edge of the rink. That's when I realize I'm not alone. There's already someone out there.

A dark figure moves in and out of the crease with almost mechanical precision. With broad shoulders, black jersey, and a presence that commands the space between the pipes, there's a cold, controlled intensity in every movement that's unmistakable.

I'm watching Griffin Price in action.

I'm rooted to the spot, captivated as he drops into a butterfly. His knees hit the ice with a dull thud before he slides effort-lessly to his left, pads skimming the surface. He snaps upright, his stick tapping the ice in a rhythm that seems to echo in the silence.

His movements are sharp, purposeful. No wasted effort. Every shift of his body is calculated, every slide and push deliberate.

My eyes trace the muscles of his legs, visible even beneath his goalie gear, the strength in his shoulders as he snaps his stick up to deflect an invisible puck. His agility is unreal, like he's more animal than man in how he moves—quick, predatory, unrelenting.

And his skin—God, his skin practically glows under the dim lights, slick with sweat despite the cold. The memory of seeing him in the gym earlier, his muscles taut and his focus absolute, lingers in the back of my mind. Seeing it in action now, how every ounce of power is being put to use, is...*hot*.

Heady in a way it has no business being.

I force myself to blink, tearing my gaze away. *Focus, Dylan. You didn't come here to gawk.*

Moving to sit on the edge of the nearest bench, I lace up my skates before stepping onto the ice. The familiar bite of the blades against the frozen surface grounds me. I glide slowly at first, letting my legs find their rhythm as I move to the opposite end of the rink.

Griffin doesn't look up, doesn't acknowledge me, but somehow—don't ask me how—I know he's aware I'm here. Turning my back to him, I block him out as effectively as he is blocking me.

Starting with puck control drills, I position the net close to the boards and line up at an angle. Firing the puck against the boards behind the net, I practice catching the rebound and snapping it into the net. The slap of the puck ricocheting off the boards echoes across the rink, loud and sharp. With each *bang* of the rebound, the tension in my shoulders loosens. The world around me fades until it's just me, the ice, and the puck in front of me.

After a while, I shift to sprints. I'd typically do goal line to goal line, but I don't want to encroach on Griffin's space. The shorter distance across the rink makes for a fun challenge as I'm forced to pick up speed faster before slamming to a stop at the other side. Ice kicks up in sprays around me, and my lungs burn, my legs aching as I push myself harder.

From the corner of my eye, I catch Griffin still performing his own drills. He drops low, his stick flashing as he imagines blocking a breakaway shot.

As time ticks on and I move to practice puck handling, a strange kind of camaraderie forms between us. Neither of us speaks. We don't even glance at each other, but there's an energy between us. An understanding. A common goal.

Two players, both driven by the same relentless need to improve. To be better than yesterday. To be better than anyone else.

An hour later, the soft scrape of my skates against the ice is the only noise besides the thrum of my pulse, still buzzing in my ears from the drills I was doing as I gather the cones I scattered around my half of the rink.

Spotting movement in my periphery, I glance in Griffin's direction as he skates toward the gate. He doesn't look over. Doesn't acknowledge me at all, much like when we're in the gym.

The absence of any snide comment or challenge is strange, but it feels...good. Better than it has any right to feel.

I nod to myself, barely holding back a grin. The silence between us, the lack of a demand for me to leave, or an attempt to make me feel out of place—it feels like a small victory. A win. For just a moment, there's peace.

Perhaps we truly do have an unspoken truce.

I can't imagine any of the other guys on the team would have let me be like this. Regardless of Ethan's *ignore her* rule, I doubt anyone else would have let the opportunity pass without making it clear what they really think of my presence on their team.

I guess Griffin doesn't care enough to make a fuss. Goalies are a breed of their own. While they play on a team, they aren't a *part* of it the way the other players are. Their job is individual. It's entirely up to them if they save or let in a goal. There's no group effort. It's one hundred percent solely on them to stop the puck from entering that net. Team dynamics mean fuck all so long as he's performing his job to the best of his capabilities.

Whatever his reason, I don't care. I can live very comfortably in this amnesty we seem to have silently agreed on.

Once off the ice, Griffin quickly removes his skates and grabs his duffel before he's out the door. He doesn't glance back, but I don't expect him to. He's just...gone.

Alone, I dump my cones at the edge before doing an aimless skate around the rink. It's stupid. I know it's stupid, but something about Griffin not giving me trouble feels like a win.

Breathing the cold air deeply into my lungs, I relish having the rink to myself. No pressure. No one telling me where I belong. I'm good here—on my own.

Eventually, I force myself off the ice.

After all, I have roommates to avoid, game tape to review, and reading to do before tomorrow.

SIX

I'M SITTING in the cafeteria on Wednesday morning, enjoying a quiet breakfast after a particularly grueling practice. I poke at my scrambled eggs, tuning out the chatter of students around me, the clattering of plates, and scraping of cutlery as I replay the fiasco.

It was a simple drill. Passing under pressure, keeping the puck moving in tight quarters. One-touch passes. Quick hands; clean execution. Kyle and I were paired up, supposed to work together. It's not the first time I've been paired with other players, or even with Kyle.

But today...I sent him a pass, tape to tape, but instead of taking it cleanly, the puck ricocheted off his stick and skittered across the ice. And because Kyle will look for any excuse to make me look bad, he didn't chase after it. Instead, he rounded on me, his voice cutting through the rink like a slap.

"*Jesus*, Dylan. What did the puck ever do to you? You're supposed to *pass* it, not attempt to take me out with it."

Before I could tell him I didn't hit it *that* hard, he was away on a tangent.

"Thank God your accuracy is shit. You could have done

some serious damage if that had hit me. What if you'd clocked me in the face, huh?" Shaking his head, he'd tacked on, "You seriously need to work on your sloppy passes."

Sloppy.

He called *my* passes sloppy. Even now, I squeeze my fork tighter, wishing I could jam the utensil into Kyle's throat. In my head, I've played that pass a hundred times since this morning. It was clean. The puck was right on target—and no, it wasn't going *too fast.* Kyle just couldn't handle it.

Loosening my grip and focusing on the pile of food in front of me, my fork scrapes across the plate, the sound sharp and grating. It wasn't just what he said, it was the way he said it— loud, pointed, like he wanted everyone in the rink to hear. Like he wanted to make sure I knew my place. And it worked, didn't it? Every guy on the ice stopped what they were doing to look at me like I'd done something wrong.

I chew mechanically on my toast, appetite long gone as I silently fume. I can still feel the weight of their stares, the silent judgment. Like Kyle's words were a confirmation of every single doubt they had about me.

The idea of the drill might have been to build chemistry, to get used to working with a teammate under game-like conditions, but all it did was prove what I already knew—that I'm not welcome in the Steelhawks' arena.

Not in their locker room.

Not on their team.

And definitely not on their ice.

I'm still stewing over the fact that Kyle went on and on until Ethan came over and dragged him away, cheeks flaming just remembering the look Bea—Coach—gave me as I skated off the ice, when the sound of someone clearing their throat drags me back into the here and now.

I blink into the present, finding three girls standing over me.

What is it with this school and everyone walking around in threes and towering over me? Each of them is holding a tray containing food, and for a second, I think they're about to ask if they can sit with me. I've been eating alone all week—not that I mind. I'm plenty used to it.

But, of course, they aren't here to join me. That becomes apparent as I take in the mirroring sneers on each of their faces.

"You think you're better than us?" the one in the middle snarks. Her hair is a perfectly straight bleach-bottle blonde, falling halfway down her back. She's wearing a tight, white, short-sleeved sweater that only enhances the double-D rack she's got going for her. A sliver of creamy skin is visible above the waistband of her baby pink miniskirt, her long legs accentuated by the six-inch heels she's wearing.

Seriously, who wears six-inch heels to class? You're just asking for a broken ankle.

Her friends are similarly dressed—for fashion or attention, I don't know which. Certainly not for comfort or academics. Since I have no idea *who* she or her friends are, I keep my lips tightly sealed.

Twirling a lock of that sunshine blonde hair around her perfectly manicured finger, she continues, "What sort of person goes to such lengths just to get close to *them?*" I still have no clue what she's rambling on about. "If you're not pretty enough to be a puck bunny—which, honey, you're not—then accept your calling in life."

A...what now?

Her minions titter, like her insult is the funniest thing they've ever heard.

"Don't resort to such desperate lengths as to try and get on the same *team* as them."

Ah, of course. I should have known this had to do with a woman being on the all-boys team—*previously* all-boys team.

It takes a moment for her words to penetrate, and when they do, I can't help but laugh. It's a sharp, loud noise that draws the attention of nearby tables, including the one where most of the team is currently situated. I feel their eyes on me, but I don't look away from the girl in front of me.

Smugness bleeds into my expression as I curl one side of my lips in a smirk. "Jealous?"

Lips parted, an undignified scoff escapes her. "Of you?" She makes a point to lower her gaze over my body. I'm wearing sweats and a loose-fitted T-shirt. So no, I don't look anything close to as good as she does, but if she'd gotten up at 5 a.m., ran, and done weights before a two-hour session on the ice, she wouldn't be walking around in that getup either. "Never."

"Then why are you interrupting my breakfast?" My brow furrows in confusion as I make a point of fixing scrambled eggs on top of my toast and taking a massive bite.

With her tray clutched in her hands, she leans in until we're nose to nose. I can smell the sickly-sweet odor of her perfume. It's...gag-worthy.

"Not *one* of them is interested in you."

Slowly chewing my mouthful of food, I raise my eyebrows, eyes going wide in a, *So? What's your point?*

"You might be their plaything on the ice, but *we* are their playthings in bed."

Ewww, nope. I gag around my mouthful of food, and it takes everything in me to swallow and not spit it out. *Bet she doesn't struggle with swallowing. She'd have probably made it look effortless. Even added a fake moan for extra credit.*

She turns to walk away but throws one last parting shot over her shoulder. "Have fun pretending you're one of them, *Bench Bunny.*"

Mouth agape, I don't get the chance to tell her that she can have every single guy on that team. They're all hers. Looks like she already got the memo, though, as she drops her tray in the spot beside Finn. Of course it's Finn she sits beside—playboy extraordinaire. He drapes an arm around her waist like it's second nature to him, turning to face her with that same cheeky smile he used on me that first day when he answered the door.

A smile he hasn't directed my way once since finding out why I'm here. Although it would be pretty hard for him to do that while pretending I don't exist. My gut twists, but I promptly ignore it, tearing my gaze away from Finn.

The other two girls have cozied up beside Kyle and a junior defenseman. I only glance at their table long enough to make my breakfast churn unpleasantly in my stomach before grabbing my things and hightailing it out of the cafeteria.

Bowl of popcorn in hand, I absently shove another handful into my mouth. My eyes are glued to the TV, the dim light illuminating the otherwise dark living room as I lean against the couch cushions, a blanket draped over my lap.

The sound of the movie fills the space. I hadn't planned on watching a movie tonight, but when I saw *A League of Their Own* while flipping through the channels, I couldn't resist.

A night off. Just me, the couch, and a young Tom Hanks. It's been a while since I let myself do something that didn't feel like a calculated move toward a goal.

My hand stalls halfway to my mouth, and I lean forward. Anticipation thrums through my veins as my favorite part of the movie approaches, and I mouth the words as Jimmy Dugan tells Dottie Hinson, "It's supposed to be hard. If it wasn't hard, everyone would do it. The hard is what makes it great."

I internally squeal!

That line gets me every time.

Moisture burns the backs of my eyes, a pang of nostalgia hitting me square in the chest.

The front door slams, yanking me out of the moment. My heart jumps, and I sit up straighter. The blanket slips off my lap, exposing my bare thighs beneath the pajama shorts I'm wearing. Heavy footsteps thud closer before the guys fill the doorway one by one.

Ethan is carrying a stack of pizzas, his expression unreadable as he takes me in, sitting on the couch. Finn is right behind him, his face blank, but his eyes flicker briefly over me before darting away. Kyle follows him in, stopping in his tracks when he spots me.

"What the fuck are you doing?"

Charming as ever. Seems he still hasn't gotten over his *sloppy* stickhandling yesterday.

I raise an eyebrow, returning my focus to the TV and dismissing all of them as I grab a handful of popcorn from the bowl on my lap. "What does it look like I'm doing?"

"Well, you can piss off. We're having a guys' night."

I shrug, popping a kernel into my mouth. "Cool. Enjoy."

From the corner of my eye, I see Kyle's face darken. It's noticeable, even in the low lighting. He's practically vibrating with fury, realizing that he isn't going to get a rise out of me.

Ethan must realize that he's about to blow as he gestures upstairs and mutters, "Just go. We'll deal with this."

Kyle huffs, shifting on his feet before he stomps toward the stairs. "Call me when the she-bitch is gone," he calls over his shoulder before stalking up them. His footsteps smack loudly against each step until a door slams in the distance.

No one moves for a moment before Finn strides forward. He moves faster than I expect, catching me off guard as he snatches the bowl of popcorn from my lap while simultaneously scooping up the remote control before collapsing onto the vacant sofa. His long legs stretch out across the couch, and he rests one hand behind his head on the cushion, the bowl balanced on the hard plane of his abs as he flicks between channels.

"Wha— Hey!" I protest, leaning forward to snatch the remote back.

Focus intent on the TV screen, he acts like I'm an annoying fly buzzing around him as he holds the controller out of my reach.

"Give me that!" I snarl, pushing to my feet to stand over him. "Finn!" He still doesn't acknowledge me, and this time, when I try to grab the remote from him, he stuffs it down the front of his jeans.

I gape at his crotch for a full five seconds before snapping my gaze to his face, my expression one of horror and disgust. "That's just nasty," I hiss at him.

He still doesn't spare me a single glance. Not the flicker of an eye movement. The slight uptilt of his lip. If he pulled that stunt on anyone else, he'd be grinning like a proud momma bear at his own idiocy.

Whirling on Ethan, I point a furious finger at him. "You!"

Lips flattened into a straight line, he arches an eyebrow as if to say, *What?* He's moved farther into the room, depositing the pizza boxes on the coffee table before he stands to face me once again.

"This *pretend I don't exist* rule is bullshit," I tell him. "It's one thing for the team to ignore me when we're at practice, but it doesn't work outside of that." I gesture around us. "How are we supposed to live together when you ignore my very presence?" My throat goes tight, and I have to force out the next words. "You don't get to act like I'm invisible. This is my house, too!"

There is the barest hitch in my voice, and I snap my mouth

shut, moving to fold my arms over my chest and stare him down like I didn't nearly show him or the others a hint of weakness.

Shoving back my shoulders, I lift my chin and, in a haughty voice, say, "Unless you all plan on moving out?"

His nose wrinkles, the only reaction he gives. Still, I can tell he's considering what I said. Finn must see it, too, as he finally unglues his eyes from the TV to look at his captain.

When it seems as though Ethan isn't going to say anything at all—some captain he is—Jax's voice cuts through the silence from the doorway where he has been leaning casually against the frame, a silent observer to our interaction. "She's not wrong."

Ethan's jaw tightens, but he nods begrudgingly. "No, unfortunately, she isn't," he agrees, tone clipped. His gaze remains on me. "What do you suggest instead?"

I shuffle beneath the scrutiny of his stare, not having expected him to ask my opinion. He's the type to take charge, to make a decision and expect everyone to agree wholeheartedly.

"House rules," I respond after giving it a moment's thought. "We set rules for within this house, and if one of us breaks them, there are consequences."

After a moment of deliberation, he nods his agreement.

"Are you two happy with that?" he asks, flicking his gaze toward Finn and Jax.

"All good here," Jax immediately agrees.

"Sure," Finn says, his tone much more blasé.

"We'll set some house rules, then." Striding over to the stairs, Ethan calls up to Kyle. "Get down here. Now."

A few minutes later, Kyle reappears. "Is she go—" Seeing me standing there, his glare turns as sharp as ever. "Guess not," he mutters under his breath.

Ethan points to the cuddle chair, and Kyle practically storms over to it. "What now?" he sighs, dropping dramatically onto the seat.

Ethan surveys the room, looking each of us in the eye, before saying, "None of us are happy about this situation, but Dylan is right." Oh, I bet that hurt to say. "Regardless of what happens with the team, we are roommates, and we need to get along." Oh, that looks like it hurt even more.

I suck my lips between my teeth to smother my smirk, but Jax notices, raising a single eyebrow, but I swear I catch a glint of amusement in his deep gaze.

I quickly look away, frowning as I focus back on Ethan's speech.

"Let's keep this simple," he continues, widening his stance and crossing his arms over his chest as he surveys the room. "Common spaces are neutral. No fighting. No messing with someone else's stuff. If you've got a problem, bring it to me, and we'll get it resolved."

He waits until the guys nod before piercing me with his gray-blue stare. "That about cover it?" he taunts.

Giving him a tight smile, I hold up my index finger. "I just have one more addition. What happens on the ice, stays on the ice."

Kyle scoffs, but Ethan holds eye contact with me before nodding.

"I also want to know what you're going to do about your little 'ignore me' rule after Roster Day." Crossing my arms over my chest, I stare Ethan down, blocking out Kyle's shuffling or the fact Finn is now sitting upright on the sofa, his feet planted and elbows resting on his knees as he listens.

"I don't think we should worry about that just yet," he responds diplomatically.

"Easy for you to say." Raising my chin, I know I'm going to incite Kyle's wrath as I dare to ask, "What happens if I get a spot on the team?"

Right on cue, Kyle scoffs, but I still don't give him any of my attention. He's not important. He's as insignificant as a blade of grass. *Ethan* is the one who matters. The one who will make the decision, the leader who the team will look up to for guidance.

There's a tightness to his jaw, a pursing of his lips before he says, "Don't you think you're getting ahead of yourself?"

I arch an eyebrow in return. He, along with the rest of the team, have been scrutinizing my every move, every pass, for nearly two weeks now. He knows what I can do. He knows I'm not going to be warming the bench all year—he's just in fucking denial.

"It's a bridge we'll cross when we come to it," he states with finality.

I shake my head, not surprised yet finding myself disappointed all the same. I'd hoped he was better, but perhaps I read him wrong.

"What about tonight?" Finn interjects, clearly focused on the more pressing issue. "Who gets the living room?"

Grabbing my blanket from the floor, I snatch the bowl of popcorn from Finn's greedy fingers, all the while glowering at him. "Living room is all yours," I tell him before marching toward the stairs. They've already ruined my peaceful night.

As I approach Ethan, I slow, deliberately meeting his gaze. My voice is low as I stab him with my words. "Excellent decision making, *Captain*."

I brush past him and up the stairs. However, as I reach the top, he calls my name. I turn slowly, finding him standing at the bottom of the steps, his silhouette cast in shadow from the lights behind. "We're hosting a party here next Friday after the roster is announced. Just wanted to be a good *roommate* and let you know."

I scoff internally. Yeah, right. A good roommate would have *asked*.

He turns away, but stops. "Oh, and as your captain, attendance is mandatory."

Pasting a smile on my face, my tone is acerbic as I respond, "Can't wait to celebrate my new position as a Steelhawk."

I only get a brief moment of satisfaction, as his expression clouds over, before I turn my back to him and hurry to my room.

AFTER A WEEK of being gawked at like I'm the latest zoo animal, I decided to skip the cafeteria for lunch on Friday afternoon. Wide eyes and whispers have followed me everywhere all week. I knew to expect it once the semester started, but that doesn't make it easier to adjust to.

Especially with the new addition of *Bench Bunny* that I've heard multiple people whispering when I walk past or when they are sitting *right behind me* in class.

The first time I heard the dickwad two seats away from me mutter those words in my sports marketing and branding class, I nearly stabbed him in the eye with my pen.

I'd zoned out the rest of that class, too busy cursing out the fucking puck bunnies who interrogated me at lunch. Naturally, they'd be the ones to spread such bullshit. Whatever. Once the season starts, everyone here will realize I'm not here to ride the bench. And I'm sure as hell not here to bag myself a Steelhawks idiot for a boyfriend—or husband.

Anyway, I've had enough of the staring and the whispering and the goddamn name-calling for one week, so instead of subjecting myself to more of it in the cafeteria, I grab a sandwich from the on-campus shop and decide to explore a little. I have yet to venture away from the athletics area where the sports center, arena, and the building with all my classes are situated, but as I walk, I remember that there is an entire campus beyond the athletic department.

With all the sports-related stuff being contained to the east side of campus, sometimes it feels like it's just us here. But the farther west I head, the more the view around me changes. Gone are guys in sweats and team jackets. No girls wearing tight spandex or people juggling backpacks and oversized duffel bags weighed down with sports gear.

Instead, preppy kids wear shirts and ties, girls in plaid and Mary Jane's, their backpacks swinging from both shoulders and books clutched against their chests. There are Goth kids dressed in all black, smoking what is most definitely weed under a tree. Two students walk past, and I overhear part of their conversation about what clubs they are going to sign up for this year.

I might only be a quarter mile from the sports center but it's like I've stepped into an alternate universe.

One where sports don't come before classes. Where students' days aren't so bogged down with practices and team meetings and gym sessions that they have time for hobbies and extracurricular activities.

For the first time all week, I inhale and relax.

There's something reassuring about knowing I can walk five minutes away and enter a whole new world. One where no one knows who I am or belittles me for what I'm attempting to do, even though it's having absolutely no recourse on their lives, so why the hell do they even care?

Sometimes, I wonder what my life would be like if I weren't so hockey-obsessed. What clubs would I join? Who would my friends be? Life would probably be a hundred times easier, but no matter what I've had to endure, the challenges I've had to face, and hardships I've overcome, I wouldn't change a single second of it.

It's nice to have a break from the hockey ecosystem, but hockey is who I am. It's in my blood. I'd be lost without it.

I wander aimlessly around the campus, enjoying the bright early September day until, eventually, I come across a tall, old building with stone steps and columns on either side of a large wooden door. Above it, engraved in stone, is written *Blackstone University Library*.

There's a library in the sports center for athletes, but I haven't stepped foot in it yet—for obvious reasons. However, casting a glance around, I ascend the steps and enter the historic building.

The door shuts with a *snick,* and silence greets me. Heavenly, blissful silence. Before me is a wide, open space filled with individual and group study tables. Rows of book-shelves line the sides and back of the room, with a sweeping staircase along both side walls leading up to a balcony and second floor where I catch a peek of more tables and book-shelves.

A reception desk is off to my right, a petite, auburn-haired girl with oversized glasses sitting behind it. Her head is down, reading a book, but she looks up at the sound of someone entering.

She gives me a bland smile before glancing down again, but immediately, her head snaps back up, her jaw parting. I'm instantly on edge.

"Holy crap," she murmurs breathlessly. Her honey-brown eyes are wide as she pushes her glasses up her nose, as though that will help her see better.

In the next second, she's on her feet, mouth still agape.

"Holy crap!" she exclaims, louder this time.

I glance nervously around. This chick clearly knows who I am, but that doesn't mean I want anyone else in here to know.

Noticing, she waves dismissively as she moves out from

behind the desk. "It's the first week of term. You and I are literally the only two people in here."

"Oh." I take a step backward, ready to flee. Pointing over my shoulder toward the door, I mutter, "I'll just—"

"No, wait." She reaches out toward me with her hand but doesn't move closer. "Sorry." She shakes her head. "I'm being a total psycho weirdo right now. Forgive me." She's still staring at me with wide, rounded eyes. I don't think she's blinked since I walked in. Her cheeks blush even as she fans herself with her hand, her face splitting into a wide grin. "I'm totally fangirling right now. Give me a moment, I swear I'll get my shit together in a second, it's just...holy crap, you're Dylan Carter, right?"

When I merely blink at her, having no clue whether confirming or denying is the better option, she blushes harder. "Oh God, please tell me you are, and I'm not making a bigger fool of myself than I already am." Her gaze wanders over me but not in a leering or assessing way like the guys who ambushed me after class or the bitch bunnies in the cafeteria. "I'm used to seeing you all geared up. I heard you'd switched to BSU, but I never thought for the life of me that we'd cross paths. Never mind that you'd ever walk into my library. I need to pinch myself. Maybe I fell asleep at the desk, and this is all a dream—"

"You're not dreaming." Finally finding my voice, I cut her off from her rambling. "And yes, I'm Dylan."

"Oh my God!" Her voice reaches a screeching decibel, her hands flying to her mouth as she jumps on the spot. "Sorry. I'm sorry." She rushes forward so fast that I flinch. Holding her hand out for me to shake, she beams at me. It's only now that she's standing directly in front of me that I realize she's a decent bit shorter than I am. Not much over five feet, if I had to guess. "I'm Wren." Hesitantly, I reach out to shake her hand. "I am such a big fan. Like, the biggest fan."

"You...are?"

She nods emphatically. "I've been following you since you played BSU my freshman year. A girl on the boys' team...the rumor mill was abuzz, but when I saw you play..."

My brow furrows as I think back to that game. It was one of my first as a college player. The NSU team hadn't classified me as a threat yet, so it was one of the few games I actually got to play without being sabotaged by my own teammates. Still, I'd only gotten a few minutes of ice time.

"The way you intercepted that pass." She shakes her head as though in awe. "And that deke!" She groans as though the mere memory of it is orgasm-inducing. "I went home that night and checked your stats and highlight reels." She shrugs, blush returning in full force. "I've been a little obsessed ever since. *Especially* when I heard you'd be playing for BSU this season."

"I...don't know what to say." I've never met a fan before.

Pretty sure I've never even *had* a fan before.

Well, none beyond my family and Bear.

Noticing my awkwardness, she steps back, grimacing slightly. "I'm sorry. You came here to study or chill, and I totally accosted you. I'm sorry. I'll just go back to my reading and leave you be."

Glancing around the library, I ask, "Is this where you hang out?"

She nods. "I'm the student librarian here."

"Does it get busy during term time?"

"A bit. Mostly in the run-up to exams. Most students prefer to use their inter-departmental libraries for studying, so it's never packed."

Nodding absently, I chew on my lower lip before asking, "Would you mind if I came back tomorrow?" My next class is starting soon, and I'll have to hightail it across campus to make it in time.

"Uh, n-no. Not at all." Holding her hands up in front of her, she offers me an apologetic smile. "I promise not to drool all over you tomorrow."

I can't help but laugh. The first genuine one since I set foot on campus. Hell, the first real one in longer than I care to admit.

"It's not a problem at all. Perhaps we can chat some more. I'd love to hear how far you think the Steelhawks will go this season."

Her eyes do that wide, shocked thing again before she nods like a bobblehead. "Y-yeah. That sounds great. Oh, I'll bring my spreadsheets." Her cheeks flush impossibly darker, and she cringes. "I'm a bit of a stats nerd."

My grin only widens. *Oh yeah, I think I like this girl.* "Me too. Give me all the spreadsheets and charts."

She chuckles, still nodding.

"I've gotta run," I say, turning halfway toward the exit. "But I'll see you tomorrow."

"Tomorrow," she confirms before I'm out the door.

Rushing down the steps, there's a grin on my face.

I might have just found my first college friend.

SEVEN

I FIRE a puck hard off the boards, watching the rebound angle as it careens toward the crease. Sliding to meet it, I drop my glove over the puck and trap it against the ice.

Quick reset. Another puck. Another rebound.

The key is control. When the puck ricochets wide, I extend a pad to deflect it. When it rebounds into my space, I snap it up with my glove or block it with my stick. No wasted movement. No room for error.

Except my control keeps slipping...

She's here.

Dylan Carter.

She slipped onto the ice not long after I did, her presence quiet but impossible to ignore. It's been like this for over a week now. The same time, the same rink, the same silent coexistence. She doesn't speak to me, doesn't try to engage. She just goes about her business, and I go about mine.

That's how I like it. Everyone on the team knows this is when I practice. They know better than to interrupt—or God forbid, *join* me.

But clearly, Dylan Carter never got the memo...or tossed it in the trash, if she did.

And every time she shows up, my focus fractures.

It's *infuriating*.

Huffing under my breath, I steal a glance as I adjust my mask and shuffle back into position. She's at the far end of the rink, just inside the blue line, practicing the same shot over and over. I've watched her miss that damn net at least a dozen times, and after each one, she skates after the puck, sets it up, and tries again.

Same angle.

Same motion.

Same outcome.

It's starting to piss me off.

If she'd just... I shake my head, turning my back to her.

Not my problem, I remind myself.

Focusing on my own drills, I push off, skating toward the boards to collect my puck. I go through the motions again. Slap. Catch. Reset. Repeat.

It's all muscle memory—anticipating rebounds and making the save before the puck even has a chance to breathe.

Still, far too soon, I find my attention waning. Shifting to the petite fireball *still* missing the net.

My teeth grind, my focus diverted enough that the next time I smack the puck into the boards, I don't get the angle quite right. The puck goes wide, and not just *extend the pad to deflect it* wide. *Wide* wide.

Now I'm really pissed off.

I tell myself to leave it. To let her figure it out—or not. It's not my problem. I've never cared to help anyone else on the team.

Despite my internal protests, the words are out of my mouth before I can stop them.

"You're leaning too far back."

Her head snaps up, and she stares at me from behind the cage of her helmet like I just grew a second head.

I stop at the boards, leaning casually on my stick as I meet her gaze. In for a penny, in for a pound. "You're pulling your weight off the shot," I explain. God fucking knows why. "That's why it keeps going wide."

She blinks at me, her brow furrowing. For a moment, we just stare at each other, the silence stretching thin. Then, without a word, she adjusts her stance, rolls her weight forward, and takes the shot.

The puck...goes wide.

Her shoulders slump, her audible sigh making it all the way to where I stand on the opposite side of the rink. With a defeated push of her legs, she skates after the puck. Her head is bent, not looking at me as she mutters something too low for me to hear.

I should just go. Leave her to it. She'll either get it or she won't. I've already told her what her problem is. Not my fault if she can't make the shot.

Except, I seem to have left all common sense at home today because instead of opening the gate and getting off the ice, I press down on my toes and skate across the rink...toward her.

She stiffens as I stop beside her, pulling off my gloves before dropping them onto the ice with a dull thud.

"What are you doing?" She's staring at me warily, watching my every move.

"I'm showing you how to do it," I grunt. "Get into position."

She stares at me for so long I nearly tell her to forget it. Fuck knows I've better things to do than have a silent stare-off with a girl I don't know in the middle of the rink.

However, she eventually, achingly slowly, turns to face the net, getting herself into position just like I asked.

She stays there, and I move to stand behind her. There's distance between us, but I notice the way her body tenses. I can't put my finger on why, but something tells me to take it slowly with this girl. She's like a wild horse, and if I move too fast, I'll spook her.

Slowly, deliberately, I lift my hands to hover just above her arms, a breath away from touching her.

"May I?" My voice is gruff, an odd scratchiness to it.

She nods—barely—and I press my palms against her forearms, slightly adjusting her position. My fingers are light but firm as I fix the angle of her stick, then shift her weight slightly forward over her skates.

"Go again," I murmur, stepping back.

She exhales, tightening her grip before she takes the shot. The puck ricochets off the post—a near miss.

"Better." I nod in approval before pushing off to retrieve the puck, placing it down with deliberate precision in front of her. "Don't overthink it this time. There's just you, the puck, and the net. Focus on that. Nothing else matters."

She nods, all of her attention focused on the round black rubber disk in front of her. Rolling her shoulders, she takes her stance without requiring any correction from me. This time, as she shifts her weight, driving the stick forward, her movements are fluid, confident. The sharp crack of her stick connecting with the puck is followed by a satisfying smack as it hits the back of the net.

She freezes for a moment, gaping at the net as she processes what just happened. Then, suddenly, she throws her arms in the air and lets out a cheer, her excitement filling the empty rink.

"Yes! Finally!" she exclaims, spinning to face me.

Before I can process what's happening, she's launched herself at me, arms wrapping around me in a spontaneous hug.

Her gloves thud softly against my padded back, her helmeted head bumping my shoulder. "Do you know how long I've been trying to master that shot?!"

I stiffen in her embrace, completely caught off guard. My first instinct is to step back, to push her away, but I don't. Awkwardness floods my chest, but it's quickly replaced by something else—a heat curling low in my stomach. Her energy is infectious, her joy so raw and unguarded that it feels like it's brushing against parts of me I didn't know existed anymore.

She pulls back almost as quickly, sliding a few feet away on her skates. Her cheeks are flushed beneath her helmet as she ducks her head, not quite meeting my eye. "Sorry," she mumbles, her voice small. "I got carried away."

I don't know what to say. So instead, I clear my throat, gesturing toward the puck. "Go again."

She nods, clearly grateful for the shift in focus, and lines up to take another shot. Her movements are smoother this time, her confidence bleeding into every step. The puck sails into the net, and she lets out another triumphant sound, this time keeping her excitement in check.

We fall into a rhythm—her shooting, me retrieving—without another word spoken. Every time she lines up a shot, my eyes track her movements, analyzing every detail. She's good. Better than I even realized. And relentless.

Just like me.

For the first time, I feel something like respect creeping in.

And I hate it.

Finally, I nod and skate to the edge of the rink, ready to leave.

"Griffin," she calls after me.

I pause, glancing over my shoulder.

"Thanks."

I hold her gaze for a beat, then grunt a quiet acknowledgement before stepping off the ice. The gate clangs shut behind me, the sound echoing in the empty space.

I tell myself it means nothing. Just a moment. Just hockey. But as I step into the cold air outside, her laughter and energy still linger in the back of my mind.

EIGHT

EVERY ONE OF my senses is on alert. I'm aware of the position of every single player on this ice—teammate and opponent—as I set up the play.

I see Monroe—a rookie center—coming from a mile away, and before he can make his move, I knock the puck sideways. It glides smoothly along the ice before Jax intercepts the pass, skating backward with steady control as he waits for his opening.

Reed moves into position on the left, ready for the pass. It's a golden moment of opportunity. I can already taste the sweetness of the win on the tip of my tongue. This might be a game between teammates to test our abilities and see how we work together on the ice, but it may as well be the Stanley Cup Finals. Doesn't matter how small or insignificant the game; if you aren't going to give it a hundred and ten percent, why even bother getting on the ice?

I expect the absolute best from myself—*and* my team. No less will do. Give it your all or get the fuck off my ice.

This is a play we've practiced hundreds of times. With light-ning-quick movements, Jax passes the puck back to me. I immediately send it on to Reed. All he has to do is pick it up, shield it from Dylan, and keep moving.

I'm pushing toward the net before the puck even meets his stick.

Except his timing is off. His stick catches the puck awkwardly, and it bounces loose.

God fucking dammit.

Like an eagle swooping in for the kill, Dylan snatches it up. She cuts past Reed with surgical precision. There's no hesitation. No adjusting. She's away, skating hard down the ice.

I tear after her. My legs burn as I push myself to go faster, but it's like she's got a turbo engine strapped to her feet, and she knows exactly where she's going.

Finn is waiting on the right. Why the hell isn't someone covering him? Dylan passes to him in stride, and he doesn't waste the opportunity. His shot rockets past our goalie and slams into the back of the net.

The whistle blows.

"Hell yeah!" Finn cheers, skating past me with a smirk he does fuck all to hide. His hand is raised for a high five as he approaches Dylan, but at the last second, realization dawns. The smile slides off his face. At the same time, his hand drops to his side, and he does a one-eighty, skating away from her, before moving to celebrate the win with some of the others on the team.

However, my gaze remains focused on her. On how her eyes lit up with delight as Finn approached...and how they dimmed in disappointment when he changed course. A tightness forms in my chest, and I force myself to turn away.

It's for the best. Laying down the law of ignoring her is the best way to appease everyone—at least until the roster is announced. After that...fuck, it's going to be a shitshow. One I haven't found a solution to. I might have told Dylan I'd cross that bridge when we got there, but the truth is, I spend every waking moment trying to figure out how I'm going to stop the team from imploding when Coach inevitably hands her a spot. One I can begrudgingly admit she will have earned, even if it does completely fuck with the team and my ability to captain.

Only two more days until shit hits the fan.

Feeling the weight of responsibility pressing down on me, I skate back to the bench. Even though my expression is neutral, inside, I'm fuming over our loss. I *hate* losing. Especially when I know we had it in the bag. Doesn't matter that it was a meaningless scrimmage.

Reed skates in behind me, at I turn to confront him. "What was that?"

His brows dip low over his eyes. "Fucking bitch tripped me."

My gaze narrows on him before I shake my head.

Before I can call bullshit, though, Griffin beats me to it. "That was no trip," he states evenly, leaning against his stick and staring Reed down. "You lost the puck all on your own."

"What the fuck would you know?" Reed retorts. "You couldn't see jack shit from all the way back in your net." He pauses, a gleam entering his gaze. "Unless you were too busy checking out that piece of ass..."

"Kyle," I warn. "Shut the fuck up."

Unbothered, Kyle shrugs before moving past me to his spot on the bench.

My gaze meets Griffin's, holding it for a moment before he skates off. I have no idea what that was about, but it only adds to the sense of doom clouding over me. I force myself to inhale deeply, shaking off the frustration from Reed's screwup. It's annoying that he cost us the goal, but Dylan? She played it perfectly. The problem here isn't her, as much as I wish it were.

Tuning out the rest of the team, I splash water over my face before drinking the rest of my bottle. When Coach steps up to offer his critique, I'm only half listening.

The rest of my attention is focused on her. Sitting farther down the bench, her helmet is off, and her cheeks are flushed as she listens intently to the coach. She looks completely unfazed, no smugness at their win or pride over how she played. It was just another training session for her, another day at the rink.

Grabbing her helmet, she gets to her feet. For a moment, I just watch as she clambers over the boards and onto the ice. Then a sharp dig into my side has my attention whirling on Jax sitting beside me. He juts his chin toward the ice in a clear, *Aren't you going out there?* And I realize Coach has ordered Reed, Dylan, and me onto the ice for forward drills.

Hurrying to catch up, I notice Reed looks like he's on the verge of imploding. His jaw is tight, eyes darting toward Dylan like she personally stole his chance at the NHL. I try to shove down the unease brewing in my gut and focus on the play, but I already know this isn't going to end well.

Hell, Coach probably shouldn't even be putting them together on the ice. No doubt he has seen the tension between them as blatantly as I have and is hoping teamwork will resolve it.

I wish it were that straightforward.

Coach barks out the drill, a simple cycle with quick passes between us. It's basic, something we've done a thousand times, and yet the second we start, Reed's making it difficult. His passes to Dylan are either rockets aimed at her skates or lazy lobs that barely reach her stick. It's deliberate and petty as hell.

I throw him a glare, silently ordering him to wise up and focus on the drill. He merely smirks in return, but I catch something in his gaze. A hardness. He's convinced himself that Dylan made him look like a fool, and now he's set on returning the favor.

It doesn't help that Dylan handles every single one of his passes with practiced ease. She doesn't get pissy or rise to his pettiness. She simply moves to catch the puck on the tip of her blade, adjusting mid-stride and keeping the drill moving.

Honestly, I respect her all the more for it.

Mostly because I don't believe she's doing it so she can rise above, but because she's as intent on this drill as I am.

Reed's frustration only mounts with every recovery she makes, and by the time the drill ends, his face is beet red—and not from exertion. He's practically vibrating with anger.

"You see that, Cap?" Kyle spits, loud enough for everyone, including Coach, to hear. "She's a liability!"

I clench my jaw and force my gaze forward, refusing to take the bait. Reed's always had a mouth on him, and engaging with him only feeds the fire.

"Screwing up plays like she's got something to prove," he continues.

I'm watching Dylan from the corner of my eye. I see the twitching of her eye, the tic of her jaw. The way her gloved hand tightens around her stick.

Don't do it, Dylan. Don't get sucked into his games, I silently beg of her.

I try to catch her eye, but she's not looking my way, staring intently at the wall on the far side of the arena as we skate back to the bench.

For a moment, I think she's going to let it wash over her. We're nearly off the ice when Reed just has to send her careening over the ledge of her self-control.

"You think the other teams will take it easy on her?" he spouts. "She's gonna get herself killed out there, and we'll be the ones left to clean up the mess."

Without looking his way, I snap, "That's enough, Reed!"

Ice sprays as Dylan whirls on him, her glare cutting. "No,

no." She gestures toward Reed. "Let it all out, Kyle. Tell us what you really think."

"I think you're a liability who is going to cost us games—cost us our futures—all so you can, what? Live out some childhood fantasy of playing with the big boys?"

Despite Reed's sneering tone, Dylan appears entirely unfazed as she stares at him. There's about a yard of ice separating them, but the tension fizzles and pops in the space between like the atmosphere before an impending lightning storm. "That's big talk for someone who can't handle a simple pass."

I internally groan. *Way to poke the bear, Carter.*

"You're kidding me, right?" Reed retorts, spine straightening as he glides closer to her on his skates. "You were out of position—"

"I was exactly where I was supposed to be," Dylan snaps, pushing forward so they are skate to skate. Since Reed is one of the shorter players on the team, it brings them nearly face to face in the middle of the ice. Their sticks hang forgotten at their sides, legs planted hip-width apart. "You screwed up your play all on your own," Dylan continues, driving the knife deeper. "You couldn't handle a simple pass, and somehow that's my fault?" Her laugh is bitter. "Maybe focus less on whining and more on actually playing."

"You don't belong here," Reed hisses. I can feel the eyes of everyone on the team—including Coach—on the back of my neck. The tension on the ice is suffocating, everyone having stopped to watch the ongoing train wreck. I'm not sure whether to intervene or let Reed get it out of his system. Maybe then he'll calm down and stop running his mouth.

"You're a joke." Reed's gaze slowly drops over her, lips curling in a sneer. "You think Coach is gonna pick you over me?"

"He will if you keep playing like *that*," Dylan shoots back without hesitation, her eyes blazing. Sliding right into his space, their helmets nearly touch as she pokes him in the chest. "Maybe if you put as much effort into your plays as you do bitching about me, you wouldn't feel so threatened by a girl."

I can see the venom in Reed's eyes. The way his hands twitch at his sides. I know that look. I've seen it right before he's slammed someone into the boards. Right before the gloves come off.

Shit.

I shoot forward, wedging myself between them before things can boil over. I shove them apart, one hand on Reed's chest, the other pressing against Dylan's shoulder.

"Enough!" My voice is sharp, cutting through the escalating chaos.

Reed glares at me, his chest heaving, but I don't let up. I point a finger in his face, my tone leaving no room for argument. "Skate it off. Now."

For a moment, he doesn't move, his jaw working like he's biting back every curse word in his arsenal. Then he finally turns, muttering loud enough for me to catch as he skates away, "Traitorous teammates."

The words hit me like a punch to the gut, but I don't react. I can't. Not here, not now. I exhale through my nose, forcing myself to focus on Dylan, who's still glaring at Reed's retreating form.

"You good?" I ask her, my voice quieter but still firm.

She blinks, dragging her gaze back to me, then nods. "Yeah. I'm good."

I nod once and skate toward the bench, my mind already racing. Reed's temper is bad enough in normal circumstances, but this is something else entirely.

Coach meets me at the gate. His expression is like stone as

he stares me down, one eyebrow arched in a way that tells me he's not impressed.

He tilts his chin toward Reed, who's at the far end of the rink, still fuming. His voice is low, meant solely for me. "Can you handle that, or do I need to?"

The words hit harder than they should. My jaw tightens, and I force myself to meet his gaze without flinching. It pisses me off, the implication that Reed's inability to keep his temper— or just play the damn game—is making Coach question my leadership. My ability to keep this team in line.

My ability to *captain* this team.

"I can handle it." My voice is steady, sure, even though my pulse pounds in my ears.

Coach studies me for a moment, his eyes hard, before he questions, "This *ignore* rule you've put in place regarding Carter, do you feel that's the best approach?"

I bite down on my tongue to keep my initial response from leaking out. Why is everyone questioning me about this? What the hell else do they suggest I do?

Feeling defensive, I cross my arms over my chest as I shuffle back and forth on my skates. "What's the point in instigating World War Three when she could be riding the bench all season?"

He cocks a brow, and his expression is eerily similar to the one Dylan used on me the other night. "Do you truly think she will be?"

Once again, I have to resist the urge to grind my teeth.

That's the fucking problem, isn't it? Because, no. I do not believe she's going to be sitting on the bench all season. I don't think she's going to be on the bench at all. And I haven't the first fucking clue what to do about that.

I don't know if he can read the answer in my expression, or if he doesn't feel he needs one, but he doesn't wait for a verbal response from me. With a clap of my shoulder, he moves past me, and I turn to watch him stride toward his office.

An itch prickles at my skin. Not having Coach's unwavering trust. Not having my players' respect. Having people thwart the rules *I* put in place...

The itching grows incessant. Nope. No, can't have it. I *need* to be in control. I *need* to be the one calling the shots. The one they all listen to—abide by.

A player marches past me toward the locker room, the name printed on the back of their jersey catching my eye. "Carter!" I call.

She stops in her skates, helmet clutched in her hand. Her shoulders tense before she slowly turns to face me.

"Captain." There's a stiffness to her tone that I don't like, but I don't call her out on it as I wave her over. She cautiously approaches.

"If Reed baits you like that again," I begin, voice low but firm, "ignore him."

She reels back, mouth dropping open as her eyes widen. "Ignore him?" she repeats, as though double-checking she heard me right.

"He's looking for a reaction out of you. He *wants* you to do something that will mess up your game."

"And your solution is for *me* to ignore *him*. Not to tell him to stop acting like a petulant three-year-old or give him consequences for starting shit during practice? Have I got that right, *Captain*?"

My teeth grind. *Goddamn this woman.*

"Are you going to do as I say or not, Carter?" I snap, straightening to my full height.

She taps her finger against her chin as though thinking about it. The action alone sends my blood pressure through the roof. *This fucking woman.* A goddamn thorn in my side. I don't have the same issues with her as Kyle, but my God, is she starting to get under my skin. Her absolute lack of respect for authority. For the chain of command. For *my* command.

"I am the captain of this team," I remind her sternly. "I am *your* captain."

Dylan drops her act, staring me straight in the eye. The flecks of gold in her irises spark to life beneath the bright lights of the arena, burning with a raw intensity. "Until you earn my respect, you're not my anything. I value you as a player, as a teammate, but, so far, you haven't done anything as a captain that I find worth respecting."

With that, she stomps off in her skates, leaving me practically billowing steam in her wake. My hands clench at my sides, and I close my eyes, forcing myself to take a breath. To calm the blood pumping through my system. To just breathe.

Snapping them open, I look up to find Griffin staring at me. Jesus, how long has he been doing that for? "Got a problem, Price?"

He smirks, shaking his head. I get the strange sense he's laughing at me, but you never quite know with Griffin. He's a bit of an oddball. Shoots the shit, plays the part, but I've always sensed something...off about him.

"Nope."

Before I can ask him what the hell he's looking at then, he walks off.

Jesus, what a shitshow of a day.

"Everyone hit the showers!" I bark, rounding up the stragglers still hanging around the rink. I follow them down the tunnel, yanking off my helmet and running my fingers through my sweat-slicked hair as I push it out of my face. Before I step into the locker room, I force out a breath, trying to regain control over my emotions. To find some semblance of control.

I'm pissed at Coach for putting me in this situation. At Reed for being a grade-A asshole. At Dylan for choosing *my* team to make her stand. Why the hell couldn't she just have stayed at her old college?

This is a complete disaster, and I fear it's only going to get worse. Reed's already teetering on the edge, and if Friday doesn't go the way he expects, he's going to blow. I'm not the only one who realizes that. I can feel the rest of the team exchanging glances as I step into the locker room, wondering the same thing I am—what the hell is going to happen come Roster Day?

And how the hell do I keep this team from blowing up with him?

NINE

THE CONFRONTATION with Kyle and my argument with Ethan still burns under my skin as I trudge into the locker room. My legs feel like lead, and my arms ache from practice, but none of it compares to the frustration boiling in my chest.

"Such a menace," Jax whispers under his breath as he stalks past me. "Causing trouble wherever you go." His eyes latch on to mine, amusement dancing in his dark depths.

He's marching over to his own locker before I can say anything. And perhaps that's for the best, given my altercation with Ethan by the rink. Not that I regret what I said. He was the one in the wrong. He's *been* making the wrong calls, starting with his stupid *ignore me* rule. What sort of harebrained nonsense is that, anyway? Stupidest advice I've ever heard. Since when does burying your head in the sand and pretending something doesn't exist actually solve anything?

Shaking my head, I keep my eyes down, ignoring the stares from other players as they glance over my skin. Despite how he reacted, Ethan was right about one thing. I shouldn't have let Kyle get to me like that. I know better. Ignore the shit they say. Tune it out. Let it slide off. But it's hard—*so damn hard*—to pretend it doesn't prickle when someone's constantly talking shit about you, blaming you for things you didn't do.

My throat tightens as my fingers fumble with the straps on my gear, but I shove it down. Stripping off my pads, I set them aside in neat piles. Beneath my gear, I've got on a sports bra and tight shorts that I'll strip off once I'm in the shower cubicle. My skin is damp with sweat, which quickly cools in the locker room's air conditioning. However, I barely notice.

What I do notice is Ethan. I watch him strip out of his gear from the corner of my eye, still unable to wrap my head around the fact that he stepped in between me and Kyle. Kyle was about to lose it—I could see it in the way his eyes narrowed and his shoulders hunched. I've seen that look before. I know what happens next. I was already bracing myself, ready to shove him off if he tried something.

That's what I've always had to do. My old team? No one ever stepped in. Not the players, not the coach, and definitely not the captain. He didn't care if the guys cornered me after practice or slammed me into the boards during drills.

At least, not until last year...

I shake my head, jaw clenched tight.

Definitely not fucking going there.

But Ethan...his stepping in today feels strange. I don't trust it.

Of course, he acted like a douche afterward, but still...

With more force than necessary, I yank the polyester pants over my hips before kicking them off. As I bend to retrieve them, the noise rises sharply around me, pulling me from my thoughts. I glance up, my brow furrowing as the tension in the room thickens.

Kyle is in Griffin's face, his voice loud and cutting, and the other guys have gathered around them in a loose circle.

"What's it like, Griffin?" Kyle taunts. "Playing hero for her?

Thought we weren't supposed to acknowledge her, yet you've been helping her improve her skills in your private, late-night lessons."

My stomach pitches.

He saw us.

He must have been watching our practice yesterday. It's the *only* time we've interacted, spoken a single word to each other. I *hate* that Kyle was privy to that. Hate that he was there, watching me when I didn't know it.

Griffin doesn't flinch, doesn't react to the accusation. He just stands there, calm and unbothered, unpeeling the tape from his stick.

Kyle steps closer, his words dripping venom. "What's the deal? Trying to impress her? Hoping she'll spread her legs in some grand prize? Or are you just desperate to be her white knight because no one else will bother?"

Griffin's blank stare breaks into a mocking grin stretching across his face. It's infuriatingly calm, like Kyle is just another minor inconvenience in his day. He laughs lightly, the sound completely devoid of warmth.

"For someone who talks so much shit about her, you're sounding pretty fucking jealous right now."

Kyle's face flushes red, and his fists curl. He looks ready to explode at Griffin's insinuation.

Griffin's grin only widens, like he's enjoying pushing Kyle to the edge. Toying with him. "Nah, you're not jealous 'cause you want her." His tone turns sharp as glass. "You're mad 'cause she's better than you, and everyone in here knows it."

That's it. Kyle snaps. He shoves Griffin hard, the sound of his hands hitting Griffin's chest protector echoing off the walls.

Griffin doesn't move an inch. He's only fractionally taller than Kyle, but he's had years of defending his corner, never deviating from the crease. However, his expression shifts so fast it sends a chill racing through me. The easy grin vanishes, replaced with something cold and lethal. His typically guarded light blue eyes harden into shards of ice.

"Lay a finger on me again, and I'll break you so thoroughly they won't even know *how* to piece you back together." Griffin's voice is low and deadly. There's no bluster, no anger—just pure, calm calculation. It should be frightening. I mean, it is. I sense he isn't just being dramatic—he means it. And yet, I find myself curious more than anything else.

I tilt my head slightly, studying him. This version of him is so different from the Griffin I typically see laughing and joking in the locker room, the one who wears boyish charm like a second skin. Now, he's all sharp edges and quiet menace, and I can't tell which version of him is more real.

Something in my gut tells me *this* is the real Griffin.

The one more in line with the reserved, quiet version I share the rink and gym with out of hours. Does that mean that the smiles and jokes are all a front? A mask he wears for the world?

The air in the room has been stretched thin, every player stopping what they were doing to watch. I swear, you could hear a pin drop.

"Then you won't have to worry about Dylan stealing your spot. It'll be all hers for the taking." He finishes delivering his threat. Am I the only one who has goosebumps?

Kyle steps closer, fists clenched as the tension in the air turns thunderous. However, before he can do something monumentally stupid, Ethan storms over.

"I'm getting seriously fucking sick of pulling teammates apart like they are misbehaving toddlers throwing a tantrum," he yells, grabbing Kyle by the back of his jersey and yanking him away.

Kyle stumbles, chest heaving as he glares at Ethan, but Ethan's face is pure stone as he stares him down. It's clear he has reached his daily limit for the amount of bullshit he will tolerate.

"Get back on the ice," he orders Kyle, voice like steel as he shoves him toward the door. "Skate suicides until your legs give out, then bag drills until you can't even hold your stick upright."

I lift my hand to cover the smirk I can't—and don't want to—squash.

Kyle's mouth gapes, indignation clear to read on his face, but Ethan doesn't give him a chance to argue. "You've done nothing but pick fights today, Kyle."

"Yeah, but—"

"*I* am the captain." The lockers literally shake with the force of Ethan's voice as it echoes off the walls. "You *will* obey me, or you can walk out that door, but if you do, don't bother coming back."

The locker room is dead silent now. Even Griffin, who'd gone back to peeling the tape from his stick, has gone still, his sharp gaze flicking between Ethan and Kyle.

Kyle's glare hardens, his lips pressed into a tight line. For a moment, I think he's going to storm out. I'm hoping he does. But then his jaw works as though chewing on something particularly bitter before he nods, not quite meeting Ethan's eye. Turning on his heel, he throws open the door and stomps toward the ice.

A heavy silence settles over the room in Kyle's wake. Ethan exhales slowly, his shoulders still tense as he turns back to the team. "Anyone else got a problem they want to work out?" His voice is calm now, but there's an edge to it that makes it clear he's done taking anyone's crap.

No one says a word.

Ethan nods once, sharp and decisive. "Good. Hit the showers then get the fuck out of here."

My gaze slides back to Griffin, finding him already staring at me. He holds my gaze for a moment, something passing between us that I can't grasp, before that charming grin slips back into place like a well-worn mask.

I look away, shaking my head as I grab my towel and head for the showers. But I can't help glancing back at him one last time, that icy look still burning in my mind.

MY PHONE PINGS as I step out the stadium doors, the fresh air blowing away some of the exhaustion from a grueling practice, followed by a self-inflicted skate around the ice to blow off steam. Rolling out the ache in my shoulders that tells me I've pushed myself too hard today, I fish my phone from my bag, finding a message from Wren. For the first time all day, a smile graces my lips.

Despite her fangirling, I returned to the library the next day, finding Wren in the same spot behind the reception desk. We ate lunch together, and it has become a near-daily routine, when our schedules align. I've opened up to her somewhat regarding the conflict between myself and my new team members, so I'm not surprised when I see her question.

WREN

How was practice?

I IMMEDIATELY TYPE OUT A RESPONSE, as I slowly make my way down the stadium steps, leg muscles straining. *Ugh, I'm going to have to soak in the bath when I get home if I want to avoid being stiff as hell tomorrow.*

ME

Went about as well as a root canal with no
anesthetic.

WREN

Ouch. Did someone swap your stick out
again?

My LIPS PRESS TOGETHER, recalling that practice several days
ago when some asshole swapped my stick out during a water
break for one that had a different curve. It took me long enough
to realize it wasn't mine and adapt to the different handling that
I let enough pucks skate by to make me look like a first-degree
idiot. Not to mention the hour I spent after practice hunting
down my *actual* stick in a storage closet on an admin floor of the
stadium.

Of course, that's not the only prank that has been pulled.
I've had trash dumped in my locker, gear wrapped in tape so
thoroughly that I've been late to practice, plus a dozen other
little things that only serve to drive me crazy.

Not to mention the whispers and shoves in the hallway
between classes, the side-eyes knowingly telling me I don't
belong. The team is playing at psychological warfare. What
they don't realize is that I've been surviving this game for years
already. It's going to take a hell of a lot more than stolen gear
and dirty looks to get me to back down.

Shaking off the hazing I've endured so far, I respond to
Wren.

ME

Nah. Just Kyle being his typical asshole self.

WREN

Kyle's a grade A douche.

Have you tried talking to your Captain about any of it?

I SNORT to myself at that, casting a surreptitious glance around the parking lot as I cross it, before walking out the gates of BSU and heading down the sidewalk to Athletes Row.

ME

Not sure Ethan is any better. He stopped me on the ice after practice and basically tried to demand respect without earning it. Like being made Captain means respect is automatic. Not impressed!

WREN

He is a good guy, Dylan. Probably just trying to flex the "C" on his jersey, show everyone what kind of Captain he's going to be.

ME

The kind that has a stick up his ass and lets his team get away with absolute bullshit? Some Captain he is!

WREN

I get that he hasn't made the best first impression, but I've only ever heard people say good things about him.

ME

Good and nice are two different things!

> In my experience, Captains don't stay neutral. I
> can handle the team on my own. Trust me, this
> is nothing.

THE SMELL of something savory hits me the moment I step through the door, a warm, tantalizing aroma that makes my stomach growl in protest. I pause, dropping my duffel on the floor and toeing off my Converse. My muscles ache from the drills I ran this evening—*alone* since Griffin was noticeably absent.

I hadn't gotten the same enjoyment from it that I usually do. I was distracted. I thought I kept feeling eyes on me, and my attention kept shifting to the stands, searching, wondering if someone was there watching me. If *Kyle* was.

It's the first time I've felt that way at BSU, and I hated it.

I hated feeling like I had to be on guard the entire time, mentally preparing myself for an ambush of some sort. I'd ended up calling it quits early and coming home.

The scent of whatever is cooking pulls me forward. When I reach the threshold of the kitchen, I stop short. Ethan stands at the counter, slicing vegetables with precision, his brow furrowed in concentration. Finn is at the stove, stirring a pot that steams in front of him, while Jax moves around the table, setting out plates. It's a picture of domesticity I wasn't expecting from a bunch of college hockey players.

Ethan glances up, noticing me lingering in the doorway. "There you are." He makes it sound like he's been waiting for me.

I blink. "What's going on?"

"House dinner," he says, as though it's the most obvious thing in the world.

"Well, have fun with that." Ignoring the enticing smell of whatever they are cooking and the grumble of my stomach, I turn on my heel to head up to my room.

"Nu-uh," Ethan calls, stopping me in my tracks. "You too."

I go to tell him it's all right, he doesn't have to include me. I'm used to doing things on my own, but he talks over me.

"It's tradition," he says, pointing his vegetable knife at me. "Night before Roster Day, we sit down together as a house and eat. Since you're a part of this house now, that includes you." He sets the knife down and meets my eyes. "And no, it's not optional."

Damn.

I debate arguing with him, but something in his tone tells me I'd be wasting my breath. I've seen what happens when Ethan is pushed to his limit. There's no need to be faced with his wrath two days in a row. Instead, I sigh, stepping fully into the kitchen. "What do you want me to do?"

He grins, and I'm momentarily taken aback by how pretty he looks when he smiles. Ethan is the picture-perfect guy next door with his dark, messy hair and kind gray-blue eyes, but he's strung as tight as I am—hell, maybe even tighter, which would be saying something. I'm fairly certain this is the first time I've seen him drop his guard and just be in the moment.

Gesturing toward Jax, who is setting out glasses beside each plate, he says, "You can help Jax set the table."

Nodding, I cross the room to the correct cabinet. The glasses, of course, are on the top shelf—because when you're a head taller than I am, everyday convenience doesn't require the bottom two shelves. I stretch up onto my toes, my fingers brushing the edge of one of the glasses but not quite getting a grip on it.

Heat suddenly radiates up my back, and I suck in a gasp. "Here," a low voice murmurs behind me.

I freeze as Jax reaches an arm up and over me, his chest brushing against my shoulder, the heat of him curling along my spine. His other hand finds my waist—firm, steady, far too intentional to be casual.

He grabs the glass with ease, but makes no move to step back. His voice, low and smooth, spills against my neck. "I got it."

For a second, I forget how to breathe. The proximity, the warmth, the quiet authority in his tone—it all sends my nerves into overdrive. My body reacts before my brain can catch up, my heart thudding in a way I wish it wouldn't. I can't want this. Not after everything that happened last year.

Clearing my throat, I step away, putting distance between us as I grab the cutlery instead. "Thanks," I mutter, keeping my head down.

Jax doesn't say anything, just resumes setting the table as if the moment hadn't happened. But I can still feel the lingering warmth where he'd stood too close. Shaking it off, I focus on grabbing silverware from the drawer and laying it out on the table.

The thundering of footsteps down the stairs announces Kyle's presence before he appears in the doorway, hair still damp from his shower. He's dressed in dark pants and a collared shirt, hair slicked back and looking like he's about to dine at a fancy restaurant. The rest of us are all casually dressed in sweats or shorts.

Then I realize he's always dressed the same way when I see him in the cafeteria on campus. Always so polished and put-together like he's trying to compensate for something.

Gaze sliding to Finn, I recall he typically prefers jeans and formfitting T-shirts that don't even try to disguise his six-pack abs and bulging biceps that threaten to rip the sleeves at the seams. Although he's gone casual tonight in low-hanging gray sweats and a loose sleeveless top that shows off the intricate web of tribal tattoos decorating his left arm.

I've never seen Jax in anything other than sweats. Even that night he came home after being at a bar with the rest of the team. And why should he wear anything else? He looks fine as hell the way he's dressed.

Ethan straddles the line between Finn and Kyle. Not as polished as Kyle, but you can tell he takes pride in his appearance. He sticks to T-shirts and dark denim jeans or pants, pairing them with sneakers, but there's never a wrinkle in sight. Although no matter how smart he looks, his hair is never anything but messy. There is just no taming that beast. It's like his hair deliberately refuses to stay in place just to prove to Ethan that no matter how hard he tries, he can't control everything.

I always find it oddly amusing to watch him shove it away from his face, only for a strand to immediately flop across his forehead.

Kyle stalks into the kitchen, his expression neutral but eyes flashing with tension. *Oh joy, isn't this going to be a fun night.* He hasn't spoken a word to me since yesterday's confrontation, and I'm not exactly eager to start a conversation with him.

Ethan, as usual, takes control of the situation. "I invited Griff," he says casually, holding Kyle's gaze. There's the slight flaring of Kyle's nostrils, but that's his only tell. "I want *everyone* to clear the air before tomorrow."

"Fine," Kyle grumbles. His lack of protest takes me by surprise, and I narrow my eyes, watching him. He doesn't seem happy about it, but he isn't fighting back either. Perhaps Ethan's punishment yesterday knocked some sense into him.

The doorbell rings a few minutes later, announcing Griffin's arrival, and we all sit down to eat. The atmosphere is oddly relaxed. Uncomfortable in places, and I can tell the guys are put out by having someone new in their space, but as they fall into easy conversation, rehashing stories about their teenage antics, any lingering tension bleeds out of the air.

"Kyle and I were at this camp when we were, what, fourteen?" Finn is saying, glancing over at Kyle, who nods, a faint smirk tugging at his lips. "Anyway, we had this coach who was, like, military-level strict. Dude had us up at dawn every day, skating suicides until we puked."

Kyle leans back in his chair, arms folded across his chest, and a mischievous glint lighting up his eyes. "Coach Bradley. The guy didn't have an off button. He'd yell at you for breathing too loud."

"Exactly." Finn nods sagely, pointing his fork in agreement. "So one day, Kyle gets it into his head that we should pull a little payback prank. You remember that, Kyle?" Finn grins at his co-conspirator.

Kyle snorts. "Pretty sure it was your idea, Finn. I was just along for the ride."

"Sure, sure, whatever." Finn waves him off, with a laugh. "Anyway, we sneak out of our cabin at, like, midnight and grab his whistle—the one he used to blow directly in our faces every morning. We rig it up to the showerhead in the coaches' locker room. Took us forever to figure out how to tie it up so the water pressure would blow it like a foghorn."

Kyle chuckles, shaking his head. "And by 'forever', he means we spent half the night arguing over the physics of a whistle. I still don't know how we got it to work."

Finn ignores the interruption, his grin growing. His face is alight with devilry as he reaches the climax of his story. "So, the next morning, Coach goes in for his shower, and we're all waiting outside, trying not to laugh. Then—BOOM!" He smacks his hands together for emphasis. "The whistle goes off like an air raid siren. The guy comes flying out of the locker room, half soapy, yelling his head off about vandals and discipline and who the hell touched his whistle."

Kyle leans forward, smirking. "And then he trips over his own duffel bag and lands flat on his ass."

The table erupts in laughter. Even Ethan chuckles as Finn doubles over, tears in his eyes. "Oh, man, I forgot about that," he wheezes.

"You forgot?" Kyle raises an eyebrow. "You almost got us both kicked out when you couldn't stop laughing during morning skate."

The banter continues, easy and natural between the group of boys. For the first time, I catch a glimpse of Kyle without the perpetual scowl and hostility. Around the guys, he's different. There's a sharp humor to him, a dry wit that fits perfectly into the rhythm of their friendship. It's strange to see him like this, relaxed and at ease, as though he's shed the weight of his animosity toward me. For a moment, I almost understand why they're friends with him. Almost.

Pushing his empty plate aside, Ethan leans back, a slight smile playing at his lips as the laughter dies down. His gaze shifts to me, and I tense, already dreading what's coming. "I'm sure you've got a story or two," he says, voice warm and inviting.

The table falls quiet, all eyes turning to me. My throat tightens, and I force myself to swallow past the lump that's suddenly formed there.

My mind flickers back to my old team. How I was shunned and ignored. The way my captain used to laugh while I shoved off another teammate's cheap shot. How I was made to feel like an outsider even when I wore the same jersey as everyone else. Definitely no fun memories there.

Instead, I land on something safer, a story from high school. "Uh...we were in the playoffs in high school, and one of my teammates—she was a defenseman—accidentally scored on our own net. Like, a perfect shot. Top shelf."

Griffin snickers, and I let out a shaky laugh, the memory easing the knot in my chest. "She was so pissed at herself, but then she came back in the third and got a hat trick. Completely redeemed herself."

"That's badass," Jax says, grinning.

Finn chuckles, his gaze colliding with mine. For a minute, I'm blinded beneath the full weight of his focus. His dazzling smile and dancing eyes. Then, something shifts in his expression, a wall slamming down over his features and blocking me out so suddenly that I feel almost breathless. It stings more than I want to admit. Ethan's rule about ignoring me doesn't apply in the house, so why is he so intent on freezing me out?

"She..." Kyle's voice has lost any amusement it held earlier, his eyes slicing through me. "So you *can* play on a girls' team."

My body goes rigid, the easy humor evaporating in an instant. The air shifts, the atmosphere turning heavy.

Before Kyle can say anything else, Ethan cuts him off, his voice calm but firm. "Nope. We're not doing this." His tone carries the kind of authority that makes you sit up straighter, even when you're not the one in trouble. He leans forward slightly, his sharp gaze pinning Finn first, then Jax and Griffin, before landing on Kyle. "Tomorrow is Roster Day. We've all done our best, worked our hardest, and Coach will make whatever decision is best for the team."

Kyle scoffs. "Easy for you to say. Your position isn't at risk, all for a pathetic PR stunt."

"*And*," Ethan continues, raising his voice and talking over Kyle as though he never spoke. "We will *all* respect his decision." His voice hardens, lingering on Kyle a beat too long, a warning simmering just beneath the surface. "Regardless of our individual positions, all of us are a team. We work together to do what's right *for the team*. So, from here on, there will be no more fighting. Not on the ice, not in the locker room, and not here. Understood?"

A murmur of agreement goes up around the table, but Ethan isn't done yet. Fixing Griffin with his piercing stare, he gestures toward Kyle and inquires, "Are you two good?"

"If Reed doesn't have a problem with me, then I don't have a problem with him. I'm here to make sure when you idiots fuck up, the other team doesn't get a goal." He softens his statement with a crooked smile.

"Har har." Jax jabs him with his elbow, rolling his eyes.

"Please," Finn teases. "The only reason you're the number one goalie in the state is because we make your job a breeze."

The mood lightens somewhat, but the damage is done. The easy atmosphere from before dissipating like smoke in the air.

"Thanks for dinner," Griffin says a short while later as he pushes his chair back and stands, glancing briefly around the table. His gaze lingers on Kyle for half a second, some of that boyish charm hardening into steel, before he looks away, waving goodbye as he walks out of the room.

I watch him go, my fingers fiddling with my knife. I should probably say something—acknowledge what he did for me yesterday in the locker room. Except...what would I even say? Thanks? For what? All he said was that I'm better than Kyle, which isn't exactly a groundbreaking statement. Everyone knows that, even if they are unwilling to say it aloud. It's a low bar if I'm going to start thanking anyone who gives me the mildest compliment.

Maybe I should apologize? But again, for what? It's not like I asked Kyle to start shit with him. None of this is my fault. Griffin doesn't seem like the type who wants pity, and an apology from me would probably come across as just that.

In the end, I decide not to say anything. If Griffin shows up in the sports center or on the ice tomorrow, we'll go back to the routine we've established—ignoring each other unless absolutely necessary. And if he doesn't...well, I'm used to being alone.

Shaking off the thought, I focus on the clinking of dishes. Kyle has disappeared upstairs, and I can hear the TV on in the living room, along with Ethan's and Jax's low voices as they watch the highlight reel of a recent game.

Forcing myself to move, I grab a dish towel and join Finn at the sink. He is already elbow deep in soapy water, scrubbing a plate.

"I'll dry," I tell him, keeping my voice neutral.

He tenses beside me, his shoulders stiffening at my close proximity, but he doesn't tell me to leave. I pick up a clean plate, drying it methodically while the silence stretches between us.

Eventually, I glance at him from beneath my eyelashes, my frustration bubbling over. "What's your problem with me?"

The only response I get is the tightening of his jaw as he scrubs harder at a pot.

"The rule doesn't apply in the house," I press, my voice sharpening. "So, why are you giving me the cold shoulder?"

Still nothing.

"Is it because I didn't tell you who I was right away that first day? 'Cause, if so, that's unfair. I was caught completely off guard. I didn't know what to do, what was—"

Finn slams the pot down, the loud clang making me jump. Before I can react, he moves.

In a blur, he closes the distance between us, his wet hands gripping the edge of the countertop on either side of me. The hard edge presses into my back as he pins me there, our chests barely brushing. His face is inches from mine, and I can feel his breath, warm and ragged, fanning over my cheek.

My own breathing turns shallow, my pulse hammering in my ears. "Finn..."

His gaze drops to my lips, green eyes turning molten. When he finally speaks, his voice is low and gravelly. "You're about to destroy my best friend," he says, his words cutting and raw. "And instead of worrying about him, all I can think about is doing this."

His mouth crashes against mine. It's quick—just a press of lips, firm and demanding—but it sends a jolt through me, leaving me shaken.

Then, as quickly as it began, it's over. He abruptly pulls back, his eyes not quite meeting mine as he turns to pick up the pot he'd dropped.

Dazed, confused, and shocked, I blink at him for a full minute before I shove out of the kitchen. My hands tremble as I sprint for the stairs, and my heart is still racing when I reach the relative safety of my room.

Inside, I lean against the door as I bring my fingers to my lips. The memory of his touch lingers as I try to make sense of what happened.

But no matter how hard I try, I can't.

TEN

ROSTER DAY

STEELHAWKS MEN'S **Hockey Team**
2025-2026 Season Roster

FIRST LINE
#17 Center: Ethan Maddox
#91 Right Wing: Finn O'Rourke
#12 Left Wing: Dylan Carter
#4 Defense: Jaxon Keller
#6 Defense: Marcus Hayes
#31 Goalie: Griffin Price

SECOND LINE:
#19 Center: Tyler Briggs
#22 Right Wing: Leo Chen
#11 Left Wing: Kyle Reed
#2 Defense: Noah Donaldson
#5 Defense: Liam Connors
#30 Goalie: Stuart Philips

. . .

THIRD LINE:
   #15 Center: Travis Bell
   #24 Right Wing: Sam Miller
   #27 Left Wing: Thomas Matthews
   #7 Defense: Andrew Reid
   #3 Defense: Lee Palmer
   #33 Goalie: Ben Taylor

EXTRAS/PRACTICE Squad:
   #23 Forward: Harris Monroe
   #28 Defense: Reggie Fletcher
   #35 Goalie: Derek Young

ELEVEN

"D-GIRL!" Bear pulls me through the front door of his modest two-story home and straight into his arms. "Congratulations."

His words are muffled against my shoulder. Still, they bring a smile to my lips.

First-line left wing for the Steelhawks!

I might have been confident but seeing my name on the first-line list was...everything.

Releasing him, I step back, a wide, toothy grin splitting my face. Bear is wearing his usual getup—an old flannel and jeans—his hands squeezing my upper arms as he beams back at me.

"I knew you had it in you."

This might be my third season playing college hockey but it's my first on the first line. The coach on my old team never started me above third, even though I was better than every other left wing on the team.

Smirking, I taunt, "It helps that I've got an in with the coach."

Shaking his head, his expression grows more serious, eyes softening as they hold mine. "That was all you, D-Girl. You put in the work, and it showed. You know I wouldn't have given it to you if you hadn't proved yourself—and not just to me." Yeah, I'm not sure I've really proven myself to the team, yet. I mean, my ability on the ice should be enough, but sadly it doesn't seem to be. I've deliberately avoided the entire team since the roster was put up, but I doubt any of them are pleased.

Coach squeezes my shoulder, regaining my attention as he brings his face level with mine. As if sensing where my thoughts have gone, his expression is hard, intent. "More than that, I wouldn't have given you the spot if I didn't think you could handle it."

I swallow roughly, my responding smile soft and genuine, as I move in to give him another quick squeeze around his middle. "I know, Bear. I won't let you down."

"You never have, D-Girl. Never."

I bury my face in his shoulder. *Oh, how I've missed this.*

My stomach chooses that moment to grumble loud enough to be mistaken for a nearby earthquake, and for the first time, I register the warm aroma of roasted chicken and garlic.

Bear chuckles. "Hungry?"

"Starved," I agree, following him through the living room and into the kitchen. "Something smells good."

With every step deeper into the familiar old home, swarming with photos whitened with age and knickknacks that tell a lifetime of stories, my shoulders relax. For the first time since I stepped foot on the BSU campus, I'm at peace.

No roommate confrontations.

No teammate glares.

No whispers hidden behind hands as I walk through campus.

A roast chicken is cooling on the counter, two plates, a pitcher of water, and a bowl of mashed potatoes so big I think he's forgotten it's just the two of us, are set out on the table.

Bear's house isn't fancy, but it's homey in a way I haven't

felt in years. Bear's been like family for as long as I can remember, and looking around the dated kitchen, I get caught up in memories of old. Playing with the bubbles in the sink. Zooming around in the brand-new roller skates he bought me for my eighth birthday. My gaze catches on the deformed figure of a unicorn drawn in red pen on the wall beside the table, and a laugh rips out of me. "I can't believe you still have that," I tell him, pointing to the drawing I naughtily drew on the wall instead of on the perfectly acceptable piece of paper I was given alongside some crayons when I was five. "Haven't you ever repainted in here?"

Bear simply grins, glancing toward the crude drawing as he loads up our plates. "Like I'd ever paint over such a masterpiece. For all I know, it could be worth a fortune one day. *The primitive artwork of a five-year-old Dylan Callahan, NHL All-Star champ,*" he states as though reading a news headline.

I snort, but my cheeks flush anyway. It's been a while since anyone had such confidence in me. Since anyone believed my ridiculously far-fetched dreams could ever possibly be a reality. It's bittersweet.

Plus hearing my dad's last name alongside mine. The hope that one day I can skate onto the ice beneath the heat of the spotlights and be Dylan Callahan instead of Dylan Carter, my mom's maiden name, is almost too much to bear. I made the difficult decision to drop Callahan when I started college. I wanted to be recognized for *my* talent—not the Callahan name. Not my *dad's* success. As much as I appreciate everything he has given me in life, including my talent, I want to carve my own path. Want to be seen for who I am and what I'm capable of and not because I'm Patrick Callahan's daughter.

Still, I wish it could be different. I wish I could honor his name every time I step out onto the ice.

Someday, I promise.

"This looks amazing," I tell Bear, changing the subject as I move to take my seat at the table. He sits down opposite, and we pile food on our plates. We keep the conversation light, easy, while we eat. He asks me about my classes, and the workload, and if I'm juggling everything okay. All the questions a concerned parent would ask, and while each one fills me with warmth at the reminder that someone still cares, it also inflicts a stabbing pain in my chest every time.

"How are things between you and the team?" he eventually asks, clearing his throat. I wondered when we'd get round to talking about the team. I sense he's been dying to ask that since I walked through the door, and I have to give him credit for holding back for this long.

"As expected," I respond vaguely with a nonchalant shrug.

"That standoff with Reed the other day..."

"Nothing I can't handle," I assure him, unable to meet his eyes as I wave his concern away.

I can feel his sharp stare on me, though. "Are you sure? 'Cause I can—"

"You can't do anything," I interrupt, tone soft to ease the blow of my words. "It'll only make me look weak if you step in. Like I can't fight my own battles." I arch a brow, giving him a knowing look. "When we both know I can."

That earns me a smile. "You're the strongest person I know, D."

Reaching over, I squeeze his hand resting on top of the table. "So have faith that I can handle this."

Blowing out a breath, he reluctantly nods. "I do, I do, it's just...it was one thing to see what those old asshole teammates did to you on the ice, but it's another to watch it going on behind the scenes. To see it happening on *my* rink." He shakes his head. "The season hasn't even started yet, and my tongue is at risk of falling off from the number of times I've had to bite it to keep my mouth shut."

I chuckle. "Well, that might actually earn me some brownie points with some of the guys if you can no longer chew their asses off."

His lips lift in a semblance of a smile, but concern still swims in those wise, aged eyes of his. "Just keep an eye out for Kyle. He's not going to be happy."

Now that I've officially taken his starting spot.

Perhaps I should be more concerned about what he'll do, but all I feel is smugness. Maybe if he'd taken my advice and focused on his game instead of mine...except I know that's not true. Kyle could have dedicated every waking moment to hockey these past three weeks, and yes, it would have been a closer competition, but I still would have come out on top. Kyle's good, but he doesn't have the raw talent to be the best. He doesn't have the drive and determination necessary to succeed at this level of competition.

I suspect he's not used to having to work for what he wants in life. He was obviously good enough in high school to get a place on a college team, but college hockey is an entirely different arena. The competition is fierce. It's at this level that you distinguish those who have the talent, who are willing to put in the work and improve, from those who simply view hockey as a hobby.

If you don't have the talent *and* the dedication, then you're just not going to cut it on the first line. It's as simple as that.

"You know," Bear begins, setting down his fork and leaning back in his chair, the flicker of a memory softening the lines on his face. "I believe it was the challenges your dad faced in college that made him the resilient player he was."

I pause mid-bite, surprised. Bear doesn't usually talk about my dad's struggles—just how talented he was, how dominant on the ice. The legend of him, not the man.

"Most of the kids I coach are carefree college students, spreading their wings for the first time and excited to sample everything life has to offer. But that wasn't Patrick. Even at eighteen, he was just a man—a dad—trying to make it work. Trying to juggle you and classes and hockey. Just wanting to be the best at everything all at once."

A lump forms in my throat. Of course, I know my mom and dad got pregnant with me in high school. I always thought their love story was one fairy tales were created from. There can't be many high school sweethearts who end up accidentally pregnant and actually make it all the way—graduate college, dominate in their chosen career path, and somehow manage to love each other unconditionally.

They had the perfect life. The perfect love story...

Until they didn't.

I lose myself to the overwhelming grief and regret and aching sadness that weighs on me constantly. Another battle I'm forever fighting to keep at bay.

"It was a different fight," Bear says, dragging my mind back into his kitchen. "Your dad had different obstacles to overcome."

Admittedly, I've never really thought about my dad that way. I know he worked his ass off, but the main memories I have of him are after college. I've never really thought about the fact that he had to fight for his place too. In my mind, he's always just been...great.

"Your mom was a godsend, of course," Bear continues. "Supported his dream no matter the sacrifices." My throat goes dry at the mention of my mom. I really should try to call her this week...assuming she'll even answer the phone.

"But your dad," Bear shakes his head, eyes glinting with that familiar fondness, "he never backed down from it. Never complained. Never blamed you for making it more difficult for him to reach his dream. If anything, you were his reason for fighting as hard as he did. He poured everything he had into hockey, into being the best. He fought for it every day."

I swallow hard, emotions I've buried deep for so long now threatening to bubble over and completely destroy me.

"Sounds like Dad." My throat is hoarse, scratchy.

Bear nods. "That drive?" he says, leaning forward slightly on his chair. "That refusal to give up no matter how much was on his shoulders? No matter the odds? That's what made him so damn good. The best I ever coached." He lets the weight of that settle for a moment before adding with a teasing glint in his eye, "Until now, maybe."

A laugh escapes me, shaky but real. "Don't start comparing me to him, Bear. I'm not even close."

"Not yet, but you've got the same fire, D-Girl. You just don't let up. You're stubborn as hell, just like he was. And if you keep at it, no one's gonna touch you."

His words land somewhere deep inside me, echoing in places I usually try to ignore. I feel it now, though, the connection. If Dad could overcome those odds, if he could carry it all and still become one of the greats, then maybe I can too.

No matter what Kyle and the team throw at me.

THE SECOND I step onto Athletes Row, I groan. It's barely past nine, but the street looks like a scene from a music video: girls in barely-there dresses totter on sky-high heels, boys whoop and shout with red Solo cups in hand, and every lawn pulses with the heavy bass of a different song. Someone's dragged speakers onto their porch, and the thrum of music vibrates in my chest.

I'm so not in the mood for this.

I'd far rather have spent the entire night at Bear's and avoided this stupid party, and the rest of the team, but that would have raised questions I don't have suitable answers for. And the last thing I want anyone looking into is my relationship with the coach. It's paramount that everyone believes we have nothing beyond a coach-player relationship, just like everyone else on the team.

With leaden feet, I make my way up the street, skirting around a group of drunk girls yelling at each other before dodging a guy in a football jersey sprinting with a keg hoisted over his shoulder. In jeans, Converse, and an old, well-worn, Timberwolves T-shirt, I'm not even dressed for a party.

By the time I reach our house, it's clear that we are the epicenter of the chaos. *That's just perfect.* I should have expected no less from the Steelhawks hockey team.

Every light blazes downstairs, the windows rattling with the music. The yard is packed, and there's a bottleneck at the front door.

Sighing, I trudge up the drive. I wish Wren were here. At least then I'd have one ally. One person I could talk to. We could huddle in a corner of the house and ignore everyone else. I tried inviting her. Alas, while hockey is her thing, parties apparently are not.

I finally squeeze my way through the front door. Inside, it's *worse.* Bodies move together in a writhing mass in what used to be our living room. The sofas have been shoved against the walls to allow enough space for a makeshift dance floor. People are pressed into every corner, making out, shouting over the music, and spilling drinks all around themselves.

I am *so* not having any part in cleaning up this mess.

I scan the room, spotting Ethan leaning against the back wall like a king surveying his court. Jax is beside him, one shoulder pressed against the wall, his focus intent on Ethan—as if he can block out the rest of the room by sheer willpower alone.

Damn, maybe I should ask him if that's possible. It would be a convenient skill to have right now.

As if sensing my eyes on him, he glances over. Our gazes collide, and he stops mid-sentence. Ethan gives him a quizzical look before following his line of sight until I'm caught in both of their stares. Gray-blue and deep brown pools act like a vortex, glueing my feet to the floor despite people shuffling past me.

It's the first time I've set eyes on either of them since the lineup was announced, and as my gaze roams over their faces, I try to get a read on their expressions—are they pissed? Resentful? Out for revenge?

After a moment, Jax's lips curve into the faintest smile, and he lifts his Solo cup in a silent toast. The gesture catches me off guard, and I know I'm wide-eyed as I gape at him. I expected indifference at best, hostility at worst. Not...whatever sort of *go you* gesture that was.

Confused, my focus shifts to Ethan. He's as stoic as always, giving nothing away regarding how he feels. He's most likely in damage control mode, figuring out how he can stop the team from imploding and ensure everyone focuses on what's important—the game. I don't envy him for having that job, but I'm not about to shrink just to make room for their egos—or make it easier for him to keep the peace.

Dismissing them both, I turn toward the kitchen, but something flashes in my peripheral vision—red hair. I freeze and scan the crowd, finally spotting Finn in the middle of the dance floor. He's holding a plastic cup over his head, his other hand wrapped around the waist of a girl pressed against him, their hips gyrating in time to the beat. He's wearing one of those tank tops with the massive arm holes that show more of his toned chest and abs than it hides, the white contrasting beautifully with the black ink visible along his left arm. I trail the dark swirls until they disappear around the petite blonde pressed up against him.

Her face is turned away from me, so I can't see who she is, but then she shifts, tilting her face up to his, and I get a clear view. The puck bunny. The one who came up to me in the cafeteria and started the whole *Bench Bunny* whispers.

My gut twists, and the spot where Finn's lips met mine in a quick kiss last night *burns*. A reminder of how foolish I'd be to assume that a kiss meant anything. Finn can't be trusted. *None* of them can.

Jaw tight, I shove my way into the kitchen and grab a soda from the counter. It hisses as I pop it open, downing a third of it. It does nothing to calm the heat I can feel in my cheeks. The rage burning in my chest. The embarrassment eating at my core.

Shaking my head, I turn so my back is against the counter and look out over the busy kitchen without taking any of it in. The noise, the lights, the stifling heat of too many bodies packed into one place—it's too much. Suffocating.

I need air.

Pushing off the counter, I stride toward the back door and out into the night. A fire burns in the center of the backyard, a circle of chairs surrounding it. Most of them are occupied by my teammates. Girls are draped over some of them while others sit and talk, their laughter cutting through the night.

I spot an empty seat on the far side of the fire, but I already know my presence won't be welcome. Nor am I in the mood to deal with shit about my position on the roster. Instead, I move toward an empty bench to the side of the back door, half hidden in shadows, and sit down, cradling my drink.

The fresh air helps to clear my head, to calm the irritation that had been prickling at my skin. Irritation at seeing Finn with another girl, that I have no right feeling. It was one kiss. A one-second touching of lips. That doesn't make Finn mine or me his. Nor should I want it to. And yet, the irrational jealousy I felt at seeing him pressed up against another girl...

"Get a grip of yourself, Dyl," I mutter frustratingly, shaking my head in disappointment.

Instead of getting lost in my head, I scan the backyard. Couples are tangled in shadowed corners, and there's a knot of people by the back door. The rest are drawn to the bonfire like moths to a flame.

From where I'm seated, I can see Griffin, cast in firelight on the far side of the flames. He's leaning back in his fold-up chair, legs spread, and soda can in hand. Relaxed for all the world to see. My gaze dips lower, noting the dark colored jeans he's wearing, paired with black boots, and a matching T-shirt that stretches beautifully across his broad chest. If I squint hard enough, I swear I can make out his nipple rings pressing against the inside of the fabric.

His body is angled toward a group of other players who appear deep in conversation. However, Griffin is quiet, mostly nodding along or listening to the others. Every now and then, he says something that makes them laugh, that crooked grin of his making an appearance. But when he thinks no one is looking, his face changes. The easy grin slips, and I see *him*—the real Griffin.

The one I caught a glimpse of in the locker room. The one I sense on the opposite side of the rink when we're alone.

The one I'm curious to know more about despite every instinct telling me to stay away.

Eventually, he gets up, saying something to the ones he's with before stalking away. I trail him with my eyes until he steps outside of the ring of light cast by the fire, swallowed up by shadows. I squint through the darkness, trying to spot him for a moment longer, before giving up. He's probably gone inside to grab a drink or chat with others from the team. Hell, perhaps he's gone to find a hookup for the night.

Returning my attention to the fire, I stare into the flames, allowing my thoughts to drift away into nothing until a sudden presence appears at my side.

I stiffen. "You didn't think I missed you sneaking out of the house, did you?" Griffin's voice is low, and despite my better judgment, I find myself relaxing, my shoulders dropping from my ears.

I still don't look at him, keeping my focus on the sparks that occasionally hiss and spit as they rise into the air, gleaming brightly before burning out.

He doesn't say anything, the two of us falling into a companionable silence. It's...nice. When was the last time I just sat with someone? No pressure to talk. No tension or hostility tainting the air.

"Shouldn't you be inside getting your rocks off?" I ask, still not looking at him.

From the corner of my eye, I notice his lips quirk in the hint of a smile. "Nah, not really my thing."

Finally turning, I arch a brow. "Isn't it?"

I overhear enough locker room talk to know that it is. Or, at least, he *pretends* it is. Now, I can't help but wonder if that's a part of his mask as well.

He only smirks, but it's not like the smug ones I saw him give the team earlier. More like, we're sharing a secret. One I don't fully understand.

Dropping my stare, I fiddle with the tab on my soda can, debating whether to say anything before finally asking, "So, what's the damage?"

Griffin raises a thick, blond eyebrow.

"With the team," I clarify. "How much do they hate me?"

He shrugs, tilting his head from side to side. "Most of them are reserving judgment. They've seen how good you are on the ice, but they want to know how you'll perform in a game situation."

"If I can hold my own or if I'll be a weak spot," I conclude.

He nods in agreement.

Okay, that's not awful. I can deal with that.

Of course, it's not the entire team who feel that way. I know for a fact Kyle won't be so understanding—so accepting of Coach's decision.

"What about you?" I dare to ask. For some reason, I find myself even more nervous to hear his answer than I was to know what the rest of the team thought.

He's silent for a long time, intense blue eyes hidden by the darkness boring into me. I can feel his stare raking over my face. Can feel it seeing more than it should. More than I'd like it to.

After what feels like a lifetime, he finally looks away, glancing toward the fire. My stare lingers on his profile a moment longer before I follow his gaze. Most of the team are still sitting around the fire, chatting or making out with whatever girl is in their lap.

He's silent for so long that I assume he isn't going to respond. My attention has drifted, the silence dropping over me like a warm blanket as I get lost in the flickering of the flames once more.

Like a ripple in still water, his voice breaks through my trance, low and smooth, like top-shelf bourbon. "I think you scare them," he says, not looking at me. Yet, I sense his entire awareness is attuned to my every move. He pauses, and I'm about to ask what he means when he turns, stealing the air from my lungs with the intensity in his eyes. "You scare them because they know you're better than they will ever be."

TWELVE

SPEECHLESS.

Griffin Price has rendered me speechless.

I stare at him, mouth parted in a silent O as his words reverberate inside my skull.

My dad was always my number one supporter, encouraging me, pushing me. Bear, too, made it clear earlier that he believes in me. But I've never—*never*—had another teammate say something so...earnest about me. About my abilities. About what I'm capable of.

The silence stretches between us, something unspoken in the air, something I can't quite put my finger on. I don't trust anyone on this team, not really, but with Griffin, I feel... something.

Perhaps it's because he's the goalie—more removed from the rest of the team. My presence doesn't affect him the same way it does the others so he doesn't take the same offense to me being here.

Yet, I don't think that's it. At least, it's not the entire reason.

Before I can put my finger on what it is, the moment is shattered.

Kyle storms out of the house, shoving a vacant folding chair out of his way as he marches toward the fire. "Where is she?" His voice echoes around the yard, drawing the attention of everyone out here. Some of the guys around the fire push to their feet, glancing at one another, but we all know who he means.

Tension has my body snapping upright, spine straight and hardened with steel. Kyle whirls, eyes scanning the yard. I catch the fury twisting his face before those blazing eyes find me in the darkness.

"You," he snarls, pointing a finger as he marches in my direction. There's a group of younger players trailing behind him, looking just as pissed off. "You stole my position."

His voice is loud enough to be heard by those in the kitchen, more partygoers spilling outside to watch the drama unfold. A crowd quickly forms. I spot Finn at the back, brows dipped low over narrowed eyes, but it's not Kyle he's glaring at. It's me.

I quickly sweep the other faces, but I don't see Ethan or Jax amongst the spectators before I focus back on the threat directly in front of me.

Kyle makes a point of looking around where I'm sitting, his lips hitching in a cruel smirk. "Let me guess," he drawls, grin sharp and predatory. "You're out here hiding because you know you don't deserve to be on the first line."

My teeth grind. I hate being in the middle of this shit. The center of attention while boys like Kyle try to tear me down for simply being myself. They couldn't possibly use my presence as an opportunity to better themselves. To beat me by working harder.

That would be far too upstanding.

My nails dig into my palms, the bite helping to ground me as I push to my feet. Griffin rises with me, a wall of strength at my side, but he doesn't move to intervene, letting me take control.

"I earned my spot fair and square," I state in a loud, clear voice. If Kyle wants an audience, then they're damn well going to hear what I have to say too. "Just like every other member on this team." Pinning him with my glare, I say, "You *earned* your second-line position."

The crowd mutters, and Kyle's face darkens. He stalks closer, fists curling at his sides. "You think you're hot shit, don't you?" he sneers.

I shake my head. "I'm no better than anyone else on this team."

"Damn fucking straight." He shoves a finger in my face. "You're nobody. An attention-seeking whore who thought she could spread her legs and have the entire hockey team begging for more."

When the fuck have I ever given anyone on this team the impression I want to sleep with them? Okay, there was that little slipup when Finn kissed me, but in my defense, he caught me completely by surprise. Now my guard is up, and that little *mistake* won't happen again.

Still, against my will, my gaze finds him in the crowd. His eyes are hard, lips pressed into a flat line. With his arms folded across his chest, it's clear he has no intention of intervening. My head tilts slightly as I stare at him. Did he tell Kyle about that kiss? Did he make it sound like *I* came on to *him*? Is that why Kyle thinks I want to bag the entire team?

My view of Finn is cut off as Kyle steps into my space. Everything in me wants to recoil, but the bench presses into the back of my calves, a warning that there's nowhere to go. His bloodshot eyes bore into me, burning me alive with the intensity of the rage living in those cold depths. "I'm going to destroy you," he hisses. Spittle hits my cheek, and I have to force myself to remain still, not to wipe it away. "I'm going to show *everyone* that you don't belong in *my* spot. On *my* team."

Bending so the bitter stench of his breath sticks to my skin, he speaks only loud enough so I can hear. "I'm going to make you regret ever coming to BSU."

The threat in his tone sends shivers skating down my spine, and my breath catches in my throat. I swallow roughly, my mouth opening and closing, but I have no response. No words that will change his mind.

As if sensing I need an assist, Griffin steps up beside me. His arm brushes mine as he shoves Kyle in the chest. "Step back, Reed."

Stumbling back a step, Kyle's fierce glare snaps to Griffin. I don't think he'd realized he was standing there this entire time, but now, he barks out a laugh, frigid and sharp. "Of course you're coming to her rescue." His lip curls in a sneer. "How many fucks did she offer in exchange for being her lap dog?"

My cheeks flame, and I'm grateful for the lack of lighting out here. Hopefully no one else can see my embarrassment. I realize Finn didn't have to tell Kyle about our kiss. The fact that he saw Griffin and I together on the ice that night, that Griffin has come to my defense not once but *twice* now, is enough for Kyle. In his mind, that *obviously* means I must be fucking him. Why else would Griffin help me? Stand up for me?

I can feel the eyes of the crowd on us, bouncing back and forth as they drink in every second of drama.

Griffin's jaw tightens, and for a second, I see the fire behind his calm exterior, the dangerous edge lurking beneath. But then he fixes his usual mocking grin in place. "Have you already forgotten my promise to you in the locker room?" His voice is a taunt, and unlike Kyle's, his words don't carry to the gathered crowd. They're intended solely for Kyle.

Snorting a laugh, Kyle shakes his head. "I haven't fucking touched you, man."

"Consider this your only warning, then. That promise extends to her." Griffin tilts his head in my direction. "Touch her, fuck with her, and it'll be *you* who doesn't see any ice time this season."

Like the idiot he is, Kyle waves off Griffin's warning like he's swatting a fly. "Fuck off, Griff. This isn't your fight." Raking his gaze pointedly over me, he tacks on, "She's not worth it."

I bristle. *Fucking asshole.* But I know better than to rise to the bait. I already caved once to him, I won't give him that satisfaction again. Won't give him the opportunity to tell Coach that I'm starting shit. Causing issues.

Griffin doesn't move. He shows no outward response to Kyle's words. He may as well not have spoken at all. Not that Kyle waits long for a retort, before raising his voice, once again appealing to the crowd, hungry for drama.

"You want to know how she got that spot?" He asks loudly, smirking menacingly at me before he spins to address those gathered behind him. His voice drips with mockery as he declares, "It's because she slept with the coach."

The yard erupts. Gasps, laughter, murmurs—all blending together to form a twisted symphony.

My vision tilts, the world around me stuttering in and out of focus. I can't feel the ground beneath my feet, and my ears ring, my shallow breaths all that I can hear.

Not again.

This can't be happening again.

I shove past Kyle, unsteady on my feet and nausea churning precariously in my stomach. I have to get out of here.

"She didn't even deny it," he calls after me, voice smug with triumph. His words slice through the ringing in my ears. I don't look back. I can't.

I shove through the crowd, uncaring of who I'm crashing into. Faces twist as I push past, disgust curling lips, eyes narrowing in judgment, sneers cracking across mouths I don't recognize. Someone spits the word *"Slut"* under their breath. Another snorts, *"Figures."* A girl glares at me like I've confirmed every nasty rumor she's ever heard.

I crash into someone and mutter a frantic apology before I look up. My breath catches in my throat. It's Finn. His face is hard, brows dipped in confusion. I find myself scouring his face, hoping for...something. Whatever it is I'm looking for, I don't find it. His lips are pressed in a flat line, eyes shuttered. Disappointment sinks like a weight in my stomach. He believes Kyle's lies.

We stare at each other for a beat, and as time stretches, something shifts in his eyes, the pulling back of a curtain. Concern, tentative and unsure, seeps through the hardness. Lifting his head, his gaze darts around us, as if only just realizing the mob of people pushing in, baying for my blood.

He steps forward, fingers reaching out for me, but the pressure of the bodies around me surges forward, pushing me away. I lose sight of him as hands shove me back. The crowd closes in, bodies pressing in from all sides. My throat burns. My skin itches. My lungs won't expand.

I can't breathe. I can't—

There's the sound of scuffling and an *oomph* from somewhere behind me. A fight, maybe. I don't stop to look.

I keep pushing forward. *Away. Away.*

Half blind, I stumble through the house and out the front door, practically falling into the street. People mill about, wandering between house parties, oblivious to the wreckage inside, but it's quieter out here than the backyard.

I suck in lungfuls of air, my vision still spotty, and as I fumble to pull my phone from my back pocket, I realize my hands are trembling. I stare at them for a long moment before shifting my focus to the black screen.

Then, I call the only number I can think of.

"I swear to God, Dylan," Wren fumes, waving her arms around as she marches back and forth in front of the sofa I'm curled up on. She was the only person I could think of to call—the only BSU student I know and trust enough to consider a friend. Being the awesome person that she is, she immediately told me to come over.

I'd expected her to give me a dorm name and room number, but it turns out Wren lives alone in a tiny apartment tucked in the heart of Blackstone, on a quiet street lined with cobblestones and tall stone buildings. Independent bookshops and cozy little cafés press in around her building like something out of a postcard. It's the kind of place that feels removed from everything, like the rest of the world can't quite reach it.

If only that were true.

My knees are pulled up to my chest, arms wrapped around them, with my chin resting on top as I watch her fume.

"If I ever see that asshole, I'm going to—" She breaks off, fists clenched and practically vibrating with rage. "No. You know what? I *am* going to see him. I'm going to hunt his sorry ass down, and I'll—I don't know—slash his tires? Superglue his helmet to his head? Shove a stick so far up his ass he whistles through his teeth?"

Despite everything, a laugh escapes me—weak, but real. "I think that last one might be a felony."

She stops pacing, rounding on me with wide, furious eyes. "Don't laugh! He humiliated you in front of everyone. If you think I'm letting him get away with this—"

"I know," I interject, voice pathetically defeated. "I was there, remember?" Shaking my head, I force strength into my next words. "It's fine," I tell her. *God, how I wish I believed that.* "It's not like there's any proof."

Except they didn't need proof last time, either.

"Exactly!" Wren points at me like I've made a ground-breaking discovery. "There's no proof. When people realize that, they'll get bored and move on to the next bit of hot goss."

My nose scrunches, lips pressed flat as I stare intently at my knees.

Wren must catch my look of skepticism. "Unless..." she hedges. "Oh my God. Did you—did you *sleep* with the coach?!"

My head whips up so fast I feel something twinge in my neck. "What? No. NO! Of course not!" I look at her with such horror and revulsion that she takes a small step back.

"Okay, okay." She holds her hands up in mock surrender. "Just checking. But then, what was that face about?"

Sinking my teeth into my bottom lip, my gaze jumps back and forth between her eyes.

"I've...lived through this before," I confess. When her brows dip lower over her eyes, I explain, "The same rumor was started at my old school."

Her mouth drops open.

I shake my head, a fresh wave of tears burning the backs of my eyes. "Why do men do this? A woman does better than them, and they automatically assume we must be sleeping our way to the top. It's...infuriating." It's so much more than that. I feel so much that I can't even put it into words. Anger. Resentment. Hurt. Exhaustion.

I'm tired. I'm so fucking tired of working my hardest, doing my best, and being told my achievements are only possible because I must have spread my legs for the right person.

"It's disgusting," Wren spits. "Pathetic. Weak." Dropping

onto the sofa beside me, she moves straight into my space, cuddling up beside me.

Feeling completely defeated, I sigh, leaning into her. I always have some fight left in me, even when I've had to scrape the bottom of the barrel to find it, but now...I'm empty.

"I feel like I'm having déjà vu," I admit in a small voice that sounds nothing like me. "I'm in my own version of *Groundhog Day*, doomed to repeat the same fragile male masculinity bullshit over and over until I lose my mind."

Wren shifts on the sofa so I can see her face, see the determination etched into her expression. "Those lies say more about them than they do about you."

I snort. "Tell that to the rest of NSU who believed their bullshit and taunted me with it at every opportunity."

Squeezing my arm, she says empathically, "But *you* know the truth. And your skills on the ice speak for themselves."

I nod. I know she's right, to an extent. But rumors matter—false or not.

"If scouts or teams got wind of any of it, I'd never get drafted. I could lose any opportunity I have to play professionally. At even working—"

"Hey!" Wren cuts off my ramble. "Let's not spiral out of control, yeah? This is a stupid college rumor spread at a party. Most of the people there were drinking and probably don't even remember who they hooked up with, never mind what one douche canoe said."

One side of my lips quirks in the shadow of a smile. Still, I shake my head. "What if this is only the beginning—*again*? It only got worse last time until I was forced to leave—"

"Stop!" Wren says firmly, holding up a hand. "That's not going to happen. You know why?"

There's such determination on her face, such fire in her eyes.

I shake my head, biting my lip.

"Because this time, you have me."

She sits up straighter, and I don't know if it's her simple statement or the confidence in her posture, but the weight of it hits me like a slap. I've never had anyone before. Not someone I could actually talk to or confide in. Someone who would have my back.

Leaning in, I wrap my arm around her shoulders. "Thank you," I murmur into her ear.

"Good, now that that's settled, we need hot chocolate."

"We do?"

She looks at me like I'm crazy. "Duh. Hot chocolate fixes boy trouble like ice cream fixes cramps."

I snort, watching as she moves over to her tiny kitchen, pulling mugs down from the shelf and lifting out the cocoa powder. Blowing out a breath, some of the tension eases from my shoulders as I sink deeper into her old, cozy sofa.

Wren's apartment has an open-plan kitchen and living area, with a door off it for the bathroom and another one that leads to her bedroom. The place is furnished with mismatched furniture that should look odd but somehow works. It's very... Wren. Large windows flood the space with sunlight during the day, and now, as I stare out, I catch the warm glow of apartments across the street and the shimmer of the town beyond.

"Here you go," she says, handing me a large mug. It's overflowing with whipped cream and marshmallows, steam billowing off the top.

I nurse it as she gets comfortable beside me, throwing a blanket over us. She has several lamps on around the room, bathing it in a soft, warm glow that casts shadows along the walls. It's cozy, peaceful. Exactly what I needed after tonight.

"I think Griffin stood up for me tonight." I'm not sure I

intended to say those words aloud. I hadn't actually given him a second thought until just now.

Lowering her mug, cream lines her upper lip, creating a comical moustache as Wren gapes wide-eyed at me.

"Griffin?" She clarifies, "Griffin Price, the Steelhawks' starting goalie and best in the conference?"

I nod. "That's the one."

"And you're only telling me this now?!" She leans forward so abruptly that she nearly spills her hot chocolate.

"I'd forgotten," I admit, chagrined.

"You *forgot* that Griffin Price stood up to your archnemesis." She shakes her head, turning to look at...absolutely nothing. "What are we going to do with her? She's completely hopeless!"

Barking a laugh, I question, "*Who* are you talking to?"

She simply waves me away. "*That* is not what's important right now. Tell me *everything*. Don't spare a single detail. What was he wearing? How hot did he look?" She clutches a cushion to her chest and sighs dramatically. "Griffin has that whole charming-on-the-surface, danger-underneath thing going for him—the kind of guy who smiles just enough to distract you from the fact he might ruin your life."

I know. Believe me, I know.

And after tonight, I think I'm past the point of distraction.

Her gaze meets mine, a smirk tilting her lips. "I don't think I'd mind being ruined by Griffin Price."

Girl, I don't think I would either!

She playfully slaps my leg when I don't immediately jump into regaling her with every detail. Just to tease her, I lift my mug to my lips first, taking a long gulp as the rich chocolate glides over my tongue.

Okay, yeah. That's amazing. I'm now a firm believer that any life crisis requires hot chocolate.

"He was with me when Kyle stormed outside," I eventually share with her.

"Wait, he was already with you?" she interrupts, eyes wide. "As in, already talking to you, or you happened to be standing beside one another, but he was in a conversation with someone else and had no idea you were there?"

"We were talking—"

"Oh my God! You were *talking* to Griffin Price."

"If you keep interrupting me, I'm not telling you what happened."

Huffing, she mimes zipping her lips before gesturing for me to continue.

I smirk at her, but I do admit that when Kyle threatened me, Griffin stepped in and threatened him right back.

"That is so hot," Wren states in a dreamy voice before straightening. "Wait, does this mean he likes you?"

"What?" I question, startled by her conclusion. "No. Of course not. It means he recognizes my talent and wasn't going to let Kyle steamroll me."

"Hmm, I'm not so sure." The certainty behind her tone has me scoffing and rolling my eyes at the extent of her delusion.

"It didn't mean anything," I tell her. "He was just..."

"Just what?" she interrupts, tilting her head to one side and studying me closely. "Being a decent human being?" she muses, clearly not needing any actual input from me. "Maybe. But also, he didn't have to. In fact, from what I've heard of Griffin, he doesn't make a point of inserting himself anywhere he doesn't want to be. And yet, he *chose* to stick up for you."

Before I can get a word in, she keeps going.

"More than that, he did it in front of the entire team. Kyle might have spouted off bullshit rumors, but the whole team also saw Griffin take *your* side. Griffin's respected amongst all of them. If he's got your back, that counts for something."

I pause, letting her words sink in. She's not wrong. Griffin *is* respected amongst the team. And they all saw him take my side over Kyle's.

I'm just not entirely sure what that means—or if it's good or bad for me.

Shifting beside me, Wren grabs the remote from the coffee table and turns on the TV, flicking through the channels until she lands on a rom-com.

I'm only half watching, but by the time we're halfway through it, the knot in my chest has loosened.

We end up falling asleep on the sofa, her head on my shoulder, the movie credits rolling. For the first time in what feels like forever, I feel just a little less alone.

THIRTEEN

THE HOUSE IS EERILY quiet when I step inside the next morning. It's so early that it's barely light out. But I wanted to get back and grab my gym gear before anyone woke up.

There is still the faint hint of beer lingering in the air, but peeking into the kitchen, I'm surprised to find it sparkling clean. Not a single red Solo cup or spirit bottle in sight. The floors have been mopped and trash taken out like the party never happened.

If only it were that easy to clear the reminder of it from my memories.

The squeaking of a spring has my head snapping toward the living room as Ethan rises to his feet. He's wearing the same dark jeans and pale blue shirt that brings out the color in his eyes that he had on last night. Except this morning, those eyes are dull, exhaustion clouding them of their usual light. His hair is a mess, too. Well, messier than it usually is—sticking up in every direction as though he spent the entire night running his fingers through it.

If I had to guess, I'd say he still hasn't been to bed. Did he stay up all night cleaning? *Why?*

As I stand there, his gaze slowly drops over my body, sharp and thorough. My skin prickles beneath the intensity of it, but I have no idea what he's searching for.

"Where the hell have you been?" he demands, finally lifting his gaze to my face. His voice is deeper than usual, threaded almost with...concern? No, that can't be right. I must be misinterpreting it. It's most likely from lack of sleep.

I blink at him, in absolutely no mood for whatever this is. I need to burn off the lingering tension from last night before starting an entirely new fight this morning. "I didn't realize I had to run my every decision past you," I snark, folding my arms across my chest as I stare back at him. "You're the captain of my team, not my life."

His nostrils flare, his jaw tightening. "You disappeared," he says through gritted teeth. "No one knew where you were or how to contact you. Do you even realize how not okay that is?"

I rear back, shocked at being scolded like a child by someone only one year older.

"I'm not a kid, Ethan. I don't need a babysitter."

"Dylan," he snaps. Those gray-blue eyes blaze with a frigid fire, scalding me to the bone. "Anything could have happened to you. Do you have any idea how reckless that was? I was up all night wondering if—" He cuts himself off, scrubbing a hand down his face.

My brows hitch at his near admission. Still...

"I can take care of myself, thanks."

"That's not the point." His words are a growl as he takes a step closer, face hardening. "Give me your number."

It's not a question. It's a demand.

"Absolutely not." I shake my head vehemently.

He blinks, visibly thrown. Guess he wasn't expecting me to deny him. "Why the hell not?" He looks incredulous, like he can't fathom why I wouldn't want him to have my number. Well, if he'd endured what I had, he'd understand.

"Because I don't want anyone on the team to have my number."

His frustration flares, his long legs eating up the distance between us. "It wouldn't be *the team*," he growls when he's standing directly in front of me. "It would be me. *Only* me."

Staring up into those thunderous eyes of his, I hold my ground. "It's still a no."

"Jesus Christ." He throws his hands up. "You ran out of here like a bat out of hell! We couldn't find you anywhere."

I'd love to know who this *we* is.

"Yes," I droll. "I'm sure the entire team was frantically searching for the unwanted player." Pinching the bridge of my nose, I exhale heavily. *Sarcasm will get me nowhere.*

The day hasn't even begun and I already feel a headache coming on.

Wearily, I ask, "Why do you even care?"

"Because," Ethan grinds, face hard with thunder. "You're a Steelhawk." There's fire behind his declaration. "And that makes you my responsibility."

I'm stunned into silence. *A Steelhawk.* He just said I'm one of them, and not in a condescending way. In a *you're truly a part of the team* way. In a way I've never experienced before, and it's...so many things. Triumphant. Jarring. Like coming home but still unsure if anyone booby-trapped the house while you were away.

I swallow around the sudden lump that has formed in my throat. "Does this mean there's no more ignoring me?" I do my best to mask the vulnerability, the hint of hope, but I sense he hears it anyway.

Ethan shakes his head, his gaze steady on mine. "No. Coach

wouldn't have put you in the first line if he didn't think you deserved it."

"Do *you* think I deserve it?"

He blows out a breath, head falling forward on his shoulders as though wishing I hadn't asked that question. He stares at the ground beneath his feet for a long moment, and I sense he's gathering his thoughts.

Eventually, he lifts his head, and I'm once again sucked into the vortex of his eyes, held captive as I await his response with bated breath. I don't know why I care what he thinks. I *shouldn't* care—and yet, for some unknown reason, I *want* Ethan's approval.

"I think no one else on the team deserved it more." Before I can let *that* go to my head, he tacks on, "But, I also think you're going to have to prove that you can hold your own on the ice against an opponent."

That gets a smirk out of me. "I don't know why you all assume being taller and broader means it'll be easier to corner me. Or why no one has realized yet that being lighter and smaller makes me quicker on my feet, so less likely to get pinned and easier to wriggle out when I do."

His gaze drops to my lips, the corners lifting as amusement glitters in his eyes. It only lasts a moment, though, before it's snuffed out.

"I heard about what happened. With Reed."

I freeze. My stomach clenches, and the blood drains from my face.

Ethan notices. He always notices. His expression shifts—less stern, more cautious. "I...I'm sorry," he says quietly. So much so that I'm convinced for a second that I heard him wrong.

"What?"

"I'm sorry," he repeats, rubbing the back of his neck. "It

should never have happened. I should've been there—should've stopped it before it started."

An apology from Ethan Maddox is the last thing I expected to hear this morning, and I'm stunned into silence.

Shaking his head, he continues, "I pulled him aside after the roster was announced. Told him to keep his head on straight. I even had someone from the team keep an eye on him last night, but—" He shakes his head, expression tight with regret. "That should never have happened."

No, it shouldn't, but...

"Kyle's actions are not your fault, nor your responsibility."

The tension in his posture doesn't ease. He looks like he's carrying the weight of the entire team on his back—and I guess, in a way, he is.

He snorts. "This entire team is my responsibility—every single one of you. I don't care if you think you can handle yourself—*I* care that you're safe. And last night..." He trails off, jaw tightening. "Last night, I failed."

I don't know what to say. Part of me wants to tell him he's overreacting, but another part of me—the part that's still reeling from what happened—takes solace from his apology.

The moment grows between us, twisting and bending until it feels like a pin could pop it.

My sigh echoes like the thud of a stick against a drum. "Fine," I relent. "I'll give you my number—but only you. You don't put me in a group chat. You don't give it out to anyone else on the team. If I get so much as a random message from an unknown number, I'm coming after you, and it won't be pretty."

I swear one corner of his lips quirks, the tension between us fizzling out.

"Scout's honor," he says, holding up his index, middle, and ring fingers.

I roll my eyes. "Of course you were a Boy Scout."

Grinning, he even seems to stand straighter, as though, by apologizing, he shed the weight of his guilt.

Exhaling heavily, I rattle off my number, and he punches it into his phone, relief flickering briefly in his eyes.

"For the record," I say, my voice quieter now. "I spent the night with a friend."

Ethan nods, slipping his phone into his pocket a second after mine vibrates against my ass. I'm guessing he texted me, so I have his number too. "Good."

"You should get some sleep," I add when the moment grows fraught between us once more. "You look like shit."

He scoffs, a faint smirk tugging at his lips. "Thanks, Carter. Quite a way with words, you've got there."

Despite everything, I smile. It's small, fleeting, but it's there. For the first time since the party, it feels like I can breathe.

Maybe I can rely on more than just Wren to help me survive this season.

Maybe, for the first time, I can trust my captain.

And if I'm lucky, perhaps by the end of the year, I'll have the support of my team.

FOURTEEN

THE CROWD IS ROARING, but I can't hear it. All I hear is the scrape of blades, the slap of the puck, and the dull *thud* of bodies slamming into the boards. My blood's already running hot, and it's not just because this is our first game of the season.

It's *them.*

Our greatest rivals: Northern Summit Glaciers.

I hate everything about them—their smug attitudes, dirty hits, and how they skate around like they own the ice. They think they're hot shit, when really, all they are is...shit. It used to give me a sick sense of satisfaction, knowing that they had a girl on the team—how much it likely pissed them off.

But now the roles are reversed.

Guess the joke is on me.

With the stick in my hand and the hint of blood, metal, and cold ice in my nostrils, I'm at home. This is where I thrive. Where chaos reigns. As I push down on my skates, chasing the puck down the rink, the roar of the crowd is muted, like it's happening underwater. There's nothing but the sound of my steady breath in my ears, the hollow clunk of the puck as it collides with my stick, and the blue crease up ahead.

Except tonight, something feels...off.

One of the Glaciers crashes into me before I can line up the shot, sending me tumbling into the boards while another snatches up the puck before I can recover.

Cursing, I take chase.

The Glaciers have always been our biggest rivals. Not because they are as good as we are—which they aren't—but because our universities are situated a measly twenty miles apart. It has created an intense rivalry that has withstood the centuries. Even during an exhibition game, such as tonight.

However, this year, there's something different.

This year, there's Dylan.

I don't recall playing against her before, but her low stats and vague comment about having to fight her teammates for the puck suggest that she didn't see much ice time at NSU.

The same can't be said for her time as a Steelhawk.

I dart across the blue line, catching a pass from Ethan. No way am I letting this one go. I take off like a bullet released from its chamber. My stick flexes as I slap the puck toward the net, but their goalie smothers it easily. The whistle blows.

Goddammit. My head falls back, and I groan to the rafters as I slowly circle back to the center ice for the face-off. We're tied nil-nil with less than fifteen minutes left on the clock. Not a great start to the year.

I notice Dylan from the corner of my eye. She's a few feet away, standing on Ethan's other side, tapping the ice like she's ready to go.

It's weird seeing her there. Correction: it's weird *not* seeing Reed there. It's been the three of us since freshman year. It's been me and Reed for even longer. I met him at peewee hockey camp when we were eleven, and for four weeks every summer, we'd dominate the ice, showing off whatever new tricks we'd learned that year.

Both of us talked about playing in college together, making it to the championships together, and eventually going pro— *together*.

Then, here comes Dylan, disturbing the status quo and changing everything we talked about doing.

My gaze flicks to the bench where Reed sits, geared up, stick fisted in his hand, and ready to go. His expression is one of pure concentration—and rage. There's always rage there nowadays—not that I can blame him. I'd be pissed too.

I immediately feel bad because, no matter how much it sucks for my friend, Dylan has been doing a surprisingly good job of holding her own. Which hasn't been easy. The Glaciers have been going after her like she's some sort of punching bag, slamming her into the boards at every opportunity, crowding her with their sticks and elbows whenever she has the puck. It's obvious to anyone watching that she's their target, regardless of whether or not she has possession of the puck.

When I first saw how hard they were going for her, I expected her to ask Coach to switch her out, but I was wrong. She's been holding her own like a pro. She doesn't expect any of us to come to her aid, doesn't flinch when an opponent shoves her, and doesn't hesitate to go after the puck even when it's in the thick of the scrum. She's as fierce as any other Steelhawk on the ice.

"So, Blackstone took our sloppy seconds." My head snaps in the direction of the Glaciers' captain. Lucas Tremble grins like the asshole he is, leaning over his stick as he talks low enough that only the forwards can hear—Dylan included. "Guess it's your turn to be bottom of the conference."

The whistle blows, and I mentally cheer Ethan on as he wins the face-off. The puck comes loose, and I race for it.

The Glaciers swarm us, and it's brutal. Every pass is contested, every shot blocked. And when Dylan makes an opening and gets the puck, it's like a pack of wolves has descended on her. Three of them pin her against the boards, their sticks hacking at her like they're trying to break her in half.

One of them wrestles the puck free and takes off.

Every instinct says chase him down, but something about leaving Dylan, still pinned to the glass, grates under my skin.

Catching my eye, her voice cuts through the noise. "Go, Finn!"

I grit my teeth—then go.

Still, unease twists my gut as I break down the ice. The way they're ganging up on her is excessive, like they're using her as a punching bag for their frustrations. She's finally on an opposing team, and now they're making sure she feels every bit of the frustration they've bottled for the past two years.

Fuck, are we going to feel the same way by the end of the season?

Will we resent her too?

When the games get harder, when the pressure mounts—will we turn on her like they have?

I want to believe we're better than they are, but I'm not sure that we are.

By the time we rotate off the ice, we're losing 1–0. Ethan slumps next to me on the bench, muttering under his breath.

"NSU's not holding back tonight."

"They're out for blood," I agree, spraying cold water from my bottle over my face.

I inadvertently spot Dylan sitting farther down the line, catching her breath. What snags my attention is the bright red on her chin, blood that has trickled from a split lip.

I hate myself for noticing, but more than that, I hate myself for the quick jolt of concern.

Ethan must see where my attention is as he mutters low for only me to hear, "They're targeting her."

I simply nod, forcing my gaze away from her and back on the ice where it *should* be. I fist my stick in my gloved grip, taking my frustrations out on it.

Kyle would be devastated if he thought for one second I was *worried* about her. She knew what she was signing up for when she joined the team. The rest of it isn't my problem. My loyalties lie with my friend. My teammate who is currently on the ice kicking ass.

Reed flies toward the net like the hounds of hell are on his ass. "Go, Reed!" I call, getting pumped as he sets up for a goal. *Fuck, yes!* We need to start pulling ahead of these assholes.

The crowd is on their feet, screaming him on.

Come on, Reed. You've got this.

He has the perfect shot at the net, but he fumbles the puck and it goes wide.

I slump back on the bench, my groan of frustration turning into outright cursing when NSU steals possession and takes it all the way home. It's a cheap deflection that somehow finds the back of Griffin's net, but still. 2–0. *Fuck.*

The first line is called up for our last shift of the game. It's a slugfest, with both teams refusing to back down. Bodies collide, sticks clash, and the air is thick with the sound of skates carving into the ice. I maneuver through the fray, my eyes darting, searching for an opportunity. The Glaciers' defense is relentless, their aggression intensifying as they aim to maintain their lead.

Dylan seizes the puck. Immediately, she is swarmed by NSU players who back her into the boards. One player twice her size rams into her so hard that her head snaps back against the plexiglass with a sickening thud.

Red flashes across my vision, teeth grinding as I do a sweep of the ice for the ref. He should be blowing his fucking whistle, announcing a penalty—*something*. Except the useless fucking prick has his back to the scene, missing the whole damn thing.

Anger simmers in my veins, and instead of positioning myself for an opening, I start toward her, instincts overriding reason when I see her slumped against the boards, head down.

She could be seriously fucking injured. *This* is why women shouldn't play men's hockey. It's not that she's not capable; it's that she can't stand up to two-hundred pounds of pure muscle. It's that she'll get herself *hurt*. Fucking *killed*, even.

However, before I make it to her, her head snaps up, and I catch a flash of menace, of unwavering determination, before she pushes off the boards. In a move so fast I barely catch it, she breaks free from the players who had her pinned. The puck's still on her stick—untouched. Almost like *she* was the target all along.

She pivots sharply, her agility leaving defenders grasping at empty air as she charges toward the goal. The roar of the arena dulls to a distant hum, as everything narrows to her. Every stride is sharp, controlled—cutting up the ice with a speed no one can match. She weaves through the opposition like they aren't even there, all instinct and fire. It's impossible to look away from. *She's* impossible to look away from.

Time slows to a crawl as she approaches the goal, her focus unyielding. I find myself mesmerized, air lodged in my throat as, with a swift, decisive motion, she takes the shot.

The puck sails past the goalie and into the net. A singular point on the scoreboard, yet it feels monumental. The arena erupts, but I'm ensnared in a moment of clarity. Where Kyle fumbled his easy goal earlier, Dylan came back from the brink and *dominated*. She proved to every single person here tonight—player and fan alike—exactly what she's capable of. She proved that she *earned* her first-line spot.

Not slept her way into it like Kyle vindictively implied.

I admit, there'd been a split second where I wondered if he was telling the truth. Until Ethan came out after Dylan had already fled and shut that shit down. I should have known. Kyle was wasted and feeling sorry for himself, but that's no excuse to start harmful rumors. I thought Ethan was going to rip him a new one when he found out.

I can empathize with Kyle. I can feel bad for him, but there's no denying that he just can't live up to Dylan. He's not in the same league as her at all. Not even close to her level. What Dylan just pulled off is a thing of beauty.

She is a thing of beauty.

I itch with the need to go to her now. To lift her off her feet and celebrate that epic goal, but I hold myself back, my fingers flexing around my stick as I watch her tilt her head back and grin to the floodlights far above us. Ethan approaches, patting her on the back and likely congratulating her. A few other players follow his lead. No one has known what to do with her since she made the roster, but I imagine that will be changing after tonight. With that goal, Dylan will have earned more than just my respect.

I force myself to turn away. I can't look at her for another second and not go to her. She might deserve her position on the team, but accepting her as anything other than a teammate would be a betrayal to my friendship with Kyle.

So I really need to get the unabating desire to kiss her again out of my head.

The final buzzer sounds, cementing our loss. Despite Dylan's show-stopping last-minute goal, defeat makes my muscles heavy as I watch NSU celebrate like they've won the Stanley Cup and not a stupid exhibition game.

"We played well," Ethan says, coming over and clapping me on the back. "It's just one of those things. We'll get them next time."

I nod, but his words barely penetrate. It's a shitty way to start the year. I know this game doesn't count for anything, but that doesn't mean NSU isn't going to hold it over our heads or that the entire team won't feel the loss as strongly as if it were a championship game.

Begrudgingly, I join the rest of the team, getting in line for the handshake. Dylan is slightly ahead of me, and despite putting her hand out each time, every single Glacier skips over her like she's not there. Like she doesn't even exist.

Something about it pisses me off. Every player on the ice, regardless of whether they are an opponent, should have respect for that goal she just pulled off. She was as good as out, but she rallied, gliding down the rink like she had wings on her back instead of skates on her feet. Still, every single NSU player looks at her like she's nothing more than worn tape—used, discarded, beneath consideration.

My teeth grind, and I have to look away before I snap the finger of the next NSU player to shake my hand. Not because I care about her, but because it's unsportsmanlike. It's just fucking respectful to shake hands with the team you played against. To say congratulations even if what you really want to do is drive your fist into their face and knock a tooth loose.

After clapping gloves with the final Glacier, I do a loop around the ice, needing to skate off some of this frustration. The adrenaline from the game. The disappointment of the loss.

Most of the team has already left the rink, probably wanting to drown their sorrows in the nearest pint or pussy they can find. That leaves mainly Glaciers still lingering. I notice several of them talking to Ethan, so I skate over.

"...fucking liability," I catch Lucas saying. "Only thing she's good for is relieving the stress after a loss, if you know what I mean." The sleazeball winks. *What the fuck is that supposed to mean?* Memories flicker, of how good her lips felt, how perfectly her body fit against mine, and my blood instantly boils. Does this asshole know how fucking sweet she tastes?

I skate to a stop beside Ethan, spraying shards of ice over Lucas's skates. He glowers and I smirk right back at the dick-wad, making a mental note to go after him with the same ferocity the entire Glaciers unleashed on Dylan the next time we face off on the ice.

Dropping his irritation, his mouth twists in faux sympathy as he glances between us. "Too bad you won't be making it to the championships. Senior year, and all." He shakes his head, but triumph gleams in his beady little eyes.

I scoff. "Blame a girl for your shitty performance all you want, Tremble, but what's your excuse going to be this year when we kick your ass—again?"

"Kick our asses?" He barks a cold laugh. "Is that what you thought you were doing out there?" He shakes his head. "We're going to slaughter you at every single game this season," he taunts. "And I can't fucking wait." He smirks cockily. "That she-hawk is going to drag you down into the dirt with her, and I'm going to enjoy watching every second of it."

Grinning like the cat that got the cream, he skates off the ice with the last of his team.

"I hate that guy," Ethan mutters as we watch them disappear down the tunnel toward the guest locker rooms.

"Yeah, him and the rest of them."

The thing I can't shake, though? What if he's right? I know Dylan can hold her own, but what if she's the spark that sets the rest of the team off balance? And that might be enough to cost us everything.

FIFTEEN

MY HANDS SHAKE as I shove my gear into my bag with more force than necessary. The adrenaline I relied on to hold it together on the ice has worn off, replaced by a sickening knot in my stomach. I knew it would be hard to face them—*him*—but nothing could have prepared me for the onslaught of memories.

And not just bad ones, either.

Quiet moments. Sweet gestures. Soft touches.

My heart squeezes painfully in my chest, and I close my eyes. Breathe in, breathe out. *None of it was real*, I remind myself for the umpteenth time. However, that doesn't eliminate the very real feelings I'd felt at the time, even if distance and a crash-landing into reality now makes me see that those feelings were born from grief and loneliness. From feeling like I was all alone in the world, drowning in the weight of everything, and desperate for a lifeline to cling to.

Fiery rage lances through the still raw hurt, and I shove my helmet into the locker, imagining I'm smashing it into Lucas Tremble's smirking face. There is truly no one I hate more than him. No one that disgusts me more.

Seeing him tonight...it brought everything back. Everything that I've buried deep and successfully avoided since fleeing the NSU campus to start over. Now, I can feel it all pressing beneath the surface of my skin, demanding to be acknowledged. All that hurt. The embarrassment. The self-loathing and disgust. The chastising at how I could be so fucking naive and stupid...

I change faster than I ever have, barely registering the bruises already forming on my arms and legs, the dull ache at the back of my head from where those jackasses deliberately drove me into the boards, or the sting of my split lip as I shower and throw on my clothes.

While Coach gives his post-game speech, I sit impatiently, my knee bouncing and head resting against the locker behind me. I don't hear a single word, and the second he dismisses us, I'm up. Half the guys are still in their gear, or have towels wrapped around their waists, but I'm ready to get the fuck out of here.

Slinging my bag over my shoulder, I duck out of the locker room without so much as a glance around or wave goodbye. An amicable sort of peace might have been reached this past week, with only Kyle and some third-line guys glaring at me from a distance, but that doesn't mean I'm about to join them at The Stanley to commiserate. Hell, I bet Kyle is just waiting to get a drink in him so he can blame our loss on me despite the fact that I'm the only player who scored a goal tonight.

A rare, arrogant smile curls the corners of my lip as I recall the air whipping in my face, the smooth glide of ice beneath my skates. That feeling of being unstoppable. Invincible. It's the best feeling in the world, surpassed only by scoring that last-minute goal. It might not have won us the game, but I think it won me some respect amongst the team. It showed them why I'm here, on the first line. Proved that I can do more than run drills and play scrimmages. Maybe now they'll realize I'm here to fucking play. To win.

"Babe."

I freeze barely ten steps from the locker room door. That voice. I'd recognize it anywhere. Where the smooth baritone was once a source of comfort, a sanctuary from my grief, it now scrapes up my spine like nails on a chalkboard.

I slowly turn on my heel, already bracing myself. There he is, in all his arrogant, hot-as-shit glory. Lucas Tremble leans casually against the wall, arms crossed like he's got all the time in the world. He's still wearing his hockey gear...almost like he was waiting for me.

As far as I'm concerned, we have nothing to say to one another.

"Don't call me that," I snap, tightening my grip on the strap of my bag.

His smirk only deepens before he pushes off the wall, closing the distance between us. I bet he deliberately kept his skates on so he'd tower over me. Without them, we're basically the same height, but as it is, I have to crane my neck to look up at him.

"But you used to love when I called you that."

"Yeah, well, I used to love a lot of things that I eventually learned were toxic for me."

He chuckles, low and condescending, not the least bit fazed at my insulting him. "Still feisty, huh? I always did like that about you."

"You never liked a damn thing about me, Lucas."

"Hmm, wrong." His eyes rake over me, stripping me bare as he stalks closer. I back up, hating how I feel when he's this close —small, weak, stupid. Like I'm right back in the worst time of my life. "I always liked it when you moaned my name—*begged* it —while I was pounding into that sweet little pussy."

Shaking my head fervently, I step back farther. My strap slides over my shoulder, the bag knocking against my hip before falling to my feet, and I realize my back is literally against the wall.

"Leave me alone, Lucas."

I force steel into my voice, but he takes no heed as he reaches out, twirling a strand of damp hair that has escaped the bun I scraped it into between his fingers. "You've missed me. Admit it."

I slap his hand away, glaring. "About as much as I'd miss a UTI."

His smirk twists into something darker, his eyes narrowing. This is the *real* Lucas. The one who gets off on messing with a grieving girl. Of stringing her along. Toying with her. Fucking her up so badly that she no longer knows up from down.

"You're still so much fun to mess with."

"I'm done playing your twisted games," I tell him. "You got what you wanted, so leave me the hell alone."

He pouts. An outsider looking in would think it was the cutest expression on his stereotypically handsome face, but I see it for the manipulation tactic it is.

Leaning in, I recoil as his warm, repugnant breath sticks to my skin. "Did I, though? I might have gotten you off my team, but it looks like you still haven't figured out you aren't wanted here." His cold gaze flicks over my face. "Maybe I'll keep playing with you until you're nothing but a shattered mess. Until the thought of stepping onto the ice makes you sick. Until just seeing a hockey stick sends you spiraling, crying in some dark corner where you belong."

My stomach churns, bile rising up my throat. I'm on the verge of shoving past him and hoping he trips over his skates, when a voice cuts through the tension.

"Everything okay here?"

I glance past Lucas's shoulder to see Jax standing a few feet away. His expression is deceptively calm, but his dark eyes are locked on Lucas, sharp and unyielding.

Lucas steps back, but those hard, hateful eyes stay pinned on mine for a moment longer before his entire demeanor shifts. His body relaxes, his lips hooking up in his characteristic smirk. "Just catching up with my girl, here," he says easily.

"I'm not your girl," I snap, at the end of my tether.

"Mm, we'll see." Lucas finally backs off, turning his attention to Jax and flashing him a practiced, charismatic grin.

Jax doesn't return it. He doesn't say a word, just stares Lucas down until he chuckles, taking several steps backward down the tunnel.

"All right, I'm going. Got me some celebrating to do tonight." He glances at me one last time, smirking. "I'll see you around, babe."

It's not a throwaway comment. It's a promise. One that chills me to the core.

I don't breathe until he's gone.

"You okay?" Jax asks when we're alone, his voice low as he steps closer, moving into the spot Lucas just vacated. Except his close proximity doesn't send me spiraling—at least, not in the same way. It doesn't feel like he's closing in around me, trapping me, kicking me until I'm two feet tall. However, the hint of cedarwood and something minty-fresh as Jax takes up my entire field of vision makes me lightheaded. Dizzy. The menacing darkness from a moment ago lifts, and instead, I feel safely cocooned in Jax's presence.

Which...makes zero sense considering I know next to nothing about this guy.

Not trusting myself to speak, my head jerks in a quick nod.

He studies me for a moment, his brow furrowing. "You used to date that clown?"

He sounds so put out at the notion that, somehow, magically, it actually makes me laugh. It's a sharp, high-pitched sound, but it's far better than the fear I was drowning in a moment ago.

"Yeah, not my best decision ever."

He grunts an agreement before silence descends over the hallway like the first snowfall of winter—muted yet peaceful.

"Well, I should probably go—"

"You played well tonight."

We both speak at the same time, catching ourselves before chuckling.

"The whole team played well," I tell him.

"Sure, but those assholes—" He points with his thumb over his shoulder in the vague direction of the away team's locker room. "—had it out for *you*. They were going after you hard out there." He studies me, those astute eyes seeing more than I want him to. More than I'm ready for. "Pretty clear you and your old team don't get along."

I shrug, avoiding his gaze. "It's old news."

"Didn't look like it."

My eyes snap to his, and I swallow. "Lucas is...he has no power over me anymore."

I'm not sure whether I'm saying those words for Jax or myself, but there's something empowering about saying that out loud. I'm no longer in Lucas's orbit, beneath his thumb, at his college, or on his team.

He can say what he wants, but the truth is...I'm free of him.

Jax's penetrating stare holds me captive. I could swear he understands more than what I'm saying. Can dig deeper than anyone has cared to look before.

There's something so bold and strangely comforting about it. About the fact that he *cares* to look deeper, even if I don't understand why. However, it also makes me feel naked, exposed in a way that has me shuffling my feet.

"The team's heading out to drown their sorrows. You going?"

"Ha, no." I shake my head. "I'd rather paint my nails pink and watch the *Barbie* movie on repeat than suffer Kyle's shitty mood after tonight's game."

"Not a girly girl?" he teases. "Huh, I'd never have known."

I laugh. We both know that, with my nails bitten to the quick, my love of Converse and sweats, and hair that is either scraped back from my face or hanging limply around my face after a shower because I'm too lazy to dry it, I'm the furthest thing from a girly girl.

Jax grins, the action changing his entire face. It leaves me momentarily stunned. He's like a dark prince, all stoic, radiating silent danger, but when he smiles like that...*wow*. It catches on the faint scar on his cheek, and I have the sudden urge to trace it with my finger. To feel the sliced edge beneath my tongue.

Wait, *what*?

Where the hell did that come from?

Jax is hot, but he's my *teammate*.

More than that, he's my *roommate*.

I've been burned once by crossing that line with someone on the same team as me.

I'm not dumb enough to make the same mistake twice.

Not when the first time is still cornering me in hallways and threatening to take the only thing I have left.

"I'll walk you home."

"Oh, you don't have to do that," I stammer. God, I can feel the heat in my cheeks. *Get it together, Dylan!* "Go out with the team. I'm perfectly capable of walking myself home."

He smirks, and God, why do I get the sense that he can see

how flustered he's making me? If the ground could just swallow me up now, that would be great, thanks.

"I'm actually heading back to the house, too."

"Drowning your sorrows in a bottle of beer not your thing?" I tease.

The corner of his lip lifts slightly. "Not in a crowded bar where every Tom, Dick, and Harry wants their photo taken with us."

"You mean every Tomilina, Dictoria, and Henrietta," I retort with a smirk.

"Ha."

I bend to retrieve my bag from where it fell, but he beats me to it, slinging it onto his back. A folded-up piece of paper flutters out of the netting at the side. Frowning, I reach for it, unsure what it is as I open it.

You were fucking fearless out there. Unstoppable.

I read the note again before glancing around. Did Lucas leave this for me to find? It's the kind of thing the person he pretended to be would do. Is this just another way for him to fuck with me?

But...it doesn't fit.

Looking back down at it, the handwriting, although messy as if written in a hurry, isn't familiar.

So if it wasn't Lucas, then who?

Bear might rain down praise on me but he'd do it to my face, not in a cryptic note. And anyone else on the team...they might be looking at me with a newfound respect after that goal, but that doesn't mean they're about to blow smoke up my ass.

"You coming?" Jax asks.

I look up, startled. He's standing a few steps ahead, waiting on me. Casting a final glance over my shoulder, I stuff the note in my pocket and jog to catch up to him. "Yeah, I'm coming."

We fall into step, the fluorescent lights humming overhead as we make our way through the arena halls.

"If you don't hang out with the team, what do you do after a loss?" I ask as we step outside, Jax barely fitting through the door with both our bags slung over his shoulders. The crowd from the game has already dissipated, with only a few stragglers hanging around in front of the building.

"Same thing I do after a win," he responds with a shrug. "Go home, decompress, play some video games."

"The violent kind where you pretend you're shooting the opposing team, or like the racing, sports kind?"

I catch a flash of his straight white teeth before he says, "Depends on how badly we lost."

"Losing the first game of the year, I'd say that's a pretty bad one."

"Yeah, but it was only an exhibition game."

"I'm not sure everyone else on the team will see it that way."

"Unlikely. Ethan's probably replaying every minute, trying to figure out what we could have done differently. Finn will be itching to get to the bar to down a few beers before hooking up with the first girl who hits on him and forget about the loss." Thankfully Jax doesn't notice when my face involuntarily scrunches at that image. "And Reed..." He cuts himself off, grimacing. "Sorry."

"Don't be." I wave him away as we walk through the campus gates and onto the sidewalk toward Athletes Row. "We both know Reed is most likely blaming me and making sure everyone else knows it's my fault, too."

He sighs, the sound heavy in the otherwise still night. "Kyle's always a dick at the start of the year when fresh meat comes along. He'll ease up as the season gets underway."

I arch a brow at him. "I bet none of that *fresh meat* ever beat him out for his spot."

Jax's lips practically disappear, he flattens them so hard.

"That's what I thought." I nod, silence falling between us. The only noise is the sound of our footsteps against the ground and the mewling of a cat nearby.

"Look," I sigh. "I don't care. I'm plenty used to being hated." I catch the dipping of Jax's eyebrows but push on before he can ask any probing questions. "But I earned my spot fair and square. I proved tonight that I can handle myself against bigger, tougher opponents, and I'll keep proving it. If the Steelhawks don't make it to the Frozen Four, it won't be because you had *a girl on the team*. Just like the reason the Glaciers didn't make it the past two years wasn't because of me. I was a convenient scapegoat for them to dump all their blame and frustration on, but I know the truth." In a smaller, softer voice, I add, "With time, I hope you all will too."

Jax doesn't say anything until we turn onto Athletes Row.

"You never told me how you unwind after a game."

I'm taken aback by the change in subject, but truthfully, I'm grateful for it. I shrug, knowing he's going to make fun of me. Still, I admit, "I work out. Or if I'm beat, I fall into Ethan's camp. I search for footage of the game online, then replay it, mentally changing plays and seeing what outcome that might have provided instead."

"Of course you do," Jax drolls, shaking his head, before glancing at me from the corner of his eye as we climb the porch steps of the house. "Can I ask you a question?" He pauses at the front door, turning to face me instead of heading inside.

"Uh, sure."

"Do you ever give yourself a night off?"

My lips part, but no answer forms.

I used to. I used to take time off to do non-hockey-related

things with my parents. Or, most likely, hockey-related activities that didn't revolve around me or developing my skills and ensuring I'm the best.

"That's what I thought." He nods knowingly. "Come on." He gestures toward the door. "Take a night off with me."

"But—" I protest, lingering on the threshold.

"One night, Carter." His voice is firm, brokering no argument as he turns to look at me over his shoulder. "If you really need to dissect the game, we can do it while we kill some zombies."

Honestly, that doesn't sound half bad.

Especially if I imagine Lucas's ugly mug on every zombie and get to take him out over and over again.

Huh, this night might actually be shaping up to be pretty decent.

SIXTEEN

"WOW. Steady there, Menace, you nearly took me out!"

I chuckle as I turn my character on the screen so I'm no longer shooting *at* Jax but *with* him, as we take on a hoard of zombies.

"Sorry about that, got a little carried away."

"You think?" he teases. "I should have known you'd be just as violent in a video game as you are on the ice."

Is it weird that I take that as a compliment? Maybe, but oh well. I still like the way he said that—with admiration. Like he's impressed.

I'm curled into the corner of the sofa, feet tucked under me and a controller in my hands as I furiously tap buttons, killing any zombie—and apparently Jax—who comes near me in the game. The rapid-fire pops of headshots and the gory splatters on the screen are strangely satisfying.

Jax is beside me, his legs stretched out, his posture more relaxed than I've ever seen. This really is his way to turn off and just chill.

And I can understand why. I'm fully unwound from the game earlier, the tension melting away as we fight our way through the digital apocalypse. Over the past hour of working side by side, a strange camaraderie has formed between us—one I hadn't expected. One you'd think would form on the ice where working together actually makes a real-life difference. But that also comes with a hell of a lot more strings, more challenges than a simple video game where it doesn't truly matter whether you make it to the beginning of a new post-apocalyptic era or get eaten alive by flesh-consuming zombies.

"Oh God, there's a whole army of them," I groan as a fresh wave of zombies appears over the hill, racing down it toward us.

We shoot manically into the crowd, but we're soon overrun. "I'm dead," Jax states, as blood drips down his side of the screen.

"Ugh, me too." I toss my controller onto the table, flopping back on the sofa with a groan.

"Want a drink?" Jax asks, getting to his feet.

"Sure. Whatever is in the fridge."

"Anything to eat?" he calls from the kitchen.

"I'm good."

He returns with two cans of fizzy drinks, handing one over to me before taking a sip of the other and setting it on the coffee table. We're silent for a moment. Truthfully, other than the occasional comment or critique about our loss tonight, we haven't talked much since we got home, both of us too intent on the video game. But Jax isn't much of a talker anyway, and I find I actually enjoy just sitting in the silence with him. I always thought it would feel strange, awkward, but not with him.

Instead, it's...comforting. Knowing we're both processing our emotions about tonight's game in our own way, but together. It makes me feel not so...alone.

I've always just gone back to my dorm after a game, knowing everyone else was out celebrating or commiserating. I'd climb into my comfiest set of pajamas and call my dad up and rehash the game until well into the night.

Pain lances through my chest. It's been a long time since I've had anyone to do that with. No one else has ever cared enough to listen, but Jax does. He pauses the game or lets the zombies override us, uncaring if we die as he gives me his entire focus while I dissect this play or that.

He suggests critiques or points out things I missed. It's a real conversation—a true meeting of the minds.

It reminds me of the chats I used to have with my dad.

"Hey." He nudges my shoulder. "Where did you go?"

I shake off the grief that's always lingering just beneath the surface, no matter how much time passes. Pasting on a smile, I gesture toward the TV. "Want to go again?"

He studies me a moment longer before answering. "Only if you promise not to shoot me this time."

I laugh, the weighted moment leaving me. "I can't make such a promise. Clearly, I get a little gung-ho with a gun in my hand and zombies in my face."

"Note to self, don't trust Dylan with a gun if the apocalypse ever arrives."

"Har har." I stick my tongue out at him playfully before shifting to pick up my controller from the coffee table.

Jax moves at the same time, our arms brushing. It's a fleeting touch, but it sends a jolt of awareness through me. He notices it, too; I see the way his fingers still on the controller, his gaze dropping to where our skin touched.

As a new game loads, I'm acutely aware of how close we're sitting. Did his leg always press against mine, or did he move closer after getting our drinks? And has his cedarwood scent clung to me all night, or has a fresh wave hit? It's all I can smell now. Every deep inhale to cool my blood is thick with it— with *him*.

The next group of zombies hits, but I barely register it. My focus is on him—on the way his profile is illuminated by the glow of the TV, on the quiet intensity that seems to radiate from him even when he's sitting still.

He must feel my gaze on him, as his lips quirk at one side, and his voice has dipped an octave lower when he asks, "You good over there?"

"Fine," I answer quickly, forcing my eyes back to the screen.

But the air between us has shifted. I feel it crackling, electric and unspoken.

I try to ignore his suddenly all-consuming presence beside me, the heat radiating from him in waves. Feeling as though I can't breathe, I lean forward. I'm staring at the screen, but I'm not intent on the game the way I was before.

A moment later, he leans forward too, bracing his elbows on his knees. Our shoulders brush once more, but this time, neither of us moves away. I glance at him out of the corner of my eye and catch him looking at me.

Illuminated only by the light from the TV, I can't decipher his expression, but the tension radiating between us makes my breath hitch anyway. I wrench my gaze away, feeling unsteady as I stare unblinkingly at the screen and put all my focus into shooting zombies and ignoring the lingering stare of the too-attractive-for-his-own-good man pressed flush against me.

Finally, he looks away, returning his attention to the game.

I manage to push past the sudden heat that has flooded my body, the shallowness of my breathing, and the heightened awareness of how close we're sitting as I focus on the game.

"Wow! Next level!" Grinning, I face Jax. He holds his hand out between us for a high five, and I slap my palm against his. His fingers curl around mine, entwining our hands together.

And that awareness is back.

That tingling where his palm is pressed against mine.

He shifts slightly to face me, his gaze searching mine before dropping to my lips. We're so close. Too close. And yet, some-how, we aren't close enough.

"Jax."

His name is a whisper on my lips, but I have no idea what I'm asking for. No, *begging* for.

To stop this or...

To kiss me.

To ravish me.

To give me everything he's got.

Honestly, I don't know who moves first, but the next thing I know, his lips are on mine, his fingers sliding through the hair at the nape of my neck and pulling me impossibly closer.

He wraps around me like a blanket, devouring me. Consuming me. Making it so I never want to come up for air.

Jax kisses exactly as you'd expect, soft yet sure. Firm but not dominating. The heat between us builds with every slide of his lips over mine. My mouth parting to grant him entry as I moan.

Desire builds in my core, rushing through my blood as I pull him closer, unable to get enough.

In the next moment, my back is being pressed into the couch cushions, and Jax's weight settles over me. I'm burning up. Need like nothing I've felt before builds with such ferocity that I don't know what to do other than claw and paw at him.

My hands are everywhere, sliding up the back of his T-shirt and gliding over the rough denim of his jeans as I cup his firm ass cheek in my palm.

More. I need more.

His touch is gasoline to a starved flame as he pushes up my top, his palms coarse and rough against my smooth skin as he easily wraps his large hands around my narrow waist and slides them up my back. I arch into him, shivering at the hard length that presses firmly against my core.

A pulsing starts up between my thighs, and suddenly all I

can think about is the two of us stripped naked, Jax above me as he drives into my clenching pussy in hard, long strokes that catapult me into oblivion. I know without a doubt that he would be insane in bed. Everything I've never experienced before. Sure and confident. Demanding yet reassuring. Rough yet gentle.

I want it all.

I want all of *him*.

I'm seconds from ripping his clothes off when the front door slams.

It jolts me out of my fever trance so abruptly that I nearly fall off the sofa in my haste to put distance between us. He moves to help me, but my gaze is stuck on the smirking, arrogant asshole who just walked in.

"Oops. Didn't mean to interrupt." His tone is taunting. "Can see why you didn't come out with us tonight, man. No need to work for pussy when you've got it right here at home."

"Fuck off, Kyle," Jax growls, not even looking at him. His focus is still intent on me, but I can't even look at him. I can't look at either of them. I can feel the heat in my cheeks, embarrassment and self-loathing warring with the unsated need still running rampant through my lower region.

Kyle scoffs, muttering something too low for me to hear but sounds suspiciously like "As easy as they said she was," before he walks into the kitchen.

"Are you okay?" Jax asks, keeping his voice low in case Kyle is eavesdropping, which he most definitely is. His face is threaded with concern, and his hand hovers in between us like he wants to touch me, but he's not sure if that's what I want right now.

Hell, *I'm* not even sure.

His hands on me were electrifying, but no.

I shift away from him, coughing to clear my throat. I keep my gaze deliberately lowered. "I'm fine. I think I'm—"

"You missed one hell of a night, man," Kyle says, returning to the room. Instead of beating a hasty retreat like I was just about to, I grab the controller I'd dropped and resume the game. I don't even care if Jax's character is standing there, primed to die. I need the distraction. I need to get myself under control. I need to find wherever the hell my sanity ran off to so I can scream at it for letting me do something so reckless. So dangerous. So...fucking stupid.

Haven't I learned from my past mistakes?

Stupid. Stupid. Stupid.

Jax and Kyle's conversation is white noise as I stare fixedly at the screen. Focused solely on shooting zombies like it's the only thing that matters right now. That is until Kyle steps directly in front of me, blocking my view. Frowning, I snap my gaze to him, barely noting the pointed sip he takes from a mug before I lean to the side to see around him.

My gaze snaps immediately back to him. "What are you doing?" I demand, my grip on the controller going slack and the game all but forgotten as I dart my gaze back and forth between the smug look on his punchable face and the mug in his hand.

The mug that is supposed to be on a shelf in my bedroom, along with all the others.

"What are you doing with that?" My voice is a little higher-pitched than usual. My heart beating just a little too fast—and not in the fun, exciting way it was a moment ago.

No, this is pure panic.

Fear.

Terror.

"This?" Kyle holds up the mug like he's showing it off. "I found it. It's nice, right?"

My breathing starts to change. "Why do you have my mug, Kyle?" There's a firmness behind my words now, but he either doesn't notice or doesn't care.

"What's going on?" Jax interjects, looking between us in confusion.

"That's my mug," I tell him, not once taking my eyes off the bright yellow-and-orange mug with the words San Francisco and a painting of the Golden Gate Bridge. "I... Kyle's not supposed to have it. I keep it in my room."

"It's just a mug," he retorts, rolling his eyes like I'm being dramatic.

"You went into her room?" Jax accuses, sounding peeved as he glares at Kyle.

"It's mine, Kyle," I demand, getting to my feet and holding out my hand. "Give it back!" I just... I need it out of Kyle's hands. I need to know it's safe.

He smirks, fingers flexing around the handle, but he makes no move to hand it over.

"Just give her the mug, man," Jax urges. "There are plenty of others in the kitchen."

"Yeah, but I like this one."

"I'm not playing. Hand it over!" I sound nearly hysterical now, and Kyle's flash of victory lets me know I'm playing right into his hands, but I don't care.

"Jesus, fine." He rolls his eyes. "If you're going to go all psycho, you can have it."

He thrusts the mug out toward me, and I grasp for it, but just as my fingers brush the ceramic, he lets go. I inhale sharply as the mug slips through my fingers. Wide-eyed and with a silent scream, I watch as it seemingly falls in slow motion, hitting the edge of the coffee table with a dull thud before crashing to the floor...where it shatters into pieces.

For a moment, the world is still. I stare at the broken shards, my chest tight, unable to breathe.

"Oops. Butterfingers," Kyle mocks with a sly grin.

Jax shoves him out of the room, his voice low and furious,

but I don't hear the words. I can't hear anything. All I can do is stare at the broken remnants of the first mug my dad ever brought home.

The memories wash over me, consuming me.

"I've got a gift for you, Princess."

The excitement I felt as my tiny little fingers wedged open the box before Dad helped me lift out the mug, warning me to be careful because it was breakable.

Breakable.

And now it's broken.

I sink to my knees, tears streaming down my face as I reach for the scattered pieces with trembling hands, then hesitate, afraid to touch them. My chest feels like it's caving in as a sob is wrenched from my throat.

It sounds ridiculous, but I feel as though I just lost another piece of him. My mugs are all I have left of my dad, and now one of them is gone. How long until none of them remain and all I'm left with are faded, distant memories? Ones where I can't recall the exact baritone of his laugh or shade of his eyes.

A hand brushes my shoulder, and I instinctively flinch away.

"It's okay," Jax murmurs, voice low and smooth as he lowers himself to the floor beside me—close, but not touching. "Kyle's gone. It's just us."

I don't look his way. I can't. Can't do anything but stare at the shattered remnants of my mug. Tears track silently down my cheeks, warm against skin gone numb.

Jax doesn't speak. Doesn't rush me. He just sits there, close enough for me to know he's here, but still allowing me the space I need to process. The only sound is my sniffles, the occasional sob of devastation.

Eventually, his voice breaks the solemn silence, raw and

pleading. "Please," he rasps, like he can't stand another moment of seeing me upset, "Just let me hold you."

It's the kindness in his tone that undoes me. The gentle way he asks. The quiet care in every word.

Still crying, I nod.

He exhales, then wraps me in his arms, slow and careful like he's afraid I'll shatter next. I fold into him, burying my face into his chest, and the sob that leaves me is sharp and broken. His fingers slide tenderly through my hair, his voice low and reassuring in my ear. "I've got you."

Only when my tears have dried up, leaving a hollow vessel in his arms, does he speak. "Talk to me, Little Menace." He pulls back so he can see my face, puffy and red from crying. "This wasn't just any mug, was it?"

I shake my head, inhaling the hint of his aftershave. "No." My voice cracks, and I press my hands against my face, trying to stifle the shuddering gasps that follow.

When I finally feel like I have myself under control, I lower them and meet his gaze. I'm sure I look like a complete mess, but Jax just swipes my tears away with the pad of his thumb, his eyes filled with nothing but concern.

"My dad gave it to me," I confess, throat scratchy. "He used to travel a lot for work, and he'd always bring me a mug from whatever city he was in... It was our thing."

"Used to?"

"He's dead now," I admit, the words hollow.

Jax releases a harsh breath. He doesn't say anything; he just holds me tighter. I lean into him, my body shaking, and he doesn't let go.

It hits me then, how long it's been since I let someone hold me like this. Since I let myself fall apart. Even at the funeral, I had to keep my shit together—for Mom. I've never, not once, let myself give in to those emotions.

I've never had a shoulder to cry on. Someone to ease the burden. To share the load.

And now I'm buckling beneath the weight of it all.

I've been moving forward, pretending I'm fine when I'm anything but.

For what feels like a long time, we simply sit there. Jax doesn't rush me, doesn't tell me to pull myself together or stop crying. He just holds me, like he's afraid I'll break if he lets go.

Eventually, he shifts, rubbing a hand in slow circles along my back. "Come on," he murmurs gently. "Let's get you off the floor."

I let him help me up, my legs shaky as he steadies me. He keeps his hand on my elbow as we move toward the stairs, guiding me up them and along the hallway to my room.

"The mug," I start, not even wanting to say the words but knowing we can't just leave it there. If one of the others comes in after too many drinks, they might hurt themselves.

"I'll sort it out," Jax promises as I lower myself onto the edge of the bed. "And I'll bring you some tea."

"Do we have hot chocolate?" I ask, feeling like a boulder has replaced my head as I lift it to meet his eyes. It did help after the party that night, so I'm hoping it will work its magic again.

"I'll find some," Jax declares, sounding like he's about to go off on a mission. "You just get into bed, and I'll bring it up."

He turns toward the door.

"Jax," I call when he's standing on the threshold. He doesn't look back, but he stops, waiting. "Thank you."

His shoulders visibly drop, the dark hair on the back of his head bobbing before he ducks out the door.

When he returns, he's carrying a steaming mug topped with cream and marshmallows. I blink at it, surprised. It's possible there could have been a tin of hot chocolate powder buried at the back of a drawer, but there is no way we had marshmallows and cream in the house.

"Where did you find those?" I ask, giving him a skeptical look.

"The girls across the street."

My eyebrows jump up my forehead, and I can't look away from his face as I take the drink from his outstretched hand and bring it to my lips. "Mmm, delicious. Thank you."

It tastes like heaven, and I sink back against my pillows as I sigh. Hot chocolate might not fix everything, but it helps. And so does the way Jax sits with me until I finally fall asleep.

SEVENTEEN

MY EYELIDS STICK TOGETHER, and the slight pounding in my temples serves as a not-so-subtle reminder of last night. Groaning, I roll over onto my back, covering my face with my hands.

I kissed Jaxon Keller.

And then I promptly fell apart in his arms.

How embarrassing!

And yet, even now, my body melts at the reminder of how good it felt to have his solid weight pressing me into the couch cushions, his lips trailing across my skin. A heated thrill pulses through me. One I shouldn't feel.

"You're such an idiot," I mumble to myself.

I swore off teammates, and yet here I've gone and kissed not one but *two* Steelhawks players. Is self-sabotage one of the ten stages of grief, because that is clearly what I'm attempting to do.

As the reminder of how good Jax's lips felt on mine fades, my gut twists, remembering what came after—Kyle holding my dad's mug, smirking like the smug asshole he is before he dropped it.

I *know* he dropped it on purpose. No way was that a simple

accident, no matter what he'll proclaim. A heavy sadness descends, and a sigh escapes me as I drag myself upright, resting my back against the headboard and scrubbing my hands down my face. There's a team meeting this morning, and I need to get ready.

When I turn to grab my phone off the nightstand, I pause. The mug is sitting there—the one Kyle broke last night.

Except...it's been pieced back together. Cracks run across the surface like a fractured mosaic, and some pieces are so tiny they're missing altogether. It's not perfect—not even close—but it's *whole*.

Jax.

A lump wedges in my throat. It has to be him. He's the only one who would've done this. Sitting up straighter, my hand shakes as I reach for the mug. The cracks are rough under my fingers, but they're solid, glued carefully with the kind of patience I can't even fathom. Jax didn't have to do this. Most people would have swept the pieces into the trash. But he did, because he understood how much the mug meant to me. Because he *listened*.

God, this must have taken him all night to painstakingly glue back together. Tears sting my eyes as I cradle it gently in my hands, unable to fully process that this is real life and that I'm not still dreaming.

Swallowing hard, I get out of bed, my bare feet sinking into the carpet as I cross the room to where I have all of my other mugs set out on a shelf. The morning light spills over each one, carefully chosen, illuminating the colors as I slide the glued one cautiously into its place. My hand lingers there for a moment before I step back, doing a quick survey of the rest of the room.

My bedroom is small but cozy. A twin bed shoved into the corner with plain white bedding on it. A desk cluttered with notebooks, a few pens, and an empty water bottle is pushed against the wall beneath the window, and my favorite hoodie hangs off the back of my desk chair. It's not much, but it's mine. Or it was—until Kyle stepped into it without me knowing.

I shiver, my face scrunching as my gaze flickers toward the door. The idea of him being in here, touching my things, makes my skin crawl. It suddenly crosses my mind that he could have done *anything* when he was in here.

With a shiver skating down my spine, I rip my bedsheets off the bed and dump them in a pile by the door to wash. Next, I go through my bookshelves, ensuring he hasn't messed with anything—or worse, *planted* something. It would be easy enough to hide a recording device among my belongings.

I rip my room apart before putting it back together again, not finding anything. Still, I feel like there is a layer of slime covering my skin. One a hot shower won't wash off. I frown at the door, an ache in my chest as I wonder if I'll ever feel safe in this room again.

Kyle broke something fundamental by violating my privacy.

No way am I letting him steal anything else.

After the team meeting this morning, I'm going to buy a lock for my door.

THE SOLES of my Converse slap against the stairs as I descend while simultaneously scraping my hair back into a ponytail. I've been at BSU for an entire month already. It's the end of September now, and fall is starting to seep in—leaves changing from green to burnt orange, a crisp freshness entering the air. However, today is gorgeous. The sun is shining, and I've decided to brave it in shorts and a tank. I'm pretty sure it's the last chance I'll get to wear them before autumn fully arrives, and the snow will soon follow.

Hitting the bottom of the stairs, I tie a hoodie around my waist as I beeline for the kitchen to grab a quick breakfast before our team meeting. As soon as I round the corner, I bump nose to chest with Ethan. "Jesus, what are you doing lurking around corners?" I grumble, rubbing at my nose. Is his chest made of granite or something? I mean, I know, like most hockey players, Ethan is ninety percent muscle, but *damn*, that hurt.

"Sorry. I heard you coming—"

"And you thought you'd break my nose before breakfast?"

He pins me with a *don't be dramatic* stare, but clearly Ethan has no idea just how freaking solid his body is.

"No," he drolls. "I wanted to check in with you. Jax told me about last night."

Miraculously, the pain in my nose is forgotten as I straighten, searching Ethan's gaze as if that will be enough to tell me exactly what he knows *about last night.*

"Did he now?" I hedge.

He nods. "I'll have another word with Kyle."

I scoff, shaking my head. *Seriously?* "Yeah, 'cause that approach is clearly working so well."

Ethan's jaw tightens. "What would you have me do?" he demands, folding his arms across his chest and staring me down.

Exhaling harshly, I pinch the bridge of my nose. "Kyle can come at me on the ice all he wants, but what he did last night crossed a hard line." Meeting Ethan's unwavering stare, I ask bluntly, "Do you have any idea how uncomfortable it makes me to have to live under the same roof as *four* guys? Men who are essentially strangers to me? Men who hate me because I dared to break societal norms?" I shake my head. "And now I can't even relax in my own room. Kyle stole that solitude from me by going in there without my permission or knowledge. The only safe space I had in this house—on this whole campus—and it's gone—"

"Kyle went into your room?" The absolute fury behind Ethan's words cuts me off, and I blink at him before slowly nodding.

"I thought you said Jax told you what happened?"

His teeth grind, jaw flexing. "He told me Kyle went at you, but he didn't give me any specifics. He sure as fuck didn't tell me Kyle invaded your privacy."

I shrug like it's no big deal when, in reality, it fucking is. "Well, he did. I'm going into town after the team meeting to get a lock for the door, and I don't care what you have to say about that being against policy. I don't give a—"

"Don't." Ethan pierces me with a look so severe that it would have me running for the hills if I didn't have the distinct impression that it's not aimed *at* me but *for* me. "*I'll* get one and fit it for you."

"I..." I trail off, momentarily lost for words. I'd expected him to argue with me. To tell me it was against our rental agreement and we'd risk losing our deposit. "You don't need to do that," I eventually manage to respond in a slightly breathless tone.

Ethan's jaw grinds like he's chewing on wasps. "I do, actually." His gaze drops, but not before I see the flash of guilt and disappointment that darkens his eyes, making them look like dark clouds on a stormy day. "It never occurred to me that you might not be...comfortable here. I wish I could promise you that you have nothing to fear—" That same weightedness enters his eyes before he looks away. He seems to stare at nothing for a long moment. I don't say anything, don't wave off whatever he's trying to say, because this is important. It's not something to be dismissed.

Blowing out a breath, he returns that heavy stare to me. "We don't hate you—*I* don't hate you," he corrects when I go to argue. "When you first showed up, I didn't like what your presence meant for the team. Admittedly," he rubs awkwardly at the back of his neck, "I didn't think you could hack it, but every time you get on that ice, you prove me wrong." I'm once again sucked into the swirling vortex of Ethan's gaze. "You held your own last night, and I know that can't have been easy—to play against your old team.

"I still think it would be easier if you weren't here, but I can see now why Coach vouched for you."

My eyebrows hitch, my lips curling in a tease. "Did Ethan Maddox just say he liked me?"

"What?!" he splutters, an adorable redness dusting his cheeks. "Absolutely not."

"I'm pretty sure I just heard you say you liked me."

Huffing an exaggerated breath, he shakes his head at my shenanigans. "I said no such thing. You're a pain in my ass, Thorn. One I could definitely live without."

"You can't live without me?" I gape at him, fighting back the laughter sitting at the back of my throat as he grows increasingly exasperated with me. "Wow, Ethan, hold your horses. Next, you're going to tell me you're head over heels in love with me."

"Forget it," he grumbles, lifting a hand as he turns on his heel and stalks into the kitchen. I follow after him, grinning. It's incredible to believe that after how last night ended, I'm able to smile this morning. That, *thanks to my roommates*, I'm capable of smiling at all. "You can deal with Kyle on your own."

I scoff as I grab a mug from the cupboard and fill it with coffee from the pot. "I was planning to." I take a deep gulp, sighing softly as the warmth slides down my throat and settles in my belly. "I've known guys like Kyle my whole life. I know how to handle them."

Turning, Ethan leans against the kitchen counter as he arches a brow. "You mean, guys like Lucas Tremble."

I grimace, looking away and taking another sip from my

mug. It doesn't taste as good this time, though. "Yeah, guys like him."

"He had some choice words to say about you last night."

I attempt a tight smile over the lip of my mug. "I'm sure he did."

Pushing off the counter, Ethan closes the distance between us. "The Steelhawks aren't the Glaciers. I won't tolerate shit like that on my team. I don't tolerate people like *Lucas* on my team. Kyle has always had an issue when there is fresh competition, but he's never crossed a line before." At least, not one Ethan is aware of, but I keep my lips shut as he continues. "Having said that, what he did—invading your privacy—is not okay, and I'll make sure he knows what will happen if he goes anywhere near your room again."

My throat bobs, emotion lodged thick and unmoving in the back of it. "And what's that?"

Lifting his head, Ethan's stormy eyes pierce mine, as though boring into my soul. "He'll have to find somewhere else to live because he'll no longer be welcome in this house."

HEAD DOWN, I'm bent over my phone, ignoring the rest of the team as they trickle into the room ahead of our team meeting. Conversations buzz around me, but I pay them no heed as I write out a text to Wren. She messaged last night asking for a minute-by-minute play of the game. She'd wanted to be there in person, but she works part-time at The Stanley bar on campus and couldn't get her shift switched. With everything that happened after the game, I never got a chance to respond, and she's blown up my phone overnight with a kazillion messages. I skim over most of them before typing out a reply.

We lost.

I GLANCE up as a broad frame fills the doorway. Lips pressed into a hard line, Griffin scans the room, stopping when he spots me sitting in the far corner. He stalks toward me, and I hastily rip my gaze away, absently scrolling through my phone. We've barely spoken since the night of the party, going back to our amicable silence when we're in the gym or doing our late-night practices on the ice. Although I swear I see him around campus more than I used to—striding past my classrooms as I happen to walk out, entering the coffee shop shortly after I do. I even thought I saw him lingering outside the library after my lunch date with Wren one day, but when I looked back, he was gone, so it's entirely possible I imagined it. I don't know if I'm just more attuned to his presence or...well, actually, there's no logical alternative, so it must be that I just didn't notice him before. Though with the intensity of his presence drawing every eye in the vicinity, that seems impossible.

Truth be told, after what he did at the party, I don't know what to say to him. He stuck up for me against Kyle—a warning that clearly the whole team has heeded. Not once since the party has anyone whispered about me sleeping with the coach. It's a miracle, really.

My shoulders stiffen as I sense him approach, but I keep my gaze down, pretending not to notice until he moves past me, his arm brushing along my back between my shoulder blades. I struggle to swallow, my entire body becoming attuned to his close proximity as he plops down on the seat directly behind me.

I dare to flick a glance over my shoulder, finding him

slouching in his chair, legs sprawled out, his arms resting on the armrests like he owns the place.

"Hurricane." He nods in greeting, and I blink at him before going back to my phone.

Hurricane.

Menace.

Thorn.

What is with these guys giving me less-than-flattering nicknames that make it seem like *I'm* the troublemaker? Why do I need a nickname at all? Using my name is perfectly acceptable.

My phone buzzes in my hand, and I glance down, huffing a laugh as I read Wren's response.

WREN

You lost?! That's all you have to say to me after 11 hours of silence? I can't believe you made me wait all night for a measly two-word response. Don't you understand the meaning of play-by-play?

I'VE BARELY FINISHED READING when another message from her pops up on the screen.

WREN

And don't think you can get away with not telling me how it felt to go up against your old team.

I GRIMACE, a shiver rolling down my spine at the memory of Lucas towering over me, *threatening* me. How did I not see what a grade-A asshole he was?

Except, no, that wasn't the case. I *knew* he was an asshole, but when he stopped being an asshole to me, I was foolish enough to think I was privy to another side of him—a soft, sweet center that he didn't show anyone else. I was naively stupid enough to think I was the exception. That I was special.

After losing the most important man in my life, the one who made me feel like I was his everything, I wanted to be something to someone else. I wanted it so badly that I ignored all of Lucas's red flags, eating up every crumb of attention he gave me like I'd spent months starving at sea.

I should have realized I could never recreate something so unique and special. Especially not with someone so spiteful and vindictive.

Ignoring Wren's comment, I slip my phone into the pocket of my shorts and glance around. It's only then that I realize most of the team has arrived. Jax and Ethan are seated a couple of chairs down from me in the same row—closer than usual. I frown slightly. *Strange.* Normally, they'd sit nearer the front.

Coach strides in, a clipboard tucked under one arm and lips set in a grim line. "Last night wasn't great," he bellows, getting straight into it as he levels his gaze on every single player in the room until we all fall silent, listening to our leader. "But there's no point in wasting energy crying about it. What we *are* going to do is learn from it."

He's interrupted when the door slams open, and Kyle stomps in. I immediately note the dark scowl on his face, and the reason for it...

Kyle Reed has one hell of a purple-black shiner.

The room bursts into life.

"Jesus, Reed, what happened to your face?" Matthews jeers.

"Fall on your ass and hit the boards too hard?" another player teases.

"Did you finally mouth off to the wrong guy, or is that just your new makeup routine?"

The comments come from all corners, the laughter sharp and quick, but Kyle ignores them all, his expression thunderous as he sinks into a chair beside Finn at the front of the room.

"Nice of you to join us, Reed," Coach says dryly.

Kyle doesn't reply, just slouches lower in his chair and crosses his arms like a sulking toddler.

My gaze flicks between him and Jax, whose face is impassive as he stares straight ahead. But the longer I look at him, the more I'm convinced—*Jax* gave him that black eye.

Coach claps his hands once. It's enough to have everyone settling down and focusing on the front of the room once more. He clicks a button on the remote in his hand, and the projector flicks to life, displaying a paused frame from last night's game. "Here's the first breakdown," he says, pointing to the screen. "This play right here—lazy. No other word for it. If we're not getting sticks on the puck in the neutral zone, we're giving them a free pass to set up their offense."

He goes on, dissecting the game piece by piece. I try to focus, to soak in his critiques and make mental notes about what I need to improve, but I can't stop glancing at Jax.

It's during one such glance that I feel eyes on me. I stiffen in my chair, subtly scanning everyone else in the room, but no one else is looking this way. They're all facing forward—toward Coach.

It's then that I feel the prick of awareness on the back of my neck. Looking to the side, I notice that Griffin is still slouched in his chair behind me—the only one in the back row. However, he's not intent on Coach, but on *me*.

"...and that's what we're doing at practice tonight," Coach

finishes. "Shake off last night and come ready to work. Dismissed."

The guys start filing out, chairs scraping against the floor, voices rising in chatter. I stand, making my way toward Jax with one question poised on my tongue—*Why? Why did he sit up all night gluing my mug back together? Why did he punch his teammate, roommate, and friend for me? Why does he care?*—but Griffin steps into my path, blocking me.

His face is blank, unreadable, the way it always is, and his voice is sharp when he demands, "Why does Reed have a black eye?"

I blink, caught off guard, before flattening my lips. A refusal to tell him anything.

"Does it have anything to do with the fact you couldn't keep your eyes off Keller for the past hour?"

It takes all of my self-control to keep from denying that. He was sitting right behind me; of course, he saw every furtive glance. Instead, I narrow my gaze on Griffin, a silent *none of your business*.

He studies me a moment longer before one side of his lips hitches in a feral smirk. As though my silence has confirmed something for him, and he's delighted at the outcome. "Got it."

He tucks his hands into his pockets and walks away, whistling a tune I don't recognize but is somehow both upbeat and eerie. Like the tune in a horror movie right before shit gets gruesome. It sends shivers skating down my spine as I watch him leave, an ominous weight settling in my stomach.

Deciding that Griffin Price will do whatever Griffin Price wants to do and there is absolutely nothing I can do about it, I shake off the weird interaction before heading for the door. I'm hoping to still chase down Jax. However, when I make it outside, Ethan's car is pulling out of the lot, Jax sitting beside him in the passenger seat.

I stop in the parking lot, staring as the car disappears down the street. Perhaps it's better this way. Better to leave last night in the past. Jax did a sweet thing, helping me in a raw moment, but that kiss...

That kiss was dangerous. If I let it, it could ruin everything.

As much as I might wish to feel Jax's firm lips on mine, his hands sliding over my skin, I can't risk it.

I can't risk my position on this team.

I can't risk my reputation.

And I can't risk the shredded remains of my heart.

EIGHTEEN

WREN RUMMAGES THROUGH MY CLOSET, throwing clothes over her shoulder with a disgusted look on her face. "Seriously, Dyl, do you not own anything that's not a hoodie, sweats, or leggings?"

"It's called being comfortable," I protest from my spot on the bed.

She makes a noise of disagreement. "What are you supposed to wear when you go out?"

"Easy. I don't go out."

She sighs, sounding as though she doesn't quite know what to do with me. "Just as well I brought extras," she mutters cryptically to herself as she moves to unzip the bag she brought with her.

"I thought we were just going to a bar?" I ask, glancing down at the black leggings and oversized top I have on. "What's wrong with what I'm wearing?"

She gives me a look as though I'm a three-headed alien. "It doesn't matter *where* we're going. It's a girls' night out. The rules of girls' night dictate that you must wear a short-ass dress and heels."

It's my turn to gape at her. "You never mentioned anything about a dress and heels!"

She shrugs. "I am now." Rummaging through her bag, she pulls out a small, baby-blue dress that looks like it wouldn't have fit me when I was five, never mind twenty-one. Holding it up in front of me, she glances at it, then me. "This will be perfect."

"Yeah, perfect to strangle you with," I snark.

She only laughs as if she thinks I'm joking. I'm not. I grew up watching hockey. Playing hockey. I am all about the violence when necessary, and if Wren comes even one step closer to me with that thing, it *will* be necessary.

She pulls out another, equally miniature dress, this one red, as well as a pair of silver and a pair of black heels. "Which do you prefer?" she asks.

"Neither, since I'm not changing."

Her head bobs thoughtfully. "I agree. The black is a bit heavy for your dress. Silver it is."

She tosses the silver heels on my bed before stripping out of her clothes and shimmying into the skintight number she picked for herself. "What are you doing?" she demands as she pulls it down over her ass. "Get ready!"

"I am," I insist.

"Dylan." She sighs in exasperation. "It'll be fun, I promise." Pinning me with pleading eyes, she says, "Do this for me, and I promise we will go somewhere that I know you're going to love." I arch a brow at her. She just pins me with a flat look. "Don't and I'm going to pick the loudest, rowdiest club to go to."

I groan, my head falling back. "Why am I friends with you?" I mutter, mostly to myself.

She grins, knowing she's won.

Sighing, I reluctantly drag the horrific ensemble across the bed toward me. "Where is it we're going anyway? I thought you didn't like parties."

"This is no party, my friend. This is beer, good food, and the best entertainment you can get in Blackstone."

I give her a skeptical look.

"Okay, fine." She rolls her eyes. "We're going to The Stanley."

I freeze. "The hockey bar on campus?"

Wren grins, hands on her hips. "The very one, and before you start with your Debbie Downer bullshit, Wednesday night is Cup Night which means reruns of classic championship games—the greats like Gretzky, Orr, and Yzerman."

She spots the flicker of interest before I can hide it.

"See!" she exclaims, pointing a painted fingernail in my direction. "Told you, you'd love it."

"Drinking a beer and watching some of the best players to ever live on TV? Sounds like my kind of night," I agree. "But do we really have to dress up?"

"Yes!" she states emphatically. "You've got legs for days, woman. Show them off a little!"

I grumble but give in, slipping into the outfit. Wren insists on doing my hair, looking absolutely horrified when I suggest simply tying it back, and applying a minimal but undeniably flattering touch of makeup. When she's done, I barely recognize myself.

"Damn, I'm good," Wren says, smirking as she surveys her handiwork.

When we're ready, we head to The Stanley. The bar is buzzing with energy when we walk in. Wren waves to one of the bartenders behind the bar as she leads us to a reserved high-top table right in front of the biggest TV in the room. "Perks of working here," she says smugly, before disappearing to order our drinks.

I've only taken a few sips of my beer when a ruckus at the door grabs my attention. The rest of the team spills into the bar, loud and boisterous as they claim what are clearly their usual seats along the back wall.

I watch them for a moment, my chest tightening. They're relaxed, at ease with each other in a way I envy. Despite feeling more a part of the Steelhawks than I ever did the Glaciers, this moment serves as a reminder that I'm still on the outside looking in.

Jax catches my eye and lifts his drink with a smile. My stomach flips, but before I can react, Finn follows Jax's gaze across the room to where I'm sitting. His eyes roam over my legs, lingering just a little too long on the short hemline of my dress before he scowls, wrenching his gaze away as he knocks back his beer.

I roll my eyes and shift my attention to the TV just as the game starts. My breath catches when I realize which one it is— the championship cup game from six years ago. Timberwolves versus Penguins. The night my dad made history with a goal so impossible, it turned him into a legend.

I was at that game. Up in the family box beside my mom, the two of us cheering him on. The bittersweet nostalgia threatens to drown me. *Oh, how times have changed.* The family I once thought could withstand anything has crumbled in the face of loss and devastation.

Despite the tightness in my chest, I'm hooked to the screen as the game unfolds, watching moments I don't remember happening and plays I recall like it was only yesterday I was standing in that box watching the Timberwolves go all the way for the first time in twenty-five years.

I'm so invested in what's happening on screen that I don't notice Wren has left the table, or that I'm alone, until a familiar presence appears at my shoulder.

I know before I meet those piercing eyes that it's Ethan. His confident, sure presence is like a beacon. I blink out of the stupor I've been in, glancing first at Wren's empty seat—I vaguely recall her mentioning needing to use the bathroom—before returning my attention to Ethan.

He doesn't look at me, his attention on the TV as my dad makes a jaw-dropping play.

"He was one hell of a player," he muses.

Turning back to the screen, I swallow roughly. "Yeah," I agree softly, my chest tight.

"I met him once."

That makes me turn in my seat to look at him, eyebrows raised. "You did?"

Ethan nods, his expression wistful. "He made a guest appearance at a summer camp I went to. Spent an entire day with us—running drills, giving pointers. He took the time to talk to every single kid there; even signed all our sticks." His lips quirk. "I've still got it, actually. I refused to play with it again after that for fear that I'd sweat all over his signature and smear it."

I can't help my soft chuckle.

"Patrick Callahan made us feel like we mattered," he continues, gaze distant, like he's back at that day at camp. "Like every single player at that camp had the potential to go all the way to the Stanley Cup."

My throat tightens, warmth spreading in my chest. *That was just like my dad.* His love for hockey was infectious, and he wanted to spread it to everyone he came in contact with. He believed in everyone, never tore anyone down.

He was just...perfect.

"You and your friend should come sit with us." Ethan's words jolt me out of my trip down memory lane, and I look up to find him already watching me. I slide my gaze to the team's tables, hesitating. "I don't want to ruin the mood."

Ethan leans his forearms on the high-top table, his stormy

gaze steady on me. "You're a part of this team, Dylan," he says, voice calm but firm. It almost feels like he's *reminding* me of that fact.

Before I can tell him that I know that, he continues. "That means more than showing up to practice and giving your all on the ice."

My brow furrows, lips thinning.

"It means bantering with one another in the locker room. It means going out to celebrate a win or commiserate a loss together—as a team. It means helping one of our own out when they're in a bind or studying together if someone is falling behind. It's *supporting* one another.

"Not everyone will do that for every single player, but it's showing up as a *team*. It's being there for one another. *As. A. Team.*"

Those gray-blue eyes of his bore into my soul. "So, answer me this, Dylan, *are you a part of this team?*"

"They don't want—"

Ethan cuts me off, arching his brow as he challenges, "How do you know that?"

I blink, caught off guard by his question.

"You've never given them the chance to get to know you," he states, tone kind but firm. "You don't talk to anyone in the locker room, don't stick around after practice. You keep to yourself. And, yeah, I get it. Shit obviously went down with your old team, but we aren't them."

His words hit harder than I expect, a quiet truth beneath the surface.

"You showed up out of nowhere, demanding we give you a chance," he says, his gaze unwavering as it holds mine captive. "But you've never given us the same opportunity. Maybe if you actually get to know some of the guys, they'll surprise you."

I glance over toward the back of the bar, my gaze settling

first on the table Ethan had been sitting at. Jax, Finn, and Griffin are there, leaning back in their seats, beers in hand. They look relaxed, comfortable with each other in a way I've never allowed myself to be.

My gaze slides over the players at the other tables until I spot Kyle sitting with a couple of third-line guys. I recognize some of their faces as ones that usually have a sneer fixed in place when staring in my direction during practice, and I don't miss the smug look on Kyle's face as he says something that makes the others laugh.

"So, what's it going to be?" Ethan asks, his voice drawing my attention back to him.

I don't have a chance to answer before Wren returns, sliding up beside me and catching the tail end of the conversation. "We'd love to," she says cheerfully, all but cutting off any refusal I was about to make.

Although, was I?

Being part of a team is all I want, but the vulnerability of opening myself up, of daring to hope a team would accept me, especially after how the Glaciers made sure to destroy any trust I have in hockey players, is almost more than I can handle.

Wren flashes Ethan a bright smile, holding out her hand. "I'm Wren."

Ethan chuckles, shaking her hand. For some reason, my gaze focuses on that. On his large, calloused palm in her small, dainty one. The contact between them is brief, but for those few seconds, I find myself wondering what it would feel like to have those strong, confident hands on *my* body.

"Oh, I know who you are." Wren grins widely up at Ethan, snapping my thoughts back to the conversation at hand as she rattles off his full name, position, and stats like she's reading off a trading card.

Ethan arches a brow, his amused gaze flicking to mine

briefly, and I wonder if he's recalling when I did the same thing the first time I properly met him and the other guys.

We follow him over to his table, and when he steps aside to let one of us into the booth, Wren all but shoves me into the seat, so I'm boxed in beside Jax, with Ethan sliding into the free spot beside me.

Grinning like the Cheshire cat, Wren takes the empty seat at the end of the booth next to Finn. Of course, that means Finn is sitting opposite me, which makes it next to impossible for me to ignore the dark glower he levels in my direction.

Beside him is Griffin, who just blatantly stares at me as I squirm in my seat. *Isn't this comfortable?* I'm going to murder Wren for dragging us over here.

Ethan and Wren fall into an in-depth conversation regarding which NHL team is going all the way this season, while Finn quietly broods and Griffin just keeps staring, a hint of a smirk curling at one corner of his mouth as though he can see how uncomfortable I am and is amused by it. Jackass.

"You've been avoiding me," Jax murmurs, leaning in close so his breath brushes my ear.

"No, I haven't."

Lips tilted, he just hums, not buying my lie. After failing to catch up with him after our team meeting on Saturday, I've decided to keep him at arm's length instead. That way I won't be tempted to remind myself of how good his lips felt on mine. I won't be drawn to get to know the man behind the silent, watchful demeanor. I won't be curious to find anything about Jax that could put me at risk of actually falling for him.

"What I can't figure out is if it's because I saw behind that tough exterior of yours." His nose brushes along the column of my throat, sending shivers racing down my spine. "Or because I kissed you."

My face heats, my breath growing shallow.

He makes a noise under his breath, like he just received the answer to that question.

I jump when the backs of his knuckles brush down the outside of my thigh, and I once again curse Wren for making me wear such a revealing outfit.

Jax chuckles breathlessly, the sound barely audible to my own ears, never mind anyone else's at the table. Still, I glance up from beneath my eyelashes. Finn has been pulled into a conversation with Wren and Ethan—thank God—but Griffin...Griffin is looking directly at *me*. There's a rare heat in his gaze, like he somehow knows exactly what Jax is doing to me.

I can't seem to look away as Jax grows bolder, the tips of his fingers circling my knee before skimming up the inside of my thigh. He moves them in a slow, teasing pattern, back and forth, that leaves tingles in its wake. My core clenches, a ball of heat growing steadily brighter with every sweep of his fingers.

"I keep wondering," he rasps in my ear, voice thick. It jolts me out of my trance, and I wrench my gaze from Griffin, slamming my eyes shut instead as I force myself to gain control. "What would have happened if we hadn't been interrupted?"

The memory unfolds on the backs of my eyelids. Jax's hands on my body; my hands on his. His lips bruising mine. The desire I felt. The need for more. How close I'd been to pulling his shirt off, to shoving down his sweats.

God, my throat is parched.

"What I would give to hear the sweet noises you'd make as I made you come," Jax murmurs, and I'm just about ready to combust. Seriously, if he moved his fingers an inch higher, he'd literally just have to tap my clit and I'd come. "The way you'd feel wrapped around me."

I shoot upright, practically knocking Ethan out of the booth in my haste to escape. I mutter an excuse about needing the bathroom before practically steamrolling over him and fleeing the table.

At the sink, I stare at the flushed cheeks of my reflection. There's a rosiness to them, a glow in my eyes. I look more alive than I have in a long time. Blowing out a breath, I run the tap and splash cold water on the backs of my wrists and neck in a bid to calm the fire Jax ignited.

The fact that he is the one to instill such life back into me...I don't know what to make of that.

I hide out in the bathroom for as long as I can, and when I finally muster the courage to leave, Finn is waiting in the hallway outside. He pushes off the opposite wall as soon as I appear. There's a tic in his jaw, and he looks absolutely furious as he takes me in. I barely get a chance to acknowledge how hot he looks in his formfitting jeans that hug his muscular thighs and shirt that stretches across his toned chest, hinting at the layers of muscle hidden underneath, the intoxicating clash of red hair and green eyes before he rushes forward, crowding me against the wall.

His palms are on either side of my head, elbows locked as he stares down at me with twin emerald pools of liquid lust, his gaze hot and heavy against my skin. "You're driving me insane, showing up here dressed like that." His voice is a thick rasp that scrapes against my skin, much like I imagine the hint of stubble along his chin would scratch my inner thighs. "Letting my friend and teammate turn you on right in front of me." My cheeks blaze red as his gaze slowly drops over me. Everywhere his eyes touch, goosebumps pebble in his wake. My breathing shallows; my chest heaves. All I can focus on is the heat of his body searing into mine.

"You're a temptation I'm trying to resist." His voice cracks, strain evident in the lines of his face, the way his palms flatten against the wall beside my head, nails scraping along the paint like he's desperate to be touching something else...to be touching *me*. "But fuck, when you look like that, I can't stay away."

Finn's mouth crashes down on mine in a kiss so rough and demanding that it leaves me dazed. The fire I'd managed to douse rages back to life stronger and more dangerous than before. I'm engulfed in it, burning alive, and I don't even care.

However, I can't forget how cold he has been toward me. His kiss might be searing, but his attitude has been arctic. Balling my fists, I go to shove him away when suddenly, his touch is gone. The warmth of him vanishes in an instant, slipping away like the final notes of a song fading into silence, leaving only the echo of what was. I sway where I stand, unsteady in the absence of him as my eyes slowly flutter open, and I stare at his retreating back. The ghost of his lips haunts mine as I watch him storm away.

Asshole. He has *got* to stop doing that to me.

Alone, I collapse against the wall. My lips tingle, and my heart is crashing against my chest like I just skated suicides for the past hour. I decide there is absolutely no way I can return to the table and act like everything is normal. Pulling my phone out of my purse, I send Wren a quick text to let her know I'm leaving. I hesitate for a second before sending the same message to Ethan, knowing he'll probably worry if I just disappear.

Before anyone can come looking for me, I slip through the crowded bar toward the exit. Of course, Griffin is waiting by the door.

"Don't start," I warn, marching past him and throwing open the door.

He falls into step beside me as I move down the sidewalk. "Easy, Hurricane. Just making sure you get home."

I glance at him, but his face gives nothing away as he strolls casually beside me, his long legs easily keeping up with my fast pace. Frustrated and shaken, I turn my gaze forward, deciding to ignore him as I keep walking.

NINETEEN

IT'S BEEN A RELENTLESS WEEK. Coach has been pushing us hard after our exhibition loss, and I've been pushing myself harder still. Mostly because I want to be the best. I want to play to the best of my abilities.

But I've also been pushing myself harder, practicing more, to avoid being at the house. To avoid having to face Jax after I nearly went up in flames beneath his touch the other night. Evading Ethan after he kept his word and put a lock on my bedroom door. I've even been going to the gym and using the rink at different times to avoid Griffin and whatever is going on there.

I came here for a fresh start, and instead, I've found myself tangled up with three different guys—four if you include Finn, who has been avoiding me as much as I've been avoiding everyone else since that out-of-the-blue kiss in the back hallway of The Stanley.

"Ready to give me back my position?" Kyle sneers as he skates past me, slow and deliberate. He speaks from the corner of his mouth, careful to make sure he doesn't get caught talking to me by Ethan.

My grip on my stick tightens, the only outward sign that I heard him at all, but in my head, I'm imagining slamming him into the boards hard enough to break his nose. I force myself to focus on the puck, on the drill we're *supposed* to be doing, instead of the urge to rearrange his face.

With Ethan riding his ass, Kyle has been forced to rally a couple of the third-liners and extras to his side, and they've been going after me all week. It's not obvious, not to anyone else, but I'm attuned to these things. I've taught myself to look out for them. To notice when I'm shoved into the boards harder than necessary during practice or slashed at with a stick.

They're trying to mess with me. To trip me into making a mistake.

As we break into teams for a scrimmage, I'm on my guard as I streak down the ice toward the net. A wiry third-liner named Thomas hooks his stick around my ankle. I don't even have the puck. It's a blatant trip, one that could have sent me flying face-first into the boards if I hadn't caught my balance at the last second.

I whirl around, my blood boiling, but before I can say anything, Jax is there. He body-slams the third-liner so hard I swear I hear something pop. "The fuck is your problem?" Jax growls, sounding feral as he pins Thomas in place against the boards.

"What the hell, man? It was an accident!" Thomas stammers, holding up his hands.

"Bullshit." Jax shoves him again.

Ethan arrives a second later, and I curse under my breath at how rapidly this entire situation is growing out of control. Yeah, he pulled a dirty move, but Jesus. It's hockey. This shit happens all the time.

He steps between Jax and Thomas. "Jax, back off. Thomas, save moves like that for our opponents, not our teammates."

Coach's whistle cuts through the air. "Is this a tea party or are we playing hockey?" he barks.

I barely smother my groan as he skates this way.

"I don't care what happened or who started it. Unless you want to skate suicides after practice, get back out there and show me you can actually function as a team."

"Yes, Coach," we all mutter, though Jax's jaw is still tight.

Thankfully there are no issues for the rest of the scrimmage, and when it ends, Coach calls us to the bench for a quick debrief. I'm still fuming as we gather around, barely managing to keep myself from fidgeting as Coach talks.

The moment he dismisses us, I'm up and storming over to Jax. "What the hell was that?" I demand.

"What?" he says, like he doesn't already know.

"You can't do that," I snap, gesturing toward the ice. "You can't fight my battles for me."

"Dylan—"

"No," I cut him off, jabbing a finger at him. "You doing that? It only makes *me* look weak. You might *think* you were helping, but you did that for *you*. You didn't stop to think how your actions might affect *me*."

I shake my head, teeth grinding. "I've dealt with far worse than someone hooking my skates. I sure as hell don't need you stepping in and making me look like I can't handle myself."

His face hardens, but I don't stick around to hear whatever comeback he's working on. I spin on my skates and march toward the locker room, my anger simmering just beneath the surface.

A cacophony of noise hits me as I step into the sweaty, male-dominated room. Lockers slam. Music is playing from some-one's phone. Guys yell over one another about a botched play during practice. I weave through the chaos, heading to my corner, already peeling off my gear. As I pull my jersey over my head, there's an almighty pop that reverberates through the locker room, drowning out all other noises.

My gaze snaps to Kyle, along with everyone else's, as a spray of glitter detonates out of his locker, bursting in waves of pink and gold goo that cover him from head to toe. As it sticks to him in globules, I realize it's not *just* glitter. Thick, sparkly glue drips down his face, streaks through his hair, and coats every inch of his practice jersey. Not to mention absolutely everything he had stashed in his locker, including the clothes he was wearing this morning.

The room goes silent. Kyle stands frozen in front of his locker, fingers clenching around the open door so hard it rattles. For a split second, everyone is in shock—until the laughter starts.

The entire room breaks into fits of hysterics.

"Oh my God, dude!" Noah shouts, doubling over.

"Reed, you look like a piñata at a five-year-old's birthday party!"

"Bro, are those...hearts?!" Ben points out the glitter chunks now embedded in Kyle's hair.

Kyle stumbles back, eyes wide and arms outstretched, as if trying to figure out what the hell just happened. His feet squelch in the puddle of glue that has formed onto the floor. He glares down at himself and then into his locker, where glitter bomb remnants hang precariously, goo still dripping from them.

"What the fuck?" At first, it's muttered, but as the shock wears off, he rounds on the room. "What the fuck?!" he roars furiously, cutting through the laughter. "Who did this?"

No one answers, the sound of muffled—and not so muffled—snickers all that can be heard.

Kyle spins in a circle, glaring at everyone in turn. He slams his hand into the locker beside his. "Tell me who did this!"

"Dude, it was just a joke," Finn says, pitching his voice low, but we all hear.

"No." Kyle shakes his head fervently. "Switching out my athletic tape for a unicorn one might have been a joke. Or changing my laces to bright pink ones, but now this? Someone is hazing me."

As if sensing the accusation coming my way, I stiffen. The slight movement has Kyle's gaze locking on to me. "You!" he snarls, pointing an accusing finger my way.

I blink at him, holding up my hands. "Me? Seriously? I've been on the ice the whole time. Pretty sure I didn't have time to set up a glue bomb mid-practice."

"She's right," Ethan cuts in, stepping between us. His voice is calm, but his stare at Kyle is hard enough to shut him up. "Dylan's not your problem here, Kyle."

"Then who the hell did this?" Kyle demands, waving toward his ruined locker.

Ethan lifts a shoulder in a lazy shrug. "Perhaps you pissed off the wrong chick. Sleep with anyone and not call them recently? Or sleep with someone's roommate or sister or best friend?"

Kyle's jaw hardens, but doubt flickers in his gaze. He's not certain. He can't be, since it wasn't actually me. His face is flushed deep red beneath the glitter, his fist clenching at his side, before he grabs his ruined clothes and towel from his locker and stomps toward the showers.

As soon as he disappears, the muffled chuckles and not-so-quiet whispers break out into full-blown belly laughs and taunts. Ethan turns back to his own locker, and as everyone goes back to getting changed, I shift my gaze to Griffin. He's leaning casually against the wall, already showered and dressed. He catches me looking and gives me a sly wink.

I narrow my eyes, my mind spinning. I don't know for sure

it's him, but...who else would it be? Who else would be hazing Kyle? I don't know how he could have pulled this one off, though...

Pushing off the wall, Griffin slings his duffel over his shoulder and strides toward me. As he steps past, he leans close enough that his breath grazes my ear. "More subtle than Jax's approach, don't you think, Hurricane?"

My stomach twists, equal parts irritation and intrigue. What is with these guys thinking they need to step in and fight my battles for me? At least Griffin's approach doesn't make me look weak.

The question is: why? Why is he defending me? Why is he taking on my problems as though they are his to solve?

He's out of the room, the door swinging softly shut behind him before I can question him. I don't have time to figure out what the hell Griffin's game is, though, because the sound of Kyle's yell from the showers carries back into the locker room.

"It won't come out of my hair!"

The entire room erupts into laughter again, but I shake my head and move to get changed.

However, later that day, when I spot Kyle stomping through campus with his white top streaked in glitter glue and a murderous look on his pink-stained face, I can't stop the smile that tugs at my lips.

Karma *is* a bitch, isn't she?

TWENTY

"EEK, I can't believe we're doing this." Wren is practically vibrating with excitement beside me as we walk into the cafeteria in the sports center. I, on the other hand, feel faintly nauseous. Although I shouldn't. After our win against the Waves on Saturday, I went out with the team to celebrate. Partly because Ethan was giving me that look—you know, the captain one that says *I'm always right* and dares you to doubt him—and partly because I was *terrified* that if I went home there would be a repeat of last week, and I know if I let Jax touch me again...let myself fall into him, I won't be able to stop it.

So best to simply avoid, avoid, avoid.

I actually ended up having a good time. In a bid to evade my roommates and Griffin, and Kyle and his minions, I sat at a table with a bunch of juniors I've barely spoken a word to before. Instead of offhand comments about my being on the team and not-so-subtle glares at my presence at their table, they easily drew me into their conversation about what teams they think will pick up Cam Fowler now that his tenure with the Anaheim Ducks is nearing its end.

It ended up being a surprisingly good evening, but that still doesn't mean I'm not nervous as Wren links her arm through mine and practically drags me into the cafeteria. I already regret telling her what Ethan said about how I should give the team a chance. She immediately packed up her belongings in the library and ushered me out of my quiet sanctuary.

"*I* can't believe you're making me do this," I grumble.

"Yes, yes." Wren waves away my foul attitude like it's nothing more than a bad smell in the air. "I know you'd far rather hide away in your cave of solitude."

"I don't hide," I protest.

Wren simply gives me a look.

Exhaling through my nose, I say nothing as the cafeteria doors close behind us. The place is packed with athletes—hockey players, football players, a few members of the swim team. The hockey guys have taken over a long table near the center of the room, their loud and obnoxious behavior drawing many eyes from around the room, including mine.

I scour the table as we step in line to grab our food, spotting Finn first. I groan at the sight of the blonde puck bunny practically in his lap. My only saving grace is that Finn doesn't seem to be paying her any attention, too absorbed in his conversation with the player on his other side.

Ripping my gaze away before the sight of her clinging to him like a leech can put me off my lunch, I decide to forgo the plates of hot food and grab a chicken salad wrap instead, before leading the way over to the hockey players' table. If I'm doing this, I might as well *do* it. Noting Griffin's and Jax's positions around the table, I opt for the empty seat at the end of the row beside Ethan.

Leo, one of the second-liners I was chatting with on Saturday, is sitting opposite him, and he lifts his chin in greeting as I sit down. Noticing Wren behind me, he gives her a friendly smile before sliding down a seat and immediately pulling her into conversation.

"Good to see you've come out of hiding," Ethan murmurs low enough for only me to hear.

"I was not *hiding*," I hiss between gritted teeth. "The testosterone is too much to deal with twenty-four seven. A girl needs a break sometimes, you know?"

His lips quirk up in a teasing smirk. "Can't say I do. Being part of the testosterone problem and all," he retorts dryly.

I blink, caught off guard. It's not the response I expected from him, not from Captain Control. "Wow." I gasp, feigning shock. "Was that...a joke?"

He rolls his eyes, but I catch the glint of humor in his pale blue depths.

"Who knew you were capable of one?"

His smirk returns, sharper this time, with a hint of something else beneath it. Leaning in, his voice is pitched lower than before as he says, "I'm capable of a lot of things that you don't know about."

A flicker of heat curls low in my stomach. My pulse stutters.

Was that...flirting? From *Ethan*?

I study him, trying to read the line of his mouth, the look in his eyes—but, as always, he gives nothing away.

"Well, aren't you just full of surprises, Captain."

Flashing me a grin, he stuffs the end of his sandwich into his mouth, and I turn my focus to unwrapping mine.

I'm chewing on my first bite when I sense someone watching me. Glancing up, my gaze collides with Griffin's from farther down the table. He's talking to the guy next to him, but his attention is locked on me. When I catch him staring, he tilts his head slightly, eyes narrowing like he's sizing me up—and liking what he sees.

Heat flickers low in my stomach, sharp and unwelcome. My

breath catches before I can stop it, and for a second, I forget to look away.

I rip my gaze from his, frowning. *What the hell is that?* I seriously have no idea what is up with that guy or why he keeps looking at me like that, like he's daring me to look back. Or why it always feels like my body's two seconds behind my brain every time he does.

Turning to say something to the player seated opposite him, Finn stops mid-sentence, his jaw tightening when he notes mine and Wren's presence at the table. And then, because he's the definition of an emotionally stunted caveman, he turns his full attention to the blonde still draped over him. She practically has hearts in her eyes as she soaks up every second of his focus like it's a spotlight, her hand sliding up the front of his chest to wrap around the back of his neck as he lowers his head.

His eyes flash to mine at the last second, and I sneer, flipping him the middle finger. *What an asshole.* Finn's smirk is smug before he buries his face in the side of her neck.

I gag—loudly—the sound one hundred percent fake. Yup, not even a little bit real as I mentally shove the memory of his lips on mine out of my mind. Forever.

Unfortunately, though, the noise garners the blonde's attention. She turns, flipping her long, perfectly straight hair over her shoulder as her eyes narrow on me. It takes a second, but then recognition clicks.

"Oh," she drawls, lips curving in a cruel mockery of a smile. "It's the bench bunny."

Giving her a deadpan stare, I flick my gaze purposefully to Finn before fixing her with a look of faux sympathy. "Could you *be* any more obvious?"

Her lips curl. "Excuse me?"

"You heard me." I gesture between her and Finn. "You're laying it on so thick it's actually painful to watch."

Her eyes narrow, her hand sliding up Finn's arm. "Jealous much?"

I bark out a laugh. "Of what, exactly?"

Her nails tighten on Finn's bicep, and I swear, for just a second, he winces. "Oh, I don't know," she says airily. "The fact that some of us don't have to degrade ourselves for attention?"

I freeze. The entire table goes silent, and I can feel them all listening in.

She smirks, taking my silence as an opening. "I mean, I can't imagine how humiliating it must be. No talent, no real skill—just a girl desperate for a spot on a team full of guys who don't even want her there." She taps her finger deliberately against her chin. "You have to wonder what she did to get it."

There it is. The implication. The nasty, ugly rumor Kyle tried to start at the roster party.

Heat rushes through me, fury burning up my spine. I feel Ethan go rigid beside me, his hand coming up like he's about to cut in, but I'm already moving, clapping my hand over his as I lean forward, voice deadly soft.

"You think I slept my way onto this team? Into my position?"

She shrugs, fiddling with the end of her hair. "Well, it's not like you earned it."

A slow, vicious smile spreads across my lips. "And yet here you are, plastered against Finn like a human leech, trying to suck your way into relevance. Tell me, what's it like being the living embodiment of a cliché?"

Her face reddens. "Bitch."

I tilt my head. "No, see, if I were really a bitch, I'd point out the fact that Finn isn't the least bit interested in you. You fill a void for him. You're a distraction. A toy." Her lips part in a protest. "And you know how I know that? Because he wasn't paying you a lick of attention until I sat down. Because, despite all your desperate little touches, he hasn't reacted once." I throw my hands wide. "And here you are, talking to me instead of sitting in his lap like you so badly want to be."

Smacking her hands against the table, she rises, glaring at me a final time before storming off.

I wave my fingers at her retreating back. "We always have the best conversations."

Hand clamped over her mouth, Wren giggles. "That was badass."

I flash her a triumphant grin, before my face scrunches. "I should really learn her name." I turn expectant eyes on Finn, who gapes at me.

"Uhh, Linda? Or Laura? Lisa?" I'm pretty sure he was asking himself that last one. Shaking my head, I turn away from him, only to be met with Ethan's unimpressed stare.

"Really?" he says dryly.

"What?" I ask innocently.

"You antagonized her on purpose."

"She started it."

"You escalated it." I roll my eyes, finally digging back into my wrap, but Ethan isn't done. "This isn't middle school, Dylan."

"No, because in middle school, I would've shoved her into a locker."

Ethan pinches the bridge of his nose. "Always such a thorn in my side."

"Relax, Captain," I soothe, rolling my eyes. "I'm not actually going to fight your puck bunny."

"She's not *my* puck bunny!"

"She's someone's," I drawl, unable to help the way my gaze flicks back to Finn. "Maybe you should have a word with your boy over there. Make sure he doesn't choke on all that desperation."

"Jesus Christ." Ethan exhales through his nose. "Pretty sure you did a decent job of making sure she doesn't come around for a while."

I flash him a wide grin. "Why, thank you."

"It wasn't a compliment."

"Huh." Snatching a chip from his tray, I chew on the end of it. "Sounded like one to me."

He shakes his head, but there's something almost amused in his expression. "You're exhausting."

"I know. It's fun, isn't it?"

"Not the word I would use—"

Whatever Ethan was going to say is cut off by the chime of notifications. Not just a few—*everyone's*. The entire cafeteria erupts into murmurs and the rustle of movement as people start pulling out their phones. Then the snapping silence—just for a second—before the first choked-off laugh breaks it.

Then another.

And another.

Until the entire cafeteria is roaring.

Across from me, Wren nearly spits out her drink, eyes blown wide. The guys at the table are losing their shit, shoulders shaking as they shove their phones at each other, jaws hanging open.

"What the fuck?" someone breathes.

A guy at the next table is crying, gripping his stomach as he wheezes out, "No way—holy shit—"

Eyes wide and throat dry, I pull my phone from my back pocket. I don't expect to see anything, no one on this campus other than Ethan has my number. And yet, as soon as I look at the screen, a single alert catches my eye.

Hands shaking, my finger hovers over the notification, unsure if I really want to know what it is.

Before I can make a decision, Kyle's roar shatters through the chaos.

"WHAT THE FUCK?!"

My head whips up, every eye in the cafeteria zeroing in on him. Guys across the room point and laugh. I frown, taking in Kyle's wild, panicked expression.

"Oh my God, is that Kyle?" I hear Wren murmur quietly as she squints at her phone. "Is that...Kyle?"

Kyle? Whatever it is, is about...Kyle?

It takes a long moment for that to sink in. For me to realize it's not about me. Not this time.

A tray slamming against the table startles me. I jump, Kyle's voice like a fire alarm blasting through the noise in the cafeteria. "Who the fuck is doing this to me?"

My gaze inadvertently falls from Kyle to Griffin, who is leaning back in his chair, arms folded, completely unbothered by the chaos unfolding all around him. His expression gives nothing away—no smirk, no arrogance, no admission of guilt.

But I see it.

I *feel* it.

The smugness radiating from him.

"TELL ME!" Kyle bellows, screaming now. "WHO THE FUCK IS DOING THIS?!'

He lunges, his chair screeching back, but before he can do anything stupid, Ethan's voice cracks like a whip. "Sit the fuck down!"

Kyle whirls, vibrating with rage, but Ethan doesn't move. Doesn't flinch. He just stares, unyielding. "Now."

Kyle's chest heaves. His fists clench. His face is bright red—whether from anger or humiliation, I don't know.

Then slowly, jaw grinding, he draws in a deep breath. His eyes breathe fire, and murder radiates from his every pore, before he turns on his heel and storms toward the exit.

I exhale the breath I didn't realize I was holding.

And when I glance back at Griffin, he's already looking at me.

Watching. Waiting.

For what, I don't know.

When Ethan catches our silent exchange, his brow furrows, and he leans in as I break eye contact. His voice is low as he all but demands, "What was that about?"

I take a sip of my drink, keeping my expression blank.

"No idea."

Liar. Liar. Liar.

TWENTY-ONE

THE AIR inside the rink is sharp with cold and rubber and that faint chemical sting of the Zamboni. The kind of familiar that settles in my bones.

I move through my warm-up like I always do—methodical, focused, efficient. Tight circles first, edge control sharp and clean, carving into the ice like I'm drawing lines around the chaos in my head. My shoulders stay loose, stick gripped light in my hands, eyes ahead, locked in.

Then crossovers, forward and backward, knees bent, stride compact. I count the beats in my head—four forward, pivot, four back. Again. Again. It's not about speed. It's about precision. Repetition. Getting every part of me firing the way it's supposed to.

Pivots next—open hip, dig in, rotate, explode out. Then transitions. Tight feet, quick turns, shoulders squared. Balance steady, blade to blade, motion into stillness and back again.

Stops and starts. Accelerations. Sharp turns.

Everything drilled into me through years of routine and discipline.

It's not purely about getting my body ready—it's about switching on. Blocking everything else out.

Tuning in to the rhythm.

Control.

I've always needed it more than most.

I'm halfway through my routine when I hear it—soft at first, then sharper, brighter.

A laugh.

Hers.

It slices through the ambient noise of blades scraping and pucks hitting boards, straight into my bloodstream like a shot of adrenaline.

She flashes a grin at Jax as they stretch at the boards, her lips moving, forming the words of what I imagine is some cocky little comment or teasing dig at his expense. Jax volleys right back with something that has her throwing her head back.

Watching them together, the easygoing camaraderie, sets something off in my chest. She's coming out of her shell.

Slowly. Cautiously. But it's there.

I've been watching it unfold over the last week—since that night at The Stanley, when I told her she needed to give us a chance. I hadn't expected her to actually listen. Honestly, I thought she'd keep her distance, keep to her little bubble of steel and solitude.

But she has showed up.

She has tried.

She came out with us after the game, even spent a large portion of the night talking to some of the juniors on the team. She's made an effort to talk to players after practice. And the cafeteria today? That was a first. Seeing her and Wren walk toward our table took me by surprise. I'd been mid-conversation with Leo and completely lost my train of thought when I caught sight of her moving through the cafeteria, shoulders back, chin up, that same focused intensity she wears on the ice.

Her hair was down for once, the brunette locks loose around her shoulders, and even dressed in simple leggings and a hoodie, with the Converse she's always sporting, she still managed to pull every inch of my attention.

I hadn't expected to get pulled so far into her orbit that I didn't want lunch to end.

Typically, I spend my lunch hour managing egos or helping someone sort out their latest crisis. Or worse, stuck in my own head, running through drills or schedules or everything that could go wrong with this season.

But today was different.

She *made* it different.

The way she needled me, challenging me with that sharp wit and sharper grin. It got under my skin in the worst way. Or maybe the best.

I hadn't meant to flirt with her when I'd told her I was capable of a lot more than she knew of. It had just...slipped out.

And the look on her face? Not rejection. Not annoyance.

Surprise. Interest.

A spark that lit up something in me I've spent weeks trying to suppress.

And then there was the way she stood her ground with Finn's puck bunny, not even breaking a sweat. I shouldn't be surprised—Dylan Carter is nothing if not fierce. She's relentless on the ice. Of course she'd be the same off it.

She's going to be a pain in my ass, though.

That much is clear.

I knew it from the moment I came face to face with her in the locker room that first day. But now, after watching her go toe to toe with myself, Kyle, Finn, and now some airbrushed girl with fake lashes and claws? Yeah, I need to keep an eye on her.

And not just on the ice.

All the damn time.

"Bring it in!" Coach's voice booms from the bench, pulling me out of my thoughts.

Hell, I just wasted the last ten minutes, daydreaming about a fellow teammate instead of finishing my warm-ups.

Shaking my head at myself, I skate toward the group, jaw tight, eyes forward.

Don't look in her direction, I mentally chastise as I feel her and Jax come to a stop nearby.

I force my focus on Coach as he explains the first drill of practice, nodding along even though I already know it. I've known it since I was twelve. That's the point—repetition, discipline, precision. The structure that keeps everything in line.

The structure that Dylan's presence is threatening to ruin.

She doesn't follow rules. Not really. She pokes and pushes and questions, and worse—she enjoys it. She enjoys getting under my skin.

And lately, I've been letting her.

God knows why. I wouldn't tolerate the shit she's pulled from any other player. If any one of them spoke to me the way she has, called bullshit on my decisions, I'd be sending them to skate suicides. But not her.

Dammit, there I go thinking about her again.

Except, even when I focus on the ice in front of me, she's *there.* Sliding into the drill line across from me. Her braid is a little messy, and catching my eyes she flashes me a grin that is all teeth.

"Try not to eat ice this time, Captain," she says low enough that only I hear.

My jaw tics.

I should shut it down. Tell her to focus. Set an example.

Instead, my mouth moves without permission.

"Worry about your own edge control, Carter."

Her smile deepens like I've just proven her point.

And damn it, I like it. I like the way she fights back, the way she challenges me without crossing the line. I like that she doesn't defer to me the way the others do.

I like it too much.

She flies through the drill with that fast, aggressive grace of hers. Sharp turns. Quick hands. Reckless as hell. And when she stops beside me, cheeks flushed from the exertion, she tosses a smug glance my way.

It should annoy me. Instead, my chest tightens.

I look away again.

I can't want her. She's a player on *my* team. She's under *my* leadership. And after what she's hinted about her last team—the betrayal, the lack of safety—I know what I represent. I know what crossing that line would mean.

I'm not that guy. I won't be that guy.

She deserves better from a captain. And I'd rather rip this interest out of my chest with a skate blade than risk being someone she can't trust.

So I put blinders on, ones I've been donning for every practice recently. I tune her out. When she says something else, something that earns a low laugh from another player, I don't turn. I stare straight ahead, counting my breaths, biting the inside of my cheek.

I have a job to do. And it's not getting distracted by the girl who's been a thorn in my side since day one.

And it works...almost.

We're nearly done with practice for the day, and I'm about to pat myself on the back for managing to avoid looking in her direction, to shut down all thoughts of her when they started to creep in, when a thump against the boards catches my attention.

I turn in time to see Dylan skating away from Fletcher,

rolling her shoulder out like it stings. My brows dip low, my stomach knotting.

"You good?" I call.

She shrugs, not looking back. "Yeah. It's nothing."

I watch her a moment longer, before ripping my gaze away and pulling those blinders back on once more.

The last few minutes of practice blurs, all of it running on autopilot while I force my brain to stay in the lane I've carved out. No distractions. No slipping.

By the time Coach blows the final whistle, my shirt clings to my back with sweat and my lungs burn. The guys start peeling off toward the benches, the air thick with the usual end-of-practice chatter, but there's a weight pressing down on the back of my neck that won't shake loose.

I coast toward the boards, falling in beside Jax, who's unusually silent. His jaw's tight, brows pulled low, like he's one wrong look away from snapping.

"You look like you're ready to murder someone," I mutter, half a breathless joke as I push my helmet up and glide toward the tunnel with him.

He doesn't laugh. Doesn't even glance at me. Just mutters something under his breath and skates a little harder, like the ice might be able to take what he's holding in.

What the hell crawled up his ass?

I WAIT near the back hallway, just outside the rink. The others have long since cleared out—bags slung over shoulders, gear rattling, loud voices fading into the night. But I stay.

Griffin didn't get off the ice after practice, staying on to skate drills like he wasn't already dripping with sweat. Typically, I'd admire his dedication. He's the most driven player on the team

—at least, he was until Dylan came along. Now, they're neck and neck, each vying for the top spot of who is the most devoted Steelhawk.

However, tonight, I just want to go home.

It's been a long day in a sea of long days, each one marked by the same silent, exhausting battle. Fighting off thoughts I shouldn't be having about my teammate. My roommate.

Dylan is everywhere. She's in my space, under my skin, and every time I think I've put enough distance between us, she says something or smirks at me, and the fucking challenge in her eyes nearly snaps my self-control. But I always regroup. Rein it in. Shore up my defenses and remind myself why I can't want her. Why I *shouldn't*.

She's a player. I'm her captain. It's a line I don't get to cross.

Tonight, though? I'm too damn tired of all of it.

Every muscle in my body aches. My brain's fried. I just want to drag myself home, climb into bed, shove in my earbuds, and let some mindless podcast drown out the noise in my head.

The thud of skates hitting rubber pulls me back to the present, reminding me why I'm still here, still standing in the damn rink after hours. His gaze latches on to mine. I suspect he's known I've been here the whole damn time, and deliberately kept me waiting. He's an ass like that.

"We need to talk," I tell him.

He doesn't respond as he stomps over, peeling his jersey off. His hair is damp, stick tucked under one arm, his sharp gaze focused on me, stare cool and unreadable.

"Yeah? What about?" His words are a near grunt.

"You know what," I clip. "Unicorn tape. Glitter bombs. Spamming micropenis photos. Ring any bells?"

That gets a flicker of something—satisfaction, maybe. He tries to smother it, but it's there.

"You think that's funny?"

He shrugs, like none of this is worth getting worked up over. "I think the punishment fits the crime."

My jaw tightens. "That's not your place. You're a goalie—your job is to stop pucks. You don't get to decide how this team runs."

He finally meets my gaze, all trace of a smirk gone.

"No, you're right. That's supposed to be your job." His eyes are hard on mine. "But from where I'm standing, you're too busy looking the other way, *ignoring* the one person on the team who needs you most."

My teeth grind. The silence crackles between us. Loud. Heavy.

Shuffling on his skates, his lips curl in a cruel sneer. "Hate to break it to you, Cap, but ignoring her isn't going to make her go away, and it isn't going to do a damn thing to extinguish those feelings you have. All you're doing is leaving her vulnerable. Unprotected." His shoulder shoves against mine as he steps past me, but he stops before moving down the hall toward the locker room. "You do your job, and I won't have to do mine."

Fisting my hands at my sides, I ignore the urge to shove him into the wall. I want to scream that I *am* trying, that every decision I've made is about keeping this team from falling apart—that I'm doing what I was *trained* to do. Keep your distance. Lead from above. Stay objective.

But Dylan isn't just another player, and maybe that's the fucking problem.

I listen as he stomps away, but even after he's gone, his words hang in the air, clinging like smoke I can't clear.

The one person on the team who needs you most.

Is that true? Have I missed something? Digs Kyle's aimed at her when I wasn't looking? Hits I didn't question because she got back up?

I don't know.

And that's what's eating me.

What I do know—what I *hate* knowing—is that ignoring her isn't working.

Not for this team.

Not for me.

She's in my head more than I want to admit, and the more I try to shut it down, the worse it gets.

I'm supposed to lead.

To protect.

To hold everything together.

But right now, I feel like I'm failing at all of it.

And I don't know how to fix it.

TWENTY-TWO

ROLLING MY SHOULDERS, I stretch my neck from side to side as I make my way down the dark corridor toward the gym. It's so early that only strips of lighting on either side of the floor light my path. The muscles in my back pop with tension, and my confrontation with Ethan last night plays out in my head. Of course the ever-watchful captain saw my exchange with Dylan in the cafeteria yesterday, and he demanded to know if I was the one pulling this shit on Kyle.

I didn't say a word, obviously. Straitlaced, rule-abiding, good boy Ethan would never approve. But then, if he were doing his job as captain and keeping Kyle in line—and him and his goons away from Dylan—I wouldn't have to step in.

Am I the only one who notices the way he looks at those two dumb fuckers, Monroe and Fletcher, before one of them invariably goes after Dylan? Did Ethan not see how Fletcher nearly snapped Dylan's arm in practice? He had her flat against the boards, her arm bent so far back I was waiting anxiously to hear it pop any second. Thank fuck my girl's a fighter and managed to get herself out of there, but I saw the way she favored her right side after that, babying her arm for the rest of practice. So how the fuck did Ethan not?!

Ethan is a decent enough guy. A fine captain, but I came so fucking close to punching him in the face last night. He's so fucking busy ignoring Dylan and pretending that she doesn't exist, that she doesn't take up more of his focus than she should, that he's missing the fucking obvious.

Jax sees it. Or he sees some of it. After Dylan's ass-chewing last week, he's backed off. He has to turn away when he sees one of them go after her. Honestly, I'm fighting the same urges he is whenever I see one of them tackling her, but I know Dylan can handle her own. She proves it every damn time she's on the ice.

Stepping into the gym, I find the woman of my obsession pacing back and forth in front of the weight rack. I stop at the threshold, held captive for a moment. Dylan Carter always looks hot as sin when she is working out—Lycra shorts that mold to the lean muscles of her upper thighs and accentuate the firm globes of her ass and her sports bra that leaves nothing except the exact color of her nipples to the imagination. A color that I am dying to find out. I'm rock hard in my basketball shorts just staring at her. If the guys had any idea how she dressed when working out, they'd all be in here at the ass crack of dawn. But then I'd have to kill every single one of my teammates, so yeah, I'll be keeping that tidbit to myself. This is *my* secret. *My* time to have Dylan all to myself.

An obsession is exactly what Dylan has become. I've always been prone to bouts of fixation and compulsion. It's why I'm the best goalie in the league. I give it every single ounce of my focus and attention, and I have done so since a stick was first slapped in my hand at the age of five.

But for the first time ever, something else has superseded that obsession. Some*one* else. Dylan. From the moment I saw her in that locker room wearing the Steelhawks gear, I haven't been able to look away. I fought it initially. Tried to ignore her, to ignore the pull toward her, but it was fucking impossible.

Ever since I watched her struggling that night on the ice...I saw her resilience, her determination to succeed, and her drive to keep going. I recognized a part of myself in her. With every interaction since, that obsession has only grown stronger, more potent, until she's become all that I can focus on.

Dylan has torn through my life like a hurricane I never saw coming. She came in fast, fierce, and unstoppable, upending the careful order of my world. Now, in the aftermath, all I see is her.

I'm drawn to her like the tide to the shore. Every time she lifts her chin and that defiant gleam enters her eyes, or when she thinks no one is looking and she finally drops her guard, allowing me to catch a glimpse of the well of sadness that resides within. It only pulls me closer. I'm so invested in this girl that I'd do absolutely anything for her—all she has to do is ask.

I've watched every bit of game footage of her I can find online. I've memorized her schedule and make a point of walking past her classroom or seeking her out from a distance during the day to make sure she's okay and no one is harassing her, and dole out retribution if they are. And since no one else is bothering to help her out with her Kyle problem, I've taken that upon myself too.

Dylan is my crease—my territory, my purpose. No matter where I am, how far I stray, I always find myself back in the blue, ready to defend what's mine.

Today, though, my hurricane is spitting mad. I take a moment to soak in all that fire. I love seeing her like this—nostrils flaring, a hint of fury in her cheeks, every sharp move-ment crackling with frustration. It's a far cry from the moments when the fight drains out of her, and she looks like she's sinking beneath the weight of whatever she's carrying. Like when I spotted her sitting on that bench at the roster party, lost in her head and staring at nothing.

I couldn't stand to see her suffering like that, all alone.

I shift in the doorway. The movement catches her attention, and she whirls toward me. Those hazel eyes of hers flare, the flecks of gold sparking like the embers of a fire.

"Looking fierce this morning, Hurricane."

Ignoring my greeting, she marches toward me. Hands out, she smacks her palms against my chest. "What the hell is wrong with you?!" she growls, and *damn*, it's sexy as hell. That spark. The twin flames in her eyes. The burn of her hands as they sear into my chest. My entire life has been ice—cold, clinical, and calculated. Hockey, routine, order. The same drills, the same structure, the same predictable patterns. But Dylan is the ember buried in the frost. She is heat and passion and chaos, turning everything I know to ash. I spent years thinking I had everything I needed, but now I know better. Now I know what it means to *crave*.

I wonder how she'd react if I kissed her right now?

Before I can find out, she hits me again with those dainty little hands of hers. How can a hockey player have such nice hands? Mine are rough and calloused from hours spent gripping my stick and catching pucks going 90 mph.

"You went too far, Griffin!" With one final smack of her hands against my chest, she stomps away, huffing and spitting fire before whirling on me again. "What you did to Kyle, it was too far."

I tilt my head, watching her like a predator sizing up its prey. "Too far?" I repeat, letting the words roll off my tongue, testing them. "I warned him, Dylan. Told him exactly what would happen if he kept fucking with you. He made his choice."

Her jaw clenches, and I see the moment she realizes arguing with me won't be easy, but my hurricane never backs down from a fight. "You humiliated him," she bites out, her hands curling into fists. "Publicly. You made him a joke."

"So?" I say, unbothered. Honestly, he's lucky I didn't do fucking worse. If he continues to fucking mess with her, what I did in the cafeteria will look like child's play in comparison to what happens next. It's only going to get worse for Kyle until he stops. Even then, I might completely destroy him just for daring to ruin what's mine. "He's been gunning for you since the minute you showed up here. Don't think I don't know that he's got those dumb-ass freshmen going after you too. One of them nearly snapped your fucking arm!"

Her breath hitches, eyes widening in surprise. *Yeah, sweetheart, I saw that. I see everything.* She shakes her head, refusing to let me sway her. "That's not the point."

"It's *exactly* the point," I snap, taking a large step closer. "You can ignore him all you want, but he's not going to stop coming after you, Dylan. Not until you're incapacitated. Until he's wiped you from the board—for good." Another step forward has me close enough to catch a whiff of her shampoo—peach and bergamot. It's perfectly Dylan—sweet and fresh with a zesty tinge. But sometimes that sharp edge of hers just needs an extra *bite*. "People like Kyle only understand one thing—power. And right now, he knows you have none."

She glares up at me, furious, but I see something else beneath it. Something raw. Fear? Pain? I can't tell, but I hate it.

"I know exactly what people like Kyle understand," she seethes, damn near bristling as her eyes burn into mine. Still, her fury only coaxes me closer, her throat bobbing at my proximity. "And I don't need you, or anyone else, fighting my battles." There's not the same grit behind her words this time, not the same conviction.

It tugs at me, the hint of weariness in her tone. How many

other fuckers like Kyle has she had to go up against? To fight on her own.

I laugh. Actually laugh. Low and dark and mocking. "Yeah, you do, Hurricane. You just don't want to admit it."

Her breath shudders, and I take a final step forward, crowding her and forcing her to crane her neck to meet my stare. "I protect what's mine," I tell her, my voice dropping to something rough and unyielding. "And you? You are mine."

Her lips part, a shaky breath escaping, but she doesn't pull away.

I reach out, skimming my fingers along her jaw, my touch light but possessive. "You stormed into my life, wrecking every ounce of control I had, and you think I'm just going to stand by while someone else tries to tear you down?" My voice drops lower. "Not a chance in hell, sweetheart."

I trail my fingers down the side of her throat, feeling the unsteady thud of her pulse beneath my fingertips. She should push me away. Tell me to fuck off. But she doesn't. Instead, she sways closer, just enough for me to feel the warmth of her breath against my lips.

It's all the permission I need.

I crush my mouth to hers, swallowing her startled gasp. There's nothing soft about my claiming. Nothing tentative about the way I drive my tongue into her mouth. I kiss her like I own her—and I'm just reminding her who she belongs to.

At first, she's rigid beneath me, but then her hand comes up to fist the front of my hoodie. A broken little sound escapes her throat, and *fuck*, it drives me insane. It's the sound of surrender, of frustration, of need, and it snaps whatever control I have left.

I dive deeper into her, wrapping an arm around her waist and walking her backward until we hit the nearest wall. She gasps, breaking our kiss. Breathing hard, I rest my forehead against hers. "You're mine, Dylan," I murmur, voice rough and possessive. "Mine to watch. Mine to protect. Just goddamn *mine*."

Lips swollen and breathing haggard, she shakes her head, defiant as ever, but I can feel the way her body betrays her—her sharp intake of breath, the shiver that runs through her when I press my thigh between hers. "I belong to no one," she argues, but the hitch in her breath betrays her.

I drag my mouth down the side of her neck, letting my teeth scrape her pulse point. "Fight me all you want, Hurricane, but I know the truth. I see it every time you look at me—the lust. The intrigue. You want this as badly as I do."

Licking into her mouth, I kiss her again, deeper this time. I don't ease in, don't take my time. I take what I want, tilting her head back and swallowing her moan like it belongs to me. Because it *does*.

I slide a hand up her side, feeling the dip of her waist, the way she fits against me like she was fucking made for this—for me.

"Admit it," I growl against her lips.

Her fingers tangle in my hair, nails scraping my scalp, and I groan, pressing harder against her. I can feel how wrecked she is, how torn between whatever war she's fighting in her own head and the way her body is begging for more.

"Fine." I chuckle darkly as my lips skim the angle of her jaw, my fingers sliding into her hair and tugging just hard enough to move her into the position I want. "I don't need your words when your body is screaming loud and clear just how badly it wants this."

She huffs out a shaky breath, her chest heaving as it brushes against mine. "You're impossible."

I smirk darkly down at her. "And you love it."

I bite her lip, then soothe it with my tongue, teasing her, testing her. Although she doesn't push me away, she glares up at me, her breathing uneven and her body tight, like she's holding herself back. Like she's still trying to fight me.

"You don't need someone to fight your battles," I murmur, dragging my knuckles down her side and relishing the way she shudders beneath my touch. "But that doesn't mean you don't *want* someone to fight for you."

Her brows pinch together.

"You like the thought of my hands around Kyle's fucking throat. That I'm making him suffer for every time he's gone after you. Every time he's tried to tear you down." I shift impossibly closer. Every ridge of my body pressed up against her soft edges as I let my lips brush the shell of her ear, my breath ghosting over her skin. "Pretend you hate it all you want, but you *like* knowing I'll hurt him for you."

Her hands fist in my hoodie, her breath coming in rapid pants.

"Tell me I'm wrong," I challenge, pressing my forehead to hers. My hands grab her hips possessively, yanking her into me. I can feel the heat emanating from her core as I drag it along the thick outline of my hardness. "*Lie to me.*"

Those hazel eyes call to me, liquid pools of green and gold boring into me as her nails dig into my shoulders. To hold me back; to hold herself back—does she even know which?

A fierce battle rages in her eyes.

One second.

Two.

Until she lifts onto her toes and kisses me back with enough force to knock the breath from my lungs.

She kisses me like it's the only truth she has left, and I take it for what it is. Surrender.

TWENTY-THREE

I HAVE COMPLETELY LOST my mind. That, or I managed to knock myself out with a weight plate and this is all some concussion-induced dream. How else can I explain going from ready to kill Griffin one second to practically throwing myself at him? One minute, I'm burning with fury, ready to slap that cocky smirk off his face, and the next, my lips are on his with an urgency I don't recognize. I'm kissing him like I've been starved for it—wild, unrestrained, and without any goddamn sense.

The world spins before I'm pressed against the cold surface of the mirrored wall that runs the full length of the gym. My nipples peak as Griffin crowds me from behind. My gaze meets his heated one in the reflective surface, and what's staring back at me should scare me. The raw possession. The hunger.

It only makes me want him more.

My initial gasp turns into a moan as he rubs his hard length against my ass. His hands are everywhere—rough and possessive as they grip my waist, my hips, my neck, and I find I like the way he touches me.

No, I *love* it.

He's not treating me like I'm fragile or breakable, like I'll shatter under his touch. He knows I won't. He's seen how I can hold my own on the ice. Clearly, he's seen more than anyone else has—he's seen how Fletcher and Monroe come after me. Which means he's also seen me effectively get out of every hold, every cornering, and every hard slam against the boards. He trusts me to hold my own, and there's something about that trust that sends a wave of heat crashing through me.

Griffin's lips sear a path along the column of my neck, teeth scraping across the back of my shoulder. His hands are everywhere—shifting, pulling, pushing me deeper into him. Everything about Griffin is rough and demanding, and I'm suffocating in the heat of it. His breath is hot on my skin as he growls dirty things in my ear, things that should disgust me, but all they do is light the fire inside me, pushing me closer to the edge.

The battle that has been raging inside me is slowly being smothered, the flames extinguished with every squeeze of Griffin's hands, every brush of his lips against my skin. I know I shouldn't be letting myself get lost in him—in any of them—but I'm so fucking tired of fighting.

This need, this craving has been building inside me for weeks now, stoked by every incinerating interaction with Jax, each time I catch Griffin staring at me, even the back-and-forth banter with Ethan and Finn's short but searing kisses. It's reaching a breaking point, and I'm in need of a release. Desperately.

No more words are shared between us, but wetness gushes between my thighs as I recall the way he growled with all the arrogance of a hockey player, "You *like* knowing I'll hurt him for you."

God damn him, he's right. It scares the hell out of me—that part of him, the way he revels in the darkness, but it also coaxes me in, draws me closer. No one has ever done what he has for me. No one has ever made me feel like I'm worth that kind of dark, twisted loyalty. He's everything I shouldn't want, yet exactly what I secretly crave.

I moan, loud and wanton, as he pushes beneath the waistband of my Lycra shorts. Thank God we are always the only ones in here at this time, and I don't need to worry about someone walking in and interrupting this. I don't think I could stop it now, even if I wanted to.

Which I don't. I really, *really* don't.

I'm *desperate* for Griffin's fingers to dip lower, to slide between my soaked folds and apply pressure where I need him most.

"Fuck, Dylan." His voice is rough, a low growl in the back of his throat as he teases along the lining of my panties. "You've been walking around in these tight little shorts for weeks, teasing me, driving me out of my fucking mind. Every time you move, every time I catch a glimpse of those legs... *Christ*." He flattens his palm over my pussy, yanking me against him as he grinds into me. His lips are hot against my ear as he confesses, "Every moment I spend in here with you has been torture." He nips at my earlobe, eliciting a gasp from me, even as heat pools in my core. "Perhaps it's time I return the favor."

His fingers curl, and I practically jump in his hold as he presses against my swollen nub. I can't help the involuntary shift of my hips as I grind along his length, my eyes hooded as I watch his arm muscles flex in the mirror. *Holy— Why is that so sexy?* His chuckle in my ear is dark and melodic as he licks a possessive path up the side of my throat. "That's it, Hurricane. Show me how much you need this."

"Please." The word falls unbidden from my lips as I arch against him, lifting my hips in a desperate plea for him to go deeper.

"Please, what?" His tone is mocking, cruel almost, but the

underscore of heat beneath it gives away how close he is to breaking too.

"Touch me. Fill me. Make me come."

"*Christ*." The curse is ripped from his mouth, all semblance of control falling by the wayside as he kicks my feet apart and shoves my panties to the side. "Hands on the mirror," he barks, already spreading my pussy lips with his fingers.

Palms pressed flat against the reflective surface and his warmth at my back, I tremble as he sinks a finger inside me. "Fuck," he hisses. "You're so warm and tight." His voice is pitched low, like he's talking to himself as he steadily moves in and out of me. My shorts are so restrictive that it doesn't allow for much movement, keeping his palm pressed firmly against my clit as he sinks back into my wet heat.

He meets my gaze in the mirror, a fresh wave of desire crashing through me at the *want* I see there. The *need*. "You look so fucking hot, squeezing my fingers, Hurricane."

I can only moan in response, my head dropping forward as he continues to fill me.

"More," I plead.

He chuckles against my skin. "Greedy little thing."

Thankfully, he obeys, adding a second finger and curling them inside me as I grind down. The movement has my ass rubbing against his cock as my clit drags along his palm. Fireworks go off behind my eyelids, my breathing growing erratic as he pushes me higher.

"Faster," I pant, feeling myself growing close.

A hand comes up to squeeze my breast, plucking hard at my nipple until I gasp. "I don't think so, Little Steelhawk. I'm the one in charge here. We're going at my pace, and you'll come when I say you can come."

Fuck, that should not be so hot, but it is.

I've never had a sexual experience like this. Typically, it's fumbling under sheets or in the dark, or a quick climb on, do the deed, and get off.

Nothing this heightened.

Nothing this consuming.

It's too much and not enough all at once. I feel like I'm soaring and falling apart all at the same time.

A tug on my ponytail has my head being forced up until my gaze meets his once more. "I want all of you, Dylan." Griffin's words are a possessive demand whispered in my ear. A dirty promise. "Every fucking inch. Every whimper. Every moan. Every tear. I want the fire in your eyes and the loneliness you run from." My breathing hitches. *How did he know?* "I *will* have it all." His lips wrap around my earlobe, sucking on it before he releases it with a pop. "I know you're not there yet. You don't yet realize that you're mine, but you will. I'll make sure of it." As if to prove his point, he licks along my jaw, his hand sliding up the center of my chest and along my throat until he twists my face to his. The intensity blazing in those blue eyes of his leaves me breathless. "Until then, I'll settle for swallowing your cries while you come on my fingers."

His lips crash down on mine, his tongue invading my mouth. His hips rock against mine, encouraging me to grind down on his hand, and he picks up the pace, fucking me roughly with his fingers until I can't fight off the impending release. "Now," he growls against my lips before capturing them with his own, and primed to release, I come.

One arm bands around my waist as my legs tremble, my fingernails clawing into the mirror's hard surface as I convulse around him, and he swallows every single one of my cries. Every heady moan. Every pleasurable whimper.

He kisses me the entire way through my orgasm, teasing out aftershocks with his talented fingers until I'm on the verge of collapse. Easing his hand from my shorts, his touch is surprisingly gentle as he turns me, so my back is to the mirror, his strength holding me up.

"Even better than I expected," he murmurs. His eyes are closed, savoring the moment. It gives me a rare opportunity to drink him in. Gone is his hard mask, the lines on his face smoothed out. Without conscious thought, my hand rises, my fingers tracing the side of his face. He sighs, leaning into my touch like he's spent his whole life bracing for a hit, and I'm the first thing he's ever let himself fall into.

When he finally peels his eyes open, there's a clarity there I haven't seen before. Neither of us says a word, our breaths mingling in the scant space between our lips. It feels like the entire world has shifted beneath my feet. Like, when I step outside, the sky will no longer be blue. Everything is different, and I don't know if I want to fight it or fall into it.

My skates carve through the ice, but I don't feel the usual release I get from practice. My body moves on autopilot, my focus elsewhere. On *him.*

Griffin's on the other end of the rink, working through his own drills, but I feel his presence like a weight pressing into my skin. He hasn't looked my way once—at least, not that I've caught—but I know he's watching. I can *feel* it. That unrelenting intensity. It's like a wire pulled taut between us, humming with something I don't know how to name. Or perhaps I'm just afraid to look too closely. Especially after what happened between us in the gym this morning.

I haven't been able to shake the feel of his hands on my body all day. Just thinking about him has my gaze sliding his way for the hundredth time since he stepped onto the ice an hour ago.

However, unlike every other time I've inadvertently found

myself staring in his direction, this time, he's staring right back. Our gazes collide, and he doesn't look away, doesn't flinch, just stands there, stick resting against his leg, mask pushed up, eyes burning into mine. My stomach tightens, and I force my focus back to my drills. This is stupid. I should be thinking about my shot, my speed—anything but the way my body reacts when he's near. It's like, by letting my guard down this morning and giving in to the pull I feel toward him, I've heightened everything. I sense him all the time. Where I felt his eyes on me like a gentle caress before, now they burn into me, hungry and possessive and impossible to ignore.

It's not long later when I give up on attempting to focus on my drills and step off the ice. Despite my half-assed attempt tonight, my limbs are exhausted, but my mind won't quit. I unlace my skates, feeling his gaze but not looking back as I hook my duffel over my shoulder and head for the exit. It's only when I'm out the door that I breathe a breath of relief.

Outside, the air is crisp, the night quiet except for the distant hum of traffic from town. Most of campus has cleared out, leaving the parking lot nearly empty except for a few scattered cars, some shrouded in darkness while others are illuminated brightly from overhead streetlights. A chill wraps around me, a sure sign that we're officially in autumn, as I bury my hands in the pockets of my hoodie and set off across the parking lot toward the gate. I probably should have driven this morning, but I wanted to enjoy the last of the good weather. Soon the snow will come in, and I'll relish the heat blasting from inside my car as I drive to campus.

Perhaps it's because I'm too lost in my head, still obsessing over my loss of sanity this morning and Griffin's intoxicating touch, but I don't initially notice the shadows starting to shift and form in the dim light, growing taller until three guys step out from behind a parked car, their feet scuffing against the asphalt.

My heart slams against my ribs as I take in the three hooded, silent figures, my pace slowing to a crawl. Keep moving. Act normal. My fingers tighten on the strap of my bag, and I keep my head down, but my focus stays on them as I attempt to hurry past.

They start to spread out, and my body locks up. I'm unable to keep all three of them in my sights. Giving up any pretense of not noticing them, my head snaps up. "What do y—" The words tumble into a strangled scream as they launch at me.

I spin, trying to use my bag as a buffer and a weapon, but three on one is not a fair fight. The bag is wrenched from my shoulder. Pain explodes through my side as something hard slams into my ribs. I stagger, the air punched from my lungs. Before I can regain my equilibrium, another blow lands. Then another.

A kick to my thigh. A punch to my stomach. I collapse to my knees, gasping for breath. Pain radiates outward through my entire body. I wrap my arms around my head, curling in on myself as I try to protect what I can.

I don't understand what's happening. *Why*. All I can do is get through. Breathe and survive. A boot connects with my ribs. I bite back a cry as I curl up in a ball on my side, as tight as I can get. I squeeze my eyes shut, willing it to be over. For the pain to end.

Another kick lands on my back, this one ripping a scream from my throat. In a final attempt to flee, I try to crawl across the parking lot on my hands and knees. I barely make it a foot before another shove sends me whirling onto my back. My head cracks against the asphalt. Pain bursts behind my eyes, before the world around me grows dark, and unconsciousness swallows me whole.

TWENTY-FOUR

I TUG my hoodie over my head as I step out of the lecture hall, shooting a grin at a couple of classmates lingering by the door. "Later, guys."

A few call back goodbyes, but I don't slow, adjusting the strap of my bag as I head for the parking lot. This is one of my later classes, and with early morning practices six days a week, while everyone else is making plans to go out for drinks afterward, I'm always heading straight home.

The night air is cool against my skin, waking me up a little as I head for the parking lot. I'm already thinking about whatever leftovers Ethan has left in the fridge that I can scarf down before grabbing a shower and jumping into bed when movement catches my eye.

I lift my head toward the parking lot, noticing the outline of three guys against the overhead streetlights. Hoods are pulled low over their faces as they kick at something on the ground.

No, not something. *Someone.*

My stomach tightens. "Hey!" I call, my voice sharp as I pick up my pace.

The guys freeze, turning my way, but I still can't make out

their faces. I'm too focused on the unmoving figure on the ground. Was this a mugging? I'm outright running now. Nudging each other, the three men take off, disappearing between the parked cars. I don't bother to chase them. My heartbeat pounds in my ears as I sprint the last few steps toward the crumpled figure on the ground.

It's only once I'm standing over the still form that I register who it is.

"Dylan—" Her name rips from my throat as I drop to my knees. *Fuck.*

Her face is half shadowed, blood drying at her temple, her arms curled around her ribs. My hands hover over her body, wanting to help but unsure where to touch her. Terrified I'll only hurt her further. Before I can figure out my next move, she shifts slightly, a groan slipping past her lips.

"You're okay." It's a poor attempt to reassure her since my voice is frantic even to my own ears. What do I do? Call an ambulance? I lift my head, scanning the vicinity for...something. Where the fuck is everyone?

"Finn." The thick rasp of her voice has me snapping my focus back to her.

"Dylan. Shit. I've got you, okay? I've got you." My hand clutches hers as relief surges through me, but it's short-lived when she doesn't respond, simply groaning as her eyelids flutter.

"Jesus, okay, okay." I suck in a deep breath, forcing myself to calm down, to think. "I'm calling for help," I tell her as I dig my phone out of my pocket. "Just hold on—"

Heavy footsteps pound against the pavement. I drop the phone, jumping to my feet and preparing to fight—to protect her —if those assholes have returned.

"Get the hell away from her!" I'm shoved aside, nearly losing my footing as Griffin falls to his knees beside her. By the time I recover, he's crouched over her still form, his body practically curled around her as he brushes strands of hair off her face.

Her eyelids flutter but don't open.

"Who did this?" Griffin's voice is lethal, his eyes burning as he lifts his head to glare at me.

I scrub a hand over my face, my pulse still racing. "I dunno, man. I was heading to my car when I saw these guys jumping someone. I didn't realize it was Dyl until I got here." I notice him scan our surroundings. "They ran off when they saw me coming."

His jaw clenches at my words, fingers flexing around Dylan's wrist like he can anchor her to him. Forcing an exhale through his nose, he then leans forward so he can press his forehead against hers, his shoulders rising and falling like he's barely holding himself together.

Fuck, *I'm* barely holding myself together.

"We need to get her to a hospital," I say, already reaching for my phone again.

"No," Dylan croaks, her voice hoarse but firm. Those eyelids flutter again, and I hold my breath, hoping to catch a glimpse of those entrancing eyes of hers, before she gives up and keeps them closed. "No hospital."

"Dylan," I argue. Griffin growls low in his throat, clearly in agreement with me that she needs to get checked out by a medical professional. What if she's hurt? She could have broken a bone or sprained something. What if she hit her head? God only knows what those assholes did to her before I showed up.

"No." This time she does manage to wrench her eyes open, but her stare isn't the typical sparking one I'm used to seeing directed my way. Her eyes are dull and unfocused. I fucking hate it. "No hospitals." The crazy woman tries to push herself upright, even though it's clear the simple movement causes her pain.

"Stop that," Griffin snaps at her. "You've probably got broken ribs."

"Not broken," she croaks, pain lacing every word as she sags back against the ground. "Just bruised, I think."

"Oh well, that's okay then," I snark, running a stressed-out hand through my hair as I pace back and forth.

Dylan has the wherewithal to roll her eyes at me. "Like you don't play with bruised ribs all the time," she gripes. She tries again to push herself upright.

"Fucking hell, Hurricane." Realizing he's not going to keep her down, Griffin helps lift Dylan to her feet, keeping one arm securely wrapped around her waist. Her face is scrunched in pain, her breathing labored.

"Are we walking or not?" Despite her snark, her face is as white as a ghost, her voice barely audible even though I'm standing right in front of her.

"Fuck no." I point toward my car. "Get in." Fetching my keys out of my pocket, I bend down to grab the duffel bag she must have been carrying when she was attacked. Jogging ahead, I open the door while Griffin helps Dylan into the back seat, before getting in with her. *I guess he's coming with us.*

Hastily throwing her bag in the trunk, I move around to the driver's side and climb in behind the wheel, adjusting the rearview mirror so I can keep an eye on her. Reversing out of the space, my attention drops to where her head has fallen back against the headrest, her eyes closed once more. I swallow roughly, hating her pale coloring and the blood staining her skin, before wrenching my gaze away and focusing on the road in front of me as I throw the car into drive.

I keep my speed slow, careful not to jostle her more than necessary, glancing back at her every few seconds as I follow the road back to the house. Each time I do, something in my chest winds tighter, until it feels like I'm going to explode.

Griffin murmurs to her, his words too low for me to hear, but I frown anyway. Since when did they become all buddy-buddy? Griffin's a lone wolf. He talks the talk, getting on with everyone on the team, but doesn't go out of his way to make friends. Frankly, beyond hockey, I don't know a damn thing about him, and I've been playing alongside him since freshman year.

My hands tighten around the steering wheel, damn near choking it to death with each little bit of insight I pick up on every time I look at them. How close his face is to hers. His dark expression. The possessiveness in the way he touches her.

A far uglier emotion bubbles to the surface. One that I can't initially place because I've never felt it before, but it boils in my gut, building in my veins. I want to hit the brakes, climb back there, and drag Griffin away from her.

I want to be the one touching her like that.

The one reassuring her. Making her feel better.

I want her full attention.

And that's not okay.

I've been fighting the same desire since the minute she showed up on my front porch, all wide eyes and long legs, and hair I could picture myself pulling on while I sucked on her skin.

Fuck, man, get it under control!

I sigh in relief when I pull into the driveway, practically diving out of the car in my haste to escape my complicated feelings and convoluted thoughts.

Wrenching the back door open, I carefully help Dylan out of the car. *Don't think about how good she feels pressed against you*, I chastise myself when a flare of awareness immediately heats my skin at her proximity. *She's hurting, you twisted fuck!*

Battling my body's reaction to her, I help shuffle her toward the house, Griffin on her other side. The second we step inside, voices explode around us. Both Ethan and Jax jump to their feet, video game controllers dropped on the coffee table as they approach.

"What the fuck happened?" Ethan storms forward, his eyes wild.

Jax is right on his tail, his eyes wide as they rake over Dylan's slumped form. "Menace," he murmurs, before shifting aside. "Get her on the couch. I'll grab the first aid kit."

He hurries off to the kitchen, and Griffin and I gently lower Dylan onto the sofa. She groans, wincing as she shifts to get herself comfortable—or as comfortable as one can be when their entire body is a giant bruise.

Griffin claims the spot beside her, not leaving an inch of space between them. There's no way I can sit still right now, so I end up pacing back and forth in front of the coffee table.

Jax returns a moment later, kneeling on the floor in front of her as he opens the first aid kit on the table. His lips are moving, but I can't hear what he's saying to her, and that's when I realize there's a whooshing in my ears. My heart races as adrenaline thunders through my body.

I swipe my hand through my hair, pulling on the ends. I feel like I can't breathe as I pace back and forth, unable to take my eyes off her for more than a second.

Ethan steps in front of me, his hands on my shoulders, stopping my pacing. It takes me a second to realize he's talking to me. Shaking my head, I force myself to take a deep breath before blowing it out. "Sorry, what did you say?"

"I want to know who did this to her," he growls, irritation evident in his voice. My gaze flicks back over to Dylan. Jax is inspecting the wound at her temple, dabbing at it with a cotton pad and antiseptic cream.

"Oh." I quickly recite the whole ordeal for him. The entire time, I'm unable to take my eyes off her. "Shouldn't we call someone?" I say, loud enough to draw Jax's attention. "A doctor or—"

"I'm fine," Dylan grouses, mustering the strength to glare at me as Jax inspects her ribs. For some reason, that settles me more than anything else. I mean, if she's capable of leveling me with that look, then she can't be about to die, right?

"Do you know who did this to you?" Ethan demands, moving to sit on the coffee table in front of her. "Did you see their faces?"

She goes to shake her head, but stops quickly, face scrunching. "No," she rasps, sighing. "They had hoods pulled low over their faces, and they never spoke."

"They didn't ask for money?" I frown. "Did they want anything?"

"You mean other than to beat the shit out of me?" A weary sigh slides past her lips, and she seems to almost sink into the couch cushions. "No. I don't know. They didn't make any demands, and I don't think they took anything." Her eyes dart around the room. "My bag—"

"It's in my car," I assure her. "Didn't look like it had been tampered with."

A thick silence settles in the room. My stomach twists as realization dawns. This wasn't a mugging. It was something else, but what? Who would target Dylan? Why?

"We'll figure it out," Ethan assures her, giving Dylan's knee a soft squeeze.

"And when we do, I'll fucking end them," Griffin vows. The possessiveness in his voice sends a shiver down my spine, and I once again wonder what the hell is going on as my gaze darts between the two of them. I notice Ethan and Jax exchanging similar looks, my own thoughts reflected in their eyes.

"For now." Ethan puts emphasis behind his words, ever the leader. "Let's just focus on Dylan. Jax, how is she looking?"

"Ribs are bruised. Maybe her kidney, too. She's got a bump at the back of her head and a few scrapes."

"Nothing we haven't all dealt with at one time or another on the ice." Dylan tries to wave away the extent of her injuries.

"Not typically all at one time, Little Menace," Jax says, his voice pitched low and smooth. "It's going to take a bit for these to heal."

The weight of that settles over us. Dylan physically deflates. For the first time since I found her lying in that parking lot, defeat drags her down. "I'm going to miss the first game of the season, aren't I?"

"There will be other games, Thorn."

Her throat bobs as she stares intently at the floor, unable to meet any of our gazes.

"Can I go to bed now?" Her voice is small, smaller than I've heard it all night, and the fact she's asking for fucking permission says everything about how affected she is. How vulnerable she's feeling. I fucking hate it. I hate all of it—this whole shitstorm of a night. I want to go back out there and track down those thugs who thought they could beat on someone smaller than them, but I don't have the first clue where to start.

Ethan's lips flatten, but his voice is soft when he responds, "Of course you can, Thorn, but don't lock your door, okay? I want to be able to get to you if your injuries worsen overnight."

Dylan hesitates before giving the briefest of nods.

Griffin and Jax are there immediately as soon as she starts to push to her feet, helping her up. "I'll stay with you," Griffin says.

"No," Ethan cuts in. "You're going to stay right here. Jax will make sure she makes it to her room and gets settled."

Griffin bristles. He goes to protest when Dylan places a hand on his arm, squeezing lightly. It's enough to stop whatever he was going to say as he glances down at her. "I'm fine. I just want to sleep."

"Fine," he grits, clearly unhappy but relenting. "I'll be here when you wake up in the morning." Bending down, he tucks his finger beneath Dylan's chin, lifting it until she has no choice but to meet his gaze. He doesn't do anything, just stares into her eyes. It's a strangely intimate moment, and I feel like I should look away, give them some privacy, but I can't seem to. "Sweet dreams, Little Steelhawk," he murmurs before pressing the briefest of kisses to her temple and watching closely as Jax leads her away.

"Are you two dating?" I spit out the question only when I hear Dylan's door close upstairs.

Standing taller, Griffin slowly turns to stare at me. Any sort of human emotion he was wearing for Dylan's sake has been shed, and in its place stands a cold, hard predator. He stares me down with the hint of a smirk curling his lips but doesn't answer the goddamn question.

"Jealous?" he taunts.

I scoff, looking away as I frown.

"No need to answer. I already know you are. Otherwise, you wouldn't be stealing secret hidden kisses at the back of The Stanley."

I whirl back to him, mouth agape. "How do you— You know what, never mind. That's none of your fucking business."

"That's enough!" Ethan interjects, moving to stand between us. "We have more important things to discuss." He levels each of us with a stern look. "Like who the fuck did this to Dylan and how we're going to find them."

TWENTY-FIVE

"SERIOUSLY?" Griffin barks a laugh that instantly grates on my nerves. It's humorless and razor-sharp. "You have *no idea who did this?*"

I frown, slowly rounding on him as I cross my arms over my chest, hiding the clenching of my fists. After tonight, I'm one argument away from losing my shit.

"Can't think of a single person who would want to do her harm? Who would *benefit* from her being unable to play?" Sneering, he shakes his head like I'm an idiot.

My gaze narrows on him, teeth grinding. I choose my next words very carefully. "What exactly are you insinuating, Griffin?"

His gaze turns sharp, calculating. "You mean other than the fact that you're a shitty captain?"

His words land like a punch—exactly like he intends. My whole body locks up, blood boiling. *"Excuse me?"*

"You heard me." Griffin's voice is low, brimming with uncontained fury now that Dylan isn't here to temper it. "How the fuck did you miss this? *Your* team. *Your* players. *You're* supposed to know what's going on."

I step forward. "Don't you dare—"

"Don't I dare what? Call you out on the fact that you've been ignoring Dylan's existence all season?" He scoffs, eyes burning into me. "First, it was because she might not make the team, so she wasn't a concern, but what's your excuse been for the past two weeks?" He tilts his head to the side, a malicious glint in his eye.

My teeth grind. No fucking way am I about to admit the truth to him. Hell, I can barely admit it to myself. Why I never spare Dylan more than a passing glance when we're on the ice. Why I make a point of not seeking her out unless I have to.

Because I'm terrified I won't be able to look away.

"I get it," he drawls. "You don't want to admit what she does to you. You think if you pretend she's not there, it'll make a difference. But while you've been busy playing fucking make-believe, Fletcher and Monroe have been targeting her. They've been going after her harder than they should, and they've been getting away with it. Because you're wearing fucking blinders!"

His words cut deep. Too deep.

I shake my head. "That's bullshit." Sure, they've gone after her a time or two, but that's just part of the game. We all get caught up in the need to win, even when it's against teammates. "There's no way. I'd have seen it."

"It's not." Jax steps forward, face set in a grim line. I hadn't realized he'd returned from sorting Dylan out. His voice isn't angry, just tired. "I've seen it too. Stepped in when I could."

I drag a hand down my face, trying to process this. To stomach my failure, all because I was intent on being the best captain possible and saw Dylan as a distraction.

"You're saying Fletcher and Monroe are the ones who attacked her tonight?" I ask, needing to focus on that instead of the twisted, sick feeling of failure threatening to eat me alive.

"They're the weapons. The puppets. Someone else is pulling their strings."

My focus narrows, putting the pieces together.

"Kyle." My gaze snaps to Griffin's. "You think Kyle is the one behind it all."

"Damn right I do."

Finn scoffs from where he's collapsed onto the sofa. "Come on. Kyle wouldn't do that."

Griffin turns on him. "Wouldn't he?"

"Kyle's got his issues," I admit, willing to believe he'd get some third-liners to do his dirty work on the ice. Especially after I told him he'd be out of here if he didn't stop going after Dylan. "But to accuse him of attacking Dylan?" I shake my head, refusing to believe it. To believe the guy I've known since we were freshmen, lived with for over three years, would go to such violent extremes.

Griffin simply arches an eyebrow. "Then where is he?"

We all fall silent.

Finn glances around the room as if expecting him to come down the stairs at any moment. I lick my dry lips. "He went out a while ago. Didn't say where he was going."

I notice Finn on his phone, and we all watch as he dials Kyle's number, putting it on speakerphone. Seconds pass. The only sound is the ringing of Kyle's phone. With every unanswered ring, my chest squeezes tighter, and Finn's expression grows shadowed. "He's not answering," he eventually admits, hanging up.

Griffin just looks at me. "Huh, I wonder why? Perhaps because he's out gloating with his new buddies."

I shake my head. "That doesn't prove anything."

His eyes are dark with certainty as he states, "I'll give you my left nut if Kyle, Fletcher, and Monroe weren't behind tonight."

No one says a word.

"No," Finn interjects, shaking his head. "No fucking way. I've known Kyle since we were kids. He wouldn't—" He can't even finish his sentence, before he abruptly gets up, redialing Kyle's number as he storms up the stairs.

Jax exhales, rubbing a hand over his jaw. "Shit."

I just stand there, mind racing. Do I believe Griffin? The problem is, I don't *not* believe him. I've seen the hatred in Kyle's eyes when he looks at Dylan. Some part of me, however small, believes Griffin might be right.

As though he wasn't ready to rip my head off mere seconds ago, Griffin drops back onto the couch. "I'm staying," he declares.

"What?" I snap my gaze to him. I don't mind Griffin but after tonight, I need space to fucking think.

"I don't trust her with any of you," he says flatly. For a moment, I regret not letting him answer Finn's question earlier. I'm curious to know, too, exactly what's going on between him and Dylan. "I can sleep here or climb in her window after you've all gone to bed. Up to you."

"Jesus fucking Christ." I pinch the bridge of my nose, listening as Jax stalks off to find some spare blankets for him. "Stay out of her bedroom," I practically growl at him, hating the way his eyebrows hitch and a smug smirk tugs at his lips. "She needs her rest."

"Uh-huh. Whatever you say, Captain."

Before I lose my cool and do something uncharacteristic, like punch Griffin in his smug fucking face, I stomp toward the back door, in need of fresh air.

The cool night is a balm to my overheated skin, and I breathe deep, trying to clear my head. It doesn't work.

At some point, I end up on the steps, elbows on my knees, head in my hands.

I don't know how long I sit like that, tonight's revelations spinning around in my head—twisting together with the fear that hit me like a freight train when Finn and Griffin carried Dylan into the house. When I saw her beaten and bruised. Knowing I hadn't been there. That I didn't protect her.

As team captain, she's my responsibility.

But she's also just...*my responsibility*.

Not because I'm the captain. Not because I'm her roommate.

But because I want her to be.

Because Griffin is fucking right—as usual—and I do feel something more for her. Something I've tried to deny...

And look at what happened!

Frustrated and no more level-headed, I head back inside. The lights are off in the kitchen and living room, and I can just about make out Griffin's form on the sofa before I head for the stairs. I take them two at a time. When I reach Dylan's door, I see it's ajar and ease it open, slipping into her room.

Jax is already inside, sitting in a chair pulled up beside her bed. His elbows rest on his knees, his gaze fixed on her sleeping form. His face is unguarded in a way I don't think I've ever seen before, showing a depth of emotion that takes me by surprise. I suspected he had feelings for her, but now I know.

"You care about her." My voice is pitched low, careful not to wake her.

Jax swallows, ducking his head. "Yeah."

It takes me a second to form the words. To find the courage, but what good has denying anything done? It's only resulted in Dylan getting hurt. "Me too."

I lean against the doorframe, staring at Dylan. She looks small like this, curled up under the blankets, her face soft in sleep. But even unconscious, she shifts slightly, like she's bracing for another hit.

The longer I stare at her, I can admit, she's upended my life in ways I never anticipated. I thought she'd cause discord among the team, upheave our chances of making it to the championships.

What I never expected was to find myself captivated by her. To admire her strength. Respect her tenacity. She's a force to be reckoned with, and I can't seem to look away. I've had to force myself to keep my distance. To walk away from her. To keep things casual. To stop myself from reaching out to touch her.

All that did was result in her getting hurt.

Guilt destroys me from the inside out.

Eventually, Jax sighs, stretching as he stands. "I'm gonna grab some sleep." He moves toward the door but pauses when he sees I haven't moved. "You coming?"

I shake my head, stepping farther into the room. "No. I'm gonna stay. Keep an eye on her. Just in case." I sink into the chair he just vacated, gaze intent on the rhythmic rise and fall of Dylan's chest.

I feel Jax's eyes on me for a second before his presence disappears from the room, leaving me alone with Dylan.

Slipping my hand into hers on top of the sheet, I make a silent promise not to let her down again. Not as a captain. Not as a roommate. Not as a friend.

I can't promise anything more. I won't. Not when my head is a mess and it's obvious Jax has feelings for her. Plus, whatever the hell is going on between her and Griffin. And if what Griffin said is true, Finn has something for her too.

I wipe a hand down my face. What a clusterfuck.

Keeping my hand in hers, I sink back into my chair and watch over her. Because, for tonight at least, that's the only thing that makes sense.

❄

CRUST LINES my lids as I groggily peel them open. I'm momentarily blinded by the first rays of morning light creeping through the window. My neck is stiff from a night spent sitting upright, and I roll it, feeling the muscles pop and grind as I work out the kinks.

Blinking the sleep from my eyes, I shift slightly, feeling the weight of exhaustion settle deep in my bones. Then my gaze lands on her.

Dylan is still sound asleep, her face turned toward me, the soft glow of dawn casting shadows over the bruises marring her skin. The darkening mark along her jaw. The scrape on her temple. The faint imprint of a boot print along her arm.

I'm not sure whether it's the light of day or the passage of time, but her injuries look even worse this morning.

A fresh wave of fury rolls through me, raw and unrelenting.

How could anyone do this to her? My teeth grind, and I have to focus on my breathing, so I don't march out of here to track down the sick fucks who did this.

If Griffin is right, that sick fuck is Kyle. Well, one of them.

I want to believe he wouldn't go this far, but the truth is, I don't know. Clearly, I don't know anything anymore.

And for that, I can only blame myself.

Guilt gnaws at me.

Dylan stirs, her breathing hitching. My eyes snap to her face as her eyelids flutter. Then, slowly, those hazel eyes of hers blink open. They're lighter in the morning sun, flecks of green and gold swirling in the amber.

I exhale, some of the tension in my chest easing. "Hey."

She swallows, shifting slightly, wincing. "Hey." Her voice is rough, barely above a whisper.

"How are you feeling?"

She blinks sluggishly, like she's taking inventory. "Like I got jumped by three guys last night."

The corner of my mouth twitches despite myself. "Yeah. That'll do it."

She exhales slowly, wincing again as she tries to push herself up. I move on instinct, reaching out to help, but she stiffens. I freeze, withdrawing my hands.

"Sorry," I murmur.

She shakes her head, avoiding my gaze. "It's fine."

A thick silence settles between us. I rub a hand over my jaw as I watch her from beneath my lashes, before finally speaking. "Griffin and Jax admitted that Kyle, Fletcher, and Monroe have been going after you during practice." Lifting my head, I meet her gaze, my chest tightening. "Why didn't you say anything?"

Dylan looks away, staring at a spot on the blanket. Her fingers twist the fabric, and I can practically see a dozen different responses forming and disintegrating on her tongue before she finally says in a tired voice, "NSU never wanted me on their team. It didn't matter how hard I worked. Whether I proved myself. I came with built-in tits and a vagina so I was automatically excommunicated, regardless of my abilities on the ice." She pauses, swallowing roughly, still not looking up from that spot on the blanket as she twists the fabric tighter between her fingers. "Maybe it would have been different if Lucas wasn't their captain." My nostrils flare. I get the sick sense I know where this is going.

"He encouraged their tormenting," I fill in when it seems as though Dylan can't quite get the words out.

She nods, and it seems as though it takes every ounce of strength she has left to lift her head to meet my gaze. "He didn't just encourage it. He instigated it. He propagated the bullying." Her lips twist. So much heartache and wistfulness shines from those hazel depths. "I've never been able to trust my captain before." Her words land like a gut punch. "I've only ever had myself to rely on. And I know you're not Lucas, but—"

"You're not used to asking for help."

She nods.

It shouldn't cut as deep as it does, but her words slay me. It's not just hearing that she doesn't trust me. It's knowing what she's been through. What she had to put up with at the hands of that misogynistic piece of shit.

I might not have wanted Dylan on my team at the start of the year, but I would never *ever* have encouraged other team members to go after her. I would never have turned a blind eye—

Except that's what I did.

Not for the same fucked-up reasons as Lucas, but I still looked the other way. I might not have known what was going on, but what happened to Dylan—last night and in the weeks since Roster Day—are as much my fault as Reed's, Fletcher's, and Monroe's.

It's a fight to keep my expression blank, to not let her see how badly her words have affected me. How much I hate myself right now.

I inhale slowly before I speak. "I wish I could say I'm not him—"

"You're not," she cuts me off, her hand lifting from the blanket. It hovers over where mine rests on the edge of the bed before she tentatively lowers it. The heat of her skin engulfs me as she gives my hand a squeeze. "You're nothing like him. I —I know that, but that doesn't make it any easier for me to trust."

I shake my head. "I had no idea they were going after you so hard." Fury—at myself—vibrates through me. "I'd seen the occasional hard hit, intervened when I caught an illegal move, but I didn't know..." I blow out a frustrated breath before lifting my gaze. I'd been staring at the point where her skin rests against mine, lingering in the spark that innocent touch ignited, but now I rake my eyes over her face, memorizing every scrape and bruise so I never forget.

Never forget the part I played in this.

My role in her getting hurt.

"You should never have had to deal with someone like Lucas Tremble," I say fiercely. "You've no idea how sorry I am that I've let you down. That I failed you. That was never my intention." Cracks appear in my armor. I know she sees them because she squeezes my hand tighter. I push on. "But I swear to you, Dylan, I'll be better. I'll be the captain you need—that you deserve. I'll be someone you can trust."

Dylan doesn't respond right away. Her eyes bounce over my face, taking me in, in much the same way I just did to her. As she does, I can see the war being waged inside her.

She wants to believe me. Wants to trust in what I'm saying, but the instinct to protect herself, to rely on no one but herself, is stronger. It's written in the tightness of her jaw, the flicker of doubt in her hazel eyes.

And that's on me.

I've done nothing to deserve her trust, nothing to prove I'm any different from Lucas or her old teammates. But I will.

I vow to earn her trust. To be worthy of it.

As much as she lets me see her hesitance, her vulnerability, her *want* to believe in me, I show her how determined I am to prove myself to her.

I've been telling her since the second she showed up in our locker room that she had to prove herself to me and the team. Well, now it's my turn.

Turning my hand over, I slide my fingers between hers. This time, I squeeze *her* hand. A silent promise that she is no longer alone.

"Have they done anything else?" There's a rawness, a grittiness to my voice as I hold my breath, hoping the answer is no.

Her hand goes stiff against mine, and for a moment I think she's going to shrug me off, but then she sighs.

"Small things," she mutters. "Most of it is on the ice, but they pull other shit too. Stealing my tape at practice. More than once, a piece of my gear has gone missing, only to turn up in the laundry bin or some other hiding place."

"What about outside of practice?" I inquire, sensing there is more.

She huffs a breath. It's clear she doesn't want to be talking about this, sharing it with me, but I'm thankful that she's opening up to me—finally.

"They shoulder-check me when passing by between class-es." She shrugs, acting as though it's no big deal, but I can see how much all of it has been weighing on her. One little thing might not get to her, but when you add each little insult together, it stacks up to be overwhelming. "Or block my way past altogether if we're in a corridor or on the stairs."

I nod absently. Everything they are doing is petty, but annoying. Small enough that unless you were looking for it, you probably wouldn't notice.

"It's nothing like how it was at NSU." She gives another infuriating shrug, like it's nothing. I don't give a shit if it's not as bad as how it was at NSU, it's still happening under my nose, when it fucking shouldn't be.

Gritting my teeth, I force myself to calm down.

"Griffin knows, doesn't he?" I already know he does. It explains the unicorn tape that Kyle's normal one was switched out for. The glitter bomb in his locker. The other shit he's been grousing about. Not to mention his public shaming in the cafeteria.

Dylan hesitates before giving a jerky nod.

"Do you think they were the ones to attack you last night?" I ask carefully, watching her closely for any reaction.

Her face scrunches, something flashing across her face, there and gone before I can make heads or tails of it.

"I didn't see their faces," she admits. "And none of them spoke." A deliberate act, I imagine...because they knew Dylan would be able to identify them? Lifting her gaze to mine, Dylan swallows. I can see she doesn't want to admit it out loud, but her eyes say it all anyway. "I wasn't mugged. They didn't take anything. It was a senseless act of violence." Her free hand lifts to her chest as she presses her palm over her heart. "I can't prove it was them, but I know the truth in here. There's no one else it could have been."

Fuck.

I exhale heavily, sagging back against my chair. "This shit stops now. If anything else happens to you, no matter how small or insignificant, you tell me." I pierce her with a hard stare until she nods. "One of us will be with you at all times when you're on campus."

She scoffs at that. "I don't need babysitters."

I arch a brow, slowly lowering my gaze over her battered form. "Clearly, you do."

She glowers at me, and something settles, seeing that fire back in her eyes. "I would think the better solution would be to deal with Kyle and the others."

"Yes," I agree heavily. "But without any proof, there's not a whole hell of a lot I can do." I eye her curiously. "You could report it to the police."

Her head falls back against the headboard, as though it suddenly requires too much effort to keep it upright. "You said it yourself, there's no proof. What are they going to do?"

I swallow. "Either way, you need to let one of our trainers check you out.

She exhales, sinking deeper into the pillow. "I'm not playing in Friday's game, am I?"

I hesitate, hating the disappointment in her voice. "That's Coach's call, but I wouldn't think so. You're pretty beat up. It's going to take a week or two for all of that to heal."

She nods, quiet for a moment.

"First, you need to eat." I push to my feet, looking down at her.

Dylan blinks up at me, looking exhausted but amused. "You cooking for me, Captain?"

I smirk. "Only because I need my best left wing back on the ice."

TWENTY-SIX

THE TRAINER'S hands are careful but firm as he presses along my ribs, feeling for anything more serious than bruising. I wince when he prods at my side, a dull ache radiating through me.

"Careful," Ethan snaps from where he stands a few feet away, arms crossed, watching everything with a hard-set jaw. The trainer tenses, glancing from me to him and back to me.

"You good?"

I nod, before flashing Ethan a hard stare. He simply meets it with a glare of his own until I roll my eyes and focus back on the trainer. While he completes his assessment, my mind drifts back to this morning. The way Ethan looked at me in the soft light filtering through my bedroom window. The vow he made. *I'll be someone you can trust.*

I don't have many of those—people I can trust. And *God*, I want to believe him. I *want* to trust in Ethan. I could see how torn up he was that he didn't see what Kyle and the others were doing, even though that was the whole point. They deliberately kept their attacks subtle enough that no one else would notice.

Griffin was the only one who did, and I'm pretty sure that's only because the psycho watches my every move. He'd probably know if something was wrong with me before I did, *that's* how closely he pays attention.

But trust isn't something I give easily, and no matter how much I may want to trust in Ethan, I need him to show me he's not another Lucas.

I already know he doesn't have Lucas's hateful intent. That he doesn't view me the same way, but I need him to prove to me that he won't just turn a blind eye. That he won't let Kyle and the others get away with what they've been doing.

The door to the training room slams open, cutting through my thoughts.

"Jesus Christ, Carter."

Bear's voice is sharp, rough with something I don't want to name. His eyes rake over me, taking in the bruises along my arms, the cut on my temple, the way I'm sitting gingerly on the table. His fingers twitch at his sides like he's holding himself back from storming across the room. I don't think I've ever seen Bear so...livid.

Ethan straightens, stepping partially in front of me...as if to block Bear. "Coach—"

Bear's eyes snap to him, and just like that, his expression hardens, locking away every ounce of emotion that was just etched into the lines of his face. He doesn't acknowledge Ethan beyond a nod, turning instead to the trainer. "What's the damage?"

The trainer clears his throat. "Bruised ribs, possible bruised kidney. She needs to rest and avoid anything that puts strain on her core for at least a week. After that, light activity before easing back into full-contact practice. No games until she's completely cleared."

My shoulders slump. "How long is that likely to be?"

"Two, maybe three weeks."

"But—"

"You heard the man, Carter. You're benched until you've healed."

Coach's order lands with a crushing blow. Friday is the first game of the season. The first time I get to start on the first line in a season game...and I'm fucking benched. Which means fucking *Kyle* will be starting in my spot. My teeth grind, fury numbing the pain I feel with every inhale. Or perhaps that's the ibuprofen Ethan made me swallow before we left the house.

Coach exhales sharply, rubbing a hand down his face. "I want a moment alone with Dylan." He looks pointedly at Ethan and the trainer. With a nod, the trainer leaves, but Ethan hesitates, his weight shifting as he looks between me and Coach. "I should stay—"

"I'll be fine," I cut in before Bear can lose it, which he looks like he's two seconds away from doing. And judging by the look on his face, it wouldn't be just words he'd use on Ethan. I meet Ethan's gaze, offering him a reassuring smile. "I could actually really do with a coffee—one of the ones from the café, with lots of syrup and cinnamon sprinkled on top." I flutter my eyelashes, giving him my best *please* look.

He studies me, his jaw working, before he finally huffs an exhale. "Fine." He gives Coach a long look, although I have no idea what he thinks Bear is going to do to me. It's almost...amusing. "I'll be right back," he says before finally stepping out of the room.

The moment the door closes, Bear exhales, closing the distance between us. He goes to wrap me in an infamous Bear hug, but he pauses, hesitating out of fear of hurting me. I roll my eyes. "Come here. I'm not going to break."

Next thing, I'm wrapped up tight in his arms. It hurts. My ribs scream at me, but I don't care. Nothing beats a Bear hug. His chin rests on top of my head, and I can feel the rigidity in his shoulders. "Kid..." His voice is rough but not like before. This time, it's tainted with worry.

I bite the inside of my cheek, ignoring the burn of tears in my eyes. I've been doing a pretty stellar job of keeping it together, but in Bear's arms, all I want to do is fall apart. "It looks worse than it is." My own voice is husky, watery with the extent of the emotions I'm struggling to keep at bay.

He moves back just enough to meet my gaze, and the look in his eyes nearly undoes me. This isn't my coach standing in front of me. This is the man who has looked out for me since my dad died. Who gave me a place to land when I fucked up at NSU. Who has treated me like a daughter since the day and hour I was born.

"I hate that I had to find out from Ethan. You should have called me."

I swallow. "There wasn't time."

He pulls me in for another hug. "I can't believe you were attacked right outside. I'm going to speak to the dean about upping security. There's no excuse for what happened."

When he pulls back, his hands linger on my arms, his gaze scanning my face. "Are the guys taking care of you? Are you safe in that house? You could come stay with me."

I shake my head, ignoring the slight pounding in my temples. "That'd only make things worse. Ethan and the others have been taking care of me," I assure him. "I'm fine."

His lips press into a hard line, but he nods. "If anything changes..."

"I know."

His grip tightens for a second before he finally lets me go, stepping back. He exhales and scrubs a hand over his face, dragging his fingers through his hair. "And you didn't see who it was?"

I shake my head, hating that that's my response every time

someone asks that question. "There were three of them. Guys, based on their height and build, but that's all I got."

His jaw tics, before he exhales harshly, turning away, like he's struggling to get himself under control. "Have you talked to your mother?" he asks, turning back around to face me.

"No. I didn't want to worry her."

His eyes soften with sympathy. "She'd want to know—"

"She's got enough on her plate," I cut in, ending the discussion. Bear knows what things are like now, but he doesn't know the full extent. He doesn't know that most of the time, my mom doesn't even take my calls. And when she does, she's a blubbering mess down the phone or so spaced out on meds that she has no idea who she's talking to. "You're not to tell her, either," I warn him.

His lips purse, and I can tell he wants to argue, but thankfully he chooses to let it go. "I won't," he promises. "It's your call."

"She doesn't need to know."

He doesn't argue, but the look on his face says he disagrees. Whatever, I know I'm making the right call. After our stare-off has dragged out for a long, tedious moment, he huffs an exhale and marches over toward the door. Throwing it open, he gestures for the trainer to come back in.

Coach takes up Ethan's former stance beside me while the trainer runs through various exercises and we discuss a physio plan for the rest of the week. By the time Ethan returns with my coffee in hand, Bear is back to being our formidable coach.

However, before we leave, Bear steps up to Ethan, his expression hard and stance brimming with authority, and there's an edge to him that wasn't there before.

"It's your responsibility to take care of her," he barks at Ethan. I open my mouth to tell him that it's really not. Regardless of his demeanor, Bear is not acting as our coach right now.

He's behaving like a scared parent, and even though it warms my heart, it's unnecessary. What he is asking of Ethan is beyond captain duties. Beyond roommate duties, too.

Except before I can say any of that, Ethan agrees. "I promise, she will be well taken care of."

Despite the pain and exhaustion pulling at me, I can't help but roll my eyes.

"She shouldn't be alone on campus," Bear continues with his ludicrous demands. "Not after this. And at the house—" His jaw tightens. "You make damn sure she's not left alone. If whoever did this comes back..."

A shiver rakes down my spine. My fingers curl tighter around the hot drink Ethan just handed me, but the warmth does nothing to chase away the ice forming in my chest.

Because my attackers weren't just some faceless threat.

One of them was Kyle. I know it was.

And he doesn't need to *come back*.

He never left.

He sleeps under the same roof as me. He moves through the same spaces. He's a fox in the hen house, and from here on out, I'm going to be sleeping with one eye open. Is the lock on my door enough to keep him out? Something tells me not for long.

Bear's gaze cuts to me, sharp but unreadable. He must see something on my face, though, because his expression darkens. His next words are for Ethan, but I swear they're meant for me too.

"She's not alone. Not for one damn second."

Ethan nods, stiff and solemn. "Understood."

Bear lingers for a beat longer before exhaling sharply. I can tell he doesn't want to leave me, but he's got no excuse to stay. Not one that wouldn't give away the fact that we have more than a coach-player relationship. I offer him a tight smile, the best that I can do. Without another word, he turns and strides out the door, leaving just me and Ethan in the suddenly too quiet room.

I stare down at my coffee, my pulse thrumming hard in my throat. I hear the sound of Ethan's footsteps before his sneakers appear in my field of vision. "Thorn?"

I force myself to look at him. His brows are drawn together, his concern unmistakable, but it's the steadiness in his eyes that almost undoes me. He's waiting—patient, unwavering—for whatever I have to say.

I swallow hard. "What are we going to do about Kyle?"

His jaw flexes, but he doesn't answer right away.

I keep going. "He *lives* in the same house. Under the same roof, and I—I *know* it was him." My voice shakes, but I don't care. "I haven't seen him since, and I..." I exhale shakily, my fingers tightening around the cup to the point that I have to force the muscles to relax or spill the hot liquid all over myself. "I can't— I don't know how to face him."

Ethan swears under his breath before carefully extracting the cup from my trembling grip. Setting it aside, he clasps my hands in his, engulfing my smaller ones in his large, strong grip. "You're not going to be left alone with him for a second, okay? Not in the house, not in the locker room, not anywhere. I'll sleep in that chair right beside your bed every night if I have to. If it means you're safe."

"Now you're starting to sound like Griffin," I tease, before the weight of the moment settles over me once more. "You can't keep that up long term."

"No," he agrees. "But if Kyle wants you incapacitated so badly, then he'll make another move. And this time, we'll catch him." Ethan's eyes darken with the depth of his promise.

"And then what?"

When he speaks, his voice is low and lethal. "Then he's done. Hockey. School. All of it."

✳

I WAKE GROGGILY, my limbs heavy, my head swimming from the lingering effects of the painkillers I took earlier. The dull ache in my ribs is still there, a persistent throb under my skin, but it's more manageable than it was this morning.

My stomach growls. Loudly.

With a sigh, I push myself up, wincing as my body protests the movement. The room is dim, shadows stretching long across the walls. Dusk has fallen while I was asleep, and a glance at the clock tells me it's early evening.

I force my legs over the edge of the bed, standing slowly as the movement pulls on my bruised skin and battered muscles. The floor is cool beneath my bare feet as I pull on a pair of leggings and fluffy socks, before dragging a baggy hoodie over my head.

Easing open the bedroom door, I listen for any noises in the hall before creeping out and across to the bathroom. The brightness stings my eyes as I turn on the light, before I adjust.

My gaze immediately lands on the mirror hanging above the sink as I shuffle forward. It's not the first time I've seen my reflection today, but I swear every time I do, I look worse.

And I hate what I see.

Splotches of purple and red bleed across my cheek, and the cut along my temple is an angry slash. A shadow of a bruise colors my jawline, another peeking from the collar of my hoodie. The harsh light makes everything look particularly gruesome, but it's not even my red, swollen skin that gets to me.

It's the fear that has taken up residence in my eyes.

Bruises aren't new to me—I've taken my fair share of hits on the ice. I'm used to dealing with guys who have no problem knocking me around, but that is nothing like last night. They never *jumped* me. Never had me so afraid for my life that I wasn't sure if I was going to walk away.

The reflection in the mirror blurs. Memories from the night before creep in, unbidden. The harsh grip on my arms. The slam of my body against the pavement. The suffocating terror that stole the air from my lungs as I realized—*really* realized—I was trapped. That there was no escape. No way out but through the pain.

My breathing grows erratic, and I squeeze my eyes shut.

Breathe. In. Out.

I will *not* let them keep me there.

I force my fingers to unclench from the sink. Force my shoulders to loosen as I tear my gaze from the mirror. I do my best to shake off the sticky residue of the memory, ignoring the lingering tremor in my hands as I use the toilet before heading downstairs.

Halfway down, voices drift up from the living room. I slow my steps, stopping just out of sight at the sound of Ethan's voice.

"...one of us with her at all times when she's on campus. She shouldn't have to walk anywhere alone right now."

"Agreed," Jax says. "We can split it up. Take shifts to ensure someone is always with her."

"I'm not worried about when she's on campus." My eyebrows climb my forehead at hearing Griffin's voice. What is he doing here? "What about when she's *here*? There's no fucking way she's sleeping beneath the same roof as that fucker."

"And what do you propose?" Ethan drawls. "That she moves in with you?"

"Exactly." Unlike the scoff that accompanied Ethan's words, Griffin is dead serious.

"Wait, what?" Jax chimes in. "Dylan isn't moving in with you. You don't even have a spare room."

I'm a little bit offended at the fact that they are fighting over me like dogs over a bone.

"Yeah, but Liam or Noah could move in here, and Dylan can take their room."

Okay, well now I'm even more offended that they are talking about me like I'm a baseball card to trade.

"That seems extreme," Finn states. "I still don't believe it was Kyle behind the attack."

My stomach drops.

Of course, he doesn't.

I've seen how close he and Kyle are. Heard the stories about them attending summer camps together. They've known each other since they were little kids.

But just because he's in denial doesn't mean it's not true.

I clutch the railing, listening as the conversation shifts.

"Pull your head out of your ass, Finn." Griffin sounds like he's seconds from pulling it out for him. "If you weren't so busy moon-eyeing your buddy, you'd see the shit he's pulling."

"I do not *moon-eye* Kyle, you fucker. He's my *friend*. I *know* him, and I know he wouldn't go that far."

"Then you clearly don't—"

The front door swings open.

I freeze, gaze snapping forward.

From where I stand, I have a direct line of sight to the entry-way. Kyle steps inside, shaking rain from his hair as he shrugs out of his coat. He turns, his gaze lifting...and landing on me.

The moment our eyes lock, my blood runs cold.

Something dark flashes across his face and his mouth lifts in a cruel tilt, before his eyes drag over me, cataloging the damage. His gaze lingers on every cut, every bruise, like he's *proud* of what he did.

My breath catches in my throat. I don't need to hear the words from his mouth to confirm what I already knew. *He* did this to me. I can't move. Can't speak. Fear lashes through me, fast and sharp. It's a battle to keep my reaction off my face, but I refuse to let him see what his sheer presence does to me.

Kyle Reed won't take anything else from me.

He steps forward, and I fight the urge to flee, but then he notices the guys in the living room. The shift is instant. His whole demeanor changes, shoulder's loosening, expression smoothing into something easy and unbothered. He barely even hesitates before flashing a smile.

"What's up?"

Ethan pushes off the couch, stepping toward him. "Where have you been?" There's an accusation there. "No one has seen you since last night."

Kyle snorts. "What is this, the Spanish Inquisition?"

Griffin leans forward, eyes fixed on Kyle. When he speaks, his voice is calm—*too* calm. "Dylan was attacked outside the arena last night."

Kyle tilts his head, expression carefully fixed into one of surprise. "Is that so?"

"You wouldn't know anything about that, would you?" Griffin's tone is still neutral, but there's an edge to it now, sharp enough to cut.

"Me?" Kyle scoffs. "Why would I know anything about *that*?" He shrugs. "I was at The Stanley with a few of the guys last night." A cocky smirk lifts his lips. "Hooked up with some chick. I'd say you could ask her if you want an alibi, but I didn't exactly catch her name."

Ewww. I just vomited in my mouth.

"Which guys?" Ethan pushes.

This time, Kyle's surprise is genuine. "Seriously, man?" His gaze moves over all four of the guys. "You all think I had something to do with that bench bunny getting attacked?"

"Watch it," Griffin growls, rising to his feet and prowling closer.

"Finn?" Kyle presses, ignoring Griffin entirely. "You can't seriously be buying this bullshit?"

I hold my breath as Finn sighs, dragging a hand down his face as though trying to give himself a few minutes to think before he answers. "Just answer the question, Reed. Who were you with last night?"

"This is fucking bullshit," Kyle sneers, shaking his head. "Not that it's any of your fucking business, but I was with Andrew, Sam, and Travis."

"Were Fletcher or Monroe there?" Griffin asks—well, demands would be more accurate.

Kyle throws his hands into the air in protest. "Yeah, I think I remember seeing them at one point. Not like I was following them around all night. Now, are we fucking done here? I need to shower and grab a nap before practice."

"Yeah." Ethan exhales, gesturing for Kyle to leave.

With a final glower and a look of disappointment cast Finn's way, he moves toward the stairs. I hurry to descend the last few steps, wanting to get out of his way. However, before I'm in the clear, he's there. His arm grazes mine as he brushes past, his fingers just barely ghosting over my side.

Those cold eyes and cruel lips bore into me.

A threat. A promise. A warning.

My throat burns. Ice solidifies in my veins.

He keeps walking like nothing passed between us, meanwhile, I'm frozen in place. Unable to move. To breathe. To think.

Pressure lands on my shoulders, firm but gentle. "Dylan."

Jax's voice grounds me back in the present, sending the fear from Kyle's presence skittering into the shadows.

I blink, dragging in a sharp breath as I focus on the deep

brown of his eyes. They aren't as dark as I'd initially assumed. This close, I see tiny flecks of amber sparking within, like fire-flies dancing in the night, calling to me.

His touch is steady but not confining as he guides me to the sofa, his hands light on my arms like he's afraid I'll break. Fuck, if he lets me go, maybe I will. It's been a long time since I've felt this fragile. Weak. Helpless.

I practically fall onto the couch cushions, still in a bit of a daze. Finn is watching me closely, his expression tight with something that looks like concern. Confusion flickers in his gaze, too. Doubt. I can't look at him for more than a second before tearing my gaze away.

He makes some excuse to the others before pushing to his feet, and I hear him disappearing up the stairs. To think or to apologize to Kyle, who fucking knows.

"Here." Kneeling in front of me, Ethan presses a ceramic mug into my hands. The heat seeps into my fingers but does little to ease the faint tremble. "Drink this."

I take a small sip, savoring the calming flavor of the chamomile tea. It works, a little. At least until Griffin shifts forward to the edge of his seat and clears his throat. "We think you should switch rooms with one of the guys at my house."

I don't meet his gaze for another moment, taking another sip of my drink before looking around at the group of men gathered around me. They'd been arguing about this before Kyle arrived. Jax had opposed his idea, but now, he's oddly silent. Is he in agreement?

My focus shifts to Ethan. He typically gives the orders, but he doesn't pipe up, letting *me* make the decision.

What do *I* want?

I don't want to sleep under the same roof as Kyle.

But if I leave, Kyle wins.

First, he runs me out of my house, then he runs me off the team, and finally, he chases me out of BSU.

I already let Lucas take everything from me once.

I won't do it again.

Setting the mug down on the coffee table, I lift my chin, meeting each of their gazes. "No."

"Hurricane—"

"I'm *not* leaving," I say firmly, cutting Griffin off. "This is *my* house, too. I won't let him scare me off."

The guys exchange looks, and I can feel Ethan watching me, his stare burning. But I don't waver. If Kyle wants me out of the house, off the team, then he's going to have to do a hell of a lot better than that.

Because I'm not giving up without a fight.

TWENTY-SEVEN

I'M BACK at practice the next morning, despite my body's protests. But it's miserable. I'm stuck on the bench, watching. Watching my teammates fly across the rink, watching the first-line practice plays I should be a part of, watching Kyle fucking Reed skate like he's not the reason I'm sitting on this stupid fucking bench in the first place.

My fingers dig into my thighs as I glare at him. He shouldn't even be on the team. Shouldn't get to walk away from what he did like it was nothing. I suck in a sharp breath and force my gaze away before anyone notices.

It clashes instead with Griffin across the ice. He stands tall, a force of padded gear in the crease, but his focus is pinned on me more than the puck. Thankfully, he's the only one who seems to have noticed the way I scowl at Kyle while I envision ripping his head from his shoulders every time he rushes past.

Jax skates by, slowing just enough to glance my way. His gaze rakes over my skin assessingly, as though checking there is no new damage. "You good?"

I nod before he skates off, rejoining the scrimmage. He's fucking lucky the guys on the opposing team didn't take his distraction for the opening it was and slam him into the boards. Idiot.

As soon as the scrimmage ends, he's back with a bottle of water, handing it over to me without a word. I sigh, twisting the cap open. At least he's subtle about it.

The freshman sitting beside me isn't so smooth. "Uh, do you need anything?" he flusters. "Ethan said...well, he told me to make sure you're okay. And, uh, get you anything."

I glance at the kid. He looks nervous, like he's afraid of screwing up his first real assignment on the team. Poor guy. I almost feel bad for him.

"I'm good, thanks. You don't have to babysit me."

"Uh, yeah, I do. Ethan was really specific."

I huff out a frustrated laugh. Of course he was. "Fine. You can sit here, but you don't have to act like my personal servant."

The kid nods quickly, and I focus back on the drills the forwards are currently running. Practice has been running for over an hour now, and my ass has grown numb. I shift, wincing as the slight movement jostles my ribs, sending pain flaring through them.

"You!" Ethan barks from across the ice, pointing a gloved finger at the freshman beside me. "Get her painkillers and a heat pad. Now!"

The kid practically jumps to his feet, stuttering out apologies.

"It's fine," I try to say. "I've got— And he's gone," I say to myself as I watch the kid race along the bench.

"Be right back!" he calls before disappearing to do Ethan's bidding.

I whip my head back to glare at the asshole but he's already focused back on his drills. I don't even know how he fucking saw that, given it appears as though his full attention is on the ice.

"Jesus, Ethan," I mutter, shaking my head as I glance around at the other players. Some of them are watching me, and I offer them tight smiles. "Overkill much?"

I'm still cursing him out under my breath as I reach into my backpack to retrieve some pain meds. Not because Ethan all but demanded it, but because I am a little sore. As my fingers wrap around the pain med bottle, they also catch on a loose piece of paper in my bag. I pull it all out, setting the bottle in my lap as I look at the paper in confusion. It's all neatly folded up, and I carefully unfold it.

Still fearless. Still fucking beautiful.

The air stalls in my lungs. It's just like the last note I received. The one I've tucked in an old journal of mine and occasionally pull out late at night, wondering who wrote such words about me. Who is looking so closely? Who sees me in this light?

"Finn!" Ethan barks. "Focus."

My head snaps up as Finn turns away, going back to his drills. I stare at him for a long moment, but he never once looks my way. I do catch him staring at his best friend, though, head tilted and eyes clouded with questions. I hope that means he's questioning his behavior, that he's considering my version of events to be the truth. However, only time will tell. Time and proof—if I can get it.

Not entirely sure what to make of these notes, I tuck it away in my backpack and pop my pills, swallowing them down with cold water. When the freshman returns with a heat pad, I give him a tight smile, and we don't talk again until the end of practice.

As the rest of the team stomps off the ice and toward the locker room to change, Bear approaches, clipboard in hand. "How you holding up?" he asks, looking me over with scrutiny.

"Fine," I lie.

I notice the guys slow, glancing my way as they pass. Bear turns to look at them, before returning his attention to me, his expression knowing. "They're protective."

I roll my eyes. "They live with me. Ethan's the captain. You practically ordered him to babysit my ass, so that's what he's doing."

Bear grunts. "Good to hear." He rubs at the back of his neck, seeming to think something over before lifting his head. "I know I offered before and you said no, but I want you to know the offer still stands. Come live with me. I can sort it all out with the dean—explain the situation..."

I'm already shaking my head, reaching out to squeeze his arm. "You know how much I appreciate you sticking your neck out for me, but it's not necessary."

"I worry about you," he admits, concern bleeding into his words.

"Then it's a good thing you like to torture us with daily practices, so you can see for yourself how I'm doing."

Ethan appears then, already changed in record time as he strides over. Stopping a foot away from Coach, the two of them seem to square off in some silent macho man dance I'm not privy to, before Bear grunts, "Keep her safe."

Ethan simply nods before Bear steps past him and walks away, leaving us alone.

Tilting his head toward the exit, he asks, "Ready to get out of here?" He's already bending down to grab my bag from the floorboards before I can move.

"I can carry my own shit," I grouse, cautiously pushing to my feet.

"Sure you can." He marches off, my bag slung over his shoulder, without a second glance.

"Asshole," I mutter, scrambling to catch up with him. "Please tell me I'm not going to be stuck with you all day."

His responding grin is not reassuring as he pushes open the door and we step out onto the BSU campus, and I already foretell that it's going to be a long day.

"I'm just as uncomfortable standing as I am sitting," I snap at Ethan, swatting him away.

"Perhaps if you took your pain meds when you're supposed to," he grouses in return.

"I'm fine."

"Yes, clearly." His tone drips with sarcasm. "That's why you're white as a sheet and breathing heavily."

"Maybe if you'd just back the fuck off and leave me be for two fucking seconds."

"Wow, the tension is sizzling out here," Wren interrupts— thank the fucking gods. Ethan and his hovering are driving me in-fucking-sane, and it's only been one morning. Someone else better be on *protection detail* soon, or we're going to be minus one captain this season.

"You weren't kidding when you said you had bodyguards," she adds, eyeing Ethan with a teasing smirk.

"Trust me," I tell her, glaring in Ethan's direction. "It's not as fun as it sounds."

"Mm, but it sure is pretty to look at. Hi, Ethan."

"Wren," Ethan greets politely, his exasperation from a moment ago suddenly nowhere to be found.

"Ready to eat?" I ask Wren, already linking my arm through hers and pulling her down the path, leaving Ethan to trail behind us. I called Wren last night to update her on what had happened, although I have kept my suspicions about who I believe attacked me to myself. I don't need to drag her into that mess. I also sent her a text earlier informing her that if one more person asked how I was doing today, I was liable to incite a massacre on campus.

So she sensibly doesn't ask how I'm feeling, although I can tell she's concerned as she runs her gaze over me, cataloging the cacophony of bruises that have drawn more than a few eyes this morning. It's been awesome.

"I'm sensing some hot and heavy enemies to lovers vibes," she comments while we walk, and I could fucking kiss her for skipping over all talk of the attack. However, I do side-eye her like she's crazy—which, clearly she is.

"You're sensing my supreme restraint to not rip his balls off."

"Oh, kinky. I didn't know Ethan was into ball play."

"What?!" I splutter. "No. I mean..." I shake my head. "Ethan's kinks are none of my concern."

Wren grins at my flustering before wagging her brows. "But you want them to be."

"I... Please shut up."

She cackles like a true-to-life witch, before glancing over her shoulder and bringing her head closer to mine. Lowering her voice, she whispers, "For real, though, is anything going on between you two? Between *any* of them?"

I choke on absolutely nothing, nearly tripping over my own feet. I cast a furtive glance back at Ethan, thankful to see he's several steps behind us, surveying our surroundings with the scrutiny of a general navigating a war zone.

"I mean, come on," she continues. "You have an entire lineup of walking sin babysitting you. Not to mention that you live with *three* of them. Don't tell me you haven't at least thought about it."

Oh, I've thought about it, all right. That's the problem!

I look away, but the heat creeping up my neck betrays me.

"Oh my God!" Wren squeals, and I snap my face back to hers, giving her wide eyes as I dig my fingers into her forearm in a warning to *shut the fuck up right now*.

Mouthing, *sorry*, she drops her voice to a hushed whisper. "Something *has* happened, hasn't it?" Another glance back at Ethan. "With which one?"

I hesitate, unsure whether I should admit to anything, but it's exhausting keeping this secret to myself, not having someone to talk it through with.

With a sigh, I lower my voice. "I've kissed three of them."

Behind us, Ethan coughs, a hacking noise like he's just swallowed a fly.

Wide-eyed, I snap my head back toward him at the same time Wren does, but he waves us away. Maybe he really did choke on a bug or something.

I frown but force myself to ignore him. Wren and I bring our heads closer together so we can keep our conversation between us.

She's beaming like she just won a Golden Globe. "Three out of four? Damn, Dylan. Let me guess..." She taps her finger against her chin. "Griffin, definitely. The way that man looks at you, I'm surprised he hasn't already hauled you off to his cave and claimed you as his own."

Her words are startlingly close to the truth. Instead of a cave, it was the gym, but Griffin has made a claiming that I have yet to acknowledge or really think too deeply about, because I have absolutely no idea what the hell to do with that information.

She side-eyes me, and I nod my confirmation.

"Finn?" she guesses next, surprising me.

"How did you guess?"

She chuckles. "He has this permanent *hate to want you* scowl in place any time you're around."

"Gee, thanks," I droll. "Talk about flattering."

She waves away my dramatics. "It's a process. I'm sure he will get there in the end."

The question is, do I want him to get there? What do I want from Finn? From any of them?

"As for guy number three." She hums, eyes flicking between me and Ethan as she debates. "Jax or Ethan..." She trails off. Then, after another glance at Ethan—who seems to be making a point of looking anywhere but at us, but I swear I can *feel* his attention on my back—she smirks. "Ethan."

I bark out a laugh. "Wrong."

Her eyebrows lift. "Really?" She sounds shocked. "Because given that lovers' quarrel I walked into back there, I'd bet my tuition I'm right."

I shake my head. "You're totally misreading that. Ethan is just protective. I'm a Steelhawk, and he feels responsible for every player on the team."

Wren gives me a *look*. "Uh-huh. Sure. And that's why he's staring at you like he's debating throwing you over his shoulder and running off into the woods."

I scoff. "You've got it all wrong. He's the captain. It's his *job* to make sure I'm okay. He was basically ordered to by Coach. That's it. Nothing more."

Wren scans my face before she smirks wickedly. "But you want there to be something more."

"What— I— No," I splutter, before sighing. "I'm not supposed to want anything with any of them. They're my teammates. My *roommates*," I spell out—for her benefit as well as my own. *And yet, you keep kissing one, you let the other feel you up at every opportunity, and the third is getting you off in the gym. Jesus, when did my life become such a mess?*

"So, who was the best kisser?" Wren wags her eyebrows suggestively.

I snort, shaking my head and refusing to answer. I'm thankful when we reach the cafeteria, although I admit I feel lighter for sharing that with her. Even if it hasn't done much to unjumble my chaotic thoughts when it comes to the guys.

Wren pulls open the cafeteria door, stepping inside. I move to follow, but Ethan's hand wraps around my wrist, pulling me back.

I turn, glancing down at where his fingers have a firm yet gentle grip on me, noting the buzzing beneath my skin. Slowly, I lift my gaze to meet his. His eyes, dark and unreadable, lock on mine as he steps closer. Too close, until the warmth of his body is pressing into mine.

Lowering his head, his breath brushes my ear, sending a shiver down my spine.

"Careful, Dylan. You're playing a dangerous game."

His words are a caress across my skin. A taunt. A warning, but for me or for himself, I'm not sure. Does this mean he heard my conversation with Wren? Does he know I've kissed three of his friends—his teammates? Do I want him to?

He lingers a moment longer, his lips ghosting over my jaw, just barely, before he releases me and steps back. His eyes continue to hold mine captive as he reaches above my head to grab ahold of the door to the cafeteria and keep it open, and his voice is an octave deeper than normal as he gestures inside. "After you."

Stepping into the room, he follows behind, the heat of his body warm at my back and his palm pressing possessively against the base of my spine as he directs me toward the table of loud, raucous hockey players in the middle of the room.

Conversation dulls as we approach, nerves fluttering in my belly. Some of the guys shoot me glances, a few offering quick nods or murmured greetings, but the atmosphere feels different. Heavier.

Ethan directs me to a free seat beside Jax, before sitting beside me and leaving Wren to sit opposite.

"Hey," Noah greets as I lower myself into the seat, careful not to jostle my sore ribs. "It sucked not having you on the ice this morning."

"Yeah, we were worried when we heard what happened to you," Tyler, the second-line center, adds with a friendly smile.

"Seriously," Marcus, a first-line defenseman alongside Jax, nods. "Shit's fucked. It's good to see you didn't let it get you down."

Others echo the sentiment, and I give the table my best attempt at a smile. "Thanks."

"Did you see who it was?" Ben, our third-line goalie, asks me.

I hesitate, fingers curling into a fist in my lap. Kyle's gaze burns into me, like a brand being seared into the side of my head. I swallow, keeping my expression neutral. "Not really. It was dark, and they wore hoods."

"Cowards," one of the other guys spits, shaking his head. "Ganging up on someone—a girl, no less—alone and in the dark. That's weak as shit."

Several others murmur their agreement, and my gaze inadvertently flicks to Kyle in time to catch the thinning of his lips, how his eyebrows draw low over his eyes. He's pissed. Because his teammates essentially called him a coward, or because they are actually bothered that I was attacked?

"I hope campus security is stepping up after this," Marcus states, lips pressed into a firm line. "My sister is a freshman here. I'd hate to think something like this could happen to her."

"It was hopefully just a one-time thing." I don't want him to worry about his sister, especially since, unless she plans on joining the men's hockey team, she won't be a target.

"What if they try it again?" someone farther down the table asks.

A shiver goes through me at the notion of being in that situation again. Scared, helpless, trapped.

A growl rumbles through Jax's chest, his hands forming fists on the table beside me.

"They won't get the chance." Ethan's voice is cold, edged with a warning as he surveys the rest of the team. "We look after our own."

"For real." Noah nods, face lined with determination, like Ethan is imparting once-in-a-lifetime wisdom. "You let us know if you need anything." His gaze is set on Ethan, but then it slides to mine, and he flashes me a warm smile while other players vocalize their agreement. Their ease to help chokes me up. A few weeks ago, most of these guys would probably have rejoiced at me being unable to play, and now they're offering to help however they can. I don't have words.

Thankfully, Ethan jumps in to save me. "Thanks, guys. We're working on a schedule so Dylan isn't alone on campus or at the arena. I think we have it covered, but if we run into any issues, we'll let you know."

The guys all respond to their captain with eager nods and words of affirmation.

Kyle pipes up for the first time since I sat down. "Come on," he scoffs. "It was a random attack. Everyone's acting like she was personally victimized."

The air shifts. Finn stares at Kyle, like he can't believe what just came out of his mouth. "Dude, that's cold. Regardless of whether it was a one-off or not, *she was attacked.*"

Kyle shrugs, tearing a bite off his sandwich. "I just think it sounds like a bigger deal is being made of it than necessary."

Griffin, who has strategically placed himself where he has an unobstructed view of where I'm sitting and also a clear line of sight to Kyle, Fletcher, and Monroe, leans forward. His stare sharpens, eyes locked on to Kyle like he's peeling back layers, looking for what's underneath. "Who's to say she isn't being targeted?"

Tension thrums through the table like a live wire, some of the guys exchanging confused and wary glances.

"How the hell would I know?" is Kyle's blasé response before he goes back to his food.

"Shit, you think one of our fans could have targeted her for being on the team?" another player directs to Griffin.

His response is to shrug. "Anything is possible."

Conversation shifts after that ominous response, but I'm not really listening.

"Here." I glance up as a tray of food is placed in front of me, but it's not the delightful smell that has my mouth dropping open. It's the person handing it to me. Finn. Finn got me food. "You need to keep your energy up."

"T-thanks."

He nods before sauntering back to where he was sitting. There's a severe look of consternation on his face as he picks at his plate, his gaze occasionally flicking up to Kyle. He doesn't engage in conversation with him the way he typically does at lunch, and I notice there is no puck bunny trying to climb into his lap today. While it's strange and a little sad not to see him being his typical charismatic, happy-go-lucky self, a tiny, minuscule part of me is glad he's starting to question things.

And the jealous witch inside of me preens at the lack of a puck bunny at his side. Although I shut her up real quick. I may be starting to see that I can trust these guys, that I'm not hated here the way I was at NSU, but that doesn't mean I can allow myself to fall for any of them. They are still my teammates, maybe even my friends, and we have a long way to go to the championships. The last thing I want to do is fuck everything up by letting feelings or sex get in the way.

As I return my attention to my tray in front of me, I catch Wren's gaze from across the table. She arches a brow, her lips quirking in a smirk. *Plot thickens,* she mouths. I shake my head, ignoring her as I dive into my food.

TWENTY-EIGHT

TONIGHT'S the first time in forever that I haven't had a practice or gotten on the ice. The amount of extra time I have is insane. I'm all caught up on my assignments, I've read ahead in most of my classes, and there's literally nothing left for me to do except stare at my ceiling in utter boredom. It's stupid, but I'm reluctant to leave my room. I should've asked Wren about doing something tonight or hanging out at her place, but I'm exhausted after my first full day back on campus.

A knock on my door makes me jolt.

"Dylan?" Jax's voice filters through the wood. "Ethan and I made dinner."

I hesitate, staring at the door like it might suddenly dissolve. I don't have anything else to do, and I do need to eat. Better to go downstairs when I know there's no risk of getting caught alone with Kyle. Besides, the thought of sitting in my room alone all night feels suffocating.

"Yeah, okay," I say, pulling open the door.

Jax smiles, a small quirk of his lips, and steps aside to let me through. I feel his presence at my back, like a protective shield against the world, as I make my way down the hall.

Downstairs, the scent of garlic and something rich and savory fills the air. Ethan is at the stove, dishing out pasta onto plates, his broad shoulders tense with focus.

"You guys actually cooked?" I ask, a little skeptical. I just assumed they grabbed most of their meals on campus—like I do. Although, the food we ate the night before the roster was announced was home-cooked, so I probably shouldn't be surprised.

Jax scoffs, nudging me lightly with his elbow toward the table while he grabs drinks for us. "Ethan cooked. I supervised."

Ethan huffs, dumping a pot into the sink. "You sat on the counter and scrolled through your phone the whole time."

Jax shrugs, looking over his shoulder at me as he retrieves glasses from the cupboard. He winks, and that simple action is like a live wire aimed directly at my core. "Like I said—supervised."

Despite my laugh, I stand behind one of the chairs at the table, my hands clenched around the wood as I glance around the open-plan living-kitchen area.

"He's not here," Ethan says, noticing my not-so-subtle search when he carries two plates over. "He and Finn went out earlier."

"Oh." It's stupid how my stomach drops.

Ethan's gaze meets mine before he gestures to the chair. "Sit." There's a hint of an order there, but it's hidden beneath gentle concern. I do as he says, but any appetite I had has fled, knowing Finn voluntarily went out with Kyle. With the way he responded to Kyle at lunch today, I thought perhaps... But that was stupid of me. Kyle is his friend.

Jax must see something on my face as he and Ethan share a glance. "We told Finn to take him out for a while so you wouldn't have to hide away in your room all night. He...wasn't as excited about it as you might think."

My eyebrows hit my hairline, my gaze bouncing between the two men who have taken it upon themselves to be my protectors. Warmth spreads through my chest. "Thank you," I murmur quietly.

The two of them join me at the table, Ethan taking the seat beside me and Jax sitting opposite. A strange sense of normalcy settles over us as we dig into our food. Other than my dinners with Bear and the occasional one with Wren, I usually eat alone. Jax and Ethan banter back and forth, joking and teasing one another. It reminds me of family dinners. Ones I haven't allowed myself to look at too closely ever since my dad died.

At first, we keep the conversation light—hockey, classes, practice, but as our plates empty and the warmth of the meal settles in our bellies, Ethan asks, "So, how did you first get into hockey?"

I shrug, feeling his stare on me but not able to meet his gaze. "My dad used to play. He basically raised me on the ice. Pretty sure I learned to skate before I could walk."

Jax hums, setting his fork down. He's the only one who knows my dad is dead. Who knows what a sensitive subject this is for me. "He played college or pro?"

I hesitate, reaching for my water. "College." It's not a lie, it's just not the full truth either. I shift in my seat. "I think, even if he hadn't played, I still would have ended up on the ice. It was just...always home, you know?"

Ethan nods like he gets it. "You still close with him?"

The question lodges in my chest. I swallow, forcing my voice to stay even. "He died last year."

"Shit, Thorn," Ethan mutters, regret deepening his voice. "Sorry."

"What about your mom?" Jax questions, and I sense he's been wanting to ask that since the night I fell apart in his arms.

"My mom and dad...their love was like a fairy tale." There's a heaviness to my words, the weight of grief tugging them down. "Losing him broke something in her." I shake my head. "I've barely seen her since... She's more of a ghost than a parent anymore."

Neither of them says anything for a moment, but I don't feel pity from them. Just...understanding.

Jax leans forward, resting his elbows on the table. "Yeah. I know what that's like."

I glance at him, waiting.

He shrugs. "I didn't really have parents growing up. They were in and out, and when they were around, they were more into each other's drama than they were into raising me. I lived with my aunt for a while. My uncle after that. Spent most of my childhood bouncing between them until I got old enough to look after myself." He flicks a crumb off his plate. "Never really felt like I belonged anywhere."

"What age were you when you started looking after yourself?" I ask, curiously, my heart aching at the thought of a young Jax getting himself dressed, making himself breakfast, going to school in wrinkled, day-old clothes.

"Ten."

I frown. That's even younger than I'd expected. I don't know what to say to that, but I don't think he expects anything.

Ethan exhales, shaking his head. "Jesus. This got depressing fast."

Jax smirks. "Don't act like you're exempt from the shitty family stories."

Ethan rolls his eyes but doesn't argue. "Fine. My dad owns a mechanic shop. Been working there since I was a kid, cleaning up oil spills and handing him tools. He made me earn every penny I needed for hockey gear, lessons, and camp."

I tilt my head. "That doesn't sound so bad."

Ethan's jaw tenses. "It wouldn't have been. If he didn't

spend every second reminding me I'd never amount to anything more than he did. Laughing at me for thinking I could ever do better. Ever be anything more than a lowly mechanic—the guy with grease under his nails." His fingers drum against the table, giving away his agitation. "It never mattered how good I was, how well I played. He's just waiting for me to fail and come crawling back."

Jax lets out a low whistle. "Holidays must be a real treat."

Ethan snorts. "Which is why I typically spend them here."

That thick silence settles in again. It's strange. I don't think I've ever sat with them like this—no teasing, no sharp edges. Just *them*. Just *me*.

Ethan stretches back in his chair, and I don't miss the way his T-shirt rides up as he lifts his arms above his head, the flash of white skin and taut muscle before it falls back down. "Jesus, we sound like a bad therapy group."

I chuckle. "Same time next week?"

Jax huffs a laugh while Ethan flashes me that boy-next-door grin of his. Pushing back his chair, he grabs my plate along with his. "I'll tidy this up. You and Jax go pick a movie?"

Dinner *and* a movie? This is beginning to look a little bit like a date. Admittedly, a weird-ass one where there are *two* guys. "Uh, sure."

We're interrupted by a knock at the front door. Jax glares in that direction, not looking pleased at the interruption. "Who the hell is that?" he grumbles, setting his plate back on the table before stalking toward the hall.

Moving to help Ethan while Jax talks to whoever is at the door, I've just added Jax's plate to the pile of dirty dishes when voices and the stomping of feet have me spinning.

"By all means, invite yourself inside," Jax grouses, each word dripping with sarcasm as Griffin marches into the kitchen. His sharp gaze darts around the room before locking on me.

Ethan bristles immediately. "What are you doing here?"

"Why aren't you at practice?" I ask, knowing this is the time when he's typically on the ice.

"Like I could focus on anything else when I know you're under the same roof as *him*." He jerks his chin toward the stairs.

Ethan makes an exasperated noise. "We're perfectly capable—"

"Is he here?" Griffin demands. His hands clench at his sides as though pitching for a fight.

Jax sighs, the sound born from frustration more than anything else. "No. Finn took him out."

Griffin nods, seeming somewhat satisfied by that at least.

A standoff ensues.

"Well, thanks for stopping by." Jax attempts to usher Griffin out of the house.

"I'm not leaving." Folding his arms over his chest, Griffin becomes the immovable man as he glowers at Ethan and Jax, just daring them to try and kick him out.

I sigh, stepping forward. The movement catches Griffin's attention, his glower softening, even though his lips are still pressed in a flat line. "We were going to watch a movie, if you want to join us?"

It's not really in my nature to be the peacekeeper, but I'm equally aware that each of these guys is fighting over protecting me. Plus, there's that strange pull...

Ethan and Jax exchange a look, but they both remain silent, letting me take the lead.

Griffin stares at me a moment longer, the room seeming to hold its collective breath, before he gestures toward the living room. "Lead the way."

As I walk past, he steps forward so my arm brushes against his chest. Static fills the air. My breath catches, and he notices, if the flash of his eyes is anything to go by. He's not unaffected either, though. His throat moves, and he doesn't dare blink as I pass. Even as I stride to the living room, I feel his gaze heavy and wanton on my back.

I plop down onto the middle of the sofa. Jax drops onto the empty spot beside me and, oh-so casually, drapes his arm along the back of the sofa behind me. Griffin notices, something dark and possessive flashing in his startlingly blue eyes. Before Ethan can claim the spot on my other side, Griffin is there, shoving him out of the way and taking the seat.

"Seriously?" Ethan drawls, glowering at him before moving to sit elsewhere. "This is *my* house."

Griffin simply shrugs. "You snooze, you lose."

I roll my eyes, ignoring their bickering as Jax flicks through the channels before finding a new sci-fi movie. As the opening credits begin, I'm acutely aware of how boxed in I am. Jax's thigh brushes against mine while, on my other side, Griffin's body heat sears into me, even through the leggings and T-shirt I'm wearing.

I'm barely paying attention to the movie as the hero starts off on his wild quest. All I can focus on is how *close* Jax and Griffin are. The way Jax's arm rests along the back of the couch, fingertips ghosting over my shoulder every so often like he just can't help but touch me in some small way. Or how Griffin's arm presses solidly against mine—a silent claim. His focus is intent on the screen, but I suspect he's as attuned to me as I am to both of them.

Heat licks up my spine, my skin hyperaware of every shift of their bodies, every touch. It drives me steadily insane as the movie plays out.

While Griffin plays at watching the movie, Jax is the opposite. With every moment we sit there, he grows bolder. Subtle brushes of his fingers against my shoulder turn into him playing with a strand of my hair. His other hand reaches across his body to skim along my arm before coming to rest on my thigh. It's a blatantly possessive touch. One that makes me squirm. Heat bleeds from where he touches me, creeping up my thigh and settling in my core until it becomes impossible for me to sit still.

Torture. Sweet, agonizing torture.

I stew in it for what feels like *hours*. Growing restless, and hot, and *desperate*.

The second the end credits roll down the screen, I bolt upright so fast that I nearly trip over my own feet. "Well, that was..." Lifting my arms above my head, I fake a loud yawn while I stretch, ignoring the stiffness in my muscles. The ache from sitting still too long. "I think I'm going to call it a night."

"Good night," Ethan says, staring at me with an unreadable expression so I can't tell whether he knew damn well what was going on during the movie or if he was completely clueless.

"Yeah, sweet dreams." Jax's smirk is so damn smug, that I can't help but glower at him. I don't dare look Griffin's way at all, for fear that I might self-combust.

Three sets of eyes follow me as I practically flee up the stairs. But even when they are out of sight, I can still feel their heat, their weight, pressing against my skin.

I duck into the bathroom and run the tap, turning the water as cold as it will go before splashing it on my face. When I finally feel more in control of myself, I brush my teeth, then move to my bedroom and exchange my clothes for an oversized Timberwolves T-shirt before slipping into bed.

The sheets are a balm to my still overheated skin, and I sigh as I close my eyes. Still, sleep evades me. I toss and turn, unable to get comfortable. Unable to forget the roughness of Jax's hands, Griffin's possessive stare, even Ethan's furtive glances every time I shifted on that sofa. He *knew*. Knew what the others were doing to me. Knew how their close proximity affected me.

What would have happened if I'd leaned into Jax's touch? If I'd reached out for Griffin? I might not be able to have any of these guys in real life, but what harm is there in indulging in a little fantasy? Especially if it will burn off this need coursing relentlessly through me and enable me to sleep.

Eyes closed, I recreate that moment on the couch as my hand pushes between the lining of my panties. In my head, I respond to Jax's touch, encouraging him to go further, to be bolder as he trails his hand possessively up my thigh, pulling my legs apart.

Griffin turns in his seat, his lips capturing mine in a passionate kiss. Between his tongue and Jax's hands, I go up in flames. Every moment trapped between them is kindling that feeds my desire.

Ripping his lips from mine, Griffin bites and licks along my jaw. My head falls back, eyes falling to half-mast. My gaze catches on Ethan. He's no longer looking at the TV. Instead, he's turned in his seat so he's staring directly at *me*. Need burns hot in his eyes, turning them molten. His entire body is rigid, as though it's taking all of his self-control to hold himself in place. To not join in.

I rake my gaze over his broad chest, lingering on the corded muscles of his upper arms, before trailing south to his trim waist. My throat goes dry, and I have to swallow as I stare boldly at the long, hard outline pressing against his jean's zipper. Oh, how I want him to take it out.

To touch himself while his teammates touch me.

To get himself off while they are getting *me* off.

My fingers slide through the wetness gathered amongst my folds, and I pretend it's Jax's hand as I push inside. His thick fingers, rough with callouses and oh-so talented, driving me higher up the peak.

Beneath their ministrations and Ethan's hot stare, I soar.

Tap. Tap.

"Dylan." Griffin's voice is guttural in my ear, and I clench around Jax's fingers as they pump into me, making me moan.

Tap. Tap.

"Dylan!" Something about Griffin's tone slides through my fantasy. I jolt upright, hand still buried between my legs as I blink back into my empty bedroom.

Tap. Tap.

Rapping against the window startles me, and I damn near fall out of the bed at the sight of a figure perched on the ledge outside. Griffin paints a stoic picture, dressed all in black with the moonlight glinting off his sweep of blond hair and piercing eyes boring into me.

For a moment, all I can do is stare at him, unsure as to whether what I'm seeing is real or if I'm actually dreaming now.

"Let me in, Hurricane!"

I throw off the bedsheets and hurry to slide open the window. "What do you think you're doing?" I chastise. "You could fall and hurt yourself."

The idiot flashes me one of those boyish grins of his. "I knew you cared about me."

God, if those devilishly good looks don't immediately remind me of what I was doing before he so rudely interrupted.

I scoff, "Please, I don't need any more reason for anyone on the team to hate me—which is exactly what would happen if you broke your leg attempting to climb in *my* window." Despite my words, I move aside so he can step into my room.

Except, it's only when his boots are planted on the ground and his intoxicating presence has infiltrated the air that I realize what a huge mistake that was. Now, Griffin Price is in my bedroom, seeming larger than life as he takes up far more space than any human has a right to, and I'm suddenly realizing how little clothing I have on.

He notices too. His gaze turns predatory as he drinks me in like I'm a tall glass of cold water and it's the height of summer. I go to step back, to put space between us, but I'm too slow. He catches my wrist, nostrils flaring as he brings my hand to his face.

"What filth are you up to in here, Little Steelhawk?"

He drags my fingers beneath his nose, eyes closing as he inhales. I should be embarrassed. Should be pulling my hand from his grip. But for some disturbing reason, the whole thing only turns me on more. Perhaps it's Griffin's desperate groan, or the hunger that turns his eyes a steely gray, or the possessive hold he has on my wrist. Whatever it is, it does it for me.

I lose all common sense. All rational thought is caught up in a gust of wind and driven straight out the open window, leaving nothing but my primed body and my dirty thoughts behind.

He steps into me, the hard planes of his body pressing against mine as he drives me backward. On bare feet, I back-track across my room, unable to look away from Griffin's shadowed expression. My arm is wedged between us, his grip on my wrist firm and unrelenting, like it's the only thing grounding him. All that's stopping him from going absolutely feral.

The backs of my legs hit the mattress before I fall onto the bed. Griffin comes with me, his body folding at the waist so he's leaning over me. Every cell in my body buzzes with awareness. My core clenches, need gathering between my thighs.

"Finish yourself off."

"W-what?"

Bringing my hand to his mouth, he runs his tongue along my fingers. "Don't play coy, Hurricane. You spent all night squirming like you were left sitting in wet panties. Now, I want to watch while you finally give your body what it's been begging for."

His breath fans over my skin as he brings his face closer

while lowering my hand between us. His fingers cup mine as he lays them over my damp panties. He gives me a knowing look. "I want to taste how sweet you are before I stretch this wet little pussy and mark you as mine."

My breathing hitches.

"What if I don't want to be yours?"

Through some sort of miracle, I manage to keep the blatant desire I feel for him out of my voice.

His responding grin is nothing short of merciless.

Ducking his head, his nose drags up the column of my throat. "I'm afraid it's far too late for that." His tongue slides around the shell of my ear, a shiver cascading down my spine. "Don't get me wrong, I tried to stay away. Tried to ignore your allure. For your sake." He exhales a dark chuckle. "But I don't have that kind of restraint. Never did."

His fingers skate down my side, slow and deliberate. "When I want something, I take it. And I want *you*, Dylan." His teeth graze my jaw, his grip tightening. "So, you can fight it all you want, Hurricane. Pretend you don't feel this." His thumb drags over my racing pulse. "But we both know the truth. You're already mine."

As if to emphasize his point, he pushes against my fingers, forcing them to drag over the evidence of how *little* I feel for him before scraping against my swollen clit.

I can't help the gasp that leaves me. The molten desire that floods me.

"Fuck your fingers, Little Steelhawk. I want to watch while you come."

He's already dragging my panties down my legs, and I'm helpless to obey, because I want this too. I *need* it. With my gaze locked on his, I use the pads of my fingers to rub my clit, my breathing coming in short pants at the delicious friction, before I push a finger inside.

Griffin's gaze drops to between my spread thighs, and the groan that rips from his lips is strained and gritty, only ratcheting my desire higher. I add a second finger, the wet sounds of my excitement mingling with our heavy breathing in the otherwise silent room.

"That's it, sweetheart. Fuck yourself for me."

I rock beneath him. His fingers clench the sheet on either side of my head, the muscles in his forearms bulging with the restraint of holding himself back. But that's not what I want. I can't be the only one letting go.

"Touch me."

His eyes blaze as they snap back to mine. "Where?"

I'm so hot. So on edge. "Anywhere. *Everywhere.*"

One hand immediately comes to the outside of my knee, sliding over my skin as he climbs upward. Palming the back of my thigh, he hitches it over his hip, opening me up further and enabling me to go deeper. The searing heat of his palm glides over my ass next, squeezing the globe, and we both groan.

"More."

I'm breathless, the wet squelching sound between my thighs growing louder with every inch of skin he claims as his. The entire time, he doesn't look away from my face, as my eyes roll back and I arch my spine. "I'm so close." I don't know if it's a warning or a plea.

"Come for me, Hurricane. All I've been able to think about is the look on your face and the noises you make, and I need a second fix."

His other hand joins the fray, sliding beneath my top until he cups my breast. He kneads the skin, squeezing as I reach the peak. When he pinches my nipple, I explode. My head falls back, teeth clenched to keep from screaming as my body grinds on nothing and I chase my release.

Before I can catch my breath, his lips are on mine. Hungry. Devouring. "Fuck, I don't think I'll ever get enough of that."

His body lowers over mine, the rough fabric of his jeans dragging over my swollen, sensitive clit and eliciting a moan. I could totally go for round two, and a dark, dirty part of me has wanted to know what it would feel like to have Griffin inside of me since he got me off in the gym.

However, I gather enough self-control to press a palm against his chest and push. He lifts up, staring down at me with that unreadable expression. It's mildly terrifying. "We can't." I attempt to push myself upright, but he doesn't move back any farther, so it only brings our faces an inch apart. "Not tonight."

Mostly because I don't know what to make of his declaration, and also a little bit because there isn't just him. I've kissed Jax and Finn. More so, I have somewhat complicated feelings for not only them, but Ethan too. It's...a mess. One I'm not looking to add to by jumping into bed with Griffin.

He stares at me for so long that I expect him to go full caveman and say no and claim me anyway. It's also super fucked up how turned on I get at the thought of that. But eventually, he backs away. "Not tonight," is all he says. He bends to retrieve my panties off the floor, and thinking he's going to help me back into them, I'm about to tell him I'll just grab a fresh pair, when he brings them to his nose and inhales. "These are mine now." His words are mostly a growl as he stuffs the fabric in his jeans pocket.

All I can do is gape at him. *Okay, that was super fucking hot!* But also... "You owe me a new pair."

He simply shrugs. "Get into bed."

Still riding the endorphin high, I do as he says, slipping beneath the sheets.

"Uh, what are you doing?" I question when he begins stripping out of his clothes.

"As much as I enjoyed that little show, I didn't risk breaking my neck climbing in your window so I could get you off. Now, move over."

"You're not staying."

"That's exactly what I'm doing," he counters. "No way am I letting you sleep alone when that fuck could come into your room at any time."

I gesture toward my door. "I have a lock."

He scoffs. "Not enough."

"So what, you're going to sneak into my room every night?" I argue, incredulous.

"Until he's out of here or I can convince you to move into my place, yes."

I shake my head. "Griffin, that's not practical."

"And yet, it's what's happening. So move over. We have practice in the morning."

I know how immovable Griffin is when he sets his mind to something, so instead of wasting more time arguing, I simply slide over, giving him space to climb in beside me.

Turning my back to him, I move all the way to the edge of the bed, making it clear that I don't agree with this arrangement and that nothing other than sleep is going to happen.

He chuckles, showing a complete lack for personal boundaries as he follows me across the bed until his heat envelops my back and his body is wrapped around mine. His arm tightens around my waist, pulling me flush against him, his breath hot in my ear as he whispers, "Sweet dreams, Hurricane."

Perhaps it's Griffin's presence beside me or knowing I'm not alone, after everything that has happened, but I sleep like a baby that night.

TWENTY-NINE

THE MOMENT I step out of class and see Jax leaning against the opposite wall, arms crossed and an easy smirk playing at his lips, I roll my eyes.

"This is stupid," I tell him, adjusting the strap of my bag over my shoulder. "Surely you have something better to be doing than waiting for me?" It's only been a couple of days and I'm already over having the guys wait on me. It can't be fun for them, and not having a moment to myself throughout the day is grating on my nerves.

He shrugs, pushing off the wall and falling into step beside me as we leave the building and move out into the crisp autumn day. It's early afternoon, and I stare up at the trees whose leaves have turned a vibrant red and orange as I pull up the zipper of my jacket to combat the cold chill in the air.

"Can't think of anything better I could be doing than making sure you're safe," Jax says easily. I know he doesn't mean anything by it, but his words sting nonetheless. Like this is just an obligation, another shift in the babysitting rotation. Which is the crux of the problem, because it niggles at me that the only reason any of them are spending time with me is because they feel obligated to. Because Ethan has *told* them to.

My stomach knots, a frown slipping over my face before I hurriedly wipe it blank. "I don't need you guys hanging around because you think you have to. If you don't want to be here, then don't." I flick my fingers over our surroundings in a *go, be free* motion.

Instead of accepting my dismissal, Jax stops in his tracks, uncaring that we are in the middle of a busy path and he is forcing students to divert around us.

He snatches my wrist, forcing me to stop and face him. His brown eyes darken, any trace of amusement vanishing. "You think I'm here because I have to be?" That gaze holds mine, rich and intense, his hand coming to rest possessively on the side of my throat as he brings his face close to mine. "Dylan, I'm here because I want to be. Because I need to be. Because your safety matters to me. *You* matter to me."

My breath catches. Everything about Jax is deep, raw...all or nothing. He's not the kind of guy to do something half-assed. When he sets his sights on something, he's all in.

I don't know how to respond, so I don't. I just hold his gaze, my pulse hammering beneath his touch.

His fingers squeeze against my skin, a reflex, a need.

"You're important to me, Menace. More important than you can even imagine. More important than *I* even realized until you walked into the house the other night, battered and bruised and barely conscious, scaring the absolute shit out of me." His fingers stroke across my skin, soft and coaxing. Comforting. "I don't give a shit what you've got going on with Griffin. Or with the others. All I want is you. Nothing is going to change that."

He doesn't give me the chance to process his words, never mind respond, before he leans in and kisses me. Right there, in the middle of campus, for anyone to see. It's not soft or tentative

—it's a public claiming. A declaration. His lips move against mine with a confidence that leaves me dizzy, and for a moment, I forget everything. Forget the people walking past, forget the bruises that still mark my skin, forget the mess of emotions tangling inside me.

Jax pulls back, his breath warm against my lips. "So, what now?" I murmur, my voice unsteady.

His smirk returns, this time edged with something wicked. "How long until your next class?"

"I've got a couple of hours."

"That should be enough time."

Sliding his fingers between mine, he tugs me along the path behind him. "Enough time for what?" I call after him, lengthening my stride to keep up with his long legs.

Turning to meet my gaze, he winks. "You'll see."

Increasing his pace, I practically have to jog to keep up with him as he leads me through campus and toward the hockey arena. It's empty at this time of day, the quiet stretching around us as we slip inside.

"Jax, what—"

"Nope. No questions," he orders, pushing me toward the locker room. "You keep a swimsuit in your locker, right?"

"Yeah?"

"Damn," he teases with a smirk. "There goes any ideas about skinny dipping."

"What?" I'm thoroughly confused about what's happening.

Shaking his head, he nudges me toward my locker. "Just get changed."

Shaking my head, I do as he says, stripping down and pulling on my black swimsuit. When I turn around, I freeze. All of the saliva in my mouth dries up.

Jax is shirtless, wearing only a pair of swimming trunks that hang low on his hips. My gaze trails over his broad shoulders, the defined cut of his abs, and the way his muscles flex as he runs a hand through his hair. My stomach flips, heat curling low as my eyes travel south, to the powerful thighs and sharp V-line disappearing beneath his waistband.

Holy hotcakes. He is a fucking *Adonis.*

He catches me staring and smirks. "See something you like?"

I force my face into a scowl, snapping my gaze to his. "Obnoxiousness is not a pretty quality."

His grin only broadens, a twinkle sparking in his eyes. "And yet, *you* find it attractive."

"Pretty sure that's not what has my attention right now."

He swaggers closer with all the confidence of a man who knows exactly how hot he is. It should be disgusting, a total turn-off, but his confidence is sexy as hell.

"Well, you better find something else to focus on or we're not leaving this locker room before your next class."

"Mm. You make that sound like a bad thing."

"Definitely not," he disagrees, flicking a strand of hair off my face. "But I have something else in mind for right now."

I huff, but before I can verbalize my protest, he takes my hand again and leads me down the hall and into a room lined with hot and cold therapy tubs. He flips a switch, filling one with steaming water.

"This will help with muscle recovery," he explains. "Improve your mobility and ease the tension you're carrying."

I don't argue. A warm bath sounds like heaven. Moving toward the tub, I throw my leg over the side and step into the hot water. A sigh slips from my lips as I sink into the warm heat. Immediately, I can feel it melting the stiffness from my body, and I let my head tip back, eyes closing as Jax joins me.

A comforting silence settles between us, the only sound the faint hum of the heater and occasional ripple as Jax shifts in the water. I allow myself to fall into the soothing comfort, to focus on relaxing my muscles and letting the heat of the water work its magic.

All the while, the weight of Jax's gaze presses into me, warm and unwavering. Eventually, I peel my eyes open. He didn't turn on the bright overhead lights when we came in, and his brown eyes are molten in the dim light, their depths swirling with something unreadable. They trace over my face, lingering on my cheekbones, my lips, the bruises still staining my skin.

"What?" I ask, feeling somewhat self-conscious.

His voice is quiet, but heavy with meaning. "You."

I scoff, gesturing at my beat-up face. "Right. I'm a fucking masterpiece."

Jax doesn't smile. Doesn't look away as he shifts closer in the water. "You are." His hand lifts, fingers ghosting over a particularly dark mark near my jaw. "These don't diminish you. They don't take away from who you are. If anything, they show how goddamn strong you are. I saw it that first day in the locker room and again when you marched into our house like you owned the place." He shakes his head, a fond smile playing at the corners of his lips. "You faced down an entire team of guys who were determined to prove you wrong, and you basically told us all to fuck off. That takes balls."

I snort-laugh, the sound cutting off as he inches closer. The water shifts between us, swishing as he moves to crouch in front of me, so close that his thighs brush mine as he brackets my legs. His hands land just above my knees, rough and reassuring as he squeezes them before sliding them higher.

His gaze remains steadfast on mine as his sure, confident hands reach my hips, fingers curling around my waist and holding tight. Surging forward, he lifts himself out of the water until he's hovering over me.

I follow the path of a droplet as it slides down his chest

before dripping onto my skin, right beneath my clavicle. It ignites a spark of heat that spreads outward, and when I glance up, I find Jax staring at the same spot. Desire has his pupils blown wide before he ducks his head.

When his lips meet my skin, it knocks the air from my lungs. His tongue flicks out to catch the droplet, and I gasp, one hand coming to rest on his broad shoulder while the other slides into the soft, short strands of his hair. "Oh," I moan, tilting my head to grant him access as he licks higher.

My blood heats with every stroke, every rough drag of his tongue over my sensitive skin. His tongue is nothing short of explosive. My grip on him tightens, fingernails digging into his scalp as though fearful he might retreat and leave me hungry for more. We've been dancing around this flame for so long now, and I'm sick of dampening it. I want to add gasoline to the fire and feel every singe, to burn as it blazes.

His hands slide up my sides, light and careful over my bruises. He skims the sides of my breasts, his touch teasing, before running his palms over my shoulders and up my neck. I sink lower in the water, spreading my legs as far as he'll let me. It's a blatant invitation, one I hope he will accept because I am fucking *dying* for his touch where I need it most.

"Jax," I murmur. A prayer. A plea.

Lifting his face to mine, our gazes clash before he captures my lips with his. This kiss is different. Slower, deeper. It's a kiss that says everything words can't. That I'm not broken. That he sees me. That he wants me, bruises and all.

That maybe, just maybe, I'm not as alone as I thought.

My hands slide down the front of his chest, fingers trailing over the ridges of his abdomen before slipping beneath the fabric of his trunks. I pull on the elastic, letting it snap back against his skin.

He leans back just enough to look me in the eye, arching a brow. "More," I demand.

He huffs a chuckle. "You're bruised," he reminds me.

Holding his gaze, I play along the waistband of his trunks before grabbing a firm hold of the wet fabric. "With all due respect, I don't give a fuck." Then I yank them down his legs. His cock springs free, thick and engorged and begging to be sucked.

For a moment, I just stare at it, licking my lips. *Oh yeah, this is exactly what I needed.*

Reaching down, Jax wraps his hand around the base of his cock. Slowly, erotically, he pumps himself while I unashamedly drool. "This what you want?" he taunts, fisting himself as precum beads at his tip.

I nod.

"Are you planning to just stare at it, or are you going to deal with this problem you've created?"

Wetting my lips, I lean forward. Mouth parted, I flick my tongue over the smooth head of his cock. Saltiness sparks over the surface before I drag my lips down his shaft. I take as much of him as I can, moaning when I can't physically fit any more of him in my mouth.

"Fuck," he hisses, one hand sliding into my hair. "Do you have any idea how gorgeous you look right now?" I flick my gaze up to meet his, and he smirks. "Go on then, Little Menace. Show me just how dirty this mouth of yours can get."

Challenge accepted.

Planting my feet on the bottom of the tub, I dig my fingernails into the tight globes of his ass, making him chuckle before it turns into a pained hiss when I hollow my cheeks and suck on all six inches of his erection that I can feasibly fit in my mouth.

"Shit, Menace. Fuck." His hand tightens in my hair as I work him over, his hips shifting as he struggles to keep himself still. That's not what I want, though. I want him to let go. To use me. To show me the dark, dominant side I know is hidden beneath that reserved facade he wears.

When he fails to give me what I want, I slap his ass. Hard.

He chuckles, the sound dark and intoxicating. Pulling on my hair, he purrs, "You want it rough, baby?"

My responding yes is in the form of my teeth scraping lightly over the sensitive skin of his dick.

His smirk is a filthy promise before he says, "Hold on."

With my fingers digging into his hips, he thrusts forward. My air is cut off, tears gathering along my lash line as drool trickles down my chin.

"That's it, Menace. You're doing so good," he praises, thrusting into my mouth. "So fucking tight. You feel so fucking good, baby. No idea how many times I've got myself off just thinking about these fucking lips wrapped around me."

My nipples are rock hard, and I shift uncomfortably. I'm so turned on by him taking what he wants, by the dirty mouth on him.

"Am I coming down your throat or on your face, Menace?" His voice is strained, betraying how close he is. I tap my finger once against his hip.

"Filthy girl," he praises, before burying himself in the back of my throat and unloading.

I swallow every drop of his cum as he strokes my hair and murmurs words of affection. Cleaning him up, I release him with a pop. He doesn't give me a second before sliding his hands beneath my thighs and spinning us. I squeal in surprise, clinging to him with a death grip. Water sloshes as he drops down where I was just sitting and pulls me onto his lap.

Fingers pinching my chin, he pulls my face to his. His tongue sweeps into my mouth, and his moan is the hottest thing ever as he tastes himself.

I meet each stroke of his tongue with a hungry one of my own as I settle onto his lap. Our moans entwine in a symphony of sound as I grind against him. I feel when he grows hard again, smirking into his kiss.

"Someone's feeling cocky," he teases, nipping at my lips.

"I've got a good reason to be."

"Mmm." He pulls me back in for another kiss, this one hungry and desperate.

I reach between us, pulling the fabric of my swimsuit aside.

"We don't need to—" he begins, pushing me back enough to slow our pace. His gaze searches mine. "This isn't about sex for me."

"I know," I assure him, stroking a finger down the side of his face. "Which is exactly why I want to." I push back the strand of hair that is always falling into his eyes. "I trust you, Jax. I trust you with my body. I trust you to make me feel good."

His hand is already skimming my thigh beneath the water, before sliding to cup my pussy. Stroking his fingers through my folds, he pushes two inside me while promising, "I'm going to make you feel so good, Menace."

With that, the slow pace between us is obliterated. Our mouths crash together in a clash of teeth while he fucks me with his fingers, and I grind against his hard cock.

"Oh God, Jax," I moan, arching my back and pushing my tits into his face. Frantic and hungry, he pulls at the strap of my swimsuit. Something tears, but neither of us gives a shit as my breast pops free and he wraps his lips around my nipple, sucking on the sensitive flesh. "Yes."

Head thrown back, I chase my release as it creeps closer with every curl of Jax's fingers, every swirl of his tongue, and press of his lips. He knows how to play my body perfectly.

He licks a path up my chest. "I'm right there, Jax," I pant. "Don't stop."

His fingers wrap around my throat, pulling me forward until our eyes connect. Grinding the heel of his palm against my clit, he wiggles a third finger inside me and growls, "Come for me, Menace." I can't look away from the sheer intensity brimming in his eyes. The passion, the lust, the affection. It holds me captive as I unravel before him, mouth parting on a cry as every muscle in my body contracts and pleasure explodes along my nerves.

"Fuck, Menace," Jax groans, burying his face in my neck. He lines himself up at my entrance, and I clench in anticipation. "You need to tell me right now if you want me to stop—"

"Don't you fucking dare." Pulling him back by his hair, I hold him captive, staring him straight in the eye as I sink onto him.

"Ooh," I moan as he groans.

"Dyl." His voice is pulled thin, his entire body locked up tight. "Holy fuck."

"Agreed." I slowly lift onto my knees before lowering myself back down. We both sigh.

Leaning back, I rest my hands on his knees. I watch his face as I lift and lower myself onto his cock. The entire time, he stares, transfixed at where we connect. His hands slide up and down my thighs, and when he lifts his gaze, his palms follow, gliding over my hips and up my abdomen.

"You're a fucking vision," he murmurs, enraptured.

Dragging my other strap down my arm, he pulls on the stretchy fabric of my swimsuit until my other breast spills out, before cupping them in his hands, kneading and squeezing until I'm moaning and clenching around him.

"You look so fucking sexy getting yourself off on my cock. Do you feel good, Menace?"

His gaze lifts to mine. "So good."

Plucking my nipple with rough fingers, his other hand falls

to where his cock is filling me, and he begins to rub circles around my clit.

"Oh God," I whimper, my rhythm faltering. "Yes. Jax. Right there."

His hand on my hip encourages my movements as he thrusts deeper, the two of us circling that peak. Water sloshes around us, the noise mixing with the sounds of our pleasure.

"Baby, I'm so close," Jax rasps.

"Me too."

"Fuck." He hisses, taking over control as he grabs both my hips and holds me still while he thrusts up into me. He fucks me hard. Relentlessly, until I'm clamping down around him and my fingernails are scraping along his skin, and I can't contain it any longer.

With one more thrust, he explodes inside of me. It triggers my own release, and I cry out as pleasure radiates through my body, leaving me boneless and panting in its wake.

I collapse against him, heaving and exhausted. His arms casually wrap around me, fingers drawing light circles on my damp skin. The pull of bruised muscles that I'd managed to block out comes racing back with a vengeance, and I groan as I drag myself upright.

"You okay?" Jax asks, pushing hair back from my face and looking me over with concern.

"Worth it." I give him a crooked smile.

Shaking his head, he chastises, "I didn't invite you in here to get into your pants. This was supposed to be relaxing."

"I dunno about you," I say, sliding off him and curling into his side. "But I'm feeling pretty damn relaxed."

With a sigh, he gives up, draping his arm around me and pulling me in against him while we catch our breaths. In no hurry to leave, we curl up in the warm water. Every so often, his lips brush my hairline, and I relax into him with a soft smile on my lips, thinking it's been a long time since I've felt this content.

"Oh shit," Jax curses when we finally make it back to the locker room. He shows me his phone screen, or more specifically, the thirteen missed calls from Ethan.

"Someone's in trouble," I tease, grabbing my own phone from where I left it. I cringe when I see I have a similar number of missed calls.

Glancing over my shoulder, Jax scoffs, "At least I won't be alone in the doghouse." He presses a quick kiss to my shoulder before dialing Ethan.

"Hey, man." He doesn't get a chance to say anything more before I hear Ethan's voice on the other end, most likely chewing Jax out for not answering his phone. "Yeah, yeah, she's fine. She was...we were working on some easy stretches."

Glancing at him over my shoulder, I arch a brow, and he smirks in return.

"It was on silent. As soon as I realized, I called you back." He rolls his eyes before turning away. "Ethan, man. She's fine. I wouldn't let anything happen to her."

I grimace. Ethan has become a tad overbearing, checking in constantly. He was probably on the verge of an aneurysm before Jax called him back.

Leaving him to his telling off, I grab my clothes and duck into the shower to rinse off. When I return, Jax is off the phone and has a towel wrapped around his waist.

"Get your ass chewed out?"

He grins, stepping forward and kissing my lips before parroting my words from earlier. "Worth it."

THIRTY

I WAKE WITH A START. The hard wood of the doorframe digs into my spine, the stiffness in my neck a sharp reminder that I haven't slept in a bed for too many nights in a row. But how could I sleep peacefully knowing I've left Dylan unprotected?

I groan as I roll my shoulders, stretching out the aches and pains that are becoming a familiar part of my morning routine. I'm scrubbing a hand over my face when the door creaks open. Dylan steps out, her eyes widening when she sees me slumped there.

"Ethan?" She glances around in search of some explanation. "Uh, what are you doing out here?"

I shift, getting to my feet and wiping the last remnants of sleep from my eyes. "I was waiting for Kyle to get home last night," I mutter by way of explanation. She doesn't need to know that I've slept outside her door like a puppy begging for scraps since the night of her attack, even when I know Kyle is tucked up in his own bed down the hall. "Must've dozed off."

Crossing her arms, she scowls at me in displeasure. "You shouldn't be sleeping out here. You've got a game on Friday; you need your rest."

"It was one night, Thorn. Won't kill me." I look away, swiping a hand through my mussed-up hair so she won't see the lie on my face.

Her lips flatten, and she holds my gaze for a moment. It affords me the opportunity to analyze the bruising on her face. While it's healing, it still looks painful, and it's an effort not to wince. I wish I could take away her pain, the reminder she must experience every time she looks in the mirror.

Before I can do something stupid like apologize—*again*—something that only serves to rile her up every time I do, she shakes her head before moving past me and heading down the stairs. Breathing out a sigh, I head into the bathroom to shower off the stiff ache in my muscles before getting dressed for the day.

Guilt gnaws on my bones the entire time. It's become a constant companion, a shadow that follows me everywhere. I should have seen it coming. I should have known what Reed, Fletcher, and Monroe were doing wasn't just regular locker room shit.

I should have stopped it before it got this far.

Making my way downstairs, I hear voices in the kitchen. Dylan's and—

Shit.

I speed up, skipping the last few steps altogether.

"You should pack up and leave BSU while you still can," I hear Kyle say before I make my presence known.

I step into the room, gaze narrowed on Reed as I place myself between him and Dylan. "Walk away, Kyle."

He smirks, that arrogant one he's always worn that says *you can't touch me*. Unlike me, Kyle comes from money. It bought him his spot at BSU, although thankfully not his position on the team. Coach would never sell out like that. However, it did afford him the best hockey coaches and trainers money can buy.

Enough to make him a solid hockey player. He's not exceptional. Not like Finn, Jax, Griffin, or Dylan. He doesn't have the raw talent or drive that they do—like *we* do. He's used to money buying him whatever he wants, and for the first time in his life, he's discovering that money can't buy everything. It can't buy Coach, and it won't buy him his way back onto the starting lineup. Not at BSU, anyway.

"Relax, Cap. We're just having a friendly chat."

"I *said* walk away. Now, Reed."

For a second, he holds my gaze, like he's debating pushing his luck. Then, with a scoff, he grabs his coffee and saunters out, leaving me standing there, vibrating with barely restrained fury.

I'm wound so tight that when someone shoves my shoulder, I whirl on them, ready to put them in their place. That is, until I'm met with all five-foot-eight of lean, brown-haired fierceness.

"What the hell was that?" Dylan demands with a wicked glower. "I had that perfectly under control before you came barging in here all caveman-like."

"I was not—"

"I don't need you stepping in every time he opens his goddamn mouth."

"I'm not letting him get in your head."

She lets out a bitter laugh. "He's been in my head for weeks, Ethan. It's not something you can fix by playing bodyguard."

Crowding her, I growl, "I can make sure he doesn't get another chance to hurt you."

"I can take care of myself," she insists, infuriating me further.

"Yeah? And look how that turned out." The second the words leave my mouth, I know they're the wrong thing to say. Dylan goes still, her jaw tightening as hurt flashes in her eyes before she locks it down.

"Screw you," she mutters before stalking out of the kitchen.

"Shit." I slap my hand against the countertop, shoulders hunched as I bow my head. I shouldn't have said that. I let my own fears, my own insecurities, get the better of me. It probably doesn't help that I haven't had a decent sleep for three consecutive nights.

Raking a hand through my hair, I check the time before breathing out hard. *Great.* I don't even have time to apologize right now because we need to leave for class. I'll just have to find time later to pull her aside and make up for my idiocy.

SEVERAL MINUTES after I told them to arrive, Fletcher and Monroe walk into the meeting room. "Where is everyone?" Monroe muses. Like clueless chickens, they both look around the empty room.

I make my presence known. Not giving them time to process, I shove Fletcher against the wall, forearm pressing hard against his throat. He lets out a grunt, eyes flashing with shock before it turns to anger. Monroe takes a step forward, but I cut him a look that stops him cold.

"Don't even think about it."

The air in the room shifts, the weight of my authority settling over them like a threat. Pinning each of them with my stare, I keep my voice even, but there's no mistaking the edge in it, as I demand, "Where were you the night Dylan was attacked?"

Fletcher's brow furrows. "What?"

I press harder against his windpipe. "Don't play dumb with me," I hiss, spittle hitting his cheek. "Where the hell were you?" Glancing Monroe's way, I add, "Both of you."

"Dude," Monroe protests. "We don't even know what night you're talking about."

I'm two fucking seconds away from punching one of them in the fucking face. Shoving my arm into Fletcher's throat until he chokes, I step back, worried I will do exactly that and cause an even greater mess. In-fighting is not something I tolerate. It's not something Coach will tolerate, and there's already enough fucking hostility without adding to it.

Fletcher's eyes flick to the side, the two of them sharing a fleeting look. Then Monroe shrugs. "We were at The Stanley."

My jaw tics. It's the answer I expected. The party line Reed has been touting. Doesn't mean it doesn't piss me off. Not when I highly suspect Dylan is right that these two were involved in her attack. Nothing else makes sense and they are the type of pathetic pissants to be pissed at a girl joining the team and immediately being better than them.

"You've been hassling Dylan all season," I spit. "On and off the ice."

Fletcher scoffs, rubbing at his throat. "Since when was hazing against the rules?"

"You know damn fucking well what you're doing goes beyond hazing," I snap, glaring at each of them. "Not to mention that it went against my orders to leave her be."

"She can't just come in here and take our spots!" Monroe stupidly protests.

"She can and has," I retort, giving him a less-than-impressed once-over. "And last I checked, you could barely maintain your position on the third line, never mind riding the first." I glance between them, knowingly. "Or are we specifically talking about Kyle's spot?"

The crack of Monroe's jaw snapping shut is audible. Strangely, neither of them has anything to say about that. Their silence says everything I need to know.

"It is not our place to question Coach's decision. He wants Dylan on the team; it's our job to include her and ensure we have the best team possible so we can go all the way this year. From what I've seen so far of Dylan's talent and skill, Coach made the right call. If Kyle has a problem with that, he can bring it to me or to Coach. He should *not* be getting you two idiots to carry out his dirty work, and he sure as shit should not be targeting Dylan." I shake my head, sneering at the two of them. "The fact that you'd go after a defenseless woman and attack her in a dark parking lot is disgusting. You should be locked up in a jail cell."

"We didn't—" Fletcher splutters. Panic widens his eyes. Good. He deserves to feel even a minuscule amount of the fear Dylan must have felt that night. If it were up to me, they'd each find out exactly what it feels like to be targeted like that, alone and outnumbered.

"Don't finish that fucking sentence!" I bellow, jabbing a finger his way. "Don't finish that *fucking sentence* unless you want to lose some teeth today." I spare Monroe a glance, ensuring he knows he's included in my threat. "If I find out you were involved in her attack in any way or that you've continued to harass her, you'll both be done."

Monroe glares. "You can't—"

"Try me," I snap. "You so much as look at her funny, and you won't set foot on the ice for the rest of the season."

Fletcher sneers. "You can't make that call."

My hands fist at my sides. "You think Coach won't back me on this? Go ahead. Test it. See what happens."

Neither of them speaks. They know I mean every word.

They share an uneasy look, sparing me a final glance before they move toward the door.

I step into their path. My expression is one of pure menace, the threat in my tone very fucking real. "I just want to clarify. When I say you'll be done, I don't just mean on the ice. I mean at this university." I step closer. "On this fucking planet. You won't breathe another breath of fucking air if I find out you've laid a single fucking finger on that girl. Disobey my order again and see what fucking happens."

Wide-eyed, they race out of the room like the hounds of hell are on their asses. Alone, I blow out a harsh breath.

The sound of slow clapping has me whirling toward the door as Griffin steps into view. "That was beautiful," he taunts with a triumphant smirk. "Didn't know you had it in you."

"Fuck off," I grumble, half-heartedly. "You've seen me go after guys on the ice."

"Sure," Griffin shrugs. "But I don't see skates on your feet right now, Mr. Diplomatic."

Twisting my head, I crack my neck in a bid to relieve some of the tension. "Yeah, well, some people heed action better than words."

And I have no fucking problem going as far as I need to when it comes to protecting Dylan.

THIRTY-ONE

THURSDAY NIGHT and it's the first night since my attack that I've been left by myself. I feel like that kid in *Home Alone*. The parents are out of town, and there's so much I could get up to that I don't even know where to start.

Perhaps that's why I've made plans to go to Wren's.

Or maybe it's because I've gotten used to sitting on the couch playing video games with Jax or dissecting a game with Ethan before crawling into bed beside Griffin, and with none of them here, the house feels strangely empty.

With the first game of the season tomorrow night, there is a team meeting and final practice this evening, which has them all busy. Since Kyle, Fletcher, and Monroe will all be there, they determined it would be *safe* for me to stay home alone. Although it was clear Ethan did *not* like the idea. Pretty sure, if it were up to him, he'd have dragged me to the meeting with them. But there's no need for me to be there. Honestly, it just pisses me off every time I have to sit on that bench and watch Kyle skate by with his smug fucking smirk that I want to slice straight off his face. It's making me homicidal, which is not a good thing, especially for a hockey player. Our temperaments already run high, I don't need to add gasoline to the flames.

Dressed in leggings, boots, and an oversized, slouchy sweater, I check myself in the mirror before grabbing my phone and keys off my desk and heading out of my room. I'm careful to lock my bedroom door in case Kyle gets home before me, before leaving the house.

Starting the engine of my car, I'm halfway down the street when my phone starts ringing. The noise comes through the entertainment system, and I check the screen to see it's Ethan calling me. I frown because he should be in the middle of their meeting right now.

For a second, I consider not answering. I'm still pissed at him for what he said this morning. Although, if I'm being honest, I'm mostly pissed that he wasn't wrong. His delivery lacked any sort of tact, but, sadly...he wasn't wrong.

I hate that he wasn't. That I couldn't take care of myself. That once again, I found myself in a position of weakness.

The fact that we argued over the fact he wants to protect me is stupid. He just...pisses me off sometimes. Most of the time. I'm in a constant war between fighting for my independence and letting them help.

Blowing out a breath, I answer the call before it rings out. "Everything okay?"

"You tell me. Where are you going, Thorn?"

I hit the brakes, pulling over to the curb and looking around me. *What the fuck?*

"Do you have someone watching me?" I accuse, feeling the rage mount. "Is it that little freshman? Is he watching the house?"

He scoffs. "I don't need to have anyone watching the house."

"Then how?"

"Where are you going, Thorn?" he repeats.

"None of your fucking business," I snap, throwing the car in gear and continuing down the street, fuming. Did I just say arguing with him was stupid, 'cause I change my mind. Arguing with him is a necessity to ensure he doesn't take control of my entire fucking life. My hands clench around the wheel, and my foot definitely presses down on the pedal harder than usual.

A few minutes later, I pull up outside Wren's.

"Ah, Wren's. You could have just said that." There's a hint of smugness in his voice that has me wishing we were face to face so I could slap him.

"How do you fucking know that?" I demand, looking around me once more, before my gaze latches on to my phone. Tilting my head, I glare at it. "Are you tracking me right now?!"

"Shouldn't leave your phone unattended."

I rack my brain before remembering I left my phone on the coffee table while I ran to the bathroom during a video game marathon the other night.

"It's password protected," I argue futilely, since clearly he managed to get past it.

"Yeah, you should really be more careful about who you let see you type in your password. Your social awareness skills are terrifying."

Are you fucking kidding me right now?

"Fuck you," I snap, irritated beyond belief as I snatch up my phone and go to change the password so a certain controlling psychopath of a captain can't have unfettered access to my personal crap.

"There," I state triumphantly when I'm done. "Try getting in now, asshole."

"I don't need access to your phone, Thorn. I already know where you are at all times."

"You do realize how insane that sounds, right? You sound like a deranged stalker."

"I'm just trying to keep you safe," he argues, frustration bleeding through.

"Yeah, by invading my personal space."

"Well, clearly I can't trust you. You said you were staying in tonight."

I throw my hands up. "Plans change. What's it matter since the three guys we know attacked me are *with you*?"

"It matters because if something happened to you, I wouldn't know about it." For the first time since I answered his call, he loses his cool and snaps at me, his voice downright menacing. It actually leaves me speechless, gaping at my phone in shock. "I wouldn't know where you are or be able to get to you. I don't give a fuck if it invades your privacy," he continues. "I don't give a fuck how it makes me look. If it keeps you safe, then you can bet your ass I'm going to do it."

I still haven't located my voice when he snaps, "Stay at Wren's until one of us comes to get you."

"I don't need—"

"So help me, Dylan, if you disobey me on this, I'm going to bend you over my knee and smack your ass until it's red."

Now I'm speechless *and* turned on.

"Enjoy your night," he says, all signs of hostility gone before he hangs up.

Well, fuck me. That was...unexpected.

I'm still reeling from our conversation when I step into Wren's apartment.

"What's wrong?" she demands upon seeing my face.

"Ethan has been tracking my phone. He called as soon as I left the house tonight, demanding to know where I was going."

Her eyes round in surprise. "Well, that's..." I expect her to say fucked up, insane, over the top. One of the many thoughts that went through my head, but instead she shocks the shit out of me by saying, "So hot."

"Wait, what?" I must have heard her wrong.

"The guy is *so* into you that he broke into your phone so he could track you?" she explains. "That's like." She begins fanning herself. "Stupid sexy."

"You need help," I tell her bluntly, moving to collapse onto her sofa. "Like real, psychiatric help."

Unfazed by my assessment of her, Wren shrugs, before grabbing the margarita she poured for herself and offering me a bottle of beer from her fridge. I typically try not to drink during the season, but since I'm not playing this week, I accept it. Besides, I think I'm owed a drink after this fucking week and tonight's revelation.

"He's only doing it because he thinks it's his duty to protect me," I tell her. "I think he blames himself for what happened."

"*Or,*" she emphasizes, "and hear me out here. But he might be doing it because he actually *likes* you."

After my admission to her the other day, she has been on a mission to convince me Ethan has feelings and that I should start some sort of group relationship with them all. Ha. As if that sort of thing actually works in real life.

I groan, my head falling back against the sofa as I nurse my beer. "You need to stop with that. Ethan hasn't once hinted at anything beyond friendship. I need to be focused on him as my captain—on building trust there. Especially after Lucas."

Wren makes a fake gagging noise. "That wretched snake. Let's not ruin a perfectly good night by talking about *that* asshole." Reaching forward to grab the remote, I see she's already got a movie lined up for us. "Time will tell with Ethan, and when it does, you can expect my *I told you so*," is her final remark before she presses play, cutting off any denial on my part.

I fall asleep halfway through the movie, thanks to the pain meds I'm on and the one beer I drank. I wake to the buzzing of my phone. Yawning, I blink my eyes open as I stretch. Wren is curled up beside me, a blanket tucked over us, while she scrolls through her phone.

"Sorry." I cringe, feeling bad for falling asleep on her.

"Don't worry about it. You've had a long week."

Pulling my phone from my pocket, I find a text from Finn in the group chat Ethan set up after the attack—with him, Finn, Jax, Griffin, and now me.

> FINN
>
> Time to go. Get your ass down here.

CHARMING. Just for that, I take my sweet time using the bathroom and drinking a glass of water to wake myself up before saying goodbye to Wren and making my way downstairs.

"Finally," he grunts, pushing himself off the side of my car when he spots me. "Took you long enough."

"I didn't ask you to come get me," I snap at him, not appreciating his attitude for one second. "If you've got a problem with it, take it up with Ethan since he's the one who deems me incapable of driving myself home alone, even though—news flash!—I've been driving myself to and from places for *years* without issue."

"Can we just get in the car?" he says tiredly. "I'm too fucking exhausted for this."

Without saying another word, I unlock the doors and we both climb in. His head falls back against the headrest, eyes drifting shut as I turn on the engine.

"Rough practice?" I ask as I pull onto the road.

"Long," he mumbles in response. He rubs at his eyes before pushing himself more upright and staring steadfastly out the windshield. "I was up half the night completing an assignment for my kinesiology class."

I simply nod as I navigate the quiet streets back to the house.

We're nearly home when I feel his eyes on me. "Did you have a good night?"

His question catches me by surprise. The few times Finn has been waiting for me outside class, he's been like a shadow, silently trailing me through campus and rarely engaging in conversation. He'll answer questions if I ask them, but he never asks his own, other than to know where or when my next class is.

"If you can call falling asleep and drooling all over Wren's sofa a good night, then sure."

"Your body is still healing," he says. It could be my imagination, but I swear his voice is a tad softer than before. "You need all the rest you can get."

My response is terse, born from frustration. "Yeah."

We're quiet, neither of us saying another word until I pull into the driveway. "Another few days and you'll be back on the ice." I know he means for his words to be reassuring, but they aren't.

Turning in my seat, I face him across the center console. Light from the porch casts his face half in shadow. "And then what? I wait for Kyle to come after me again? What if he doesn't stop at beating me this time? What if he breaks my arm or leg and I'm out for *weeks*? Hell, he could fracture my back or give me a concussion so bad that it has me out for the rest of the season. The rest of *my life!*"

Finn's face is pinched, anguish, concern, and skepticism all warring for first place. His lips part, but no words come out. He doesn't know what the fuck to say, because he doesn't know *who* to believe. And I get it, I do, but it doesn't make the situation any more palatable.

Giving him a free pass, I push open my door and move to climb out. He reaches across the space between us, his fingers tightening around my wrist. I pause, looking back at him. "We're not going to let them hurt you again." I can tell he means it. That it bothers him that I think he would.

"That's the problem, though, isn't it?" I say, looking him in the eye. "You shouldn't even have to promise me that. I shouldn't have to be afraid for my safety all because I want to play a game. I shouldn't have to be scared to fall asleep at night. To be left in the house alone." Leaning in, I let him see the stark fear I refuse to even let myself acknowledge most days, never mind let anyone else see. "I shouldn't have to stare into the faces of the men who attacked me every single day and know that they got away with it, and yet that's the reality we live in. Worse, it's one I don't envision changing anytime soon."

When I tug against his hold, he lets me go, and I leave him behind in the car as I walk into the house.

THIRTY-TWO

THE GYM IS empty when I step inside. It's late—super fucking late. I should be in bed, especially given my lack of sleep last night, brutal practice tonight, and the fact that we have a game tomorrow.

However, as soon as Dylan delivered her killing blow before getting out of the car, I knew I wouldn't be getting any sleep anytime soon. Instead, I'd texted Kyle to meet me at the gym and made the short walk to campus on foot.

"I shouldn't have to be afraid for my safety all because I want to play a game."

"I shouldn't have to be scared to fall asleep at night. To be left in the house alone."

"I shouldn't have to stare into the faces of the men who attacked me every single day and know that they got away with it, and yet that's the reality we live in. Worse, it's one I don't envision changing anytime soon."

Dylan's words play on repeat in my head, ripping me open and burrowing deeper with every loop.

I need to know.

I need to hear Kyle say it. That he didn't attack Dylan.

Because the truth is, I'm starting to believe Dylan's version. I'm starting to think he *could* have done it.

And what sort of shitty friend does that make me?

I met Kyle at peewee hockey camp when we were eleven, and sure, he has a bit of a temper and an arrogance issue, but introduce me to a single hockey player who doesn't have either of those things.

I know he doesn't like Dylan, but neither would I if it were my position she'd been gunning for. Disliking her doesn't mean he *attacked* her.

So yeah, I just...need to know. I need to hear it from Kyle's mouth because this tug-of-war I'm playing with myself is getting pretty fucking exhausting. I'm like an addict who keeps relapsing, going back for a fix of Dylan, only to wise up and back off until the next backslide.

While I wait for Kyle, I load up the barbell with weights before lying on the bench. Wrapping my fingers around the bar, my muscles strain as I press it up before lowering it. It's not long before my arms begin to burn, however, the repetition does nothing to clear my mind, nothing to silence the voice in my head that's been getting louder ever since Dylan shoved out of the car.

"I shouldn't have to be scared."

No. She shouldn't, and the truth is, it fucking shredded me to hear that she is. Dylan is so strong. So tough, never truly letting anyone see how she's feeling. Bar that night she was attacked, she's never once shown any fear, but I swear I caught a flicker of it in her gaze tonight.

I push myself harder, doing more reps than I'd typically do. I lose myself in the monotony of it, forcing myself to focus on the screaming of my muscles, the burn searing up my arms, the sweat dripping down my face.

A weight drops onto the bench beside me, snapping me out of my state.

"You're not going to be able to lift your stick tomorrow, never mind hold off an opponent," he comments casually.

I rack the bar, sitting up, and he tosses me a towel.

"So what has you pumping iron in the middle of the night like you're trying out for the World's Strongest Man?"

I wipe at the sweat along my forehead, my pulse pounding in my ears, though I don't know if it's from the workout or the conversation I'm about to start. "I need to ask you something."

Kyle nods as he leans forward, resting his elbows on his knees. "Shoot."

Shifting so I'm facing him, I study his expression. The sharp jawline, the confident smirk that I very rarely see him drop, even when we're alone like this. I heave out a long sigh, holding his gaze. "I need to know if you did it," I state bluntly.

His expression doesn't change. Doesn't flicker, doesn't falter. He blinks at me, head slightly cocked. "Did what?"

I grit my teeth. "You know what. Dylan. Did you—"

"Jesus, Finn." He exhales sharply, shifting on the bench as he shakes his head. He's quiet for a moment, looking off into space while his jaw tics. He rubs at his chin with his hand, huffing a humorless laugh under his breath. "I knew the others believed that little—" He cuts himself off, gaze whipping my way. "But you?" He shakes his head again, eyes still boring into mine. "I never thought you'd take a girl's word over that of your best friend." Hurt flashes across his expression, stabbing me right in the heart.

Fuck.

"Do you really think I could do something like that?" he presses.

I don't answer because the truth is, I don't know what I think anymore. A part of me genuinely thought he might confess to attacking Dylan, but sitting here looking at him, hearing the hurt in his voice, makes me second-guess myself.

Kyle sits up, lips pursing as he seems to deliberate something before saying, "Look, I know you've been playing babysitter for her. And I know she's been feeding you all sorts of bullshit, but come on, man. It's me. Do you really believe I'd throw away everything? My spot on the team, my future, my fucking life, just to go after some chick who stole my place?"

Well, fuck, when he puts it like that, it does sound extreme.

Perhaps Dylan is wrong. She saw Kyle's aggression on the ice and incorrectly assumed he'd be capable of that—and more—off of it, when in reality, she was just in the wrong place at the wrong time.

I saw for myself how mad he was when Dylan took his first-line spot. Saw the way he targeted her on the ice. And yeah, he's always been aggressive, always played on the edge of dirty, but off the ice? He's never been that guy.

At my continued silence, Kyle sighs. "I get it," he says, sounding resigned. "You don't know who to trust. She's got you all twisted up. But let me ask you something, Finn. Do you even really know this girl?"

My stomach knots, my brow furrowing. "What is that supposed to mean?"

He leans back on his hands, his posture open and relaxed now. "I got talking with Lucas after the exhibition game."

I scoff, "You expect me to believe anything *Lucas* says?"

Kyle shrugs. "I know he's a dick, but he had no reason to lie. He said Dylan was the same back when she was at NSU. She was dating Lucas, but she was also hooking up with other players on the team."

I frown, recalling my brief lapses in judgment when I've kissed her, along with other snippets I've noticed—her and Jax curled up on the sofa, the way she looks at Ethan sometimes, the feral possession in Griffin's eyes when she's in the room. Except, she's not dating any of them—of us. Not that I'm aware of anyway.

"Sound familiar?" Kyle questions, a lilt to his voice that makes me feel as though I've been a blind idiot.

"Sounds to me like Lucas is a scorned ex-boyfriend," I retort.

"Maybe," he responds easily. "But look at what she's doing here. Cracks have been forming in the team ever since she arrived. Hell, you and I have barely spoken since Roster Day, and throughout it all, she comes out smelling like roses."

I frown but remain quiet.

Kyle sighs. "I'm not trying to tell you what to do. But she's got Ethan, Jax, and Griffin wrapped around her finger. Don't let her do the same to you."

I exhale, dragging a hand through my hair. I don't want to believe him, but the doubt is already there, gnawing at the edges of my mind. Dylan is different, I know she is. But I also thought Kyle was different.

And now? I'm even more confused than I was before this little chat.

Rising, Kyle claps a hand on my shoulder, giving it a squeeze. "Just...be careful, all right? I don't want to see you get played."

I nod, but the unease in my gut doesn't go away.

Because now, not only do I not know who to believe, but I feel as though I can't even trust myself.

THIRTY-THREE

I SWEAR TO GOD, if I hear Ethan sigh one more time, I'm going to whip him with my resistance band. I do my best not to look at him through the mirror as I go through my exercises with Nolan, the trainer I've been working with the past couple of days. However, every now and again, I catch glimpses of him between reps. He looks far sexier than he has any right to in a pair of loose black, knee-length shorts that show off his muscular calves and an oversized white workout top with the large arm holes. It's a mouthwatering sight, to say the least.

Still, I'm too aggravated with him to let myself be distracted by the amount of skin he has on display. His hovering all week is driving me in-fucking-sane. Not to mention, I'm still fuming over his blatant disrespect for my privacy. He was in his room last night when I got home, so I didn't get to chew him out, and it felt wrong to do it today—what with it being game day and all.

I get why he did it—he's worried. They all are in their own way, but Ethan has taken it to a whole new level. All week, he's barely let me out of his sight. When he does, it's only because he's handed me off to Finn, Jax, or Griffin, like I'm some delicate package that needs to be constantly monitored. And when

Kyle's around? He acts like he's Ethan Hunt in *Mission Impossible*, diving in to control the situation before I can even process it.

He treats me like I'm his problem to fix. His to protect. Especially when he looks at me the way he is right now, gray-blue eyes boring into me, seeing everything, assessing, scrutinizing, analyzing. It messes with my head when he looks at me like that.

The problem is, it's not just that he invaded my privacy. It's that, a part of me fucking *liked* it. Yes, I'm as fucked up as Wren because, although I didn't say it aloud, I *did* get a stupid little flutter at the fact he would go that far to ensure I'm safe. A bigger part than I care to acknowledge wants to wave the white flag and let him do his macho bullshit and come to my rescue every time. My whole body reacts when he does. My stomach tightens, and my pulse jumps when his body shields mine and his voice drops into something dark and commanding. However, the logical part of my brain realizes that I can't let myself get used to his protection. Just like I can't get used to Griffin sleeping in my bed every night or feeling Jax's comforting stare throughout the day. I can't allow myself to drop my guard and let these guys in. I *won't*. I've already learned the hard way that those you let in, those you love, leave. Whether by choice or not. I need to be able to stand on my own two feet. The one and only time I dropped my guard and allowed someone else to hold me up, I severely learned my lesson.

It's not one I need to be taught twice.

Of course, that does little to subdue the all-out battle being waged inside me. It's a goddamn war zone inside my head. And every minute spent around Ethan, Griffin, Jax, or Finn only escalates the conflict.

I push through another rep, my muscles burning, sweat prickling against my skin. We're focusing on keeping my muscles loose and active, since I can't participate in on-ice drills or scrimmages. Although I'm hoping to be back on the ice for practices, if not games, next week. I don't think I can stand another week of sitting on the sidelines, *watching* instead of participating.

"You're favoring your right side."

My gaze snaps to the mirror. Ethan is watching me with narrowed eyes, giving a barely-there shake of his head. "Straighten your back."

I inhale sharply through my nose, but adjust my stance, ignoring the pull of fatigued, overworked, bruised muscle. "I'm *aware*," I grit out.

Ethan tilts his head. "Then fix it."

I slam my arm back down, letting the resistance band I've been working with for the past hour go slack as I glare at him through the mirror.

"Don't you have your own training to focus on?" I snap. "Warm-ups or some pre-game routine to carry out?"

"Nope." He pops the *p*, folding his arms across his chest as he makes himself comfortable against the wall. It only irritates me more.

"She's doing fine, Ethan," Nolan interjects, his tone even but firm. "She's still working through the stiffness in her ribs. It's about activation, not overexertion.

Ethan doesn't look away from me. "Overexertion isn't the problem. She's holding back."

My fingers twitch. *I swear to God—*

Before I can say anything, another trainer walks over, calling Nolan's name.

"Hey, can I grab you for a sec?" the guy asks.

Nolan glances between me and Ethan before nodding. "Yeah, just a minute." He looks back at me. "Keep going, I'll be right back."

He walks off, leaving me alone with Ethan.

The moment the door swings shut behind them, I explode. "What are you doing here, Ethan?"

Now that we're alone, he pushes off the wall and moves closer.

"It's my shift," he counters, like that explains it, except Jax and Finn haven't felt the need to sit in on my physio sessions. Admittedly, I can't envision Griffin doing anything other than staring unblinking at me throughout the entire session, but thankfully, he hasn't been *on duty* when I've had one.

"Then go wait outside." I fling my arm toward the door. "You don't need to be by my side every second of the day." Instead of heading out of the room, he moves closer. His long legs eat up the distance between us, even as I step back in a bid to maintain it. "I can't breathe with you constantly in my space," I toss at him. "I can't think. I can't—"

His hand snaps out, fingers curling around my throat as he drags me closer. I gasp as my body collides with his, his chest rising and falling unevenly.

"You think I want this?" he grits out, voice dark and strained. "You think I *like* being stuck in this fucking hell where I can't let you out of my sight? Where I wake up every damn day knowing that if I let my guard down for even a second, something could happen to you?" His fingers flex against my throat. "Because I don't."

I stare up at him, chest heaving, pulse rioting against my ribs.

His grip tightens.

My core clenches.

And then he snaps.

In a blur of movement, my back hits the wall. I barely feel the coolness against my overheated skin before his mouth crashes against mine.

I let out a sharp gasp, but he doesn't give me room to breathe. His hands bracket my face, fingers digging in, controlling the angle, the pace. It's all-consuming, this kiss—heated and desperate, a battle neither of us can win. His teeth scrape against my bottom lip before his tongue sweeps inside, taking, claiming, *owning*.

"Do you have any idea how often I've thought about this?" he rasps, ripping his lips away but remaining fully in my space, taking up all of my oxygen. "Even though I shouldn't. You're a player and I'm the captain, and if you were anyone else I wouldn't, but it has been driving me *insane* knowing that my friends, my roommates, my *teammates* have tasted your lips, and I haven't." His nostrils flare, pale blue eyes boring into mine with so much raw heat that it leaves me parched.

His words slowly penetrate, and my eyes widen, realizing he overheard my conversation with Wren. *"Careful, Dylan. You're playing a dangerous game."* At the time, I'd thought he was referencing me kissing the other guys, but now I wonder, did he mean himself? Was Ethan...jealous? My lips part, and Ethan takes that as an invitation, ducking his head and sweeping his tongue inside my mouth. He kisses me until all I see, all I think of, is *him*.

My hands fist in the pathetic excuse of a top that he's wearing. I intend to push him away. That's exactly what I *should* do, but instead I end up pulling him closer.

Fuck it. Breathing is overrated anyway.

I arch into him, my breasts dragging along the hard planes of his chest as my hands roam freely over the expanse of smooth skin. His muscles flex and tighten beneath my touch, while my own body turns soft and pliable.

I'm two seconds from wrapping my legs around his waist and clinging to him like a spider monkey when the door opens.

We spring apart like two teenagers caught doing something they shouldn't.

"How's it going in here?" Nolan asks, lifting his head from the clipboard in his hand.

Clearing his throat, Ethan turns away, keeping his back to Nolan as he adjusts the obvious erection tenting the thin fabric of his shorts.

"Fine." My voice sounds anything but, and I focus on the resistance band, going back to my movements as I try again. "Think I've got the muscles in my chest and back all worked out."

"Good." Nolan appears oblivious as he moves farther into the room, dropping the clipboard before approaching me. "Let's move on to your legs then."

For the next hour, tension crackles in the air and my lips tingle like they've been stung by a dozen bees, and any time I accidentally catch Ethan's eyes, everything in the room ceases to exist.

I've done it again—kissed another Steelhawk I have no business wanting. And I'm starting to think I don't want to stop.

I'm well and truly fucked.

THIRTY-FOUR

THE ENERGY in the arena is electric, buzzing with the kind of intensity only opening night can bring. The Steelhawks are dominating, and even though I'm stuck on the bench, unable to play, my heart still races with every shift, every pass, every shot on goal.

I'm cheering along with the rest of the team when Finn buries the puck in the back of the net, but beneath the excitement, my mind won't stop wandering.

To Ethan.

To the escalating tension that has been culminating between us all week, swelling and growing until it couldn't be contained. Until it resulted in him kissing me like he could consume me whole and still not be satisfied. I still feel the bruising on my lips, the hard planes of him pressed against me, while I wonder what would have happened if Nolan hadn't interrupted.

To Griffin.

To the fact that he's been sneaking into my bed every night since the attack. He doesn't say anything about it, never asks, nor does he seem to expect anything. But he's there, and disturbingly, I find comfort in that. No one has ever gone out of their way, risking their health, to climb through my window every night just to ensure I'm safe. Not to mention he's a surprisingly good cuddler—not that I'd ever tell him that. But every time I roll over, he follows, pulling me right back into his chest so his arms are a steel cage around me. And I let him.

To Jax.

And the undeniably inappropriate hot tub sex we had. I will never step foot in that room again without feeling how deliciously my walls stretched around him, the feel of him coming inside me, his lips on my skin and hands in my hair. Once wasn't enough. Instead of getting him out of my system, he's burrowed so deep now that I fear I'll never not want a taste of him. The chemistry between us is off the charts, crackling like a live wire every time we're near.

Finn, though, he's an entirely different problem. On one hand, I feel on stable ground with him in a way I don't with the others. I know where I stand with him, even if his impulse-driven kisses haunt my dreams at night. During the day, all I want to do is shake some sense into him. I want to scream at him that his best friend is a misogynistic asshole and how can he not see that. But I can't force him to see something he doesn't, and if I could figure out a way to get Kyle to confess, then I'd have done it by now. I have to hope that Kyle will slip up and show Finn his true colors. At this point, it's the only thing that will make him understand who he's really protecting. Who he's choosing to side with. And until such a day, I guess I'm stuck living in a world where I simultaneously want to kiss the asshole and shake the living daylights out of him.

Exhaling sharply, I force myself to refocus on the game. Graywater Lightning has the puck and is closing in on Griffin in the net. Bodies shift. Sticks clash. My fingers dig into my thighs as I watch them set up a perfect one-timer, but Griffin tracks the shot and snags it out of the air like it's nothing.

A loud whistle. A roar from the crowd.

I grin, clapping along with everyone else as players rotate off the ice. Movement in my periphery catches my eye, and when I glance to the left, Kyle is climbing over the boards as his replacement takes the ice. His body language drips smug arrogance despite the fact that he fumbled a couple of simple passes earlier. His gaze finds mine almost instantly, like he was expecting me to look his way.

The smirk that curls at his mouth is razor-sharp, full of something taunting, something cruel. A reminder. A warning. I've been doing everything possible to avoid him all week, with the guys running interference when we have to be around each other, but any time we're alone like this, no one else present, I witness the Kyle who is capable of attacking an unsuspecting woman in a dark parking lot.

I don't take the bait.

Instead, I keep my expression blank, my posture loose, even as goosebumps pebble along my arm.

Kyle exhales a quiet chuckle, barely audible over the roar of the crowd, and then, without another word, he turns his back to me. Dismissive. Like I'm nothing.

The irritation pinches, hot and pulsing beneath my skin. Gritting my teeth, I turn my attention back to the ice just as the final buzzer sounds.

The Steelhawks win.

The guys are all celebrating, shouting, and hollering as they clear the ice. And even though I didn't play a single second, I still clap, still offer my congratulations as they file past me toward the locker room.

Jax slows as he reaches me, pushing his helmet up onto his head. Sweat makes his hair stick to his forehead, and the helmet only enhances his strong jaw and draws my eye to the faint scar on his cheek. For a moment, I lose all track of time as I drink him in. He is so effortlessly hot. Moody and mysterious with a panty-melting smile.

Before I can swoon entirely and embarrass myself, I wrench my gaze to his. I suck in a breath when I find him staring blatantly at my lips. "You have no idea how badly I want to kiss you right now." His voice is thick, gravelly, piercing straight through me as my body involuntarily leans closer to his.

The words *"yes please"* are on the tip of my tongue. As if sensing that, Jax clears his throat, pulling back just enough for me to remember where we are and who is looking on.

Right. Making out with a team member in front of an entire arena of fans, plus the rest of the Steelhawks, definitely isn't a smart move. Especially when I have no idea what is happening with *three other Steelhawks,* and I have Kyle just itching for dirt on me.

"Good game," I tell him as I wrangle my hormones back under control.

He flashes me a cocky smirk. "You coming out tonight?" His voice is still gruff, pupils dilated, likely with adrenaline from the win.

"Are you?"

The corner of his mouth tugs up. "I'll go if you go."

Before I can answer, Ethan skates over to stand beside Jax. He's got his helmet tucked under his arm, and his damp hair sticks up in all directions when he runs his fingers through it. It shouldn't be hot, but it is. It *so* is.

"She's going," he states, making the decision for me.

"Is that so?" I challenge with an arched brow.

He pierces me with a no-nonsense look. You'd think that kiss yesterday might have burnt off some of his controlling energy, but unsurprisingly, no, it did not. "The whole team is going out—and that includes you."

"If the whole team is going out, then that sounds like the perfect opportunity to get the house to myself."

Jax laughs. "Good one, Menace. Like Ethan would let you stay home alone after last night."

I huff, knowing he's right. "I didn't do anything wrong," I argue, "and I feel the need to remind you both that I'm not a child."

Reaching over, Jax wraps his gloved hand around mine. "We just want to make sure you're safe."

My gaze drops to where the coarse fabric rubs back and forth across my skin. "I know." I'm frustrated. I hate that this is how it is. I hate how weak it makes me feel to rely on others. And I hate the niggling voice in my head that says the guys are only spending time with me out of obligation.

I hate everything about this situation, and worst of all, I don't know how to change it. Short of giving Kyle what he wants —me off the team—there is no other solution. No way to stop him and his minions from coming after me again.

"Come on," Jax encourages, as if sensing my plummeting mood. "It'll be fun. Then we can go home, and I'll kick your ass at COD."

I scoff, "You mean, I'll kick *your* ass."

Once Coach has debriefed the team and everyone is show-ered and changed, we all pile into The Stanley. It is loud, packed with the usual Friday night crowd of students, hockey fans, and locals. The team walks in like they own the place, everyone patting backs and high-fiving. The energy is contagious.

Unlike last time I was here, I'm dressed casually in black leggings and matching ankle boots, and a cream-colored loose, flowing top. Since I wasn't playing tonight, my hair is down, swishing around my shoulders as I push onto my toes to see behind the bar.

I spot Wren immediately, serving the three-person deep crowd surrounding her. At the commotion of the team's entrance, she looks up, scanning the crowd until she sees me. I wave, and she grins before going back to work.

"I'll grab us a round of drinks," Jax says. The crowd divides like the Red Sea to let him through. Flanked by Griffin and Ethan, with Finn ahead of us, lapping up the attention, we make our way through the crowd and toward the booths at the back of the room that quickly emptied as soon as the team walked in.

I end up sitting beside Ethan, with Griffin opposite. Finn initially diverted to talk to some of the guys at another table, but he returns when Jax appears with beers for each of us before claiming the open spot at my side.

It's not long before the puck bunnies start circling. I catch sight of the blonde who is always hanging off Finn, and groan. Hearing it, Ethan glances my way before following my line of sight.

"Selena incoming," he announces as the bunny's—Selena's —gaze lands on Finn with the precision of a sniper homing in on his target, and she starts moving this way. *Great.*

Dressed in a crop top and skintight leather pants that I swear give her a fucking camel-toe, she slides right up to him, oblivious to anyone else at the table as she presses her hands against his chest like she has every right to touch him.

"Congratulations," she purrs, batting her fake eyelashes at him. "You looked incredible out there tonight."

Not, you *played* incredibly, but you *looked* incredible. Does she even know the rules of hockey? How the game is played? Or is she too busy eyeing up every person on the ice like they are pieces of meat for her to drool over?

Finn catches my look of distaste, before giving her a tight

smile. "Thanks, Selena." He doesn't pull her onto his lap or even shift over for her to sit beside him. In fact, he barely acknowledges her, but she doesn't take the hint. Instead, she leans closer, fingers tracing over his shoulders.

I take a sip of my drink, forcing my gaze elsewhere. I try to engage in the conversation happening around me, but like passing the scene of a car crash, my eyes keep flitting back to Finn and Selena.

She's squeezed herself into the end of the booth now, and I watch with a morbid curiosity as she angles her body so her breasts are pressed against his arm. She drags a pink-polished nail over the cord of muscles on his arm, slow and deliberate. My nostrils flare. The sudden desire to grab her by her perfectly straight hair and wrench her away from him is potent and unwelcome. Finn isn't mine, and I'm not even sure I'd want him to be. Not that it's an issue. *He* doesn't want to be mine, so it's a moot point.

Catching me staring, Finn must read something in my expression as his emerald green eyes darken. I quickly look away.

My gaze accidentally collides with Griffin's instead. He arches a questioning brow, glancing back and forth between me and Finn knowingly. I scowl at him before focusing on my drink instead.

"I was thinking..." Selena's voice pierces through the deep rumble of male tones. I tell myself not to listen, but it's like I'm attuned to her voice. I can't *not* listen. Or look, apparently, as my gaze slides in their direction. Selena is twirling a strand of blonde hair around her finger, staring up at Finn with lust-colored love hearts in her eyes. Oh no, wait. It's green dollar signs I see in her mud-brown depths. My bad. "We should celebrate your big win properly tonight." Her voice drips with suggestion. "Just the two of us." She bats her eyelashes seductively. "It's been a while since we... I'll do that thing you like—"

My glass hits the table harder than intended. I'm pretty sure I just threw up a little in my mouth.

It's not my business, I tell myself. Finn can do whatever the hell he wants.

And yet, there's an acrid burn in my gut.

As if sensing my inner turmoil, his eyes flick toward me, sharp and aware. The bastard smirks. It makes me want to stab him with the nearest sharp object.

And then, just to drive the knife in deeper, he *touches her.*

His hand skims down her back, featherlight, before settling on her hip. His fingers flex, a slow drag up and down over her bare skin.

It's calculated.

A test.

Because he knows I'm watching.

Selena practically melts into him, pressing closer, her lips brushing his ear as she murmurs something I can't hear. Something ugly curls in my chest. My nails dig into my palm, jaw locked so tight it aches. I shouldn't care.

I *don't* care.

Except, for some stupid reason, I do.

And Finn knows it.

"Dylan."

Ethan's voice snaps me out of my disturbingly violent thoughts. I barely registered him watching me, but now his eyes flick between Finn and me, his expression unreadable. "You good?"

I exhale sharply, schooling my features into something neutral. "Yeah. Just need another drink." I push up from the booth, forcing Jax to move to let me out.

"I'll go with you," Ethan presses.

I shake my head. "I just need a second." I point toward the bar. "I'll be right over there. You can see me, no problem."

Ethan doesn't look happy, but after a beat, he gives a tight nod.

I turn on my heel and head straight for the bar, feeling Finn's—the entire table's—eyes on me the entire time.

"You look like you're having fun." Wren has to shout to be heard over the music, which is much louder closer to the bar and dance floor than at the back of the room.

I just shake my head. "Boys."

She grins. "I have a cure for that." Moving away, she grabs a beer from the chiller, popping the top off before handing it over. "Sorry, I can't hang around and chat," she says after I've paid, indicating the busy crowd.

"Don't worry. You go do your thing." I wave her away with the promise that we will catch up tomorrow. Taking a sip of my beer, I will my frustration to settle. It doesn't.

"You're Dylan Carter, right?"

I glance sideways at the guy beside me. I recognize him from one of my classes—innovative marketing, maybe? Tall, dark-haired, sharp jawline. He's cute, in a frat-boy sort of way.

"That's me," I respond, voice light, neutral.

He smirks, watching me over the top of his bottle as he takes a sip of his beer. "The girl playing on the men's team. Ballsy move."

I stiffen, although he doesn't say it with judgment. If anything, there's an edge of intrigue. I recognize the way his gaze skims over me, lingering a second too long.

"Yeah, well, I guess I like a challenge."

I don't mean anything specific by the words, but the guy's dark eyes flash, and he sits up straighter. His smirk turns more coy, and I mentally curse myself for giving him the wrong idea. I'm not playing hard to get. I'm not *playing* at all.

Although as the guy flirts with me, I kinda wish I was playing. That I could. He's cute. Charming. And most importantly, *he's not a Steelhawk hockey player*.

And yet, I feel nothing for him. No spark. No chemistry.

I wish I could be drawn to someone like him. Someone untangled from my team, from my life, from the constant push-pull of everything happening with Ethan, Finn, Jax, and Griffin.

It only makes me more frustrated that I'm not.

I force a small smile, sipping my beer as he keeps talking, telling me about himself. I'm nodding along as he gripes about the number of assignments in our marketing class when a shadow falls over us. I look up as Finn sidles up to me, close—too close. His arm slides around my waist, possessive and territorial as he practically yanks me against his hard, firm body. His hand lands heavy on my hip, squeezing as if in warning. As though he's silently telling me to behave.

My teeth grind.

He lowers his head, and I go rigid as his lips brush my temple. "You've been over here for too long, babe," he says, loud enough that there's no way the guy beside me doesn't hear.

I tighten my fingers around my beer as I twist my head to glare up at him. *Babe?*

Despite his playful smirk, his eyes are dark, locked on the guy beside me, and a muscle jumps in his cheek. His irritation simmers just beneath the surface—but why? He was just flirting with his puck bunny, so what the hell is he doing over here, staking a claim on something that isn't his?

The guy beside me stiffens. "Oh. I didn't realize—"

I go to tell him it's not what he thinks, mostly just to piss Finn off, but the asshole beats me to it. "She gets off on keeping us a secret," he says, tilting his head my way. "Likes it when I catch her flirting with other guys, then drag her into a back room and remind her how good I can make her feel."

I choke on nothing but air, my cheeks flaming from embarrassment. *What the fuck?!*

"Oh." The guy looks completely speechless, and who can blame him? I'm going to have to hide from him in class now. "Well, I should just—" He doesn't even hang around long enough to finish his sentence.

The second we're alone, I whirl on Finn. Thankfully, it dislodges his arm from my waist, and I blatantly ignore the cold that seeps in, in its wake. "What the hell was that?" I demand.

"What was what?" he questions, playing innocent.

"Don't *what* me!" I'm so angry, I can feel steam coming out of my ears. Not wanting to get into this in front of a bar full of strangers who are most likely eavesdropping and looking for juicy gossip, I grab Finn's arm and drag him toward the back corridor, where the bathrooms are.

The moment we're out of view of the rest of the bar, I let go and shove him. Hard.

He barely stumbles, just tilts his head, lips curling into a smirk that pisses me off even more.

"I'm not the one flirting it up with some guy while you've got three others drooling over you." His smirk turns into a sneer.

I blink, stunned for a moment before scoffing, "Oh, I'm sorry, I didn't realize I needed your fucking permission to talk to someone."

"I didn't realize you needed *more* when you've got the whole team wrapped around your finger."

I shove him again. "Fuck you, Finn. Go back to Selena and stay out of my life."

His eyes darken, amusement flickering there now. "Jealous, Carter?"

I laugh sharply, shaking my head. "If anyone's jealous, it's you. I mean, what else could that ridiculous posturing have been?" I throw my hand out in the direction of the bar.

Finn moves before I can process it—a step forward, crowding into my space, forcing me back against the wall. His hands cage me in, palms braced on either side of my head.

My pulse hammers, my breath short, and I get the strongest sense of déjà vu.

The air between us crackles, just like the last time he had me pressed against the wall in this exact same spot. Anger and something else, something even more volatile, hisses and spits between us.

His gaze drops to my mouth, then back up. "You have no idea how much it fucking kills me."

My throat tightens.

His jaw clenches, his voice a low rasp. "That I can't flirt with you in a bar. That I can't touch you."

His fingers brush my arm as he says it, a slow, deliberate caress. My skin prickles, heat curling in my stomach. I don't think. I lift my chin, defiant, daring. "What's stopping you?"

It's the final fucking straw.

Finn surges forward, his lips crashing onto mine, swallowing my gasp. It's fire and fury, all-consuming, devastating.

And just like every other time, it wrecks me.

But it's over too quickly.

He jerks back like he touched a live wire, cursing under his breath. His jaw is tight, chest rising and falling hard. He won't look at me.

"Finn," I start, but he shakes his head, already turning to storm off.

Oh no. Not this time. I've had enough of him kissing the sense out of me and then walking away.

I push off the wall and march after him, shoving at his shoulder. "Seriously?" I snarl. "What the *fuck* is your problem?"

He whirls on me, his face a mask of frustration and something deeper, rawer. "My problem?" He lets out a bitter laugh. "*You* are my problem, Dylan."

My breath catches.

Anguish racks his face before he turns it away, raking his fingers through his hair. His whole body is taut with tension. "You have my head so fucked, I don't know what to do. I don't know who I am anymore." His voice drops, eyes flashing. "I don't even know if my best friend is who I thought he was."

I swallow hard, my stomach twisting. "Finn—"

"I won't betray his loyalty." His voice is raw, like the words are being ripped from him. "Not without proof. Not without knowing for sure that he's not the man I once knew." Lifting his gaze, his stare is *tortured*. Wrecked. As though he can't help but reach out one more time, he rubs a strand of my hair between two fingers. "You and I are teammates, Dylan. Nothing more."

With a sigh that carries the fragments of my cracked heart, he drops his hand, holding my stare a moment longer before he turns and stalks away.

This time, I let him go.

Throat raw and limbs trembling, I sag against the wall. My heart pounds, head spins, and my eyes drift shut as I suck in a breath.

When I open them again, Kyle is standing a few feet away, watching me. His lip curls, gaze sweeping over me with clear disapproval. "You sure do get around, don't you?"

My stomach turns. Why the hell is he always showing up when I don't want him to?

Before I can react, he sneers and shoves into the men's bathroom, leaving me alone in the empty hallway.

THIRTY-FIVE

 JAXON

"CARTER, A WORD," Coach calls as practice ends and the rest of the team head toward the lockers to change. It's Monday, and after a team meeting yesterday to discuss Saturday night's game, we're back on the ice this morning, focusing on the next one. That's just how the season is. A moment of reflection before you move forward. Always improving, always adapting. I like the fact that you're constantly moving, never sitting still for too long.

But right now, I frown as Dylan stomps over to Coach in her skates. It was her first practice back on the ice, and although she did amazing, I can tell from the slump of her shoulders that it's taken it out of her. Her skin is still stained yellow from lingering bruises, and her muscles must be stiff despite her doing a few warm-up laps last night to loosen them ahead of today. What she needs is to stop moving and sit down. Maybe a warm bubble bath and a massage.

Still, I can't exactly snap at Coach for keeping her on her feet longer than she should be.

"You coming?" Finn asks, stopping beside me to pull off his helmet. His sweat-slicked hair sticks to his head, and he runs a hand through it.

"Yeah. I'll be there in a sec."

He glances between me and Dylan, but makes no comment before heading toward the locker room. I should go, too, but I can't seem to make myself move.

I want to ensure she makes it back okay. Her legs are probably sore and weary. She pushed herself to the max out there, and in her exhausted state, it would be easy for her to trip and injure herself further.

So while the team changes and heads out, I stand at the side of the rink and wait. I do my best to not stare at her the entire time she's talking to Coach, but it's hard. My gaze keeps inadvertently focusing back on her. I'm too far away to hear what they are discussing, but I can surmise Coach is checking in, making sure she's recovering okay, and assessing how she got on tonight. He'd do the same with any other player on the team.

On one of my passing glances, he reaches out to squeeze her upper arm. It takes me by surprise initially. Coach isn't a touchy-feely kinda guy, and I'm especially surprised when his touch lingers. It's not an awkward pat or reassuring clap on the shoulder—his typical go-to moves with the team. It's something more. He says something to her, and she nods, his hand falling away before she smiles at him and turns away. I watch as she stomps toward me in her skates. Coach watches her a moment longer before he moves away to talk to one of the assistant coaches.

"You didn't have to wait for me," Dylan says as she approaches.

I smile, shaking off whatever that was. It's probably because she's a girl. Sure, we're supposed to look past that, but it's hard, especially when she's hurting. With the attack happening right outside the arena, Coach is probably feeling particularly guilty, even though it's not his fault.

"Wanted to make sure you got to the locker room okay."

Shaking her head, she grumbles something about overprotective boys as she moves past me. The locker room has mostly emptied out by the time we get there, and Dylan practically collapses onto the bench, groaning as her head falls back to rest against her locker.

"You overdid it out there," I chastise. Of course, she couldn't have just eased herself back into practice. She had to give it her all, as though proving to everyone out there that she's as strong as the rest of us. Like we'd ever doubt that. She's more than proven how tough she is. Fierce and dedicated. Hell, she's more driven than half the guys on the team.

"I'm fine," she grumbles, without bothering to open her eyes.

"Yes, clearly." I roll my eyes, not that she sees. "Need help with your skates?"

"I've got it. Just give me a sec."

Lowering myself to the bench in front of my locker, I take off my skates and begin shedding my layers of protective gear. A shadow falls over me, and I look up to see Ethan standing beside me, a towel wrapped around his waist. However, his gaze is focused on the brown-haired spitfire. "What's wrong with her?"

I shake my head. "She overdid it."

Once I'm stripped down to my boxers, I wait until the last of the guys have headed out before I approach her. Ethan is changed but is clearly refusing to leave until Dylan does. Finn has just emerged from the showers, and Griffin, who has become Dylan's personal shadow, has been sitting watching her from the second she stepped into the locker room.

"Come on, Little Menace," I murmur, kneeling in front of her. "Let's get you showered and dressed."

"I can do it," she mumbles, wrenching her eyes open. They're dull with fatigue, the usual green hue and golden flecks dimmed from their usual flare.

She leans forward to start on her skates, but I swat her

hands away, doing it myself. I ease her skates off her feet, setting them aside, before rubbing my thumbs into the arch of her foot.

"Mmm, so good," she groans.

"There's more of that once we get home," I promise her. "Shower or no?"

She rubs at her eyes before stretching her arms over her head. "Shower. It'll wake me up."

I nod, helping her take off her protective gear until she's left in just her sinfully tight shorts that leave absolutely nothing to the imagination and make me instantly hard, and her equally revealing tank top. She has the attention of all four of us as she grabs her towel and shuffles into the showers.

Once he's changed, Finn flops down onto the bench with a loud sigh, folding his arms across his chest and resting his head against the locker while he waits. Everything about his posture says he's pissed off at having to wait, yet he doesn't leave.

"We'll make sure she makes it to class," Ethan states curtly, eyes narrowed on Griffin.

"I know you will, 'cause I'll be with you." Griffin's stance is equally confrontational as he squares off with Ethan from across the room.

Ethan's teeth grind. "That's really not necessary. I'm perfectly capable of looking after her."

"*We* are," I correct.

"Pretty sure she'd have all your asses for making it sound like she can't take care of herself," Finn unhelpfully points out.

"Regardless, I'm staying," Griffin states with finality. "Besides, I got her something."

I sit up straighter. "You got her a present? Why?" Shit, is it her birthday or something?

He lifts one shoulder in a casual shrug. "Because why not?"

What sort of non-answer is that?

My jaw tics, but instead of sitting here arguing with him, I snatch up my towel and head to the showers myself. Steam billows from a nearby stall, and I can hear the water running as I step into the one next door.

Throwing my towel over the door, I strip out of my boxers and flip on the water and step beneath the hot spray. It's heaven on my overexerted muscles, instantly relaxing them and easing the tension.

I don't stand under the stream for long, turning it off and grabbing my towel to wrap around my waist when I hear Dylan step out of the stall beside me.

"Feeling better?" My gaze inadvertently rakes over her towel-covered body. Even though it hides her delectable curves, it does nothing to ease the pull I constantly feel toward her. I felt it from the minute she stepped into our house that first day, with her head held high and defiance glinting in those hazel eyes of hers.

And it's only gotten stronger at every turn when she has proved us wrong. When she has shown just how much of a Steelhawk she truly is. It's in her blood.

"Much." She gifts me one of her rare, genuine smiles.

Something in me slips the moment I see it—that soft curve of her lips, unguarded and real. It hits me square in the chest.

I close the space between us.

My hand slides over the fluffy fabric of her towel, squeezing her hip as I press my lips to hers.

It's not rough. Not urgent. Just...something I've been wanting to do all morning. Her lips part, and my other hand finds the back of her head, holding her carefully—lightly— because I know she's still sore, still recovering. She melts into me anyway, and fuck if I don't feel something shift in my chest.

My fingers trail up her side and over the edge of her towel

until I'm met with warm, damp skin. I seek out the tension I know is there, and when I find the tight spot just beneath her shoulder blade, I rub gently, kneading it with slow pressure. She groans against my mouth, and it shoots straight through me.

I could easily lose myself in this. In her.

Which is exactly why I force myself to pull back, forehead resting against hers, both of us breathing hard.

I smirk at her as my thumb brushes her collarbone. "There's more of that waiting at home, too."

The tension is palpable when we walk back into the locker room. Finn looks about ready to remove Griffin's head from his shoulders. I give Ethan a questioning look, but he simply shakes his head, lips pursed in a thin line. Dylan either doesn't notice the tension or pretends not to as she moves to her locker and starts to throw on clothes.

"First practice over with," Griffin says, giving her one of his boyish grins that makes him look less like the unfeeling psychopath he is, and that frequently has girls going weak at the knees for him. I don't see it, but whatever. Pushing off the wall he was leaning against, he approaches once she's changed and packed, and ready to leave. "You'll be back in play in no time."

She gives him a small, weary sigh. "Hopefully."

"I got you something to celebrate, and help make the wait a little less dull." She perks up as he reaches into an inside pocket of the leather jacket he's wearing tonight. Unlike most of the guys on the team, myself included, Griffin doesn't live in sweats and shorts. He's always wearing all black—black jeans, black T-shirt, black leather jacket, black boots. He'd be more suited to a motorcycle club than a hockey team. I think the most casual I've ever seen him was once after an ice bath when he put on black tracksuit bottoms after he'd toweled off.

Dylan plucks a piece of paper from his outstretched hand. "You got me a ticket to see the Timberwolves game this week?"

"Yeah. They're playing against the Marauders in Burlington. Thought we could go." He waits until she lifts her gaze to his. "Make a date of it." He winks. Fucking *winks* at her. Oblivious to the clenching of my fists or the sudden tension that has permeated the air.

"You want to take her on a *date*?" I'm surprised that it's Finn who speaks first, the snarl evident on his face as he glowers at Griffin. Out of all of us, he's the one least attached to Dylan—or so I thought. "As in, just the *two of you*? *Why*?" He looks so disgusted that it would be funny if Dylan hadn't subtly flinched at his words.

Griffin notices too, based on the way his nostrils flare, and he looks at Finn like he could murder him without blinking an eye. "Because that's what grown-ass men do when they like a woman," he bites out. "Not that I'd expect you to understand."

"What the hell does that mean?" Finn spits.

Turning to square off with him, Griffin says, "It means, the only women you spend time with are puck bunnies, and there's only one thing anyone is looking for from *that* transaction." Griffin's gaze rakes over him. "Hell, you've finally found a girl you want to more than just fuck, and you've been pushing her away at every turn."

"What?" Finn splutters, mouth agape. "I don't—"

"Don't finish that fucking sentence," Griffin snarls, stepping forward to jab a finger in Finn's chest.

I notice Dylan is staring at the ticket in her hand. Her shoulders are bunched, though, so she's listening to every word these dipshits say.

"This isn't the time or place for this discussion," Ethan interjects, showing us all why he was elected to be our captain this year. He's efficient at wrangling testosterone-fueled, adrenaline-rushed men. Stepping between Griffin and Finn, he forces Griffin back a step as his gaze shifts from one to the other.

"You're both acting like children." Fixing his glare on Griffin, his jaw works as though he doesn't want to say whatever he's mulling over. "If you want to go on a date with Dylan, then it's not on us to stop you, but perhaps now isn't the right time—"

"I want to go," Dylan cuts in, lifting her head and looking between each of us. "I want to go to the game. It's been...a while since I was at one."

Ethan's shoulders lower as he turns to face her, his expression softening. "I get that, but you're exhausted." He gestures toward her. "You can barely stand on your own two feet."

Oh, Dylan doesn't like that. Not one bit. Her eyes narrow on him, defiance blazing from the hazel depths. That defiance shouldn't go straight to my dick, but it does. I have such a hard-on for her fire. It's magnetic. I could readily sit back and watch her decimate anyone who tries to tell her what to do. "Just as well it's a hockey game and not a concert we're going to," she snarks. "Plenty of seats."

Ethan sighs, dragging a hand down his face. "That's not what I meant."

Griffin holds up a hand. "We know what you meant. You're being a sour pussy because you're missing out."

"A sour what?!" Ethan splutters. "I am not!"

Ignoring him, Griffin continues with a smug look. "Guess it's a good thing that I got enough tickets for everyone, isn't it?" He pulls four tickets from his pocket, flashing them for us to see. "You didn't have to put on all this posturing bullshit." He waves the tickets back and forth between Finn and Ethan. "All you had to do was ask nicely."

"You're a real asshole," Finn grumbles.

Uncaring, Griffin just shrugs. "Does that mean you don't want to come?"

"No." Finn frowns. There's no ignoring how petulant he sounds, though.

"That is," Griffin says, "if Dylan is okay with you ruffians tagging along?"

As one, all of us look at Dylan. Sighing, she rolls her eyes. "So long as you're all done measuring dick sizes."

Griffin scoffs before anyone else can comment. "Everyone here already knows mine's the biggest," he purrs, his gaze incinerating at he stares at Dylan, pulling her in against his body and bringing his face to her neck. She shivers in his hold, and while I'm definitely jealous that he's the one touching her and not me, I'm not...totally put off by it.

It's actually kind of hot to stand back and see the pleasure she derives from his touch and whatever filth he's whispering in her ear.

THE ARENA PULSES WITH ENERGY, a steady hum of voices blending with the pounding bass of the pre-game hype video playing on the jumbotron. Fans in Timberwolves and Marauders jerseys flood the concourse, laughter and conversation bouncing off the walls as vendors call out their sales. The scent of popcorn and beer clings to the air, thick and familiar. It doesn't matter what arena I'm in or where in the world it's located. They all sound and smell the same. They all feel like home. After a childhood spent bouncing between houses, never feeling like any of them were home, my local ice rink became my one constant. The one familiar in my life when everything else was a revolving door of change.

I should be taking in the pre-game buzz, lapping up the energy the way I typically do, but my attention is locked on the girl walking in front of me. Dylan is dressed tonight in a white crop top that shows off her toned abdomen, and dark denim skinny jeans that draw my eyes to the round globes of her ass.

She's straightened her hair and left it down tonight and has even put on makeup—something I've only seen her wear once, that night at The Stanley. To say she looks beautiful would be an understatement. Dylan always looks beautiful, even when she's coming off the ice, drenched in sweat with her hair sticking to her head after a two-hour practice. But tonight...tonight she looks like something I want to make irrevocably mine.

I haven't been able to stop thinking about her since our moment in the hot tub. She was constantly on my mind before that day, but since...it's on a whole different level. To say I'm obsessed would be an understatement. I'm bordering on Griffin's level of preoccupation, and I don't even care. If anything, it only makes me understand him better. How could he *not* be stalker level consumed by her? Dylan is like a magnet pulling us all in, and I have no interest in being anywhere other than right by her side.

Griffin slings an arm around Dylan's shoulders, pulling her close as we weave through the crowd. She doesn't pull away. His fingers toy with the neckline of her crop top, his touch so casual it makes my teeth clench. Like he has the *right* to touch her so intimately. Like he's done it so many times before that it's second nature to him.

I might *understand* Griffin, but that doesn't mean I like him touching *my girl* so fucking familiarly. I don't want Dylan to be here on a date with *him*. I want her to be on a date with *me*. With *us?* I think about that for a second as I cast a glance around our group. I decide I don't fucking care, so long as I can touch her with the same carefree casualness Griffin currently is.

"Is this actually a date?" I bark, voice low and threatening as I wield a finger between the two of them. "Are you—" I want to say fucking. Based on Griffin's smug smirk, that's what he's expecting me to say. At the last moment, I manage to wrap my tongue around a more socially acceptable word. "*Dating?*"

I might have slept with Dylan, she might consume my every thought, but we've never had the *dating* conversation.

Fuck, why haven't we talked about that?

"Yup," Griffin answers with unfiltered haughty arrogance at the same time Dylan says, "No."

Her quick denial is the only thing that stops my fist from flying into Griffin's face, and based on the flash of excitement in his eyes, he fucking knows it. Sick, twisted fuck.

However, Dylan's denial doesn't seem to bother Griffin. He looks down at her with a grin, like he expected the contradiction. Like it amuses him. The way he looks at her, though... There's something in his expression that makes my stomach twist—a softness that's uncharacteristic for him. Dylan lifts her head, their gazes connecting. An intimacy passes between them that shouldn't be possible in a place this loud and chaotic. She might deny this is a date, but there's no denying there's *something* between them.

"No?" I press, a desperate need pressing against my skin. I look straight at Dylan. "So then you'd be open to dating other people?"

She shrugs, barely sparing me a glance before looking away as though surveying the crowd. "I'm focusing on hockey this year."

It's a bullshit answer. If she were really focused on hockey, she wouldn't be here with Griffin. Wouldn't be standing here with his arm around her while my skin burns from being close but not close enough.

Equally, if she were *only* interested in Griffin, she wouldn't have agreed to let us tag along on their so-called date.

A smirk curls my lips.

She might not be mine yet, but she's not his either. And that's all the invitation I need.

We find our seats just as the starting lineups are being

announced. Griffin slides into the row first, dragging Dylan behind him. I push forward, claiming the seat on her other side before Ethan can. He fixes me with a look before reluctantly sitting next to me, with Finn at the end, putting as much distance between himself and Dylan as possible, like he thinks space will fix whatever's brewing inside him. I see the way he looks at her when he thinks no one's watching, the barely masked scowl when she laughs at something someone else says, the flicker of jealousy every time Griffin touches her.

It's easy to read because I feel the same way.

I don't know when they got this close, when Griffin earned the right to be so fucking familiar with her, but I want that too. I need it. I've never felt this undeterred urge to call someone mine. When I started at BSU, I found a home with the guys. A camaraderie. A friendship. But this is different. Stronger. Like the home I've built over the past three-plus years has been missing something vital, and I'm only now realizing. Realizing there's a void—a Dylan-shaped hole that needs to be filled.

The plastic digs into the backs of my thighs as we settle into our seats. Glancing to my right, Griffin catches my gaze, a smirk curling along his lips as he sinks lower in his chair and spreads his legs. His thigh presses against Dylan's in a deliberate move while his fingers skim over the back of her seat, a barely-there brush against her hair. The entire time, he holds my stare with that knowing, smug smirk that I want to punch clean off his face.

Challenge accepted, asshole.

Slouching down, I mirror his posture. My foot nudges Dylan's, my leg pressing flush against hers. The contrast of my large thigh with her much thinner, leaner one showcases how much smaller she is than me—than any of us. Yet, she's not fragile. Hell, I suspect she might be tougher than us all. Her gaze shifts to where we're touching, before she lifts her head. She glances between me and Griffin, her eyes flickering to the way we've effectively caged her in before she shakes her head, a hint of a smile peeking through.

Yet she doesn't move away.

I smirk, victory curling through my chest.

The game gets underway, the Timberwolves facing off against the Marauders. The first period is fast, aggressive. The Timberwolves set the tone early, controlling the puck in the Marauders' zone, their forwards relentless on the forecheck. A hard hit against the boards sends the crowd into a frenzy, cheers erupting as one of the Marauders gets laid out at center ice.

The game is paused while the ref skates over to check him out.

"Wow. Wild game already," Ethan states, leaning forward to stretch out the kinks in his back.

I nod in agreement, but I'm distracted by Dylan shifting in her chair beside me. She cranes her neck, looking up toward the luxury boxes. Her gaze lingers there, as though seeking someone out, before an incomprehensible look of pain crosses her face.

I lean in. "What are you looking at?"

She jerks slightly, her eyes darting to mine before she shakes her head. "Nothing."

Liar.

I search her face but get no answers to the haunted look in her gaze. There's an ache there that she refuses to let surface, but I see it. I may not understand it, but I see it. I feel it in my chest, even though I don't know the source. She forces a smile, turning back to the ice as the game gets underway again, but the sadness etched into her face stays with me. It bothers me, the thought of her dealing with whatever it is alone.

Without thinking, I reach over and hook my pinkie around hers. It's a small gesture, barely a touch at all. She glances down, staring for a long moment at where our fingers are intertwined.

For a moment, I fear she'll pull away, but then she tightens her finger around mine. It's as though she's anchoring herself to me. Putting faith in me. She's asking me to help her keep her head above water. Which is perfectly fine.

I'll be her buoy.

I'll keep her afloat.

THIRTY-SIX

GRIFFIN HAD no idea the tornado of emotions he elicited when he gifted me those tickets. Nostalgia hit me with the force of a Mack truck. I'd instantly been overwhelmed with memories of attending past games, wearing my dad's jersey and cheering him and the team on, and after a year of avoiding anything pro hockey, I'd suddenly been itching to watch my dad's team once more.

I should have known being here, watching them play without him, would be bittersweet. Don't get me wrong, I loved seeing my dad's team out there on the ice—like old times. They absolutely dominated their opponents, but seeing someone else in my dad's position was hard. Even harder was looking up to the family box where my mom and I would sit, and knowing she wasn't there. That she'd never be there again. Not because she wouldn't be welcome. She was as integrated into the pro-hockey scene as much as my dad, and has—had—close friends in many of the WAGs.

They tried initially, bringing over food, checking in, trying to coax my mom out of the house, but nothing worked. She fell deeper and deeper into a pit of grief and loneliness until no one else in the world existed. Not even me.

A nudge on my shoulder interrupts my thoughts, and I blink up at Jax. "Where did you just go?" His brows are creased with concern, and I know I'm giving too much away. He's been watching me closely the entire game, sensing something is off and trying to figure it out.

Shaking my head, I give my best attempt at a normal smile. "Nowhere." I notice everyone is piling out of the rows, toward the exit, now that the game is over. Across the rink, the seats are all basically empty, only Timberwolves fans still lingering behind, prolonging their celebration. "We should probably move."

We file out of the row and into the concourse. Needing a moment to gather myself, I point toward the sign for the women's bathroom. "I'll be just a sec."

However, before I can duck inside, I'm whirled around, my back hitting the wall beside the door. "What the—"

"What's wrong?" Griffin demands, oblivious or uncaring to the fact that he's caging me in, in a concourse full of people.

"Nothing!"

His insightful stare scours my face. "Liar."

"I'm fine," I insist, trying and failing to push him back a step. It's like trying to move a brick wall. Huffing out a breath when he shows no signs of letting me go until I give him something, I lick my dry lips before admitting, "Hockey was something me and my dad shared." Unable to meet his piercing blue eyes as I reveal such a fragile, broken fragment of myself, I shift my gaze to the side, staring at the faceless strangers walking past as I confess, "He... died last year and this was the first game I've been to without him."

Gentle yet firm fingers capture my jaw as Griffin moves closer. His body heat wraps around me like a warm caress, his arm encasing my waist. Griffin is typically so rigid, so shut down from any real emotion, that it's a surprise to see this level of empathy from him.

He directs my face toward his and waits patiently until I muster the courage to meet his gaze. We're so close now that the world beyond him ceases to exist. His eyes hold mine captive, deep, endless pools calling to me, drawing me in until blue is all I see.

Griffin is all I see.

His fingers trail down my throat, his hand wrapping around the base of my neck as his lips connect with mine. It's not a typical Griffin kiss, brimming with possession and dominance. It's soft, coaxing. It's exactly what I need—reassuring and bolstering without expecting too much.

My lips move against his, our tongues meeting in languid strokes. The usual chemistry that always seems to exist between us simmers, but unlike every other time, it doesn't snowball until all I can think about is getting us naked as fast as humanly possible.

This kiss isn't about uncontrollable passion or inexpressible desire. It's about more. It speaks to the deeper connection forming between us. This bond that I didn't ask for, didn't want, didn't think I needed, but suddenly find myself immensely grateful for.

"I'll be waiting right here," he murmurs when we break apart, still so close that his breath is warm against my cheek. "Take as long as you need."

His gaze lingers on me until the bathroom door closes between us. I move to stand in front of the sinks, staring at my reflection in the mirror. Grief clings to me, thick and cloying. It's written in the lines at the corners of my lips and in the darker green of my eyes—like a shadow has been cast, blotting out the slightly more vibrant color I used to see when looking in the mirror.

Still, today was a milestone. An achievement—in a disgustingly sad, depressing way. There was a time, right after my dad's tragic and untimely death, that I thought I'd never step foot on the ice again. I'd wanted to pack it all in. I'd stared at my skates for weeks, resenting them as if they were to blame for the fact I was now all alone in the world. It hadn't helped that I was riding the bench at NSU, and it had felt like everything Dad and I had worked toward was for nothing. I'd already been looking at my future in professional hockey through a gloomy lens. My father's death felt like the final nail in the coffin. The sign I'd been looking for that I should accept the reality that I'd never have a true position on an NHL team.

It was actually Bear who helped me realize that hockey was all I had left of my dad now, and that when I'm on the ice, stick in hand and puck whizzing toward me, is when I'm closest to him. Now, I swear I feel his presence with me whenever I'm out there. I live for those moments.

Closing my eyes, I work to do the same now. He might no longer be out on the ice but that doesn't mean he can't still be here with me. That he wasn't watching his team from the sidelines, a spectator much like myself.

My father and hockey are synonymous. I used to believe you couldn't have one without the other. Without my father, there could be no hockey. But now, hockey is the only tether I have left to him. Not just playing hockey, but watching it, talking about it. It's how I keep the memory of him alive, especially because I've worked so hard to separate myself from his legacy. I can't talk about him directly for fear that it will raise unwanted questions, but I can talk about the thing he loved most in the world—after me and my mother.

I snap my eyes open at the sound of the door opening. A

little girl comes running in, wearing a Timberwolves jersey, and her dark hair neatly styled in pigtails. She rushes straight over to the sinks, stretching onto her tiptoes to reach the tap before sticking a stuffed wolf toy under the stream of water.

"Oh, I don't know if he's supposed to get wet." I cringe as the water seeps into the toy's fur. I have the same stuffed animal in my bedroom at my parents' house, so I know they are cheaply made, mass-produced, and I have no idea how they hold up against water.

Seemingly unbothered, the little girl looks up at me through the mirror. Still drowning her wolf beneath the water, she grins at me. "Hi."

The door flies open behind us, bouncing off the tiled walls with a crack as a red-haired woman marches in, wearing the same jersey as the little girl. "Aurora," she says in exasperation. "What have I told you about running off."

"But, Mommy," the little girl argues. "Wolfie got sticky. He needed a bath."

"And you should have waited for me to come with you, not gone off on your own." The woman approaches her daughter, grimacing when she spots the soaking wet soft toy before taking it from her daughter's hand and attempting to salvage the situation.

Aurora immediately turns her attention to me. "Are you a Timb-a-wolves fan?" I smile at her inability to say Timberwolves. I'm guessing she's maybe four or five and hasn't quite figured out how to get her mouth around the word yet.

"I am." I gesture toward her jersey. "I'm guessing you are too."

She nods emphatically. "My daddy is on the team." She turns around so I can see the name Astor written across the back.

"Your dad is Logan Astor?"

She practically beams with pride. "Yup. Well, one of them, but my other two daddies don't play hockey."

"Oh." I honestly don't know what to say to that. Is this little girl telling me she's got three dads? I mean, obviously, biologically, she doesn't. Is one of them her biological dad, and then the other two are...what, exactly?

My gaze slides to her mother.

"Really, Aurora," the woman sighs. "This poor woman doesn't want to know the complicated state of our family."

Except, if it's what I think it might be—that this woman is *with* three different men—I really, *really* do.

"It's fine," I tell her, before holding out my hand toward her. "I'm Dylan."

Her returning smile is friendly. "I'm Riley, and this is Aurora."

"My daddy really is Logan," Aurora interjects, her bottom lip pushing out in a pout. "People don't believe me sometimes when I tell them."

I crouch down in front of the little girl. "Well, I believe you. My daddy used to be a Timberwolf too."

Her eyes go wide. "He did?"

"Yup. In fact, he played alongside your daddy. I even remember meeting your dad after one of their games. He seemed like a pretty cool guy."

"He is. He's the best," she says with such love and enthusiasm. "But not more than my other daddies. They are *all* the best."

I chuckle. "I bet they are."

She tilts her head to one side, thoughtful. "Your daddy doesn't play anymore?"

My responding smile is soft. Sad. "Not anymore. He, uh, retired."

Glancing up at her mother, she asks, "What does that mean?"

When I follow her gaze, I find Riley watching me, before a knowing look enters her eyes. "Your dad was Patrick?"

I swallow before nodding. "He was."

"I'm so sorry." She shakes her head. "That was such a tragedy. I was at that game. Thankfully, Aurora was at a sleep-over, but...it was awful."

I have nothing to say in response. What is there *to* say? It was the worst game—the worst day—of my entire life. I still have nightmares about that night. The blood staining the white ice. My father's unmoving form, the entire team huddled around him, blocking him from view so we couldn't see whether he was okay or not. Whether he was still *alive*.

"I remember meeting your mother at a couple of the games," she continues, snapping me from my dark thoughts. "Such a vibrant woman. It was clear for everyone to see that she loved Patrick. I hope she's doing okay."

My throat is tight. All I can do is nod and give a half-assed smile.

"The other wives mention her often. She's thought of all the time, and I know the other women would love to see her, if she felt up to doing anything."

"Thanks," I say curtly. "I'll pass the message along."

The blare of a ringtone thankfully cuts off any further conversation, and I move away as Riley digs her vibrating phone out of her pocket.

"Don't even think about barging in here, Grayson," she answers sharply. There's a brief pause, where the other person—Grayson—says something. "Everything is fine. We'll be out in a minute."

"Sorry about that," she apologizes once she's hung up. "He's a tad overbearing."

"Not with me," Aurora interjects, making both of us laugh.

"Especially with you," her mother retorts. "Right now, you think it's funny, but wait until you're older. You're going to hate him."

Aurora gapes at her mother in horror. "I could *never* hate Grayson." Turning to me, she explains, "He's my brother-daddy."

"Dear Lord," Riley groans, eyes rolling toward the ceiling. "Please stop oversharing our family dynamics with people in bathrooms. They are going to think we're crazy." Speaking to me, she adds, "It's not as weird as it sounds." She then pauses, seeming to think. "Actually, it is. When you lay out the facts like my daughter so bluntly does, it is as weird as it sounds, but I promise it somehow all makes sense."

I hold my hands up. "No judgment here. I'm hardly in a position to comment on anyone else's situation when I'm currently here with four guys and have K-I-S-S-E-D *all of them*."

Riley just laughs, not the least bit appalled by my actions. "Oh, I do not miss those days." She shakes her head, still smil-ing. "I'm so glad we finally made it through. Only advice I can give is to not shut yourself off because you think you shouldn't want it. If these guys are worth it, then do what makes you happy. Life is too short to play by societal rules."

Aurora tugs on Riley's sleeve. "What does K-I—that word mean, Mommy?"

"That's a grown-up word that little girls don't need to worry about. What you *do* need to worry about is Grayson storming in here if we don't go find him."

"Oh no." Aurora begins pulling on Riley's sleeve, trying to drag her toward the bathroom door. "He and Mommy get all kissy-faced whenever he does that," she says, nose scrunched in disgust as she does her best to encourage her mom out the door. "It's *gross*."

I laugh, and Riley calls a quick goodbye before her daughter pulls her out of the bathroom.

Left alone, Riley's words turn over in my mind as I use the toilet and wash my hands. I've spent so much time being sad, but Riley is right. Life *is* too short. My dad is proof of that. His death is proof that life as a pro-hockey player can be taken from you at a moment's notice. I don't want to spend what time I have left on this earth grieving. Dad wouldn't want that for me. He'd want me to be happy. Just like he wouldn't have wanted me to give up hockey. I was able to find my way back to the sport we both loved. Now I need to find my way back to the life I loved too.

I EMERGE from the bathroom with a smile on my face and a pep in my step that I didn't have before. Griffin immediately notices —because, of course he does—and arches a brow as I approach where he's standing with the others. I merely shrug my shoulders and look between them. "What's the plan now?"

"We could grab some food?" Ethan suggests.

"I could eat," Jax says, while Finn and Griffin nod.

"There's a bar not far from here," I suggest. "Does the best hot wings and cheesy fries."

"Sold!" Jax claps his hands together before gesturing toward the arena doors. "Lead the way."

We dissect the game while we make the short walk to the bar. Ethan and Finn are arguing over a particular pass one of the players made. I wish I'd been able to pay better attention, but I enjoy listening to them talk around me. Hockey is the one thing that unites all of them. If it weren't for the game, I don't think any of them would be friends. That's...a sad thought.

"You having a good night?" Jax asks, moving to walk beside me. He stands so close that the backs of our hands brush before he links a finger around mine in a loose hold.

It's stupid how such a small gesture has me fighting back a smile. I'm supposedly on a date with Griffin, yet here Jax is, reminding me he doesn't give a shit about the rules. I kinda like it, how he doesn't just step aside.

"You seemed a little off back there."

I offer him a reassuring smile. "I'm good. This has been fun. We should do it again."

The corners of his lips tilt up. "Yeah? You wanna go out with us again?"

The way he says that, all deep and suggestive, has my core clenching and dirty thoughts racing through my mind. He makes it sound like I'm not simply on a date with Griffin, but with all of them.

My thoughts drift back to Riley and her insinuation that she's with multiple men. Is a relationship like that truly possible? Is it something I even want? I've found a strange sort of home with these guys—even Finn, who has gone out of his way to ensure I'm cared for even while ignoring me. However, I made a rash decision about a boy after my father's death, and it's one I'll regret for the rest of my life. I don't want to rush into a similar situation. But then, while I am still grieving—is there ever a time when I won't be?—it's not as raw and potent as it was back then. It doesn't affect my ability to make decisions the same way.

I look up into Jax's handsome face. His expression is always carefully masked, but his eyes give him away. They brim with emotion that I don't think he truly allows himself to feel.

"You know, I think I do."

I'm rewarded with a wide grin that shows off the dimple in his chin. I can count on one hand the number of times I've seen Jax express his emotions so openly—and every time, what he's feeling has been directed at me. He never allows others to see this side of him. Never truly lets anyone in. Yet, for some reason, he's been letting me in.

He pulls open the door when we reach the bar, gesturing for me to go ahead. Murphy's is your average, run-of-the-mill corner bar. If you didn't know about it, you'd walk right past it without a second thought. As I step inside, I'm greeted with dark wooden walls and dimly lit sconces which cast a soft amber glow and makes everything feel a little hazy. A handful of patrons sit at the bar, their low murmurs mixing with the occasional clink of glasses and the muted hum of a game playing on the old TV mounted in the corner. The air smells of fried food and spilled beer.

We claim an open booth near the back, Griffin sliding in beside me without hesitation. Jax takes the seat directly across from me, his sharp gaze flickering between Griffin's arm, draped casually over the back of the booth, and me before stretching his legs out under the table so they tangle with mine. I fight back a smile, something warming inside me at his jealousy and the fact that he isn't put off by Griffin's open posturing. It makes me wonder again if something more could be possible between me and them.

Ethan joins him, while Finn settles at the end, keeping as much distance as possible between us. I roll my eyes at that.

A server swings by, dropping off sticky menus and taking our drink orders. We order a round of beers before each taking a moment to decide what we want to eat.

"Everyone up for sharing the platter of hot wings and fries?" Jax asks, looking around the table. Everyone murmurs their agreement, and we place the order when the waitress returns with our drinks.

Sitting back in my seat, I ask, "So, what are each of you studying?" I've lived and played alongside these guys for nearly two months, but I don't even know that basic thing about them. Sure, I've overheard them talk about a particularly difficult class or some assignment they are working on, but I don't know their majors, their plans for after college, or five years from now.

Unsurprisingly, they each rattle off something sports related —broadcasting, sports management, physiotherapy.

I snort at their answers. "I'm assuming the ultimate plan is to go pro then?"

"Obviously," Finn retorts, like it's not even a question. Like making it to the NHL is a foregone conclusion. Oh, how I wish it were that certain for me.

"What about backup plans?" I challenge.

Jax waves a hand. "We'll figure it out if we need to. We know what we want, and we have our degrees for if things don't work out as planned, but why put too much focus on something that isn't what we ultimately want?"

"Going pro is the goal," Ethan tacks on. "That's where our focus needs to be."

Griffin and Finn nod, none of them looking particularly worried.

Food arrives, baskets of hot wings and curly fries filling the table. We dig in, conversation shifting again until Ethan turns his gaze on me. I can see the questions brewing there. Ones I bet he's been dying to ask since I first showed up at BSU. "What about you? What's your plan after college?"

I swallow a bite of fries and shrug. "Same as you. Go pro."

The words come out steady, but they don't carry the same easy certainty as theirs did. Because for them, it's expected. For me? It's a gamble. A near impossibility. The NHL isn't exactly welcoming to women, and there's no real alternative that offers the same level of competition, the same dream.

"For real?" Finn questions, leaning forward to look down the table at me. Intrigue and something else, something more... heady, gleams in his eyes. "You're aiming for the NHL?" He looks around the table. "Can that even be done?"

"Women have played in the NHL before," I snark back with a glare.

"Yeah, but not routinely. They're pulled out for a PR stunt in exhibition games." He arches a brow. "You don't strike me as the type to accept that. You're not a show pony."

Is that a compliment or an insult? I can't tell.

"No," I agree. "I want a permanent position. I don't care if it's on the third line, so long as I get some real, actual time on the ice."

The table falls quiet for a beat, the weight of the difference between us settling in. Ethan studies me intensely, I can practically read the thoughts on his face—the realization that I'm fighting harder than anyone else on this team because, unlike for many of them, a position on a pro team is not a guarantee. It's the slimmest of hopes, a sliver of a chance. But I'm fighting for it anyway.

"Why?" Finn asks, sounding curious rather than insulting. "The chances are so slim. Why put all this effort into it when you could dominate on a women's team?"

I don't know how to explain it to him—to any of them. They've always known what they wanted, and to them, while obviously they have had to work their asses off to achieve it, it *has* been firmly within the realm of possibility for them. For me, I'm fighting to achieve the near impossible. But it's the only thing I've ever wanted.

I grew up surrounded by the team. My dad was a lifelong Timberwolf, and his teammates were like extended family.

They were in and out of our home, like I was in and out of many of theirs. There were family days, dinners, and celebrations after big wins. I grew up in that community. It's all I've ever known, and it's all I ever wanted for myself.

Before I can figure out how to formulate that in a way these guys can understand, the door to Murphy's opens, the cool night air rushing in.

Jax's jaw drops, and Ethan murmurs, "Holy shit," under his breath. The guys beside me turn, but I don't have to look to know the Timberwolves just walked in.

I stifle a groan, mentally kicking myself. Of course they are here. The only reason *I* know about this place is because my dad brought me here once. Why the hell didn't I realize it was one of the team's go-to spots?

The guys are abuzz around me, sneaking glances toward the bar as the team makes themselves comfortable, ordering a round of drinks. I, on the other hand, shrink slightly in my seat. I need to figure out a way to slip out of here before anyone recognizes me.

Doing a sweep of the room for a back exit, I curse when I catch Vince's gaze.

"Dylan?"

The familiar voice carries across the bar, drawing more eyes than I'd like. I shut my own for half a second before forcing a smile.

"Holy shit. Guys, it's Dylan!"

Vince, a veteran player, slaps some of the guys surrounding him on the shoulder before making his way over. Several others trail behind him, all wearing bright smiles.

I can feel Ethan and the others looking between us, most likely wondering how the hell I know the Timberwolves personally. *That* is not a question I am ready to answer.

"Shit, Dylan. It's been a minute," Isaac, a defenseman and long-time player for the Timberwolves says.

"Yeah," I manage. "I guess it has."

His eyes search mine, questioningly. "How ya been?"

I lift a shoulder in a shrug. "You know. Getting by."

His lips are flat, a sorrow in his expression as he nods, understanding.

"You gonna introduce us to your friends here?" Vince prompts, eyeing up each of the guys like he's debating between holding out a hand and dragging them out of the booth. His protective nature brings a smile to my lips, even as a tightness cinches my chest.

I clear my throat. "Uh, yeah. This is Ethan, Jax, Finn, and Griffin," I introduce, going around the table and pointing out each of the guys. "They're teammates of mine." That seems about the safest explanation for how we know one another.

They exchange nods and handshakes. "We came up for the game tonight," Ethan says. "Hell of a third period."

Isaac grins. "Yeah, we had to dig deep for that one."

"Well, it paid off," Jax adds.

Vince and Isaac go back and forth with the guys for a bit, discussing the game, before Vince circles the conversation back to me.

"You still at NSU?"

I shake my head. "Switched to BSU this year."

"No shit." Vince grins. "A Steelhawk, huh? Taking after your old man."

Isaac tilts his head my way, but his question is directed at the guys. "She running circles around you yet?"

"She's trying," Griffin teases.

"Showed us all up her first week," Jax adds.

Isaac winks at me. "I wouldn't expect anything less from our D-Girl." Isaac elbows Vince in the side. "Man, do you remember how she used to wipe the ice with us, even as a scrawny teenager?"

"Hey," I protest, but there's no real heat behind it. In fact, I'm smiling at the memory.

Vince shakes his head, grinning as he addresses the guys. "She was getting shots past our forwards back when she was fourteen, half our height, and weighed about as much as a box of cereal." Ethan glances at me, eyebrows raised, but I don't acknowledge it. "This girl was born to be a hockey player." The affection behind Vince's words warms my heart, and he turns his attention my way. "The entire team is going to be right fucking there, rink side, your first NHL game, while you make history."

I can feel my cheeks heating. "Gotta make it on to a team first," I remind him.

He scoffs, and Isaac shakes his head, the two of them sharing a knowing look.

"Sweetheart," Isaac begins, "the only reason why we wouldn't be on the sidelines cheering you on is because we're standing on that ice right alongside you. One way or another, you *will* be calling yourself an NHL player, and you know you'll always have a home with the Timberwolves."

"You are one of us," Vince adds. "Whether you wear our jersey or not."

My throat is dry, tears burning behind my eyes. It takes immense effort to keep my shit together, to not break down or lunge myself at Vince and accept one of his giant hugs.

"Vince," someone calls out from the bar. "Food's here."

Vince gestures that he's coming. "You guys want to join us?"

I shake my head before the others can pipe up. "Thanks, but we should get going. Early class tomorrow."

He nods, looking at me knowingly. "All right. Well, it was great seeing you." Glancing toward the guys, he adds, "Nice meeting you all." He lingers while we all pile out of the booth, and before I can say goodbye, he's sweeping me into a hug. "It's good to see you," he murmurs, before pulling back, meeting my eyes. "You're family, Dylan. Don't be a stranger." His words are soft, meant only for me.

"I won't," I promise, giving him another quick hug before letting go.

With a final smile and nod at the guys, he heads back toward the rest of the team. Quite a few of them are watching us, and I wave their way. They call out or lift their drinks in greeting before I head toward the exit.

"Thorn," Ethan murmurs in my ear as we step out into the cool Vermont night. "You've got some explaining to do."

Fuck. How the hell do I talk my way out of this one without telling them who my dad is? What my legacy is?

"You gonna tell us how you know *the Timberwolves*?" Jax asks as soon as we're in the car and on our way back to BSU.

"She doesn't just *know* them," Finn adds, turning around in the front passenger seat. His eyes dance with intrigue as they take me in. "She's been to their practices. *Played* with them." He's practically gaping at me. "You realize that's, like, every hockey player's fantasy?"

I can feel Ethan's gaze on me through the rearview mirror. All of them have been brimming with excitement, burning with questions, since we left Murphy's. For the hundredth time, I curse myself for suggesting we go there. As great as it was to see Vince and the guys, I do not need *this*—these questions I'm not ready to answer. Facts about my life I'm not ready to share. I'm not ready to see the pity in their eyes when they realize the Timberwolves player who went down hard after a brutal hit and an accidental slip of a skate—who lay motionless on the ice as he bled out, the crowd falling into stunned silence as his teammates rushed to him, as the medics skated out too late—was my dad.

"So?" Jax prods when I remain astutely quiet. "You going to tell us?"

"I wasn't planning on it."

Griffin chuffs a laugh beside me in the back seat.

"Seriously?" Finn grouses.

Internally sighing, I can't meet any of their gazes when I say with more force than necessary, "My dad worked with the team, okay? He'd bring me along and let me watch their practices sometimes." There's a burn in my throat, one I know they all notice as I snap my gaze up, staring each of them down. "Happy?"

Murmured responses are echoed as Finn turns back in his seat, and Ethan turns up the radio. No one says a word the rest of the journey home.

Later that night, I'm sitting on my bed, a marketing textbook open in front of me. Griffin left as soon as we got back to campus, but I know he'll be knocking at my window soon enough. Kyle is out, still, so my bedroom door is open, and I glance up when a large body fills it.

Ethan leans against the doorframe, arms crossed, as his eyes peruse my bedroom. His gaze pauses on the shelf of mugs.

"I told you how Patrick Callahan came to one of my summer camps once," he says thoughtfully, focus intent on the shelf before slowly pulling his gaze to me. "He was all excited that day 'cause he was heading home to his daughter after being on the road for the past week." My mouth goes drier than the Sahara. "He said he needed to make a stop on the way because he always brought her a gift when he was away—a mug from wherever he was traveling."

I couldn't formulate words even if I tried.

Ethan's gaze holds mine, and I stare right back. I have no idea if my walls are in place or if I'm giving everything away. If he can read every line of torment in my face, or if it's a blank slate.

"I think about her sometimes, after I've watched a Timberwolves game. Wonder where she is, what she's doing, how she's coping."

My throat bobs, my swallow audible. There's a fine tremor to my hands as I move to hide them between my legs.

"I'm sure, whatever it is she's doing, he's looking down on her with love. That he's proud of everything she's accomplished."

His gaze holds my blurry one for a moment longer, before he turns. "Good night, Dylan," he murmurs before leaving my bedroom, the door snicking shut behind him as silent tears course down my cheeks.

THIRTY-SEVEN

"I'M PLAYING IN THIS GAME."

No other player could get away with talking to Coach like that. Hell, the only reason I'm getting away with it is because we're alone in his office, and even then, Bear arches a brow, letting me know I'm walking a fine line.

"I *have* to," I press. "Don't make me sit on the sidelines for this one, Coach. *Please.*"

Breathing heavily, he eyes me warily from behind his desk. "Is this because it's NSU?"

I hesitate, before nodding. It's been over two weeks since my attack. I've sat on the bench for two—*two*—games now. I can't sit on the sidelines for a third. The fact that this is our first official game of the season against my old team just makes it all the more important that I'm out there. I *have* to be on that ice. *Have* to be a part of the team when we kick their asses. I *have* to be the one to wipe that fucking smirk off my ex-boyfriend's face when he realizes the Steelhawks aren't like his misogynistic team— well, not every Steelhawks player is.

"Do you think I've forgotten the way they went after you

during the exhibition game?" Violence threads his words, and instead of cowing me, a smile teases along my lips.

"Have you forgotten how I was able to hold my own?"

A grumble of discontent rumbles in his chest, and I allow myself an affectionate smile. "Bear," I say softly, pleadingly. "I'm more than ready to be back on the ice. Even the trainers say so and you've seen me in practice. *I'm fine*. Fully healed, not a pinch of pain." It's true, I'm back to my full strength and more than ready to dominate in Friday's game.

Inhaling deeply, Bear pins me with an unreadable stare. The seconds tick by. One. Two.

"Fine," he grits. "You're right. The trainers have cleared you to play. I can't bench you simply because I worry about you."

Grin splitting my face, I race around the desk and throw my arms around his broad shoulders. Pressing a kiss to his cheek, I squeeze him tight as I say, "Thank you."

Throwing open the door to the locker room, I'm still grinning like a loon as I throw my arms in the air. "It's official!" I announce. Most of the team has already left, hightailing it as soon as practice ended, leaving just my guys—huh, *my guys*... that doesn't sound so bad, you know—behind, waiting for me. Coach will deliver the proper announcement at tomorrow's team meeting, anyway. "I'm back, baby!"

An embarrassingly girly shriek escapes as I'm hauled into strong, masculine arms. Jax's cedarwood scent envelops me, my arms coming up to squeeze his neck as he spins me around. "That's my girl," he says, low enough that only I hear.

My girl.

That sounds even better than *my guys*.

My blood heats at the affection behind those words. He's been doing little things like that since the night of the Timberwolves game, saying sweet things that make me swoon, little touches when we're out in public and more claiming, possessive ones when we're at home.

"Knew you had it in you," Ethan says, his smile broad and genuine. He pulls me in for a hug as soon as Jax sets me back on my feet, but I can still feel his warmth at my back as I bury my face in Ethan's chest for a brief moment, inhaling his sure strength and confidence.

I'm yanked from his hold as Griffin's possessive hands slide across my hips and cup the back of my neck. His steely eyes bore into mine, a hint of a smile tugging at his lips. "I can't wait to take the ice with you on Friday."

There's a hunger behind those words, a flare of heat, like chasing a puck and getting rammed into the boards is a turn-on for him. Hell, knowing I'll be on the ice right alongside him— alongside all of them—is turning *me* on.

Movement out of the corner of my eye catches my attention, and my head whips up. Finn is standing in front of his locker, hands shoved in the front pockets of his jeans. He nods when our gazes collide. "I'm glad you're back," is all he says, but I catch a hint of the relief in his eyes. He might not believe that it was Kyle who attacked me, but he's not *like* Kyle. He never wanted me hurt, never wanted me off the ice.

Ethan's hand squeezes my shoulder, garnering my attention. "We're going to need all of our best players if we're going to beat NSU."

"Oh, we *are* beating NSU."

I won't have it any other way.

ONE SIDE EFFECT from Coach announcing that I was starting on the front line on Friday's game that I hadn't foreseen was the guys ramping up their protection detail.

The second Coach made the announcement and Kyle stormed out of the room, cursing up a storm, they've barely left my side. It's a miracle I can use the bathroom without one of them standing in the stall with me.

Ethan was able to wield his power as captain and get Kyle to stay elsewhere, meaning it's just been me and the guys at the house all week. The weight that has lifted from my shoulders at knowing Kyle isn't going to walk in the door at any second, that he isn't sleeping just down the hall, or could creep up on me whenever, is indescribable. I hadn't realized until now how stressed that had me all the time.

Even though Kyle isn't here, it hasn't stopped Griffin from creeping in my window every night. It's become such an ingrained habit that I don't know what I'd do if he stopped. Am I even capable of falling asleep on my own anymore? I'm not so sure.

His chest rises and falls beneath me, the steady rhythm grounding me as we lie tangled together in the dim light of my bedroom. His bare skin is warm under my cheek, the soft drag of his fingertips tracing idle circles over my spine and sending lazy shivers down my back. Perhaps it should feel suffocating, the weight of his protection, the intensity of his presence, but it doesn't. It steadies me in a way I hadn't expected. There's a comfort to it, a reassurance.

It's late, and we've been lying like this for a while, neither of us speaking, lost in the quiet before tomorrow's storm.

The game. My return to the ice.

He shifts slightly, angling his head so his lips ghost over my hair. The motion is so simple, so intimate, so casual, like he's always done it, like he always *will* do it. These quiet moments alone with him in my bed at night, it's the only time Griffin is completely relaxed, entirely himself. There's no show for the team. No keeping up appearances on campus or posturing in front of the guys.

His expression is always that hard, granite mask, but I've come to realize that's the real him. Not the version of himself who smirks at jokes and plays the fool in front of the team. Although, why he feels the need to put on the act is beyond me. It feels wrong to ask. Hopefully, one day, he'll feel comfortable telling me.

Breaking the silence, his deep voice rumbles through the night. "What happened with Tremble?"

My breath catches.

I don't lift my head. Don't look at him. Just focus on the feel of his skin under my fingertips, the slow, even rise and fall of his chest.

For a moment, I don't answer. The memories press in, sharp and jagged, but I force my body to stay loose against his. If he senses how uncomfortable this topic makes me, he's unlikely to wait until tomorrow to go after Lucas.

Finally, I exhale softly, swallowing around my suddenly dry throat as I struggle to find the words to answer his question. I want to shrug it off and not answer at all, but perhaps there's a catharsis in sharing it with someone, and I can only hope that if I open up to Griffin that he will feel as though he can open up to me in return.

"He hated me from the moment I joined the team," I tell him, lips trembling even though my voice doesn't shake.

Still, Griffin stills, sensing my unease. His fingers halt against my back. I press on before he can speak.

"He couldn't stand the idea of a girl on the team. Of a girl being good enough to *qualify* for the team." I let out a quiet, humorless laugh. "And he made sure I knew it, too." I swallow roughly. "The whole team made it clear I didn't belong."

Griffin's hand tightens around my waist. His silence is dangerous, his stillness lethal.

I push on, my voice cracking over my next words. "Then my dad died."

His exhale is sharp, like the words physically wound him. His hand starts moving again, this time over my ribs, like he's trying to soothe away something he can't touch.

"He did a complete one-eighty," I tell him, staring pointedly at the rhythmic movements of his chest. I use that to center me, to focus me while I bare one of the worst hurts of my soul to him. "He started being nice to me after that. He'd shut down the guys when they got too bad. Defend me when they said I should quit. He listened. He let me talk about my dad when I couldn't talk to anyone else. He was…kind." I hate to use that word to describe him, but it's true. "I—" The words catch in my throat. "I thought he cared." I shake my head, my cheek rubbing against Griffin's warm skin. "I needed someone, and he was there."

His chest rumbles beneath me. "He used you."

I nod, my throat tight. He's right. "It was all an act," I admit, my voice hardening as anger curls beneath my ribs. "He never gave a shit about me. He saw my grief, my weakness, and he played it against me. I was a joke." I pause. "Even worse, the whole team knew, and they let me believe it was real."

Griffin's breathing turns shallow, his entire body going rigid beneath me. He's quiet for so long that I finally lift my head, meeting his gaze. His eyes are black. Not with rage. Not with fury. With something deeper. Something…lethal.

"I'll kill him." The words are quiet. Steady. A promise, one I have no doubt he will follow through on.

I shake my head again, leaning up onto my elbow as I push my hand against his chest. "No, you won't."

His jaw tics.

"I'm not letting you get suspended—or worse—over me." I

force my voice to stay calm. "I don't need you to fight my battles, Griff."

His fingers tighten at my waist, not in anger, but like he's holding himself back. "You think this is about fighting your battles?" He shifts, rolling us until I'm on my back and he's above me, arms braced on either side of my head. My hands wrap around his biceps, fingers digging into the skin as though I can anchor him to me and keep him from going after Lucas—not that the asshole wouldn't deserve Griffin's wrath.

"This isn't about him hurting you," Griffin says, voice low and deadly. "It's about them *all* hurting you." He leans closer, his breath hot against my lips. "You're *mine*, Dylan." His voice drops lower, his eyes taking on a carnal burn. "And no one hurts what's mine."

Heat coils in my stomach. It should be terrifying how absolute he is. How obsessed. But it's not. It never is with Griffin.

I reach up, trailing my fingers along his jaw. "Then let me handle it."

His eyes flick between mine, searching. War raging behind them. He vibrates with barely restrained fury, every muscle locked, his breathing ragged.

Indecision battles in his gaze, the torment cutting through him like a blade. I can see it—he's seconds from storming out of here, from hunting Lucas down, from destroying him and anyone who stands in his way.

I fist my hands in his hair, tugging him closer. "Stay with me," I whisper.

A muscle jumps in his jaw. "If you don't want me to kill them all," he growls, voice rough, "then you better find a way to distract me."

Dark, exhilarating heat crackles between us.

I arch beneath him, my lips parting, my pulse hammering against my ribs. Reaching up, my tongue flicks out to run along his lower lip before I nip at the flesh. "I can think of a few ideas."

Griffin's restraint snaps, and all of that anger and adrenaline unleashes as he surges forward. His weight presses me deeper into the mattress, and his lips are bruising against mine. Our tongues clash, and I can feel him along every inch of my skin. The oversized Timberwolves T-shirt I'm wearing rides up when I hitch a leg over his hip, the fabric of my panties dragging along the hard erection in his boxers. His hands are everywhere, stroking, kneading, squeezing. I feel like I've been set on fire, and Griffin is the only one capable of dousing the flames.

His hand slips beneath my T-shirt, gliding over skin. He growls against my lips when my breast fills his palm. Heat envelops me, hot and heavy as I grind against him.

"Fuck, Hurricane," he rasps, ripping his lips away to trail a path down my throat. I arch my back, craning my neck to give him better access. He pulls the neckline of my T-shirt over my shoulder before lapping at the exposed skin.

But I need more.

With my leg over his hip, I flip us. He lands on his back on the mattress with a surprised, but equally dark and intoxicating, chuckle, his hands instantly coming to rest on my exposed thighs.

He looks up at me with so much carnal heat. That, mixed with the darkness that permanently resides around him, leaves me breathless. Griffin is everything you shouldn't want in a man and everything I *crave*.

"What are you going to do now, Hurricane?" he taunts, arching a thick eyebrow.

I meet that challenging stare with one of my own. "You told me to distract you."

He nods, and I smirk.

"I figured, what better way to distract you than by sitting on your face?"

He groans, hands squeezing my thighs possessively.

"If there is a better one, I can't think of it." His words are more animal than human as he kneads my skin and stares me down with that starved look in his eyes.

I go to climb off him so I can pull down my panties, but he stops me, grabbing my arm as he sits upright. "If you get off me right now, I'm liable to storm out that door."

"But—" I'm rendered speechless by the tearing of fabric, followed by a sharp sting along my hip before my panties fall away.

"Did you—"

"Yup." His smirk is one born of pure male arrogance, and it's shameless of me to say that it's hot as fucking hell.

"This goes too," he growls, already tugging at the hem of my T-shirt as he pulls it over my head. Another rumble vibrates through his chest as his eyes slowly lower over my naked form.

"Get the fuck up here already, my mouth is watering at the thought of tasting you."

He collapses back onto the bed, pulling me with him until I'm hovering over his face. His hands knead my thighs before grabbing my ass, squeezing the skin as he stares at my bare pussy with unadulterated need.

Gliding his fingers between my thighs, he spreads my pussy lips as he pulls me down onto his mouth. A jolt of electricity zaps up my spine at the first swipe of his tongue, followed by a moan as he swirls around my clit before diving back down.

"Oh God, that feels really good," I tell him, hands snapping out to grab the headboard as everything inside me clenches.

Before I know it, I'm riding his face. He growls in approval while he laps and sucks at me, until I'm a wound-up ball of need and desire on the precipice of destruction.

"Griffin," I gasp before sparks dance across the backs of my eyes, and everything inside me goes tight before pleasure barrels through me.

It takes everything in me not to cry out, to alert everyone else in the house to what is happening in here. Hands loosely clasped around the headboard, I slump forward, boneless as I catch my breath.

With firm, confident hands, Griffin slides me down his bare body, leaving a wet trail that glistens against the warm skin of his chest and hard planes of his abs. Somehow, it only adds to the appeal, already enhanced by his nipple piercings and the hint of tattoo running up his side that I can spot from this angle.

My heart is still hammering against my ribs when he surges upward, one hand sliding to the back of my head while his other grasps possessively at my hips, pulling me closer. His lips descend on mine, wanting. I can taste myself on him as his tongue invades my mouth, both of us moaning.

"Need you," he growls against my lips. "Right fucking now." Holding on to me with one hand as though I might disappear—like I'm going anywhere, I couldn't walk even if I *wanted* to—his other shoves his boxers down enough to grasp his cock.

It springs free, thick and engorged, the blunt head slick already.

"Ride my cock, Hurricane," he practically orders, fisting himself as he uses his hand on my hip to push me lower until his tip nudges at my entrance. "I need to feel you around me."

You don't have to tell me twice.

Hands perched on his shoulders, my fingers dig into the thick cords of muscle there as I seat myself on him. I whimper at the painful stretch of my inner walls. He's so damn *thick*. Larger than anyone I've been with before, but I welcome the bite of pain.

"That's it," he encourages as another inch slips inside me. "You're doing so good, Hurricane. Nearly there."

Rocking my hips, I gasp when he fully penetrates me, my hips hitting his.

Chest rising with deep inhales, my fingers play with the light blond strands at the base of his neck, and I stare into those captivating pale blue eyes of his while I catch my breath.

I can feel his fingers pressing into my skin, the flexing of his muscles as he fights not to move. Chemistry crackles in the air between us, but also something more, something deeper, something that terrifies me to look too closely at. So, instead, I lean forward and press my lips to his.

Our kiss is dirty and brimming with desire. With the undeniable attraction between us. The yearning. The impossible, ever-present *ache*.

"Need you to move," he grunts, hips bucking as he thrusts up into me. Hands on my hips, he helps to lift me, before I tilt my hips and slam back down. We both groan at the impact, the connection, the sizzling along our nerves.

My hands are everywhere, roaming over his broad shoulders, fingernails scraping along his chest, palms gliding up his muscular arms before I pluck at the rings piercing his nipples making him buck and groan. I can't get enough. The need to touch him everywhere consumes me as our hips knock together, and the feel of him deep inside me, sliding over that spot, rocketing me higher and higher.

Sweat slicks along my skin, and I can feel his heart hammering against his chest in time with mine as my release races forward.

"Griffin."

"I'm here, Hurricane. I'm right here with you." His hands move to my ass, moving me faster, deeper. My hips buck, but he keeps me moving as I sink forward, my breasts pressing against his chest as my mouth meets his and I cry into his kiss as I come around him hard enough that I'm pretty sure I momentarily black out.

His deep groans reach me over the thundering of my pulse, his fingers pressing hard enough to leave bruises on my hips as he thrusts up into me, burying himself deep before he comes.

"Fuck," he rasps breathlessly, fingers still pressing into me as we remain close. My head falls to his shoulder, the rise and fall of his chest rhythmic as we both catch our breaths. His lips continue to brush along my damp skin, like he can't bring himself to stop.

I don't know how long we stay like that, wrapped up in one another, in this intimate moment between us. Only when I feel him growing inside me do I lift my head, my shocked stare meeting his smug one.

"I hope you weren't planning on getting any sleep tonight, 'cause I am nowhere near done with you."

With that, he flips me onto my back and proceeds to prove his point until the sky outside streaks purple with the first light of day.

THIRTY-EIGHT

THE LOCKER ROOM hums with quiet energy, the kind that settles deep into your bones before a big game. I pull my jersey over my head, the familiar weight of it grounding me as I shift on the bench. The guys move around me, finishing their own pre-game rituals, but my gaze keeps drifting to the other side of the room.

Kyle sits on the far bench, lacing up his skates with slow, methodical movements. He hasn't said a word, hasn't so much as looked in my direction. And that's what unnerves me the most.

Since the moment Coach announced I was playing, we all expected him to retaliate. I almost *wanted* him to. To try, at least. I don't believe Ethan, Griffin, or Jax would let him get anywhere near me, but a failed attempt to target me would open Finn's eyes to who Kyle truly is at his core. Something I find myself wishing for more and more frequently.

However, instead of the attack I'd anticipated, there's been... nothing. Not a single spitted word or harsh glare. No discreet shoves or veiled trips. Certainly no cornering on dark nights or trying to get me alone. He—or his minions—haven't even gone after me during practice.

There has been nothing but silence.

And that's what worries me.

I look away before he catches me staring, rolling out my shoulders to shake the tension building there. It doesn't help that Griffin kept me up most of the night. Not that I'm complaining. I would do it all again in a heartbeat. What is a little tiredness when I had multiple moments of pleasure last night? By our last time, I was so out of it that he had to hold his hand over my mouth while I came because I was incapable of keeping quiet any longer.

I shiver, just remembering the delicious stretch of him inside me, the feel of his slick skin sliding over mine, our breaths and heartbeats in sync.

That's now two Steelhawks I've slept with, and perhaps I should feel guilty about that, but remembering both last night and my time with Jax, I can't bring myself to regret a single thing.

The only thing I want is to do it again.

"Attention, everyone." Ethan's voice snaps me out of my wandering thoughts. He's standing in front of the room now, his gaze sweeping over us. He waits until everyone quiets down, all heads turned toward him. "This is it. Our first game of the season against our biggest rival. You all know how much this game means, not just for points but for pride. They think they can push us around. They think they own this conference." He smirks, the reminder of how they dominated us and rubbed it in during the exhibition game boiling in our blood. "We're about to remind them whose ice this is."

A few of the guys let out quiet cheers, fists knocking against pads. The energy shifts, turning sharp, focused.

Bear steps up next, giving his usual pre-game words about discipline and execution. Ethan moves to stand beside me, his voice pitched low when he says, "They're going to come after you."

I keep my gaze straight ahead, jaw hard as I stare at where Bear stands. "I know."

I feel the other guys move to crowd around us, the five of us forming a group at the back of the room. Even Finn is here—although why, I don't fully understand.

"You're not alone."

I'm not sure if Ethan understands how significant those words are. How deeply they bury themselves in my heart. Wrapping around the organ like vines and permanently latching on.

In agreement, Jax's pinkie curls around mine, and Griffin's hand squeezes my shoulder. Even Finn seems to shuffle closer. I glance his way, our gazes meeting, and he gives a subtle nod. We might not be on the same page when it comes to Kyle, but in this —against NSU—we are aligned.

"Steelhawks hunt—" Ethan calls, stepping forward and moving through the locker room when Coach has finished his speech.

"And never fall!" we all recite.

"Steelhawks strike—" Ethan bellows, reaching the front of the room and turning to face us all with a look of severe consternation. The charming boy next door is gone, and in his place is a competitor who hates to lose. A champion who knows nothing else.

"And take it all!" we shout in return. Our voices bounce off the walls, every single player getting to their feet.

"Steelhawks on three," Ethan calls. The buzz of anticipation has my pulse kicking up, my body already humming with adrenaline. "One, two, three!"

"Steelhawks!"

We are united in our determination, in our desire to win as we pile out of the locker room and stomp down the tunnel.

It's time.

We step out of the tunnel, onto the ice, and the arena erupts. The home crowd roars, the sound vibrating in my chest as we take our warm-up laps. The moment my skates touch the ice, the rest of the world fades away. This is what I've been waiting for. What I fought to get back to.

Across the rink, Lucas watches me, a smirk playing on his lips. He tries to get in my head right away. A few choice words as soon as we're all lined up for the start of the game. A sneer when I ignore him altogether. But it's different this time.

This time, I'm not alone.

"Keep running your mouth, Tremble," Ethan interjects, jaw ticking even though his voice comes out even, calm. "See how long you last on your feet."

Lucas laughs. "Protecting your girl, Maddox? Cute."

Instead of getting annoyed, Ethan chuckles, a smugness entering his gaze as he faces off against Lucas. "If you knew *anything* about Dylan, you'd know she doesn't need protecting." He skates an inch closer, the humor draining from his expression as his gaze turns hard, deadly. "But if you touch her, I'll make you regret it."

Lucas looks like he wants to push it, but before he can, the ref's whistle cuts through the air, and we drop into position for the face-off.

The game is brutal. NSU is aggressive, taking every chance to check me hard, slash at my stick, and make their presence known. But every time they try to take me out, one of my guys is there. Never undermining my position but backing me up when needed.

Even Finn is a force on the ice. He clears space for me, knocking Lucas against the boards so hard the glass rattles.

I give as good as I get, landing hits of my own, digging deep to keep the advantage. By the time the second period ends, we're up by two points.

We head back to the locker room, the guys bumping shoulders and hyping each other up. I towel the sweat off my face, my hands still shaking with adrenaline. We're doing it. We're winning.

Coach goes over strategies for the second half, his voice steady, but the energy in the room is electric. We know NSU won't go down easily, but we've got them on their heels.

When we return to the ice, the roar of the crowd is deafening. I glance up, taking in the smiling faces, the blue-and-silver flags and scarves being waved. My own smile makes an appearance. Typically, I'm so focused on the game that I pay little to no attention to those here to cheer us on, but for a moment, I allow myself to bask in their support. But then—

The deafening thump of the music cuts off.

An eerie quiet settles over the arena, spectators turning to one another as cheers turn into whispers and looks of confusion. Someone points toward the jumbotron hanging above the ice, and I glance up.

My stomach drops.

I blink at the screen, unsure if what I'm seeing is actually real.

I'm looking at myself, standing on this very rink, except the lights are dim, the seats in the audience vacant. And taking up the brunt of the screen is me...and Griffin. My helmet dangles from one hand, Griffin's mask discarded on the ground, but what has my insides shriveling is the fact his hand is in my hair, mine fisting the front of his practice jersey, while our lips are interlocked.

Our kiss is hot and passionate, the way it always is between us.

Before I can wrap my mind around the scene unfolding before me, it changes. Instead of Griffin I'm kissing, it's Finn. The background is dark, but it looks like the back hallway of The Stanley.

The clip changes again. I recognize the team's physio room. Finn's body becomes Ethan's, and for a moment, I'm back in that room, Ethan's lips on mine, my hands tangled in his shirt.

A final transition, and I already know what's coming before it materializes. Me and Jax in the hot tub, his fingers tangled in my hair, his mouth moving over mine. I can feel the heat in my cheeks, the stares directed my way, and fingers being pointed. I don't dare look away from the jumbotron even though it makes me sick to my stomach to continue watching.

Expecting that to be the end of it, I wrench my gaze away. It clashes with Kyle's across the ice, and the sourness in my gut boils into fury. Even without the dark smirk curling his lips, I know this is his doing.

A flicker from the jumbotron has me glancing back, and I suck in a breath. This time, I'm entwined with someone wearing a white-and-glacial-blue jersey—NSU colors. Lucas.

More clips play out. I recognize the moments, remember them with unease, but the face in each of them has been altered. Each of these moments are private ones I shared with Lucas, but the clips have been doctored to make it seem as though I was intimate with most of the NSU team.

A montage of faked moments spliced in with real ones, painting a picture that isn't real but looks damningly convincing.

Image after image blends together in a sickening display until acid burns in my mouth and my muscles scream at me to run.

The crowd gasps, murmurs turning into a deafening roar. NSU fans jeer and laughter echoes from their bench.

I can't move. Can't breathe. My entire body feels numb as I stare up at the screen, watching my humiliation play out in front of thousands of people.

Slowly, I turn to the guys, both dreading and hoping...

Ethan's face is unreadable.

Jax grips his stick so tight his knuckles go white, but still, I can't get a read on his thoughts.

Finn's face is a blank slate.

And Griffin—Griffin looks as though he's contemplating murder, but whether it's whoever did this or mine, I can't be sure.

When the vile, incriminating video is finished, the screen returns to the typical Steelhawks promo. I'm not sure if the arena goes quiet or if the rushing of my pulse in my ears drowns out all other noise. Only the high-pitched blow of the ref's whistle jolts me back into the present. The reality that I am now left to rise or crumble in.

Despite the interruption, a game is in progress, and we are expected to continue on as if nothing happened.

I swallow hard, my hands shaking as I grip my stick.

A hand comes to rest on my shoulder, and I flinch.

"Dyl—" Bear's worried tone has me sucking in a grounding breath.

Before he can say anything else, I shake my head. "I'm fine."

I'm anything but, but I refuse to let Kyle and Lucas see any hint of weakness. I will play. I will fight. And I will win. Even if they've won the war, I will win this battle.

The third period starts. I try to catch the guys' gazes, but they avoid looking my way. Any spare moment, I search for some kind of reassurance, but their faces remain unreadable.

Anxiety knots in my stomach, clawing up my throat. What if they believe what they saw? What if they think I'm a slut?

That I played them all? That whatever we were starting to build is already over?

With every question unanswered, I push myself harder. Faster. I channel the sick churn of emotions inside me into every shift, every play. I crash into my opponents with unrelenting force, steal pucks with ruthless efficiency, and fire shots at the net like my life depends on it.

I check Lucas so hard he stumbles, my shoulder slamming into his ribs. When he snarls, I just skate away. I don't even feel triumphant over besting him. I'm numb to it all.

I deke through the Glaciers' defense, driving the puck forward, weaving past bodies like they're nothing. When I finally get my chance, I take the shot—and score. The horn blares. The crowd erupts.

I don't celebrate. I don't stop. I demand the puck on every shift, pushing my body beyond its limits, refusing to let them take this from me.

They can try to ruin my name, but they will never take my game.

THIRTY-NINE

CELEBRATIONS ARE GOING on all around me in the locker room, but I am immune to it all. For the first time, I'm not joining in with the rest of the team, not celebrating our win against NSU.

Instead of being sweet with victory, the air around me is thick, suffocating. I'm distantly aware of skates clattering on the floor, the snap of a towel as the guys change out of their gear, but I barely register any of it. It's background noise to the questions flying like loose pucks inside my head.

The only thing in the room I am aware of is Dylan's absence. She was hauled into Coach's office the second the final buzzer went. That, and the fact that Griffin, Ethan, and Jax are as quiet as I am. Like me, they aren't partaking in the celebrations, not caught up in the high of the win. Heck, looking at the four of us, you'd think the Steelhawks lost tonight when we fucking dominated.

Even if it was Dylan who was ultimately responsible for our destroying win. She was on fire out there tonight, especially in that third period. Until that video, I'd been loving every second of being on the ice with her. Watching her do her thing. *Helping* her. We were a solid team, and it showed.

But after? My body was in the game, going through the motions, but my head was elsewhere.

I drop onto the bench, ignoring the pumping music from someone's phone and the general buzz of laughter around me as I rest my elbows on my knees and lean forward, closing my eyes. The images from the jumbotron play on a loop in my head.

I knew Dylan was getting close with the others, that lines had been crossed. But seeing her doing the exact same thing with guys from NSU...

What the fuck does that mean? Was she using us—them? Does she get off on screwing her teammates? I don't understand. All I know is the bitter taste of the acidic bile that crawled up my throat as clip after clip played out before me.

I shake my head, willing the pictures away, but they are burned into my retinas.

Kyle was right.

He warned me. Fucking *warned* me and I didn't listen. Continued to get close to her, unable to physically stay away. I groan into my hands.

I should have *trusted* him—my best fucking friend.

Whatever Dylan's game is, it's clear none of us meant a goddamn thing to her.

I was foolish to believe she was different. She'd wholly captured my attention that day she rocked up to the porch in her little denim shorts and Converse, and I wanted to believe that maybe, just maybe, she was the kind of girl who meant the things she said.

But I was wrong.

So. Fucking. Wrong.

My head snaps up as a hand claps my shoulder, and I look up at Kyle's pinched, sympathetic expression. "Come on." He gestures toward the door, and barely sparing the others a glance, I grab my things and follow.

I'm not paying any attention to our surroundings as we leave the arena, as I drop into the passenger seat of Kyle's Mercedes. The small town of Blackstone blurs past my window.

"I'm sorry, man," he says, glancing my way. "I tried to warn you."

My stomach knots. He did. And like the idiot I am, I ignored him.

"I just—I don't get it," I mutter. "She seemed—"

"Convincing?" Kyle fills in, huffing a quiet laugh. "Yeah. I'm sure she did." He shakes his head, another soft chuckle escaping. "Bench bunny suddenly sounds a lot more fitting."

I grimace, turning away to stare absently out the window. Even now, the thought of him—of anyone—referring to her that way pisses me off. I hated it when Selena did it, although telling her to stop only made her do it more, but the thought of all that shit starting all over again pisses me off. Even though it shouldn't. Dylan's true colors have been revealed now.

And I should be fucking done. Done with her. Done with this tangled mess of emotions gnawing on my gut any time I think of her, scent her bodywash in the bathroom, spy her from across the room.

"I hate that it had to happen this way," he says a while later as we pull up to a lookout spot halfway up the mountain that overlooks Blackstone. Lights sparkle against the night sky, the lights of civilization competing with the stars above. "But at least now you know the truth."

The truth. The word tastes bitter in my mouth.

And yet, something in his voice gives me pause.

Had to happen this way.

I frown, turning those words over in my head.

"Did *you* put together that video?" All the pieces slot into place. Our conversation the other week. Running into him in The Stanley right after that kiss with Dylan, The lack of surprise when the music cut out right before third period. "You did, didn't you?"

There's no contrition on his face. No guilt or shame. Equally, there's no smugness either. He just stares expectantly back at me. Waiting.

"Why?"

"Because I need you to see—*all of you to see*—who she is. She doesn't care about you. Hell, I wouldn't be surprised if she's trying to fracture the team from the inside so when scouts come, she looks like the best one of us on the ice."

My brow furrows, but I don't say anything.

He shakes his head. "I didn't even share the worst of it, man."

"What do you mean?" I ask almost nervously. How can there be *more?*

He hesitates just long enough to make my pulse spike. Then he pulls out his phone, taps the screen, and turns it toward me. The video plays, shaky and grainy, but clear enough. Dylan and Coach.

Coach's hand on her back, lingering just a second too long. Dylan standing too close, her expression one of joy and affection I've never seen on her before. Coach hugging her on the front stoop of his house, late enough at night that the lights inside glow through his windows.

"I don't—" I cut myself off, unable to say any more.

Kyle sighs, the sound heavy. "Apparently she was sleeping with her old coach too. It's just what she does." He shrugs casually, like he's not destroying every single image of the girl I thought I knew. "She might be a great player—I'm not disputing that—but she's got some serious issues."

The recording he's taken plays again, and I stare at the screen in shock. Every muscle in my body is locked up tight.

She played us. Lied to us. And we fell for it.

Anger flares hot in my chest, burying away whatever was left of the doubt I'd been harboring. I look up at Kyle, my jaw tight. "We need to tell the others. They need to see this."

Kyle nods, his expression solemn. "Yeah. They do."

FORTY

"THERE MUST BE some sort of explanation."

The words fall out of my mouth before I can stop them, shattering the silence that's been weighing down the locker room like a fucking tomb since the rest of the team piled out, heading to The Stanley to celebrate our win. Unsurprisingly, no one stopped to ask if we were coming, probably sensing that we weren't in the mood. Even Ethan didn't try to muster the enthusiasm to go, even though usually, if the team is out, he is too, wanting to keep an eye on everyone and make sure no one celebrates too hard.

He hasn't said a word since we got off the ice. Even now, his arms are crossed as he sits on the bench farther down from me, his jaw clenched so tightly I swear I can hear his teeth grinding.

Griffin doesn't hesitate. "Of course there is." His tone is firm, leaving no room for doubt. I glance his way, wondering how he can be so confident. He saw what I did—what the entire arena did.

I want to believe him, but my mind won't stop churning. Dylan told us she had issues with her old team. That they didn't get along. But she also dated Lucas. What if there were others?

What if, once she burned bridges, she just started fresh at a new school—new team, new guys, new game?

All this time, I've been thinking we have something special —not only between myself and Dylan but between the five of us. I've sat back and watched as she got closer to my friends, catching glimpses of a future where she is *ours*. I've even accepted Griffin's role in all of this.

And now I'm wondering if she's done this before, with her old team. If it means nothing to her at all. If *I* mean nothing to her. It hurts. My entire life, the only thing I've ever had, the only thing I could call my own, was hockey.

Until Dylan.

I never had a stable home growing up, never a place where I felt like I truly belonged, but when I was around Dylan, I felt at peace in a way I never thought possible. *She* was my home—the one I'd longed for as a kid, convinced myself I didn't need as an anguished teen, had found the beginnings of in Ethan and Finn.

The thought that we—that *I*—didn't mean the same to her... makes my stomach churn. Makes my blood feel like it's burning under my skin. I *liked* Dylan. Hell, I was fucking falling for her. Based on how fucking wretched I feel right now, I'd go so far as to say I was nearly in fucking *love* with her.

And now, after weeks of watching her, learning her, getting pulled deeper and deeper into whatever this thing is between us, I'm starting to wonder if any of it was real.

There's a swoosh as the door swings open.

Dylan walks in, skates digging into the floor, helmet dangling from her loose grip. Her shoulders are rounded, her head low. But the second she spots the three of us sitting there, her spine snaps straight. There's a sheen to her eyes that makes them sparkle beneath the bright overhead lights—a flash of raw, unfiltered emotion—before it vanishes behind a cold, unreadable mask.

Her gaze slowly sweeps over us before flicking around the otherwise empty room, looking for someone else. Looking for Finn.

"What are you still doing here?" she asks, returning her focus to us. There's an edge to her voice, something wary, closed off. Like she's suddenly realized she's alone in an empty locker room with three guys who might not be on her side anymore.

Before I can say anything, Ethan steps forward, his expression hard. "We need to hear your side."

Dylan scoffs, lifting her chin as she defiantly stares Ethan down. "You need to hear that I'm not a slut? That I didn't make out with half the fucking NSU team? Or do you need to hear that I haven't been playing you?"

Her gaze locks on to me, then Ethan, then Griffin. "We've been living in and out of each other's pockets for two months. We live together. Train together. Play together. One of you is with me every moment I'm on campus. If a ten-second video is enough to make you think I'm someone else, then we never had a chance of being anything."

Silence stretches tight. Her words dig under my skin, planting themselves there like barbed wire.

Then Griffin moves. One step. Another. Until he's standing directly in front of her. With her skates on, it puts her at nearly the same height as him. Her throat bobs as she waits for him to speak, but he seems content to drink her in for a moment, his gaze roaming over her face as though committing it to memory. "I know exactly whose bed I've been sleeping in every night," he murmurs, voice pitched low, but the words carry nonetheless. "Whose lips I've been kissing. Whose body has been wrapped around mine. Anyone who believes that amateur soft porn is an idiot undeserving of you."

Her gaze softens with hope, but she doesn't truly allow herself to relax until his arm curls around her, pulling her against him. She buries her face in his chest, and a shudder rolls through her as she relaxes into his hold.

After placing a chaste kiss on the top of her head, he shifts, moving to stand behind her. One arm snakes around her waist, the other banding around the front of her chest as he pulls her flush against him.

They both stare at Ethan and I. Dylan with a shuddered, albeit slightly nervous expression, and Griffin with hard, unyielding eyes that promise pain and retribution. It's clear whose side he's on. Without a single moment of hesitation, he has chosen Dylan.

I envy him. I wish I could so blindingly move to her side. Wish I didn't have these questions and doubts. And yet, seeing how resolutely he stands with her makes me wonder if he's right. What did that video on the jumbotron really tell us? That Dylan has kissed a few guys? It would make each of us a hypocrite to say we hadn't gotten around with other girls before her. Some of us more than others, but there have been puck bunnies a plenty since we started at BSU.

There's bound to be some reasonable explanation. Hell, even if it's just that she hooked up with a few guys after a win or on a night out. That doesn't have to diminish what we have. Her past shouldn't be held against her.

My foot moves forward.

My weight shifts.

Dylan's keen gaze zeros in on the movement.

And then the door bangs open, and we all turn as Kyle strolls in, Finn at his side.

"The gang's all here," Kyle sneers, his gaze landing on Dylan. "Even the whore."

Griffin is on him in seconds, shoving him back against the wall so hard Kyle grunts in pain. However, he still finds it in him to smirk—cocky and sure.

My gaze catches on Dylan and Finn. The two of them are locked in a silent battle, seemingly oblivious to everything going on around them as they just...stare at one another. Even with his jaw ticking, Finn looks broken.

As for Dylan? She just looks resigned.

"Say that again," Griffin's menacing growl draws my attention back to his confrontation with Kyle. A vein pulses along his temple, his hold on Reed's shirt unrelenting. "I fucking dare you." A vehement snarl rumbles from his chest, his lip curling. "*Please*, do," he taunts, voice low and deadly. "I'm looking for *any* excuse to rip you limb from limb."

Kyle remains smug, quiet, satisfaction glinting in his eyes because he knows he's getting under Griffin's skin.

Griffin sneers, his rage only intensifying as he leans in closer. However, he doesn't lower his voice as he snarls, "That jumbotron stunt, that was you, wasn't it?"

Kyle's smirk widens. "You needed to see who she truly was."

Griffin doesn't hesitate. His fist slams into Kyle's face with a brutal crack.

Dylan's gasp slices through the air as Kyle stumbles, clutching at his face. Bent over with a hand on his knee, he breathes heavily before lifting his gaze to Griffin. Hatred darkens his eyes. "You and Dylan are perfect for one another." He spits blood onto the white floor, the bright red stark and offensive, before he stands up. There's a fresh cut along his lower lip. "Crazy attracts crazy, I guess. But have the common decency to leave the rest of us out of it."

"It's laughable that you think you're *any* part of this," Griffin sneers.

Ignoring him, Kyle fixes each of us in his sights. "You should all walk away while you still can." Focusing on Ethan, his voice is edged with insistence. "Don't you see who she is now? She's a user. She does this for attention, to divide the team. And you're all falling for it."

His accusations snap the last of Dylan's restraint. She surges forward, fury blazing in her eyes, ready to pick up where Griffin left off and land her own blow on Kyle. I step in without thinking. My hand wraps around her arm, stopping her before she can throw a punch and hurt herself in the process.

The second our bodies connect, sparks ignite along my fingertips. My breath hitches, and I don't think I'll ever get used to how potently my body responds to hers.

She jerks her head toward me, eyes rounding in surprise. I'm a little shocked, myself, that I intervened. But I'm also pissed off at Kyle. He was behind the jumbotron stunt? I should have suspected. It hadn't even crossed my mind to question *who* was responsible. To publicly humiliate Dylan so casually—it makes me *murderous*, even amidst all this chaos.

However, I don't wish to see Dylan hurt. As entertaining as it would be to watch her give Kyle a black eye, the last thing she needs is to be benched for another game because she broke her hand on his smug face.

Ethan steps forward then, his face impassive. "I think it's best if you go, Kyle. Before you end up with a broken nose to match your busted lip."

Kyle smirks, glancing at Finn. "I'll catch you at The Stanley." Then, like a hurricane that leaves nothing but destruction in its wake, he's gone.

However, with him gone, the buzz of tension that's been residing in the air since she first walked in only escalates. Like the static that precedes a thunderstorm. You can't see it, but you can *feel* the storm coming.

Whirling on Dylan, Ethan's face is still set in that hard mask. "We need to talk about what happened tonight."

As if realizing I still have her in my grip, Dylan glares at me, yanking her arm free before turning sharply to face Ethan. "Why?" she snaps. "What difference does it make? You've already made up your mind."

Folding his arms across his chest, Ethan arches a brow in challenge. "Are you saying that wasn't you in those clips?"

Her jaw tightens, her posture equally as stubborn. "It was me." A wound rips open inside me at that admission, so painful that I nearly double over. Gritting my teeth, I force myself to breathe through my nose. Out of the corner of my eye, Ethan stiffens, and Finn's nostrils flare. "But it wasn't what you think," she tacks on defensively. "The photos were doctored. All of it, every single photo, was me with *one guy*—Lucas."

"What?" That one word tumbles from my lips, hope and hurt clashing brutally inside me. Is she saying what I think she is? Was she set up?

Finn doesn't seem to buy it, based on his derisive scoff. "And what about your old coach?" he challenges. "I'm guessing you didn't fuck him either?" Dylan blanches, but Finn keeps going. "What's your excuse for that one? Your long-lost twin did it?"

Advancing on her like a predator stalking his prey, Finn sneers. "Was she the one sleeping with our coach too?" Holding his phone up in front of his face, Dylan's face drains of all color. "You can't bullshit your way out of this one, Dylan. You fucked your old captain. You fucked your old team. And you're pulling the exact same shit here."

"What the hell are you talking about?" Ethan demands, snatching the phone from Finn. I move to look at the screen over his shoulder, brows pulling lower over my eyes as each strangely intimate scene with our coach unfolds.

I blink at the screen in confusion as I recall instances of catching Coach and Dylan standing closer than a typical player and coach. Times when it seemed as though Coach wanted to hug her.

My stomach twists dangerously.

Everything I've noticed—the way she and Coach interact, the familiarity, the looks—suddenly it all makes sense. The puzzle pieces slide into place with striking clarity.

Griffin snatches the phone from my grip, barely glancing at the screen before he scoffs, "You're all fucking idiots. This video? The jumbotron? None of it tells you shit."

And yet, Dylan is strangely quiet about the whole thing. Looking at her, she's white as a ghost, her hands trembling. Unlike when she first walked in here, defiant and ready to take on whatever we unleashed, she now looks...*guilty*.

Yeah, that's *exactly* how she looks.

And there's only one reason why she'd feel that way.

At our resolute silence, Griffin shakes his head. He turns to Dylan, easing her catatonic form onto a bench and removing her skates with fluid efficiency before helping her into her sneakers, not bothering to change her out of the rest of her gear. Instead, he stuffs her belongings into a duffel. Throwing it over his shoulder, he grasps her hand tightly and pulls her to her feet. With an arm wrapped around her shoulders, he pulls her into the supporting strength of his body. Leveling each of us with a ferocious glare that chills me to the bone, he escorts her toward the door.

Ethan just can't help himself, though. "Where are you going?" he demands.

"Anywhere but here." Griffin doesn't stop as he closes in on the door.

"Fine," Ethan harrumphs. "We'll have this discussion at home."

That garners Dylan's attention. She goes rigid, forcing Griffin to stop. Slowly, her head turns, so she's glowering at Ethan over her shoulder. Despite her pale skin, her eyes *burn* with a fire that looks nowhere close to being extinguished.

"I'm not going *home.*" There's a terrifying calmness to her words. "I'll be staying at Wren's—indefinitely. And your body-guard duties? Consider them no longer necessary." Her gaze sweeps over all of us. "Outside of practice, I don't want to see *any* of you."

With that, she's gone, whisked out the door and out of my life, leaving a cold, dark, gaping hole in my chest.

FORTY-ONE

THE STREET outside Wren's apartment is alive. Students spill out of bars, laughing, stumbling, swaying. A couple leans against a lamppost, tangled in each other, oblivious to the world around them.

I watch it all through the windshield, feeling...absolutely nothing. I'm so far removed from being able to understand these students' carefree lives that I may as well be on a different plane of existence.

I'm...numb. Disconnected. *Gutted*.

BSU had been starting to feel like home, like where I belonged. Where I should have been all along. And now...I'm beginning to think I don't belong anywhere. Nowhere can replace the home I lost. Perhaps I'm destined to roam this world alone for the rest of my days.

Except, I'm not entirely alone.

Griffin sits beside me inside the car, silent except for the muted tapping of his fingers drumming absently on the steering wheel. His presence is the only thing tethering me to reality. The only thing keeping me from unraveling completely.

I swallow against the tightness in my throat. My voice

comes out hoarse, barely above a whisper. "Why?" He turns to face me, and I force myself to look at him. "Why did you believe me over everything you saw? Over Kyle's accusations?"

His jaw clenches, dark violence flashing across his striking blue eyes, momentarily darkening them. It's there and gone so quickly that I almost wonder if I imagined it as he reaches forward, eliminating the space between us. His thumb traces along my jaw and down the side of my neck before his fingers curl possessively around my throat. My breaths turn heavy as he pulls me toward him until only a slither of space exists between us. When he speaks, his voice is low, rough. "Because you. Are. Mine."

A growl accompanies those words. One that sends a shiver racing through me. His eyes burn into mine, intense, unrelenting.

"I don't give a fuck what you did or didn't do. If you slept with your old team, if you fucked your coach—I. Don't. Care." His grip around my throat flexes. "You're still mine. End of story."

A shudder runs through me at the force he puts behind those words, the volatile flicker.

"For what it's worth, I will always believe you, Dylan. Always choose you. No matter how hard it gets, no matter what kind of shitstorm we're in the middle of." He leans in, his breath warm against my lips. "You're it for me."

Then his mouth crashes into mine.

It's not gentle. It's desperate, consuming, a raw collision of lips and teeth and tongue. A sealing of his promise. The fingers of his free hand tangle in my hair, and he uses his hold on my neck to drag me impossibly closer. I melt into him, letting him steal my breath, letting him erase everything else.

When we finally break apart, I'm panting, my fingers fisted

in his hoodie. His forehead rests against mine, his hands still holding me like he's afraid I'll disappear.

His steady, unmoving gaze is all I see as I force myself to speak. "Lucas compiled the video. I mean, I'm assuming Kyle got the footage of all of us, but the stuff from my old team came from Lucas. They must have been working together."

Griffin's body goes rigid, fine shakes vibrating through him like it's taking considerable restraint to keep himself still. To not move to find both of them and tear them apart, just like he swore earlier.

I keep going, though, needing to get it all out. "He used footage from when we were together. Photoshopped things to make it look like I was—" My voice breaks, Griffin's fingers massaging soothingly over my skin as I push through. "He used it to blackmail me into leaving. I was terrified of what it would do to my reputation, to my mom. She was barely holding on after my dad died, drowning in pills and alcohol. If she saw that..."

Whether it's my words or the devastation I can feel shredding me, Griffin's stance turns predatory. Rage consumes him, blazing out of his eyes with such intensity that I'd be absolutely fucking terrified if I were Kyle or Lucas right now.

"I'll kill him." The words are an animalistic snarl, barely coherent. "I swear to fucking God, I'll end him. Both of them." His voice is guttural, dark, and a twisted shiver of delight skitters through me. It's been a long time since someone has been so vehemently on my side, and, hell, I've missed it. Missed having that unquestionable support. That irrefutable love.

Not that I'm saying Griffin and I are in love.

Although, staring at him now, the devil who would never forsake me, I can't help but think I might be a little in love with him.

"While I'm at it," he continues darkly, "I should strangle Ethan, Jax, and Finn for how they treated you tonight."

A sad smile tilts my lips upward, the action not quite meeting my eyes, and my throat is thick as I run my fingers reassuringly down the ropey muscles of his arms. "They're entitled to feel what they feel and think what they think."

His nostrils flare. "They fucking betrayed you."

I swallow hard, the hurt still so fresh and painful. "Maybe, but I guess I can't fully blame them after everything they saw."

"I can!" His eyes flash with malice.

Despite the warmth that blooms in my chest at his words, I redirect the conversation. "I never slept with my coach—old or current."

He scoffs like the fact that I'm even having to say that is ludicrous. "Of course you didn't. Why would you sleep with someone who is like an uncle to you?"

I still. *How the hell does he know that? Does he know everything about my past—about who I am?*

Catching my wide-eyed look of shock, he chuckles darkly, seductively. "Hurricane, don't you know by now that I know everything there is to know about you?" He leans in, inhaling as his nose trails up the column of my neck. "When I say I'm obsessed with you, I don't just mean your body. Although, believe me, I am absolutely in love with every inch of your skin. But it's not just the sex I'm after. It's *you*. All of you. Your mind, your talent, your family, your history, your future. I want it all."

"God forbid you just *ask* me about any of it," I drawl, needing a bit of levity as my heart slams against my chest like it's trying to jump from my body and launch itself into his.

He smiles against the crook of my neck. "Where would the fun in that be?"

He chases the question with taunting, open-mouthed kisses that send my pulse skyrocketing. "Come home with me," he rasps. "You can stay in my bed. I've got plenty of ideas that will keep you distracted."

As if to demonstrate, he swirls his tongue over my skin, and I moan. My core is already clenching, hips tilting upward in an open invitation. Who needs a bed? I'd shamelessly let him take me right here, on the side of the road, for all of Blackstone to witness.

For a moment, I lose myself in the fog that always descends when Griffin is touching me, looking at me.

"I can't." I have to force the words out, my body protesting every syllable that leaves my lips. I don't *want* to leave. I could easily lose myself wrapped up in Griffin for the remainder of the weekend.

Tugging down the neckline of my gear, he continues his blazing trail along my shoulder. I didn't even get a chance to shower after the game. I'm covered in dry sweat and probably stink, but Griffin doesn't seem to care. If anything, the taste of salt on my skin only seems to encourage him.

"I-I need girl time." It's a struggle just to maintain a logical thought process when he's playing my body like it's his own personal toy. "T-to think."

"You think too much," he grunts, hands sliding beneath my clothing and...*oh, God.* "You need to feel."

Feel him worshipping every inch of my body.

Feel him spreading me open and claiming what's his.

Feel him pumping me full of his cum.

Another moan rips free, and I squeeze my legs together.

"Stay with me."

His words are a plea, a demand, an order from someone who doesn't expect to be denied.

In a single moment of clarity, I push on his shoulders, putting enough distance between us so I can think clearly. My chest heaves with my labored breaths as I stare into his dark, hungry eyes.

I shake my head, partly in a no to his words and also to clear it of the lusty fog. His face morphs into a scowl, one that is part terrifying, part adorable. Or maybe I'm just entirely fucked in the head.

"I could just drive off with you." Darkness laces his words as he reaches to push the button for the central locking.

I arch a brow. "You're going to kidnap me?"

He shrugs, entirely unbothered. "If that's what it takes."

Crossing my arms over my chest, I stare back at him, headstrong, even as I fight back a laugh at the notion of bargaining with a crazy man. "How about I text you during the night?"

He grumbles, not looking entirely appeased.

"And we can do something tomorrow—grab dinner or whatever."

His fingers flex. "Not enough."

I sigh, giving him an exasperated look. "Breakfast then. You can pick me up first thing."

"Fine." It's clear he's still not happy, but he relents.

Grinning at him, I keep one hand on the door handle as I lean over to press a brief kiss to his lips. "Good night, Griffin."

I hurriedly scurry out of the car before he can tempt me to stay—or trap me. He growls at my hasty retreat, eliciting a laugh from me.

Grabbing my bag from his back seat, a thought strikes me before I close the door. "First thing does not mean you show up here at 6 a.m.," I tell him sternly. "Nine, at the earliest."

"Six. Be ready, or I'll break down Wren's door to get to you."

He's gone, the door closing as he pulls away from the curb, before I can argue. *Dumb, territorial males.*

I'm still shaking my head at his ridiculousness when I knock on Wren's door. However, the moment she opens it, the weight of everything from today cracks the dam. My face crumples.

"Oh, honey." She pulls me into a hug, and the tears I'd held back since the locker room come rushing forward. For the first time tonight, I don't try to stop them. I just let myself fall apart in the safety of Wren's arms.

THE CREDITS ROLL across the screen, the soft hum of the movie's soundtrack filling Wren's small apartment. Empty bowls of ice cream sit on the coffee table, remnants of melted chocolate and sprinkles pooling at the bottom. A warmth has settled over me—not just from the hot chocolate, but from the safety of this space, of Wren. The weight in my chest feels a little lighter, the pain of the night dulled by her rants about the guys and the way she all but knighted Griffin for actually using his brain.

I shift slightly, curling deeper into the couch, my gaze flicking her way. "There's one thing I never told you." I've been debating over this all night. Since she vowed that the next time any of them came into The Stanley she was going to serve them spittle beer. I mean, if that's not true friendship, what is?

She turns to me, instantly alert, the kind of friend who never half listens. "What?"

I chew on the inside of my cheek, then exhale. If I'm doing this, I may as well rip off the Band-Aid. One I've been wearing since I started college. "Patrick Callahan is my dad."

For a moment, she just stares at me, her lips parted in shock. Then her eyes widen, and it's a flurry of blankets as she untangles herself and shoots upright, letting out a sound that can only be described as a screech. I swear dogs respond to the other-worldly noise. "WHAT?!"

Her hands clap as she practically vibrates with excitement. "You do mean *the* Patrick Callahan, right? As in, Hall of Famer, three-time Stanley Cup winner, and one of the best centers to ever play the game." Her face takes on a crushing expression. "Please God, tell me you're not talking about some random, middle-management, beer-belly, scratches-his-balls-in-public Patrick Callahan that nobody has ever heard of?"

The laugh that tears out of me is free and genuine. One only Wren is capable of eliciting after such an emotionally exhausting day.

"I'm talking about the Hall of Famer, Stanley Cup winner."

Another ear-splitting screech has me covering my head for fear of a burst eardrum.

"Oh. My. God." She clutches my wrist, shaking me slightly as her excitement overwhelms her. "Dylan. Dylan! You are actually hockey royalty. I feel like I should bow."

I groan. "Please don't."

She ignores me, still gaping. "This explains so much. Your instincts, your skating, your absolute murder-for-blood style of play. Holy shit, it's genetic."

I let out a breathless laugh. "I mean, maybe."

She leans closer, excitement still gleaming in her eyes. "Do the guys know?"

I hesitate. "Ethan figured it out, and I think Griffin knows."

Wren smirks. "Of course he does. He probably has the phases of your cycle memorized."

I scrunch my nose. "God, I hope not."

"What about Finn and Jax?"

I shake my head. "I debated telling Jax a couple of times, but...now I'm glad I didn't."

Something shifts in her expression, understanding settling in. Finding a modicum of self-restraint, she nibbles on her bottom lip, staring at me with wide eyes full of questions.

I chuckle, gesturing toward her. "You can ask."

She flashes me a grin. "So why change your name to Carter? When?"

I nod, running my fingers along the seam of my sweatshirt. I showered and changed as soon as I managed to stem the flow of tears that just wouldn't stop after I arrived. "When I started college. I wanted to carve out my own career, my own legacy. If I kept my dad's name, I'd never just be Dylan. I'd always be Patrick Callahan's daughter."

Wren's face softens, something that looks like understanding flashing in her eyes. "That make sense, and honestly? That's badass."

A warmth blooms in my chest. "Thanks."

She's quiet for a moment before she speaks again, "Since we're sharing truths..." She glances my way, her lower lip caught between her teeth. "I don't think I ever told you my last name."

I arch a brow, confused as to where she's going with this.

"It's Winslow." I just blink at her, clearly not getting whatever it is she's trying to say. "As in the *Atlantic City Serpents* Winslow."

My mouth falls open. My jaw hits the ground.

I splutter, at a loss for words. "Are you telling me your family *own* an NHL team?"

Her face scrunches before she nods.

"Holy shit...and you said *I* was hockey royalty?"

She scoffs. "You are. I'm like...management royalty. Ownership royalty?" She tilts her head in consideration before shrugging. "Whatever. My family could own anything, it just so happens to be a hockey team. Your dad—you—actually play the sport. Ergo, you are *proper* hockey royalty."

I shake my head, struggling to fathom why *that* is what we're hung up on right now.

"Is that why you're so into hockey? Because of your parents?"

She shrugs. "I mean, I guess so. I grew up surrounded by it. My brother is actually a rookie on the team this year, but that's not why I love it."

I nod, understanding. We're the same. We grew up surrounded by the sport, but that constant availability doesn't foster love. You could grow up in our shoes and end up hating the sport. Loving it is something more. It's ingrained in you. It's in your blood. In your very soul. It's a part of you that you can't deny.

"Well, holy crap. I was not expecting that," I say, collapsing back on the sofa, stunned.

"I don't tell many people," she admits, not looking at me. "People get funny when they find out who I am—who my family is."

"Yeah." Reaching over, I squeeze her hand. "Your secret is safe with me."

She gives me a very *Wren* grin. "Ditto, babe."

I chuckle, the two of us falling into silence.

"Is it hard? Being here, at BSU—his alma mater?" she eventually asks, voice soft.

I think about it, letting the question settle in my bones. Then, finally, I shake my head. "No. It feels right. Like I was always meant to end up here. Going to NSU was part of me creating my own path, but...now, I kinda wish I'd been here from the start. He would've loved to see me in Steelhawks colors, wearing his old jersey.

She squeezes my hand, her fingers warm and reassuring. "I bet he's looking down on you. Pumping a fist every time you show up one of the guys on the ice."

A laugh breaks free, but there's a lump in my throat, the

sting of grief not as sharp as it used to be but still there, still woven into me. "Yeah. Maybe."

She squeezes my hand again. "Definitely."

And for the first time in a long time, I let myself believe it.

FORTY-TWO

THUD. *Thud. Thud.*

A relentless pounding on the door drags me from my thin veil of sleep. My head throbs, the dull ache of exhaustion pressing against my skull. I groan, rolling over, but the knocking persists, loud and insistent.

"Fuck's sake. Does no one answer the goddamn door in this house?!"

With a grunt, I swing my legs over the side of the bed, barely registering the fact that I'm only in my boxers as I shuffle barefoot down the hall. *Fuck it, if some asshole insists on banging on the door at the ass crack of dawn, then they can deal with me wearing fucking boxers.*

Stomping down the stairs, I swipe a hand through my mussed-up hair, probably only messing it up more. What I need is a shower.

And five more hours in bed.

And for my brain to stop replaying images of Dylan kissing her old fucking teammates.

"Ugh."

Still feeling groggy, I yank open the door, intent on telling whoever is on the other side to piss off. Except the words lodge in my throat.

"Uhh...Coach?" Confusion slams into me. I glance past him, although I have no idea who the fuck I'm looking for, before snapping my gaze back to his. "Umm...what are you doing here?"

His arms are crossed over his chest, his expression carved from stone. I'd say it's a typical stance for Coach except, he looks about as fucked in the head as I feel. His eyes are blood-shot, day-old stubble darkening his jaw. I don't think I've ever seen him anything other than clean-shaven.

Astute, yet dulled with fatigue, eyes sweep over me once, lips flattening in clear disapproval. Well, fuck, now I wish I'd taken the two seconds to pull on a pair of sweatpants. Maybe a T-shirt, too.

"Where is she?" he all but demands in his typical no-nonsense, do-as-I-say tone.

I cringe. *Shit.*

Scrubbing a hand over my face, I mutter, "She's not here." He tenses immediately. "She stayed the night at Wren's."

I don't know if he knows who Wren is, but he doesn't appear overly concerned at the news, so I'm guessing he's at least heard of her. Except, isn't that weird as fuck? If Dylan was *just another player*, he wouldn't have a clue who her friends are outside of the team. Just like he'd have no idea who *my* friends are outside of the team. Same for any player.

Fuck, my headache is back.

I just can't make sense of any of this.

I'm scrutinizing Coach's face, trying to piece it all together, to understand, so I notice the way his lips press together—in concern? Irritation? I can't fucking tell. He nods once, the motion sharp and curt. I expect that to be the end of this awkward interaction, however, he makes no move to leave.

There's a flicker of something unreadable in his eyes before he asks, "Can I come in?" For the first time in years, I hear hesitancy in his voice.

Surprised, I blink at him, but I find myself stepping aside to let him in. "Yeah, sure."

Coach steps through the doorway, his presence making the hall feel smaller, heavier. "How is she?" His voice is gruff, but there's something in it—guilt or worry—that catches me off guard.

It's just so...out of character for Coach.

Not to mention showing up at a player's house.

It sends my thoughts spinning again...

But then I glance sideways at him, and *seriously*? Dylan and Coach? Maybe I'm too close to the entire situation, but I just don't see it.

There was a moment last night, when my emotions where high, anger and confusion were clouding my judgment, and Finn had just added more wood to the bonfire by telling me she'd fucked her old coach, where I assumed it to be the truth... but in the stark light of day, I just don't fucking get it.

"She was upset when she left the arena," I finally answer, watching him closely, trying to get a read on what he's thinking. If the jumbotron stunt happened to any other player, he wouldn't be on their doorstep with the first streaks of daylight. So why is he here? What makes Dylan different? Is it just because she's a girl? He's been preaching all season about how we shouldn't treat her differently, but maybe seeing her hurt or upset got his instincts all screwed up.

Or could it be something more?

Silence stretches between us, thick and awkward. I don't have the first fucking clue what to say or do, so I blurt out the only thing that comes to mind. "Want a coffee?" I sure as hell need one.

He exhales, some of the tension in his shoulders easing. "Yeah."

With a tilt of my head, I lead him toward the kitchen. As we step over the threshold, my gaze lands on Finn, my footsteps slowing. He's sitting at the table, dark circles staining the skin beneath his eyes, a scowl twisting his face. I didn't even notice him sitting there when I came downstairs. Shows just how in my head I am. He's not looking at me, though.

Finn's glare is locked on Coach, his ire focused and burning. He doesn't even acknowledge me as I move toward the coffeepot.

"What are *you* doing here?" he sneers, lip curled in obvious disgust.

It's so unlike him—unlike anyone on the team. No one talks to Coach that way. Not only because he'd flay us alive but because we each respect him. At least, we used to. If that footage we saw yesterday is true, Finn's respect isn't the only one he'll lose.

Coach arches a brow, his expression cooling into something sharp. "Mind your tone, O'Rourke."

Finn doesn't blink, doesn't flinch at Coach's uncompromising tone. If anything, his gaze only narrows further on the man we all unquestioningly obeyed—until today.

"So, it's true then." He doesn't phrase it as a question. It's a statement of fact. "You are sleeping with Dylan."

Coach blanches so hard that I'm surprised he manages to stay on his feet. He physically recoils from Finn's accusation, color draining from his face as his expression morphs into one of absolute horror. All thoughts of coffee are abandoned as I turn to face him fully, cataloging his reaction with interest and more than a few questions of my own.

In the next second, Coach's face is red with fury, and he plants his feet before staring Finn down. "Are you drunk,

O'Rourke?" He practically vibrates with rage. "How dare you so casually throw around such an accusation. Do you have any idea of the consequences of such lies?"

Unperturbed, Finn fires back, "Are they lies, though?"

Spluttering, Coach's gaze flashes to mine. "Maddox, what is the meaning of this?"

"I think he's talking about the fact you and Dylan seem particularly...comfortable with one another," Jax explains, rubbing a hand over his face as he steps into the kitchen. Sweats hang low on his hips, and his hair is an absolute disaster. Behind him, I notice the mess of blankets on the sofa in the living room. Apparently he distracted himself with video games until he passed out last night. Better than Finn, I guess, who doesn't look like he has had a wink of sleep all night. He went out with Kyle and the team after Griffin dragged Dylan out of the locker room, and I didn't hear him come home, so it must have been super late—or early, I guess. "And the fact she's been seen leaving your house late at night," Jax tacks on, looking more awake now as he leans against the kitchen counter, eyeing Coach in the same shrewd way I am.

For the first time in as long as I've known him, Coach is speechless. His mouth opens and closes a number of times before he manages to spit anything out. When he does, what he says leaves all of us reeling.

"Dylan is like a daughter to me!"

Those words, along with the intensity behind them, nearly knock me off my feet. I'm not the only one blown back by his unexpected response. Jax rears back, and Finn's mouth drops open in surprise.

"I've known that girl since she was little more than a baby," he fumes, the words tumbling over one another. "Whoever is spreading such disgusting rumors, they are baseless, and frankly, they are *wrong*."

My ears ring in the pursuing silence. My thoughts spin in a dozen different directions, trying to make sense of any of this and coming up empty.

"A daughter?" Finn asks, quizzical. Sounding just as confused as I feel, as Jax looks.

"I don't understand," I add, watching Coach's shoulders rise and fall with his heavy breaths. "You knew Dylan before she came to BSU?"

He exhales sharply, dragging a hand down his face. I'd put Coach in his mid-fifties. Despite the lines that have started to appear on his face, his salt-and-pepper hair that becomes more abundant every season, I've never considered him as *old* until now. In the span of thirty seconds, he's gone from being the strong coach I've known since freshman year to looking...old. Tired. *Human.*

Wrapping his hand around the back of a chair at the kitchen table, he sinks into it, pinching the bridge of his nose. "Her parents were college freshmen with a baby."

"Her dad was a Steelhawk." Even if I hadn't figured out exactly who her dad was, his teammates said as much that night at the bar.

Coach nods. "He was a good man. Struggling to make it to practice and classes and be there for Lorraine and the baby. So, I stepped in sometimes. Helped out when they needed it. Looked after Dylan during practice when a sitter fell through. Kept her at my place when they both had to study for exams. By the time they both graduated, I was like an uncle to that kid. I was at every single one of her birthday parties, at her high school graduation." He swallows, emotion overwhelming him. "After her dad died..." He falters for a split second before he clears his throat, pressing on. "She's been to hell and back this past year. Between her dad, and the shit she was dealing with at NSU." He shakes his head, and I'm pretty sure he's talking mostly to himself when he mutters, "I hadn't realized it was that bad. I should have... she wouldn't have taken the out unless she was desperate. Unless she had no other choice. She'd been so adamant that she had to pave her own path that when she accepted my offer to come here, I didn't question it." He sighs heavily before the room falls silent.

I sense he's lost in his own thoughts, in what he considers his own failures, but my mind spins with the nuggets of information he's given us. Nuggets that, along with the tidbits we've gotten from Dylan, suggest she was being bullied, badly, by her own team. To the extent that she was *forced* to leave. That left her feeling, like Coach said, like she had no other choice. Dylan is *strong*. She has more than proven that. Which begs the question, how fucking bad were things for her at NSU before she left? How fucking bad did *Lucas* make things for her?

Jax and I share a look, but it's Finn who questions, "What happened at NSU?"

That seems to snap Coach from his thoughts, and he gives Finn a hard look. "Don't think I don't know there's something going on between Dylan and each of you. If she hasn't shared her past with you, then I certainly won't."

"You brought her to BSU because she was being bullied," I interject.

Coach's glare shifts to me. "That girl was a Steelhawk from the day and hour she was born. She'd have been here from freshman year if it wasn't for her stubborn pride." He pins each of us with a look. "She *deserves* to be here as much as anyone else. NSU couldn't see that her potential was wasted sitting on the bench every game, but *I knew*."

I'm not disputing that. I don't believe any of us are. Dylan has more than proven herself on the ice. I'm beginning to think she's proven herself off the ice, too, and we were the dumb shits who believed some pictures over her word.

She even said herself that the photos were Photoshopped.

Is that part of the bullying Coach referred to? Did Lucas pull that shit on her last year? My teeth grind at that notion, even though I have no right to feel anger on her behalf, to feel protective of her. Not after how majorly I'm beginning to realize I fucked up last night.

How majorly *we* fucked up.

Certainly if Kyle was wrong about this, it reasons that he was wrong about her sleeping with her old coach. Which means that all of it, every moment that played out on the jumbotron last night, was fake.

Except for the ones between each of us.

That was the only real thing displayed on the jumbotron.

And we fucked it all up.

I made the biggest mistake of my life by not believing her. By doubting her.

God, I'm a fucking idiot.

I exchange a look with Finn, then Jax, each of them wearing mirroring guilt-ridden, panicked expressions.

"I agree," I tell Coach, facing him with a newfound determination. "Dylan is a Steelhawk through and through, and Steelhawks take care of their own."

Coach nods. From the corner of my eye, Jax straightens, a similar look of resolve settling on his face. Even Finn sits upright in his chair.

Even if Dylan doesn't want our help. Even if she despises us now. She *is* a Steelhawk, and Kyle has just proven that he isn't.

I'M SITTING on the sofa that afternoon, still reeling from our chat with Coach earlier. All of us are. Jax has chosen to distract himself with video games while Finn took himself upstairs after Coach left, looking like he'd just been informed he'd never play hockey again. He came down half an hour ago, grabbing the roll of trash bags under the sink before storming back upstairs without looking our way. God only knows what he's doing up there. His room is a bit of a pigsty, so hopefully he's on a rampage clean. I've been on at him to keep it organized for years now, but he never does listen. If it takes fucking up with Dylan to get him to do it, then who am I to say anything?

We all have our own coping mechanisms for dealing with the fact that we fucked up. Our own ways of passing the time until Dylan comes home. So we can talk. Fix things. Can we fix things? Fuck, I hope so. Once again, I've let her down. Let her down as her captain. As her friend. As a guy who is wholly consumed by her and wants everything she's willing to give.

I let petty emotions, jealousy and insecurity, get the better of me instead of trusting the woman who has been slowly opening up to me—to us. *Fuck, I'm an idiot.*

"Why do you think Griffin was so quick to defend Dylan?" Jax asks, his mind clearly stuck on the same loop as mine, even as he steers a Formula One racing car around a track on the screen. "Do you think he knew, about what happened at her old school?"

Sighing, I scrub my hands down my face, running them down the cotton fabric of my sweats while I lean back on the sofa and turn over his question. "No clue. Maybe. Or maybe he's just a better guy than we are."

Jax scoffs, then seems to think about it and his lips purse. "Things are bad when Griffin is the one doing the right thing and *we* are fucking up."

"At least she had someone last night." That's all I can think about. At least she wasn't alone. Griffin took care of her. He got her out of that locker room, and I have no doubt he will have made sure she made it to Wren's okay—assuming he left her side at all.

The red car Jax is driving makes it over the finish line and he tosses his controller on the table with a weary sigh. "Assuming we manage to fix this, what then?" Leaning back, he brings his feet up to rest on the edge of the table as he meets my gaze. "We've never actually talked about it. Each of us has just pursued her, knowing the others are too."

I shrug, having even less of an answer for that than his previous question.

"All I know is I want her. She makes me strive to be better. A better player, a better captain. A better man."

Jax nods knowingly. "Same. She gets me out of my head. She makes me laugh. When she's around I'm...lighter."

"You are," I agree. "You've spent less time holed up in your room or absorbed in video games, and you've come out with the team more than normal. You don't hide away the same way you used to. It finally feels like you're an active member of the team off the ice. It's good."

He smirks. "Well, I hate to break it to you, man, but she does nothing for your control issues. You've turned into a rabid bear since Dylan showed up. I bet you spent all night staring at that tracker app, making sure she was at Wren's."

Guilty as charged.

He barks a laugh, reading the answer all over my face.

"Griffin's not going to let her go," he says, growing serious again.

"Would you?" I arch a brow at him, already knowing his answer. It's the same as mine.

"If I can salvage what we had, then fuck no." He tilts his chin toward the ceiling. "What about Finn?"

"Pretty sure he's just up there grappling with his come-to-

Jesus moment. He's been so busy denying his feelings for her, using excuse after excuse to build a wall between them."

"And now that wall's just been bulldozed."

"Yup."

"So, assuming she forgives us, are the four of us just going to...share her?" Jax sounds curious more than anything, his gaze staring off with a slight furrow between his brows like he's trying to envision that future.

"I mean, we're used to working as a team," I say. I've been giving the situation a lot of thought this past twenty-four hours. "We're stronger together. Yeah, I wasn't sure how Griffin fit in, but after yesterday, I can see that Dylan needs him."

"Are we planning on fucking up that often?" Jax retorts with a hint of a teasing smile. "We're going to get real good at groveling if that's the case."

"Griffin proved himself yesterday. To be honest, he earned my respect when he unquestioningly stood by her. When he ushered her out of that locker room and took care of her."

Jax nods his agreement. "He didn't have to invite us to the Timberwolves game," he adds, cringing as he rubs the back of his neck. "I don't think I even would have thought of inviting you guys if I had the opportunity to get her all to myself for a night."

I huff a chuckle, but I totally get it. It's a rarity to have Dylan alone. I'm not sure I'd have been so eager to share her with anyone else either. That night, Griffin had the chance to take her out, just the two of them. He could have used that opportunity to keep her for himself, to put a wedge between her and us, and yet, he hadn't. For a possessive asshole, he sure seems open to sharing the one person who has come to mean the most to all of us.

The sound of the front door being opened has me jumping to my feet, Jax straightening as our heads whip toward the sound. My breath lodges in my throat as I wait in hope for Dylan to appear. To see with my own eyes that she's safe.

"Oh, it's you." Jax physically deflates as Griffin stomps into the room, looking like a man possessed. My own shoulders deflate in disappointment.

He doesn't acknowledge Jax's words, doesn't so much as slow down as he storms toward us. "Tell me what the fuck you're going to do to fix this, 'cause if I have to look at Dylan's tearstained face one more time, I'm going to castrate each and every one of you, and I'll fucking enjoy doing it."

Jax looks like he's been slapped. "She's been crying?" He cringes, his hand coming up to rub at his chest.

"She never cries," I muse aloud, voice quiet, devastated.

"Only when the people she thought she could trust throw her away like she's dog shit," Griffin snarls, sounding feral. Stopping in front of us, he crosses his arms over his chest. He's wearing his standard all black gear, the muscles of his forearms straining against the seams of his leather jacket. "So tell me how the fuck you're planning on fixing it."

Jax and I share a look. One that makes Griffin growl in irritation.

"Do I need to go get a knife from the kitchen?" he snarls. His body is strung so tight that I'd well believe he's a split second's hesitation away from following through on that threat.

Undeterred, Jax rolls his eyes. "Don't be so dramatic."

It's apparently the wrong thing to say. Any self-control he possessed is obliterated. Griffin's eyes flash with menace as he takes a threatening step toward Jax, who abruptly stands, planting his feet and squaring his shoulders. Before I can intervene, Griffin's lip curls back and he hisses, "Dramatic? I can guarantee, you'd be feeling downright *murderous* too if you'd spent the morning with the woman who is a mere fucking *shell* of who she was yesterday. And if you didn't," he continues, looking Jax over with contempt, "then you never fucking deserved her."

Well, holy shit. I think it's safe to say Griffin Price is in love.

And it's downright terrifying.

"So either you dipshits have a plan or I'm packing up her room and she's moving in with me."

"Dylan isn't going anywhere." We all turn as Finn appears at the bottom of the stairs, a trash bag thrown over his shoulder and another dangling from his hand. He drops them on the ground by the door, planting his hands on his hips. "Kyle is."

And now I know what's in the bags.

"Look who finally pulled his head out of his ass." Griffin slow claps.

Ignoring him, Finn's gaze slides to mine. "Dylan can't live under the same roof as him. Not after the shit he pulled last night."

Griffin snarls, but wisely keeps his mouth shut. I know what he's thinking. She shouldn't have had to endure living under the same roof as him after he attacked her. There's no point in bringing that up now, though. Finn is finally seeing Kyle for who he is; is finally onboard with protecting Dylan. I'm not about to argue with that.

"I agree." I look Jax's way.

"So do I," he says, face lined with resolve.

Clapping his hands together, Griffin says, "It's settled then. I'll move in here and take Kyle's room, and he can have my old one."

Finn's head whips in his direction, eyes narrowing. "We didn't agree to that."

"I wasn't giving you a choice," Griffin drawls. I swear, he lives to antagonize those around him.

"It's the best solution," I say, holding up my hands and

pinning Finn with a glare. "It's him or someone else on the team. Who do you think Dylan would choose?"

That seems to get through to him, and he snaps his jaw shut. Turning his sharp stare to Griffin, he jerks his head toward the stairs. "In that case, you can help me carry down the rest of his shit before he gets home."

"Where is he anyway?" Griffin inquires, a gleam entering his gaze. "I want to make sure I'm here when he gets back."

"He went home with some girl he picked up at The Stanley last night," Finn informs us. "He'll be back soon."

"Don't think this will be enough to make things right with Dylan—or with me," Griffin states with a touch of warning as he eyes each of us.

"What the fuck did we do to you?" Finn barks.

The look Griffin levels him would have lesser men pissing themselves. But we're hockey players. We don't balk in the face of pain. We stand taller.

"You hurt the only thing on this planet that I care more for than hockey." There's a possession behind his words, a level of loyalty that runs so deep I don't believe even death could sever it. "And I will make sure you get on your knees and fucking *beg* for her forgiveness before she gives it to you."

I can already see what a fucking blast it's going to be having Griffin living here. Don't get me wrong, I will willingly get on my knees before Dylan and beg her to forgive me. I just didn't expect to be doing it with Griffin smirking down at me. Asshole.

FORTY-THREE

I CHECK the time on my phone, my stomach twisting tighter with every passing second. 7:57 a.m. The team meeting starts in three minutes, and I'm still tucked in an alcove down the corridor, heart hammering against my ribs. I really, *really* don't want to go in there. I haven't seen Ethan, Finn, or Jax since Friday night. Haven't spoken to a single soul besides Wren, Griffin, and Bear, choosing to hide out at Wren's all weekend. However, Monday has now rolled around, dragging reality with it.

Not showing up to this morning's meeting isn't an option. Missing it and practice afterward would mean sitting out the games this weekend, and there is no fucking way I'm letting some humiliating stunt and a shattered heart keep me off the ice.

7:59 a.m.

I dig deep for my big girl pants.

Exhaling sharply, I shove my phone in my pocket and force myself forward. Every step toward the team room feels heavier than the last, but I keep moving, fingers curled into fists at my sides. I've got this. They can't say or do anything worse than what has already been done.

The second I step through the doorway, the room goes silent, all eyes swiveling my way like they've been waiting for me. I duck my head, keeping my gaze on the floor as I maneuver through the room. I expect whispers to break out. Hushed laughter. Slurs hissed just loud enough for me to hear. But nothing comes.

Silence clamps over the room like a vise.

I can feel the weight of every gaze pressing into me, but no one says a word. No one smirks. No one sneers. The unease coils tighter inside my chest, but I don't stop, moving quickly to the back of the room where Griffin always sits. He's waiting there for me, his hand moving to rest possessively, protectively on my knee as soon as I sit down.

No sooner has my ass hit the chair when Coach marches into the room. If the vicious scowl on his face wasn't an indicator of his piss-poor mood, the fact that he slams the door so hard the glass rattles in its pane would be.

All heads snap toward the front of the room, players sitting straighter in their chairs, shoulders squared like they are soldiers lined up waiting for their commanding officer's orders.

Fury rolls off Coach in waves, his expression a mask of unrelenting authority as he glares out over the room with eyes sharp as flint. Even the air crackles with the extent of his contempt as he takes his time, sweeping his gaze over each individual player like he's committing every face to memory. I fight the urge to scan the room, not wanting to see where Ethan, Finn, or Jax are seated. If they are beside Kyle and his cronies. I definitely do not want to see the smug look on their disgusting fucking faces.

When Coach finally speaks, his voice is a blade, slicing through the air with finely crafted precision. "What happened Friday was a *disgrace*." The words land like a slap, several players around me flinching from the verbal blow. "I don't know which one of you thought it would be funny to humiliate one of your teammates, but let me be clear—if you choose to spend your spare time crafting high school pranks, *you don't belong on this team.*" His fist bangs against the top of his clipboard.

No one moves. No one speaks. No one dares to even breathe.

My pulse stumbles. Even knowing Bear wouldn't let this slide, I wasn't prepared for the force of his anger. The sheer authority in his voice.

"*I do not tolerate bullying.*" His jaw flexes. "I do not accept hatred amongst teammates. If you have a problem with another player, you bring it to me. We handle it like fucking *adults.*" His grip on his control falters as he smacks his clipboard against a nearby table, the sound reverberating through the room and bouncing off the walls.

"When you wear your jersey, when you step onto *my ice*, you represent me. You represent this program. You represent this university." He shakes his head, his voice quieter now. "Friday night was an embarrassment. Not just for the player you humiliated, but for every single one of you." I struggle not to slide lower in my chair. *I am strong. I have survived worse.* Instead, I lift my chin an inch higher as Coach glares out over the room and declares, "An attack against one of our players is an attack against us all."

A slow, suffocating wave of shame crashes over the room. Shoulders stiffen. A few heads dip. The air is thick with tension.

Something hot pricks at the back of my throat.

Coach exhales sharply, nostrils flaring as he drags a hand through his thinning hair. When he speaks again, the rage is still there, but underneath it is something heavier.

Disappointment.

He lets the silence stretch, lets the weight of his words settle like concrete while he scans the team one last time before shaking his head. "I expected better—from all of you."

The weight of his words, his disapproval, sits there, festering, bubbling, lingering like a bruise. When the tension in the room is pulled so taut it's about to snap, he straightens.

"I *will* find out who was behind this," he declares in a quiet, dangerous promise. "And when I do, you will be stripped of your jersey. *You will no longer be a Steelhawk.*"

If the silence was deafening before, it's nothing like the pressure I feel against my eardrums after that statement.

A warm hand squeezes my thigh, grounding me, as Coach moves on to analyze Friday's game. I don't hear a single word he says as I glance over, meeting Griffin's unreadable gaze. However, there is something steady there, something solid.

For the first time since that horrible video began playing on the jumbotron, I don't feel so alone, so isolated. Things don't feel so hopeless.

I might have lost three out of four of the guys.

But I still have Griffin on my side.

And this time, I have a coach who's got my back. I've got Bear.

I KEPT my head down during practice, ignoring the feel of eyes on me. From the team, but most prominently from the guys. Them and Kyle. *Fucking Kyle.* I never met his gaze purely so I wouldn't see the smugness residing there, and he couldn't see the devastation I hid in mine. I focused on my drills, on being the best player out there, and on being part of a team even if I was back to being an outsider. No one spoke to me, but I equally didn't get any hostile vibes from anyone. Well, other than Kyle and his goons, but I'm so used to it, that it rolls off me like water.

By the time the end of the day comes around, I'm ready to

fall into bed. Gathering my things after my last class of the day, I sling my bag over my shoulder and exit the classroom.

"Watch it!" someone sneers as something hard connects with my shoulder, and I fall back against the door. My head whips up, meeting Kyle's incensed gaze. He's glaring down at me, lip curled back. It's a far cry from the smug expression I expected him to be sporting after his stunt on Friday. "Bench Bunny," he hisses. It immediately gets my hackles up, but I don't let him see that.

Unfortunately, instead of moving on, he lingers, moving closer. Students file past us, no one paying us any attention as they head out of the building, ready to get home after a long day on campus.

"I don't know what you did to wrap them so tightly around your finger," he snarls, deliberately dropping his gaze to linger on my breasts and between my legs. "Your pussy must be made of gold or some shit." His gaze snaps back to mine, hardening into something cold and cruel. "Either way, I *will* prove that you don't belong here." Another curl of his lips. "Women don't belong in men's hockey. Especially not bench bunny sluts."

Misogynistic prick.

He disappears back into the crowd like he was never here. I watch him go before blowing out the breath I was holding. I have no idea what has him so pissed now. Was it Coach's speech this morning? Except that doesn't make sense. Whatever has his panties in a bunch, I sense it's no longer purely about getting his spot back. It's about getting me off the team. About proving I don't belong.

One thing's for sure, I'm going to have to watch my back.

A pang goes through my chest, knowing I'll no longer have the guys as my bodyguards. Sure, I might have disliked having them constantly watching me—Ethan always knowing my whereabouts—but there was a sense of safety in it too. Now, I feel exposed.

A shiver runs down my spine, and I cast a glance over my shoulder, doing a sweep of the hallway, but other than the odd straggler, I'm alone.

Fixing my bag on my shoulder, I quicken my steps as I head out of the building, suddenly all too keen to get out of here myself. Except, the idea of going home stalls me on the steps outside.

I want to go back to that house about as much as I wanted to step foot in that meeting this morning. As much as I want to remain here after Kyle's delightful little threat. What I *really* want is to go to Wren's. I want to cuddle up beneath a blanket on her sofa and listen to her bitch the guys out and yell at the characters on the TV like somehow she can make them make different decisions. I want to pretend that I didn't lose the only people, other than Wren and Griffin, who have come to mean something to me. People who have been steadily plugging the deep, gut-wrenching hole left inside me after my father's death.

I want to pretend like I don't already miss playing video games with Jax, Finn's stealth kisses, or Ethan's overprotective-ness—even if it did piss me off at the time, at least it showed that he cared and it had been so, *so* long since I'd had someone truly *worry* about me. In their own ways, they made me feel like I belonged. They included me, looked out for me, ensured I was fed and safe. They...made me happy.

And now I feel truly fucking miserable without them.

"You look like you just found out we lost the season to NSU."

Lifting my head at the sound of his voice, my lips quirk as Griffin strides up the steps toward me.

"Over my dead body will that be happening."

He growls, shadows curling around his features. It's fucked

up how that look sends a shiver through me, and not one of fear or discontent. One of *excitement. Exhilaration.*

"Over *my* dead body will *that* be happening."

I roll my eyes, my grin growing wider. He immediately drops his arm over my shoulders, pulling me into his side before leading me down the steps.

We catch each other up on our days as we pass through campus before walking down the sidewalk toward Athletes Row. However, as soon as we turn onto the street, my stomach seizes, and my steps slow.

Reaching the house I've been sharing with the guys and Kyle for the past two months, I stop. I don't know if I can make myself go in there. It was challenging enough when it was just Kyle I had to avoid, but now I have to avoid all *four* of them. That's impossible!

And yet, what choice do I have?

I can try searching for somewhere else to stay, but that isn't going to happen today. So, for right now, I need to make myself go in there.

It'll be fine. You can stay in your room the entire time, go back to eating meals on campus, and hang out with Griffin or Wren in the evenings. I literally just need to sleep here.

As if sensing my resolve, Griffin steps forward. "You don't have to come in," I tell him. Probably better that he's not here for this. He's already seen the evidence of my tears and a restless night's sleep the past two days when he picked me up at fucking dawn to get breakfast. I swear it nearly sent him on a homicidal rampage. I kinda dread what might happen if he sees me break down over these guys. He might actually kill them, and as much as I'm hurt by them, disappointed by their actions, even I don't want them *dead*.

At least, not yet. Let's see how the rest of today goes. I reserve the right to change my mind tomorrow.

Instead of leaving, Griffin's arm falls from my shoulders as he takes another step forward. He turns to face me, his backpack swinging as he throws his arms out. He begins to walk backward toward the house, a sly grin stretching across his face. "What do you mean? I live here."

My brow furrows, and I watch as he continues to back up to the house. At the bottom of the stairs, he spins around, climbing them to the porch. He's at the front door before I find my words. "Wait," I call, taking a step forward, then another. "What do you mean?"

He's already opening the front door, and I hurry to catch up. "Griffin! What do you mean *you live here*? Since when?!"

He's gone, disappearing inside and leaving me to chase after him.

Hastily dropping my bag inside the door, my Converse slap against the wooden floors as I move deeper into the house. "Griffin! What are you—"

I come to a stop at the entrance to the living room, finding not only Griffin but all four of the guys standing there as though waiting for me.

My next breath lodges in my throat, a sudden case of nerves assaulting me, even as I internally balk at how fucking hot the four of them look standing there together. Even as tired and worn down as Ethan, Finn, and Jax look, they paint the most breathtaking picture of strong, athletic, should-absolutely-be-in-a-dirty-calendar men.

Forcing myself to go three days without seeing them is like witnessing them up close and in person outside of their hockey gear for the first time. I'm left just as stunned, just as speechless now, as I was that first day on campus.

Ethan steps forward, brow creased and eyes soft, pleading. "He means we kicked Kyle out."

They did?

Wait, is *that* why Kyle felt the need to pull his little intimi- dation act?

But... "Why?"

Jax steps up beside Ethan, their shoulders brushing, but his gaze is zeroed in on me. "Because we're fucking idiots. We should have listened to you. Should have given you the opportu- nity to explain." He ducks his head, running a hand through his hair, before glancing at me through his thick, lush eyelashes. "We let our emotions overrule common sense. Let *jealousy* blind us. We momentarily forgot the type of person you truly are and that you'd never do something like that."

"What, kiss multiple guys?" It's a defensive response, one primed from years of being on guard, years of being let down, of being bullied, hated on.

Jax shakes his head. "Betray us."

"But we betrayed you," Finn finally speaks up, joining the line on Ethan's other side. Pain flashes across his face, and for the first time, I catch a glimpse of Finn's true feelings, instead of hiding them behind the mask he typically wears in my presence. "Me, most of all." He shakes his head, stuffing his hands in the front pockets of his jeans. "I didn't want to believe it, but Kyle showed his true colors on Friday night with that stunt."

I notice he doesn't mention the attack, and I don't needle him with it. Now isn't the time, but I firmly believe a time will come when Kyle will show just how far he's willing to go—and it's well beyond public humiliation.

My eyes rake over each of them before flitting to Griffin who is standing off to the side. "Did you put them up to this?"

Before he can answer, Ethan does. "Coach made us realize what idiots we'd been." I stiffen. "He told us that you were basi- cally family."

He pauses as if waiting for confirmation, and licking my dry lips, I croak, "We are. He's like an uncle to me."

"Yeah, that's what he said." Finn's face scrunches. "Although, I, uh, might have accused him of fucking you first."

I grimace. It was disgusting the first time that was thrown in my face, and it's equally as disturbing now.

"Yeah, he made that exact same face," Finn says. "Right before telling us the truth."

Fuck, hopefully not the whole truth, although I'm guessing by the fact no one is bringing up the fact that Patrick Callahan is my father, that he didn't.

"That's when we realized, if Kyle lied about that, he could have lied about the whole thing."

"Could have." There's a strange robotic tone to my voice.

"Did," Ethan corrects. "But even if every single kiss on that jumbotron was real, who are we to judge? We had no right getting angry at you over it."

"No," I say curtly. "You didn't."

He nods, lips pursed.

"We know he was behind the entire thing," Jax interjects, as if sensing their opportunity slipping through their fingers. "Coach might not be able to do anything without proof, but we can."

By kicking him out.

"Kyle and I swapped rooms," Griffin states, talking for the first time. His face splits into a wide grin, so at odds with the tension in the room. "We're roommates now."

"We don't expect you to forgive us," Ethan informs me, drawing my attention back to him. "But please say you'll stay."

My gaze lingers on Ethan, the dark circles beneath his eyes, the haggard look on his face, before flicking to Finn. He looks equally as disheveled, his gaze tortured, before I shift my attention to Jax. His deep brown eyes seem to bore into me, pleading, begging, and his voice is rough when he speaks.

"Please, Little Menace. Who am I going to play video games with?"

There's the slightest quirk of his lips, a hint of a smile that I know he reserves solely for me.

It's my downfall.

"Fine," I relent. "I'll stay, but don't think this means all is forgiven. You hurt me. You broke my trust in you, and that's going to take time to earn back."

All three give sharp, serious nods.

"We understand." Ethan.

"We'll earn your trust back." Jax.

"We won't break it again."

The intensity in Finn's eyes nearly bowls me over, and I strangely find myself believing him. Believing all three of them.

At the very least, I *want* to believe them.

FORTY-FOUR

I'M nervous the next day as we carpool to campus. So far, the morning has gone like any other, each of us rushing through our morning routines to get out the door so we're on time for practice. It takes until we're pulling through the gates onto campus before I figure out *why* I'm a ball of nerves.

I feel like I'm waiting for the other shoe to drop.

I'm half expecting one of them to turn around and tell me this is all some cosmic joke. That they're actually pissed and this is all some twisted plan to get back at me.

I don't believe that they've suddenly gone from being as hurt and confused as they looked on Friday night to being on my side. It just doesn't feel real. I glance at each guy as the four of them banter back and forth while Ethan pulls into a parking space outside the arena.

This all feels too smooth.

It's too easy to fall into this sense of camaraderie.

And yet, I find myself soaking up every minute of it.

Getting out of the car, we grab our bags from the trunk before making our way inside. Griffin is immediately at my side, no hesitation as he slides his hand into mine. I can feel the other guys watching us, but nobody says anything as they crowd around, the five of us forming a unit as we navigate the arena hallways.

Heads lift as we walk into the locker room, greetings exchanged. I'm cautious at first, until our teammates greet me with the same warmth and easy *"Mornin'"* the guys receive.

I make a beeline toward my locker, but my steps slow when I notice the guys who occupy the lockers on either side of mine are now sitting elsewhere.

"What's going on?" I ask when Griffin and Ethan step up to the lockers beside mine, dumping their bags on the bench in front of them like this is where they've always gotten changed. Finn and Jax have moved to their other sides, the four of them fanning out beside me.

The crease between my brows deepens.

"Everyone already knows we're all together," Griffin says with such casualness that it takes a second for his words to penetrate.

"We figure, what's the point in hiding it any longer?" Ethan tacks on.

"Not that that's what we were doing," Finn quickly adds, flashing me a crooked smile. He's been doing that all morning —smiling at me. Gone are his surly scowls and forbidden glances of longing. Instead, he openly dropped his heated gaze over me when I came down the stairs this morning, before flashing me a toothy grin and pressing a bagel and cup of coffee into my hand. I was left in such a state of shock that he had to actually tell me to inhale it all before Ethan ordered us out of the house.

"No," Jax says, elbowing him. "You were too busy living in denial."

Finn rolls his eyes as he shrugs out of his top, baring all that glorious tanned and inked skin. Just like the others, he's all lean muscle. I could lose hours, days even, tracing every ridge and dip with my fingers.

"Funny," I say, ripping my gaze away before he notices, and it goes to his head. "I don't recall a single one of you asking me out."

Instead of being put off by my snark, Griffin grins. Flattening his arm across his locker in a move that has the hem of his top riding up to flash a slither of sculpted skin, he leans into me until his lips are a hair's breadth away, and I can smell the crisp minty freshness of his toothpaste as his breath dances over my cheek. The world comes to a standstill, everything beyond this moment ceasing to exist. I can feel the eyes of others in the locker room on us, but right here, in this moment, I don't care. "If I recall correctly, *I* asked you on a date."

Air whooshes out of my lungs as I poke him in his ridiculously hard chest. "Not the same thing, and you know it."

He just smirks. "What's the point in asking when we already know the answer?"

This time, I shove at him, rolling my eyes as I turn my back to him and begin changing into my gear. "Cocky."

And yet, something settles in me. Some of that unease I've been feeling all morning calms. As ridiculous and possessive as it is, I needed this outward display of acceptance from them.

And it only feels better when Kyle slips into the locker room to find his locker has been moved. One of the guys points him to the far corner of the room beside the showers, away from the thick of the bantering and celebrating, to an empty locker beside Fletcher and Monroe. His fury at being randomly moved makes my entire fucking day.

❄

By THE END OF PRACTICE, it's clear that Kyle is being shunned. Not just by me and my guys but by the entire team. Every single Steelhawk snubs him, interacting only enough to get through a drill and navigate a practice game.

There's only one person other than Coach who has the power to achieve that, so as we're crossing campus toward the athletes' dining hall, I move to walk beside Ethan.

"What did you do?"

He arches a brow. "Not sure I know what you're referring to."

"Bullshit. You're the only one who could get lockers switched and the entire team to rebuff Kyle."

His lips quirk, a rare smugness lighting up his face. Ethan isn't one to gloat about his actions, but he's clearly proud of what he's achieved.

"Coach might not have the evidence he needs to kick Kyle off the team, but the guys don't need proof. All they needed was my word."

"You told them to shun him?"

He shakes his head, his grin turning genuine. "That's the best part. I didn't have to. I told them Kyle was the one responsible for the jumbotron, and they were all instantly furious on your behalf. They made the decision to freeze him out themselves. I didn't have to say a word."

My mouth drops open in shock, and a softness enters Ethan's gaze as he stares at me. He reaches out, his hand hesitating in midair like he's not sure if he's allowed to touch me or not, before he traces a line down my temple, pushing a loose strand of hair out of my face. It might not be the intimate touch my body craves, but his hand lingers, like he can't quite bring himself to pull away.

"I don't think you realize just how much the team cares

about you. You're one of us—a Steelhawk. Coach was right when he said an attack on one of us was an attack on us all, except the team isn't doing this out of a sense of loyalty or team obligation, but because they are genuinely furious for you. They have your back. *We* have your back, and I'll be forever sorry that I made you question otherwise."

I'm still speechless, still turning his words over in my head when we reach the cafeteria and head inside to our usual table in the middle of the room. No sooner have I sat down, when a tray is placed in front of me, the plate loaded with scrambled eggs, bacon, and toast.

Typically, Finn drops off my food before hightailing it as far down the table as he can get, but today, he slides into the empty seat beside me. He flashes me another one of those charismatic smiles, this time following it up with a cheeky wink that has my insides fluttering traitorously.

I look away before he can notice the heat in my cheeks. *What am I doing, I'm acting like a schoolgirl with a crush!*

"Thanks," I mumble before diving in. Despite my pre-workout bagel this morning, I'm *starving*. There's a temporary lull in conversation while everyone stuffs their faces, before conversation turns to this week's hot topic—Halloween.

Just like on Roster Day, Athletes Row is hosting a street party this Saturday for Halloween. I spent a good portion of my week trying to convince Wren to go since apparently attendance is mandatory for all hockey players—cue eye roll—but no matter what I offered her, she wouldn't budge. Honestly, it surprises me that she's so anti-house party. Wren is so outgoing. She loves a fun night out and getting drinks at The Stanley, but she absolutely refuses to attend an Athletes Row party. Makes me wonder if there is someone on the street she is trying to avoid —and if so, who and why?

"What are you dressing up as for Halloween?" Finn asks casually.

I shrug, not having given it much thought. I'm not exactly buzzing to go, given how my last Athletes Row party went.

"Probably just throw on my Steelhawks jersey and call it a day."

"Original." Finn smirks. "Is it dressing up if you go as yourself, though?"

"All right, I'll put on your jersey and walk around with an arrogant swagger, flirting with anything in a skirt."

Throwing back his head, he barks out a loud, carefree laugh. It's the first time he's done that—with me, at least—and it warms my chest. I realize that for the first time since I arrived at BSU, we're having an actual conversation. Not one where we're throwing barbs at one another or riling the other up, but an actual, genuine conversation.

"Nah, I wouldn't be wearing a jersey." Lifting the hem of the navy top he's wearing, he smacks a palm against his rock-hard abs. "Would be a shame to hide all this from the ladies."

Leaning in, his voice dips an octave as he rasps, "I wouldn't mind seeing *you* in my jersey, though. But not at the party." His gaze dips lower before flicking back to my face. "I wouldn't be able to stop myself from pouncing on you, and I wouldn't give a shit who all was watching."

My entire body flushes. I grow uncomfortably warm as I shift in my seat, pressure gathering between my legs. I'm momentarily speechless, struggling to remember to breathe, never mind form a coherent sentence.

When I finally recover enough brain cells to make my lips move, my voice comes out breathless. "Oh." Yup, that's what I came up with. Oh. *Real smooth, Dylan.*

My teeth sink into my lower lip, and he tracks the motion,

the green of his eyes deepening as desire flashes across them. It seems to take physical effort for him to drag his eyes up from my lips, but when he finally does, he smirks mischievously.

Of course, Kyle chooses that moment to walk past. He scoffs, looking between us, seeing how we're both leaning into one another. No doubt he can taste the pheromones in the air. God knows, I can. His lip curls in disgust before he addresses Finn. "So, this is what eleven years of friendship amounts to, huh?"

Shaking his head, Finn simply says, "I'm not doing this with you, man."

Kyle makes a noise in the back of his throat. "What happened to bros before hoes?"

The insult rolls off my back, but Finn straightens, turning fully to face Kyle. "What happened to focusing on the sport? The love of the game?"

"The love of the game isn't enough to get me onto a pro team. I thought we had a dream—you and me playing pro hockey together."

"We do," Finn argues, wincing before correcting himself. "We did."

Leaning in, Kyle hisses, "That was never going to happen with *her* in my spot. You think second-line picks get drafted?" he scoffs. "'Cause they don't."

"So instead of improving your game, you chose to publicly humiliate her off the team?" Finn frowns. "What happened to you, man? You never used to be like this."

Kyle scoffs in disagreement. "I was just doing what had to be done." He glances my way almost dismissively, before focusing back on Finn. "*You're* the one who has changed. Let some girl whisper in your ear while you're balls deep inside her, and all of a sudden your priorities are her priorities."

Finn is on his feet in the next second, chair legs scraping

across the floor loud enough to draw the attention of the rest of the table. Hell, the entire cafeteria.

"I would *never* target another player because they're better than me." He gives Kyle a hard look. "I never thought you would either."

At Finn's obvious disappointment, Kyle loses his cool. "She's a *girl*," he snaps, loud enough that those listening hear him. "She shouldn't even *be* on the team."

"Now isn't the time or the place, Reed," Ethan states, voice loud and authoritative. He doesn't even glance up from his tray, completely dismissing Kyle. "Go sit down."

Teeth grinding, Kyle glares first at the top of Ethan's head and then at me, before storming off with his tray in hand. At the far end of the table, beside Fletcher and Monroe, he drops it with a loud clatter before glaring at his food until conversations start up once again.

Sighing, Finn ducks his head, elbows resting on the table.

"I'm sorry," he murmurs, so quietly that I nearly miss it. "I don't know what's gotten into him. He never used to be like that. Competitive, sure, what hockey player isn't, but not to the point of going after a player off the ice."

"Some men just can't handle the fact that a woman is better than they are."

Finn looks up at me, brows furrowed low over his eyes. "I don't think—"

"You said it yourself," I cut him off. "He's never gone after any other player, then suddenly a woman shows up who is better than him. Sure, the stakes are higher—it's college and you're in your senior year—but even if I hadn't shown up, Kyle *still* isn't good enough to go pro. Best he could hope for is a farm team, but you and I both know he doesn't have the skill, the drive, or the passion to make it big."

Finn purses his lips, but he doesn't disagree. If anything, I can tell he's really thinking over what I've said, perhaps seeing Kyle in a new light—seeing the *real* Kyle instead of the preteen version he knew once upon a time.

THE OVERHEAD LIGHTS cast long shadows across the ice, the silence of the empty stands pressing in around us. The arena is ours for the taking.

This has become my favorite part of the week. Something that I used to partake in alone. Then there was Griffin—at first a silent witness to my self-directed practices, then as an ally on the ice. Now, it's all of us.

Five bodies moving across the ice, five players working in sync. No one keeping score. No one holding back. Just us, training, refining, and bettering each other.

Every night after dinner this week, we have come out here. When the guys first suggested it, I'd been nervous. This was *my* thing. My quiet time away from the world. Sure, Griffin had wormed his way into it, but Griffin is quiet. He keeps to himself. I knew the others wouldn't be like that, and I was right. Ethan immediately went into captain mode, ordering everyone to warm up before putting us through drills.

Even though my previous solitude has become loud chaos, I find myself stopping frequently to watch Jax and Griffin walk through plays, Finn showing off, and Ethan frowning while he completes a move. Often with a small smile on my face. Solitary practices weren't my norm growing up. It was always me and my dad—maybe another kid or two skating about. They were loud, filled with laughter amongst the teachings. Somewhere along the way, I'd forgotten that while playing hockey, I was supposed to be having fun.

These nights, these practices with just the five of us...they are the most fun I've had in years.

"Come on, Menace. Try and get past me," Jax calls as he skates past. Grin on my face, I race after him. He flips so he's skating backward, smirking cockily as I close the distance between us.

"What do I get when I win?" I ask, deliberately holding back, moving the puck side to side as we glide across the ice.

He smirks. "You can touch me anywhere you want."

Despite the cold, my body heats. He's been doing that all week—taunting me, teasing, saying dirty things that he knows get a reaction out of me. However, he has yet to actually follow through. Instead, he gets me all worked up to leave me hanging. Sadistic asshole.

I scoff. "Like you'd protest to my hands on your body."

He winks, and I love this playful side to him. He keeps it carefully tucked away, only really bringing it out when we're alone or with the guys. I never see it on campus, when we are surrounded by students or the rest of the team. It makes it that much more special. Makes *me* feel special.

"All right," I say with a roll of my eyes. "And what do you get if you win? Which you won't, but hypothetically speaking."

"Hypothetically speaking, I get to touch *you* anywhere *I* want."

A shiver rolls through me, before I smirk coyly. "Too bad you won't be winning."

I put on a burst of speed. Dropping my shoulder, I explode forward, faking right before cutting left, slipping past him before he can react.

"Fuck," I hear him curse before spinning to chase me down. My triumphant laugh turns into a squeal as I push faster. Despite his size, Jax is lightning on the ice. I'm fast, but somehow he manages to catch up. I feel the whisper of his fingers against the back of my jersey before his arms band around me from behind, lifting me off the ice before slowly setting me back down. He keeps his arms wrapped around my waist, his skates framing mine as we glide across the ice together.

Reaching the boards, he turns me to face him, backing me against the glass. "I won," I say, breathless, and not just from the burst of exertion. Tapping my gloves against his, where his hands are bracketing my hips, I whisper, "That means *I* get to touch *you*."

Unfazed by his loss, he smirks, letting go of me only so he can plant his hands on the glass above my head. It only serves to bring him closer, his stance widening as his body comes within inches of mine. His cedarwood and mint scent invades my space, and for the first time ever in hockey, I find myself wishing I'd lost. That's how insane these boys make me.

Ducking his head, his breath fans across my cheek as he brings his lips to my ear. "Go ahead, then. *Claim your prize.*"

I shiver. The notion of Jax as a prize, a present to unwrap...it has me clenching my thighs. I blink up at him through my lashes. I must look anything other than sexy in my oversized hockey gear and wearing a helmet, sweat glistening on my skin, but he looks at me like I'm all he sees. Like I'm the only thing *worth* seeing. It momentarily stalls the air in my lungs and makes my brain glitch.

Lifting my hand, my glove hovers inches above his chest. His gaze shifts to watch, his chest rising and falling heavily, like he's as anxious to feel my touch as I am to touch him. We've been playing video games, talking, spending time together all week, but neither of us has initiated anything physical. None of them have, except Griffin, who avails of every opportunity to drape himself over me, kiss me publicly, and tease me when we're at home. I'm pretty sure he's getting a kick out of pissing the guys off.

Holding my hand there, I flick my gaze to his, waiting until he looks at me. "Hmm, I don't recall there being a time limit on this deal." Ducking under his arm, I spin to face him, grinning impishly. "I think I'll *claim my prize* another time."

He growls, desire darkening his features as he pushes off the boards as though intent on chasing me again. Part of me wants him to. Wants him to chase me, to pin me down, to get me so wound up that I can't consider anything *other* than touching him.

"Let's get back to it," Ethan interjects, pushing Jax's stick into his hands before pointing him into position across the ice. "Drink," he says more softly, handing me a bottle of water that I greedily accept.

He nods in satisfaction when I'm done, taking back the empty bottle, the plastic crinkling in his grip.

"We going again?" Griffin calls from the net, flipping his mask up.

"Yeah," Ethan returns. "Run the play again. This time Finn and Dylan on offense." Bringing his gaze back to mine, he checks, "If that's good with you?"

I nod, adjusting my gloves, and he skates off. Before I can move, though, Finn is suddenly there, tugging my helmet strap tighter. "Loose," he murmurs, voice rough, like the thought of me getting hit unsettles him. "Can't have that."

My pulse jumps, throat bobbing. "I can do it."

His smirk is slow, lazy. "I know."

After he's finished adjusting the straps, his fingers linger, his gaze locked on mine. "Ready to show them how it's done?"

I flash him a grin. "Let's bring it."

Excitement flashes across his green eyes, adrenaline, the thrill of the play flushing his skin. We work in tandem, barely even needing to communicate. Our bodies do all the talking as we pass the puck back and forth, closing the distance between us and the net.

I can feel Ethan's gaze on us, critical, assessing. Feel the tension in Jax's body as he waits for us to get closer, the surety in Griffin's stance as he makes himself as large as possible, covering as much of the net as he physically can.

When we're in the zone, Finn goes off with the puck, drawing Jax toward him. Jax crowds him, the two of them battling for possession. Without so much as sparing me a glance, Finn knocks the puck in my direction. It sails straight toward my blade, and I catch it with ease as I line it up for the shot.

"Dammit," I grumble, when Griffin deflects it with a sharp, practiced motion.

"Good attempt," he says, skating out from the crease. "But I saw it coming a mile away."

"So did I," Ethan adds, skating up beside me. His hand brushes my hip like it's nothing. Casual. Something he does all the time. In fairness, it's something he does frequently now, and I have to admit, I like it quite a bit—this casual display of affection. "You hesitated a second before the shot," he points out. "Don't give the goalie that advantage."

I nod, absorbing the advice.

"Let's go again," I say, sharp, focused.

"Fine, but Ethan's on defense," Jax states, before grumbling, "two against one is just cruel."

We break up, running through the play again and again, switching positions so either Ethan, Finn, or I are playing defense, while the other two run offense.

With every pass, every shift, something inside me settles. It's the rhythm of it, the ease. The way we push each other and challenge one another, but never in a way that feels cruel or punishing. It's effortless, like it's always been, like it was always meant to be.

Griffin taunts Ethan for getting deked. Jax shoves Finn when he cuts too close. It's easy. Fun.

Because this? This is what I've been missing. This is what I *love*.

The ice, the game, the camaraderie and—despite everything —perhaps even these boys. My boys.

FORTY-FIVE

FRIDAY IS AN AWAY GAME. The parking lot is a riot of cars as I approach the coach that will transport us to Dunhaven. "Thanks," I say to the driver as he takes my duffel to stow in the storage area beneath the coach, before turning to search the sea of players for one of my guys.

They are easy to spot, huddled together, and I make my way toward them with a small backpack containing some snacks and my earbuds for the journey in hand and my travel hoodie loose around my frame.

"We need to decide who is sitting beside Dylan," I overhear Griffin say.

"I will," Jax is quick to put forth.

"Nope." Finn shakes his head, scowling. "We need to decide like men."

"By asking the woman who *she* wants to sit with?" I butt in, arching a brow as I survey each of them. Ethan shuffles to the side so I can join their huddle.

"All right, then. Who are you picking, Thorn?" he asks.

I scour Ethan's face, noting he's freshly shaven and his eyes are sharp, ready for tonight's game. Shifting my attention to Jax, he smirks at me, eyes dancing with hidden mirth. Before I can lose myself in those dark depths, I turn to Finn. Unlike Jax, he doesn't bother to hide his amusement.

"You know I'll be the best company," he teases, knocking my shoulder. "It's a *long* ride to Dunhaven. I'll even let you drool on my shoulder."

"So chivalrous." Rolling my eyes, I turn lastly to Griffin. His expression is what it always is, unreadable, yet there's a steadiness in it, a stability that has fostered over the past number of weeks. One I'd be lost without.

"On second thought, I'm not sure this is something I want to get in the middle of. Perhaps there are some things you should agree on amongst yourselves."

"Coward," Finn teases, before focusing on the guys. "Rock, paper, scissors it is. Single elimination."

With serious expressions, they go at it. It's ridiculous, truthfully. Hands fly and curses are muttered. Griffin is eliminated first, followed by Finn, who groans dramatically and claims it's rigged. Jax and Ethan stare each other down in the final showdown.

"Rock, paper, scissors—shoot."

Ethan's fist clenches in triumph. "Hell yeah!"

Jax huffs, muttering about an unfair system as we all pile onto the coach.

"Window or aisle seat?" Ethan asks as we slowly make our way up toward a set of free seats.

"She likes the window seat," Griffin interjects before I can tell Ethan that I don't mind where I sit.

"Window it is then."

I roll my eyes, sending a mock glare Griffin's way that he completely ignores.

Finding three empty rows, I slide into the middle one, Ethan dropping into the chair beside mine. Jax and Finn claim the seats in the row in front while Griffin stretches out in the row behind, all of them effectively boxing me in.

Laughter bubbles up from our group as Finn and Jax continue to bicker over the legitimacy of Ethan's win. Griffin makes a dry remark that has them groaning, and even Ethan smirks at the exchange.

That's when Kyle appears. Spotting us, he slows, expression darkening as his gaze bounces from Ethan, to Jax, to Finn, lingering the longest on his former friend. His lips curl in growing disgust, and when his gaze meets mine, pure, venomous hatred radiates from his dark eyes. I still in my seat. Outwardly, I keep my expression blank, but inside, I'm ice cold, my stomach twisting with unease. That look...it terrifies me.

His stare lingers for a beat too long, his presence thick with menace. "Keep walking." Ethan's voice is like steel, devoid of emotion yet dripping with warning as he flicks his attention up to Kyle's face. Tearing his gaze away, Kyle stares at Ethan, then Finn, Jax, and Griffin—all watching him now, their easy camaraderie vanishing in an instant. He sneers but says nothing, continuing down the aisle to claim his seat. It's only when he's gone that I realize I've been gripping the edge of my hoodie in a tight fist. I force my fingers to relax, inhaling a slow breath, but I don't miss the way Ethan watches me, his jaw tight, nor the way Griffin's gaze lingers, assessing.

"We need to do something about him," Griffin says, voice low but no less menacing. "Shunning him isn't enough."

"Agreed," Jax says, turning around in his seat.

Finn turns too, his lips pursed, but he keeps quiet. However, his eyes rake over me, as though searching for... What, I don't know.

"I know," Ethan says, voice equally as quiet yet strung tight. "I'm just not sure what." Glancing my way, he adds, "You're not to be left alone. One of us will be with you at all times. I don't trust him not to try something."

Neither do I.

Sighing, I mutter, "I know," before dismissing them all and turning to look out the window.

It's no hardship to spend time with any of them. I enjoy being around each of the guys, but I equally like to have time alone. I want us all to spend time together of our own free will and not because we're forced into it. Is that too much to ask? Apparently.

They leave me alone to sulk until everyone is on the bus and we're ready to leave.

"Have you ever heard of *The Infinite Monkey Cage*?" Ethan asks, the question obscure enough that I turn to face him. He's holding an earbud out toward me in invitation. It sounds like the name of some 70s teenage rock band who failed to make it beyond their garage.

"Uhh, should I have?" I hesitate on my way to pluck the earbud from his hand.

He smirks. "Probably not. It's an obscure, British, science-based podcast. Some of the episodes are really weird, like wondering what the universe would be without stars, or what aliens look like if they exist."

"So, it's space related?"

He shakes his head. "No, they cover all things weird and wonderful. I listened to one recently about the secret life of sharks. Did you know they're even older than dinosaurs?"

Fighting back a smile, I say, "I did not."

"I swear, I'm not a nerd," he argues.

"Are you sure?" I tease. "I feel like I'm seeing a whole new side of Ethan Maddox. I can just picture you with oversized glasses and an *I love science* T-shirt."

"I could totally pull that off," he banters.

I nod in agreement. "You'd make one hot nerd." There is absolutely zero doubt about that.

He shakes his head, but he's smiling as he pushes the earbud into my hand. "I promise, it's mostly scientists talking nonsense. Give it a go, and no offense taken if you're bored out of your skull."

"How did you start listening to it?"

"Our captain, my freshman year, was originally from England. His parents moved here when he was young. His dad was a physicist or something and went to college with one of the podcasters. He listened to the podcast every week. I was sitting beside Glen, the captain at the time, on the way to an away game, and we got to talking about it. I gave it a listen, and I've been hooked ever since. I might be a jock, but I enjoy learning new things, and the blend of humor and knowledge keeps me interested."

Well, now he's got *me* interested.

"What is this week's podcast about?" I ask, popping the bud into my ear.

Checking his phone, he says, "Egyptian mummies."

Can't say that's a topic I know anything about. I settle into my seat as he presses play, the opening theme tune of the podcast beginning. It's quickly followed by a British accent as the presenters introduce themselves.

We get on the road, and I'm soon laughing at the wit and out-there remarks made by the podcasters and their guests. It's not just scientists but comedians too, and I soon realize that it's not the droll scientific podcast I'd been picturing. Still, it's an interesting insight into Ethan beyond hockey and his role as captain, and I gobble it up.

Each episode is only twenty minutes long, and as soon as we reach the end of the first one, I'm asking if there's another.

Heads together, we scroll through his phone, picking out various topics of interest to listen to.

The entire time, his warmth seeps into me, his leg pressing firmly against mine. At some point, my head tips back against the seat, the rhythmic swaying of the bus lulling me to sleep. The last thing I register is the sound of Ethan's podcast in my ear and the feel of his body, hard yet warm.

I WAKE to the slow realization that I'm leaning into solid warmth. Blinking blearily, I find my head resting against Ethan's shoulder, my body curled toward his, and his arm draped casually over my back.

Licking my lips, I swipe at my mouth while silently praying I didn't drool in my sleep. And if I did, that Ethan is sleeping too and didn't notice.

With a flick of my gaze, I realize there's no such luck. Ethan is looking down at me, something achingly soft in his expression. It leaves me momentarily speechless.

"Hey," he murmurs.

I straighten, rolling my shoulders to stretch them out and feeling the loss of his warmth immediately. "How long was I out?"

"Long enough to make a wet patch on my T-shirt."

I sit up fully, horrified. "I *did not*—"

Eyeing his bone-dry shoulder, I smack him on the chest, and he chuckles, loose and carefree. "Kidding."

"We will be arriving at the hotel within the next ten minutes," Coach calls out from the front of the bus.

Ten minutes later, we're disembarking and piling into the hotel. It's nothing fancy, but it's not a shithole either. Just your average hotel. More than suitable for a bunch of jocks for one night.

We grab our duffels from beneath the coach before heading inside. The lobby buzzes with the low murmur of teammates as we wait around while Coach checks us all in.

"All right, listen up!" Coach raises his voice over the noise, waiting until the chatter silences. "Come collect your keys from me. You're doubled up, two to a room. Swapping is not optional, so I don't want to hear your whining. You've got two hours to unpack, settle in, do whatever you need to for your pre-game routine. Be back down here at six sharp. *Don't be late.*"

A chorus of "Yes, Coach," echoes through the lobby as guys gather round to get their room assignments and keys. When it's my turn, Bear hands it over, saying, "You've got your own room. It's across the hall from mine, and I've put these guys on the same floor." He gestures to Griffin, Finn, Ethan, and Jax surrounding me.

"Thanks, Bear. I appreciate it."

He nods, before fixing each of the guys with a stern look. He holds their keys hostage for a moment. "I don't want any shenanigans," he half growls. "No banging doors or switching rooms in the middle of the night. We're here to play a game. To win. That's it, got it?"

With serious expressions and backs straight, the guys murmur, "Yes, sir," before Bear surrenders their keys. With a roll of his eyes and a soft smile directed my way, he dismisses us.

"Bear, huh?" Finn says when we're all inside the elevator. "Because he's growly like a grizzly?"

I shake my head, grinning. "Because he's cuddly like a teddy bear."

His face scrunches into the most hilarious expression. "I don't see it."

"Same," the others chorus.

"I've not once ever gotten that vibe from him," Jax states as the elevator rises. "I'd rather attempt to hug this one than Coach." He flicks his thumb Griffin's way, and Griffin gnashes his teeth savagely.

"I'd sooner rip your head from its shoulders. Only person I want touching me is Hurricane."

Jax fixes me with an arched brow and thinned lips. *See?*

"What do you reckon the chances are of my balls remaining attached to my body if I called him Bear?" Finn muses aloud.

"Zero," Ethan says without missing a beat.

"Nil," Jax adds.

"He'd probably ram them so far down your throat, you'll never speak again." Finn visibly pales at Griffin's graphic image.

"I dunno, I think you should try it," I say with faux innocence. Turning toward him, I flutter my lashes before dragging the tip of my index finger down the front of his shirt, noting the hardness of his muscles beneath. "I'll make it worth your while, if you do."

For a second, his eyelids droop, pupils becoming hazy with lust, before he blinks it away. Instead, a lascivious smirk transforms his face into something mischievous.

"Careful, Hellion. You're playing with fire." He steps closer, seemingly bringing the walls of the elevator with him, until it feels as though all the oxygen has been sucked out of the air, leaving only a hint of his aftershave—something rich and oaky—behind.

I forget about the others' presence as he reaches up, tugging on a loose strand of hair before tucking it behind my ear. It's a strangely intimate gesture, especially from Finn. Especially after he's worked so hard to stay away from me these past weeks. For him to suddenly touch me so effortlessly feels...strange, and yet, my insides rejoice at the contact. At the breaking down of barriers. At the realization that we're moving beyond secret back room kisses laden with guilt and shame and moving into the light. Into something real. Something we both acknowledge and accept. Something that could last?

Only time will tell.

"As tempting of an offer as that is," he murmurs, voice flowing over me like warm whiskey, "I like my balls where they are." His lips skim the corner of my jaw. "And I think that's where you'd prefer they stay too."

The *ding* of the elevator announcing that we've reached our floor saves me from melting into a puddle of steaming goo. Still, the guys give me knowing, heated looks as they file past me. However, there is no jealousy, no sharp barbs, or cutting remarks. Only mirrored expressions of lust. Want. *Need.*

Fucking hell, what have I gotten myself in for with these guys?!

Taking a moment, I fan my heated face before following them off the elevator. As a group, we head down the hall in search of our rooms. We come across mine first, and the guys all wait while I drop my bag off.

Grabbing my phone, I do a quick scan of the basic room—king-size bed, TV on the wall, window overlooking the street below—before I lock my door behind me and follow the guys to their rooms.

Just like before we got on the coach, I can see the argument coming before it unfolds. So can Finn. We've no sooner slowed to a stop in the hallway outside their rooms when he grabs my arm and drags me through the door on the left.

Protests start up behind us, and glancing over his shoulder, he calls, "You got her on the bus. Only fair we get her until the game."

"I didn't—" The door slams closed behind us, cutting off Jax's protest.

Glancing around the room, it's similar to mine, with plain

white walls and artwork typical of that found in generic hotels. A TV hangs on one wall, and a window overlooks the parking lot. The primary difference is the two double beds instead of the one large king in my room.

Dropping his duffel, Finn launches himself onto the bed by the window with a loud sigh, starfishing so he's taking up the whole thing. My lips twist in a semblance of a smile as I watch him. A click from behind has me turning as Griffin slips into the room. "We'll meet up with them just before six and go down together."

Nodding absently, I find myself feeling strangely awkward alone with the two of them. Finn is scrolling on his phone while Griffin moves to the other bed and begins lifting things out of his duffel. I'm an interloper in their usual routine, and I find myself shuffling my feet, unsure of what to do. My skin still tingles from Finn's flirting in the elevator but now is not the time to fall down *that* rabbit hole. I need to be getting myself in the mindset to crush the Krakens tonight.

"So, umm, what are your pre-game rituals?" I ask, already going through my mental to-do list.

"Nap. Chill. Eat." Finn waves a hand in the air lazily. "I wouldn't call it a routine per se. Not like the insanity this guy does. Superstitious asshat."

Cocking a brow, I shift my attention to Griffin.

"It's not about superstition," he states simply, like he's explained this a hundred times before. "It's calibration. Control. The routine strips it all down—thoughts, nerves, bullshit. I clear the noise, focus the mind, get my body in sync. By the time I hit the ice, I've already been in the net for hours." He taps the side of his head. "Up here."

"And what exactly is this *insane* routine?" I tease curiously.

Griffin shrugs casually. "Thirty-minute steam shower. Then I eat a meal of two hard-boiled eggs, a bowl of plain oatmeal, and half a banana." He lifts out a stack of Tupperware containers as my eyes go wide. "Plus twelve ounces of room-temperature water." He shakes his water bottle. "Then forty-five minutes of stretching while listening to *The Rite of Spring* by Stravinsky."

"That's it?" I question. "That's not so bad." I've heard of players doing far worse—crazy pre-game dances, wearing the same pair of underwear for every game. My dad had a teammate once who shaved his head before every game because the first time he won a championship game, he'd lost a dare and had to shave all his hair off. He literally spent the entire season with a buzz cut, then grew it out in the off-season, only to shave it all off again.

"Except he left out the best bit," Finn says with a shit-eating grin. Before Griffin can fill me in, Finn blurts, "You can't speak to him the entire time. He nearly knocked out a freshman last year who shared a room with him and had the *audacity* to ask him a question."

"How dare he," I tease.

"He had it coming," Griffin grunts, unrepentant. "He knew the rules."

Finn throws his head back, laughing.

Shaking my head, I wave my hand toward the attached bathroom. "Well, go get your shower on. I promise not to breathe in your direction until after the game."

Growling, Griffin stalks over to me, a white towel now thrown over his shoulder. He looks sexy as hell, dressed in a tight black tee and loose matching sweats that enhance the sky blue of his eyes.

When we're standing toe to toe, he reaches up to trail the tip of a finger along the seam of my lips. The backs of his knuckles glance along my skin, eliciting shivers and making my heart trip over itself. "Hurricane, you're the only variable I'd rewrite every routine for."

I stand frozen, stunned by the gravity of his words as he disappears into the bathroom, the door closing with a soft *click* behind him. With my pulse a riot, my breathing is caught somewhere between disbelief and something far more dangerous.

The only variable.

What the hell am I supposed to do with that? Other than fall headfirst in love with Griffin Price and never recover.

FORTY-SIX

"COME WATCH SOMETHING STUPID WITH ME," Finn says, shaking me out of the stupor Griffin left me in. He pats the spot beside him on the bed. I kick my shoes off and pull my hoodie over my head, leaving me in leggings and a crop top as I flop down beside him.

He pulls up YouTube on his phone, scrolling through a mix of hockey highlights, absurd prank videos, and chaotic animal clips until we settle on a compilation of fails. Side by side on the bed, our shoulders brushing, our heads close together, we laugh at the ridiculousness of people launching themselves off trampolines, slipping on ice, and getting tackled by dogs.

At some point, a notification comes through on his phone, someone named Emmy sending him a photo. I tense, acting as though I didn't notice the alert as I continue to blindly stare at the reel we were watching. Out of all the guys, Finn is the player. He probably has a catalog of girls sending him all sorts of photos, and I hate how that notion irritates me.

"Sorry," he mumbles, pulling the phone closer. "That's my sister."

His *sister*.

The relief I feel at that is monumental—and insane.

"Oh."

"She had a competition today," he explains as he clicks into the chat. I turn my head away to give him some privacy. "And I'm guessing she won," he says with a laugh, tilting his phone toward me so I can see the scrawny, younger female version of Finn, dressed in soccer gear and holding a trophy over her head, grinning into the camera.

"She's the spitting image of you."

Finn grins. "I know. Much to my mom's dismay. We both look exactly like our dad. His dominant, red-haired gene, but we also have his eyes, and facial structure. Mom often jokes that if she hadn't given birth to us both, she'd wonder if we were even hers."

"Sounds like you've got a good family."

"Yeah, they are pretty great." Turning his head, his phone is forgotten as he asks, "What about you? You mentioned your dad, but what about your mom?"

I swallow roughly, unable to meet his piercing stare. I'm not used to having Finn's undivided attention for longer than a quick, desperate kiss, and I'm discovering it can be as heavy and intense as Griffin's, despite his mischievous, lighthearted personality.

"My family used to be pretty great too," I tell him, allowing myself to soak in those memories for a moment. To remember the warmth of Dad's smile, the comfort of Mom's hugs. "Since Dad died, she's been drowning in grief. I barely— She never takes my calls nowadays." I shake my head. "I don't even remember the last time I spoke to her."

Rolling onto his side, Finn shuffles over on the bed, eliminating any space between us. The heat of his body seeps into mine, relaxing the muscles and calming the flurry of stress over my mother.

With his head propped in his hand, his elbow digging into the pillow, he reaches over. My hands are clasped on top of the bare skin of my abdomen, above my leggings, and he rests his on top, the heat suffusing my skin.

"I can't imagine what your mom is going through—what you've *both* endured. The agony of losing a parent. Of losing the other half of your soul."

That's precisely what my dad was to my mom. What my mom was to my dad. They were two halves of one soul, and without one another, my mother is left adrift. Lost. Unable to anchor herself to stable ground.

Truthfully, I'm not sure she'll ever find her way again. Although I'm not ready yet to say those words aloud. To face that grim reality.

A soft, gentle touch down the side of my face and neck draws me out of my thoughts, and my gaze connects with Finn's brilliant green one. I swear his eyes are the color of grass on a summer's day. Of tree leaves and open fields, with the flecks of gold sunshine reflecting off their surface. I could get lost in those eyes. In the heat of summer. In the hope of better, brighter days.

"I already know my life would be emptier without you in it," he murmurs, voice soft and low, caressing like silk over my skin. "You've consumed me from the second I opened the door to you standing on my porch, all dark, wavy hair and hypnotizing eyes, wearing those little shorts that showed off those long, lean legs of yours, and your cute-as-hell Converse." He flashes me a cheeky grin before growing more serious. His eyes flash with some emotion I can't decipher, something sharp and soul deep. Goosebumps ripple along my arms when he strokes the back of my hands.

"Try as I might, I couldn't stay away. I was drawn into your orbit, no matter how hard I tried to resist." He pauses, a slight quirk of his lips drawing my eyes to his mouth. "Although, admittedly, I didn't try as hard as I could have. Even though I felt like it was wrong to give in, every time I laid eyes on you, I'd tell myself just one more. One more touch. One more kiss." He swallows, his Adam's apple bobbing. "I'd tell myself it was the last time, then I'd see you again and know I'd been fooling myself. There could never be a *last time*. When it comes to you, I'll always want more."

At some point, his hand drifted to the bare skin of my abdomen, his fingers trailing a tantalizing path. Too caught up in his vulnerable declaration, I hadn't noticed, but now my breath hitches.

His face lowers, breath fanning over my flushed skin. My pulse thunders, and I find myself suddenly starved for Finn's touch. Is it crazy of me to admit that I've missed his desperate, rogue kisses?

"You have no idea how badly I want to kiss you."

I can feel my breasts straining against the confines of my bra, nipples pebbling in a cry for his attention. Licking my suddenly dry lips, my voice comes out husky and wanton. "So why haven't you?"

Dear God, man. Kiss me already.

A nearly imperceptible groan rumbles through him— agonized. His features pinch, the restraint palpable in the air between us before he blows out a breath. Collapsing backward, the whole bed bounces, the tension snapping like a band between us.

I'm still reeling, trying to process why his lips aren't on mine, my hands in his hair, and our bodies pressed together, when he speaks. "I can't."

I must react physically to his words, because he's leaning over me in the next second, hand on my face, drawing my eyes to his. "I didn't mean it like that," he says, looking pained. "Everything between us to date has been me kissing you."

"So you want me to kiss *you*?" I question.

One side of his lips twitches. "Me kissing you and then walking away," he expands. "But secret, impulsive kisses aren't what I want. They aren't *all* that I want," he clarifies at my confused expression. Closing his eyes, he blows out a frustrated breath before muttering, "I'm not explaining this very well."

Focusing back on me, he tries again. "I'm trying to make up for being an ass to you," he states plainly. "But more than that, I need you to know without a shadow of a doubt that I'm interested in you for more than furtive make-out sessions." A softness enters his gaze as it roams over my face. "I want to chill out together while we watch stupid YouTube videos. I want to tell you about my family, even introduce you one day. I want you to feel safe enough to open up about your mom."

Brushing his fingers through my hair in a move that presses his body more thoroughly against mine and brings his face close enough that I can see the flecks of gold in his irises, he adds, "It's not solely your body I want, Dylan. It's *you*—all of you. It's quiet moments and inside jokes. Waking up beside you and having comfortable dinners where we don't feel the need to fill the silence. It's game days and lazy Sundays. The highs and lows. The wins and the losses."

"It's a relationship you want." The words come out oddly breathless, but I can't seem to get air into my lungs.

"It is," he states resolutely. "Never been in one before, so I can't promise to be very good at it, but a relationship with you is *exactly* what I want."

"You've..." I blink up at him in shock. "You've never been in a relationship before? Not even when you were eleven and did the whole '*Will you be my boyfriend? Will you be my girlfriend?*' But by the end of recess, you'd both gone your separate ways, and the next day you were dating some other girl on the playground?"

Mirth dances in his eyes. "Is that what you did?" he teases. "Did some tween douche break your heart in the school yard? Need me to beat him up for you?"

"Shut up." I shove at his shoulder, shaking my head even as a smile blooms across my face.

Bringing his hand to my face, he grasps my chin between his fingers and drags my attention back to him. His expression has grown stoic, vulnerable. "Be mine, Hellion."

It's not really a question. It's not in Finn's nature—in any of their natures—to ask permission. Still, he lingers, hesitates, waiting for a response. "Let me make up to you the wrongs I've done."

"We don't need to date for you to do that."

"No," he agrees, still looking at me with that soft, open expression. "But like I said, I *want* to date you. The question is, do you want to date me?" Staring into his eyes, I can see the vulnerability lying there. The nerves. Unlike ever before, Finn is putting himself out there. Making his feelings clear and telling me *precisely* where he stands.

"What about the others?" I ask in a quiet voice. My heart is lodged in my throat while I wait for his reply. It's make or break, because despite how drawn I am to Finn, I'm basically already dating Griffin. Even if I chose to let him go, I'm pretty sure he wouldn't let me—not that I have any intention of doing that. He's been my grounding force in all of this. My stable place to land. I wouldn't let him go for anything.

And then there's Ethan and Jax. There's no way I could give either of them up. Not playing video games with Jax or the little insights I've been getting into Ethan.

Just...nope. Not happening. As selfish as it might sound, I need them all.

"Baby, if hockey has taught me anything, it's how to be a team player."

When I merely roll my eyes, he nudges his nose against mine. "What do you say, Hellion?" he murmurs, shifting to hover over me as he drags his lips down the side of my neck. I tilt my chin, granting him better access, my body heating as his tongue occasionally flicks out to wet my skin, sending my mind spinning. "Be mine."

There's an edge to his voice. A plea that has me responding, "Yes," without a single bit of doubt or hesitation. For as much as Finn says he wants me, I want him too. This chemistry between us is undeniable, but more than that, Finn makes me laugh, and despite keeping his distance, he's shown that he cares for me. He brings me lunch and ensures I eat before practice and throughout the day. It's a surprisingly sweet side of him that I imagine very few have the privilege to experience. "Yes," I repeat, turning my head toward him. I breathe in a hint of his aftershave, something rich and oaky. It's a combination that fits Finn to a T. Playful but brooding. "I'll be yours."

He half moans, half groans into my skin. "Three words have never sounded so perfect." He's still on top of me, his hands skimming my skin, mouth pressed to my throat. I can feel the hard ridge of his cock against my hip. Oh, how I want to spread my legs, to have him settle between them. Kiss me. Suck on my skin. Stroke this heat that is steadily building.

"Fuck," he murmurs, sounding as dazed as I am. His hips jerk before he stills. His breaths are heavy against my skin, strained as he forces himself to calm. With one final deep inhale, as though he's breathing my scent into his lungs, tattooing it to the lining so he never forgets, he pulls away. Our gazes lock. "I need to get out of this room or I'm going to forget everything I just promised and fuck you into this mattress."

I mean, I wouldn't complain if he did.

He must see exactly how much I want him, because he shakes his head, backing away. "Nope. No. None of that." He points an accusing finger at me as he crawls to the end of the bed. I sit up on my elbows, sucking my lips into my mouth to keep from grinning when he unashamedly adjusts himself in front of me. "I'm going to check on Ethan and Jax. You just stay here. Do whatever you do to prepare for a game. I'll be back in a bit." He's already out the door, moving like there are flames licking at his heels.

Alone, I flop back down onto the bed. My sigh is loud in the otherwise silent room, and my body still pulses with the need Finn stirred. I'm horny as hell and there's no way I can focus on getting in the mindset necessary for tonight's game while feeling this way.

I *could* sort myself out.

Or...

My head tilts to the side, staring at the bathroom door as I strain my ears for sounds of the shower running. As I'm listening, the water cuts off, and images form in my head of Griffin, dripping wet, towel wrapped low around his hips, all that gorgeous, taut skin on display.

I'm off the bed and stalking toward the bathroom before I can second guess myself. I slip into the room without knocking, the door still damp from steam and the air thick with the smell of Griffin's bodywash—clean, woodsy, dangerous.

He's standing in front of the fogged-up mirror, white towel circling his hips as he runs another over his wet hair. Slowly, passionately, my eyes trail over him, lingering on the droplets of water that carve paths down the ridges of his back, catching in the valleys of muscle, slipping lower, before disappearing into the folds of white at his waist. He's all sinew and strength, every inch of him honed and effortless. It makes saliva form in my mouth as I envision tracing the lines and grooves with my tongue, and heat blooms low in my stomach, spreading outward like a lit fuse.

My gaze snags on the ink slashing down his ribs—a single black line, thin and stark, bending into sharp, deliberate angles. What I initially stared at across the gym floor, I've now seen up close and personal countless times.

It isn't a decorative tattoo. Not one intended to be pretty, but it doesn't need to be. That jagged, unyielding line is Griffin. Unforgiving. Exact. A warning etched into skin.

On quiet feet, I move in behind him, my fingers brushing his damp skin before sliding around to the front of his abdomen. Solid muscles press against my palm, tensing and flexing beneath my touch. Leaning in, I press a kiss to the back of his shoulder, soft and slow, just enough to make him still.

He turns, the towel in his hand falling to his side, and his eyes find mine, narrowed and skeptical.

"What are you up to?" he asks suspiciously, yet his blue eyes sparkle with intrigue beneath the bathroom lights.

I shrug, the picture of innocence. Stepping back, I click the door shut behind me and turn the lock with a quiet *snick*.

Turning to face me, his head tilts slightly, that predatory gaze observing my every move. "Hurricane..."

Lifting both my eyebrows, I tap my finger against my lips—a silent reminder of *his* rules.

A minute passes, the two of us simply taking the other in, before he arches a brow. It's a question. A challenge. One I'm ready to step up to the plate and meet.

My answering grin is slow and deliberate before I fall to my knees in front of him. His knuckles tighten around the towel at his waist, the one in his other hand falling to the floor, forgotten.

His eyes blaze with heat, and he does nothing to stop me as I reach up and tug on the edge of the towel. He lets go, and it drops. He's already hard and ready beneath it, his engorged cock bobbing in front of my face.

"Is this what you wanted, Hurricane?" he purrs, fisting himself with slow, sultry movements that coax a bead of precum to his tip. My tongue is heavy in my mouth with the desire to flick out and lick it, to taste him. I nod, sucking my lower lip between my teeth as I watch him work himself over, heat pooling between my thighs.

"If you're so set on not talking," he murmurs, eyes dark as they drop to my mouth before he brings his hand to my face, tugging my lip free, "I guess I better keep your mouth busy, huh?"

Applying slight pressure to my jaw, he coaxes my mouth open, and I lean forward to meet him as he pushes the blunt head between my lips.

My tongue drags over his silken skin, and he groans. Salty mustiness washes over my tongue, and when he slips down the back of my throat, momentarily obscuring my airway, I moan. My hands come up to grip his thighs, the muscles tense beneath my palms as I dig my fingers in.

I flick my gaze up the hard planes of his body, until I fall, enraptured, into his glazed-over eyes. Watching Griffin shed the mask he constantly wears, knowing *I'm* the one responsible... It's empowering. I always thought nothing could feel better than skating toward the crease, the puck at my feet, and knowing without a shadow of a doubt that I'm going to make that shot. But this...this moment, having this strong-willed, reserved, domineering man falling apart at the seams all because of me... yeah, this feels infinitely superior.

It's the hottest thing, watching him shudder and fracture before me, and I soon find myself shifting on my heels, squeezing my thighs together in a desperate need for friction while I suck him deeper into my mouth.

Hot and needy, I slip my hand down the front of my leggings, but I barely make it past the waistline before a sharp slap to my cheek makes me freeze. It's not sore, it's more the surprise of it that catches me off guard.

"None of that," Griffin says, pumping his hips with shallow thrusts.

I moan around his thick shaft, blinking my teary eyelashes in a plea for release.

"This is *my* routine you're interrupting, so you'll do as *I* say, and I'm telling you *not to come.* I want you to think about this moment, to remember how frustrated you're feeling right now for every shift you play tonight. Every time you have possession of the puck. Every goal you make." He runs his fingers possessively down the side of my face, before wrapping his hand around the front of my throat—firm, but not tight.

"Only when we win tonight's game—only when you've *earned it*—will I let you come. And it won't be by your hands." Saliva dribbles out the side of my mouth, and he scoops it up with a finger before pushing it back in, stretching my lips thin. "It'll be by mine. My fingers. My tongue. My cock. You understand, Hurricane?"

All I can do is moan in response, even as my panties disintegrate and my nipples chafe against the inside of my bra.

He smirks down at me, looking like a dark king atop his throne. "Now show me what a good girl you can be and let me fuck your mouth."

There's no waiting for permission. No easing into it. Griffin grabs the back of my head, and in the next second, I'm choking on his cock. Tears stream from my eyes and my fingernails leave half-moon indents in his thighs, but the grunts that fall from his lips and the way he uses me, like he'll fucking *die* if he doesn't come in my mouth this second, has me hornier than I've ever been in my life.

My lungs burn and my jaw aches, and I swear, I could probably get off on the friction I get from my leggings. With a sharp tug on my hair, Griffin throws his head back and roars my name as his seed spills into my mouth, washing over my tongue, and dripping down my chin before I can swallow.

Dragging me to my feet, he kisses me with abandon. "You realize, if we win, you're going to have to get on your knees for me before every game?"

With my hair a mess and cum on my face, I grin at him.

Totally. Fucking. Worth. It.

FORTY-SEVEN

THE LOCKER ROOM buzzes from our win—half-dressed bodies moving between the showers and benches, towels snapping, someone blasting a too loud victory playlist on a Bluetooth speaker. The air reeks of sweat, soap, and adrenaline. Everyone's riding the high.

I sit at my stall, towel around my neck, laces undone, half listening as the guys go back and forth, debating on which club we should hit up to celebrate.

I'm already calculating how much bullshit I'll have to suffer through before I can get Dylan back to the hotel. The only way I want to celebrate is by stripping her bare before making good on my pre-game promise.

I glance up just as she steps out of the shower room, dressed in tiny black boy short panties that cling to her curves like sin and a fitted tank that leaves nothing to the imagination. Every head turns. She doesn't notice—or maybe she just doesn't care—but I do. I growl at those closest to me, promising a painful, torturous end as I glare down everyone else until they quickly avert their eyes.

She's rifling through her bag for her jeans when something

slips out. A small, folded piece of paper flutters to the ground, skidding across the slick floor until it stops right at the toe of Kyle's sneaker.

I tense. "Dylan—" I start, but Kyle's already bending.

She whirls toward him, eyes widening in horror. "Don't!" Her voice slides through the locker room like a puck to the glass. It has everyone stopping what they were doing, chatter cutting off abruptly, as everyone turns to soak up the drama.

The only person who appears wholly unperturbed is Kyle. With casual ease and absolutely zero regard for personal privacy, he unfolds the note. The entire locker room seems to be holding its breath as he scans it, expression morphing into something ugly and smug all at once. Then he chuckles, one of those slow, venomous sounds that spreads like oil on water.

"Oh, that's rich," he says, loud enough to cut through the last of the locker room noise.

"Kyle, give that back!"

Dylan's demand goes unheard as Kyle snaps his gaze to Finn's, lips curling in a cruel sneer. "Really, Finn? *This* is how low you've fallen?"

Confusion ripples through me as I glance at Finn. He stands frozen at his locker, shirt half on, staring at Kyle like he's watching a car crash in slow motion.

What the hell is going on?

And then, just to twist the knife deeper, Kyle flicks his gaze back to the piece of paper and starts to read it aloud.

"I used to think I knew what I wanted. Then you came along and changed the rules. Watching you out there tonight—sharp, fast, fearless—I couldn't look away. I'm not scared of what this is anymore. I want it. I want you. All of you."

Laughter ripples through the locker room, some guys confused, others clearly entertained. I glance at Dylan, and she's rooted in place. Face pale. Eyes locked on Finn.

Realization dawns—Finn's been leaving the little Steelhawk love notes. Love notes she never told me about. Given Dylan's reaction when the paper first fell out of her bag, this wasn't the first note that had been left.

And she just kept them. *Kept them.*

Based on her current shocked expression, she had no idea they were from Finn. Anger spikes through me like a wire pulled too tight. What if they hadn't been from him? What if it had been some creep, some obsessed stalker leaving her notes? What if it were someone like *me*?

I don't *like* not knowing something about her. Especially not something like this. It doesn't matter that it was Finn. It *could* have been someone else. Someone dangerous. Someone who presented a threat to *my* hurricane. Someone interacting with her beneath my nose and I never fucking knew. My jaw tics, teeth grinding. It's my job to know everything about her. To protect her. Protect what's *mine*.

Finn shifts on his feet, drawing my attention. He's staring at Kyle like he might commit murder with his bare hands, while Kyle waves the note in front of him like it's a victory flag.

"Jesus, Finn. Didn't realize you'd turned into such *a little bitch.*" Kyle's voice is thick with venom. "I mean, I knew she had you whipped, but this? You write her *cute little love notes* now?"

Finn still doesn't speak. Doesn't blink. But his jaw clenches so tight I hear it grind from across the room.

Kyle turns to the rest of the team. "Who'd have thought Finn O'Rourke, the great Casanova, would fall so far off his pedestal?" There are some laughs, but for the most part, the team looks between Kyle, Finn, and Ethan, unsure how to react. "The question is," Kyle continues, menace bleeding into his tone as he fixes Finn in his sights once more. "How long can sappy Finn last? We all know you're a flirt. A hit-it-and-quit-it kind of guy. One girl's never going to be enough for you." His gaze flicks to Dylan, expression mocking. "You really think *you're* the exception?" The disgust underlying his words as he trails his eyes over her, making sure she's aware that he's less than impressed by what he sees, has me seeing red.

Despite her blank expression and rigid stance, Dylan flinches. Her gaze slides in Finn's direction, and I catch sight of the pain Kyle just inflicted. The moment of doubt. I move to intervene, because *fuck no* will someone hurt my girl. Not when I'm standing right fucking here.

Except Finn beats me to it.

He steps up to Kyle, chest to chest. "Don't fucking talk to her," he snarls, face thunderous in the way it is when he's facing off against an opponent on the ice.

Kyle smirks, egging him on. "What? Gonna punch me, lover boy? Gonna hit your best friend since childhood?"

Finn doesn't launch at him—*yet*. But he's *vibrating* with the urge to. "You, Kyle Reed, are no friend of mine."

What looks suspiciously like hurt flashes across Kyle's eyes before he buries it beneath his rising fury. "Then don't come crying to me when she chooses one of these other idiots and leaves you lying in the dirt." He scoffs. "She's got you so tightly wound around her finger that you're writing her fucking love letters. I mean, do you even remember who you used to be?"

"Do you?" Finn tosses back accusingly. "You lose out on your position to a better player and all of a sudden you're a spiteful dickhead? Instead of *working* to be better, you try to sabotage that player instead? Who even are you, Kyle, because you sure as shit aren't the friend I grew up with."

Sneering, Kyle snaps, "She's a manipulative, lying, power-hungry whore, and you're just too fucking blind to see it."

A growl erupts from my chest.

Finn's already moving before his last word lands. He *explodes*—a full-body launch. He tackles Kyle backward into the row of lockers. A sharp *crack* of metal rings out, followed by the unmistakable thud of fist to flesh. The room erupts in chaos, jeers, and whistles, egging the two of them on as the team forms a circle around the brawling pair.

I shove closer, satisfaction thrumming through my veins at the sight of blood dripping from a cut to Kyle's eyebrow. Folding my arms over my chest, I'm happy to watch as Finn gives Kyle the beating he's been deserving of for quite some time.

Kyle doesn't take it lying down, getting his own punches in too, but they only seem to fuel Finn's fury. Catching my attention, Ethan gestures for us to intervene. Face scrunching, I shake my head. Fuck no. This is the best entertainment I've had in ages. Karma has finally come for Kyle, and I want to bask in every bloodthirsty moment of it.

Tilting his head toward Dylan, I follow his gaze, and my lips purse. Dylan isn't averse to violence. Fights break out all the time on the ice. Hell, frequently, Jax or Finn will be caught up in one. But something about seeing Finn embroiled in one off-ice has her worried. Her wide gaze darts back and forth between the fighting pair, her lower lip tugged between her teeth in a sign of stress.

Shit.

Meeting Ethan's gaze again, I reluctantly nod, and the two of us move in to pull Finn off Kyle, but not before he gets a final hit in—right to Kyle's jaw. A loud, satisfying *crack* renders the air as his head whips to the side, blood spraying from his mouth.

"You're a fucking piece of shit," Finn spits, fighting against me and Ethan. *Jesus.* I don't think I've ever seen him this worked up. Not even when Sions' captain threw a dirty check last year during the championship semi-finals.

"Get Kyle out of here," Ethan barks at a couple of rookies. "Now."

Rushing forward, two of them prop Kyle up as they usher

him out of the room. The door slams behind them, the echo of it clanging through the silence like an aftershock.

No one moves.

No one speaks.

Then Ethan's voice cuts through the tension like a blade. "Get dressed and get the hell out."

It's not a shout. It's worse—it's cold, sharp, *final*. Ethan is exerting his authority in a way he never has before.

Just like that, the room jolts to life. Guys scramble, shoving their gear into bags, throwing on clothes. No one's talking anymore. No jokes. No plans. Just eyes averted and movements stiff, like they don't want to catch whatever just happened. Within minutes, the room clears out, the space emptying until it's just me, Ethan, Finn, Jax...and Dylan.

Finn's still in my grip, arms trembling with residual rage, a fresh split blooming on his lower lip. Ethan stands firm on his other side, Jax hovering behind Dylan, who hasn't taken her eyes off Finn since we pulled him off Kyle. I'm not sure she's even aware that the room has emptied out.

She steps forward. Quiet. Calm. But there's something tight in her face, like her skin is stretched too thin over everything she's holding in. Lifting her hand, she brushes her thumb through the trail of blood from his lip to his chin. She doesn't flinch at the smear of red. Doesn't say anything.

And neither does he.

They just *look* at each other, like the chaos around them has quieted into something private. Unspoken. Intimate in a way that has the rest of the world falling away. It's as though none of the rest of us exist.

An entire conversation passes between them unspoken, until finally Dylan steps back, dropping her gaze. "I'll go dampen a paper towel."

She turns and walks toward the showers, the sound of her footsteps echoing in the now hollow space.

When she's gone, Finn exhales, slow and ragged, before muttering, "I need a fucking drink."

"Seriously?" I side-eye him. So much for hoping to skip out on the club and take Dylan straight back to the hotel.

He nods, extracting himself from mine and Ethan's hold as he stretches out his neck. "On second thought, I need an entire fucking bottle."

Meeting Jax's and Ethan's gazes, I begrudgingly murmur, "I guess we're going clubbing."

Just. Fucking. Great.

THE CLUB PULSES AROUND ME. Bass-heavy and dripping in sweat, smoke, and sin. Lights flash like lightning across the ceiling, casting people in silhouettes—writhing, grinding, blurring into one another. But my eyes don't move.

They haven't since she stepped onto that dance floor in that tiny black dress that hugs her like it was painted on.

Dylan.

She moves like the music is hers. Head tipped back, dark hair swinging, skin glowing in the strobe light. Every now and then, she throws her arms around Jax's neck, laughing at something he says, dragging him closer as they dance. And I know I should look away. Give her space. Pretend I'm not three seconds from tearing through the crowd like a predator with a scent. But I can't. Not with her.

She's too fucking radiant. Too magnetic. Like she was carved into existence just to ruin me. I bring my bottle of beer to my lips, the lukewarm liquid spilling over my tongue, but it does fuck all to quench my thirst because I'm not thirsty for alcohol.

I'm thirsty for *her*. Insatiably so.

A night after a game, I'd typically be hanging out with the guys from the team, shooting the shit, playing the pretense of normal, but since meeting Dylan, I've started to wonder why I fucking bothered.

The truth is, I've always worn a mask. Easy charm. Sharp jokes. Camaraderie on demand. It's easier to pretend to be normal than to let people glimpse your true nature. It made things smoother—kept the coaches happy, the team tight, and no one looking too close. Something that was especially important after I emancipated myself at sixteen, leaving my drug addict mom and abusive dad in the dust. But it wasn't me. It never was. I don't give a fuck about parties or post-game banter. I care about hockey. About winning. About staying sharp. Everything else was an act I got too good at playing.

Until Dylan happened. And suddenly, I can't stomach pretending anymore. Not when I've seen what it's like to want someone with every twisted part of me. She cracked me open, and instead of trying to shove the pieces back in place, I've stopped fighting it. I want her. I want this. Her and hockey— that's it. That's the whole list.

I truly don't give a shit about anyone else. But I *do* give a shit about *her*. And, unfortunately, she gives a shit about *them*. So I've tried to care, too. And if I'm being honest, outside of their dumb-ass response to the jumbotron fiasco, they've earned my respect. Well, maybe not Finn—I'm still waiting on that fucker to pull his head out of his ass and prove his worth—but the others. They have her back. They protect her. Look out for her. But most of all, they make her happy. And who the fuck am I to intervene with that?

It also helps that they're damn good hockey players. I couldn't have tolerated their presence if they were like fucking Kyle—all talk and unwarranted arrogance. Like me, they have a true love of the game, a dedication, and drive. Hockey is as much a part of them as it is me—a vital organ necessary for survival. We might not all bleed the same, but on the ice, we speak the same language, and that counts for something.

A nudge at my arm draws my attention for the first time since we arrived at this hellscape of a club, and I turn to glare at Ethan. Ignoring me, he jerks his chin toward a table not far from the bar. "Finn's fucked."

"Yeah, no shit." He was off his face within half an hour of getting here. The first thing he did was march up to the bar and order Jägermeister shots for the whole team...only to down most of them himself.

Following Ethan's gaze, Finn is slumped in a booth with a few of the rookies who have been put on babysitting duty. There's a shot glass in his hand, another five already emptied in front of him.

"Jesus," I mutter.

"Yeah," Ethan agrees with a grimace. "I'm getting him out of here before he ends up in ER getting his stomach pumped."

I nod. "Wise."

"You'll stay with her?" he asks, gaze cutting across the dance floor to where Dylan is partially visible through the crowd, her hands running over her curves as she sways to the beat. Her head is thrown back, her eyes closed, blocking everything out except for how she feels in this exact moment. As I watch, she twirls to face Jax, dragging her hand down his chest as she smiles up at him. She's oblivious to the danger, which is exactly the way I want it. It's precisely why Ethan and I have taken up protective stances, always keeping her in sight, why I've been sucking on this one beer since we arrived. So she can have this blissful moment of peace. She deserves it after tonight. After everything she's endured. After all the shit she's had to take from the guys, the team, and everyone else in this crap pack of a world who can't see that Dylan isn't like the rest of us. She's meant for greater things. Most of us are placed on this earth for no grand reason, but every once in a while, someone comes along who is meant for greatness. To change the course of existence. Dylan is one of those people. I have no doubts about it. She is going to change the entire trajectory of sports. She's going to break through the glass ceiling and transcend barriers. It's not a matter of how, but when. And I can't wait to be there at her side when she leaves all these suckers fucking gobsmacked.

"Always," I tell Ethan.

As if our thoughts are aligned, we both turn in tandem toward the bar, where Kyle is standing, flirting it up with a couple of girls like he isn't responsible for the massive showdown in the locker room only a few hours ago. I shake my head and have to avert my gaze before I do something reckless like give him a broken nose to go with his split brow and black eye.

The satisfaction I felt when he walked in here looking like he'd gotten into a fight with The Rock was euphoric. It might have only sent Finn spiraling further, but it beat out the shutdown I secured tonight, which guaranteed us our epic win—which is saying something!

Clapping my shoulder, Ethan's parting words are, "Keep her close," before he pushes his way through the crowd toward Finn. Hauling him out of his seat, he drags him like a fallen soldier out of the club.

With a glance in Kyle's direction, content to see him getting it on with the blonde at the bar who will most definitely wake up with regrets tomorrow, I set my mostly empty beer bottle on a nearby table before slowly threading my way through the crowd.

I don't rush. I don't stalk. I weave through the drunken mess of bodies and heat when the bass hits harder, until I'm behind her.

Static buzzes over my palms as I reach out to touch her, hands gliding over her hips and around her waist until I can pull her into me. She fits against my larger frame like she belongs there—because she fucking does. My face presses into the curve of her neck, just under her hairline, and I breathe her in. Peach and sweat, and the last trace of whatever body lotion she used earlier. My pulse spikes. My cock stirs. It's ridiculous how much I need her. How much I *always* need her. Like I haven't been watching her all night. Like I didn't have her on her knees for me hours ago. Like I haven't heard her call out my name in pleasure a dozen times before.

Her soft gasp melts into a smile as she leans back into me, one arm reaching up to hook around my neck. Her other hand reaches blindly, entangling in the front of Jax's shirt and tugging until she's caught between the two of us. A Dylan sandwich. A mouthwatering, could-live-on-it-for-the-rest-of-my-life kind of sandwich.

The music throbs. She rolls her hips in time with it—against me, against him. Her dress rides higher with every twist of her body. My hands find her hips, anchoring her in place.

"Fuck, Hurricane," I murmur against her ear, voice low and wrecked. "You're gonna kill me."

She grinds back harder in response.

I run one hand down her side, slow and possessive, tracking every inch of skin from her waist to her thigh. She shivers beneath my palm but doesn't stop moving. Her hands roam over Jax's large frame, and he stares down at her with heat-filled eyes. It's hard to tell in the strobe lights, but I'd swear he isn't even blinking, too afraid to miss a single moment of rapture on her face. His hands are all over her too, up her sides, along her arms, brushing the sides of her ass.

We're no longer dancing—we're *devouring*. Lost in the music, in the heat, in *her*. Our bodies locked together in a rhythm that isn't choreographed but instinctual. The beat pulses through the floor, through our veins, into the space between our lips and skin, dragging us deeper.

Dylan leans into me like I'm gravity, her lips seeking out Jax's. Right now, we're one unit. Moving together. Breathing each other in. Lips swollen and pupils dilated, her head tips back to rest on my shoulder. Her body arches, caught in the push and pull between us. I lock eyes with Jax over her head—heat, want, understanding. Words aren't necessary as he ducks, burying his face in her neck, lips skimming her sweat-slicked skin. I feel the breath she exhales against the side of my face, feel the way her knees falter slightly.

My hand trails down her side until I find the hem of her dress again. My fingers graze soft, warm skin as I slip them between her thighs. Her breath catches, and I smile into her hair, my lips brushing the shell of her ear as I murmur, low and rough, "I believe I have a promise to uphold."

Her body tenses, then melts, a soft sound escaping her—half gasp, half moan. Jax's hands move in tandem with mine, one of his fingers drawing lazy circles just above her knee while mine slide higher, closer, until her hips jerk and her heat engulfs me.

And I'm lost.

To the music. To the dark. To her.

Right now, there's no one else in this club. No prying eyes. No past. No Kyle. No games.

Just us.

The music thickens, bass low and pounding like a second heartbeat. Or maybe that's just mine. Lights strobe red across Dylan's skin, casting a glow that makes her look half temptress, half angel. And she's mine. Ours. But *mine* first.

My fingers slide over the damp fabric of her panties, causing her to tremble between us, and the sound she lets out? Sinful. My blood roars.

I can't hold back any longer. I'm going to burst a vein or have a heart attack or go fucking insane if I don't get inside her right now. What I want more than anything is to rip off the pathetic excuse of a barrier, bend her over, and fuck her right here in front of everyone so they can know *exactly* who she belongs to. So the entire goddamn club knows that she's *mine*.

But fucking decorum and all that, so I settle for shoving her panties aside and burying two fingers inside her wet cunt. Her gasp is drowned out by the heavy bass. "Such a good girl, Menace," Jax purrs, his words only audible because of how close we all are. His breath is hot on the other side of her throat before he lifts his head enough to meet my gaze. "Tell me, is she wet for us?"

"Fucking soaked."

He groans, diving in to claim her lips in a hungry, frantic kiss. I never thought I'd be into watching, but with my girl pressed up against me, and feeling how hot he gets her, how her hips buck and a gush of excitement coats my fingers, I'm fucking hypnotized. Entranced. The only thing hotter would be if she were clenching around my dick instead of my fingers. One day. Soon. Very fucking soon.

Releasing her lips, Jax drags his mouth down her neck. Her head drops back against my shoulder, and she whimpers. Her eyes are glazed over, lids at half-mast, and cheeks rosy as she trembles against me, completely wrecked between us.

I feel Jax's hand brush mine as he moves to circle her clit, and she practically comes apart.

"Tell Jax the rules," I murmur in her ear. She blinks up at me, dazed. "Who owns this orgasm?"

"You do." Her voice is barely a whisper.

"And when do you get to come?"

Her lips part, but instead of words, a moan rips free, her

eyes falling closed as she arches her back. "Please," she whimpers. "I need to come."

"Not until I tell you," I growl, bending to nip at her earlobe. She yelps at the bite of pain, a sound that soon transforms into one of pleasure as Jax continues to rub her clit and I stroke the raw bundle of nerves inside her. "You'll come on *my* fingers. With *my* name on your tongue."

"Say his name, D," Jax coaxes, finger moving faster against her clit.

Her breath catches. "Griffin..."

"Louder," I demand, scraping my teeth along the sensitive skin of her neck and making her shiver. "You're not ashamed to take what I give you—what *we* give you—are you?"

"No—*Griffin.*"

Her voice is loud enough to have a few heads turning our direction, but a glare from Jax and me has them quickly looking away.

"That's right," I purr encouragingly. "This body belongs to me. Every moan. Every fucking drop of you. Don't forget it."

"Fuck, Griff, she's so close," Jax says, his voice all dark amusement. "She's about to come."

"Not yet," I snap, slowing my pace just enough to draw a strangled moan from her throat.

Jax chuckles, seeming to enjoy this form of torture as much as I am. *Interesting.*

"You're starving for it. Aren't you, sweetheart?" My words are barely more than a possessive, wild growl, my chest vibrating as she clings to both of us. We're the only things holding her up. She is so close to the edge that I can feel it in the way her thighs twitch, the way she tries to grind down on us like she's forgotten we're in a public place.

"I need—Griff—Jax—*please*—"

I bite back a groan. My free hand grabs her jaw and turns

her to face me. "You gonna come for us, right here in this fucking club? Let the music drown out the sounds you make when we ruin you?"

"She's about to make a mess all over your hand," Jax warns.

"Let her," I snap, thrusting my fingers hard. Jax matches my relentless pace until she shatters between us, silent and staggering, held up only by our arms. Her body spasms, helpless and beautiful, and her nails dig into my neck as I smother her gasps with my mouth.

Jax watches her fall apart like he's addicted to it.

We both are.

When she finally sags boneless between us, I pull my hand from between her thighs, slick with her. I raise it to my mouth, sucking one finger into my mouth as I watch her pupils expand and her cheeks blaze red. "You taste like fucking heaven," I tell her.

Before I can lick her essence from the rest of my fingers, Jax's hand snaps out to grab my wrist. Bringing my hand to his mouth, he doesn't hesitate before wrapping his tongue around my middle finger and sucking the juices off it. "Divine," he murmurs, savoring the taste of her.

Glancing around, Dylan's eyes go wide, reality breaking through as she brings a hand up to smother her gasp. "I can't believe we just did that in a club."

I shrug, not giving one iota of a shit. "Considering I wanted to fuck you right here in front of everyone, I think we showed incredible restraint."

She gapes at me. Jax just laughs, shaking his head as he pulls her close and kisses her cheek.

"Let's get the fuck out of here," I grunt, looking around and noticing most of the team have already left—or are hidden in a dark corner. I don't really give a fuck. Kyle is nowhere to be found, and now that I've had a taste of my hurricane, I want more. Now.

With Jax and I flanking her, the three of us push through the crowd and out of the club. It's only a ten-minute cab ride back to the hotel, and we walk Dylan to her door. Her cheeks are still flushed, her stance unsteady. Jax rubs a hand down her back, his gaze lingering on hers before he murmurs, "I'm gonna check on Finn. He was really knocking the shots back earlier, and I wanna make sure he hasn't drowned in his own puke."

Dylan's nose scrunches adorably, but concern bleeds into her expression as her gaze flicks toward the door of the room I'm sharing with Finn. She worries her bottom lip before Jax tugs it free. "Let me know if there's anything I can do," she offers.

He flashes her a grin before moving away, and I step into her field of view. "I'll grab a few things from my room," I tell her, brushing a knuckle under her chin. "Then I'll be back."

"You don't have to—"

I cut her off with a press of my finger over her lips. "If you think for one second I'd leave you to spend the night alone in a hotel, you clearly have no idea the lengths I'd go to keep you safe."

She rolls her eyes but huffs out a breath. "Fine." Waving toward the door behind her, she says, "I guess I'll be here."

I wait until she's safely tucked away behind her door before striding after Jax. Stepping into my room, I'm hit with a wall of sweat and tequila. *Delightful.* Ethan is sitting at the head of my bed, legs stretched out in front of him, with Jax standing nearby, the two of them looking at a passed-out Finn.

"He's fine," Ethan assures. "Just dead to the world. He'll feel it tomorrow."

"Bus journey home will be some fun," Jax mutters, dragging a hand through his hair.

"It's late," Ethan says, moving to stand. "We should all get some rest."

They both head out the door, but just as I'm about to close it behind them, I notice Ethan isn't moving toward his door across the hall, but to one farther down. To Dylan's. He stops outside, and, curious, I watch as he just stands there, frowning at the door like it's offended him.

"Jesus Christ," I mutter, sighing loudly. "What is this, the waiting room for purgatory?"

Ethan doesn't look at me. "I just... I fucked up twice already." His face twists in a grimace, shoulders slumping. "I need to make it up to her first."

I bark out a humorless laugh. "You planning to do that telepathically? She's not a mind reader, Maddox."

Still, he doesn't move. Just continues staring at the bit of wood separating him from Dylan. The guy's got more self-control than anyone I know, and yet it's driving him fucking crazy.

"Well," I drawl, "If you're planning on sleeping outside her door, just know I'll be sleeping *inside* it. And if Dylan and I are sharing that bed, you can guarantee there will be very little actual *sleeping* involved."

He flinches. I smirk. "Thin walls, remember."

With that, I turn to go. I've barely shut the door when I hear it—a soft knock. Then the low murmur of voices.

When I crack the door open and peek into the hallway, Ethan's gone.

FORTY-EIGHT

I WAKE SLOWLY, the kind of lazy, drifting wake-up that makes it easy to forget where I am. For a second, I think I'm back in my room on Athletes Row, sunlight warming my comforter, and a practice I'm probably running late for waiting in the distance.

A knock sounds at the door, soft yet persistent, and I realize that's what woke me up. "Menace," Jax says through the wood.

"Jax?" I murmur, brain foggy from sleep. I reach up to rub my eyes. "What time is it?" I go to grab my phone from the bedside table, but something tightens around my middle, preventing me from moving.

Glancing down, a heavy arm is slung over my waist, warm breath ghosting against the back of my neck, and the solid weight of a body curled protectively behind me.

At first, I assume it's Griffin. I'm so used to him sneaking into my room at night that I don't think twice about it, but then memories of last night creep to the forefront of my mind. Being out at the club. Dancing with Griffin and Jax. Ethan knocking on my door...

Twisting carefully, I glance over my shoulder.

Ethan's face is relaxed in sleep, mouth slightly parted, lashes fanned over flushed cheeks. The golden morning light drips over the high angles of his cheekbone and the strong line of his jaw. He looks...soft. Human in a way he rarely lets himself be. Not the overprotective, broody captain he so frequently is during the day.

My heart does a little flip.

I'd been surprised to see him on the other side of my door last night. He claimed he was just checking on me. Making sure I had everything for the night, but even after I confirmed I was fine, he lingered, like he couldn't bring himself to walk away.

So I invited him inside.

I thought we'd maybe watch TV for a bit, then I'd pass out and he'd leave, but we ended up talking for hours—about nothing and everything. He didn't make a move or try to touch me, but he made an effort to get to know me, to connect. I learned more about the enigma that is Ethan Maddox in one night than I have in several months of living together. He's so reserved, keeping to himself, that it can make it difficult to get to know him. Truthfully, all of the guys are a little like that. Jax would be the most forthcoming.

In the predawn hours, we must have passed out from exhaustion. I don't even remember climbing beneath the covers. I hadn't intended for Ethan to spend the night sleeping beside me, but then again, I hadn't intended to nearly mount Finn yesterday or get hot and heavy with Griffin and Jax on the dance floor like some kind of reckless exhibitionist.

My brain might still be guarded, but my body's clearly staging a rebellion.

It's just...when they touch me, I melt. When they look at me like that, I lean in. Every time I tell myself to hold the line, I find myself caving anyway.

And then there are the letters.

For weeks, I've been wondering who's been sending them.

Leaving folded words of color and quiet devotion tucked inside my locker or slipped into my notebook. I thought maybe Ethan. Jax, even. But never Finn. He was last on my list of potentials.

He's the one who's pushed me away the most. Who's been hot and cold like it's a sport. And yet I saw the resignation on his face when Kyle outed him yesterday.

All of them came from him.

Every note that has made me smile after a long practice or preen after we've won a game, that has picked me up when I've had a crappy day...every single one came from Finn.

From the boy who fought tooth and nail to keep me at arm's length. To push me away at every turn.

Kyle claims he's incapable of sticking to one girl, but those notes, the things he said to me in the hotel room yesterday, they paint a picture of a very different man from the one Kyle claims to know.

Maybe Kyle never knew Finn at all.

The *real* Finn.

The one who's been trying to protect me in his own maddening, roundabout way.

Another knock on my door, this one more persistent, jolts me out of my thoughts, and I scramble out of bed, careful not to wake Ethan. Creeping across the carpet in my bare feet, I crack the door.

Jax is right there, arm resting above the doorframe, pools of brown instantly pulling me in. His gaze rakes over me, a crooked smile lifting his lips. I immediately lift a hand to try and flatten my obvious bedhead.

"How can you look so...alive this early in the morning?" I grumble, glaring at him.

He chuckles. "I know it's early, but I wanna take you some-where before the bus leaves."

My eyebrows hitch. "Where?"

"It's a surprise," is all he says, still smiling.

My eyes narrow on him, but he simply shoos me away to get changed. Closing the door on him, I hurry to grab my clothes and change quickly in the bathroom, before slipping back out of the room and leaving Ethan asleep in my bed.

"Musical beds?" Jax muses, noticing me silently closing the door behind me before we take off down the hall.

"Mm?" I'm still only half awake. I couldn't have gotten more than a handful of hours' sleep last night, and I'm already hoping I can conk out on the bus on the way home.

"Griffin keep you up all night?" There's a velvety undertone to his words, and I wonder if he's remembering our tryst on the dance floor. "Now I'm regretting being a gentleman and not joining you, but I wanted to show you what I have planned for today before we go any further." Slipping his hand into mine, he says softly, "I'm hoping today helps show you how serious I am. That I want you in my life, as a part of my future."

My eyes widen, but I can't deny my hand feels perfect in his. I love how easy it is to be around Jax. He's closed off to most of the world, but he's never really been that way with me. Not since that night we first played video games together. He dropped a wall that night, and it hasn't been erected around me since.

"It was Ethan, actually, in my bed last night."

His eyebrows shoot up. "Seriously? I assumed he'd slept in Griffin and Finn's room to keep an eye on Finn."

I shrug, stepping into the elevator. He follows, pushing the button for the ground floor. "He just crashed. We talked."

"*Talked.*"

The way he says it—the obvious connotation. I roll my eyes. "It wasn't...like that."

"So, no shirtless cuddling? No spooning with benefits?"

Thankfully, there's a soft *ding* followed by the opening of the elevator doors saving me from having to answer that. While there were no *benefits*, considering I woke up wrapped up in Ethan, there was definitely cuddling and spooning.

It's early morning in November, and the city's just starting to stir as we step out onto the street. A cool breeze nips at my cheeks, and golden sunlight stretches long across the sidewalk. The trees are on fire with color, red and oranges and dusky golds that shimmer in the breeze. A couple of joggers pass us, earbuds in. A man with a shopping bag and a coffee gives us a nod as we walk by.

My hand is safely tucked in Jax's, our shoulders brushing as we walk side by side down the sidewalk. It's peaceful. Normal. In a routine where hockey trumps all and any moment we're not on the ice or in the gym is spent cramming or studying, there's very little time for chilled Saturday morning walks.

"So, where are we going?" I ask when we're a couple of blocks from the hotel.

He glances down at me and winks. "You'll see."

"So cryptic," I murmur, making him chuckle.

"Not a fan of surprises, huh?"

I shrug. "I don't mind surprises. I guess I'm just more like Ethan—I prefer to be in control."

"I get that," he says, voice softer now. "Growing up, control was something I never really had. I was at the mercy of someone else's decisions—bounced between my aunt and uncle, which-ever one was willing to deal with me that year. Shuffled between houses without any say in what *I* wanted." He shrugs like it's no big deal, but I can't imagine how hard that must have been. How lonely. "I guess I got used to the chaos. Learned to roll with it. It taught me to let go a little. Not everything has to be planned or perfect—although don't tell Ethan that, he might have an aneurysm." He huffs a laugh, and I smile in reply.

Holding my gaze, he finishes, "Sometimes the unknown is where the good stuff happens."

I can feel my cheeks heat. "I can't say I disagree with that. I thought I had everything worked out when I moved here." I make a gesture with my hands. "Hockey was the focus. The *only* focus. No relationships. No boys. No distractions."

He smirks. "That's because you like your lines clear. Your decisions measured."

"Is that your way of saying I'm uptight?" I shove his shoulder, quirking a brow at him.

"No," he says with a slow grin. "It's my way of saying you're brave enough to try and steer the storm. Me? I just lean into it."

As we walk past a cute corner café, the scent of fresh coffee curls out into the morning air, and I moan aloud, making him laugh. "Need your morning fix?"

"Please." I practically groan as he tugs me inside. We order our drinks, and not long later, we're back on the sidewalk, warm drinks in hand as steam curls into the crisp air. I can't keep the smile off my face, and tilting my head toward the sky, I let myself enjoy this—just being with him. No drama. No rushing. Just us. Our footsteps in sync, and his fingers laced through mine like it's the most natural thing in the world.

Eventually, we stop in front of a quaint little boutique with display shelves full of handmade pottery and delicate ceramics.

"A pottery shop?" Confusion colors my voice as I glance up at him.

"C'mon." He drags me inside before I can question him further. We're met with soft music and shelves upon shelves of silty-toned mugs, quirky bowls, and tiny ceramic creatures line the walls. It smells like clay and something earthy, and a friendly woman waves from behind the counter.

"Just let me know if you need anything."

We wander the shelves for a few minutes. I run my fingers

along a glossy, deep blue mug with little gold flecks. Jax picks up one shaped like a fox's face.

I raise a brow at him. "This is adorable but...why are we in a pottery shop?"

Setting the mug carefully back in its place, he turns to face me. For the first time since I've known him, he looks...nervous. My head cocks as I watch him, trying to understand why he seems so uncertain all of a sudden.

He scratches the back of his neck, eyes flitting to the window. "I just... I had this idea that we could keep your dad's tradition going."

I freeze. My heart skips, and my ears ring.

He pushes on, voice even more hesitant and slightly panicked sounding. "Not the same, obviously. But, like...our own version. You and me. Every away game, we pick out a mug together. Something dumb or weird or cool. Keep the memory of your dad alive but...but make it ours too."

I stare at him, emotions a chaotic storm in my chest. My throat tightens. I don't even know what to say. If I can even speak.

Words can't describe...

Fisting the front of his shirt, I yank him toward me. He's so surprised that he comes, eyes wide as I plant my mouth on his. His lips are hard beneath mine, but only for a second before he caves to my touch. I run my tongue along the seam of his lips, and he parts, granting me entry. I don't deepen it. That's not what this is.

It's a thank-you. For seeing me. For listening. For...everything that I can't put into words.

My lips tingle and his are swollen when I let him go, and his eyes shine as they dart over my face. "I don't know what that means..." he confesses, voice thick. "Is it a dumb idea or—"

"Not a dumb idea." My vision is blurry before I blink the sheen of tears away. "I love it."

He hesitates, gaze meeting mine. "Yeah?"

I nod, trying *really hard* not to cry in the middle of the shop. "Losing that tradition has been one of the hardest parts." My voice catches, and I take a moment to inhale. Smiling wistfully, I share with him, "I used to get excited every time he came home with a new mug. It meant more than he probably ever knew to know that he thought of me when he was away. That I was a part of his life even when he couldn't be a part of mine. This... this means a lot."

Jax brushes his thumb across my cheek before cradling my face in a soothing gesture that I lean into.

"I'd love nothing more than to bring back his tradition and make it our own," I tell him in a thick rasp. "Thank you." My voice cracks over the words, and in the next instant, Jax has hauled me into his chest, his large arms banding around my back, his hand cupping the back of my head and holding me to him like I'm something precious to be safeguarded.

Time ticks by, but we don't move. His arms remain securely wrapped around me while I bury my nose in his chest and inhale his cedarwood and mint scent.

He remembered.

As if it wasn't enough that he fixed the mug Kyle broke, he's gone and brought my dad's tradition back to life. Breathed fresh air into it. Thought about it. Planned it. Risked my reaction to suggest it. Not because he had to, but because he *wanted* to.

The ache in my chest grows sharp and full. It's not just grief this time—it's the sudden, startling realization that I care for him. That maybe I'm already half in love with him. But this, Jax's kind of love? That's the kind that sneaks up on you. That seeps in slowly and then suddenly, all at once.

Eventually, he bumps my shoulder. "Let's find the perfect mug."

We browse the shelves together, holding up mugs, debating colors, shapes, and ridiculous designs. I snort when he shows me one shaped like a cat, and he laughs when I hand him one with a misshapen handle I can barely fit my fingers through.

After pointing out a few other ones, we both reach for the same mug—a hand-thrown one with a deep indigo glaze that catches the light like a lake at twilight.

"This one," we say at the same time before both bursting out laughing.

Jax pays, ignoring my protests, and as we walk back to the hotel, his fingers laced with mine and a paper bag swinging gently between us, something unfurls in my chest. A tiny seed of hope. Maybe I *can* trust him—all of them, even.

Fuck, I hope so, because I'm pretty sure this is what falling in love feels like.

FORTY-NINE

IT'S MID-MORNING, that quiet lull between the breakfast rush and the lunch crowd. The cafeteria's not empty, but it's not packed either—just the usual hum of students grabbing food between classes, muted chatter, and the occasional scrape of a chair against tile. I've got the end of the table the hockey team has claimed to myself, working through a late breakfast and scrolling mindlessly on my phone, earbuds in but not really listening. Just killing time. Minding my own business.

Until she shows up.

Dylan. Fucking. Carter.

She drops onto a chair several seats down like she owns the place. Like she *belongs* here.

This table—*our* table—is where the guys sit. At peak hours, it's packed with the team, loud and rowdy. Right now, it's mostly empty. Just me and a couple of others lingering before our next classes. The only *women* who should be here are puck bunnies, maybe the occasional girlfriend when someone on the team has one, but that's it.

Since Dylan is neither, nothing more than a fucking *inter-*

loper on our team, she has no right to be sitting here. It's a point I'll stand by until my last fucking breath.

As if the universe is out to personally piss me off today, Finn appears. Sliding a tray of food in front of her like she's too good to stand in line like the rest of us, before he claims the seat next to her. He doesn't even notice me sitting at the same fucking table as him. Too fucking hypnotized by Dylan's presence. Too sucked into her toxic orbit to notice if fucking Big Bird walked in.

I grip my fork tighter, knuckles whitening as I watch him give her this stupid fucking grin. The two of them are lost in their own little world, talking quietly. She laughs at something he says, and he leans in closer, their heads nearly touching. It's disgusting. The heart eyes. The shared looks.

Don't get me started on if I have to watch him tuck her hair behind her ear one more time or smile at her like she's the second coming of Christ. I'm bordering on homicidal as it is.

Finn is *my* friend. He should be sitting with *me*, the way it normally is if we have a gap between classes. Talking shit and tearing into rookies. Not giggling and flirting over goddamn turkey sandwiches. Seriously, where the fuck are his balls? And his common sense, for that matter.

He's not the only one that slut has wrapped around her finger. It's all of them. Ethan has refused to hear a bad word said against her since the beginning. He didn't give a shit that she was targeting me on the ice, going after me so she could take my spot. Then he had the fucking nerve to tell me to *work harder* when she finally did. Work harder? Like I wasn't already working hard enough. That bitch thinks just because she's got tits and a vagina that she can waltz in here, flutter her lashes, and get what she wants. And every fucking dumbass on this team *including Coach* are proving her right.

The only other one who sees her for what she is, is Lucas.

If only he'd succeeded in permanently squashing her instead of simply sending her running to *my* team. He'd been willing to help with the jumbotron showdown, giving me the video footage he had. He'd been convinced it would be enough to send her running, to get her to give up indefinitely.

But he'd been wrong.

She's way more fucking stubborn than either of us had given her credit for.

And it doesn't help that she's got Ethan, Jax, Griffin, and Finn in her corner. What should have divided them only seemed to make them fucking stronger.

The fork in my hand begins to bend, and I force myself to relax my grip, looking away from the sickening couple. I've officially lost my appetite, and I push my tray away, disgusted.

No fucking way am I going to sit back and watch this shit play out. Like this is normal. Like this is fine.

It's *not* fine.

Finn was my best fucking friend, and she's the reason he's gone.

I can't let her get away with that.

"Reed! Back the hell off! This isn't the NHL," Coach roars after I send another player—I don't even know who, they're all faceless enemies to me in this state—sprawling against the boards.

I skate off like I don't hear him, blood pumping too loud in my ears. Everything is too loud, too bright. I want to hurt something. Break something. *Someone.*

Except she's not a fucking part of this scrimmage so I have to settle for letting my anger out on everyone else. On anyone who gets in my way.

There's a blur of motion in front of me, and I go for a hip check that sends the guy flying. Clean? Maybe. Probably not.

Coach blows his whistle, barking out the end of practice. Except, before I can escape to the locker room with everyone else, he calls me aside.

"What the hell are you playing at?" he demands, Eyes sharp and jaw tight. It's clear he's not in the mood for bullshit. Well, neither am I, which is precisely what this conversation will be.

I shrug. "I'm playing hard."

"You're playing recklessly," he snaps. "That cheap shot on Chen? You could have dislocated his goddamn shoulder."

I don't respond. Just shift my weight from one skate to the other and glance past him, already done with this conversation.

"You keep this shit up and you won't be dressing Friday night. You hear me?"

"Got it," I mutter, flat as anything, and move to push past him.

He grabs my arm. Not hard, but enough to stop me. "You want to be benched?" His eyes narrow on me. "Because that's the road you're on."

I jerk my arm free. "I'm not on any road."

He sighs. "Christ, kid. What's gotten into you this season? You've been late. Skipping lifts. Half-assing drills. And now this —cheap hits, mouthing off, acting like the rules don't apply to you."

"I'm here, aren't I?" I snap. "I show up."

"Showing up isn't enough," he fires back. "Especially when you're doing everything you can to prove you *don't* give a shit."

I fall silent, grinding my teeth. He isn't going to let me leave until he says whatever he needs to say.

He blows out a breath, runs a hand over his cap. "Look...I get it. Losing your spot on the first line? That stings. I don't blame you for being pissed."

I scoff, eyes fixed on the boards.

"But Dylan earned it," he goes on, unaware of how much those words curdle my insides. "She outworked you, outplayed you. You know that. And deep down, I think you know she deserved it."

Like fuck she did, but I can't tell Coach that. He's as blinded by her as everyone else is.

"That doesn't mean I don't see how much it's eating at you," he continues. "Hell, I'd be worried if it *wasn't* bothering you. But the way you're handling it?" He shakes his head. "You're proving exactly why Dylan is the better player."

My jaw is clenched so tight it hurts. Thank fuck hockey players don't worry too much about losing their teeth cause I'm pretty sure I'm about to crack one.

"You want a shot at that first line?" he asks, piquing my interest for the first time. "Start acting like someone who *wants* it. Like someone who's still a part of this team. Take all that animosity you're feeling and channel it into something productive."

Channel it? Sure. But getting my spot back is just the beginning.

Dylan has stolen *everything* from me.

My spot. My best friend. My fucking *room*.

My respect.

No one on this team looks at me the same now.

If she'd never come to BSU, none of this would have happened. I wouldn't be angry all the goddamn time. Wouldn't feel like I'm drowning in silence, clawing to get back everything she stole.

Something twists inside me. Tight and dark.

This is her fault.

All of it.

And I'm done with the warnings. This time, I'm going to make certain she doesn't get back up.

FIFTY

THE THIRD PERIOD is almost over, and the tension is brutal. We're down one goal, and I can feel the weight of it in my chest like a puck caught under my ribs. The Eastwick Knights are playing dirty—as always. They don't give a damn about finesse. Just brute strength and whatever they can get away with when the refs aren't looking.

I clock Dylan weaving up the ice, slicing through defenders like she was born for this. She's fast, humble, light on her skates, and for a second—just one—I think she's got an opening. I think maybe, maybe she can tie the game.

It plays out in slow motion. One minute, she's lining up for the shot on a goal, and the next, a defenseman barrels toward her. He's not going for the puck. He's going for *her*.

"Dylan—"

I don't even hear the rest of what I scream. My blades dig into the ice as I pivot hard, but I'm too far away. He slams into her full force, shoulder to midsection, and she goes airborne before crashing down.

I don't know if I imagine the noise or actually hear it over the crowd and blood rushing in my ears, but the sound of her hitting the ice—fuck, I'll never forget it.

It's the worst moment of my life, followed immediately by the next...when she doesn't get up. Doesn't move.

Panic floods me. The whistle shrieks. Coach is yelling from the bench, but it's all white noise as I drop my stick and skate harder, faster than I ever have before.

"Dylan?" I drop to my knees beside her, yanking my gloves off. My hands tremble as I reach them out. "Dylan, talk to me."

She's curled onto her side, arms wrapped around her ribs. Despite the layers of protection she's wearing, I've never seen her look so small. So fragile. Is this how Finn felt that night he found her beaten up outside the arena?

Her eyes are scrunched tight, but they flutter open when I touch her shoulder, slicing right through me as our gazes connect, and I glimpse the extent of pain she's in. "I'm here." My voice is hoarse, raw, but I'll do anything to ease the pain she's in. "You're okay. You're gonna be okay."

"Menace." Jax sounds just as broken as I am, and Finn skates over a second later, falling to his knees beside me. "Shit, Dyl. Where does it hurt?"

"Ribs." She winces. "Back. Pretty much everywhere. Feels like I got taken out by a Mack truck."

"Considering the size of that fucker, it would probably have hurt less if you had," Jax grumbles, eyes blazing fury despite the gentle way he touches Dylan.

"Can you move?" I ask her.

"I think so." She moves to sit up, but she winces, her breath catching.

"What?" The demand is a near-feral snarl as it rips from my lips.

"My shoulder." She reaches up to tentatively touch it,

grimacing at the light touch. "It hurts to move." Her face falls, any color remaining draining away.

"It's probably just bruised. You took a hard hit," I assure her.

She nods, but I can tell she doesn't fully believe me.

"Hurricane." Griffin practically shoves me out of the way as he skids to a halt at her side, his goalie pads plush with the ice and his mask already discarded. He doesn't hesitate as he hauls her into his arms.

"Careful," Finn chides.

"Back up. Back up." The medic cuts through the group gathered around us—mostly team members. "Give her some space."

I nudge Jax, signaling for us to move aside, but careful to keep Dylan in my line of sight, easily within reaching distance should she need me.

We all hover while the medic does a quick assessment. She's awake, talking, and that should settle me, but flashes of the hit she took, the sound she made when she hit the ground...they play on repeat in my head, freezing me in place, making it impossible to move forward. To *breathe*.

Her dad died in a freak accident in the middle of a game.

She could have died tonight. If she'd hit the ice differently. If she'd twisted when she'd fallen...

How the fuck does she find the strength to get on the ice knowing that?

A stretcher is brought out to get her safely off the ice. Her helmet was removed at some point, and her gloves have been pulled off. Coach is over now, his jaw tight and face pale beneath the bright lights of the arena. He's talking to her. She's arguing. I hear the odd words. *Fine* and *still play*. She's doing what any one of us would do—fighting to stay in the game—but the thought of her out there, at risk of another hit, one that could have more lasting repercussions, makes me want to keel over and vomit.

"You need to get checked out," I tell her firmly. "Your shoulder needs looking at. If you continue to play with it as is, you could do more damage. Tear your rotator cuff or something, and instead of missing the last twenty minutes of a game, you could be out for the next several weeks."

I *need* her off the ice. Not just for her sake, but for my sanity.

Her lips part in an argument, but I lean in, cupping the back of her neck and bringing my forehead to hers. "Please." It's a plea. A prayer. A...I don't even know what. I have *never* been this concerned about a player. This unfocused on a game. For the first time in my life, I don't give a shit about the scoreboard. About the fact that we're losing this game. *She* is all I can think about. All I see. All I care for. "Let them check you out," I beg of her.

Whether it's the catch in my voice, the fear in my eyes, or the tight grip I have on her neck, she agrees, and the medics begin to move her off the ice.

"She's in good hands," Coach says, voice tighter than normal as he puts a hand on my shoulder.

"I should go with her—"

"You've got a job to do." His voice is firm, much like the tone I used on Dylan earlier.

"But—"

How can I possibly finish out the rest of the game? How can he expect me to run through a play, and have my head in the game when the woman I've fallen in love with is injured? I said she was fine, but I have no fucking clue. What if she tore a muscle or ripped a ligament? What if she needs surgery? Rehab? What if this affects her whole damn future? Hockey is *it* for her.

I can feel myself spiraling until a hard squeeze of my shoulder draws me back. I meet Coach's hard gaze. I can see the worry in his brown depths, but unlike me, it's not getting the better of him. "I know you're worried. I am too, but she's in good hands. She'd want you focused on the game. Living up to your role as captain." He jabs me in the chest. "So get the team focused and prove to her that you're the captain—the *player*—she believes you to be. 'Cause you know damn well as soon as you go back there, she'll be wanting to know we did everything we could to win."

Fuck. He's right.

I fucking hate that he's right.

I nod, not daring to take my eyes off Dylan until she disappears from view down the tunnel. I can feel the others at my side, all of us watching our girl be taken off the ice. My chest tightens, pulse thrumming with fear and fury. When I finally manage to tear my gaze away, it collides with another—across the ice, right at the glass.

Lucas.

He's standing there in the stands like he owns the place. Smirking.

That same smug, calculating look I've seen too many times before.

A flare of something sharp twists in my gut. I nudge Jax beside me and lift my chin toward the stands.

He follows my gaze. So do Finn and Griffin.

All three of them go still. Jax's jaw clenches. Griffin's hands curl into fists. Finn mutters a quiet, "You've got to be kidding me."

No one says it aloud, but we're all thinking the same thing.

What the hell is he doing here?

And did he have something to do with what just happened to Dylan?

The whistle blares, ripping through the moment like a blade.

Jax claps a hand on my shoulder. "We need to focus."

I force myself to turn away from Lucas, my spine rigid. Facing the rest of the team, I shove the fury down deep and push all questions regarding what he might be doing here to the back of my mind as I bark, "Huddle. Now."

The team closes in, expectant eyes on me. I meet them all, one by one, my gaze hard, determined. "You saw what they did to one of ours," I start. Murmurs go up, tones of disgust and anger. "I don't know if we can win this, but we can at least give them hell."

My words are followed by a chorus of "Hell yeah!"

"Let's show them that if you mess with one Steelhawk..."

"You mess with us all," Griffin finishes, a lethal glint in his eyes and a cruel curl to his lips.

I hold out my hand in the center of the huddle. "For Dylan."

Jax's palm slaps against mine. Then Finn. Griffin. The rest of the team.

"For Dylan."

FIFTY-ONE

I DON'T REMEMBER GOING down. Just the crack of my skull against the helmet and the white-hot pain that exploded in my shoulder and up my side.

And distant voices yelling my name.

Now I'm in the medical room—a side hallway off the main rink, all white walls and disinfectant—perched on an exam table while a trainer gently palpates my shoulder.

"Good news is, there's nothing broken," he states, voice calm but firm.

"And the bad news?" I grimace as I try to roll my shoulder.

"You're bruised, maybe some muscle strain, but your range of motion is decent, and your reflexes are intact. You got lucky."

Lucky. Sure.

I nod through the dull throb that pulses from my shoulder to my spine. Every muscle aches, and I'm still pissed I had to miss the end of the game. And even while the trainer drones on about anti-inflammatories, hot pads, and soaking, all I can think about is the game. What happened after I left?

"Thorn," Ethan growls, throwing the door open and crossing the room in three strides. Finn, Griffin, and Jax are

right behind him, all still in partial gear, skates off but pads and
jerseys askew. The panic on their faces is palpable.

"I'm fine," I assure them, lifting my hands as Ethan crouches
in front of me. His hands hover at my knees, like he wants to
touch me but isn't sure if he should.

Finn moves behind Ethan, his gaze raking over me. "You
didn't get back up." There's a tightness to his voice, the fear, the
panic, still evident. "You went down, and you didn't get back
up." He sounds accusatory, but I know it's not directed at me.
It's his fear talking, and seeing such a reaction from him, the guy
who kept himself at arm's length from me for so long, breaks my
heart.

Reaching out, I grasp his hand, squeezing hard. "I'm fine." I
put emphasis behind my words, hoping it will ease some of his
energy. He nods, the movement sharp and jerky, and his hold on
me is almost painful, but I don't let go. Don't comment. I need
this as much as he does.

Griffin is immediately at my side. He doesn't have the same
hesitation as Ethan as he wraps a hand around the front of my
throat and brings his face within inches of mine. The pads of his
fingers caress my skin lovingly, soothingly, like he needs to feel
my pulse beating in order to assure himself I'm here—with him.

"You scared the shit out of me." His voice is akin to gravel,
digging into my flesh and leaving a scar that goes farther than
skin deep.

Then, without warning, his mouth crashes down on mine.
It's not gentle or hesitant—it's searing, claiming, as if he needs to
stamp his mark on me, to remind us both that I'm alive and his.
His kiss is heat and desperation, anger and relief. By the time he
pulls back, I'm breathless, my heart hammering all over again
for an entirely different reason.

Bringing my free hand up, I cup the side of his face,
brushing my thumb over his cheekbone, the two of us sharing a

moment before I swing my gaze to Jax. He's waiting patiently but looking no less concerned than the others.

He offers me one of his rare smiles, and I know it's not possible, but it eases the throb in my shoulder. It's probably the anti-inflammatories the trainer gave me kicking in, but Jax has always had this ability to calm me, to make me feel like all will be all right in the world.

"What did I miss?" I ask, still holding his gaze, even though I'm speaking to all of them. "Did we win?"

Ripping my gaze away, I take each of them in. I see the answer in their crestfallen expressions before Ethan admits, "We lost. 1–0. Couldn't get a single goddamn shot past their goalie."

"He was a wall," Finn mutters dejectedly. "But Griffin kept them from scoring again too."

I smile at him as he smirks cockily.

"And we got the asshole who hit you," Jax adds, sending my head whipping in his direction, eyebrows climbing to my hairline. His smug grin has my gaze trailing downward until I spot the blood dusting his split knuckles.

The trainer interrupts before I can ask anything more. "All right, everyone out. Carter needs to soak, and you all need to hit the showers before you stink up my treatment room."

"We're not leaving," Griffin argues, while the others voice their own protest, but the trainer isn't hearing any of it as he stands at the open door, waving them out. "Go."

"Go," I encourage. "He's right. You all stink. How can I soak in peace with the stench of sweat clogging my nostrils?"

With some final grumbles and reluctant glances, they move toward the door. Except, before he can disappear through it, Ethan comes back, closing the distance between us with a look of determination that stalls the air in my lungs. In the blink of an eye, he's in front of me, cupping my face between his palms. "I never want to experience that again," he murmurs, voice rough. Then he leans in and kisses me—hard, deep, like he's pouring everything he feels into this one moment. His lips are insistent, desperate, and when he pulls away, his thumb sweeps across my cheek like he's memorizing me all over again. "I know I've fucked up, but *shit*, Thorn. You terrified me out there. The thought of losing you..." His expression is anguished as he shakes his head.

"Shh," I soothe, stroking his hands still cupping my face. "I'm right here. I'm okay."

He swallows audibly, intense blue eyes meeting mine. He crouches so our lips are inches apart. "I don't know when it happened, but you snuck your way under my skin and now I can't remember how it felt without you there. I don't *want* to remember."

Reaching up, my fingers trail over his lips, still swollen from our kiss. "I don't either." He leans into my touch before reluctantly pulling away. The others are hovering by the door, and he stalks over before they all file out. Griffin lingers, eyes on mine like he wants to say something. Instead, he gives me a small nod before he disappears.

The trainer helps me to my feet, leading me into a connected room that holds two large stainless-steel tubs—one for ice baths, one for hot soaks. It's a private space, tiled from floor to ceiling, the warm scent of eucalyptus wafting in the air. I can't help but recall the last time I was in here...with Jax. Entirely different circumstances—unfortunately.

He instructs me to sit in the tub for half an hour. "You can keep your base layers on," he says, nodding to the sports bra and tight shorts I wore under my gear. "Let the heat work into your muscles. If anything feels off, hit the panic button beside you. Got it?"

It's not my first injury on the ice. Not my first hot soak, so I simply nod, already moving toward the tub.

"I'll leave you to it, then," he says, already walking out the door.

Alone, I sink into the tub with a hiss. The water is hot, nearly too hot, but once I'm submerged, I melt. My sore muscles sing in relief, and I groan, letting my head fall back as the last bit of throbbing disappears.

I sit there for long minutes, half lost in the ripple of heat licking over my skin. My muscles ache, but I'm okay. Just bruised. Nothing torn. Nothing broken. Still, it rattles me how easily that could have changed. I *know* how quickly death and injury can come on the ice. I've *seen* it.

Shivering, I push away those ugly thoughts. I can't afford to dwell on that now, or I'll spiral. Instead, I force myself to focus on my breathing. On nothing at all.

As the water lulls me into a half sleep, images play out on the backs of my eyelids. Ethan's wild eyes, panicked and desperate. Jax's frantic, raw voice. Finn's trembling hand wrapped in mine. Griffin's death grip on my arm, like if he let go, I'd disappear.

I let out a slow, steady breath.

Even in pain, I feel...seen.

Cared for. Protected. Loved, even.

The hinges creak on the door as it's pushed open.

A slow smile tugs at my lips. "You just couldn't stay away, huh?"

No response, but I hear the pad of footsteps moving closer, the subtle shift of the air. I wonder which one of them it is. Griffin, maybe? He's the most likely to break the rules, but then I recall the fear in Ethan's eyes, and I think it *could* be him. He's not a rule breaker, but he is the type to check up on an injured player. He wouldn't have wanted to stray too far, to have me out of his sight for long.

"You guys are relentless," I tease, shaking my head.

There's still no response, and when I don't hear the sounds of someone stripping down, the ripple of water as someone steps into the tub, I open my eyes—

A hand slams down on my shoulder. Hard.

Another clamps the top of my head, and before I can gain purchase or scream, I'm shoved under the water.

Panic explodes in my chest.

I thrash, bubbles escaping as I try to scream. My lungs burn. I claw, scramble, twist. The weight above me is too strong. Unrelenting.

Water fills my nose and floods my mouth. My ears roar. The pressure on all sides of my face reminds me I'm in a suffocating prison. One that will soon become my tomb...

My fingers scrape along the smooth sides of the tub, but there's nothing to hold on to. My feet slip against the bottom.

The pressure builds.

The silence sets in.

My limbs grow heavy, my thrashing slows. Panic turns to fog. Darkness creeps in.

And then there's nothing at all.

FIFTY-TWO

THE LOCKER ROOM IS CHAOS, the way it always is after a game. Except this time, I'm not engaging in the banter, arguing over where we should go for drinks, and making fun of the rookies.

Running the towel through my wet hair, I glance quickly at the others. I'm in the lead in our undisclosed race, but not by much. Snatching my shirt from the bench, I wave over my shoulder at them as I stalk toward the door. "Later, fuckers."

I'm out of the room before the words have even left my mouth, jogging down the corridor in my eagerness to check on Dylan. To make sure she's okay. I know she said she was. The hit didn't look as bad on replay as it felt in real time. But I still need to see her with my own eyes. Hold her. Kiss her. Wrap her in bubble wrap if I have to.

Especially after seeing Lucas in the stands tonight.

What the hell was he doing here? Why *tonight*?

His presence alone was enough to crawl beneath my skin, but the timing of it—showing up the night Dylan gets knocked out—was too much of a damn coincidence.

I couldn't stop thinking about it. Not during the second half of the game. Not while I was throwing punches at the guy who hit her.

And sure, I felt his skin split under my knuckles. But even that wasn't enough.

Because every time I passed Lucas on the ice, he was smirking. Grinning. Laughing with his buddies like he hadn't just witnessed the most important person in my life being carried off the ice.

Like it was all a game.

And it only made the fury burn hotter.

I'm nearly at the door to the treatment room when I hear it. Yelling. Muffled, but unmistakable.

My pace quickens.

My heart slams against my ribs as I break into a sprint.

The door has been flung open, the voices louder now within. Familiar.

On the threshold, I falter, paralyzed by the sight before me.

Coach has Kyle pinned to the wall, forearm pressed to his throat, while Kyle thrashes and spits venom.

"She took everything!" he yells.

My brow furrows, my body so tense it could snap.

Time slows down as my gaze swivels to the tub. That's when I see her. Lying face-down. Floating.

Something inside me breaks. Shatters.

"No," I choke. I launch myself across the room. Water splashes everywhere as I jump into the tub, hauling her out with trembling arms.

She's limp.

Too still.

Fuck. Fuck, fuck, fuck.

Thundering footsteps sound behind me, the already open door slamming into the wall as the guys flood in. Pandemonium ensues. Griffin takes one look at Dylan, unconscious and dripping wet in my arms and barrels toward Kyle, roaring, "You fucking bastard!"

I don't have time to watch whatever violence he invokes. Panicked and working on autopilot, I set Dylan on the ground. Water seeps into my T-shirt and soaks my knees. The last thing I notice before I lean over to pinch her nose and blow air into her mouth is Ethan, frozen in the middle of the room, his face white as a ghost.

"W-what do we do?" Finn asks in a trembling voice as he drops to the floor on Dylan's other side. His hands shaking as they hover over her still form.

"Support her head," I tell him as I move to do chest compressions. My own hands shake as I press against her sternum, once, twice, again. "C'mon, Menace," I murmur, beg, then plead, "Breathe for me."

Her skin is pale, lips tinged blue.

"Come back to us," Finn whispers, leaning in to push her hair away from her face. "Please." He presses a kiss to her temple, voice rougher, more demanding when he practically orders, "Don't you dare leave us."

"Why isn't she breathing?" Griffin shouts, stomping over. Violence rolls off of him. I don't dare look up from Dylan's lifeless form, but I can see him pacing in my periphery. "If she dies—" His voice breaks over the word, and something inside me withers. No, she can't fucking die. I push down harder on her sternum. "—I'm going to fucking kill you with my bare hands."

He's already marching back across the room toward Kyle. Ethan must have finally snapped himself out of his shock to intervene, as the next thing I hear is him barking at Griffin, "Sit your ass over there and call an ambulance. Now."

I lose track of what happens next as Dylan shudders beneath me. She makes a choking, gasping, spluttering sound.

39

"Quick, get her on her side." Together, Finn and I roll her. She jerks, water spewing from her lips and onto the tiled floor.

"That's it," I soothe, while Finn pushes her hair out of her face. Relief crashes through me, raw and sharp, as I rub circles on her back. "Get it all out."

Finn practically sags in relief, the two of us sharing a look that says more than words ever could about how fucking close we just came to losing her. To losing the only woman headstrong enough to manage the four of us. How we *never* want to be in this situation again.

Once Dylan seems to have gotten the water out of her lungs, I shift to cradle her, holding her head in my lap as she gulps in air, each breath ragged and desperate.

"I got you," I whisper, stroking her soaked hair. "You're okay. You're okay."

She trembles, tears streaming silently.

A drop of water lands on her cheek, and I realize I'm crying too.

I don't even try to hide it as I curl forward, bringing my head as close to hers as I can and simply breathing in the feel of her in my arms. Hearing her ragged breath. Alive. She's alive.

She shivers, and that's when I notice the goosebumps. "Get her a blanket," I order Finn, who scrambles to obey as quickly as possible.

He's back a second later with several large towels, which he drapes over her, tucking her in and murmuring to her all the while.

"Ambulance is on its way," Griffin states, voice hollow yet calm now for the first time since he entered the room. "Security too."

Lifting my head to meet his gaze, I find him staring unblinkingly at Dylan. Griffin is always shut down. He's a blank slate. Emotionless. But right now, he's bleeding out. He's...ravaged.

Just like the rest of us. The pain blazing in those cold eyes of his mirrors my own. Mirrors Finn's. Ethan's.

We may seem like a motley crew, having not much beyond hockey keeping us together, but in this, we are united. In loving Dylan, we are allied. *She* makes us brothers.

She makes us a *family*.

Two arena security officers barrel into the room. I don't know what Griffin said to them, but they take less than a second to survey the scene before moving straight toward where Coach and Ethan have Kyle pinned to the wall.

"He was trying to drown her when I found him," Coach explains, voice deathly calm. He's nearly always shouting at us, so to hear him so even-keeled is...scary as fuck.

"She's a bitch," Kyle spits, eyes wild as the officers manhandle him toward the door. "Stole everything. I had it *all* before she came!"

What. The. Fuck.

The guy has truly lost his ever-loving mind.

Security drags him out the door, his ranting echoing down the corridor, but none of us are listening to a word of it.

With him gone, all eyes fall on Dylan. Her eyelids have fallen shut, but her heavy breathing lets me know she's still awake, or semi-conscious at least. Ethan's at her side in a second. His finger skims her stark white cheek, and her eyelids flutter before she peels them open.

"Thorn."

His voice is destroyed. Broken in ways I never thought our strong captain could be.

She looks up at him through slitted lids, and when he slides his hand into her limp one, she musters the strength to return his squeeze before he gently lifts it to his lips, pressing a kiss to the backs of her fingers.

"I'll go check on the ambulance," Coach says, face pinched as he looks down at Dylan. "Make sure they know where to go."

With that, he's gone, leaving us alone in the suddenly deafeningly quiet room. No one speaks. We barely dare to breathe, the four of us sitting in a shrine around Dylan. Her head is in my lap while Ethan clutches her hand in his. Finn's hand rests over her clavicle, like he needs the reassurance of her rising chest to know she's alive, and Griffin has a death grip on her calf beneath the layers of towels.

We sit frozen in the aftermath, not yet ready to process what almost happened. The rage, the guilt, the terror—it'll come later. For now, there's just her breathing, and us, clinging to that breath like a lifeline.

FIFTY-THREE

IT'S dark when I wake.

At first, all I register is the quiet hum of machines. The sterile scent of antiseptic. The soft hiss of air conditioning. Then the dull throb in my skull and the ache in my chest remind me I'm not in my own bed, and the memories...they come slowly. Disjointed. Like puzzle pieces I'm too afraid to put together.

My fingers twitch beneath the blanket, and I shift, wincing at the sharp twinge that slices through my side. My limbs are heavy, my throat scratchy. I blink up at the ceiling, a faded white with tiny specks, like someone forgot to finish painting.

Hospital.

The realization sinks in with a quiet dread.

I lift my head and glance around, sluggish, disoriented. A single reading light casts a soft glow over the room. There's a vase of flowers on the windowsill—tulips, I think, but it's too dark to be sure. Then my eyes catch on the figure slouched in the chair beside me.

Bear.

He's hunched forward, elbows on his knees, hands clasped

like he's praying—or trying not to break something. His head lifts the second I stir, his eyes locking on mine. He doesn't move for a beat. Just looks at me. Like he's not sure I'm real.

Then he exhales, deep and shaky, dragging a hand down his face. "Jesus Christ, kid."

I try to speak, but only a hoarse croak comes out. My throat's dry as sandpaper.

He stands immediately, grabbing the plastic cup on the tray table and angling the straw toward me. I take a slow sip, the cool water soothing the ache in my throat.

"You're in the hospital," he says quietly. "They're keeping you overnight for observation. Your vitals are good now, though. You're okay."

I nod slowly, my body still too heavy to do much else. "What...what happened?" My voice is rough, barely audible. "I remember...the tub. Someone... I couldn't breathe. I—" My chest tightens as I remember the weight pressing me under, the panic clawing through me. The struggle. My arms flailing. My lungs burning. The terror. The rage. The cold. And then...nothing. "I thought I was going to die," I whisper.

My last thought had been of the guys. And how we never had the chance to see where things went between us.

Bear's face crumples.

Not dramatically. Not like in the movies. Just this small, devastating shift. His jaw tightens. His brow draws low. He lowers himself back into the chair like his legs can't hold him anymore.

"I found him," he says, his voice raw. "Kyle. Standing over you. I didn't even realize it was you in the water at first. Just saw someone in the tub. Then I saw your hair." He shakes his head. "I thought you were dead, Dylan."

Tears spring to my eyes, hot and burning.

"I got him off you. The guys came in right after. I kept him pinned to the wall while Jax—Jax got you out. They brought you back." His voice breaks on the last word. He sucks in a shaky breath, forcing himself to hold it together. "I've never been so goddamn scared in my life."

"Bear..."

"I should've stopped him," he says, voice rising with frustration. "I knew he was spiraling. Ethan came to me, said something was off. Said Kyle had a bone to pick with you. I kept my eye on him. I tried talking to him. Tried getting through to him. I gave him warnings, threatened to bench him. I did everything I could—"

"This isn't your fault," I cut in.

His eyes snap to mine.

"No," I say, firmer this time. "It's not. You did everything you could. Kyle made his choices. This was never on you."

"He was *my* player," Bear says, shaking his head. "My responsibility. Your father would've—" He stops, pain flashing through his expression. "He would've had my head for letting this happen to you. I'm supposed to look out for you. And I almost—"

"You didn't," I whisper. "You didn't lose me. I'm still here. Because of you. Because of Jax. Because of all of them."

Silence stretches between us. I reach out, my fingers brushing his hand. He takes it, strong and warm, and for a long time, we just sit there like that. Holding on. Him to me. Me to him.

My chest aches, but for the first time since waking up, it's not fear that fills it. It's something steadier. Stronger. Like even after everything, I'm not alone.

"Where are the guys?" I ask eventually, breaking the silence.

"I sent them home to shower and rest. They were hovering over your bed like mother hens." He clucks in annoyance, but I know he doesn't really mean that. He loves his players as much as he does me. "They'll be here first thing, probably at the ass crack of dawn, if I know them."

I smirk. I wouldn't expect anything less. Honestly, I wouldn't be surprised if Griffin is hanging out in the waiting room.

Eventually, I close my eyes, exhaustion tugging at me again, but as I drift, peacefully this time, into the abyss, I keep Bear's hand safely in mine.

When I wake, the calloused hand in mine has been replaced with a much finer, more delicate one. Cracking open an eyelid, I take in the fine lines, the familiar French manicured nails, and sparkling sapphire engagement ring.

"Mom?" Thankfully, my voice isn't as wane this time, as I lift my gaze to meet hers. It's almost a shock. I haven't seen her in so long. She looks the same as always, except for the fine lines that have grown around her eyes and lips, and the fresh streaks of gray in her hair that is otherwise the same thick brunette as mine. She's...older than I remember. Fragile in a way that tugs at my chest.

The second our eyes meet, hers flood with tears. "Oh, baby." She's up in an instant, smoothing my hair back, cupping my face between her palms like she can't quite believe I'm here, breathing, alive.

"What—what are you doing here?" I'm still stunned to see her. Shocked.

She hasn't answered any of my calls in months. Hasn't reached out. Hasn't...anything.

My gaze moves past her to Bear, who is lounging in a chair nursing a cup of hospital coffee. He grimaces behind her back. "The hospital contacted her. Don't worry, I went and picked her up."

Returning my gaze to my mother, I tell her, "You didn't have to come. I'm fine." I know how much hospitals bother her—both of us—ever since...

"*Fine?!*" I wince at her screech. "Dylan Rae Callahan, from what I am told, you nearly drowned in the team's hydro pool. You are most definitely *not* fine."

I wince again, this time at the accuracy of her words.

Her face crumples. "My baby was hurt. Of course I'm going to be here. Where else would I be?"

I close my eyes, lifting my hands to squeeze her wrists, her hands still cupping my face. I'm overwhelmed by the sheer love pouring from her. When I open them again, Bear is watching us with something soft and almost broken in his eyes.

"How are you feeling?" Mom asks, brushing my hair back again, her hands trembling.

"Sore," I admit, "but better."

She gives me one of those *mom* looks, and I smile despite everything that has gone down in the past twenty-four hours. God, how I have missed that look. Her soft touch. That feeling of being loved. Tears prick the backs of my eyes.

"I swear, Mom. I'm feeling better." Bringing her hands together in mine, I give her a teary smile. "I'm so happy to see you."

"Oh, sweetheart." She finally sits down again but doesn't relinquish her tight grip on me. "It's so good to see you too." Her eyes run over me affectionately, tinged with sadness. "You look so grown up." Her smile is watery. "I swear, you look more and more like your father every day."

I can feel heat in my cheeks as my eyes drop to the bedsheet. My father is still such a sore subject, especially between us. I never know if talking about him will make her smile or set her off...

Mom squeezes my hand tighter. "He would be proud of you, baby. So, so proud."

The lump in my throat grows to an unbearable size, but before I can respond, the door bursts open and a whirlwind of noise floods in.

Ethan. Finn. Jax. Griffin.

They barrel into the room, all urgency and panic, until they come to a screeching halt, noticing my mom's presence.

For a beat, the room freezes.

Mom straightens instinctively, smoothing her hair and her shirt, eyes wide as she takes them all in. For a moment, we all just look at one another.

"Well, Dylan, dear, aren't you going to introduce me to your friends?"

I cough to hide my laugh. "Uh, Mom, these are...some of my teammates." I introduce them each in turn, and one by one, they step forward, offering polite handshakes and greetings.

"Nice to meet you, ma'am." Ethan, of course.

"Your daughter is reshaping the whole team this year," Jax tells her with a flash of that smile that always renders me speechless.

"She's keeping us on our toes," Finn admits.

Griffin steps up last. He doesn't say anything, but he nods in respect, his gaze lingering the longest on my mother before flicking to me. There are questions there, ones I can't answer now. *Later*, I mouth.

Mom's smile wobbles but holds. "It's very nice to meet you boys. Thank you...for looking after her."

They all glance at each other like they're not sure what to say to that. Mom's words dredge up bad memories, and the air in the room suddenly feels heavy with guilt. Even if I don't blame them one bit for what happened yesterday.

Thankfully, we're saved from further awkward conversation by the ringing of Bear's cell. He pulls it out and glances at the screen. "I need to take this. I'll be right outside."

The second the door swings closed behind him, the guys turn their full attention to me.

"How are you feeling?" Ethan demands, crowding closer.

"Any pain?" Jax's face is etched with concern.

"You scared the sh—eh..." Finn glances sheepishly at my mother.

"I've spent more than enough time around hockey players, dear. You don't have to censor your words for me."

"Right." He gives her an apologetic grimace before returning his focus to me. His eyes blaze with so much fear still, like he's stuck in that moment. In those feelings. "I'm so glad you're okay," he murmurs, voice much softer this time.

While they've been rapid-firing questions, Griffin has circled around them to come to my other side. He stares down at me, like if he blinks, I might disappear.

"I'm here," I tell him softly, reaching out to take his hand. "I'm here."

The grip he has on me borders on painful, but I don't dare ask him to loosen his hold. Knowing he's here—that all of them are. That they were there when I needed them most... his hand in mine is as grounding for me as I imagine it is for him.

"I'm fine." I give them the same answer I gave my mom, but unlike me, she doesn't pull any punches. The second the words are out of my mouth, she scoffs.

"She's sore, still."

Immediately, the guys' hackles are up.

"Where?" Ethan demands.

"Have you had painkillers?" Jax.

"I'll go get a nurse." Finn is halfway to the door before I call out to him to stop.

"My chest aches a bit and my head hurts," I tell them succinctly, "but I'm okay. Really. The nurses have me on a schedule for pain meds. I'm sure they will be back when I'm due the next lot."

It guts me, the way their expressions tighten, the guilt that bleeds into their eyes.

I can't stand to look at it, but we can't have the conversation we need to have with my mom in the room.

Throwing back the covers, I swing my legs over the side of the bed.

Ethan and Jax are immediately there, protesting.

"Whoa, whoa, where do you think you're going?"

"Get back in bed, Thorn."

I wave them off stubbornly. "I need to pee, not climb Mount Everest."

Griffin, ever my savior, grabs the duffel bag they brought, rifling through it until he pulls out some sweats and a fresh T-shirt. Without a word, he holds his arm out for me to lean on and helps me to the bathroom.

He sets the pile of clothes on the floor, but instead of turning toward the door, he swings toward me. His hands frame my face, and he presses his forehead to mine. "Hurricane," he breathes, like he thought he'd never get the chance to call me that again. I can hear the pain in his voice. The ache. "I'm so fucking thankful you're alive."

Then he kisses me, hot and quick, and desperate. Like he's trying to brand the feeling of me alive onto his soul. Before I can respond, he pulls back, gives me a look that says he's barely holding it together, and slips out, pulling the door quietly shut behind him.

I sag against the wall, breathing hard, ribs protesting, before forcing myself into the shower.

Once I've toweled off and changed, I step out of the bathroom, towel-drying my hair. The guys are talking quietly near the windows, but they all straighten the second they see me.

"Where's my mom?" I ask, when I don't see her.

"She went to get coffee," Finn informs me. He says it with such ease, in such contradiction to the sudden thumping of my heart.

I'm moving toward the door on autopilot, dread forming like sludge in my gut.

She doesn't cope well in hospitals...

My fingers are wrapped around the door handle when a scream comes from down the hall. I throw the door open and take off at a run. I hear the guys' footsteps thundering behind me. My breath is short, and every inhale hurts, but I keep going. I need to get to my mom.

Rounding the corner, I careen to a stop when I find her at the nurses' station, hysterical and arguing with a bewildered nurse.

"Where is he?" my mom demands. I sense more than hear the guys stopping behind me. "Patrick Callahan! How dare you not tell me where he is!"

The nurse is trying to calm her, but it's not working. She's frantic, tears streaking her cheeks, hands shaking.

I rush forward. "Mom! Mom, hey, it's okay, I'm here."

She collapses into my arms, sobbing. "I can't find him, Dyl. I can't find him."

My own tears blur my vision, but I hold her tighter, whispering soothing nonsense against her hair. "It's okay. I've got you. I've got you."

I guide her to a nearby chair, crouching at her feet while she clutches at me like I'm her lifeline. Behind me, I hear one of the guys murmur, "Anything we can do?"

I shake my head, not trusting my voice, too busy keeping her anchored to me.

Her shoulders shake, her breath stuttering as she cries against me. The entire time, I rub a soothing hand up her back and murmur softly in her ear. It's not the first time I've had to do it, and it likely won't be the last. For a futile moment there, when I woke up and saw her in my room, I thought perhaps she was getting better, but now I'm wondering if she will *ever* get better.

Without my dad, she's not whole. She *can't* get better when she's forced to live in a world where her soulmate no longer exists.

My heart falls. Breaks. Shatters.

It's a devastating scenario. One that has no happy ending.

I don't realize I'm crying silently until a presence appears, blurry and out of focus. I blink the tears away to find a frantic Bear standing there. "I'm so sorry," he murmurs, voice low. His face is grave as he slowly lowers to kneel beside me. He gently pries my mom from my arms, promising to make sure she makes it back to Oak Haven safely.

She goes easily with him, her expression blank and shut down, the way it often is after an episode. She doesn't say a final parting word before he escorts her away. I stand and watch them disappear into the elevator and out of sight.

My legs give out, but my guys are there to catch me. Surrounding me, they whisper words of comfort and support as they usher me back toward my hospital room. They get me settled back in bed before crowding around me. I'm not sure the bed can support so much weight, but I'm not about to tell any of them to get off.

I need them.

FIFTY-FOUR

"PATRICK CALLAHAN, HUH?" Jax says, finally breaking the silence. I don't know how long we've sat in it. Minutes. Hours. But I guess it's now time to explain. They all know bits and pieces, Ethan and Griffin knowing the most, and Finn the least, but it's time they all knew everything.

Rolling onto my back, I stare up at the hospital ceiling while I gather my thoughts.

"I thought your name was Carter?" Finn questions, confusion coloring his words.

Blowing out a breath, I meet each of their gazes. Finn looks the most confused. Jax has a knowing expression, so I'm guessing he's connected the dots of what I *didn't* say. Ethan offers me an encouraging smile, while Griffin just squeezes my hand, nodding. I know if I tell the guys I don't want to talk about it right now, that he'll enforce it, but it's time.

"Carter is the name I started going by when I decided to pursue college hockey," I tell them. "My *real* name is Dylan Callahan." Dropping my gaze, I confess, "Patrick Callahan was my father."

"Patrick Callahan?" It's Finn this time who asks that question. "As in, *the* Patrick Callahan. Hockey *legend*, Patrick Callahan."

"The one and only." There's a hollowness to my words. One that seems to resonate throughout the room.

No one says anything right away. It's not the kind of thing you can just brush over with a joke or a nod. It's a bomb dropped right into the middle of us, a revelation that seems to shift the air.

I run my thumb over Griffin's hand, still gripping mine, grounding myself. "After he died...it was like everything broke at once. My mom especially. She..." I trail off, swallowing hard against the lump forming in my throat.

Ethan shifts closer, his knee brushing mine in silent support.

"She fell apart," I say finally. "She couldn't eat. Couldn't sleep. Barely spoke. Some days she didn't get out of bed. Other days..." I glance up, forcing myself to meet their eyes. "Other days, she thought he was still alive. Would talk to him. Set plates for him at the table. Call his phone and get upset when he didn't answer."

Finn's expression crumples slightly, his confusion replaced by something else—something raw and understanding.

"Those days were the hardest," I admit aloud. "She'd lash out when I tried to make her see the truth. When I said anything that contradicted the bubble she'd encased herself in." I swallow roughly, shuddering as I remember those dark days. Drowning in my own grief and waking up every morning terrified that she would have joined my dad, and I'd be all alone. I'd take her throwing glasses at my head and screaming insults at me over that.

"She wasn't safe," I whisper. "Not for herself. Not for me. Eventually, Bear stepped in. Together, we found Oak Haven. It's a facility for people like her, with mental health issues. She was severely depressed, but truthfully, I think it's more than that. I think losing my dad broke her. They were..." My throat closes over momentarily. "They belonged together," I force out in a haggard tone. "One doesn't function without the other."

"I'm so sorry, Menace." The bed shifts as Jax moves, his hand landing lightly on my ankle, a silent tether.

"She seemed like she was doing okay when we arrived," Ethan says softly.

I nod. "I thought so too. She seemed...more like her old self." I shrug. "But that's the thing with grief and depression. It can hit you at any time." I gesture around the room. "Being here, in a hospital. It triggered her."

"We should never have let her leave the room alone," Finn says, voice pained.

I shake my head. "You didn't know. Honestly, it probably had more to do with seeing me than...being here."

"What do you mean?" There's an edge to Ethan's voice, like he's ready to jump up and defend me.

I can't quite meet any of their eyes when I admit aloud for the first time, "I'm a reminder of everything she lost. I'm a reminder of my dad." I press my hand against my stomach to keep it steady. "Seeing me is like ripping the scab off a wound that never healed. I always set her off. That's why I rarely go to see her now." My voice is so small by the time I finish that I'm sure they have to strain to hear.

Griffin's hand tightens over mine. "You shouldn't have to carry that," he mutters, voice fierce. Protective.

"She's my mom." My voice cracks. "I'll do whatever she needs, even if what she needs is for me to stay away."

"What about what *you* need?" Jax asks, his voice rough. He leans in closer, those deep, bottomless eyes of his holding me hostage. "Who's looking out for you?"

His question lingers heavily in the air. I've had Bear. He's done everything he can—checking up on me, getting me enrolled in BSU, and offering me a spot on his team. But it's not quite the same. I appreciate everything he's done, but I can't unload everything that's bottled up inside me onto him. Not the way I could with my dad. Not the way I can...with each of them.

"We're here now," Ethan answers, voice low but certain. "You're not alone anymore, Thorn." He moves, his hand covering mine where it's still tangled with Griffin's. Finn shifts closer too, until his thigh is pressed firmly against mine. Jax leans against my feet, his presence a warm, solid weight.

"Never again," he adds gruffly.

Finn nudges me with his shoulder, a small smile breaking through. "You're stuck with us."

Griffin presses his forehead to the back of my hand, breathing me in like he needs the reassurance too.

I laugh, watery and broken. But it's real.

They don't try to fix it. They don't make promises they can't keep. They just stay with me, anchoring me when the world feels like it's falling apart all over again. And for the first time in a long while, I let myself lean into them. All of them.

I let them prop me up when all I want to do is crumble.

"What happened to Kyle?" I finally pluck up the courage to ask as we're driving back to the house. I was medically discharged earlier with a bottle of pain pills that I'm sure Ethan is going to force down my throat if I refuse to take them, and the aggravating advice to *rest*. Ugh, all I want is to get back on the ice and prepare for this week's game. The thought of missing yet *another* game this season prickles. Yet, even as I shift in my seat, I feel the pull of bruised muscles, the tightness that still resides in my chest. None of it is as profound as when I woke up in the hospital two days ago, but it's still there, a constant niggle when

I move or breathe too deeply. Hopefully, another couple of days will see it easing up enough for me to do some light skating.

Turning round from where he's sitting in the front passenger seat, Finn flashes me a wicked grin. "He's in police custody. Coach dealt with it all. Gave a statement to the police."

"He did?" My eyebrows hit my hairline, but of course, I shouldn't be surprised.

"They might want to talk to you too," Ethan warns, his gaze meeting mine in the rearview mirror for a brief moment before he returns his focus to the road before us.

"But for now, they obviously have enough from Coach to arrest him." Jax, sitting beside me in the back seat, gives my hand a reassuring squeeze.

"So he's gone?" The relief that fills me is euphoric.

"He's gone." So caught up in the knowledge that I am finally fucking *free* of Kyle Reed—that he is gone from the house, gone from the rink, gone from campus. *Gone*—I don't even know which of the guys responds, but I feel Jax and Griffin press in on either side of me. I feel the goofy grin stretch across my skin. The weight lifts from my shoulders.

I feel...free.

"Plonk your ass on the sofa and I'll grab snacks for us all," Jax orders as soon as we make it home. Finn is already directing me toward the living room, stealing the seat beside me on the couch.

Snuggled beneath a blanket, with Finn fussing over me, the TV humming in the background, and the guys chatting amongst themselves, I let out a yawn, my eyelids suddenly feeling ridiculously heavy. How can a simple journey home make me this exhausted?

And yet, I know it's not the journey. Or, not solely the journey. It's knowing that I'm safe. That I'm surrounded by the four of them, cocooned in a fortress of warmth, loyalty, and love.

It's knowing they came for me. That they didn't hesitate. That when it mattered most, they were there—dragging me from the water, chasing off the darkness, fighting for me when I couldn't fight for myself.

I feel it in every glance, every gentle touch, every wordless exchange between them as they hover close. I'm safe with them. Safe enough to let go. Safe enough to let the weight of the past few days slip off my shoulders, to let my body surrender to sleep.

Because I know without doubt or question that they'll be here when I wake.

That they'll keep watch.

That they'll always protect me.

Even from the monsters that wear familiar faces.

I WAKE TO DARKNESS.

The flicker of the TV plays muted images across the far wall, casting faint light through the living room. I blink slowly, the heavy comfort of sleep still pulling at me. It takes a moment to orient myself, to realize the solid warmth beneath me isn't a blanket or the couch.

It's Ethan.

I'm curled in his lap, tucked into his chest, and I wonder when that happened. I'd fallen asleep with them all surrounding me, and never even stirred when he lifted me onto his lap. His arms are wrapped tight around my waist, one large hand splayed protectively over my stomach, and his heat enveloping my back. His heartbeat thrums steadily against my cheek. Glancing around the darkened room, I notice we're alone.

He must notice I'm awake as he brushes a finger down the

side of my face, and I shift slightly, just enough to see his face in the shadows. "Thorn," he murmurs, almost reverently, dark eyes boring into mine.

"Sorry. I didn't mean to just pass out."

He shakes his head. "It's fine." His arms tighten slightly, like he's afraid I might disappear now that I'm conscious. "You looked so peaceful. We didn't want to move you."

"The others?"

"They went up to bed a while ago." He's still staring at me as though too afraid to blink, to look away. Even in the dim light of the room, I can see the tension in his shoulders, the darkness behind his eyes.

"You didn't have to stay," I tell him, feeling bad that he's sat up with me when he's bound to be just as tired as the others.

His mouth twitches, but the smile never forms. "I wasn't going anywhere."

I settle against him, pressing my cheek to his chest again. We fall into silence, the kind that feels sacred. The kind that says more than words ever could. His arms remain a solid band wrapped around me. Steady. Secure. Safe. They feel like home. Like lazy Sundays and nights spent cuddling on the sofa. Like somewhere I could grow. A safe place to fall at the end of a long day.

"I never got the chance to thank you," I eventually say, breaking the silence that had cocooned us. I blink up at him, using the darkness as a blanket for the vulnerable words. "For coming for me. For...saving me."

My words seem to gut him, and his jaw flexes. His expression hardens—not in anger, but in pain—and he can't seem to meet my eyes as he admits in a rough, bitter voice, "I wasn't the one who saved you, Thorn."

Maybe not him, specifically, but he still came. He still helped. Jax might have been the one to expel the water from my lungs, but as far as I'm concerned, they *all* saved me that day.

I start to protest, but he cuts me off, finally looking at me—and the anguish in his eyes knocks the breath out of me.

"I froze, Dylan." His hands fall away from my body like he's disgusted with himself. "I walked in and saw you in Jax's arms—lifeless—and I just... I froze. Griffin went for Kyle. Finn dropped to his knees and tried to get you breathing. Jax was soaked and shaking, trying to keep you with us. And I just stood there. Watching. Doing nothing."

The self-loathing. The hatred. The disgust. All aimed at himself... It flays me open. My cocky, confident, self-assured captain should never sound so broken. So hollowed out, like he left a piece of himself in that room.

I reach for him, but he flinches, pulling back like he doesn't deserve to be touched.

"I'm their captain," he spits, voice low but shaking. "I'm supposed to lead them. To protect my teammates. To protect *you*. But I stood there like a fucking statue." He spits the words, vitriol lacing every hate-filled word.

"Ethan—" I try again, pushing myself upright on his lap and placing my hand over his heart. It thunders beneath my palm.

"I've never felt fear like that," he whispers almost brokenly. "Not once in my entire life. It was like everything collapsed in on itself. Like the world tilted, and I couldn't get my footing. I couldn't *breathe*, Dylan. Watching you, like that...I've never been so scared."

His voice breaks over the last word, a tear slipping free and racing down his cheek before he ducks his head to hide it.

I can't take it anymore. I move to straddle his lap, cupping his face between both hands and forcing him to look at me. His eyes shine in the dim light, wide and cracked with emotion.

"Stay with me," I say firmly. "Not there. Here. In this

moment. I'm okay. I'm alive." I take his hand and place it over my heart, letting him feel it beat, steady and strong. "You don't have to be in control all the time. You don't have to carry everything."

He stares at me like he's trying to memorize every inch of my face. Like he can't quite believe I'm really here.

"You're the only thing that's ever made me feel like this," he says, voice a whisper dragged from his soul. "The only one who's ever made me lose control."

"Good," I breathe. "I like you like this. When you let go. Like you did in the training room." I smirk. "I like knowing I'm the only one capable of undoing you."

"You are," he assures, eyes shining. "The only one. The only one I'd ever let see me like this."

His hand slides to the front of my throat, not tight, just enough to hold me in place as he pulls me down to him. His kiss is searing—dominant, and commanding, like he's reclaiming every piece of himself he lost that day.

Like he's anchoring himself to me for all eternity.

For every inch of control I might take from him, he claims it all back, controlling the kiss, the pace, the rhythm. His tongue glides along mine, deepening when he demands and pulling back on his orders.

My hips move without thinking, grinding against him as heat pulses between us. He groans into my mouth, and I feel the tight coil of tension unraveling in his grip. In the way his hands glide low on my abdomen and pull me tighter.

He might be losing himself in me, but he's still Ethan. Still the one in control, and I wouldn't want it any other way.

Not when his hands are on me. His teeth sinking into my lip and his tongue learning the grooves of my mouth.

My hands slide up the front of his chest, the hard planes of his abs rippling beneath my palms, before I entwine my fingers with the fine hairs at the back of his neck. His lips on mine are all heat and desperation, the air around us growing hot and electrified with every sweep of his tongue over mine. Every nip. Every suck of my lip. Every soft moan and hungry growl.

Grabbing the hem of his T-shirt, I go to lift it, but he stops me with a hand catching mine, breaking our kiss to meet my gaze.

"Please," I plead before he can say anything. I don't need to hear his words, I can see the hesitation written all over his face. "I need this," I whisper. "I need *you*. I need to feel something good. To remember what safe feels like—and that's here. With you."

For a moment, his jaw tics. War rages in his eyes. Then, decision made, he slams his lips back on mine, hungrier than before. "You'll always be safe with us," he growls against my lips.

With fast, frantic movements, I tear his shirt over his head, my heart thundering as I drink him in under the dim light of the TV. Broad shoulders, defined muscles, warmth and tension carved into every line.

Before I can do more than *look*, he catches my chin between his fingers and reclaims my mouth in a commanding kiss. I move with him, following the pull of his mouth, the way he knows exactly when to take more, when to slow, when to make me beg without ever speaking a word.

When I reach for the hem of my own shirt, his hand catches mine again.

"*I* get to take this off you," he softly demands, his tone low, coaxing, and laced with steel. A thrill rolls down my spine. "You've no idea how long I've waited to get you naked," he murmurs, eyes dropping as he slowly lifts the fabric of my T-shirt, revealing inch after inch of skin. "To see all of you. *Feel* all of you."

Despite his lust-laced words, he takes his sweet time pulling my top up. His eyes darken with every inch of milky skin he exposes, but his control remains precise. By the time the shirt clears my head and drops to the floor, I'm breathless. Exposed. His gaze devours me.

His hand finds my side, slides up to cup my breast, then the other. He strokes me deliberately, watching every reaction, drinking in the way I arch toward him. When he brushes his thumbs over my nipples, I gasp, grinding against the growing heat between my legs.

"More," I demand, breathless, needing to feel his lips on my skin, his tongue sliding over my flesh.

He gives me a look. That cool, unreadable smirk he wears when he knows he's in full control. "Patience, Thorn."

I huff, but it turns into a moan when his mouth closes around my breast. He licks, sucks, and grazes it with his teeth until I'm trembling. My fingers dig into his shoulders, leaving behind crescent moon marks as he shifts to lavish the other one with the same worshipful care.

Releasing me with a pop, his fingers follow his gaze down my stomach, teasing the waistband of my sweats. They don't dip below, just skim the edge, his knuckles brushing skin as his touch makes my breath hitch. I whimper with need. My body is burning up, my core hot and wet and needy.

And he *knows* it.

"Need something, my prickly little thorn?" His words are a taunt murmured against my overheated skin.

"Yes," I grit out, grinding against the hard length beneath me until he hisses. "I need you to make me come."

He hums, low and cocky, and presses his mouth back to mine.

"All in good time."

In contradiction to the need building inside me, this kiss is slow, languid. And it does sweet fuck all to fan the flames of my desire. If anything, the control he wields despite knowing he's as desperate for me as I am for him, only stokes them higher.

I'm a puddle of lust, breathless and pliable in his hands by the time he finally—*finally!*—releases me.

My gaze latches on to his, and something dark and possessive, so unlike the *boy-next-door* Ethan I know, flashes in his eyes. "Take my dick out, Thorn."

I shiver at the command.

Not needing to be told twice, I reach beneath the elastic of his sweats and free his hard cock from the confines of his boxers. It bobs in front of me, erect and angry, with precum beaded at the tip. I stare at it for a moment, my mouth salivating.

"Touch me, Dylan," he groans, desperate, all-consuming need, lacing the order.

My fingers wrap around the silken skin of his shaft before I slide my hand upward. He hisses between his teeth, and my gaze flicks to his face, watching it slacken in rapture as I work him over. His head falls back, but his eyes remain locked in mine, even as his chest rises and falls with rapid breaths.

His hands glide up and down my thighs, his hips thrusting shallowly beneath me. My own hips rock against his, need building into an inferno in my core. If I don't get him inside me ASAP, I'm going to lose my shit.

"Ethan," I moan, his name a plea on my tongue. "Please. I can't take any more teasing." He shudders beneath me, his pupils blown with desire, and I know he's as on edge as I am. Still, he wraps his hand over mine and keeps it pumping. His other hand delves beneath my sweats, his fingers pushing their way into my panties until he's rubbing my clit.

I'm trembling with need, moans spilling endlessly from my lips as I rock against his muscular thigh. My other hand cups my breast, pulling on my pert nipple and kneading my slick skin.

"Fuck, you look like a goddess," he hisses, unabashedly watching me.

"More, Ethan," I beg. "I need more."

Hunger flashes in his eyes, darkening them. "So needy for your captain." He nips at my lips, a growl reverberating through his chest. "I like hearing you beg. Tell me what you need," he demands, voice thick and raspy as he thrusts upward while working my hand over his hard shaft.

"You. Inside me," I pant. "I need you to fuck me so bad, Ethan, that it physically hurts. Please, Ethan. Fuck me. Fuck me so good that I forget everything else exists."

I'm rambling, begging, pleading, but whatever I say is his undoing. Like an elastic band reaching its limit, he snaps. Surging forward, he hauls me to my knees before ripping my sweats and panties down my legs. Naked and wet, he positions me over him, barely giving me a second to find purchase on his shoulders before he grasps my hips and yanks me down.

His cock drives up into me, and I'm so wet and ready for him that the stretch isn't painful as he forces his way inside, and we both sigh in relief as he bottoms out.

"Fuck," he grunts, fingers flexing over my hips and his eyes half lidded as they drink me in. His sweat-slicked skin is warm beneath my palms, and I can feel my heart thundering in tune with his.

He uses his hold on me to roll me over him, back and forth, his cock sliding in and out. Our heavy breaths and the wet noise of our fucking is the only sound in the otherwise silent room. Color from the TV dances over our bare skin, occasionally high-lighting the pale blue of his eyes and the dark scruff from his five-o'clock shadow. He hits that spot deep inside me, and I moan, arching my back and throwing my head back as I chase that high.

Before I can catch it, though, he grabs hold of my wrists,

pulling them behind my back. He effortlessly holds them in one hand, effectively restricting my movement and reducing me to small, shallow thrusts that do nothing but tease and leave me whimpering.

I should have known he wouldn't give up control for long.

Smirking, he holds my hips in place with his free hand before thrusting upward. I gasp, feeling him deeper and more prominently than I did before. "God, Ethan. Yes."

"Look at you," he rasps, watching as though enthralled as he drives his dick into me. "Taking everything I give you. So perfect for me."

His pace is harder, faster than mine was. More demanding, almost...punishing. Fireworks ignite behind my eyes, and I can feel my release barreling forth.

A sharp sting to my ass has me snapping my eyes open.

"Eyes on me," he growls. "I want to see how pretty you look when you fall apart just for me."

I moan, shaking and trembling with the onslaught of pleasure.

"Fuck, you're squeezing my dick so tight, D." His words are strained as he pumps up into me. "You're so close, aren't you?"

I nod.

"You're going to be a good girl and come for me, aren't you, Thorn?"

He groans as I clench around him. *Fuck,* who knew I had a praise kink?

The knowing glint in his eye says he loves that I do.

He pinches my skin when I don't respond. "Y-yes, Captain."

He hisses, eyes flashing. *Oh, he likes when I call him that.*

"Good girls do what their captain tells them," he grits, voice strained. "Now be good and come."

My orgasm washes over me like a tidal wave, whiting out all other noise. Everything ceases to exist except the feel of my muscles clamping down around him, his skin slick beneath mine, his breath hot on my cheek, and his murmured "Good girl" ringing in my ear.

Sweaty, limp, and exhausted, I collapse against him, sated and feeling lighter than I have in days. He wraps his arms around me, pulling me flush against him, his cock slowly softening inside me. Our hearts thunder in sync, the only sound other than the whoosh of blood in my ears.

Curled up against him, I have no desire to move—ever. I press my face against his neck and allow my eyes to drift closed, basking in his warmth, his protection, and knowing I'll never know life without that again.

"Spend the night with me?" I ask when I've finally regained my voice.

He strokes his hand along the back of my head, and I feel his lips brush my temple.

"There's nowhere else I'd rather be."

FIFTY-FIVE

DO you know something no one ever talks about? Afternoon showers. They are *hugely* underrated. Having a shower in the middle of the day just because you can? I had not realized this was something I was missing from my life until today. Typically, my showers are bleary-eyed early morning ones, exhausted end-of-day ones, or hurried ones after practice. But relaxed, midday showers, where you have time to shave your legs, body scrub, *and* moisturize? That is where the shit is at!

I have never, in my entire life, felt as primped and smooth and supple—yes, *supple*—as I do right now, as I stare in the mirror with a towel wrapped around me while I run a brush through my wet hair before pinning it back with a large claw clip. I swear, my skin is glowing, and I can't stop stroking my forearm.

"What are you grinning at, pretty girl?"

My gaze snaps to Griffin's through the large mirror hanging over the bathroom sink. He's leaning casually against the door-frame, legs crossed at the ankles as though he's been standing there for some time, watching me.

"Stalk much," I tease with a smile. "I thought you had class this afternoon?"

He lifts a shoulder in a careless shrug.

When he gives no verbal response, I roll my eyes. "I'm perfectly fine to be left home alone."

There was a whole debate about it this morning. I'm taking one more day off before heading back to classes, and while the guys wanted to play hooky and join me, they have to attend their classes if they want to play in Friday night's game.

Finn owes me twenty bucks, though. I told him Griffin would be the one to cave and cut out early for the day.

I'm actually happy to see him. As great as it's been having the house to myself, I was growing bored—hence the midday shower. Plus, it totally gives me the warm and fuzzies to know he couldn't stay away all day. Admittedly, now that Kyle isn't a constant threat hanging over my head, I'd been a little nervous. Until now, the guys have felt obligated to spend time with me. Now, though, they're free to do as they please.

However, Ethan has been demanding hourly check-ins, Finn has been messaging me nonstop, and Jax keeps sending me memes for this new apocalypse game he downloaded for us to try out.

"Maybe so," Griffin eventually says, pushing off the doorway and stalking closer. "But I wasn't fine being without you."

His voice is low and rough, curling around my spine like smoke. The towel suddenly feels far too thin for the way his hungry gaze steals over me, devouring everything in sight.

He comes to a stop behind me, his hands moving to rest on my bare shoulders. His thumbs drag across my collarbones, slow and reverent, and when our eyes meet in the mirror, the heat there is scorching.

"You smell like sugar and sin," he murmurs, nose brushing up the column of my neck. He inhales deeply, and I sense it's more than just the smell of my moisturizer he's inhaling. It's me. The scent of life. The reminder that I'm *alive*. His gaze remains on mine, and despite the desire I see there, it's masking a deeper emotion. Fear.

I lean back into him, and he sighs, like he's been waiting all day to feel me in his arms. "I'm here," I murmur, sensing he needs the reassurance as I dance my fingers over the warm skin of his forearms.

We haven't had a chance to talk one-on-one since...

"If you hadn't..." His throat bobs, and his eyes drift closed as he buries his face in my neck, breathing deeply. "If you had died..." His hands clench around my hips, his jaw locking, and the sentence cuts off abruptly as though he can't even bear to finish it. "I would have followed you straight into the fucking dark."

His declaration is practically growled out. Said with such certainty and vehemence that I know he means every dark and foreboding word.

"Griffin—"

"No!" His voice vibrates through me. "You don't get it. I didn't *exist* before you. The only thing that gave me any spark of life was hockey. Then you show up—this reckless, mouthy, stubborn little hurricane—and now I can't fucking *breathe* without you."

My breath hitches, my reflection wide-eyed in the mirror as his hands slide slowly down my arms, slipping beneath the towel and dragging it down, baring my skin inch by inch until I'm naked and exposed, on display just for him.

His mouth is at my ear now, lips brushing the shell of it. "You think I care about class? About a game?" He nips at my earlobe, an admonishment that makes me jump. "The only thing I care about is you. Living. Breathing. Safe. *Mine*."

He turns me then, his hands gripping my hips with bruising intensity. I expect him to drop his gaze over my body, but instead, he stares straight into my eyes. "I do not *exist* without you, Little Steelhawk." There's such reverence, such awe in those words that it steals the air from my lungs. "I live and breathe, and if need be, will die for you."

His words cinch my chest, pinching painfully, but I know chastising him for thinking my life is worth more than his, or for thinking that I could possibly live on without *him*, would be futile. He's not in the frame of mind to listen right now.

"You are mine, Dylan," he rasps. "And if he'd taken you from me, I would have made sure Kyle's death was slow and agonizing before chasing you into whatever comes next."

I gasp as he grasps the backs of my thighs, hoisting me up so my ass is perched on the counter, the cold surface biting into my flesh. Something primal rises in his storm-dark eyes.

"I need to feel you." His voice is like gravel, rough and frayed with emotion. "Need to feel you wrapped around me. Coming apart for me—screaming my name, alive, burning."

Any response I have goes up in smoke the second his hands slide up my thighs, pushing them apart as he steps between them. His touch is desperate and reverent all at once, alighting my skin and making me tremble.

I'm already wet by the time he reaches the apex of my thighs, his fingers sliding between my folds before he pushes them inside. My head falls back against the mirror, my eyes fixed on his as my chest heaves. My nipples are sharp peaks in the cool air of the room, and my hand fists in the front of his T-shirt. There is something highly erotic about being naked while he is fully dressed, towering over me, staring down at me like a demon possessed, while his fingers play me like a violin.

"Griffin." My spine arches, my hips rocking in time with his thrusts.

I'm whimpering and inching closer and closer to release when his gaze flicks to the mirror behind me. I glance toward the doorway, sucking in a gasp when I realize we're no longer alone.

Jax stands there, arms at his sides and molten gaze fixed on me, while Griffin gets me off. I should push Griffin away, should cover myself up, but I only grow wetter knowing he's watching us.

"Looks like I'm not the only one who couldn't stay away," Griffin purrs. The sound of my excitement grows louder, and he chuckles darkly. "Filthy little exhibitionist, you like Jax watching me finger fuck you?"

I shiver at his dirty words, my response breathless as I say, "Yes," while still looking at Jax. His jeans are stretched tight over his groin, and as I watch, he moves to adjust himself.

"He making you feel good, Little Menace?" His voice is thick and deep, sending desire rolling through me.

I nod. "So good."

He smirks, not moving from the doorway as he watches Griffin's fingers pump into me over and over. My head rolls back to face him, but he snaps out an arm. Griffin's fingers press into the flesh of my cheeks as he forces my head toward Jax. "Look at him while I make you come, Hurricane. See what you do to him while you're coming apart on my fingers."

I whimper, wholly intoxicated by the entire situation. The feel of Jax's hungry eyes on me, knowing he wants me even while Griffin is the one making me come.

Griffin's grip remains tight on my face, holding me in place while he rubs my clit with his thumb and drives me directly toward the edge with his talented fingers.

"Come for Griffin, baby," Jax purrs. "Drench his fingers so we can take you to bed and make you come all over our cocks."

Fuck.

Yup, that does it.

The thought of taking both of them at once, of having their hands all over me, lips on my skin, sends me careening over the edge. I scream Griffin's name as I clamp down on his fingers.

When I come back down, I'm being tossed onto a bed, and I open my eyes to see Jax climbing on top of me, licking his lips as he eyes me hungrily.

"You look so fucking hot when you come, Menace. Was it the thought of taking both of us that got you there?"

"Yes," I answer on a barely-there whisper.

He smirks before swooping in to steal my lips with a kiss. His tongue delves into my mouth, and I wrap myself around him, uncaring of the fact that I'm naked and *both* of them are fully dressed.

I'm so lost in Jax's kiss, I don't register where Griffin is until I feel his hands pushing my thighs apart, and my hips buck as his tongue sweeps up the length of my slit.

"Oh, God," I groan into Jax's mouth. He bites my lips before capturing them once more, swallowing down every mewl and moan as Griffin continues to eat me out. Fuck, I had no idea having the two of them together could be so intoxicating. Imagine if it were all *four* of them.

Heat rushes through me, wetness gushing between my thighs. It seems impossible, considering I *just* came, but another orgasm rips through me. I throw my head back, my back arching and legs quivering as they clench around Griffin's head.

Jax trails kisses down my chest, flicking his tongue around my nipples, and extending the shocks of pleasure until I'm sweaty, breathless, and panting.

"Oh my God," I gasp, lying completely boneless on the bed. "That was so good."

"Don't tell me you're done already, Menace?" Jax teases with a sharp nip of his teeth around my nipple. "We're only getting started."

I crack my eyes open to find both of them shucking out of their clothes. The tiredness that had washed over me quickly dissipates, and my mouth runs dry as I watch them strip down to their boxers. I've seen them in just their underwear countless times, every day after practice, but I don't think I'll ever get enough of seeing them like this. Standing tall, so much glorious skin and muscle on display, cocky smirks on their faces. I'm instantly a goner. I could be half dead, and the sight would still turn me on.

Completely naked now, Jax crawls back over me, ducking down to kiss my swollen lips before flipping us so I'm straddling him. His cock bobs, hard and erect and waiting, and I'm so damn wet that when I lower myself onto him, he slides straight in with a pleasant groan.

"Fuck, Dyl," he murmurs with a reverence, hands kneading my thighs. "I forgot how fucking good you feel."

Griffin snorts from where he's watching us at the side of the bed, his hand fisting his dick and eyes blazing with heat as he watches me ride his teammate.

"I could have dementia and I still wouldn't forget how fucking perfect she feels," he states before climbing onto the bed behind me. His knees bracket mine as his hands skate pleasurably over my skin, his lips trailing a hot path along my shoulder.

Jax's hands are firm on my hips, rocking me back and forth over his cock, my fingernails digging into the hard planes of his chest with each pleasurable jolt he elicits.

"Has anyone ever taken you here, Little Steelhawk?" Griffin

asks huskily, voice a dark promise as his fingers slide between my ass cheeks to prod at the tight ring of muscle there.

I shake my head, nerves and want warring within me.

Moving back around to my clit, he rubs until I'm a whimpering, trembling mess, bucking against Jax, and his fingers are soaked with our desire, before moving back and pushing the tip of one inside.

I gasp at the painful stretch, muscles clenching. Griffin murmurs soothing words in my ear, not pushing any farther and instead pumping the tip of his finger, while Jax rubs his hands up and down my thighs, shifting the angle slightly so his cock hits the bundle of nerves inside me, sending shock waves of pleasure outward.

Between them, they take their time, slowly stretching me, ensuring every bite of pain is followed by ricochets of pleasure until Griffin has two fingers in my ass, and my back is arching, needing more. Moans spill from my lips, and the sensation of feeling full is both strange and intoxicating. *God, why have I never done this before?*

Jax chuckles. "I think our girl is ready."

"You want my dick in your ass, Hurricane?" Griffin rumbles darkly in my ear.

"Yes." My response is heady, breathless. I can barely string words together.

There's some shuffling. Jax uses his grip on my hips to lift me off him, and I whine at the loss of him inside me.

"Shh, baby," he soothes. "We need to get Griffin all lubed up, so he doesn't hurt you."

I don't fully register his words before Griffin slides into my soaked pussy. *Oooh. I'm* the lubrication. Jax holds me in place, Griffin's hand on my shoulder bruising as he pumps hard into me. Sliding a hand between my thighs, Jax rubs at my clit, the two of them sending me blisteringly close to the end.

"I'm so close," I groan, legs trembling and breathing jagged. It feels as though my heart is about to crash right through my chest.

"I think she's ready," Jax tells Griffin, meeting his gaze over my shoulder.

He must agree, as he withdraws in the next instance. Before I have the chance to miss the loss of him, Jax is already sliding his cock back into my slick pussy.

"Come here, baby girl," he purrs, directing my face to his. Our kiss is sloppy and languid, desire and so much more burning between us.

I feel Griffin behind me, spreading my ass cheeks with his hands before his blunt head nudges at my hole. I tense on instinct, and he runs a soothing hand down my spine, squeezing my hip in a silent gesture. *Trust me.*

I do. I trust him—all of them.

No small feat, but one they have all earned.

Forcing myself to relax, I focus on the feel of Jax's tongue tangling with mine, his warm skin beneath my palms, his short shallow pumps inside me.

The burn when Griffin pushes forward makes me gasp, but Jax only tightens his hold on the back of my head, his other hand snaking between us to rub at my clit. Pleasure mingles with pain in an intoxicating blend, and I whimper into his mouth.

"Fuck, D," Griffin groans. "You're so unbelievably tight. I've never felt anything like it, you feel so fucking good, Hurricane. Do you feel good?"

I mumble my agreement into Jax's mouth before pulling back and gasping, "Yes. So full. So...I don't even know, but it's so good."

Jax's chest vibrates beneath my palm. "Want more, baby?"

I nod, and the two of them share a look before Griffin pulls back. He slams back into me, and I jerk forward, crying as pleasure different and deeper than anything I've experienced before shudders through me. "Oh God."

Jax and Griffin find a rhythm between them, one that keeps me constantly stimulated, vibrating on the edge of release, and feeling like my entire skin is about to rip apart. It just keeps building and building, I don't know how I'm going to contain it.

"I..." I pant, having no clue how to finish that sentence. I'm what? Going to come? Going to die? Going to explode?

Yes to all of the above.

"Come for us, Little Menace," Jax grunts, his own thrusts jerky as he nears his release. Griffin's grip behind me is bruising, his breath hot in my ear, and even without words, I can tell he's close too.

I can't hold it back any longer. I don't *want* to.

Pleasure barrels through me with such ferocity that it's all I can see, think, and feel. Light flashes behind my eyes. My body transcends into a plane I didn't know existed. I don't know if I scream or cry. I'm fairly certain I black out, because the next thing I know, I've collapsed on top of Jax, heart thundering like crazy, breathing like I just ran a marathon, and completely boneless. Do I even still have limbs?

"Fuck," Griffin hisses, collapsing onto the bed beside us. My eyes are heavy, and I'm barely able to keep them open as I take in his sweat-slicked skin shining in the afternoon light. He meets my gaze, and I find the energy to smile at him. I probably look delirious. "Fucking perfect," he murmurs.

"So perfect," Jax concurs, the sound vibrating through his chest and into my bones. He presses a kiss to the top of my chest before rolling us. I fall straight into Griffin's arms, my eyelids falling shut.

I'm faintly aware of the bed moving as Jax gets up, but I'm too exhausted to ask where he's going. He's back a moment later, anyway, and there's some shuffling before I'm rolled onto my back. I hum at the feel of a warm washcloth between my thighs.

"Gotta clean you up," Jax murmurs, finishing up before tossing it aside and climbing back into the bed with us.

He pulls me into his arms, and with the feel of his steady heartbeat beneath my palm and Griffin's warmth at my back, I pass the fuck out.

FIFTY-SIX

THE STUDENT-ATHLETE LIBRARY is unusually calm for a weeknight, the kind of quiet that settles in just before dinner when everyone else is either heading to the dining hall or pretending they're going to study later. Griffin, Ethan, Finn, and I have spread out over a table in the center of the room, notepads open and books strewn across the table.

While I'm all caught up on my schoolwork—the only upside to being benched and thus having nothing else to do with myself while my body heals and recovers—apparently Finn is swamped with assignments. Ethan, unsurprisingly, is as on top of his work as I am. As for Griffin...I have no idea. He's the only one who hasn't got books out in front of him, too busy staring at me for the past thirty minutes since he arrived, but that by no means suggests he doesn't have work he *should* be focusing on instead.

"Don't you have anything better to do?" I muse, nudging his shoulder. He's leaning back in his chair beside me, legs sprawled out like he owns the damn place, and his eyes on me while I finish off an assignment.

"Yes, but I didn't think you'd appreciate it if I bent you over and fucked you in the middle of the library."

Despite the traitorous flutter in my belly, I send him a withering glare.

Having overheard him, Ethan sputters while Finn laughs like it's all one big hilarious joke. It's not, I can tell by Griffin's expression that he's dead serious. Griffin doesn't joke about fucking me.

I shake my head, going back to focus on the textbook lying open in front of me. "I mean schoolwork. Don't you have any studying you need to do?"

"I'm a visual learner," he replies, voice low and unbothered. "Besides, you're my favorite subject."

Finn hums in agreement from where he's sitting across the table from me. I whip a harsh glare in his direction. Entirely unfazed, he flashes me a grin. "You're my favorite subject too, Hellion." His gaze rakes over me lasciviously, only heating my skin further. *Damn, boys.* This is why I should have studied with Wren.

Ethan doesn't look up from his laptop as he interrupts, "Try focusing on econ, idiots." His fingers fly rapidly across the keyboard. "Exams are only a few weeks away."

Finn nudges me under the table with his foot, the ball of his sneaker brushing my ankle. I shoot him a look, but his innocent expression is ruined by the mischievous twinkle in his eye. "Mm, I'm not sure I can wait a few weeks."

The insinuation in his tone is blatant, and the air grows thick and heavy.

"Seriously?" I drawl, trying to act like I'm entirely unaffected when he knows damn well I'm not.

Arching a brow, he brushes his shoe over my leg again. A little higher this time.

I subtly shift and *accidentally* kick him back. He just laughs under his breath, eyes sparkling like he's thoroughly enjoying himself.

Ethan sighs, flitting his gaze around the table before dragging his hand down his face. "Remind me why I hang out with any of you?"

"Because you love us," Finn singsongs.

"Because we're the only ones who will put up with you," Griffin says at the same time.

"Because you'd implode without the ability to micromanage everything around you," I offer sweetly.

Ethan lifts his eyes to mine, unimpressed. Of course, that's when a yawn rips out of me. He immediately sits straighter in his chair, eyes raking over my face with concern. "Are you tired? Did you not sleep well last night? Was it—"

"I'm fine." My tone is exasperated. It's been a week of him—of all of them—fussing over me, and it's safe to say that I'm over it. "I got my full eight hours of sleep. It was just a yawn."

Eyes narrowed, he continues to watch me, even after I've chosen to ignore his existence and focus back on my own work.

"Do you have a headache?"

The pen I'm clutching threatens to snap in half as I glower at him. "What?"

"You're rubbing your temple." He gestures toward where my free hand is rubbing circles into the side of my head. Shit, I hadn't realized I was doing that, and now that he mentions it, there is a slight throbbing behind my eyes.

I hastily drop my hand from my face. "It's nothing."

His expression is flat, skeptical. "You've done enough studying for today."

"I just need to finish this assignment and then I'm done," I snap at him. I'm about to lay into him for being a hovering mother hen when he reminds me why I put up with his bullshit. "How about we get in a practice session after this—just the five of us?"

The beginnings of my headache instantly fade, and the

energy that was flagging a second ago surges forward. I haven't been on the ice since...*that* game. *That* night.

"Nothing intense," Ethan presses. "Just light drills."

Griffin perks up, but it's nothing compared to the way my whole body lifts at the suggestion. "Seriously?"

Ethan nods. "Doctor cleared you to start easing back in. We're easing."

I grin. I can't help it.

Hell yeah!

Finn's leg brushes against mine, and Griffin leans into my space. I can't take my eyes off of Ethan, though. His lips lift in a smile, his eyes dancing. He knows how badly I've been dying to get back on the ice. The trainer cleared me this morning, but with classes, I haven't had a chance to actually get skates on my feet and get out there.

"Hey," Finn says, drawing my attention. "How is your mom doing?"

Internally, I wince. My mother is such a sore topic, but I don't think that's ever going to change. It's just how she is now. It's sweet of Finn to ask, though. After her meltdown at the hospital, they've all been asking about her. She's back in Oak Haven, and I made a point of switching my emergency contact number to Bear so she doesn't get called the next time I invariably end up in the hospital—hopefully for a bog-standard hockey accident and not a near-murder attempt.

"She's doing good," I tell him, offering a grateful smile. "They've upped her meds and she seems to be a bit more... balanced."

Still barely accepting any of my phone calls, though. However, the few times she has, she sounds more like the mom from the hospital. The one I remember from before. So, I haven't completely given up hope. I'm just...guarded.

The library door opens and Jax strolls in with a coffee carrier in one hand and a brown paper bag in the other.

He beelines straight for our table. "Sorry I'm late. Had to make a detour," he says, setting the cup down beside me. "I know you like the hazelnut one from the campus café, and I got you one of those muffins you like."

My heart squeezes. "You didn't have to—"

He shrugs. "I wanted to."

"You bring us anything?" Finn demands, reaching for the bag.

Jax yanks it back just in time. "Nope. Get your own."

Finn gapes. "Unbelievable. Not even a single cookie?"

"Nope."

"Not very team-player behavior," Finn continues to grouse.

Griffin flashes a wicked grin at him across the table. "Pretty sure these are particular muffin privileges. Maybe if you put out."

Finn's nose wrinkles before he retorts. "And yet, I don't see your *muffin privileges*."

Still grinning, Griffin flips him his middle finger.

"You idiots can *put out* all you want," Jax interjects, pulling out the free seat beside me and dropping into it. "There's only one person I'm interested in spooning—or being spooned by—and it sure as hell isn't either of you."

As if to hammer home his statement, he leans over and presses a kiss to my lips. It's quick, chaste, but no less tantalizing.

"Fantastic," Ethan drawls, sounding like an exasperated parent trying to corral wayward children. "Now that we've clarified that, can we get back to work?" His gaze slides to mine. "I promised Thorn we'd take her out on the ice when we're done."

Fuck yes!

"You heard the captain." I fix Griffin, Finn, and Jax with my most serious expression. "If any one of you eat into my ice time with your bullshit, nobody will be spooning anybody."

"Cold, Hellion," Finn teases with a cunning grin. "So cold."

My only response is to glare at him until he goes back to work.

Nothing, and I mean absolutely nothing, is going to stand in my way of getting back on the ice tonight.

I'M sore in that deep, bone-heavy way that tells me I'll be paying for this tomorrow, but I'm smiling so hard my cheeks hurt. My chest is burning, my muscles are screaming, and my shoulder is already starting to throb, but none of that matters.

I'm back.

The familiar scrape of my blades against the ice, the sting of cold air on my cheeks, the way the puck snapped against my stick when I finally nailed that pass—all of it has me feeling alive in a way nothing else does.

There's freedom out here. Control.

And right now, even if just for a second, I feel like myself again.

I coast to a stop at the edge of the rink, stepping off the ice and onto the bench with a groan that's half laughter, half regret. Dropping onto the seat, I lean back and roll my shoulder out slowly. Yeah. Tomorrow's going to suck.

A second later, Ethan sinks down beside me and presses a bottle of water and some pain meds into my hand. I take them gratefully and glance over at him.

Griffin, Jax, and Finn are still on the ice, finishing up a drill —quick passes, rapid pivots, laser-focused. My guys. My team.

I take a long sip of water, then glance up toward the wall of the rink. The familiar number stares back at me.

#19. Callahan.

My dad's jersey, framed beneath the spotlights above the tunnel. My throat tightens. I've looked up at that jersey a thousand times, but tonight...it feels different.

Whole.

"He'd be proud of everything you've achieved," Ethan says, his voice low, thoughtful.

I don't look at him. I can't. Not right away.

"He always wanted me to be a Steelhawk," I murmur, a soft smile tugging at my lips.

Ethan shakes his head beside me. "Not just as a player."

I blink, surprised, and finally turn to face him.

"It's the person you are that would bring him to his knees," he clarifies, eyes steady on mine, "After everything you've been through...the way you keep fighting, keep showing up, keep holding your ground—" He shrugs, like it should be obvious. "He'd be proud of the strength in you, Dylan. Not just the skates on your feet."

It hits me harder than I expect. Like a shot straight to the chest.

Everyone always talks about my dad in terms of hockey. About me making him proud because I'm chasing the dream he never got to finish. But no one ever talks about me as just...his daughter. Not the athlete. Not the legacy. Just a girl he would've been proud of—even if I never picked up a stick.

"Thank you," I whisper, and I mean it more than I've meant anything all day.

Ethan bumps my knee gently with his. "I'm only stating the truth."

A blur of motion draws my attention. Finn skates over, elbows resting on the boards as he leans forward. Behind him, Jax and Griffin are gathering up cones and gear, clearly done with their final drill of the night.

"You two done with your emotional heart-to-heart, or should I come back in a sec?" he teases, but his grin softens when his gaze lands on me.

"Har har," Ethan retorts. "You guys done?"

Finn nods. "I was thinking we could grab some ice cream before heading home. You know, the place on Main Street."

"We just ate dinner a couple of hours ago," I remind him.

Finn's grin deepens, slow and dangerous. His eyes rake over me like he's starving, and I know damn well he's no longer thinking about food. My pulse flares.

"I know, but trust me," he murmurs. "I'm starving."

My mouth goes dry. Every nerve in my body lights up like a live wire.

Because for all his heat, all the looks and tension and lingering stares...Finn hasn't touched me. Not since the hotel. Not since he kissed me like I was something worth fighting for, then backed away like he was the one who might shatter.

And now?

Now it's like some twisted version of foreplay. The kind that draws out every second until I'm going to combust from the pressure.

My body's more than ready. My brain is screaming at him to just *do something*.

But he's still standing there, cocky and calm and pretending like we're not both toeing the edge of something sharp and hot and completely inevitable.

"Did someone mention ice cream?" Jax asks, skating over.

"Yeah, but it doesn't look like Hellion is interested." There's a teasing glint in Finn's eye.

"I didn't say that," I defend.

His green eyes dance with humor. "So you *do* want ice cream?"

I huff a laugh. "Like I'd ever say no to ice cream."

"Didn't think so." He grins, pleased with himself.

As we file out of the arena, the cool night air hits my over-heated skin like a sigh of relief. My legs ache, my shoulder's stiff, and I'm dead on my feet—but I don't care. I haven't felt this alive since before...

Refusing to go there, I shove the thought away and focus on Jax's hand wrapped around mine. His thumb brushes slow, lazy strokes over my knuckles. On my other side, Griffin slings an arm over my shoulders, tugging me into his side with casual possessiveness like he's done it a hundred times before.

Finn's a step behind, carrying my backpack and shooting shit with the guys.

And Ethan's walking in front of me, leading the way with that naturally commanding stride of his. Every so often, he glances over his shoulder like he's checking I'm still here. Still with him.

It's quiet for a beat, the kind of peace that settles in when everything feels...right.

It's simple. Uncomplicated. A perfect end to a long day.

And right now, I don't want anything else.

THE CAFETERIA HUMS with the low roar of voices, the clatter of trays, and the squeak of sneakers against tile. Finn's thigh brushes mine under the table, his hand ghosting across the back of my chair like he owns the space. Ethan sits across from me, sharp blue eyes softened by the way he keeps sneaking glances at my plate as though to make sure I've eaten enough. Jax is to my left, quiet as always, but his presence at my side is steady, immovable. Griffin leans back with that calculating smirk of his, saying little but watching everything.

The rest of the team is spread out around us, shoulders

bumping, voices overlapping, the easy rhythm of inside jokes and trash talk. And for once, I'm in the middle of it—laughing, chirping back, adding my own digs when someone brags about their shot accuracy.

Ever since Kyle tried to drown me, something's shifted. The guys haven't just closed ranks—they've pulled me into them. I get texts now, random check-ins, a sophomore sending a meme at midnight just to make sure I'm okay. On the ice, someone always seems to have my back—Matthews grabbing me an extra water before drills, Donaldson quietly retying a loose strap on my pads, Connors knocking into anyone who skates too close a second late. After my first attack outside the stadium, their concern had been...distant. Removed. How anyone would feel hearing about someone they don't really know ending up in that situation. Any offer of protection or help was offered to Ethan. *For* him. But this? This is different. This isn't protection out of obligation. It's rage that one of their own would turn on me. It's worry not for the incident, but for *me*.

"Carter," Matthews calls across the table, smirking. "Tell me straight—whose shot's harder? Mine or Finn's?"

The table erupts in laughter, Finn arching a mischievous brow at me like the answer better be obvious. Heat creeps up my neck, but I grin, leaning into the easy ribbing.

"Depends. Do we count the ones that actually *hit the net*?"

A chorus of "Oooooh" follows, and Matthews clutches his chest like I've wounded him. Finn just smirks wider, smug as hell, and Ethan shakes his head like he's trying not to smile. For the first time, I don't feel like I'm trespassing at this table. I feel like I belong at it.

A thick, sweet, suffocating scent has my nose twitching, and I turn instinctively, my laughter dying on my lips as Selena glides toward us, hips swaying, eyes locked on Finn. A feline smile curves her mouth, predatory and polished. She's a viper ready to strike, every step a warning coil.

She doesn't even pause before she's pressing up against his side, fake nails grazing his chest. "Hey, babe." Her voice is syrupy, a practiced purr, and I'm still staring at her in shock when she blows my mind by lowering herself right into his lap like she belongs there.

Only she doesn't land.

Finn's hands are on her hips, but instead of holding her steady, he shoves her firmly off.

"What the hell, Finn?" Selena's voice is shrill, disbelief twisting her features.

"Not interested, Selena," he states flatly, barely sparing her a glance as he drags his chair closer to mine. His arm drapes over my shoulders, pulling me tight into his side as his lips brush the crown of my head, casual but unmistakable.

Selena stumbles back, blinking like she's been slapped. "Excuse me?"

Finn's gaze meets mine, an apology in his green depths before he sighs and turns to face her.

"I'm. Not. Interested."

Her face flames, shock crumbling into venom as her eyes cut to me, sharp enough to slice. "You've got to be kidding me. *Her?* The little Bench Bunny? What, you couldn't find anyone with an actual chest?"

Hey! Rude! Not all of us want giant tits jiggling in our face. I can't imagine anything worse than attempting to score a goal with those giant blobs of hers getting in the way.

Before I can say a word, Griffin's voice cuts through, dark and unamused. "Watch it." He leans forward, pale blue eyes glinting like a predator scenting blood. "You're about three seconds from getting dragged out of here by your hair."

Selena turns wide eyes on Griffin, backing up a step at the

vicious look shadowing his features. However, it's not enough to stop the slight sneer that curls her lips. "I bet she's sleeping with you, too." Scanning the broader table, her disgust deepens as she spits, "All of you." She laughs caustically. "That's what a Bench Bunny does, after all."

My lungs lock, eyes sweeping the room and realizing we have the attention of everyone in here. Of course we do. I can practically hear the whispers, the speculation from our onlookers. Then, the scraping of chair legs snaps my attention back to the table.

Ethan is standing now, every inch of him radiating authority as he stares Selena down. "Get out."

Another chair scrapes. Jax. His voice is quiet but thrums with warning as he mirrors Ethan. "Leave. Now."

Selena falters, but her sneer snaps back in place. "Wow. She really does have you all wrapped around her—"

"Shut. Up." Finn's tone is sharp enough to cut glass. His arm tightens around me, a vice-like squeeze before he also rises. He stares Selena down. "Funny thing, Selena," he sneers at her. "You keep calling her a Bench Bunny, but you're the only one I've ever seen hopping from lap to lap."

Like a scene from a movie, team members rise one by one. "Yup, you've definitely spent time on mine," Palmer says.

"And mine," Chen tacks on.

And on and on it goes until basically every guy at the table confesses to having been with her.

And she had the nerve to call me a slut!

When silence reigns, heavy and vindicated, Ethan's voice cuts through the air like steel. "I think I speak for the entire team when I say, we're done with you."

The rest of the guys immediately voice their agreement. No hesitation. No looks of regret. "You're not welcome here anymore," Ethan finishes, voice final. "Not at this table. Not at our games. Not with us."

Selena's mouth opens, but no words come. The silence presses in, thicker than any shout, until finally she spins on her heel and storms out, her heels clacking like gunshots.

When she's gone, the room exhales. Laughter and chatter slowly resume around us, the tension dissipating like smoke.

But me? I can't move.

I sit frozen, Finn's arm returning to its place around my shoulders, Ethan's sharp gaze steady across the table, Jax's solid bulk beside me, Griffin's smirk a promise. The rest of the team scattered around, returning to their conversations like what happened was just another day. Nothing out of the ordinary. Completely unaware of how much their support means to me.

My throat is dry, and I struggle to swallow around the lump lodged there. As if sensing how choked up I'm feeling, Jax reaches over to squeeze my hand, and when I glance up at him, there's a knowing glint in his eye, a soft curl to his lips.

For the first time in my life, I don't feel like I'm fighting alone.

For the first time, I belong.

FIFTY-SEVEN

THE SKY HANGS low and gray over the campus, heavy with the promise of snow. The cold cuts through my jeans and jacket like a blade, making me wish I'd worn something heavier. I swear the weather changed overnight, emphasizing that we are on the cusp of winter. I wrap my scarf tighter, my breath forming puffs of white in the frigid November air as Wren and I cut across the quad.

"Last night was hell," Wren grumbles, her boots crunching over the brittle grass. "Some idiot puked outside the bar entrance, I got groped twice by drunk freshmen, and to top it off, a hockey player tried to tip me with a Stanley Cup keychain like it was fucking gold."

I snort. "Ah, the dream of college life."

"Shut up." She nudges my shoulder with her own. "We can't all live out our real-life fantasies of having a harem of hot hockey guys."

"It's not all unicorns and rainbows over here." I filled her in on everything that happened with Kyle after the game as soon as I was released from the hospital. The guys had already given her the cliff notes since she'd inevitably heard about the hit I took on the ice, but we had a *long* phone call once I was released, where I told her everything. Followed by a girls' night once I was fit enough to return to campus. That was a week ago.

She links her arm through mine, squeezing as she gives me an understanding smile. "It *hasn't* been, but it will be from here on out. For the rest of the year, all you're going to have to worry about is hockey and sex."

I choke on nothing. Leave it to Wren to make me smile after everything that's happened.

"Pretty sure I have to worry about passing exams, too."

She waves her hand dismissively. "Small potatoes. Focus on the important stuff."

"Hockey and sex?"

She flashes me a white, toothy grin. "Hockey and sex."

We both laugh, the sound curling into the cold air between us. It's nice to walk campus like this again—without the guys hovering at my elbows. They're still protective, still close. One of them usually drops by between classes, we eat breakfast and lunch together on campus most days, and they text constantly. But now it's because they *want* to, not because they feel *obligated* to.

When I mentioned it to Jax, he rolled his eyes and told me no one was making them do anything. That they'd always wanted to spend time with me, and they wouldn't have been so protective if they didn't care—if they didn't want to be around me.

Still, the distinction feels important to me.

I'm not just someone they are keeping safe. I'm someone they *want*. Someone they are *choosing*.

"Seriously, Dyl. You must have snagged the only halfway decent hockey players out there," Wren continues.

"I thought you loved hockey players?" I arch a brow, glancing her way.

"No. I love *hockey*—the game. Hockey players? Not so much."

"Is that why you don't come to any Athletes Row street parties?" I tease, nudging her this time.

She throws her head back and laughs, but the sound is off. Not as carefree as normal. "Players be playin' and I'm a dating girl," she says, not meeting my questioning gaze. "Besides, my family being who they are makes it difficult."

"Never really know they're with you for you or because of who you are."

"Exactly."

I get it. My issue wasn't hockey players specifically, but more fans of my dad. I remember going on a date with one guy in high school who handed me his Timberwolves jersey at the end of it and asked if my dad could sign it. Like, seriously? He could have just asked and saved us both some time. The annoying thing was, I'd liked him. He'd been funny and easygoing, but after my dad had signed his jersey, I never heard from him again.

So, yeah. I get Wren's reluctance to go anywhere near hockey players.

I lose track of our conversation when a shadow falls over us as someone steps into our path.

"Look who we have here."

That voice is like ice water down my spine.

No. No, that's not possible.

I freeze. My lungs stop working. My body stops moving. I feel like I've been locked in place, rooted to the spot, unable to breathe.

Kyle Reed—a very free, uncuffed Kyle Reed—stands in front of us, hands in his coat pockets, and a smug grin twisting his mouth.

Wren stiffens beside me, her arm tightening around mine like a band. "What the fuck are you doing here?"

He doesn't even glance her way. His eyes are locked on me, and there's something in them that makes my stomach twist. A slow-burning fury. Glee. Madness. It makes my knees quake.

"You're supposed to be in jail." I hate how soft my voice is, how weak I sound.

Only one other man has ever made me feel this way. Made me feel so afraid. So helpless.

He laughs, the sound scraping along my skin like gravel, leaving little bloody nicks in its wake. "Cops know trumped-up, bullshit charges when they see them."

Thankfully, that snaps through the helplessness, allowing a gap for my rage to surge forth. "Bullshit?" I snarl, vibrating now. "You tried to *drown* me!" The words burst out, jagged and raw.

The fucking psychopath gapes at me, his hand coming to his chest like he's a Southern woman clutching her pearls. "Me? I tried to *help* you! I was trying to *save* you when Coach stormed in, reading the room entirely wrong."

I shake my head. "No. No. You pushed me under. You held me down."

My hands tremble, from fear, from fury...who knows.

His eyes flash with menace as he leans in, dropping his voice. "Prove it."

Hands balled into fists, I go to step forward. Oh, how I want to punch the fucking smirk off his sick, twisted face. Wren's arm, still linked through mine, yanks me back, though.

"You're fucking insane," she hisses at him.

For the first time, Kyle looks her way, giving Wren a slow and disturbing once-over, before flicking his focus back to me.

"You think you've won, huh? Got the guys, the sympathy, the team. But you haven't. You'll never beat me, Carter. You just delayed the inevitable."

I shake my head. This was never a game. Never about *beating* anyone.

My throat tightens, and I don't know if he leans in or just the rest of the world falls away, but his gleaming, menacing face takes up my entire field of vision. He sneers down at me, insanity gleaming in his pale eyes. I always knew Kyle was a misogynistic prick who couldn't stand to lose, but did I really drive him to this level of lunacy? Or was it there all along, hidden beneath arrogance and getting his own way?

Dropping his voice, his breath is warm and sickly against my cheek, twisting my stomach violently. Oh God, I think I'm going to throw up.

"I'll be seeing you around, Dylan."

The world is spinning as he walks off, like he didn't just upend my life...again.

Wren turns to me immediately, grabbing my arms. "Dylan. Are you okay? Talk to me."

But I can't speak.

I can't breathe.

The cold that nipped at my skin a moment ago has sunk deeper, rooting in my bones.

He's back.

And this time, he isn't going to go down without taking me with him.

I'M CURLED on the couch in the living room, still in a haze. Coach, Griffin, Ethan, Jax, and Finn are all here—because Wren called the guys the second Kyle walked away, and they called Coach in a demand for answers. Coach's office was too small to house four humongous hockey players with anger issues, so we're packed into the living room instead. Which, large as it is, is barely big enough to contain the fury vibrating through the floors and up the walls.

Griffin paces like a caged animal. Jax is beside me, his hand rubbing circles over my arm and shoulder. Finn and Ethan have been snapping questions at Bear since the second he showed up on the porch.

"I thought he was locked up," Ethan growls. "How the hell did he get out?"

Bear's jaw clenches, his head hanging low between his shoulders. He looks at me with such ravished pain that it twists my heart. "His lawyers are claiming he was trying to save Dylan," he states, his words a near snarl. His leg bounces with pent-up aggression. "Said he found her drowning and that I *misinterpreted* the scene."

"Are you fucking kidding me?" Finn snaps. "Why the hell would she be drowning in a shallow-ass tub she could stand up in?"

Bear throws his hands up.

"They'll say she had a concussion," Ethan answers grimly. "Or that she passed out. Seizure. We all saw the hit she took on the ice—they can claim any number of things to justify their version of the truth."

A shiver crawls up my spine.

Lies. Their version of the truth is *lies*, but I know better than anyone that the truth means jack shit. It's not a matter of what you know, it's what you can prove. I've been in this situation before—with Lucas—except the stakes weren't so high then. My life wasn't on the line—just my career, my future.

"What if she goes to the police?" Finn tries, running his hand through his messy red hair. It's something he does when he's frustrated. "She can tell them what happened. The *truth*."

Coach looks pained as he shakes his head. "It won't matter. It's her word against his. There's no evidence. No witnesses."

Griffin snarls as he turns on his heel, wearing a path in the wooden floor with his pacing. "So what, we do nothing? Let him get away with it?"

"He's off the team," Bear states firmly. "I've notified security. He's banned from the arena, from our facilities, from every game. But I can't stop him from attending class. That's out of my hands."

Finn's resounding laugh is bitter. "So that's it?"

There's silence. Defeat hangs like smoke in the air.

My eyes close, my head falling forward to rest on my bent knees. This is never going to end. I came here for a new start, and it's turning into an even bigger nightmare than at my old college.

I sense a presence before someone takes my hand in their warm one and I open my eyes to find Ethan kneeling in front of me. His eyes search mine with such intensity I feel stripped bare.

"We're not letting anything happen to you, Thorn. Not ever again. What happened in that tub—" He swallows hard. "That won't happen again. He won't get near you."

I nod, but the movement feels hollow.

The conversation buzzes around me, but I barely hear it. Bear eventually stands, grabbing his coat. "I'll do what I can. But for now...be careful."

Once he's gone, Finn drops onto the couch beside me, his head falling back against the cushions. "So we do nothing?"

It's the one question that's been asked on repeat, none of them willing to believe we're helpless. That there isn't *something* we can do.

"No," Griffin snaps. His voice is dark, feral. "We don't do nothing. We make sure he never lays a finger on her again."

His gaze finds mine, and I remember the vow he made in the bathroom. That if Kyle had taken me from him, he would have killed him before following me straight into the afterlife. His expression now tells me he still means it.

"There's only one thing you do with sick bastards like Kyle," he says coldly. "You get rid of them."

Finn gives a half laugh, more out of disbelief than humor. "What, like kill him?" he says, clearly expecting someone to scoff or call him dramatic.

Griffin doesn't blink.

The room stills. Finn's eyes go wide. "Wait, no—seriously?" He glances at the others as though searching for confirmation. "Dude! We're not the fucking mafia or some shit. We can't just go around killing people."

No one says anything. No one agrees with him. But no one tells Griffin he's wrong either. The air is thick with something heavy and dangerous. We all know Griffin. Know the quiet rage he carries like a loaded weapon. He wouldn't say it if he wasn't thinking about it. If he wasn't already planning.

Ethan exhales slowly, measured as always, the voice of reason. "Griff...his dad has money. Serious money. You make someone like Kyle disappear and there'll be consequences. Investigations. Questions." His eyes widen, intent on Griffin. "You'd go to *prison*. Your future would be over. Any chance at the league, gone."

"You think I give a fuck about hockey right now?" Griffin snarls, stepping up to Ethan. He stabs a finger in my direction. "The only thing I give a shit about is keeping my girl safe, and unlike you, I'm willing to sacrifice anything—*everything*—to do that."

He glances my way, and the amount of love I see there, the level of obsession, scares me. Not because it's too much, but because I know he means it. He would burn the world down for me. He would destroy himself just to make sure I'm safe. And I can't lose Griffin.

"I'd *gladly* go to prison for her," he states loudly, confidently, with his chin lifted high.

"No." My voice breaks over the syllable. Just the thought of... "No," I say more firmly, pushing to my feet and crossing to him. I press my body against his, grasping his face with my hands. His hands slide to my hips as though the action is involuntary. Like he can't *help* but touch me. "I can't lose you, too," I implore him. "I need you—*here*. With me. With *us*."

He softens, just barely. One hand lifts, brushing my hair back, his fingertips lingering along my jawline like a promise. "I'll do whatever it takes to keep you safe, Hurricane."

I press a hand to his chest. "Then stay. Stay here. Stay with *me*." I choke over the final words, tears momentarily blurring my vision.

Ducking his head so his forehead rests against mine, those piercing blue eyes of his threatening to swallow me whole, I see the war raging within. The internal battle he's fighting.

The fury. The loyalty. The need to protect me at any cost.

"I survived Lucas on my own," I murmur, voice low but steady. I'm aware of the others listening, and while I'm speaking to Griffin, my words are for them too. "I fought my way through it. *Alone*. And I would've kept doing it on my own if I had to. But now I know what it's like to have you—to have all of you—and I can't go back. I don't want to go back."

"Hurricane." Griffin's voice is like nothing I've ever heard before. It's soft, haggard, cracked. "You'd still have them."

I shake my head, refusing to hear his words. He sounds so set on his decision, and honestly, that scares me more than seeing Kyle today. The thought of losing Griffin is more *terrifying* than facing Kyle.

My fingers fist the front of his top as I shake him.

"Kyle's not the first guy who's hated me just because I dared to dream outside the box," I say, voice sharpening with conviction as I meet his resolute gaze with a defiant one of my own. "Because I took a spot he thought belonged to him. Because I wanted something I wasn't supposed to want. And he won't be the last. There will be others—on the ice, in the NHL, in locker rooms filled with ego and entitlement. Guys who think a girl like me shouldn't exist in their world."

That does the trick. His fingers tighten around my hips, murder flashing in his eyes—but this time it's not for Kyle. Well, not solely for him. It's for all potential future threats.

Yeah, I realize I'll have to talk him down from going after them too. But future problems and all that. I can only take on one battle at a time, and today, this is it.

"You're no good to me stuck in a prison cell. I need you out here. *With me.* Please," I murmur.

Closing his eyes, he exhales heavily before giving the slightest of nods.

The relief I feel is monumental. Still, I cling to him as though afraid that if I let him go, he'll stalk straight to wherever Kyle is and rip his head from his shoulders without a single care for the consequences.

"We do what we've always done," Jax mutters, and I look up, realizing the three of them have come to stand with us, all four of my guys surrounding me. He looks between each of the guys. "We keep our girl safe."

As though forming a pact, they all nod in agreement. "We keep her safe," Finn mutters.

I catch Ethan's gaze. "You're not to be out of our sight, Thorn. Not for a single second."

It's a promise and a warning.

And just like that, the brief taste of normalcy I had is gone. Replaced with fear. Control. Watchful eyes.

FIFTY-EIGHT

IT'S BEEN days since Kyle slithered back onto campus like the spineless snake he is. Days since our girl started flinching at shadows again. Since the light dimmed behind her eyes.

I'm going insane.

I pace the length of the living room, hands balled into fists, breathing sharp and uneven. I can still recall the absolute terror that rocked me at seeing her wet, limp, lifeless body in Jax's arms, the memory a never-ending loop in my mind. Her bruises might have faded, but the damage is done. He tried to take her from me—from us. And the fact that he walks free while Dylan curls in on herself like prey, it curdles my blood.

If it weren't for her, I'd have ended him already. Snapped his neck without a second thought and slept like a baby after. I still could. I could walk out that door right now, find him, and make him choke on everything he's done.

But I gave her my word. A fucking promise I hate myself for making.

And I regret it—God, I do—but I'd make it again if it meant she looked at me the way she did in that moment, face open and expression vulnerable, eyes shining with emotion. That's the sick part. I'd give her anything, everything, even when it costs me pieces of myself. Because if Dylan wants me at her side, if she needs me in this house instead of out there hunting him down, then here I'll fucking stay.

Even if it kills me.

The front door opens, and Finn steps inside, brushing snow off his shoulders.

I'm on him immediately. "She get there okay?"

He nods. "Yup, delivered her right into Coach's arms myself with a promise from her to message one of us when she's ready to leave."

His words do little to settle the storm inside me. One that has been constantly raging for days now and shows no signs of blowing out anytime soon.

I see a similar war being fought in Finn's eyes, too. And in Jax's and Ethan's. We're all on edge. All in need of an outlet. Friday's game was the most brutal one of the season—all of us using the excuse of the game to let out our frustrations, but it was the wrong person's blood coating my knuckles.

"So, what are our plans for the night?" Jax asks, twitchier than I've ever seen him. "I don't think I can sit in."

"Same," Finn agrees.

Ethan doesn't vocalize it, but I see the wildness in his eyes. He's struggling just as much as the rest of us.

We're all worked up. In need of a release—and sadly, not the dirty kind.

"I've got something in mind." I don't know if it's the tone I use, or the fact that they know me well enough to know if I'm suggesting an idea, it's probably not a casual drink at the bar or a night at the cinema.

Jax perks up immediately. "What kind of *something*?"

I smile, slow and sharp. "The kind that ends in blood."

He doesn't hesitate. "Fuck, yes!"

Finn grins, cracking his knuckles. "That fight the other night barely hit the spot."

Ethan, always the golden boy leader, crosses his arms, looking at me skeptically. "We're not going after Kyle."

He's a broken fucking record. It's like he thinks if he says it enough times, I'll put to bed my revenge plans for that fuckwit. I swore to my little Steelhawk that I wouldn't do anything to get myself arrested, and I won't. Ethan nattering on in my ear every fucking day isn't going to change a damn thing.

Instead of saying any of that, though, I roll my eyes at him. "Who said anything about that fucking asshole?"

His eyes narrow, lips thinned, but thankfully, he doesn't contradict me.

Arching a brow at him, I challenge, "So, are you in or not?"

"Where are we going?"

I don't answer, just keep staring at him until he huffs a breath.

"Fine. But I'm only coming to babysit your dumb asses."

Yeah, whatever you say, *Captain*.

We all pile into my car, cold air fogging up the windows as I crank the heat. No one asks questions—not yet. They know me well enough to wait. I drive out of Blackstone, into the sprawl of backroads leading toward NSU.

When the campus signs appear, Ethan finally breaks. "Why the hell are we at Northern Summit?"

Jax lets out a breathy laugh, the pieces falling into place. "Lucas Tremble," he mutters darkly. "Son of a bitch." He claps both hands on my shoulders, shaking them despite the fact that I'm driving. "You sneaky bastard. You've had this planned since the game, haven't you?"

Damn fucking right I have.

Ever since we saw his smug-ass face in the stands the night Dylan got hit.

Right before Kyle tried to drown her in the fucking therapy pool.

The timing wasn't just suspicious. It was *calculated*.

And we've been too distracted—too busy helping Dylan recover and keeping her safe—to chase the truth.

Until now.

From the back seat, Finn lets out a low whistle. When I glance at him in the rearview mirror, he's grinning, vicious and sharp. "Oh, I am so fucking in. After all the crap he's pulled on Dyl, that piece of shit has it coming."

He sure as hell does.

I side-eye Ethan as I navigate my way through the campus. He's quiet, but I see the same need for answers in his eyes that has burned in my gut since that night. Even if he was against what we're going to do—and I don't think he is—he isn't going to stop it. He needs to know as badly as I do: Did Lucas have something to do with our girl getting hit that night? Was it his fault that Kyle had the opportunity to try and take her out?

The leather steering wheel creaks beneath my white-knuckle grip, and I force myself to relax.

We're about to fucking find out.

I park in a secluded lot near the athletic dorms. At this time of night, most people are probably in the dining hall, studying, or catching up with friends. Only a few windows are lit up from within, and those who are wandering around do so with their hoods pulled up and long strides, getting them out of the cold weather as quickly as possible. No one is going to be paying any attention to us.

"What's the plan?" Ethan asks, not taking his eyes off our surroundings. "You don't even know where Lucas is."

"I know exactly where he is," I mutter. "South side rec building, basement room." I can feel all their eyes on me. "There's a regular poker night there. Lucas never misses it."

Finn scoffs. "Of course the dipshit has a gambling habit."

Not listening to any more of their rambling, I shove open the car door and climb out into the bitterly cold night.

We move like shadows through the dark, quiet campus paths. By the time we reach the building, poker night is over, and dark silhouettes spill from the door, disappearing into the night. I spot his large, hockey-made frame the second he steps outside, and once he's moved away from the others, we corner him.

"What the—"

We shove him into the hidden shadows at the side of the building.

"Evening, princess," Finn drawls, getting all up in his face and flashing a maniacal, white-toothed smile.

Lucas stiffens, looking from face to face. His smirk is delayed, forced. "If you guys wanted to see how real hockey players live it up, you just had to ask."

Ethan sneers in his face. *Knew the fucking golden boy wouldn't be able to resist.* "Have you even been looking at the ranks, Tremble? We're kicking your ass."

"Harder than we have in previous years," Jax adds, smirking.

Fisting the front of Lucas's jacket, Finn shoves him harder into the wall. "Yeah, all thanks to our brand-new *star player*." He puts on a fake pout. "Too bad you couldn't see past her gender to her potential."

All pretense of friendliness drops as Lucas sneers at each of us. "Why are you here?" he demands, wrestling to get free of Finn's grip.

I jerk my head toward the building, a silent *not here*. Peeking around to the front, it's now empty, everyone having quickly cleared out. Between the four of us, it's not difficult to haul Lucas, even with his struggling, back into the dark, quiet building. It's vacant, no sign of the hush-hush poker game that just wrapped up.

"What the fuck do you want?!"

His gaze meets mine, and I catch a flash of his fear. Good. He *should* be afraid.

"Just a friendly chat." Despite his words, Jax's tone is laced with menace.

Lucas sneers. "What, get bored playing bodyguard to that slut? Had to come all the way to NSU to get fresh pussy?"

The air turns deadly.

I step forward, closing the distance. "Cut the bullshit. Why were you at the game that night?"

His grin stretches wider. "We had the night off. Thought we'd catch some college hockey. Lucky us, right? Hell of a hit."

I clench my jaw so hard I feel it crack. "You expect me to believe that?"

He shrugs, all arrogance and ease. "Timing worked out. What can I say? We picked a good night to come watch you guys."

Ethan's voice cuts through the static in my ears. Hard. Cold. Menacing. "Were you behind it?"

Lucas lifts a brow, the picture of mock innocence, but amusement flickers in his eyes. "Behind what?"

"The hit. Did you tell him to go after her?" Ethan's voice drops lower with every word. Each one a warning. "Did you put a target on her back?"

Lucas chuckles, low and oily. "You really think I'd waste my time orchestrating a hit on a *girl*?" His gaze flicks to each of us. "You give me too much credit."

Jax's voice is quieter, but somehow hits harder. "You sat there smiling while they carried her off the ice."

Lucas doesn't answer.

Doesn't blink.

Doesn't deny it.

He just leans back and smiles like this is a game he has already won.

Finn mutters something sharp behind me, but I'm done.

I didn't come here for a confession. I came for confirmation.

And I just got it.

I lunge.

My fist slams into his jaw with a sickening crunch that echoes through the room. The snap of his tendons as his head whips to the side is music to my fucking ears. Lucas stumbles, barely catching himself before I slam into him again, this time with a gut punch that doubles him over. He gasps, but I'm not done. Not even close. Fury bleeds through my veins, only fueled by his pained grunts and labored breathing.

I grab his jacket, yank him upright, and deliver another blow to his temple. He swings back, manages to graze my chin, but then Finn's there, a blur of rage, cracking his knuckles against Lucas's ribs.

Jax joins in next, grabbing Lucas by the collar and slamming him against the wall before driving a punch into his stomach so hard Lucas wheezes.

Even Ethan, ever the voice of reason, lands a solid hit to Lucas's jaw before stepping back, eyes hard. It was only a matter of time until he joined in on the action. He might like to pretend he's 'above it', but he's a red-blooded hockey player just like the rest of us. The need for violence burns through him. That aggression. That need to punch. To bleed. To win.

Together, we dismantle the asshole who was dumb enough to go after our girl. Four furious storms descending on a single, cocky bastard who's finally realizing he picked the wrong person to fuck with.

On his knees, blood dribbling down his chin, breath coming

in ragged heaves. His face is swelling by the minute, one eye already closed over and purpling.

With effort, he lifts his head, meeting our enraged gazes with his one good eye. He sneers through bloodied lips. "You came all the way to NSU...for her?" He laughs, a wet, broken sound that means we've broken a couple of his ribs. It makes me smile. "You're more pussy-whipped than I imagined."

He spits blood onto the ground. "I don't get the appeal. Whole NSU team had her. Every guy said the same thing—forgettable. Mediocre fuck."

My vision tunnels. *Fucking idiot has a death wish.*

One I have no qualms about delivering.

I'll readily watch the light leave his dead fucking eyes.

Except Ethan blocks my path. I snarl at him.

"Don't," he says low. Then, to Lucas, "We know the video was bullshit."

Lucas chuckles, the sound cold and deranged. "Is that what she said? And you dumbasses believed her?"

Jax grabs him by the hair, yanking his head back so violently I'm surprised it doesn't snap. "The lengths you'll go to because you're jealous of her? Pathetic."

Lucas scoffs, wrestling against Jax's unrelinquishing hold. "Jealous?" he spits. "Of what?"

"Her innate talent," Finn growls.

"Her drive to succeed," Ethan adds, as though we're ticking qualities off our fingers.

"Her ambition," Jax snarls.

"Her determination," I finish, stepping closer. "Dylan is the light, and you? You are a fucking cockroach scurrying around in the dark."

He makes another noise of disagreement, but I'm fucking done listening to him.

"Finn. Get me his phone." I extend my hand.

Lucas immediately starts thrashing. "Don't touch my fucking phone!"

But Jax and Ethan have him restrained, and Finn fishes the phone out of his pocket before holding it up to Lucas's swollen face. Given the damage, I'm surprised it actually recognizes enough of him to unlock, but it must as Finn tosses it over to me.

Lucas struggles harder, shouting obscenities, but I tune him out as I dig through the device.

Texts. Dozens of messages between him and Kyle going back to the start of the season. To the first game after Dylan became a Steelhawk.

I start to read through the first few.

KYLE

She won't back off. Thinks she's untouchable now.

LUCAS

She was the same here. Arrogant little bitch.

I SCROLL past more of the same. Kyle spewing hatred and Lucas fanning the flames, until I come across an exchange not long before Dylan was attacked.

LUCAS

You want her out of the games? A few broken bones should do it. Ribs, maybe. Wrist.

KYLE'S RESPONSE several days later is a video. I know if I look at it now, I'm going to explode, and I want to see what the fuck else these two have been conspiring about.

There are more messages about the jumbotron. Lucas saying he'll send over files, which must be the videos that were played. Kyle bragging about how well it went down. Lucas wishing he could have seen the look on Dylan's face.

Fuck, I can't wait to see the look on his face when I beat him fucking unconscious.

However, it's the most recent exchanges that leave me cold. As if what little warmth Dylan has breathed into me is suddenly sucked dry from my body.

KYLE

> None of this shit is working. I need something else. Something more permanent.

LUCAS

> Do it then. You know what needs to be done. She's like a bug that refuses to just die. It's the only way.

KYLE

> ...

LUCAS

> Do the same as you did before. Or make it look like an accident. You could catch her when she's soaking in the rehab tub. It's not that deep. She's small. She'd go under fast, and everyone would think she just drowned.

THE BILE CLIMBS MY THROAT. The rage is threatening to boil over.

Before I crush the phone in my iron grip and decide to give Lucas a slow and agonizing death, I scroll back to the video, knowing it's going to send me careening right over the fucking edge and into blood-soaked darkness.

With red-tinged vision, I hit play.

The video comes to life. It's dark out, and the recording is shaky as the person carrying the phone moves. Then Dylan comes into view, curled up on her side on the ground, arms up to shield her face. The only sound is her pained grunts, her stifled sobs as three sick, twisted fucks take turns kicking her. The camera shakes with their silent laughter.

"Is that—" Finn's words are cut off when we hear his voice on the recording, calling out.

There's a hushed "Shit," too low for me to determine which asshole it came from, before the three of them hightail it out of there. Before the footage cuts, Kyle flips the camera, smirking down at it like an actual fucking psychopath. On either side of him, just visible in the light of passing streetlights, are the faces of Fletcher and Monroe.

All. Fucking. Dead. Men.

Ethan wrenches the phone from my iron-clad grip, gaping at the footage before doing something. I'm too antsy to focus on whatever it is he's doing. The need to kill every single one of these motherfuckers burns through me with such ferocity that it's painful to ignore it.

Stalking forward, I grab Lucas by the collar and drag him to his feet. Face to face, I snarl at him. My free hand grabs the switchblade in my pocket, brandishing it like a sword. The sharp edge glints as I press it against his throat, just hard enough to have a bead of blood welling. It's not nearly enough.

Panic flashes in his eyes. For the first time tonight, he looks truly afraid.

It makes my blood fucking *sing*.

Kill him, a voice urges in my head. *He deserves it.*

"I'm going to fucking *end* you."

He trembles, stammering, but I'm not listening. All I hear is the roar of fury in my head.

"I will carve you up so slowly, you'll beg me to finish the job. I'll make you bleed for every bruise on her body. For every scar on her soul."

He whimpers, eyes blown wide.

"You want to know what real pain is?" I lean in, voice a razor's edge as I twist the tip of the blade at his throat. That bead becomes a trickle that races over the white flesh of his throat. Electricity sizzles along my nerves like a lightning bolt.

Do it, that voice hisses in dark, delightful pleasure.

I'm on the precipice, perched on the knife's edge and ready to slide it through the thin barrier of his skin and into his artery until blood pumps out of him like a waterfall.

My hands shake with the effort to hold myself back, and the blade's tip slips, cutting deeper into his skin. He hisses, flinching in my grip, but all I can see is the blood. I can *feel* his lifeline pulsing between my fingers. So fragile. So... *temporary.*

And then a hand clamps heavily around my shoulder and snaps me out of it.

"Dylan," Ethan murmurs low in my ear, for only us to hear.

A reminder, as if that's not *precisely* who I'm thinking of.

"She needs you—here," he says, as though reading my mind. "You made her a promise."

Fuck. He's right.

I stare at the tip of the blade embedded in the fucker's neck for another moment before I wrench it free. Flipping it closed, I return it to my pocket. Then, because he fucking deserves the agony, I lift my leg and slam it into his knee. I hear the popping. The tearing of ligaments. I force his kneecap so far out of position that there's no fucking way it's going back into position without surgery.

The pussy screams, falling to the ground and clutching at his leg.

"Try finishing out the season now, you fucker."

"My leg," he cries, tears and snot mingling with the blood on his face. "My leg."

"I'd be worried that this could end your hockey career," I taunt, face a mask of faux sympathy. "But we both know you never had a hope of playing after college." With a wicked smirk, I finish, "Have fun finishing out your last year on the bench."

Still sniveling, he shakes his head.

That's when Ethan steps forward. I can tell by the stiffness in his shoulders that he doesn't agree with what I did. What the fuck ever. However, as a true captain, a true team member, he has my back.

Stepping in front of Lucas, he crouches in front of him, holding the asshole's phone up. "Just in case you get any ideas about telling people what happened here tonight, we're going to keep this. I've already changed your password and disconnected it from your cloud account. If anyone comes asking questions about what happened to you, you'll find *yourself* answering questions about how you have video footage of a girl being beat up and you didn't take it to the police. Obvious taunts to not only *hurt* that girl, but get her fucking killed. So I suggest you come up with a story real quick."

"Fell down the stairs," Jax supplies.

"While trying to take a heroic selfie," Finn adds. "Lost his balance mid-duck face.

"Tripped over his own ego," Jax says. "You know it's got a wide berth."

"Nah." Finn shakes his head. "Tore his ACL trying to impress a puck bunny with a cartwheel."

"Or maybe he was doing squats in the mirror and tried to wink at himself." Jax gestures toward Lucas's sobbing mess of a face. "Dropped the weight on himself."

"Ohhh." Jax cringes while flashing an evil smile. "That would get a laugh from the team.

Apparently not done with their theorizing, he claps his hands as another idea comes to mind. "Tell them you were chased by a squirrel and tripped over your feet," Jax says, dead-pan. "I mean, sure, you screamed like a five-year-old girl, but you lived."

Finn smirks.

"Oh!" Jax snaps his fingers. "Freak pogo stick accident."

Finn throws his hands up. "You can't just *say* that and not explain it."

"Exactly." Jax grins. "No one's gonna ask follow-ups to that shit. Like, what is a grown-ass man doing with a pogo stick? No one wants that answer!"

"Guys," Ethan interjects with a droll expression. "Are you done or can we go now?"

Scoffing, Finn shakes his head. "We could go on for days."

"Please don't," I groan. I'd far rather get the fuck out of here.

My chest heaves. My knuckles are bloodied. My rage is still an untamable storm. But at least there's one less threat against my little Steelhawk.

And he'll never play his beloved hockey again.

Since he's spent the last two-plus years trying to take that from Dylan, it seems fitting that *he's* the one who will be sitting out his final year, and any hope he had of being picked up by some farm team or playing abroad—because let's face it, we all know he didn't have the skill to make it in the NHL—has just been brutally shattered...exactly like his knee.

FIFTY-NINE

THE CHILL of the late fall air bites through the fabric of my coat as I wait on the front porch of Coach's house for him and Dyl to say their goodbyes. Pulling back from their embrace, she smiles up at him. It's not the kind of smile I like to see on her. It's small. Quiet.

Her spark has been dimmed. Not snuffed, not extinguished, but dulled around the edges like a blade that's seen too many battles.

It guts me.

Because I remember the hellraiser who showed up that first day with fire in her eyes and steel in her spine, ready to take on a locker room full of skeptical assholes. The girl who stared us down like we were prey.

Now, as she turns to meet my stare, that fire is...lessened. Not because she is less fierce but because Kyle and Lucas have chipped away at her, bit by bit, like the fucking cowards they are, until all that remains is a wisp of a flame that would take but a faint breeze to extinguish.

Her breath puffs in the cold air as she moves toward me.

"You look...different," she says suspiciously.

I lift an eyebrow. "Different?" Surreptitiously, I give myself a once-over. I'm certain I washed all of Lucas's blood off of me before I left the house to come get her.

She scrutinizes me for a moment, this cute little crease forming between her brows as she tries to figure it out. "I dunno. Calmer. Less...restless."

She's not wrong. I *feel* calmer. Feel less like I'm about to come out of my own skin after putting Lucas in his place. If only we could do the same to Kyle so my girl wouldn't have to worry, but I'm confident his time will come. Especially with the video we found on Lucas's phone.

A small gasp falls from her lips, and she reaches out to grab my hand, inspecting the bruised, raw knuckles.

"Finn O'Rourke, who did you get in a fight with?"

Fuck, why does her saying my full name in that angry tone make me hard as nails?

I subtly adjust myself as we make our way down Coach's driveway to the sidewalk, and when she continues to give me that *well, I'm waiting* look, I vaguely respond, "Someone who deserved it."

Her eyes narrow. "Finn—"

But I cut her off, catching her hand in mine and tugging her close. Her body melds into mine, and I wrap my arm around her shoulders, pulling her infinitely closer. Her scent of warm bergamot and something sharper wraps around me like a tether, and I breathe deeply. Violence and her—this night is shaping up to be the best one in a while.

Ignoring her murderous glare, I duck my head to murmur in her ear, "Come skate with me?"

She forgets she was grilling me, that cute little crease back between her eyes. "What?"

"Come skate with me," I repeat, this time with a grin. "No hockey. No drills. Just some good old-fashioned skating."

Her brows lift, and there's a spark of excitement—faint, but there.

"When was the last time you just went out on the ice for the hell of it?" I question her.

She shakes her head slowly. "I can't remember."

"All the more reason to say yes." I wag my eyebrows. *Come on, Hellion, say yes. You know you want to.*

She snorts. Actually snorts, the first full, genuine smile I've seen in days gracing her gorgeous, kissable lips.

"There she is," I say, smugly.

"Fine," she mutters with a roll of her eyes. "But only because I haven't spent nearly enough time on the ice this week."

Whatever you need to tell yourself, babe.

We head to the arena, grab some skates, and hit the ice. At first, we skate in circles, darting around each other, testing speed and grace. I try a spin and almost eat ice, making her laugh so hard she doubles over.

"Okay, okay," I pant, even though my face is split with a grin. I knew getting her out here would help clear her head. Just like we needed to earlier with Lucas, she just needed to blow off some steam. On the ice is her happy place. She just needed to get out here for a bit when there was no one else around, no expectations or orders barked. Just her and the ice. And I'm the lucky one who gets to witness her transformation. "Show me how it's done."

With a dramatic flair, I gesture over the rink.

"Mm." She taps her lip. "And what do I get if I can pull it off?"

Skating over to her, I grab her hands in mine and spin us in a circle. "What is it you want, Dylan Callahan?"

It's the first time I've said her full *actual* name aloud. I still can't believe she's Patrick Callahan's daughter. That she has the blood of a freakin' *legend* running through her veins.

Hell, she's a legend in her own right.

She might have inherited some talent from her father, but her skills, her dedication, her dogged determination...that's all her. She's the impressive player she is today, not because of her father, but because of the hard work *she* put in.

Needing to feel her closer, I pull her in against my chest. Her gaze drops to my lips, and I can't help but smirk. "If a kiss is what you want, Hellion, you don't need to perform some fancy figure skater move to get one."

A slight pink hue dusts her cheeks that could be mistaken by the cold air if it wasn't for the fact that it wasn't there a second ago. Despite that, she rolls her eyes at me, pushing against my chest. I refuse to let her go, tightening my hold around her waist.

"Is a kiss what you want, baby?"

For the first time in...ever...she seems almost bashful, gnawing on her lower lip before softly saying, "Maybe." She looks up at me from beneath her eyelashes, her hands sliding up the front of my chest. There might be several layers of clothing between her hands and my skin, but I swear I feel the heat of her against me. "I miss our secret, impulsive kisses."

My hand moves on instinct to cup her cheek. God, how I've missed kissing her too.

"I've been trying to make it up to you," I tell her softly.

"I don't want you to hold yourself back from me."

My hands flex around her hips.

She searches my gaze, although for what, I have no idea.

"Yeah, you were an ass about it, but I liked the way you'd drag me into a dark corner because you just *had* to kiss me. Like you couldn't stand going another second without doing so."

"I couldn't," I rasp.

I still can't, I've just gotten better at shoving the urge down.

She smiles softly up at me, and goddamn, it's the most beautiful sight.

"I'm loving this new side of you, but I want that side too. I don't want you to hold any part of yourself back from me, Finn."

"You don't know what you're asking, Hellion," I warn her, my hold on her verging on bruising.

Entirely unaware that she is waving a red flag in front of a bull, she smirks up at me.

"Oh, but I'm pretty sure I do."

With that, she pushes her way out of my arms, skating toward the center of the ice before spinning on her skates to face me.

"If I stick the landing, I can have anything I want?" she asks.

All I can do is mutely nod.

The grin she flashes me is seductive as hell. Fuck, she has never looked so beautiful. So sure of herself. Of what she wants.

"Good, 'cause what I want is you, Finn. All of you."

She turns away before I can tell her she already has all of me. She's owned every part since that first day she knocked on our door.

Doing a loop around the ice, she sets herself up to do the move I so spectacularly failed at. I hold my breath as she goes in, unable to take my eyes off of her.

And then she does it—an effortless, elegant spin, lifting one leg in perfect symmetry. She looks like a ballerina on skates, and it's a mental snapshot I'll keep for the remainder of my days.

"What the hell? How did you do that?" I demand as she skates over to me, eyes ablaze with delight and a dazzling smile on her face.

"I took figure skating when I was a kid. My dad wanted me to try it. Pretty sure he was hoping I'd prefer it over hockey and go down that route—less violence and all that—but it wasn't really my thing. I did keep at it for a few years, though. It helped my balance, sharpened my edgework. Made me better on the ice."

"Tell me about him—your dad." I pull her forward, maneuvering us around the ice and keeping her appropriately distracted while she opens up to me.

And she does. Little things at first. Trips to the rink at dawn. Him shouting encouragement from the stands. Silly rituals and game-day pancakes. She explains that the collection of mugs in her bedroom are ones he'd bring back from away games.

Her voice trembles once, but she keeps going, and I don't say anything. I just skate with her, her fingers wrapped around mine, so she knows I'm here with her.

"I miss him," she says eventually, emitting a heavy sigh, one laden with grief and loss. "So much that it hurts."

I guide us to a gentle stop and pull her into my arms, wrapping her up in everything I have. She sinks into me like she's finally found a safe space to land, and it does weird and wonderful things to me to know I make her feel that way. Make her feel safe. I don't fully believe I've earned such a privilege, but it's one I'll accept regardless.

Tilting her chin up, I lower my lips to hers. It's soft. Reverent. Nothing like the heat-fueled kisses we've shared in dark corners. It's a whisper of a promise—of comfort, of presence.

"I needed this," she murmurs, her breath dancing over my lips. Her cheeks are flushed, eyes glassy, but she's glowing.

"I know," I reply, because I did too. I needed this time with her. One-on-one.

Pushing out of my hold, she grins. That spark is back in her eyes, lighting her up from within. "Bet you can't catch me," she teases.

She skates off before I can respond, laughter trailing behind her. My heart swells.

With a barked laugh, I push off, chasing after her.

We race. We dance across the ice, dodging and weaving, playful and breathless. And when I finally catch her, I spin her around, her laughter bursting against my throat.

This time, when I kiss her, it's all fire and hunger and want. It's everything I've been holding back. Everything she's already claimed.

She's mine.

And I'm so goddamn hers.

SHE'S STILL BREATHLESS, cheeks flushed, when we step off the ice. Her fingers are wrapped around mine, and I can feel the leftover tremor of laughter in them, the echo of something lighter. Freer.

But that weightlessness between us? It's shifting. Morphing into something heavier, hungrier.

I tug her down the corridor, not toward the exit, but deeper into the arena. Into the locker room. Past the benches.

"Finn?" she asks, laughing, confused. "What are you—"

I don't give her time to finish.

With one hand on her hip, I back her into the tiled wall of the shower room and kiss her. Hard. Deep. Like I've been holding it in for far too long.

Because I have.

She gasps into my mouth, hands flying up to grab the front of my hoodie. My name—half moan, half plea—slips from her lips, and it wrecks me. Unravels whatever shred of restraint I've been holding on to.

"Finn."

Hands on the cool tile on either side of her head, I force

myself to pull back to meet her glazed eyes. "Still want all of me, Hellion?"

"Always." No hesitation. No second-guessing.

My responding smirk is instantaneous. "Good, because I can't wait any longer." My lips are already back on hers. Searching. Seeking. Needing.

Her fingers are in my hair, her body arching into mine. "Then don't."

That's all I need.

My hands move with purpose, unzipping her coat and shoving it over her shoulders, before sliding beneath the hem of her hoodie and lifting it over her head. Her tank top follows. She's still flushed from the cold, but her skin is warm beneath my hands, soft and perfect and mine.

I can't stop kissing her.

Won't.

Every inch of her I uncover, I press my lips to—her shoulder, her collarbone, the swell of her chest. She's not just letting me. She's pulling me in. Meeting me at every point with the same desperate energy that thrums through my veins.

For every item of clothing I remove, she practically tears one off me, until we're both naked, chests heaving. I break away just long enough to fumble with the shower controls, flipping the hot water on full blast. Steam begins to fill the air around us, thick and heady. The moment the spray hits the tiles, I'm back on her, pulling her into the mist, and her laugh swallowed by my mouth.

We're soaked in seconds. Her hair clings to her face. Water trickles down her skin in ways that make my pulse race. She's gorgeous, like some mythical creature sculpted from heat and flame, and she's looking at me like I'm the only thing that matters.

"Finn," she whispers, fingers tracing the lines of my chest.

"I've got you," I breathe, slipping my hands around her waist and lifting her. Her legs wrap around me like it's instinct.

The water beats down on my back as she kisses me again, slow and deep, before she pulls back just enough to murmur, "I know. I trust you."

I shudder at the depth of her words. What they truly mean. How wholly undeserving I am of them, and yet I wrap them up and store them deep, something precious to be nurtured and cared for.

Time losses all sense of meaning as I stare straight into those hazel orbs. The water is hot enough to steam the mirrors and fog the tiles around us, but nothing burns hotter than her—wrapped around me, lips parted against mine, fingers clinging like she can't get close enough.

I press her back against the unyielding wall, one hand braced beside her head, the other gripping her thigh to keep her anchored to me. She's soaked, slick skin against slick skin, her hair dripping down her back, plastered to her face in wild, messy strands.

And fuck, she's beautiful like this.

Raw. Real. Unfiltered.

"I can't hold back any longer," I growl, lowering my mouth to her neck, dragging my lips down the column of her throat. "Every damn second. Every time you walked into a room. Every time you laughed. Every time you glared at me like you wanted to set me on fire."

She gasps as my teeth graze her collarbone.

"Please, Finn," she begs, eyes wild when they connect with mine. "I need you."

I grab her wrists and lift them above her head, pinning them to the wall. She arches, pressing her chest to mine, her breath shuddering when our hips align. Her body writhes like she's trying to crawl inside my skin—and if I could let her, I would.

Her head tips back when I kiss her again. Slow and deep. My tongue sweeps into her mouth like I'm staking a claim. She meets me with the same intensity, her fingers lacing through mine, squeezing tight.

I shift so I can pin both her wrists with one hand, sliding a palm down her arm, over her waist, to the swell of her hip. My thumb traces the lines of her ribs, memorizing every curve. Her breath hitches when I dip lower, my hand skating down the backs of her thighs, lifting her again so I can press her to the wall and feel every inch of her against me.

"Finn," she whines, tightening her legs around my hips until I lift my face to hers. Staring back at me with so much need and lust and desire, she pleads, "Burn with me."

Groaning, I notch myself at her entrance, and unable to deny either of us any longer, I slide all the way home. I eliminate all remaining space between us until the only thing that exists is skin and heat and every word we're unable to say pouring out through every touch, every kiss, every shiver that rips through her when I move.

We don't speak after that.

We just feel.

Water drums down my back, masking our gasps, our groans, the sharp intake of her breath when I kiss her like it's the only thing tethering me to this earth.

And maybe it is.

Maybe *she* is.

Because when she clutches at me like she's scared to let go, I realize I'd burn the world down just to keep her in my arms like this—alive, safe, mine.

SIXTY

THE BUZZ of the locker room wraps around me like a familiar blanket—laughter, sharp chirps of tape ripping, the dull thud of gear hitting benches, and the low hum of adrenaline. My hands move on autopilot, lacing up my skates, looping them twice before pulling tight.

It's game night.

And for the first time in a long time, it feels like just that. A game. Not a war. Not survival. Just hockey.

Two weeks ago, I wouldn't have believed this peace could exist. That I could sit here, surrounded by my teammates—my guys—and feel this strange, sweet normalcy blooming in my chest.

When Finn and I got home that night after our impromptu late-night skate, I was glowing from the inside out. Not just because of the way he kissed me, not just because he made me feel safe and seen, but because he—and the others—had taken that final weight off my shoulders.

They told me everything. About Lucas. About the texts. About the video.

And together, we took it all to the police.

Between that and my statement—and Finn stepping up with his own eyewitness account—it was enough.

Kyle was arrested, along with Fletcher and Monroe.

Actually arrested. This time, Kyle didn't just walk free with a smirk on his face and a legal technicality in his back pocket. His dad's lawyers are fighting it, of course. Throwing money at the problem like it'll bury the truth. Maybe it will. Maybe it won't.

I've learned I can't control what comes next.

But he's out of my life now. Expelled. Banned. Barred from stepping foot near the rink, near the team, near me.

And I refuse to give him any more space in my mind.

These past two weeks have been...good. Really good. The kind of good that feels like sunlight pouring through a window you forgot was there. The boys—*my boys*—have been incredibly affectionate. There's still that protective edge to them, sure, but it's softened by the teasing, the casual touches, the laughter.

We've found our rhythm.

Between classes, practices, and stolen kisses between locker rows, we make time. For each other. For ourselves. For us.

Even Wren has managed to claw out sufficient space in my life amongst the chaos, with a kind of ferocity I admire. The guys have learned not to argue when she shows up at the door with a raised brow and a demand for *girl time*. Not unless they want to get scorched.

"I like seeing this smile on you," Ethan murmurs at my side, nudging me gently with his elbow.

I flash him a grin. "Good, 'cause you're going to be seeing a lot of it."

His eyes soften, and he leans closer as his lips drop to mine. I instantly melt, and we both groan, pulling back, knowing we can't get into that here, in the locker room. Where we'd never hear the end of the catcalls.

"New *Infinite Monkey Cage* episode dropped," he says instead, changing the subject. "Thought we could listen to it later."

My heart does a little flip. It's become a weekly thing. If we're not at away games, we listen to that week's new episode at home. "It's a date."

"What's this I hear about a date?" Jax interjects, shoving his way into our conversation. "You better not be planning one with him, Menace." He points an accusing finger at me. "You still haven't played this new game with me. I've been building a fortress, and it's lonely as hell without you."

"Nu-uh." I shake my head, wagging a finger between them. "I'm not getting in the middle of this. Sort it out amongst yourselves."

After many an argument, I've learnt to step back and let them argue amongst themselves when it comes to spending time with me. They always figure it out in the end—after some tussling and bloodshed.

I guess, boys will be boys.

As predicted, Ethan and Jax begin to bicker. Shaking my head in amusement, I turn back to my gear—but when I reach for my gloves, something slips out from beneath them and flutters to the bench.

A note.

Unfolding it, I already know who it's from. Finn's handwriting is a little messy, all bold strokes and slanted letters. I read it silently, biting back a smile that threatens to split my face wide open.

I love you.

Simple. Understated. Perfect.

Smiling to myself, I clutch the scrap of paper to my chest,

breathing in his words. They've become a regular thing, not just the odd one here and there. But nearly daily—in my textbooks, my skates, my coat pocket, my locker.

Always places I'll find them in random, inconspicuous moments.

And then he follows them up by seeking me out and kissing me in a dark corner like he can't help himself. Like it's a compulsion.

I lift my gaze to find him, but it's not Finn I lock eyes with.

It's Griffin.

He's across the room, sitting quietly, lacing his skates with methodical precision. But his eyes are on me. Always on me.

Silent. Watchful.

My protector, even when I don't ask him to be.

I blow him a kiss. His lips twitch, just slightly, and for Griffin, that's practically a declaration of love.

Before I can say anything else, Coach steps into the room, his voice rising over the hum.

"All right, Steelhawks. Game time."

The room shifts—tension coiling, laughter dimming, focus sharpening. I tuck the note into my gear bag and slide my gloves on, standing with the others.

It's time to show them what we're made of.

And for the first time in weeks, I feel like myself again.

Steel and fire and everything in between.

THE NOISE from the crowd dulls. Blurs. Nothing exists except my hands wrapped around my stick and the whoosh of air in my face as I lead the puck straight for the net.

My breaths are loud in my ear. The net is in sight. My focus is sharp.

I swing my arm back.

The puck hits the back of the net with a satisfying crack.

For a moment, everything is silent. That sweet blip in time when no one has registered the goal, when your body has yet to react, and you feel frozen in time. Weightless.

And then the world explodes.

Noise rushes back in, loud and chaotic. The blast of the horn announcing the end of the game. The screaming of the crowd.

Steelhawks jerseys surge toward me like a blue-and-silver tidal wave, the roar of the crowd swallowed by the crashing adrenaline in my veins. Ethan is the first to reach me, lifting me clean off the ice and spinning me while he shouts something I can't even hear over the ringing in my ears. Finn crashes into us next, followed by Jax and Griffin. "You did it!" one of them yells loudly in my ear. "You fucking did it!" Then the whole team is there, piling on, yelling, cheering, laughing.

We won!

I scored the game-winning goal!

I'm at the bottom of the dogpile, my face pressed into Griffin's chest, and I can't stop laughing. It bubbles out of me, wild and breathless and euphoric. My lungs burn and my eyes sting and my heart—God, my heart feels so full it might burst.

This is it.

This is what I've worked for. Fought for. Bled for.

Acceptance.

Belonging.

Family.

The guys peel back one by one, their faces flushed, beaming, breathless.

"That's my girl," Griffin growls in my ear, his hand a brand on the back of my neck.

"You're a fucking goddess," Finn yells, his face split in two with a wide, mischievous grin that has me wanting to kiss him.

Nipping at my earlobe, Jax rasps so low only I hear, "I'm gonna show you exactly what scoring that goal did to me later." His promise sends delicious shivers racing down my spine, and I shift my gaze to Ethan next.

He ducks down so we're at eye-level. "Hell of a finish, Thorn." His thumb presses against my lips, tugging the lower one down. "I'm so fucking proud of you."

With heat in my cheeks and love in my heart, I turn, my gaze drawn upward to the rafters, to the jersey hanging high above us.

#19—*Callahan*.

My father's name. His number. His jersey.

My chest aches in the best kind of way. The kind that cracks something open inside you and lets the light in. I imagine him up there, watching. Smiling. Proud.

Warmth spreads through my limbs, and for a moment, I sense him there, watching. I can practically feel the pride in his eyes.

Movement from the stands catches my eye and I turn my head, mouth dropping open. There in the front row, are an entire line of men in ball caps, their hats pulled low and jackets nondescript. But even without the Timberwolves logos, I'd recognize them anywhere. A smile curls my lips as I identify Vince, Isaac, and Logan amongst the rest of the Timberwolves players. My dad's former teammates.

Skating over, breath caught somewhere between disbelief and awe, I shout, "What are you doing here?"

Vince grins, that familiar crooked smile stretching across his face. "Your boyfriend sent us the schedule. Said we had an open invite." He shrugs, still grinning. "We had a week off, and none of us could think of a better way to spend it than cheering on the girl who's always cheered us on."

Tears sting the backs of my eyes before I can stop them. I shake my head, lips parted, but before I can say a single word someone grabs me from behind and suddenly I'm being dragged into the celebratory chaos, my helmet knocked askew as players jostle me from every side.

I'm still grinning as we make it back to the locker room, the air thick with sweat and victory. We change quickly, laughter echoing off the walls. Someone throws a towel at Jax, another guy pretends to interview Finn with a shampoo bottle.

We move the celebrations to The Stanley, where we're met with rowdy fans as soon as we step into the bar. We're instantly swarmed, people clapping us on the back. People cheer my name as I push past them. Gone are the looks of contempt and skepticism, the whispers about a *girl* on the men's team. Now, there's only praise. Celebration.

As if sensing the shift in my emotions, Ethan's hand comes to rest on my shoulder, squeezing the muscle there. I glance back at him over my shoulder and smile.

Wren is behind the bar, expertly pouring beers and shaking cocktails like a queen. When she sees me, she abandons her post without hesitation, pushing through the crowd to throw her arms around me.

"You legend!" she squeals. "You freaking legend!"

I hug her back tightly, breath catching in my throat.

"First round of drinks is on me," she says, pulling back with a grin. "Well. On the house, but you get the idea."

We make our way to our usual booth in the back, and unlike all those early visits where I felt like an outsider tagging along, this time, I'm at the heart of it. The guys surround me. The rest of the team fanning out to claim the tables around ours. There are backslaps and drinks clink and someone retelling the final play like we didn't all literally live it. I laugh along, cheeks aching, heart light.

At some point, Wren squeezes her way in beside me at the booth, shouting in my ear that she's got a fifteen-minute break. She smells of citrus and vodka, and I lean into her shoulder with a contented sigh.

The door swings open, and the bar hushes to low murmurs as Valehurst College hockey players walk in—our opponents from tonight's game. They're not a bad group. Their captain and Ethan had a friendly interaction on the ice, and Jax explains to me that the Steelhawks had a low-key rivalry with them, a kind of mutual respect laced with a healthy dose of trash talk.

While most of the team heads for the bar to order drinks, the captain and two others I recognize from the ice make their way toward our table.

The team's captain shakes hands with Ethan, the two of them exchanging tired grins and post-game banter. "Nice finish," he says, nodding in my direction. "Your girl here has got fire."

The second he speaks, Wren goes tense as stone beside me.

"You barely saw anything out there," Ethan replies with a proud grin directed at me.

The two of them shoot the shit, reminiscing about some Athletes Row party they all attended a couple of years ago, but the entire time, I'm aware that Wren has gone so still, I have to squint to see if she's even breathing. *What the hell?*

Her gaze bounces between the three players, face pale and brows tipped low over her eyes. While two of them are engaged in conversation with my guys, the one on the far left glances our way. His eyes lock on Wren...and go wide.

He's tall, with dark hair, and looks like a boulder couldn't take him out. He stares at Wren like he's seen a ghost.

As though she can't stand the intensity of his gaze another

moment, she bolts to her feet. "I need to get back to work," she speaks so fast that the words jumble together, her voice brittle.

Then, careful not to make contact with the players standing in front of our table, she slips past them and disappears into the crowd.

With her gone, I eye the guy she'd been staring at. Who the fuck is he and what the hell did he do to invoke such a reaction from her? My gaze narrows on him, but he's not paying me any attention, too busy flicking glances toward where Wren disappeared in between talking to the guys.

"Do you know her?" I ask, scooching over so I can keep my voice low, not wanting the entire table to hear our conversation.

He seems taken aback by my question before quickly recovering with a shake of his head. "No. Not really. We met at a party once..."

His words trail off, as if he doesn't know how to finish that sentence, but what he's said sticks with me.

Wren doesn't do parties.

I've tried all year to get her to keep me company at one of the team's *mandatory* parties, and she has made it clear that she would rather watch paint dry.

The conversation moves on while I'm lost in my thoughts, puzzling pieces that don't fit together. When I zone back in, Jax is cracking a joke with the newcomers. I shake off the strange interaction, joining in on the conversation.

I don't see Wren again for the rest of the night.

SIXTY-ONE

MY HAND SLIDES down the soft silk fabric of my dress. Smoothing out the nonexistent creases. The mid-season annual benefit dinner is everything I expect it to be—overly formal, painfully slow, and so full of ego I feel like I'm drowning in it.

I'm plenty used to grinning and bearing my way through such events, but thankfully, being surrounded by the guys, all dressed up in their sharp suits, makes it bearable.

It's been several weeks since we won against Valehurst, and we have been undefeated since. In fact, we are heading into the break and have only lost one game so far this season. The Steel-hawks have never looked stronger. Word is spreading—scouts are talking, articles are being written, and my inbox has been filling with interview requests and sports features. I've gained a small but loyal group of fans online. Most days, I still can't believe this is real.

I sit nestled at the round table between Jax and Ethan, with Griffin and Finn across from me. I've sat at plenty of fancy dinner tables on behalf of my dad and his career, his success, but this is the first I've attended that revolved around me—*my* team.

Wren worked some kind of magic with my hair and makeup, and the dress she picked for me...it's daring. Red, backless, clinging to every curve. Paired with strappy heels and a dash of perfume, I feel like another version of myself—sleek and devastating.

The version I caught reflected in their eyes the moment I descended the stairs tonight.

Griffin didn't even try to hide his reaction. His jaw clenched, his hands curled into fists at his sides like it physically pained him not to touch me. Jax cursed under his breath and muttered something about how I was going to be the death of him. Ethan blinked once, then twice, and murmured, "Christ, Thorn." Finn whistled low and told me he was seconds from saying to hell with it and dragging me back up the stairs to see if the dress was equally as devastating on my bedroom floor.

All night, they haven't been able to keep their hands off me. Light brushes of fingers down my arm. Warm palms pressed to my thigh. Jax's hand is currently resting on the small of my back, while Griffin's foot nudges mine beneath the table.

Onstage, the head of the college—President something-or-other; I forget—drags on about funding and alumni donations. The usual fluff. I tap my finger against the table, nerves building. I haven't told the guys about what's coming. I wanted it to be a surprise.

Of course, Ethan notices my fidgeting. He threads his fingers through mine and pulls my hand into his lap, grounding me with just a look.

"And now," the president says, voice booming over the mic. "I want to take a moment to acknowledge our talented players, without whom we would have no one to cheer on every weekend. The team we have amassed this year is spectacular, as our record demonstrates. However, there is one player in particular

I would like to recognize. A new addition this year who has already made a significant impact. I'll admit, I was skeptical when Coach Fitz selected this player for the team, but they have more than proved their worth in the short time they have been here." He lifts his hand, the champagne glass glinting beneath the sparkling lights of the chandelier. "Please join me in recognizing the raw talent and gritty determination of one of our own. Not only has she inherited her father's God-given talents, but she brings her own flair and hard work to the ice. Raise your glasses to Dylan Callahan."

Silence swells.

Then the room erupts into hushed murmurs and wide-eyed stares.

Players, staff, and donors alike putting the pieces together. Connecting the dots.

Whispers of *Patrick Callahan's daughter* float around the room.

The guys all look at me. Stunned.

"Did you know he was going to do that?" Jax leans in, his voice low. There's an edge to it, like if I say no, he's going to go over there and give the head of the college a piece of his mind— or his fist.

I reach over and squeeze his arm, nodding. "Bear told me. He asked what name I wanted him to use in his speech. I told him Callahan."

"Why now?" Ethan asks, head tilted in curiosity.

"I always wanted to be known for my own accomplishments. To build a name without riding my dad's coattails. But...I think I've done that. I might not have gotten into the NHL yet, but I've proven my worth. They all know what I'm capable of now."

"Hell, yeah they do, baby." Finn winks at me, his grin infectious.

"It feels right," I continue. "To carry his name. To honor him."

One by one, they reach out. Ethan squeezes my thigh. Finn grabs my hand. Jax leans his shoulder into mine, and Griffin's gaze burns into me from across the table. Their support wraps around me like a second skin.

When the speeches end and the music starts, I'm pulled into their orbit.

We dance. Laugh. Spin beneath the soft golden light. I share a slow dance with each of them—Griffin's hand possessive on my lower back, Ethan's touch reverent, Jax pressing a kiss to my temple, Finn twirling me so fast that I fall into his arms, giggling.

With sore feet and a full bladder, I excuse myself to the bathroom. Staring at myself in the mirror, my cheeks are flushed and my eyes dance. The grief is still there, but it's nothing like what it used to be. I'm...happy. I'm...a girl in love. A girl who has the world at her feet. And four strong men to see through every challenge with, every win, every loss. Four men who have my back...no matter what is thrown at us.

With a smile on my face, I head back toward the ballroom.

Thick, muscular, familiar arms grab me around the waist, sweeping me off my feet and pulling me into the shadows. My back hits the wall, and I barely have the chance to take a breath before Finn's lips crash into mine, hungry and urgent, like he's been waiting all night for this. I clutch his jacket, melting into his kiss.

"You in that dress, Hellion," he groans against my lips, like a man dying. "Trouble with a capital T."

"You're going to smear my lipstick," I chastise, but there's no heat behind it. I'd readily fix my lipstick a hundred times if it means his lips are on mine.

"Maybe that would matter if there was any chance you'd be

making it back to the party." A new voice joins us, dark like chocolate as Jax comes into view beside Finn. "I see you started the *real* party early," he directs at Finn.

Unapologetic, Finn simply shrugs. "Couldn't help it."

Two sets of searing hot eyes bore into me. "Mm." The sound rumbles through Jax's chest. They are both so close that I can feel the heat coming off them in waves. The chemistry between us crackles in the air, and my breaths are shallow, my nipples peeking through the thin fabric of my dress. Jax reaches up to brush his thumb over my swollen lips. "Can't say I blame you."

I flick my tongue over his skin, and another rumble vibrates through him.

"Unless you want to get fucked in a hotel corridor, Menace, you better put that tongue away."

It's a warning and a promise, and the thought of *anyone* walking in and seeing us only sends my pulse skittering higher. He must see what his threat does to me, as his fingers slide down my arm before linking with mine and he tugs me away from the wall.

His voice is deeper, thicker, when he rasps, "Message the others. We're leaving now."

Without waiting for Finn's confirmation, he drags me down the corridor and out of the hotel without bothering to say goodbye to anyone.

The car journey home is unbearable and seems to last a lifetime. Tension fizzles in the air, hot and heady. Hands are everywhere, and I can feel Ethan's gaze like a lightning rod on me through the rearview mirror.

By the time we get home, we barely make it through the front door before they are on me, like birds of prey descending on their dinner.

"You've ruined me in this dress," Griffin growls into my

neck. "All I've been able to think about all night is bending you over the nearest flat surface and taking you in it."

"You and me both," Finn mutters, nibbling my ear.

They share a look, heat flashing in their eyes, possession, need, before Griffin whisks me over to the sofa. I'm bent over the armrest, my ass in the air as he lifts my dress and kicks my legs apart.

Groans go up from all of them when they discover the strip of red lace I'm wearing underneath.

"Did you wear this just for us, Little Menace?" Jax purrs, fingering the edge of my thong.

"Yes."

"Such a dirty girl." His words are a praise that heats my blood. He squeezes my ass before coming to kneel at the edge of the sofa beside me. "You wanted us to fuck you, didn't you?"

The words are stolen from my lips when Griffin drags the scrap of fabric down my legs, baring me to him. "So wet already," he coos, his hands gliding over my bare skin. His fingers slip between my slick folds, and I shiver.

With his pants unbuckled, and hair disheveled, like he's spent all night running his fingers through it to stop himself from reaching for me instead, Finn moves to kneel in front of me. He kisses me slow and deep, and I groan into his mouth as Griffin's fingers slide inside me. I feel Ethan and Jax's hands on my skin, the four of them setting me alight.

I gasp into Finn's mouth when Griffin pushes into me from behind, groans falling from our lips.

"Think you can take more, baby," Finn asks, his words caked in need and darkness.

"Please."

Leaning back on his heels, he takes his cock out of his pants. I flick my tongue out, swiping it over the tip and smirking when he shivers at the simple touch. "Fuck, Hellion. I'm not going to last long in that mouth of yours."

Parting my lips, he slides into my mouth, and I fall into the heady pleasure of the two of them taking me, the feel of Ethan's hands on my skin, Jax's encouraging, filthy words in my ears.

The three of us come together in a symphony of moans and grunts and ecstasy. I'm still catching my breath when Ethan hauls me up. My legs are shaking, but he holds me close as Jax steps up to my back. His fingers trail over my skin as he lowers the zipper of my dress.

"While these Neanderthals wanted to fuck you in this, all I've wanted is to strip it off you," he whispers seductively in my ear. He peels the fabric down slowly, reverently, kissing his way down my back until it falls into a puddle at my feet. Then they switch places. Jax takes me into my arms while Ethan falls to his knees at my feet. With care, he unbuckles the straps of my heels, slipping them off my feet one at a time.

"Mmm," he groans, lifting his head and licking his lips. "I can smell you from here."

My cheeks pink. Griffin's cum coats my inner thighs, but Ethan doesn't seem to care as he pushes my legs apart and buries his face in my apex. I cry out as he swipes his tongue between my folds, flicking it over my sensitive clit. He moans into me.

While Jax's hands are a vise around my waist, Finn stalks over, his pants still undone and cock already growing hard once more. Bending at the waist, he takes a pert nipple into his mouth, sucking on the flesh until I'm arching into him, my hips bucking against Ethan's face.

"That's it, Little Steelhawk," Griffin encourages, joining us. "Be a good girl and come for Ethan."

My body reacts on impulse to the command, and I come with a cry. Boneless, Jax collapses onto the sofa, bringing me with him so I'm straddling him backward. His erect cock prods at my entrance, before he pulls me down with a firm grip on my hips.

I groan as he fills me, the aftershocks of my previous orgasms still skittering through me and heightening every sense.

"Think you can take both of us?" Jax's voice is strained, his breathing heavy as he fucks into me. I blink my eyes open, finding Ethan standing in front of us, fisting his hard cock. Images of when Griffin and Jax shared me flash before my eyes, and I nod, eager.

"Such a good girl for us," Ethan praises, leaning forward to tug at my lip with his thumb.

"A filthy dirty girl," Griffin adds.

Ethan hums his agreement.

"Yeah, but she's all ours." Finn flashes a possessive grin, his freckles glinting beneath the lights in the room.

"Damn straight, she is," Ethan agrees. "Our girl."

"Ours," the others repeat.

Jax shifts with me on his lap so we're sideways on the sofa. "Can't wait to take this tight little ass of yours, Menace. Been dreaming about it since Griffin had you."

He shifts me on his lap, lifting me so he can slip out, and instead pushes his tip against my back hole. I force myself to breathe, to relax, but Ethan is there, in front of me, his cock sliding into my soaking wet pussy and his fingers playing with my clit.

They both fill me, and it's as foreign and intoxicating as it was before.

Pressure on my chin has me opening my eyes. Griffin has a hold of me, his eyes alight with shadows and desire. "Think you can take two more, Hurricane?"

I nod, and amongst the pleasure inflicted by Ethan and Jax, I wind up with my hand around Finn's cock while Griffin fists the back of my hair and drives his dick into my mouth. It's filthy. It's hot. It's mesmerizing. It's a joining and a fragmenting all at once.

We collide.

Four big, strong hockey players and the girl who made the ice her kingdom—and claimed them as hers.

EPILOGUE
STEELHAWKS VS TITANS CHAMPIONSHIP GAME

WELCOME BACK, folks, to what is shaping up to be one of the most exhilarating college hockey championships we've seen in years. The Blackstone Steelhawks versus the Lakehurst Titans —it's a rivalry that never fails to deliver. But this year? This year is different.

All eyes have been on one player in particular—Dylan Callahan.

Yes, *that* Callahan. Daughter of Timberwolves legend Patrick Callahan, and the first woman to play on Blackstone's Division One men's hockey team. There was skepticism at the start of the season—critics calling it a PR stunt, others arguing she wouldn't be able to keep up. But game after game, Callahan has proven them wrong. She's not just keeping up. She's dominating.

And with just under a minute left in the third period, with the score tied 1–1, she's back on the ice with her infamous line. Callahan at leftwing. Finn O'Rourke on the right. Ethan Maddox at center. Jaxon Keller on defense. And Griffin Price, the Steelhawks' immovable wall, in goal.

O'Rourke moves like lightning. He's been a playmaker all

season long, and it's no wonder he was signed straight to the Timberwolves alongside Maddox. Keller and Price were traded shortly after the news broke, making this one of the most talked-about pre-draft shakeups in recent memory.

And then there's Callahan. Rumors have been swirling that she's already made a deal with the Timberwolves. Between her late father's legacy and her off-the-charts stats this season, insiders say her father's old jersey is already being dusted off in preparation for when she graduates next year.

Back on the ice, Ethan Maddox wins the face-off with brute force, knocking the puck back toward Jax Keller.

Maddox's control at center has been a cornerstone of the Steelhawks' strategy. And Keller? That man plays defense like it's personal. He clears a path with the grace of a dancer and the fury of a wrecking ball.

Keller flips the puck forward to O'Rourke, who taps it across to Callahan.

Callahan's got it! She dodges a brutal hit from the Titans' captain and cuts toward the goal. O'Rourke is right there with her. Maddox trailing. Keller on the edge of the blue line, ready to strike if needed.

Ten seconds.

Callahan passes to Maddox.

Maddox to O'Rourke.

O'Rourke feints, draws the defense—

Back to Callahan!

SHE SHOOTS!

Buzzer blares.

AND IT'S IN!

Dylan Callahan scores the game-winning goal at the buzzer! The Steelhawks take the championship in the final breath of the game!

What a storybook ending to a powerhouse season. A team

built on chemistry, grit, and magic—and a legacy that just keeps on giving.

Callahan has more than lived up to her name. And if the Timberwolves have signed her for next year, as many believe, they'll be reuniting the most electric line in college history.

This? This is history in the making.

ACKNOWLEDGMENTS

Thank you so much for reading Stick It. This book has resonated with me more than any other I have written. These characters are buried deep in my soul.

As always, there are so may people responsible for this book because of the hard work they contribute behind the scenes. Number one is my PA, Nikki. The time and feedback she gives to each book and character is invaluable. Thank you so much for being on this crazy journey with me.

I want to thank to my alpha and beta readers for their time and the feedback they provided. I always love to read their comments and guess who will be their favourite MMC.

A massive thank you to my editor and agent, Angie for dealing with every single "I know I told you I was done, but I just added this little bit" comment I dropped her after telling her it was all hers.

I also have to thank my tiktok and street teams for helping to promote and spread the word. I appreciate all your hard work every week.

I need to thank my husband who is always my rock and support.

Lastly, thank you to all of you, the readers, for picking up this book and reading it. Without you none of this would be possible!! If you loved this book, please help me spread the word by leaving a quick review.

ALSO BY R.A. SMYTH

<u>Crescentwood Series</u>

A dark, high school bully reverse harem with a stalker and gang element.

<u>Pacific Prep Series</u>

A dark, academy bully reverse harem with a taboo relationship.

<u>Black Creek Series</u>

A rival gang-mafia reverse harem with a vigilante FMC. Contains MM.

<u>The Ruthless Boys of Ridgeway</u>

A college, friends-enemies-lovers, second chance reverse harem with a stalker and secret society elements.

<u>Halston U</u>

A college, hockey, stepbrother, enemies-to-lovers reverse harem with a revenge plot.

ABOUT THE AUTHOR

R.A. Smyth is best known for writing contemporary dark romance filled with unexpected twists, mystery, and plenty of steam. Rachel lives in the UK with her husband and two golden retrievers, and when she's not busy thinking up crazy cliffhangers to drive her readers insane, she enjoys inflicting the same torture on herself by reading incomplete series.

She has always been an avid reader, starting from the Harry Potter books as a kid. It's an interest that has grown into an obsession over the years and becoming an author has been a secret lifelong dream of hers.